MINDING
FRANKIE

MINDING FRANKIE

Maeve Binchy

ALFRED A. KNOPF   NEW YORK   2011

THIS IS A BORZOI BOOK
PUBLISHED BY ALFRED A. KNOPF

Copyright © 2010 by Maeve Binchy
All rights reserved. Published in the United States by Alfred A. Knopf,
a division of Random House, Inc., New York.
www.aaknopf.com
Knopf, Borzoi Books, and the colophon are registered trademarks of
Random House, Inc.
Originally published in Great Britain by Orion Books, an imprint of the
Orion Publishing Group Ltd., a Hachette UK company, London, in 2010.

Library of Congress Cataloging-in-Publication Data
Binchy, Maeve.
Minding Frankie / by Maeve Binchy.—1st U.S. ed.
p.   cm.
ISBN 978-0-307-27356-7
1. Recovering alcoholics—Fiction.   2. Child rearing—Fiction.
3. Fatherhood—Fiction.   4. Families—Fiction.   5. Interpersonal
relations—Fiction.   6. Community life—Ireland—Fiction.   7. City and
town life—Ireland—Fiction.   8. Domestic fiction.   I. Title.
PR6052.I7728M56 2011
823'.914—dc22   2010035999

Jacket art by William Low
Jacket design by Carol Devine Carson

Manufactured in the United States of America
First United States Edition

For dear generous Gordon,
who makes life great every single day

MINDING
FRANKIE

Chapter One

Katie Finglas was coming to the end of a tiring day in the salon. Anything bad that could happen had happened. A woman had not told them about an allergy and had come out with lumps and a rash on her forehead. A bride's mother had thrown a tantrum and said that she looked like a laughingstock. A man who had wanted streaks of blond in his hair became apoplectic when, halfway through the process, he had inquired what they would cost. Katie's husband, Garry, had placed both his hands innocently on the shoulders of a sixty-year-old female client, who had then told him that she was going to sue him for sexual harassment and assault.

Katie looked now at the man standing opposite her, a big priest with sandy hair mixed with gray.

"You're Katie Finglas and I gather you run this establishment," the priest said, looking around the innocent salon nervously as if it were a high-class brothel.

"That's right, Father," Katie said with a sigh. What could be happening now?

"It's just that I was talking to some of the girls who work here, down at the center on the quays, you know, and they were telling me . . ."

Katie felt very tired. She employed a couple of high school dropouts: she paid them properly, trained them. *What* could they have been complaining about to a priest?

"Yes, Father, what exactly is the problem?" she asked.

"Well, it *is* a bit of a problem. I thought I should come to you directly, as it were." He seemed a little awkward.

"Very right, Father," Katie said. "So tell me what it is."

"It's this woman, Stella Dixon. She's in hospital, you see . . ."

"Hospital?" Katie's head reeled. What *could* this involve? Someone who had inhaled the peroxide?

"I'm sorry to hear that." She tried for a level voice.

"Yes, but she wants a hairdo."

"You mean she trusts us again?" Sometimes life was extraordinary.

"No, I don't think she was ever here before. . . ." He looked bewildered.

"And your interest in all this, Father?"

"I am Brian Flynn and I am acting chaplain at St. Brigid's Hospital at the moment, while the real chaplain is in Rome on a pilgrimage. Apart from being asked to bring in cigarettes and drink for the patients, this is the only serious request I've had."

"You want me to go and do someone's hair in hospital?"

"She's seriously ill. She's dying. I thought she needed a senior person to talk to. Not, of course, that you look very senior. You're only a girl yourself," the priest said.

"God, weren't you a sad loss to the women of Ireland when you went for the priesthood," Katie said. "Give me her details and I'll bring my magic bag of tricks in to see her."

"Thank you so much. I have it all written out here." Father Flynn handed her a note.

A middle-aged woman approached the desk. She had glasses on the tip of her nose and an anxious expression.

"I gather you teach people the tricks of hairdressing," she said.

"Yes, or more the *art* of hairdressing, as we like to call it," Katie said.

"I have a cousin coming home from America for a few weeks. She mentioned that in America there are places where you could get your hair done for near to nothing cost if you were letting people practice on you."

"Well, we do have a students' night on Tuesdays; people bring in their own towels and we give them a style. They usually contribute five euros to a charity."

"Tonight is Tuesday!" the woman cried triumphantly.

"So it is," Katie said through gritted teeth.

"So, could I book myself in? I'm Josie Lynch."

"Great, Mrs. Lynch—see you after seven o'clock," Katie said, writing down the name. Her eyes met the priest's. There was sympathy and understanding there.

It wasn't all champagne and glitter running your own hairdressing salon.

Josie and Charles Lynch had lived in 23 St. Jarlath's Crescent since they were married thirty-two years ago. They had seen many changes in the area. The corner shop had become a mini-supermarket; the old laundry, where sheets had been ironed and folded, was now a Laundromat, where people left big bags bulky with mixed clothes and asked for a service wash. There was now a proper medical practice with four doctors where once there had been just old Dr. Gillespie, who had brought everyone into the world and seen them out of it.

During the height of the economic boom, houses in St. Jarlath's Crescent had changed hands for amazing sums of money. Small houses with gardens near the city center had been much in demand. Not anymore, of course—the recession had been a great equalizer, but it was still a much more substantial area than it had been three decades ago.

After all, just look at Molly and Paddy Carroll, with their son Declan—a doctor—a real, qualified doctor! And just look at Muttie and Lizzie Scarlet's daughter Cathy. She ran a catering company that was hired for top events.

But a lot of things had changed for the worse. There was no community spirit anymore. No church processions went up and down the Crescent on the feast of Corpus Christi, as they used to. Josie and Charles Lynch felt that they were alone in the world, and certainly in St. Jarlath's Crescent, in that they knelt down at night and said the Rosary.

That had always been the way.

When they married they planned a life based on the maxim that the family that prays together stays together. They had assumed they would have eight or nine children, because God never put a mouth into this world that He didn't feed. But that wasn't to happen. After Noel, Josie had been told there would be no more children. It was hard to accept. They both came from big families; their brothers and sisters had produced big families. But then, perhaps, it was all meant to be this way.

They had always hoped Noel would be a priest. The fund to educate him for the priesthood was started before he was three. Money was put aside from Josie's wages at the biscuit factory. Every week a little more was added to the post office savings account, and when Charles got his envelope on a Friday from the hotel where he was a porter, a sum was also put into the post office. Noel would get the best of priestly educations when the time came.

So it was with great surprise and a lot of disappointment that Josie and Charles learned that their quiet son had no interest whatsoever in a religious life. The Brothers said that he showed no sign of a vocation, and when the matter had been presented to Noel as a possibility when he was fourteen, he had said if it was the last job on earth he wouldn't go for it.

That had been very definite indeed.

Not so definite, however, was what he actually *would* like to do. Noel was vague about this, except to say he might like to run an office. Not work in an office, but run one. He showed no interest in studying office management or bookkeeping or accounting or in any areas where the careers department tried to direct him. He liked art, he said, but he didn't want to paint. If pushed, he would say that he liked looking at paintings and thinking about them. He was good at drawing; he always had a notebook and a pencil with him and he was often to be found curled up in a corner sketching a face or an animal. This did not, of course, lead to any career path, but Noel had never expected it to. He did his homework at the kitchen table, sighing now and then, but rarely ever excited or enthusiastic. At the parent-teacher meetings Josie and Charles had inquired about this. They wondered, Does anything at school fire him up? Anything at all?

The teachers were at a loss. Most boys were unfathomable around fourteen or fifteen but they had usually settled down to do something. Or often to do nothing. Noel Lynch, they said, had just become even more quiet and withdrawn than he already was.

Josie and Charles wondered, Could this be right?

Noel was quiet, certainly, and it had been a great relief to them that he hadn't filled the house up with loud young lads thumping one another. But they had thought this was part of his spiritual life, a preparation for a future as a priest. Now it appeared that this was certainly not the case.

Perhaps, Josie suggested, it was only the Brothers' brand of religious life that Noel objected to. In fact, he might have a different kind of vocation and want to become a Jesuit or a missionary?

Apparently not.

And when he was fifteen he said that he didn't really want to join in the family Rosary anymore; it was only a ritual of meaningless prayers chanted in repetition. He didn't mind doing good for people, trying to make less fortunate people have a better life, but surely no God could want this fifteen minutes of drone drone drone.

By the time he was sixteen they realized that he had stopped going to Sunday Mass. Someone had seen him up by the canal when he was meant to have been to the early Mass up in the church on the corner. He told them that there was no point in his staying on at school, as there was nothing more he needed to learn from them.

They were hiring office staff up at Hall's, the big builders' merchants, and they would train him in office routine. He might as well go to work straightaway rather than hang about.

The Brothers and the teachers at his school said it was always a pity to see a boy study and leave without a qualification, but still, they said, shrugging, it was very hard trying to interest the lad in anything at all. He seemed to be sitting and waiting for his schooldays to end. Could even be for the best if he left school now. Get him into Hall's; give him a wage every week and then they might see where, if anywhere, his interest lay.

Josie and Charles thought sadly of the fund that had been growing in the post office for years. Money that would never be spent making Noel into a reverend. A kindly Brother suggested that maybe they should spend it on a holiday for themselves, but Charles and Josie were shocked. This money had been saved for God's work; it would be spent on God's work.

Noel got his place in Hall's. He met his work colleagues but without any great enthusiasm. They would not be his friends and companions any more than his fellow students at the Brothers had become mates. He didn't *want* to be alone all the time, but it was often easier.

Over the years Noel had arranged with his mother that he would not join them at meals. He would have his lunch in the middle of the day and he would make a snack for himself in the evening. This way he missed the Rosary, the socializing with pious neighbors and the interrogation about what he had done with his day, which was the natural accompaniment to mealtimes in the Lynch household.

He took to coming home later and later. He also took to visiting Casey's pub on the journey home—a big barn of a place, both comforting and anonymous at the same time. It was familiar because everyone knew his name.

"I'll drop it down to you, Noel," the loutish son of the house would say. Old Man Casey, who said little but noticed everything, would look over his spectacles as he polished the beer glasses with a clean linen cloth.

"Evening, Noel," he would say, managing to combine the courtesy of being the landlord with the sense of disapproval he had of Noel. He was, after all, an acquaintance of Noel's father. It was as if he were glad that Casey's was getting the price of the pint—or several pints—as the night went on but as well as this he seemed disappointed that Noel was not spending his wages more wisely. Yet Noel liked the place. It wasn't a trendy pub with fancy prices. It wasn't full of girls giggling and interrupting a man's drinking. People left him alone here.

That was worth a lot.

When he got home, Noel noticed that his mother looked different. He couldn't work out why. She was wearing the red knitted suit that she wore only on special occasions. At the biscuit factory where she worked they wore a uniform, which she said was wonderful because it meant you didn't wear out your good garments. Noel's mother didn't wear makeup so it couldn't be that.

Eventually he realized that it was her hair. His mother had been to a beauty salon.

"You got a new hairdo, Mam!" he said.

Josie Lynch patted her head, pleased. "They did a good job, didn't they?" She spoke like someone who frequented hairdressing salons regularly.

"Very nice, Mam," he said.

"I'll be putting a kettle on if you'd like a cup of tea," she offered.

"No, Mam, you're all right." He was anxious to be out of there, safe in his room. And then Noel remembered that his cousin Emily was coming from America the next day. His mother must be getting ready for her arrival. This Emily was going to stay for a few weeks, apparently. It hadn't been decided exactly how many weeks. . . .

Noel hadn't involved himself greatly in the visit, doing only what he had to, like helping his father to paint her room and clearing out the downstairs storage room, where they had tiled the walls and put in a new shower. He didn't know much about her; she was an older person, in her fifties, maybe, the only daughter of his father's eldest brother, Martin. She had been an art teacher but her job had ended unexpectedly and she was using her savings to see the world. She would start with a visit to Dublin, from where her father had left many years ago to seek his fortune in America.

It had not been a great fortune, Charles reported. The eldest brother of the family had worked in a bar, where he was his own best customer. He had never stayed in touch. Any Christmas cards had been sent by this Emily, who had also written to tell first of her father's death and then her mother's. She sounded remarkably businesslike and said that when she arrived in Dublin she would expect to pay a contribution to the family expenses and that since she was letting her own small apartment in New York during her absence, it was only fair. Josie and Charles were also reassured that she seemed sensible and had promised not to be in their way or looking for entertainment. She said she would find plenty to occupy her.

Noel sighed.

It would be one more trivial happening elevated to high drama by his mother and father. The woman wouldn't be in the door before she heard all about his great future at Hall's, about his mother's job at the biscuit factory and his father's role as a senior porter in a very grand hotel. She would be told about the moral decline in Ireland, the lack of attendance at Sunday Mass and that binge drinking kept the emergency departments of hospitals full to overflowing. Emily would be invited to join the family Rosary.

Noel's mother had already spent considerable time debating whether they should put a picture of the Sacred Heart or of Our Lady of Perpetual Succour in the newly painted room. Noel had managed to avoid too much further discussion of this agonizing choice by suggesting that they wait until she arrived.

"She taught art in a school, Mam. She might have brought her own pictures," he had said, and amazingly his mother had agreed immediately.

"You're quite right, Noel. I have a tendency to make all the decisions in the world. It will be nice having another woman to share all that with."

Noel mildly hoped that she was right and that this woman would not disrupt their ways. This was going to be a time of change in their household anyway. His father was going to be retired as porter in a year or two. His mother still had a few more years in the biscuit factory but she thought she might retire also and keep Charles company, with the two of them doing some good works. He hoped that Emily would make their lives less complicated rather than more complicated.

But mainly he gave the matter very little thought.

Noel got by well by not thinking too deeply on anything: not about his dead-end job in Hall's; not about the hours and money he spent in Old Man Casey's pub; not about the religious mania of his parents, who thought that the Rosary was the answer to most of the world's problems. Noel would not think about the lack of a steady girlfriend in his life. He just hadn't met anyone, that's all it was. Nor indeed did he worry about the lack of any kind of mates. Some places were easy to find friends. Hall's wasn't one of those places. Noel had decided that the very best way to cope with things not being so great was not to think about them at all. It had worked well so far.

Why fix things if they weren't broken?

Charles Lynch had been very silent. He hadn't noticed his wife's new hairdo. He hadn't guessed that his son had drunk four pints on the way home from work. He found it hard to raise any interest in the arrival next morning of his brother Martin's daughter, Emily. Martin had made it clear that he had no interest in the family back home.

Emily had certainly been a courteous correspondent over the years—even to the point of offering to pay her bed and board. That might come in very useful indeed these days. Charles Lynch had been told that morning that his services as hotel porter would no longer be needed. He and another "older" porter would leave at the end of the month. Charles had been trying to find the words to tell Josie since he got home, but the words weren't there.

He could repeat what the young man in the suit had said to him earlier in the day: a string of sentences about it being no reflection on Charles or his loyalty to the hotel. He had been there, man and boy, resplendent in his uniform and very much part of the old image. But that's exactly what it was—an old image. The new owners were insisting on a new image, and who could stand in the way of the march of progress?

Charles had thought he would grow old in that job. That one day there would be a dinner for him where Josie would go and wear a long frock. He would be presented with a gold-plated clock. Now none of this was going to happen.

He was going to be without a job in two and a half weeks' time.

There were few work opportunities for a man in his sixties who had been let go from the one hotel where he had worked since he was sixteen. Charles Lynch would have liked to have talked to his son about it all, but he and Noel didn't seem to have had a conversation for years now. If ever. The boy was always anxious to get to his room and resisted any questions or discussions. It wouldn't be fair to lay all this on him now.

Charles wouldn't find a sympathetic ear or any font of advice. Just tell Josie and get it over with, he told himself. But she was up to high doh about this woman coming from America. Maybe he should leave it for a couple of days. Charles sighed again about the bad timing of it all.

Dear Emily,

I wish that you hadn't decided to go to Ireland. I will miss you greatly.

I wish you had let me come and see you off . . . but then you were always one for the quick, impulsive decision. Why should I expect you to change now?

I know that I *should* say that I hope you will find all your heart's desire in Dublin, but in a way I don't want you to. I want you to say it was wonderful for six weeks and then for you to come back home again.

It's not going to be the same without you here. There's an exhibit opening and it's just up the street and I can't bring myself to go to it on my own. I won't go to nearly as many theater matinees as I did with you.

I'll collect your rent every Friday from the student who's renting your apartment. I'll keep an eye open in case she is growing any attitude-changing substances in your window boxes.

You must write and tell me all about the place you are staying—don't leave anything out. I am so glad you will have your laptop with you. There will be no excuse for you not to stay in touch. I'll keep telling you small bits of news about Eric in the suitcase store. He really IS interested in you, Emily, whether you believe it or not!

I'll hear all about your arrival in the land of the Shamrock when you get your laptop up and running and read this.

Love from your lonely friend,
Betsy

Hi, Betsy,

What makes you think that I would have to wait to get to Ireland to hear from you? I'm at Kennedy Airport and the machine works.

Nonsense! You won't miss me—you and your fevered imagination! You will have a thousand fantasies. Eric does not fancy me, not even remotely. He is a man of very few words and none of them are small talk. He speaks about me to you because he is too shy to speak to you. Surely you know that?

I'll miss you too, Bets, but this is something I have to do.

I swear that I will keep in touch. You'll probably get twenty e-mails from me every day and wish you hadn't encouraged me!

Love,
Emily

"I wonder, should we have gone out to the airport to meet her?" Josie Lynch said for the fifth time next morning.

"She said she would prefer to make her own way here," Charles said, as he had on the previous four occasions.

Noel just drank his mug of tea and said nothing.

"She wrote and said the plane could be in early if they got a good wind behind them." Josie spoke as if she were a frequent flyer herself.

"So she could be here any time . . . ," Charles said with a heavy heart. He hated having to go in to the hotel this morning knowing that his days there were numbered. There would be time enough to tell Josie once this woman had settled in. Martin's daughter! He hoped that she hadn't inherited her father's great thirst.

There was a ring at the doorbell. Josie's face was all alarm. She snatched Noel's mug of tea from him and swept up the empty eggcup and plate from in front of Charles. Patting her new hairdo again, she spoke in a high, false voice.

"Answer the door please, Noel, and welcome your cousin Emily in."

Noel opened the door to a small woman, forty-something, with frizzy hair and a cream-colored raincoat. She had two neat red suitcases on wheels. She looked entirely in charge of the situation. First time in the country and she had found St. Jarlath's Crescent with no difficulty.

"You must be Noel. I hope I'm not too early for the household."

"No, we were all up. We're about to go to work, you see; and you are very welcome, by the way."

"Thank you. Well, shall I come in and say hello and good-bye to them?"

Noel realized that he might have left her forever on the doorstep, but then he was only half awake. It took him until about eleven a.m., when he had his first vodka and Coke, to be fully in control of the day. Noel was absolutely certain that nobody at Hall's knew of his morning injection of alcohol and his midafternoon booster. He covered himself very carefully and always allowed a bottle of genuine Diet Coke to peek out of his duffel bag. The vodka was added from a separate source when he was alone.

He brought the small American woman into the kitchen, where his mother and father kissed her on the cheek and said this was a great day that Martin Lynch's daughter had come back to the land of her ancestors.

"See you this evening then, Noel," she called.

"Yes, of course. I might be a bit late. Lots of things to catch up on. But settle in well. . . ."

"I will, and thank you for agreeing to share your home with me."

He left them to it. As he pulled the door behind him he could hear the pride in his mother's voice as she showed off the newly decorated downstairs bedroom. And he could hear his cousin Emily cry out that it was just perfect.

Noel thought his father had been very quiet today and last night. But then he was probably just imagining it. His father didn't have a care in the world, just as long as they made a fuss of him in that hotel and while he was sure there would be the Rosary every evening, an annual visit to Lourdes to see the shrine and talk of going farther afield one day, like maybe Rome or the Holy Land. Charles Lynch was lucky enough to be a man who was content with things the way they were. He didn't need to numb himself against the dead weight of days and nights by spending long hours drinking alcohol in Old Man Casey's.

Noel walked to the end of the road, where he would catch his bus. He walked as he did every morning, nodding to people but seeing nothing, noting no details about his surroundings. He wondered mildly what that busy-looking American woman would make of it all here.

Probably she would stick to it for about a week before she gave up in despair.

At the biscuit factory Josie told them all about the arrival of Emily, who had found her own way to St. Jarlath's Crescent as if she had been born and reared there. Josie said she was an extremely nice person who had offered to make the supper for everyone that night. They were just to tell her what they liked and didn't like and point her to the market. She didn't need to go to bed and rest, apparently, because she had slept overnight on the plane coming over. She had admired everything in the house and said that gardening was her hobby so she would look out for a few plants when she went shopping. If they didn't mind, of course.

The other women said that Josie should consider herself lucky. This American could have easily turned out to be very difficult indeed.

At the hotel, Charles was his normal, pleasant self to everyone he met. He carried suitcases in from taxis, he directed tourists out towards the sights of Dublin, he looked up the times of theater performances, he looked down at the sad face of a little fat King Charles spaniel that had been tied to the hotel railing. Charles knew this little dog: Caesar. He was often attached to Mrs. Monty—an eccentric, titled old lady who wore a huge hat and three strands of pearls, a fur coat and nothing else. If anyone angered her, she opened her coat, rendering them speechless.

The fact that she had left the dog there meant she must have been taken into a psychiatric hospital. If the past was anything to go by, she would discharge herself from the hospital after about three days and come to collect Caesar and take him back to his unpredictable life with her.

Charles sighed.

Last time, he had been able to conceal the dog in the hotel until Mrs. Monty came back to get him, but things were different now. He would take the dog home at lunchtime. Josie wouldn't like it. Not at all. But St. Francis had written the book as far as animals were concerned. If it came to a big, dramatic row Josie wouldn't go against St. Francis. He hoped that his brother's daughter didn't have any allergies or attitudes towards dogs. She looked far too sensible.

Emily had spent a busy morning shopping. She was surrounded by food when Charles came in. Immediately, she made him a mug of tea and a cheese sandwich.

Charles was grateful for this. He had thought that he was about to miss lunch altogether. He introduced Emily to Caesar and told her some of the story behind his arrival in St. Jarlath's Crescent.

Emily Lynch seemed to think it was the most natural thing in the world. "I wish I had known he was coming. I could have gotten him a bone," she said. "Still, I met that nice Mr. Carroll, your neighbor. He's a butcher. He might get me one." She hadn't been here five minutes and she had got to know the neighbors!

Charles looked at her with admiration. "Well, aren't you a real bundle of energy," he said. "You took your retirement very early for someone as fit as you are."

"Oh, no, I didn't choose retirement," Emily said, as she trimmed the pastry crust around the pie. "No, indeed, I loved my job. They let me go. Well, they said I *must* go, actually."

"Why? Why did they do that?" Charles was shocked.

"Because they thought that I was old and cautious and always very much the same. It was a question of my being the old style. The old guard. I would take children to visit galleries and exhibits. They would have a sheet of paper with twenty questions on it and they would spend a morning there trying to find answers. I thought that it gave them a great grounding in how to look at a picture or a sculpture. Well, I thought so, anyway. Then came this new principal, a child himself, with the notion that teaching art was all about free expression. He really wanted a recent graduate who knew how to do this. I didn't, so I had to go."

"They can't sack you for being mature, surely?" Charles was sympathetic. His own case was different. He was the public face of the hotel, they had told him, and these times meant the hotel's face must be a young face. That was logical in a cruel sort of way. But this Emily wasn't old. She wasn't fifty yet. They must have laws against that kind of discrimination.

"No, they didn't actually say I was dismissed. They just kept me in the background doing filing, away from the children, out of the art studio. It was unbearable, so I left. But they had forced me to go."

"Were you upset?"

"Oh, yes, at the start. I was very upset indeed. It kind of made nothing of all the work I had done for years. I had gotten accustomed to meeting people at art galleries who often said, 'Miss Lynch, you started off my whole interest in art,' and so I thought it was all written off when they let me go. Like saying I had contributed nothing."

Charles felt tears in his eyes. She was describing exactly his own years as porter in the hotel. Written off. That's what he felt.

But Emily had cheered up. She put twirly bits of pastry on top of the pie and cleared the kitchen table swiftly. "But my friend Betsy told me that I was crazy to sit sulking in my corner. I should resign at once and set about doing what I had really wanted to do. Begin the rest of my life, she called it."

"And did you?" Charles asked. Wasn't America a wonderful place! *He* wouldn't be able to do that here—not in a million years.

"Yes, I did. I sat down and made a list of what I wanted to do. Betsy was right. If I had gotten a post in some other school maybe the same thing would have happened. I had a small savings account, so I could afford to be without paid work for a while. Trouble was I didn't know exactly what I wanted to do, so I did several things.

"First I took a cooking course. Tra-la-la. That's why I can make a chicken pie so quickly. And then I went to an intensive course and learned to use computers and the Internet properly so I could get a job in any office if I wanted to. Then I went to this garden center where they had window-box and planter classes. So now that I am full of skills I decided to go and see the world."

"And Betsy? Did she do that too?"

"No. She already understood the Internet and she doesn't want to cook because she's always on a diet, but she did share the window-box addiction with me."

"And suppose they asked you back to your old job. Would you go?"

"No. I can't now, even if they *did* ask. No, these days I'm much too busy," Emily said.

"I see." Charles nodded. He seemed about to say something else but stopped himself. He fussed about getting more milk for the tea.

Emily knew he wanted to say something; she knew how to listen. He would say it eventually.

"The thing is," he said slowly and with great pain, "the real thing is that these new brooms which are meant to be sweeping clean, they sweep away a lot of what was valuable and important as well as sweeping out cobwebs or whatever. . . ."

Emily saw it then. This would have to be handled carefully. She looked at him sympathetically. "Have another mug of tea, Uncle Charles."

"No, I have to get back," he said.

"Do you? I mean think about it for a moment, Uncle Charles. Do you have to? What more can they do to you? I mean that they haven't done already. . . ."

He gave her a long, level look.

She understood.

This woman he had never met until this morning realized, without having to be told, exactly what had happened to Charles Lynch. Something that his own wife and son hadn't seen at all.

. . .

The chicken pie that evening was a great success. Emily had made a salad as well. They talked easily, all three of them, and Emily introduced the subject of her own retirement.

"It's just amazing—the very thing you most dread can turn out to be a huge blessing in disguise! I never realized until it was over that I spent so much of my life on trains and crosstown buses. No wonder there were no hours left to learn the Internet and small-scale gardening."

Charles watched in admiration. Without ever appearing to have done so, she was making his path very smooth. He could tell Josie tomorrow, but maybe he would tell her now, this very minute.

It was much easier than he would ever have believed possible. He explained slowly that he had been thinking for a long time about leaving the hotel. The matter had come up recently in conversation and, amazingly, it turned out that it would suit the hotel too and so the departure would be by mutual agreement. All he had to do now was make sure that he was going to get some kind of reasonable compensation.

He said that for the whole afternoon his head had been bursting with ideas for what he would like to do.

Josie was taken aback. She looked at Charles anxiously in case this was just a front. Perhaps he was only blustering when inside he was very upset. But inasmuch as she could see he seemed to be speaking from the heart.

"I suppose it's what Our Lord wants for you," she said piously.

"Yes, and I'm grabbing it with both hands." Charles Lynch was indeed telling the truth. He had not felt so liberated for a long time. Since talking to Emily today at lunchtime, he had begun to feel that there was a whole world out there.

Emily moved in and out, clearing dishes and bringing in some dessert, and from time to time she entered the conversation easily. When her uncle said he had to walk Mrs. Monty's dog until she was released from wherever she was, Emily suggested that Charles could mind other people's dogs as well.

"That nice man Paddy Carroll, the butcher, has a huge dog named Dimples who needs to lose at least ten pounds," she said enthusiastically.

"I couldn't ask Paddy for money," Charles protested.

Josie agreed with him. "You see, Emily, Paddy and Molly Carroll are neighbors. It would be odd to ask them to pay Charles to walk that big foolish dog. It would sound very grasping."

"I see that, of course, and you wouldn't want to be grasping, but then again he might see a way to giving you some lamb chops or best ground beef from time to time." Emily was a great believer in barter, and Charles seemed to think that this was completely possible.

"But would there be a real job, Emily, you know, a *profession,* a life like Charles had in the hotel, where he was a person that mattered?" Josie asked.

"I wouldn't survive just with dog walking alone, but maybe I could get a job in a kennel—I'd really love that," Charles said.

"And if there was anything else that you had both *really* wanted to do?" Emily was gentle. "You know, I so enjoyed looking up all my roots and making a family tree. Not that I'm suggesting that to you, of course."

"Well, do you know what we always wanted to do?" Josie began tentatively.

"No. What is that?" Emily was interested in everything so she was easy to talk to.

Josie continued. "We always thought that it was a pity that St. Jarlath was never properly celebrated in this neighborhood. I mean our street is called after him, but nobody you'd meet knows a thing about him. Charles and I were thinking we might raise money to erect a statue to his memory."

"A statue to St. Jarlath! Imagine!" Emily was surprised. Perhaps she had been wrong to have encouraged them to be freethinkers. "Wasn't he rather a long time ago?" She was careful not to throw any cold water on Josie's plan, especially when she saw Charles light up with enthusiasm.

Josie waved this objection away. "Oh, that's no problem. If he's a saint, does it matter if he died only a few years back or in the sixth century?"

"The *sixth* century?" This was even worse than Emily had feared.

"Yes, he died around A.D. 540 and his Feast Day is June sixth."

"And that would be a very suitable time of the year for a little procession to his shrine." Charles was busy planning it all already.

"And was he from around these parts?" Emily asked. Apparently not. Jarlath was from the other side of the country, the Atlantic coast. He had set up the first archdiocese of Tuam. He had taught other great holy men, even other saints: St. Brendan of Clonfert and St. Colman of Cloyne. Places that were miles away.

"But there was always a devotion to him here," Charles explained.

"Why would they have named the street after him otherwise?" Josie wanted to know.

Emily wondered what would have happened if her father, Martin Lynch, had stayed here. Would he have been a simple, easily pleased person like Charles and Josie instead of the discontented drunk that he had turned into in New York? But all this business about the saint who had died miles away, hundreds of years ago, was a fantasy, surely?

"Of course, the problem would be raising the money for this statue *and* actually earning a living at the same time," Emily said.

That was apparently no problem at all. They had saved money for years, hoping to put it towards the education of Noel as a priest. To give a son to God. But it hadn't taken. They always intended that those savings be given to God in some way, and now this was the perfect opportunity.

Emily told herself that she must not try to change the world. No time now to consider all the good causes that that money could have gone towards—many of them even run by the Catholic Church. Emily would have preferred to see it all going to look after Josie and Charles, and give them a little comfort after a life of working long, hard hours for little reward. They'd had to endure what to them must have been a tragedy—their son's vocation "hadn't taken," to use their own words. But there were some irresistible forces that could never be fought with logic and practicality. Emily Lynch knew this for certain.

Noel had been through a long, bad day. Mr. Hall had asked him twice if he was all right. There was something behind the question, something menacing. When he had asked for the third time, Noel inquired politely why he was asking.

"There was an empty bottle which appears to have contained gin before it was empty," Mr. Hall said.

"And what has that to do with me and whether I'm all right or not?" Noel asked. He was confident now, emboldened, even.

Mr. Hall looked at him long and sternly from under his bushy eyebrows. "That's as may be, Noel. There's many a fellow taking the plane to some faraway part of the world who would be happy to do the job you are meant to be doing." He walked off and Noel saw other workers look away.

Noel had never known Mr. Hall like this—usually there was a kindly remark, some kind of encouragement about continuing in this work of matching dockets to sales slips, of looking through ledgers and invoices and doing the most lowly clerk duties imaginable.

Mr. Hall seemed to think that Noel could do better and had made many positive suggestions in earlier days. Times when there was some hope. But not now. This was more than a reprimand; it was a warning. It had shaken him, and on the way home he found his feet taking him into Casey's big, comforting pub. He vaguely recalled having had one too many the last time he'd been here but he hesitated for only a moment before going in.

Mossy, the son of Old Man Casey, looked nervous. "Ah, Noel, it's yourself."

"Could I have a pint, please, Mossy?"

"Ah, now, that's not such a good idea, Noel. You know you're barred. My father said . . ."

"Your father says a lot of things in the heat of the moment. That barring order is long over now."

"No, it's not, Noel. I'm sorry, but there it is."

Noel felt a tick in his forehead. He must be careful now.

"Well, that's his decision and yours. As it happens, I have given up drink and what I was actually asking for was a pint of lemonade."

Mossy looked at him openmouthed. Noel Lynch off the liquor? Wait till his father heard this!

"But if I'm not welcome in Casey's, then I'll have to take my custom elsewhere. Give my best to your father." Noel made as if to leave.

"When did you give up the gargle?" Mossy asked.

"Oh, Mossy, that's not any of your concern these days. You must go ahead serving alcohol to folks here. Am I interfering with your right to do this? I am most definitely not."

"Wait a minute, Noel," Mossy called out to him.

Noel said he was sorry but he had to go now. And he walked, head high, out of the place where he had spent so much of his leisure time.

There was a cold wind blowing down the street as Noel leaned against the wall and thought over what he had just said. He had spoken only in order to annoy Mossy, a foolish, mumbling mouthpiece for his father's decisions. Now he had to live with his words. He could never drink in Casey's again.

He would have to go to that place where Declan Carroll's father went with his huge bear of a dog. The place where nobody had friends or mates or people they met there. They called them "Associates." Muttie Scarlet was always about to confer with his Associates over the likely outcome of a big race or a soccer match. Not a place that Noel had enjoyed up to now.

Wouldn't it be much easier if he really *had* given up drink? Then Mr. Hall could find whatever bottles he liked. Mr. Casey would be regretful and apologetic, which would be a pleasure to see. Noel himself would have all the time in the world to go back to doing the things he really wanted. He might go back and get a business certificate so as to qualify for a promotion. Maybe even move out of St. Jarlath's Crescent.

Noel went for a long, thoughtful walk around Dublin, up the canal, down through the Georgian squares. He looked into restaurants where men of his own age were sitting across tables from girls. Noel wasn't a social outcast, he was just in a world of his own making where these kind of women were never available. And why was this? Because Noel was too busy with his snout in the trough.

It would not be like this anymore. He was going to give himself the twin gifts of sobriety and time: much more time. He checked his watch before letting himself into Number 23 St. Jarlath's Crescent. They would all be safely in bed by now. This was such an earthshaking decision he didn't want to muddy it all up with conversation.

He was wrong. They were all up, awake and alert at the kitchen table. Apparently his father was going to leave the hotel where he had worked all his life. They appeared to have adopted a tiny King Charles spaniel called Caesar, with enormous eyes and a soulful expression. His mother was planning to work fewer hours at the biscuit factory. His cousin Emily had met most of the people in the neighborhood and become firm friends with them all. And, most alarming of all, they were about to start a campaign to build a statue to some saint who, if he had ever existed, had died fifteen hundred years ago.

They had all been normal when he left the house this morning. What could have happened?

He wasn't able to manage his usual maneuver of sliding into his room and retrieving a bottle from the box labeled ART SUPPLIES, which contained mainly unused paintbrushes and unopened bottles of gin or wine.

Not, of course, that he was ever going to drink them again.

He had forgotten this. A sudden, heavy gloom settled over him as he sat there trying to comprehend the bizarre changes that were about to take place in his home. There would be no comforting oblivion afterwards, instead, it would be a night of trying to avoid the ART SUPPLIES box or maybe even pouring the contents down the hand basin in his room.

He struggled to make out what his father was talking about: walking dogs, minding pets, raising money, restoring St. Jarlath to his rightful place. In all his years of drinking, Noel had not come across anything as surreal and unexpected as this scene. And all this on a night when he was totally sober.

Noel shifted in his seat slightly and tried to catch the eye of his cousin Emily. She must be responsible for all this sudden change of heart: the idea that today was the first day of everybody's life. Mad, dangerous stuff in a household that had known no change for decades.

In the middle of the night, Noel woke up and decided that giving up drink was something that should not be taken lightly or casually. He would do it next week, when the world had settled down. But when he reached for the bottle in the box, he felt, with a clarity that he had not often known, that somehow next week would never come. So he poured the contents of two bottles of gin down his sink, followed by two bottles of red wine.

He went back to bed and tossed and turned until he heard his alarm clock the next morning.

In her bedroom, Emily opened her laptop and sent a message to Betsy:

> I feel that I have lived here for several years and yet I have not spent one night in the country!

> I have arrived at a time of amazing change. Everyone in this household has begun some kind of journey. My father's brother was fired from his job as a hotel porter and is now going to go into a dog-walking business, his wife is hoping to reduce *her* hours at her place of employment and set up a petition to get a statue erected to a saint who has been dead for—wait for it—fifteen hundred years!

The son of the house, who is some kind of recluse, has chosen this, of all days, to give up his love affair with alcohol. I can hear him flushing bottles of the stuff down the drain in his bedroom.

Why did I think it would be peaceful and quiet here, Betsy? Have I discovered *anything* about life or am I condemned to wander the earth learning little and understanding nothing?

Don't answer this question. It's not really a question, more a speculation. I miss you.

Love,
Emily

Chapter Two

Father Brian Flynn could not sleep in his small apartment in the heart of Dublin. He had just heard that day that he had only three weeks to find a new place to stay. He hadn't many possessions, so moving would not be a nightmare. But neither had he any money to speak of. He couldn't afford a smart place to live.

He hated leaving this little flat. His pal Johnny had found him this entirely satisfactory place to live, only minutes from his work in the immigrant center, and only seconds from one of the best pubs in Ireland. He knew everyone in the area. It was worrying to have to move.

"Couldn't the Archbishop find you a place?" Johnny was unsympathetic. He himself was going to move into his girlfriend's place. This wasn't a solution open to a middle-aged Catholic priest. Johnny was in the habit of saying to anyone who would listen that a man must be certifiably mad to be a priest in this day and age and the least the Archbishop of Dublin could do was provide lodgings for all these poor eejits who had given up anything that mattered in life and went around doing good day and night.

"Ah, it's not really the Archbishop's job. He has more important things to do," Brian Flynn said, "but it should be no trouble to find a place."

It was proving more troublesome than he had thought possible. And there were only twenty days to go.

Brian Flynn could not believe the amounts people were asking as rent. Surely they could never get sums like that? In the middle of a recession as well! Other things kept him awake too. The appalling priest who had broken his leg in Rome falling down the Spanish Steps and who was *still* out there eating grapes in an Italian hospital. Father Flynn was therefore *still* acting chaplain in St. Brigid's Hospital, with all the many complications that this added to his life.

He kept hearing reports from his old parish in Rossmore. His mother, who was already fairly confused and in a home for the elderly, was thought to have seen a vision, but it turned out she was talking about the television, and everyone in the old people's home was greatly disappointed.

He found himself increasingly brooding about the meaning of life now that he had to see so much of the end of life in St. Brigid's. Look at that poor girl Stella who seemed to like him just because he had arranged for a hairdresser to come in and visit her. She was pregnant as well as dying. She had lived a short and vaguely unsatisfactory life but then she told him that almost everyone else did as well. She seemed not even marginally interested in preparing to meet her Maker, and Father Flynn was always very firm about this; unless the patients brought the matter up themselves, it wasn't mentioned. They knew what his job description was, for heaven's sake. If they wanted intervention made, prayers said or sins forgiven, then he would do that; otherwise he wouldn't mention the topic.

He and Stella had had many good conversations about single-malt whiskey, about the quarterfinals in the soccer World Cup, about the unequal division of wealth in the world. She said that she had one more thing to do before she was off to the next world, whatever it might bring. Just one thing. But she had a sort of hope that it was all going to work out all right. And could Father Flynn kindly ask that nice hairdresser to come again fairly soon? She needed to look well when she did this one last thing.

Father Flynn paced his small apartment with the soccer posters nailed to the wall to cover the damp patches. Maybe he would ask Stella did she know anywhere for him to live. It might be tactless since he *was* going to live and she wasn't, but it would be better than looking into her ravaged face and haunted eyes and trying to make sense of it all.

In St. Jarlath's Crescent, Josie and Charles Lynch whispered long and happily into the night. Imagine—this time last night they hadn't even met Emily and now their lives had been turned right around. They had a dog, they had a lodger and, for the first time in months, Noel had sat and talked to them. They had begun a campaign to have St. Jarlath recognized properly.

Things were better on every front.

And, amazingly, things continued well on every front.

A message came to the hotel from a psychiatric hospital saying that Caesar's mother, Mrs. Monty, was unavoidably detained there and that she hoped Caesar was being adequately looked after. The hotel manager, bewildered by this, was relieved to know that the matter was all in hand and somewhat embarrassed to learn that the rescuer had been that old porter he had just made redundant. Charles Lynch seemed to bear him no ill will but let slip the fact that he was looking forward to some kind of retirement ceremony. The manager made a note to remind himself or someone to organize something for the fellow.

At the biscuit factory they were surprised to hear that Josie was going to work part-time and raise money for a statue to St. Jarlath. Most of the others who worked with her were desperate to hold on to their jobs at any cost.

"We'll have to give you a great sendoff when you finally retire, Josie," one of the women said.

"I'd really prefer a contribution to the St. Jarlath's statue fund," Josie said. And there was a silence not normally known in the biscuit factory.

. . .

Noel Lynch found the days endless in Hall's Builders' Merchants. The mornings were hard to endure without any alcohol. The nice fuzzy afternoons were gone and replaced now by hours of mind-numbing checking of delivery dockets against sales slips. His only pleasure was leaving a glass of mineral water on his desk and watching from the distance as Mr. Hall either smelled it or tasted it.

Noel could see only too well that his job could easily be done by a not-very-bright twelve-year-old. It was hard to know how the company had survived as long as it had. But in spite of everything he stuck to it, and before too long he was able to chalk up a full week without alcohol.

Matters were much helped by Emily's presence at Number 23. Every evening there was a well-cooked meal served at seven o'clock and, with no long evenings to spend in Casey's bar, Noel found himself sitting at the kitchen table eating with his parents and cousin.

They fell into an easy routine: Josie set the table and prepared the vegetables, Charles built up the fire and helped Noel to wash up. Emily had even managed to put off the Rosary on the grounds that they all needed this joint time to plan their various crusades, such as what strategy they should use to get the fund-raising started for St. Jarlath's statue and how Emily could go out and earn a living for herself and where they would find dogs for Charles to walk and if Noel should do night classes in business or accountancy in order to advance himself at Hall's.

Emily had, in one week, managed to get more information out of Noel about the nature of his work than his parents had learned in years. She had even been able to collect brochures, which she went over with Noel. This course looked good, but rather too general; the other looked more specific, but might not be relevant to his work at Hall's. Little by little, she had learned of the mundane clerical officer–type work Noel did all day—the matching of invoices, paying of suppliers and gathering of expenditure data from departments at the end of the month. She discovered that there were young fellows in the company who had "qualifications," who had a degree or a diploma, and they climbed up what passed for a corporate ladder in the old-fashioned builders' providers store that was Hall's.

Emily spent no time regretting time wasted in the past or wrong decisions or Noel's wish to leave his school and not continue with education. When they were alone one night, she said to him that the whole business of beating a dependency on alcohol was often a question of having adequate support.

"Did I ever tell you that I was battling against alcohol?" Noel asked her.

"You don't need to, Noel. I'm the daughter of an alcoholic. I know the territory. Your uncle Martin thought he could do it on his own. We lived through that one."

"Maybe he didn't choose AA. Maybe he wasn't a social man. He could have been a bit like me and didn't want a lot of other people knowing his business," Noel said in his late uncle's defense.

"He wasn't nearly as good a man as you are, Noel. He had a very closed mind."

"Oh, I think I have a closed mind too."

"No, you don't. You'll get help if you need it. I know you will."

"It's just I don't go along with this thing 'I'm Noel. I'm an alcoholic' and then they all say, 'Ho, Noel' and I'm meant to feel better."

"People have felt better for it," Emily said mildly. "They have a great success rate."

"It's all a matter of 'me and my illness'; it's making it so dramatic for them all, as if they are heroes of some kind of thing that's working itself out onstage."

Emily shrugged. "So AA doesn't do it for you. Fine. One day you might need them. They will still be there, that's for sure. Now let's look at these courses. I know what CPA means, but what are ACA and ACCA? Tell me the difference between them and what they mean."

And Noel could feel his shoulders relaxing. She wasn't going to nag him. That was the main thing. She had moved on and was asking his advice on other matters. Where could she get timber to make window boxes? Would his father be able to make them? Where might Emily get some regular paid work? She could run an office easily. Would it be a good idea to get a washing machine for the household, as they were all going to be so busy raising money for St. Jarlath's statue?

"Emily, you don't think that will really happen—the statue business, do you?"

"I was never more sure of anything in my life," Emily said.

Katie Finglas went to the hospital again. Stella Dixon looked worse than before: her face thin, her arms bony and her round stomach more noticeable.

"This has got to be a really good hairdo, Katie," Stella said, as she inhaled the cigarette down to her toes. As usual, the other patients kept watch in case a nurse or hospital official should come by and catch Stella in the act.

"Have you set your eye on someone?" Katie asked. She wished that she could take a group of her more difficult clients into this ward so they could see the skin-and-bones woman who knew nothing ahead of her except the certainty that she would die shortly after they did the cesarean section to remove her baby. It made their problems so trivial in comparison.

Stella considered the question. "It's a bit late for me to have my eye on anyone at this stage," she said. "But I *am* asking someone to do me a favor, so I have to look normal, you know, not mad or anything. That's why I thought a more settled type of hairstyle would be good."

"Right, we'll make you look settled," Katie said, taking out the plastic tray that she would put over the hand basin to wash Stella's thin, frail-looking head with its pre-Raphaelite mass of red curly hair. She had styled it already, but the curls kept coming back as if they had decided not to take any notice of the diagnosis that the rest of her body was having to cope with.

"What kind of a favor is it?" she asked, just to keep the conversation going.

"It's the biggest thing you could ever ask anyone to do," Stella said.

Katie looked at her sharply. The tone had changed and suddenly the fire and life had gone out of the girl who had entertained the ward and made people smuggle her in packets of cigarettes and do sentry duty so that she would not be discovered.

"Call for you, Noel," Mr. Hall said. Nobody ever telephoned Noel at work. The few calls he got came in through his cell phone. He went to Mr. Hall's office nervously. This was a time he would normally have had a drink; it was the low time of morning and he always liked a drink to help him cope with an unexpected event.

"Noel? Do you remember me, Stella Dixon? We met at the line dancing night last year."

"I do, indeed," he said, pleased. A lively redhead who could match him drink for drink. She had been good fun. Not someone he would want to meet now, though. Too interested in the gargle for him to meet up with her these days. "Yes, I remember you well," he added.

"We sort of drifted away from each other back then," she said.

It had been a while back. Nearly a year. Or was it six months? It was so hard to remember everything.

"That's right," Noel said evasively. Almost every friendship he had sort of drifted away, so there was nothing new about this.

"I need to see you, Noel," she said.

"I'm afraid I don't go out too much these days, Stella," he began. "Not into the old line dancing, I'm afraid."

"Me neither. I'm in the oncology ward of St. Brigid's, so in fact I don't go out at all."

He focused on trying to remember her: feisty, jokey, always playing it for a laugh. This was shocking news indeed.

"So would you like me to come and see you sometime? Is that it?"

"Please, Noel, today. At seven."

"Today . . . ?"

"I wouldn't ask unless it was important."

He saw Mr. Hall hovering. He must not be seen to dither. "See you then, Stella," he said, and wondered what on earth she wanted to see him about. But, even more urgently, he wondered how he could approach a cancer ward to visit a woman he barely remembered. *And* approach her without a drink.

It was more than any man could bear.

The corridors of St. Brigid's were crowded with visitors at seven o'clock. Noel threaded his way among them. He saw Declan Carroll, who lived up the road from him, walking ahead of him and ran to catch him up.

"Do you know where the female oncology ward is, Declan?"

"This lift over here will take you to the wing. Second floor." Declan didn't ask who Noel was visiting or why.

"I didn't know there were so many sick people," Noel said, looking at the crowds.

"Still, there's lots that can be done for them these times compared to when our parents were young." Declan was always one for the positive view.

"I suppose that's the way to look at it, all right," Noel agreed. He seemed a bit down, but then Noel was never a barrel of laughs.

"Right, Noel. Maybe I'll see you for a pint later? In Casey's, on our way home?"

"No. As a matter of fact, I don't drink anymore," Noel said in a tight little voice.

"Good man, yourself."

"And, anyway, I was actually barred from Casey's."

"Oh, well, to hell with them then. Big barn of a place anyway." Declan was being supportive, but he had a lot on his mind. Their first baby was due in the next several weeks and Fiona was up to high doh over everything. Plus his mother had knitted enough tiny garments for a multiple birth even though they knew they were going to have only one baby.

He could have done with a nice, undemanding pint with Noel. But that was obviously not on the cards now. He sighed and went purposefully towards a patient who was busy making plans to come out of hospital soon and wanted Declan to try to hurry up the process. The man's diagnosis said that he would never leave the hospital, sooner or later, and would die there within weeks. It was hard to rearrange your face to see something optimistic in this, but somehow Declan managed it.

It went with the territory.

There were six women in the ward. None of them had great, tumbling red curly hair.

One very thin woman in the corner bed was waving at him.

"Noel, Noel, it's Stella! Don't tell me I've changed *that* much!"

He was dismayed. She was skin and bone. She had clearly made a huge effort: her hair was freshly washed and blow-dried, she had a trace of lipstick on and she wore a white Victorian nightdress with a high neck and cuffs. He remembered her smile, but that was all.

"Stella. Good to see you," he mumbled.

She swung her thin legs out of the bed and gestured for him to pull the curtains around them.

"Any ciggies?" she whispered hopefully.

"In *here,* Stella?" He was shocked.

"Particularly in here. Well, you obviously didn't bring me any, so reach me my sponge bag there. The other girls will keep watch."

He looked on, horrified, as she pulled a cigarette from behind her toothpaste, lit it expertly and made a temporary ashtray out of an old envelope.

"How have you been?" he asked and instantly wished he hadn't. Of course she hadn't been well—otherwise why was she wasting away in front of his eyes in a cancer ward? "I mean, how are things?" he asked, even more foolishly.

"Things have been better, Noel, to be honest."

He tried to imagine what Emily might say in the circumstances. She had a habit of asking questions that required you to think.

"What's the very worst thing about it all, Stella?"

She paused to think, as he had known she would.

"I think the very worst thing is that you won't believe me," she said.

"Try me," he said.

She stood up and paced the tiny cubicle. It was then he realized that she was pregnant. Very pregnant. And at exactly that moment she spoke to him.

"I was hoping not to have to bother you about this, Noel, but you're the father. This is your baby."

"Ah, no, Stella, this is a mistake. This didn't happen."

"I know I'm not *very* memorable, but you must remember that weekend."

"We were wasted that weekend, both of us."

"Not too drunk to create a new life, apparently."

"I swear it can't be me. Honestly, Stella, if it were, I would accept . . . I wouldn't run away or anything . . . but . . . but . . ."

"But what, exactly?"

"There must have been lots of other people."

"Thanks a lot for that, Noel."

"You know what I mean. An attractive woman like you must have had lots of partners."

"I'm the one who knows. Do you honestly think I would pick *you* out of a list of candidates? That I'd phone you, a drunk in that mausoleum where you work, in some useless job? You live with your parents, for God's sake! Why would I ask *you*, of all people, to be the father of my child if it wasn't true?"

"Well, as you said yourself, thanks a lot for that." He looked hurt.

"So you asked me what would be the worst thing. I told you and now the worst *has* happened. You don't believe me." She had a defeated look.

"It's a fantasy. It didn't happen. I'd remember. I haven't slept with that many women in my life, and what good would I be to you anyway? I am, as you say, a useless drunk with a non-job in Hall's, living with my mother and father. I'd be no support to you. You'll be able to bring this child up fine, give him some guts, fight his battles for him, more than I would ever do. Do it yourself, Stella, and if you think I should make some contribution, and I don't want you to be short, I could give you something—not admitting anything—just to help you out."

Her eyes blazed at him.

"You are such a fool, Noel Lynch. Such a stupid fool. I won't bloody well be here to bring her up. I'm going to die in three or four weeks' time. I won't survive the operation. And the baby is not a boy, by the way, she's a girl, she's a daughter, her name is Frankie. That's what she's going to be called: Frances Stella."

"This is only a fantasy, Stella. This illness has made you very unhinged."

"Ask any of them in the ward. Ask any of the nurses. Wake up to the real world, Noel. This is happening. We have to do something about it."

"I can't raise a child, Stella. You've already listed all the things against it. Whatever chance she's going to have, it can't be with me."

"You're going to *have* to," Stella said. "Otherwise she'll have to go into care. And I'm not having that."

"But that would be the very best for her. There are families out there who are dying to have children of their own . . . ," he began, blustering slightly.

"Yes, and some other families, like the ones I met when I was in care, where the fathers and the uncles love to have a little plaything in the house. I've been through it all and Frankie's not going to have to cope with it just because she will have no mother."

"What are you asking me to do?"

"To mind your daughter, to give her a home and a secure childhood, to tell her that her mother wasn't all that bad. Fight her battles. The usual things."

"I can't do it." He stood up from his chair.

"There's so much to discuss . . . ," Stella began.

"It's not going to happen. I'm so sorry. And I'm really sorry to know how bad your illness is, but I think you're painting too black a picture. Cancer can be cured these days. Truly it can, Stella."

"Good-bye, Noel," she said.

No matter how often he said her name she would not turn towards him.

He walked to the door and looked around once more. She seemed to have shriveled even further. She looked tiny as she sat there on her bed. He fancied that the other women in the ward had heard most of their conversation. They looked at him with hostility.

On the bus home Noel realized that there was no way he could force himself to sit at the kitchen table eating a supper that Emily would have kept warm for him. Tonight was not a time to sit and talk about saints and statues and fund-raising and accountancy and business management classes. Tonight was a night to have three pints in some pub and forget everything. He headed for the pub where Paddy Carroll, Declan's father, took his huge Labrador dog every night. With any luck, at this time of night Noel might get away without being spotted.

The beer felt terrific. Like an old friend.

He had lowered four pints before he realized it.

Noel had hoped that he might have lost the taste for it, but that hadn't happened. He just felt a great sense of irritation and annoyance with himself that he had denied himself this familiar and friendly relaxation. Already he was feeling better. His hand had stopped shaking, his heart wasn't pounding as it had been.

He *must* stay clear and focused.

He would have to go back to St. Jarlath's Crescent and take up some semblance of ordinary life. Emily would, of course, see through him at once, but he could tell her later. Much later. No need to announce everything to everyone all at once. Or maybe no need to announce anything at all. It was, after all, some terrible mistake. Noel would *know* if he had fathered a child with that girl.

He would *know* it.

It had to have come from her mind having been affected by this cancer. Anybody normal would not have selected Noel, of all people, as the father of their child. Poor Stella was far from normal and he pitied her, but this was ludicrous.

It could not be his child.

He waved away the suggestion of a fifth pint and moved purposefully towards the door.

He didn't see Declan Carroll having a drink with his father and looking curiously at the man who had claimed to have given up alcohol but who had just downed four pints of beer at racing speed.

Declan sighed.

Whatever Noel had heard at the hospital, whoever he had visited, it had not made him happy.

Paddy Carroll patted his son's hand.

"In a matter of weeks it will all be behind you. You'll have a great little son and the waiting bit will be forgotten."

"Yes, Dad. Tell me what it was like when Mam was expecting me."

"I don't know how I survived it," Declan's father said, and told the old, familiar story again from the point of view of the father of the baby.

The mother's role in the birth had been merely minimal, apparently.

Noel had only opened his mouth when Emily looked up at him sharply. It was as if she had called the meeting to order.

"We're all tired now, it's late. Not a good time to discuss the running of a thrift shop."

"A what?" Noel shook his head as if that would somehow settle the collection of thoughts and ideas that were nestling in it. His parents looked disappointed. They were being carried along by the enthusiasm of Emily's planning and they were sorry to see it being cut short.

But Emily was adamant. She had the whole household ready for bed in no time.

"Noel, I saved you some Italian meatballs."

"They were just delicious," Josie said. "Emily can turn her hand to anything."

"I don't think I really want anything. I stopped on the way home, you see . . . ," Noel began.

"I did see," Emily said, "but these are good for you, Noel. Go on into your room and I'll bring a tray in to you in five minutes."

There was no escape.

He sat there waiting for her and the storm that would follow. Oddly there was no storm. She never mentioned the fact that he had taken up drinking again. And Emily had been right—he *did* feel better when he had something to eat. She was clearing up and about to go when she asked sympathetically if it had been a bad day.

"The worst ever," he said.

"Mr. Hall?"

"No, he was fine. Just something mad and upsetting happened later on in the day. That's why I went back to the pints."

"And did that help?" She seemed genuinely interested.

"At first it did a bit. It's not working now and I'm just annoyed with myself for staying off it for all those days and nights and now running straight back when I get a bit of an upset."

"Did you sort out the upset?" She was completely nonjudgmental. She looked at him, inviting him to share whatever it was, but she would have left if there was no information to hear.

"Please sit down, Emily," Noel begged, and he told the whole story, haltingly and with a lot of repetition. Mainly he said that he could not have fathered a child without remembering it.

"I have so little sex, Emily, that I'm not likely to forget the little bit I *do* have."

She was very still as she sat and listened to him. Her face changed from time to time. It was concerned and distressed when she heard how gaunt and painful Stella's face had become. She inclined her head to show sympathy as Noel told how Stella had said that if she were to choose a father from anyone in the world he would be the very last choice—a drunk who was a loser and still lived with his parents.

It was only when Noel came to the end of his tale, when he got to the part where he had walked away from Stella, the hospital and the problem, that Emily's face became confused.

"Why did you do that?" she asked.

"Well, what else could I do?" Noel was surprised. "It has nothing to do with *me*. There's no point in my being there—it's adding to the whole charade. The girl's head is unhinged."

"You walked out and left her there?"

"I *had* to, Emily. You know what a tightrope I'm walking. Things are quite bad enough already without inviting the Lord knows what kind of fantasies in on top of me."

"You say that things are bad enough for you, Noel? Right?"

"Well they *are* bad." He sounded defensive.

"Like you have terminal cancer?" she asked him. "Like you were abused when you were in foster care? Like you are going to be dead a month from now, before you see the only child you will ever have? No, indeed, Noel, none of these things has happened to you, yet you just said things are very bad for *you*."

He was stricken.

"That's all you think. You think how things are for *you*, Noel. Shame on you," she said, her face full of scorn. This was the nearest he had come to having a best friend and now she was turning against him.

"Emily, please sit down. You asked me what was wrong, so I told you."

"Yes, you did, Noel." She made no movement to sit down.

"So? Won't you stay and discuss it?"

"No. Why should I join in this charade, as you call it? Don't make faces at me, Noel. These are your words. Why should I not think of the perilous tightrope that *I* am walking in my life? I'm

sorry, but everyone in all this is becoming . . . what did you call it—
'unhinged in the head'? Why should I let people surround me with
their fantasies?" She was almost at the door.

"But they're not fantasies, Emily. It's what happened."

"That's right. They're not fantasies. It's what actually happened.
But hey, what the hell? It's got nothing to do with *you*, Noel. Good
night. I'm sorry, but that is all I feel capable of saying." And she was
gone.

He had thought that this day just couldn't get any worse. That's
why he had told her. In a few short hours two women had turned
away from him in disgust.

And somehow it had made the day worse than ever.

Betsy,

There is a drama unfolding here which we would have considered
compelling when we were kids and went to the movies on Saturday
afternoons. But oddly it's too sad to talk about just now. I will tell you
how it turns out.

OF COURSE you should go out with Eric! I told you a hundred times
he is not interested in me. He just said that as a devious way of
getting to know you better.

I know! I know! But the longer I live, the more crazy I think
everyone is.

Love,
Emily

Katie Finglas was locking up the hair salon. It had been a long day
and she was tired. It was Garry's night out. Once a week he and a
group of the lads kicked a ball around a pitch and planned strategy
for the year.

Katie would have loved to have gone home and had a long bath while he made them some French onion soup. Then they could have sat by the fire and talked about the big decision they had to make. People thought that Katie and Garry had plenty of time to talk to each other all day since they worked together in the salon. Little did people know how rarely they had a chance to snatch a five-minute coffee together. And then there were always people within earshot and it was impossible for Katie and Garry to talk about their plans.

So she was looking forward to a proper discussion. One where they would put all the arguments on one side and then the other. They would list the reasons why they *must* lease the flat over their salon: they needed to expand, they had no storage place, they had no proper staff areas, they would be able to install little manicure stations and could fit in tables and mirrors for at least six more customers, how it would mean that they would be able to compete on equal ground with the successful health and beauty salons in Dublin.

It was too much to take on. Too big and spread out so they would use only half the space upstairs. And just suppose they *did* do it— then they would have to do up some of the rooms and sublet them in order to try to get a return on their money. And just suppose that they did rent them—what kind of people would they get? Suppose they turned out to be the tenants from hell, making a lot of noise and leaving litter, making nonsense of all Katie and Garry's hard work?

Katie sighed as she set the alarm outside her premises.

Across the street she saw Father Flynn, that cheerful priest from the center down the road, the one who had introduced her to poor Stella Dixon up in St. Brigid's.

Stella had said that she didn't normally have a lot to say for the clergy, but Brian Flynn was a very decent fellow and didn't go on about sin and redemption and things. He did what a priest should do—he brought her cigarettes and did little jobs for people.

Katie called out to him and was delighted when he suggested they go for a coffee in a small Italian place on the corner.

Father Flynn spoke briefly and testily about his friend the priest who had fallen down the Spanish Steps and was still malingering in Rome. He also spoke about his greedy landlord, who had evicted him, and how it was impossible for a man of simple lifestyle, like himself, to discover any kind of budget accommodation.

"I'm such an undemanding person, really," Brian Flynn said, full of self-pity. "If people only *knew* how little I want in terms of style or comfort."

Katie looked at him thoughtfully across her cappuccino. "Exactly *how* undemanding?" she asked. She suddenly saw a solution to everything.

Father Flynn would be the perfect tenant.

"Finish up your coffee there and come with me," she said, draining her cup and heading back to the salon that she had just locked up.

By the end of the month, he had moved into his new home. His friend Johnny had put up a few bookshelves for him and Katie's husband had found him a secondhand fridge where he could keep his milk, butter and the odd can of beer. His only duty was to make sure that he locked the salon properly and put on the burglar alarm whenever he left the premises after hours. It suited everyone perfectly.

Chapter Three

Noel couldn't believe that Emily, who had recently been part of his every waking moment at St. Jarlath's Crescent, now seemed to have disappeared completely.

"Where is she?" he asked his mother on the morning after Emily had left his room in scorn and disgust. "It's not like Emily to miss breakfast."

"Oh, she's gone to find a premises for the charity shop," Josie Lynch replied, confident that Emily would have one before the day was out. There was nothing that woman couldn't do.

"She took Caesar with her. She's going to make inquiries for me about dog-walking opportunities as well." Charles was pleased too. "She said she'd have more credibility if she was accompanied by a dog herself when she went looking for business."

"She'll be back after lunch, Noel, if you wanted her for anything," Josie said. "She's going to the market for our supper later. What *did* we do before she came to stay?"

Noel hadn't known Emily to be out of the house for two meals in one day. Not since she had arrived. There was only one explanation. She was avoiding him.

He did try to stay off drink when he was at work, but the sharp pain of Stella's situation and Emily's shocked revulsion kept coming back to him as the day crawled along. When it came to midafternoon he could bear it no more and made an excuse to go out and get some more stationery supplies. He bought a half-bottle of vodka and decanted it into a bottle that already had a fizzy orange drink in it. As he drank mug after mug of it he felt the strength coming back to him and the pain receding. The familiar blur came down like a thick, comforting shawl.

Noel now felt able to face the afternoon again; but what didn't go away was the feeling that he was a loser who had let down three people: the dying Stella, his strong cousin Emily and an unborn child called Frankie, who could not possibly be his daughter.

But he should have handled it very differently.

Emily was in the Laundromat with Molly Carroll. She had brought towels for a service wash but actually she was there on a mission. On a previous visit she had noticed two large sheds that were not in use. They might form the basis of the new thrift shop that would help raise money for the statue. She had to take it one step at a time: find out who actually owned the premises first.

It had turned out to be much simpler than she had feared. Molly and Paddy Carroll had bought the sheds some years back when the owner had had some pressing gambling debts and was anxious for a quick sale. They had never needed the unused part of the premises but had been loath to sell it in case someone built a noisy takeaway food outlet.

Molly thought that a thrift shop would be perfect. She and Emily toured the place and decided to put shelves here and clothes rails there. They would have a secondhand book section and Emily said she could grow a few plants from seed and sell them too. Together they made a list of people to approach, those who might give a few hours every week to working in the charity shop.

Molly knew a man who had the unlikely name of Dingo. He was a decent soul and would help them with his van, collecting things or stacking them. Emily had met several women who said they would be happy to help, but were a little anxious in case they wouldn't be able to manage the till properly. Emily said she would check what permits they might need and if they had to apply for a change of premises; she promised she would deliver a fully planted window box to the Laundromat the following week to celebrate the whole deal. Molly said her husband Paddy's friend had a lot of Associates in the pub who could do the refurbishments.

They decided to call the place St. Jarlath's Thrift Shop, and Molly said it would be great to be partly in charge because if a nice jacket came in she could get first crack at it. Emily left with the air of someone who had completed a difficult and complicated assignment.

She stopped at a fishmonger and bought some smoked cod. Charles and Josie had not been great fish lovers or salad eaters when she arrived but, little by little, she was changing their ways. It was a pity that she couldn't do anything to direct Noel, but the boy had built a shield about himself that even she couldn't penetrate.

"Is there anything I can get you, Stella?" Father Flynn had brought her the usual pack of cigarettes.

"Not much, Brian, but thanks all the same." She looked very down, not her usual gutsy self.

He hesitated asking any more. The future was bleak for her. What helpful words could he find?

"Any visitors?" he asked.

Stella's eyes were dull. "No visitors to speak of," she said, and as he looked at her with sympathy and with the realization he had no comfort to give, he saw for the first time a tear in her eye.

"I'm no good with words, Stella," he began.

"You're fine with words, Brian, and with getting me fags and a hairdresser—for all the bloody use it was."

"Your hair looks very nice," he said hopelessly.

"Not nice enough to make that no-hoper believe me."

"Believe you about what, exactly?" Brian was confused.

"That he was the father of my child. He said he couldn't remember having sex with me. That was nice, wasn't it?"

"Ah, God, Stella, I'm so sorry." There was real compassion in his face.

"It was probably my own fault. I told him all wrong. He's a bit drinky, as I was indeed myself, and he couldn't face it. He ran out of here. *Ran,* I tell you."

"Maybe he'll come back when he sees sense."

"He won't—he literally doesn't remember. He's not making it up." She sounded resigned, defeated.

"Could you get a DNA test to prove he's the father?"

"No. I thought about it, but if he doesn't remember being there at her conception, there's no point in asking him to be a father to her. No, she'll have to take her chances like the rest of us."

"Would it help if I had a word with him?" Brian Flynn felt that he should offer anyway.

"No, Brian, thanks, but no. If he ran when I told him, he would go into orbit if I sent a priest after him." For a moment, there was a flash of the old Stella.

After supper that night in St. Jarlath's Crescent Emily was busy explaining her day's negotiations with Molly Carroll. Charles and Josie were drinking in every word.

Charles had news too. There would be a good-bye celebration for him in a few weeks' time at the hotel—finger food, wine and beer, and a presentation. And would you believe who wanted to come to it, but Mrs. Monty—who was really Lady something. The woman who wore a fur coat, a big hat and pearls and nothing else: the hotel manager was very nervous about letting her in.

Mrs. Monty was now going into a residential home where, sadly, Caesar would not be welcome; and since Charles had agreed to take him, she wanted to thank the kind employee who had given the little spaniel such a good home. She was also going to make a donation to a charity of his choice. It would be a wonderful start to the fund-raising.

Charles was allowed to bring a small number of family and friends. As well as Josie, Emily and Noel, he thought he would invite Paddy and Molly Carroll and the Scarlets, Muttie and Lizzie.

"Will Noel be able to come, do you think?" Emily's voice was slightly tart.

"Well, here he comes now—we can ask him!" Josie cried out happily.

Noel listened carefully, arranging his face in various receptive expressions as the excitement of the good-bye celebrations was revealed.

Emily knew the technique: she recognized it from her father. It was a matter of saying as little as possible and therefore cutting down on the possibility of being discovered to be drunk.

Eventually he had to speak. Slowly and carefully he said that he would be privileged to be part of the ceremony.

"It would be great to be there when they are honoring you," he said to his father.

Emily bit her lip. At least he had been able to respond adequately. He had managed not to rain on his father's parade.

"There's some lamb stew left, Noel. I'll heat it and bring it up to you," she said, giving him permission to leave before his mask of sobriety collapsed.

"Thank you, Emily, I'd love that," he said and fled to his room after shooting a grateful look in her direction.

When she went in with the tray, he was sitting in his chair with tears streaming down his face.

"Oh, Lord, Noel, what is it?" she asked, alarmed.

"I'm utterly *useless*, Emily. I've let everyone down. What's the use of my going on, waking in the morning and going to bed at night? What good does it serve?"

"Have your supper, Noel. I brought you a pot of coffee as well. We have to talk."

"I thought you didn't talk to me anymore," he said with a great sniff and wiping his eyes.

"I thought that *you* were avoiding *me*," she said.

"I didn't want to come home and have you being cold and

distant. I don't have any friends, Emily. I have no one at all to turn to. . . ." His voice sounded lost and frightened.

"Eat your supper, Noel. I'll be here," she said. And she was there while he told her how despairing he was and what a hopeless father he would be to any child.

She listened and then said simply, "I hear all that and you may well be right. But then again it might be the making of you, *and* Frankie. She might make you into the kind of person you want to be."

"They'd never let me keep her . . . the social welfare people . . ."

"You'll need to show them what you're made of."

"It's better they don't know," Noel said.

"Please, Noel, no self-pity. Think—think what you should do next. A lot of lives will be affected by it."

"I couldn't bring the child here," he said.

"It was time for you to move on anyway." Emily was as calm as if they were discussing what to have for lunch tomorrow, rather than Noel's future.

Next morning, Stella looked up from the magazine she was reading as a shadow fell on her bed. It was Noel, carrying a small bunch of flowers.

"Well, hello!" she said. "How did you get in? It isn't visiting time."

"Am I interrupting you?" he asked.

"Yes, I'm reading about how to put more zing back into my marriage, as if I knew what either zing or marriage was!"

"I came here to ask you to marry me," he said.

"Oh, Christ, Noel, don't be such an eejit. Why would I marry you? I'll be dead in a few weeks' time!"

"You wouldn't say the baby was mine if it wasn't. I would be honored to try to bring her up."

"Listen, marriage was never part of it." Stella was at a complete loss.

"I thought that's what you wanted!" He was perplexed now.

"No. I wanted you to look after her, to be a dad for her, to keep her out of the lottery of the care system."

"So will we get married, then?"

"No, Noel, of course we won't, but if you *do* want to talk about looking after her, tell me why and how."

"I'm going to change, Stella."

"Right."

"No, I am. I was up all night planning it. I'm going to go to AA today, admit I have a drink problem, and then I'm going to enroll to do a business course at a college and then I'm going to find a flat where I can bring up the baby."

"This is all so sudden. So spur-of-the-moment. Why aren't you at work today anyway?"

"My cousin Emily has gone to Hall's to say I have a personal crisis today and that I will make up the time next week by going in one hour earlier and staying one hour later every day."

"Does Emily know about all this?"

"Yes. I had to tell someone. She was very cross with me for walking out on you."

"You didn't walk, Noel. You ran."

"I am so sorry. Believe me. I *am* sorry."

"So what has changed?" She wasn't hostile, just interested.

"I want to amount to something. To do something for someone before I die. I'll be thirty soon. I've done nothing except dream and wish and drink. I want to change that."

She listened in silence.

"So tell me what you'd like if you don't want us to get married?"

"I don't know, Noel. I'd like things to have been different."

"So do most people walking around. They all wish things had been different," he said sadly.

"Then I'd like you to meet Moira Tierney, my social worker, tomorrow evening. She's coming in to discuss what she calls 'the future' with me. A fairly short discussion."

"Could I bring Emily in? She said she'd like to come and talk to you anyway."

"But is she going to be a nanny figure? Always there hovering, making all the decisions?"

"No, she'll be going back to America soon, I think, but she *has* made me see things more clearly."

"Bring her in, then. Is she dishy? Could you marry *her,* maybe?" Stella was mischievous again.

"No! She's as old as the hills. Well, fifty or forty-five or something, anyway."

"Bring her in, then," Stella said, "and she's going to have to talk well to deal with Moira."

He leaned over and put the flowers in a glass.

"Noel?"

"Yes?"

"Thanks, anyway, about the marriage proposal and all. It wasn't what I had in mind but it was decent of you."

"You might still change your mind," he said.

"I have a tame priest in here. A very nice fellow. He could do it if we were pushed, but actually I'd prefer not to."

"Whatever you think," he said, and touched her gently on the shoulder.

"Before you go, one thing . . . how *did* you get in outside visiting hours?"

"I asked Declan Carroll. He lives on my road. I said I needed a favor, so he made a phone call."

"He and his wife are having a baby at the same time as I am," Stella said. "I always thought the children might be friends."

"Well, they might easily be friends," Noel said.

When he looked around from the door he saw she was lying back in her bed, but she was smiling and seemed more relaxed than before.

He set out then to face what was going to be the most challenging day of his life.

It was hard to go into the building where the lunchtime AA meeting was taking place. Noel stood for ten minutes in the corridor watching men and women of every type walking down to the door at the end.

Eventually he could put it off no longer and followed them in.

It was still very unreal to him but, as he had said to Emily, he had to get his head around the fact that he was a father and an alcoholic.

He had faced the first and he could still recall the glow in Stella's face this morning. *She* hadn't thought he was a loser and a hopeless father for her baby.

Now he had to face the drinking.

There were about thirty people in the room. A man sat at a desk near the door. He had a tired, lined face and sandy hair. He didn't look like a person who was a heavy drinker. Maybe he was just part of the staff.

"I would actually like to join," Noel said to him, hearing, as he spoke, his own voice echoing in his ears.

"And your name?" the man asked.

"Noel Lynch."

"Right, Noel. Who referred you here?"

"I'm sorry? Referred?"

"I mean, are you coming here because of a treatment center?"

"Oh, heavens no. I haven't been having any treatment or anything. I just drink too much and I want to cut it down."

"We try to encourage each other to cut it out completely. Are you aware of that?"

"Yes, if that were possible, I would be happy to try."

"My name is Malachy. Come on in," the man said. "We're about to begin."

Later in the day Noel had to do his third confrontation.

Emily had made an appointment for him with a college admissions supervisor. He was going to sign up for a business diploma, which included marketing and finance, sales and advertising. The fees, which would have been well beyond him, were going to be paid by Emily. She said it was an interest-free loan. He would repay it when he could.

She had assured him that this was exactly what she wanted to do with her savings. She saw it as an investment. One day when he was a rich, successful man he would always remember her with gratitude and look after her in her old age.

The admissions supervisor confirmed that the fees had been paid and that the lectures would start the following week. Apart from the lectures, Noel would be expected to study on his own for at least twelve hours a week.

"Are you married?" the supervisor asked.

"No, indeed," and then almost as an afterthought Noel said, "but I'll be having a baby in a couple of weeks."

"Congratulations, but you had better get a good bit of the groundwork in before the child arrives," said the admissions supervisor, a man who seemed to know what he was talking about.

That evening at supper Josie was eager to discuss the thrift shop and its possible opening date. She was excited and alive.

Charles was in high good form too. He wasn't going to have to give Caesar back to Mrs. Monty, he was going to have this big celebration at the hotel, he had more plans for dog walking and dog exercising and he had been to a local kennel.

But before the conversation could go down either route—thrift shop or dog walking—Emily spoke firmly.

"Noel has something important to talk to us about, perhaps before we make any more plans."

Noel looked around him, trapped.

He had known that this was coming. Emily said they could not live in a shadowy world of lies and deception.

Still, he had to tell his parents that they were about to become grandparents, there was no marriage included in the plans and he would be moving into a place of his own.

It was not news he was going to find easy to break. Emily had suggested that he might pause before using the same opportunity to tell them that he was joining Alcoholics Anonymous and that he was registering as a student at the college.

She wondered whether it might not be too much for them.

But when he began his tale, sparing nothing but telling it all as it had unfolded, he felt it was easier and more fair to tell them everything.

He went through it as if he were talking about someone else, and he never once caught their eye as the story went on.

First he told of the message from the hospital, his two meetings with Stella, and her news—which he had refused to believe at first but realized must be true; then he told of his intention to meet the social worker and plan for the future of the baby girl, whose birth would also involve her mother's death.

He told them how he had tried to give up drinking on his own and had not succeeded, that he now had a sponsor in AA called Malachy and would attend a meeting every day.

He told them that his job in Hall's had been depressing and that he was constantly passed over while younger and less experienced staff were appreciated because they had diplomas or degrees.

At this point he realized his parents had been very silent, so he raised his eyes to look at them.

Their faces were frozen with horror at the story he was telling.

Everything they had feared might happen in a godless world *had* happened.

Their son had enjoyed sex outside marriage and a child had resulted and he was admitting a dependency on alcohol even to the point of getting help from Alcoholics Anonymous!

But he would not be put off. He struggled on with the explanations and his plans to get out of the situations he had brought on himself.

He accepted that it was all his own fault.

He blamed no outside circumstances.

"I feel ashamed telling you all this, Mam and Da. You have lived such good lives. You wouldn't even begin to understand, but I got myself into this and I'm going to get myself out of it."

They were still silent so he dared to look at them again.

To his amazement they both had some sympathy in their faces.

His mother's eyes were full of tears, but there were no recriminations. No mention of sex before marriage, only concern.

"Why did you never tell us this, son?" His father's voice was full of emotion.

"What could you have said? That I was a fool to have left school so early? Or that I should put up with it. You were happy at work, Da. You were respected. That's not the way it is at Hall's."

"And the baby?" Josie said. "You had no idea this Stella was expecting your child?"

"None in the wide world, Ma," Noel said. And there was something so bleak and honest in his tone that everyone believed him.

"But the drink thing, Noel . . . are you sure that it's bad enough for you to be going to the AA?"

"It is, Da, believe me."

"I never noticed you drunk. Not once. And I'm well used to dealing with drunk people up at the hotel," his father said, shaking his head.

"That's because you're normal, Da. You don't expect people to come back from work half-cut, having spent two hours in Casey's."

"That man has a lot to answer for." Charles shook his head with disapproval for Old Man Casey.

"He didn't exactly open my mouth and force it down," Noel said.

Emily spoke for the first time.

"So we are up to speed on Noel's plans now. It's going to be up to us to give him all the support we can."

"You *knew* all this?" Josie Lynch was shocked and not best pleased.

"I only knew because I can recognize a drunk at fifty feet. I've had a lifetime of knowing when people are drunk. We don't talk about him much, I know, but my father was one very unhappy man and he was miles from home with no one to help him or advise him when he had made one wrong decision that wrecked his life."

"What decision was that?" Charles asked.

This evening was full of shocks.

Since Emily's arrival there had been no mention of the late Martin Lynch's drinking.

"The decision to leave Ireland. He regretted it every day of his life."

"But that can't be right. He lost total interest in us. He never came home." Charles was astonished.

"He never came home, that's true, but he never lost interest. He probed it as if it were a sore tooth. All he *could* have done if only he had stayed here. All of it fantasy, of course, but still, if he'd had someone to talk to . . ." Her voice trailed away.

"Your mother?" Josie asked tentatively.

"No joy there, I'm afraid. She never understood what a hold drink had on him. She just told him to stay away from it, as if it were a simple thing to do."

"Could you not talk to him? You're great at talking to people," Charles said admiringly.

"No, I couldn't. You see, my father didn't have the basic decency that Noel here has. He could not accept that in the end it was all up to him. He wasn't half the man Noel is."

Josie, who had in the last half hour been facing the whole range of disgrace, mortal sin and shame, found some small comfort in this praise.

"You think that Noel will be able to do all this?" she asked Emily pitifully, as if Noel were not even there.

"It's up to us to help him, Josie," Emily said as calmly as if they were discussing the menu for tomorrow's supper.

And even to Noel it didn't seem quite as impossible as it had when he had begun his explanation.

· · ·

"Stella, I'm Emily, Noel's cousin. Noel's gone to get you some cigarettes. I came a little early in case there's anything I should know before the social worker comes."

Stella looked at the businesslike woman with the frizzy hair and the smart raincoat. Americans always dressed properly for the Irish weather. Irish people themselves were constantly being drenched with rain.

"I'm pleased to meet you, Emily. Noel says you are a rock of sense."

"I don't know that I am." Emily seemed doubtful. "I came over on a whim to learn about my late father's background. Now I seem to be up to my neck in organizing a statue for some saint who has been dead for centuries. Hardly a rock of sense . . ."

"You're very good to take all this on as well." Stella looked down somewhat ruefully at the bump in her stomach.

"You have enough problems to think about," Emily said, her voice warm and sympathetic.

"Well, this social worker is a bit of a madam. You know, interested in everything, believing nothing, always trying to trip you up."

"I suppose they have to be a bit like that on behalf of the child," Emily murmured.

"Yes, but not like the secret police. You see, I sort of implied that Noel and I were more of an item than we are. You know, in terms of seeing each other and everything."

"Sure." Emily nodded approvingly. It made sense.

There was no point in Stella telling a social worker that she hardly knew the least thing about the father of the child she was about to have.

It wouldn't look good from the start.

"I'll help to fill you in on all that," Emily said.

At that moment Noel came in, closely followed by Moira Tierney.

She was in her early thirties with dark hair swept back with a red ribbon. If not for her frown of concentration, she would have been considered attractive. But Moira was too busy to consider looking attractive.

"You are Noel Lynch?" she said briskly and without much enthusiasm.

He began to shuffle and appear defensive.

Emily moved in quickly. "Give me your parcels, Noel. I know you want to say hello to Stella properly." She nudged him towards the bed.

Stella held up her thin arms to give him an awkward combination of a hug and a peck on the cheek.

Moira watched suspiciously.

"You and Stella don't share a home, Mr. Lynch?" Moira said.

"No, not at the moment," he agreed apologetically.

"But there are active plans going ahead so that Noel can get a place of his own to raise Frankie," Emily said.

"And you are . . . ?" Moira looked at Emily inquiringly.

"Emily Lynch. Noel's cousin."

"Are you the only family he has?" Moira checked her notes.

"Lord, no! He has a mother and father, Josie and Charles . . . ," Emily began, making sure that Stella could hear the names as well.

"And they are . . . ?" Moira had an irritating habit of asking a question the wrong way round, as if she were making some kind of disapproving statement.

"They are at home organizing a fund to erect a statue to St. Jarlath in their street."

"St. *Jarlath*?" Moira was bewildered.

"I know! Aren't they wonderful? Well, you'll meet them yourself. They'll be in tomorrow to see Stella."

"They will?" Stella was startled.

"Of course they will." Emily sounded more confident than she felt.

Josie would take a lot of convincing before she arrived to see the girl who was no better than she should be. But Emily was working on it and the important thing just now was to let the social worker see that there was strong family support.

Moira absorbed it all as she was meant to.

"And where do you intend to live, Mr. Lynch, if you *are* given custody of the child?"

"Well of course he will have custody of the child," Stella snapped. "He's the child's father. We are all agreed on that!"

"There may be circumstances which might challenge this." Moira was prim.

"What kind of circumstances?" Stella was angry now.

"A background of alcohol abuse, for one thing," Moira said.

"Not from me, Noel," Stella said apologetically.

"Naturally, we make inquiries," Moira said.

"But that is all under control now," Emily said.

"Well, that will be looked into," Moira said in a clipped voice. "What kind of accommodation were you thinking of, Mr. Lynch?"

Emily spoke again. "Noel's family have been discussing nothing else but accommodation. We are looking at this apartment in Chestnut Court. It's a small block of flats not far away from where he lives now."

"Would it not be preferable to start the child off living with a ready-made family in er . . . St. Jarlath's Crescent?"

"Well, you see . . . ," Noel began.

"You see, Moira, you are very welcome to come and visit Noel's home at any time, but you will realize that it's entirely unsuited for a baby. The places in Chestnut Court are much more child-friendly. The one we are all interested in is on the ground floor. Would you like to see a picture of it here . . ."

Moira didn't seem as interested as she might have been. She was looking at Noel and seemed to spot the surprise on his face.

"What do *you* think of this as a place to move to?" she asked him directly.

Stella and Emily waited anxiously.

"As Emily said, we have talked through so many ideas and this one seems to be the most suitable so far."

Moira nodded as if in agreement, and if she heard the breath of relief from the two women, she gave no sign.

There were questions then about the rent that would be paid and the babysitting support that would be available, seeing that Noel would be at work all day.

And soon it was over.

Emily made one last statement to show how reliable her cousin Noel was.

"I don't know whether you realize that Noel is very anxious to marry Stella. He has proposed to her, but Stella would prefer not to. This is the attitude of a committed person, someone who would be reliable and responsible."

"As I said, Ms. Lynch, there are some formalities that have to be gone through. I will have to talk about it with my team and then the last word will be with the supervisor."

"But the first and most influential word will be from *you*, Moira," Emily said.

Moira gave one of her brisk little nods and was gone.

Stella waited till she was out of the ward before she started to celebrate. With a flick of her wrist she pulled the curtains and produced the cigarettes.

"Well done to the pair of you," she said, looking from Noel to Emily and back. "We have Madam Moira on the run!"

"We still have a way to go," Emily said, and they settled down to discuss further strategies.

And they continued to do this for the next few weeks. Every aspect of the effort to turn Noel into a father was discussed.

Josie and Charles were introduced to Stella and, after some awkward shuffling at the start, they found an astonishing amount of common ground. Both Noel's parents and Stella herself seemed entirely convinced that shortly Stella would be going to a better place. There was no pretense that she might recover.

Josie talked wistfully of Stella going to meet Our Lord fairly soon and Charles said that if Stella were to meet St. Jarlath, she could pass on the news that the statue would indeed be erected but it might take a little longer than they had once believed possible. They had helped by paying a deposit on the flat in Chestnut Court. St. Jarlath's image might have to wait a little, but it would happen.

"Wouldn't he be able to see that already?" Stella asked.

"Yes, I imagine he would," Charles agreed. "But it would be no harm to give him a personal message."

Noel felt ashamed that his parents took this whole idea of an afterlife so casually. They really and truly saw heaven as some kind of a big park where they would meet everyone.

Stella rolled her eyes a bit at the whole notion, but she didn't seem put out by it either. She was game to take a message to any old saint just to keep the show on the road.

But they also made plans on a more practical level. Chestnut Court was only a seven-minute walk from St. Jarlath's Crescent. Noel could wheel the baby around to his parents' home before work each morning; Josie and Charles would look after Frankie until lunchtime. Then she would go for the afternoon either to Molly Carroll's house or to this couple called Aidan and Signora, who looked after their grandchild; to Dr. Hat, who had retired recently and found time hanging heavy on his hands; or to Muttie and Lizzie Scarlet, who, quite apart from their own children, had raised twins who were no blood relations to them at all.

The three evenings a week when Noel would be at his evening classes would be covered as well. For a time Emily would go to the new apartment in Chestnut Court and do her paperwork. Noel would return after his lectures and she would cook him a meal. He had started getting lessons from the district nurse on what he would need in the new flat to welcome the baby and had been shown how to prepare a feed and the importance of sterilizing bottles. Declan Carroll's wife, Fiona, had sent a message to say that she had already received a baby's layette that would be enough for sextuplets. Stella and Noel *must* help her out and get the garments worn; their babies would arrive at around the same time. What could be more luck?

Noel was swept along in the whirl of activity of it all.

The thrift shop was up and running; he and his father had

painted it to Emily and Josie's satisfaction and already people had begun to donate items to be sold. Some of these would be useful for Noel's new flat, but Emily was adamant: a fair price must be paid for them. The money was for St. Jarlath, not to build a comfortable lifestyle for Noel.

He had little time alone with Stella. There were so many practicalities to be sorted out. Did Stella want the child to be brought up as a Catholic?

Stella shrugged. The child could abandon it once she was old enough. Possibly to please Josie and Charles, there should be a baptism and First Holy Communion and all, but nothing too "Holy Joe."

Were there *any* relations on Stella's side whom she might want to involve?

"None whatsoever." She was clipped and firm.

"Or anyone at all from the various foster homes from the past?"

"No, Noel, don't go there!"

"Right. It's just that when you're gone, I'll have no one to ask."

Her face softened. "I know. Sorry for snapping at you. I'll write her a letter telling her a bit about myself and about you and how good you've been."

"Where will you leave the letter?" Noel asked.

"With you, of course!"

"I mean, if you wanted to leave it in a bank or something . . . ," Noel offered.

"Do I look to you like someone who has a bank account, Noel? Please . . ."

"I wish you weren't going to leave, Stella," he said, covering her thin hand with his.

"Thanks, Noel. I don't want to go either," she said. And they sat there like that until Father Flynn came in for a visit. He took in the scene and the hand-holding, but made no comment.

"I was just passing," he said foolishly.

"Well, I was on my way anyway, Father." Noel stood up to leave.

"Maybe you could stay a minute, Noel. I wanted Stella to tell me what, if anything, she wanted for her funeral."

The question didn't faze Stella at all.

"Listen, Brian, ask Noel's family what *they* want. I won't be here. Let them have whatever is easiest."

"A hymn or two?" Brian Flynn asked.

"Sure, why not. I'd like a happy clappy one. You know, like a gospel choir, if possible."

"No problem," Father Flynn said. "And burial or cremation or body to science?"

"Don't think my body would tell anyone anything they didn't know already." Stella considered it. "I mean, if you smoke four packs a day, you get cancer of the lung. If you drink as much as I did, then you get cirrhosis of the liver. There isn't a part of me sound enough for a transplant, but what the hell . . . it could be an awful warning." Her eyes were very bright.

Brian Flynn swallowed.

"We don't talk about this sort of thing much, Stella, but do you want a Requiem Mass?"

"That's the one with all the bells and whistles, isn't it?"

"It gives a lot of people comfort," Father Flynn said diplomatically.

"Bring it on then, Brian," she said good-humoredly.

Chapter Four

Lisa Kelly had been very bright at school; she had been good at everything. Her English teacher encouraged her to do a degree in English literature and aim for a post in the university. Her sports teacher said that with her height—by the age of fourteen she was already nearly six feet tall—she was a natural and she could play tennis or hockey, or both, for Ireland. But when it came to it, Lisa decided to go for art. Specifically for graphic art.

She graduated from that, first in her year, and was instantly offered a position in one of the big design firms in Dublin. It was at that point that she should have left the family home.

Her younger sister, Katie, had gone three years previously, but Katie was very different. No child genius, only barely able to keep up with the class, Katie had taken a holiday job in a hairdresser's and found her life's calling. She had married Garry Finglas and together they had set up a smart salon that had gone from strength to strength. She loved to practice on Lisa's long honey-colored hair, blow-drying it and then styling it into elegant chignons and pleats.

Their mother, Di, had been very scornful about it all. "Touching people's dirty heads!" she had exclaimed in horror.

Their father, Jack Kelly, barely commented on Katie's career, any more than he had on Lisa's work.

Katie had begged Lisa to leave home. "It's not like that out in the real world, not awful silences like Mum and Dad have. Other people don't shrug at each other the way *they* do, they *talk*."

But Lisa had waved this away. Katie had always been oversensitive about the atmosphere at home. When Katie went out to friends' houses, she returned wistfully talking about happy meals at kitchen tables, places where mothers and fathers talked and laughed and argued with their children and their friends. Not like their home, where meals were eaten in silence and accompanied by a series of shrugs. And anyway, Katie had always been easily affected by people's moods. Lisa was different. If Mum was distant, then *let* her be distant. If Dad was secretive, then what of it? It was just his way.

Dad worked in a bank, where, apparently, he had been passed over for promotion; he didn't know the *right* people. No wonder he was withdrawn and didn't want to make idle chitchat. Lisa could never interest him in anything she did; if ever she showed him one of her drawings from school, he'd shrug, as if to say, "So what?"

Her mother was discontented, but she had reason to be. She worked in a very upmarket boutique, where rich, middle-aged women went to buy several outfits a year. She herself would have looked well in those kinds of clothes, but she could never have afforded them; so instead she helped to fit plumper women into them and arranged for seams to be let out and for zip fasteners to be lengthened. Even with a very generous staff discount, the clothes were way out of her league. No wonder she looked at Dad with disappointment. When she had married him at the age of eighteen he had looked like a man who was going somewhere. Now he went nowhere except to work every morning.

Lisa went to her office and worked hard all day. She had lunch with colleagues at places that were high in style and low in calories. But it was at a private lunch for a client that Lisa met Anton Moran: it was one of those moments that was frozen forever in her mind.

Lisa saw this man crossing the room, pausing at each table and talking easily with everyone. He was slight and wore his hair quite long. He looked confident and pleasant without being arrogant.

"Who's *he*?" she gasped to Miranda, who knew everyone.

"Oh, that's Anton Moran. He's the chef. He's been here for a year, but he's leaving soon. Going to open his own place, apparently. He'll do well."

"He's gorgeous," Lisa said.

"Get to the end of the line!" Miranda laughed. "There's a list as long as my arm waiting for Anton."

Lisa could see why. Anton had style like she had never seen before. He didn't hurry, yet he moved on from table to table. Soon he was at theirs.

"The lovely Miranda!" he exclaimed.

"The even lovelier Anton!" Miranda said archly. "This is my friend Lisa Kelly."

"Well, hello, Lisa," he said, as if he had been waiting all his life to meet her.

"How do you do?" Lisa said and felt awkward. Normally she knew what to say, but not this time.

"I'll be opening my own place shortly," Anton said. "Tonight is my last night here. I'm going round giving my cell phone number to everyone and I'll expect you all to be there. No excuses now." He handed a card to Miranda and then gave one to Lisa.

"Give me a couple of weeks and I'll give you the details. They'll all know I must be doing *something* right if you two gorgeous girls turn up there," he said, looking from one to the other. It was an easy patter. He might be going to say something similar at the next table.

But Lisa knew that he had meant it. He wanted to see her again.

"I work in a graphic design studio," Lisa said suddenly, "in case you ever need a logo or any designs?"

"I'm sure I will," Anton said. "I'm certain I will, actually." And then he was gone.

Lisa remembered nothing about the rest of the meal. She yearned to go to Miranda's flat and talk about him all night, check that he wasn't married, that he didn't have a partner. But Lisa had survived life so far by remaining a little aloof. She didn't go to stay with friends, as she didn't want to invite them home to her house. She didn't want to wear her heart on her sleeve and confide to someone gossipy like Miranda about Anton. She would get to know him herself in her own time. She would design him a logo that would be the talk of the town.

The important thing was not to rush it, not to make any sudden moves.

She thought about him way into the night. He wasn't conventionally handsome but he had a face that you wouldn't forget. Intense dark eyes and a marvelous smile. He had a grace like you'd expect in an athlete or a dancer.

He must be spoken for. A man like that wouldn't be available. Surely?

She was taken aback when he telephoned her the next day.

"Good. I found you," he said, sounding pleased to hear her voice.

"How many places did you try?"

"This is the third. Will you have lunch with me?"

"Today?"

"Well, yes, if you're free. . . ." And he named Quentins, one of the most highly regarded restaurants in Dublin.

Lisa had been going to have lunch with Katie. "I'm free," she said simply. Katie would understand. Eventually.

Lisa went to her boss, Kevin.

"I'm going to have lunch with a very good contact. A man who is about to open his own business and I was wondering . . ."

" . . . if you can take him to an expensive restaurant—is that it?" Kevin had seen it all, heard it all.

"No. Certainly not. *He's* paying. I thought I might offer him a glass of champagne and that I might go an hour early so that I can get my hair done and present a good image of the agency."

"Nothing wrong with your hair," Kevin grumbled.

"No, but better to make a good impression than a sort of half-hearted one."

"All right—do we have to pay for the hairdo as well?"

"No way, Kevin. I'm not greedy!" Lisa said and ran off before he could think about this.

She raced out to buy a large potted plant for Katie and turned up at the salon.

"So this is a consolation prize. You're canceling lunch!"

"Katie, *please* understand."

"Is it a man?" Katie asked.

"A man? No, of course not. Well, he is a man, but it's a business lunch and I can't get out of it. Kevin is on his knees to me. He even let me have time off so that I could have my hair done."

"What do you want done? Apart from bypassing the line of people who actually made bookings?"

"I beg you, Katie . . ."

Katie called to an assistant. "Could you take Madam to a basin and use our special shampoo? I'll be with you in a moment."

"You're too good . . . ," Lisa began.

"I know I am. It's always been my little weakness, being too good for this world. I wish it *were* for a man, you know, Lisa. I'd have done something special."

"Let's pretend it *is* for a man," Lisa begged.

"If it was a man who would get you out of that house, I'd do it for nothing!" Katie said, and Lisa smiled to herself. She yearned to tell her sister, but a lifetime of keeping her own counsel intervened.

"You look very elegant," Anton said as he stood up to greet Lisa at Quentins.

"Thank you, Anton. You don't look as if you made too late a night of it yourself."

"No, indeed. I just gave my phone number to everyone in the restaurant and then went home to my cup of cocoa and my narrow little bed." He smiled his infectious smile, which would always manage to get a return smile. Lisa didn't know what she was smiling at— cocoa, a narrow little bed, an early night . . . But it must mean that he was giving her signals that he was available.

Should she send back a similar signal or was it too early? Too early, definitely.

"I told my boss I was coming here for lunch with a man who was going into business on his own and he said that I should offer you a glass of champagne on the company."

"What a civilized boss," Anton said admiringly as Brenda Brennan, the proprietor, came over. She knew Anton Moran already. He had worked in her restaurant a while ago. He introduced Lisa to Brenda. "Lisa's company is buying us a glass of champagne each, Brenda, so could we have your delightful house sparkling to start us off, with a receipt for that to Lisa, and the rest of the meal is on me."

Brenda smiled. Her look said she had seen Anton here with several ladies before.

Lisa felt a stab of hurt, which surprised her. In twenty-five years she had never known such a feeling. It was envy, jealousy and resentment all rolled into one. This was completely ludicrous.

It wasn't as if she were a starry-eyed teenager. Lisa had had many boyfriends, and some of them had been lovers. She had never felt a really strong attraction to any of these men. But Anton was different.

His hair looked soft and silky, and she longed to reach across the table and run her hands through it. She had the most absurd wish to have his head on her shoulder while she stroked his face. She must shake herself out of this pretty sharpish and get back to the business of designing a look and styling a logo for his new company.

"What will you call the new place?" she asked, surprised that she could keep so calm.

"Well, I know it's a bit of an ego trip, but I was thinking of calling it Anton's," he said. "But let's order first. They have a really good cheese soufflé here. I should know—I made enough of them in my time!"

"That would be perfect," Lisa said. This could not be happening. She was falling in love for the very first time.

Back at the office Kevin asked her, "Any luck with Golden Boy?"

"He's very personable, certainly."

"Did you give him any outline and our rates?" Kevin was anxious there would be no gray areas.

"No—that will come later." Lisa was almost dreamy as she thought of Anton and how he had kissed her cheek when they parted.

"Yeah, well, as long as he understands it doesn't come free because he's a pretty boy," Kevin said.

"How do you know that he's a pretty boy?" Lisa asked.

"You just said that he was personable and I think he was the same guy that my niece had a nervous breakdown over."

"Your niece?"

"Yes. My brother's daughter. She went out with a chef called Anton Moran once. Nothing but tears and tantrums, then she drops out of college, *then* she goes to face him down about it all and he's gone off cooking on a cruise ship."

Lisa's heart felt like lead. Anton had told her of his wonderful year onboard a luxury liner.

"I don't think it could have been the same person." Lisa's tone was cold.

"No, maybe not . . . probably not . . ." Kevin was anxious for the least trouble possible. "Just as long as he knows he's getting nothing for free from us."

Lisa knew with a terrible certainty that there would be a lot of trouble ahead. Anton had barely the money to cover the deposit on his premises. He was relying on outstanding restaurant reviews to meet the mortgage payments and the expenses of doing the place up. He had given no thought whatsoever to the cost of a graphic artist and a campaign.

The site for the restaurant was perfect: it was in a small lane just a few yards off a main road, near to the railway station, a tram route and a taxi rank. He had suggested a picnic. Lisa brought cheese and grapes, Anton brought a bottle of wine.

They sat on packing cases and he described his great plans. She hardly took in any of them as she watched his face. His sense of excitement was contagious.

By the time they had finished the cheese and grapes she knew that she would leave Kevin and set up on her own. Perhaps she could move in with Anton, work with him—they could build the place together—but she must not rush her fences. However hard it was, she mustn't look overeager.

Anton had mentioned very little about his private life.

His mother lived abroad, his father lived in the country and his sister lived in London. He spoke well of everyone and badly of no one. She *mustn't* ask him about Kevin's niece. She must hassle him about nothing. She knew that he was totally right—this place was going to be a huge success and she wanted to be part of it and in at the very start.

She gave a sigh of pure pleasure.

"It's good, that wine, isn't it?" he said.

It might as well have been turpentine. She couldn't taste it. But she mustn't let him know at this early stage that she was sighing with pleasure at the thought of a future with him.

It would be lovely to have someone to tell—someone who would listen and ask, What did you do then? What did he say to that? But Lisa had few close friends.

She couldn't tell anyone at work, that was for sure. When she left Kevin's studio she wanted no one to suspect why. Kevin might become difficult and say she had met Anton on *his* time and that he had stood them the glasses of champagne that had clinched the deal.

Once or twice he had asked her if "Anton pretty boy" had got any further along the line in his decision-making. Lisa shrugged. It was impossible to know, she had said vaguely. You couldn't rush people.

Kevin agreed. "Just so long as he's not getting anything for free," he warned several times.

"Free? You *must* be joking!" Lisa said, outraged at the very idea.

Kevin would have been astonished had he known just how long

Lisa had spent with Anton and how many drawings she had shown him to establish a logo for his new venture. At that moment she had concentrated on the colors of the French flag, and the *A* of *Anton* was a big curly, showy letter. It could not be mistaken for anything else. She had done drawings and projections, shown him how this image would appear on a restaurant sign, on business cards, menus, table napkins and even china.

She had spent every single evening with Anton—sometimes sitting on the packing cases, sometimes in small restaurants around Dublin, where he was busy seeing what worked and what didn't. One night, he did a shift at Quentins to help them out and invited Lisa to have a meal there at a staff discount. She sat proudly, looking out from her booth, grateful that she had met this man who was now quite simply the center of her whole life. Then and there she had definitely decided to leave Kevin's office and set up business on her own.

She would shortly leave the cold, friendless home where she lived now, but would wait until Anton suggested that she move in with him. He would ask her soon.

The whole business had been brought up for discussion. As early as their fifth date he had made the first move.

"It's a great pity to go back alone to my narrow bed . . . ," he had said, his voice full of meaning as he ran his hands through her long hair.

"I know, but what are the alternatives?" Lisa had asked playfully.

"I suppose you could invite me home to *your* narrow bed?" he offered as a solution.

"Ah, but I live with my parents, you see. That kind of thing couldn't happen," she said.

"Unless you were to get your own place, of course," he grumbled.

"Or we were to explore *your* place?" Lisa said.

But he didn't go down that road. Yet.

When he brought the matter up again it was in connection with a hotel. A place thirty miles from Dublin where they might have dinner, steal some ideas for the new restaurant and stay the night.

Lisa saw nothing wrong with this plan, and it all worked out perfectly. As she lay in Anton's arms she knew she was the luckiest girl in the whole world. Soon she was going to be living and working with the man she loved. Wasn't this what every woman in the world wanted?

And it was going to happen to her, Lisa Kelly.

"I always knew you would fly the coop one day," Kevin said. "And you have been restless for the last couple of weeks. I guessed you were planning something."

"I was very happy here," Lisa said.

"Of course you were. You're very good. You'll be good anywhere. Have you decided where to go yet?"

"On my own," Lisa said simply.

"Not a good idea in this economic climate, Lisa," Kevin advised her.

"*You* took the risk, Kevin, and look how it paid off for you. . . ."

"It was different. I had a rich father and a load of contacts."

"I have a little savings and I'll make the contacts," Lisa said.

"You will in time. Have you an office?"

"I'll start from home."

"The very best of luck to you, Lisa," he said, and she managed to get out before he asked her was there any news of Anton.

Kevin, however, knew all about the place Anton had in Lisa's life and the reason for her move. He had spent a weekend in Holly's Hotel in County Wicklow and Miss Holly, forever anxious to give her customers news of one another, mentioned that one of his colleagues, Ms. Kelly, had stayed there the previous night.

"With a very attractive young man. Most knowledgeable about food, he was out in the kitchens talking to the chef."

"Was his name Anton Moran?" Kevin asked.

"That's the very man." Miss Holly clapped her hands. "He even asked us for the recipe for our special orange sauce that the chef makes with Cointreau and walnuts. Normally Chef won't tell anyone, but he told Mr. Moran because he was going to cook it for his parents."

"I'll bet he was," Kevin said grimly. "And did they share a room?"

Miss Holly sighed. "Of course they did, Kevin. But that's today for you. If you tried to apply any standards these days you'd be laughed out of business!"

Kevin thought of his niece, who was still in fragile health, and he shivered a little for what might lie ahead for Lisa Kelly, one of the brightest designers he had ever come across.

Lisa wondered were there other homes in Dublin like hers, where the communication was minimal, the conversation limited and the goodwill nonexistent. Her parents talked to each other in heavy sighs and to her hardly at all.

Every Friday, Lisa left her rent on the kitchen dresser. This entitled her to her room and to help herself to tea and coffee. No meals were served to her unless she were to buy them herself.

Lisa wasn't looking forward to telling her parents that shortly there would be no salary coming in, and therefore the rent would be hard to pay. She was even less enthusiastic about telling them that she would be using her bedroom as an office. In theory, they might offer her the formal dining room, which was never used and would have made a perfectly presentable business surrounding. But she knew not to push things too far.

Her father would say they weren't made of money. Her mother would shrug and say they didn't want strangers traipsing in and out of the place. Better do it little by little. Tell them about the job first, then gradually introduce the need to bring clients to the house as they got used to the first situation.

She wished over and over that Anton was less adamant about their living arrangements. He said that she was lovely, the loveliest thing that had ever happened to him. If this was so, why would he not let her come to live with him?

He had these endless excuses: it was a lads' place—he just had a room there, he didn't pay for it, instead he cooked for the lads once a week and that was his rent, he couldn't abuse their hospitality by bringing in someone else. Anyway, it would change the whole atmosphere of the place if a woman were to come into it.

He had sounded a little impatient. Lisa didn't mention it again. There was no way she could afford a place to live. There were new clothes, picnic meals and the two occasions she pretended to have got hotel vouchers in order to spirit him off for a night of luxury. All this had cost money.

Once or twice she wondered whether Anton might possibly be cheap? A bit *careful* with money, anyway? But no, he was endearingly honest.

"Lisa, my love, I'm a total parasite at the moment. Every euro I earn doing shifts I have to put away towards the cost of setting the place up. I'm a professional beggar just now, but in time I'll make it up to you. When you and I are sitting in the restaurant toasting our first Michelin star, *then* you'll think it was all worthwhile."

They sat together in the new kitchen, which was coming to life under their eyes. Ovens, refrigerators and hot plates were springing up around them. Soon the work would begin on the dining room. They had agreed on the logo and it was being worked into the rugs that would be scattered around the wooden floors. The place was going to be a dream, and Lisa was part of it.

Anton was only mildly surprised that she had left Kevin. He had always assumed that she would one day. He was less enthusiastic, however, about the notion that she might move into one of the spare rooms in the new building.

"I could make a bed-sitter out of *this* room and my office out of *that* one." Lisa pointed out two rooms down the corridor off the new kitchen.

"This one's the cold room and that's for linen and china," he said impatiently.

"Well, eventually, but I have to have *somewhere* to work and we agreed that I should help with the marketing as well . . . ," she began, but he started to look cross again so she dropped it.

It had to be home.

The reception was more glacial than she had expected.

"Lisa, you are twenty-five years of age. You have been well educated—expensively educated. Why can't you find a place to live and work like other girls do? Girls with none of your advantages and privileges . . ." Her father spoke to her as if she were a vagrant who had come into his bank and asked to sleep behind the counter.

"Even poor Katie, and Lord knows she never achieved much, she's at least able to look after herself," Lisa's mother said witheringly of her other daughter.

"I thought you'd be pleased that I was going out on my own," Lisa said. "I'm even thinking of taking some classes, on starting your own business and the like. I'm showing initiative."

"Mad is more like it. These days anyone who has a job holds on to it instead of throwing it up on a whim," her father said.

"And no rent for the foreseeable future," her mother sighed. "*And* you'll want the heating on during the day when there's no one else at home. *And* you want businesspeople filing in and out of this house. No, Lisa, it's not on."

"If we were to let your room to a stranger, we could get a proper rent for it," her father added.

"What about the dining room? I could put shelves and a filing system into it . . . ," Lisa began.

"And ruin the lovely dining room? I think not," her mother said.

"Why don't you forget the whole idea and stay where you are . . . in the agency," her father suggested, his tone slightly kinder as he saw her distressed face. "Do that, like a good girl, and we'll say no more about any of this."

Lisa didn't trust herself to speak anymore. She walked quickly to the front door and left the house.

She didn't *care* about money. She didn't *mind* working hard, and even though she hated self-pity she did begin to feel that the world was conspiring against her. Her own family were so unsupportive and her boyfriend impervious to any signals and hints. He *was* her boyfriend, wasn't he? He had mentioned no other woman and he had said she was lovely. Admittedly, he hadn't said he loved her, but being lovely was the same thing.

Lisa caught sight of herself in a shopwindow: she looked hunched and defeated.

This would never do. She brushed her hair, put on more makeup and held her shoulders back and strode confidently along to Anton's, to the place where a great restaurant was about to rise from the rubble and confusion that was currently there.

Later she would think about where to live and where to work. Tonight she would just drop into the gourmet shop and buy some smoked salmon and cream cheese. She wouldn't weary him with her problems. She would hate to see that impatient frown again on his handsome face.

To her great annoyance there were eight people there already, including her friend Miranda, who had been the one to introduce her to Anton in the first place. They were sitting around eating very gooey-looking pizza.

"Lisa!" Anton managed to sound delighted, welcoming and surprised at the same time, as if Lisa didn't come there every evening.

"Come on in, Lisa, and have some pizza. Isn't Miranda clever? She found *exactly* what we all wanted."

"Very clever," Lisa said through her teeth. Miranda, who looked slim like a greyhound but who ate like a hungry horse, was sitting on the ground in her pencil-slim jeans, wolfing down pizza as if she had known no other food. Some of the men were people who shared Anton's flat. The other girls were glamorous and suntanned. They looked as if they were auditioning for a musical.

None of them was broke, in debt, with nowhere to live and nowhere to work. Lisa wanted to run away and go and cry somewhere, big heaving sobs. But where could she go? She had nowhere, and this, after all, was where she wanted to be.

She slipped the smoked salmon and cream cheese into one of the fridges and came to join them.

"Anton has been singing your praises," Miranda said when she looked up momentarily from the huge pizza she was devouring. "He says you are a genius."

"That's going a bit far." Lisa smiled.

"No, it's the truth," Anton assured her. "I was telling them all about your ideas. They said I was very lucky to get you."

These were the words she had wanted to hear for so long. Why did it not seem as real and wonderful as she had hoped?

Then he said, "Everyone is here to give some ideas about marketing, so let's start straightaway. Lisa, you first . . ."

Lisa didn't want to share her ideas with this cast. She didn't want their approval or their dismissal.

"I'm last in—let's hear what everyone else has to say." She gave a huge smile at the group.

"Sly little fox," Miranda whispered, but loudly enough to be heard.

Anton didn't seem disturbed. "Right, Eddie, what do you think?" he began.

Eddie, a big bluff rugby player, was full of ideas, most of them useless. "You need to make this place a focus for the rugby set, somewhere people would lunch on the days of an International."

"That's about four days a year," Lisa heard herself say.

"Well, yes, but you could host fund-raisers for various rugby clubs," he said.

"Anton wants to *make* money, not give it away at this stage," Lisa said. She knew she sounded like someone's nanny or mother, but honestly . . .

A girl called April said that Anton could have wine appreciation classes there, followed by a dinner serving some of the most popular choices of the evening. It was so ludicrous as a moneymaker that Lisa hardly believed anyone would take it seriously, yet they were all eager and excited.

"Where's the profit?" she asked icily.

"Well, the wine manufacturers would sponsor it," April said, annoyed.

"Not until the place is up and running, they won't," Lisa said.

"Anton could have fashion shows here," Miranda suggested.

Everyone looked at Lisa to see how she would knock this one down, but she was careful. She had been too snide already.

"That's a good idea, Miranda. Have you any designers in mind?"

"No, but we could think up a few," Miranda said.

"I think it would take from the meal itself," Anton said.

"Yes, maybe you're right." Miranda didn't care; she was there only for the laughs and the pizza anyway.

"What do *you* think, Lisa? Do you have a background in marketing and business as well as graphic art?"

"No, I don't, April. In fact, I've just decided to do an evening course in management and marketing. The term starts next week, so at the moment all I have is my instinct." Lisa even managed a smile.

"Which says . . . ?" April was obviously keen.

"Just as Anton says, that the food is going to be extraordinary and everything else is second to that." She had surprised herself with the announcement about the evening class. She'd had the vague notion that such a thing would be a good idea, but being challenged by April had made up her mind. She was going to do it. She'd show them.

"You didn't tell me you were going back to college," Anton said when the others had all left. It had been touch and go as to whether April would *ever* leave, but somehow she realized that Lisa would outstay her and she did go grudgingly.

"Ah, there's lots of things I don't tell you, Anton," she said, scooping the glutinous pizza and paper plates into a refuse bag.

"Not too many, I hope," he said.

"No, not *too* many," Lisa agreed. This was the way it had to be played. She knew that now.

She signed on for the business diploma the next day. They were very helpful in the college and she gave them a check that was the very last of her savings.

"How will you support yourself?" the tutor asked her.

"It will be hard, but I'll manage," she said with a bright smile. "I have one client already, so that's a start."

"Good. That will keep you solvent," the tutor said, pleased.

Lisa wondered what he would say if he knew that the one client wasn't going to pay a cent for the job she was doing and that he was costing her a fortune because he liked a woman to smell of expensive perfume and have lacy underwear, but because he was putting everything he had into the business he was unable to buy her any of these things.

At her first lecture, she sat beside a quiet man called Noel Lynch, who seemed very worried about it all.

"Do you think it will help us, all this?" he asked her.

"God, I don't know," Lisa said. "You always hear successful people saying that qualifications don't matter, but I think they do because they give you confidence."

"Yes. I know. That's why I'm doing it too. But my cousin is paying my fees and I wouldn't want her to think it was a waste. . . ."

He was a gentle sort of fellow. Not smart and lively and vibrant like Anton's friends, but restful.

"Will we go and have a drink afterwards?" she asked him.

"No, if you don't mind. I'm actually a recovering alcoholic and I don't find myself at ease in a pub," he said.

"Well, coffee then?" Lisa said.

"I'd like that," Noel said with a smile.

Lisa went back to the bleak terraced house that she had called home for so long. *Why* was Anton so against her moving into his premises? It made absolute sense for her to be there, and once settled she could persuade him to give up his ludicrous bachelor existence with the others. After all, they were still on the prowl, while he had everything sorted: his own restaurant, his own girlfriend. What *was* the point in keeping up the charade of all being men about town?

If she could have gone back to the restaurant now and told him about the introductory lecture, it would have been great.

Mother was out somewhere and Father was watching television. He barely looked up as she came in.

"It went very well," she said to him.

"What did?" He looked up, startled.

"My first lecture at the college."

"You have qualifications already: a career, a job. This is just some kind of a *figario* you are taking." He went back to the television.

Lisa felt very, very lonely. Everyone in that lecture hall tonight had someone to talk to about it. Everyone except her.

Anton was out tonight. He and the flatmates were going to some reception, not that he would have been *very* interested, but he would have listened for a little bit anyway.

Katie would have cared, but Katie and Garry had gone away on a long weekend to Istanbul. It seemed a very long way to go just for three nights, but they were highly excited about it and regarded it as one of the great explorations of all time.

There were no other friends. None who cared. What the hell? She would call Anton. Nothing heavy, nothing clinging, just to make contact. He answered immediately.

There was a lot of noise in the background and he had to shout.

"*Lisa*, great. Where are you?"

"I'm at home."

"Oh, I thought you'd be here," he said, and he actually sounded disappointed.

Lisa brightened a little. "No, no, I was at my first lecture tonight."

"Oh, that's right. Well, why don't you come along now?"

"What is it, exactly?"

"No idea, Lisa, just lots of fun people. Everyone's here."

"You must know what it is."

She could hear him frown. Even over the phone.

"Love, I don't know who's running it, some magazine company, I think. April invited us. She said there was unlimited champagne and unlimited chances to meet people, and she was right."

"April asked you."

"Yes, she's part of the PR for it all. I was expecting you to be here too. . . ."

"No, honestly, I have to dash," she said and got off the phone just before she began to weep as if she were never going to stop crying ever again.

Katie came back from Istanbul and called Lisa to say she had a present for her. "How was it at the college?" she asked.

"You remembered?" Lisa was amazed. Nobody else had asked.

"I got you a terrific present at the bazaar," Katie said. "You'll love it!"

Lisa felt a prickling behind her nose and eyes.

She never remembered getting Katie a present from anywhere. "That's lovely," she said in a small voice.

"Will you come over this evening? Garry and I will bore you to death about all we saw."

Normally Lisa might have said that she'd have loved to but she had a million things to do. But she surprised both herself and her sister by saying that there was nothing she would like better.

"Brian might come as well, but he's no trouble."

"Brian?"

"Our tenant. We gave him the two rooms upstairs. I told you about him."

"Oh, yes, of course you did." Lisa felt guilty. Katie had indeed been wittering on about someone coming to live upstairs. She wished she had thought of asking for the rooms herself, but as usual the timing had been all wrong.

"You're not trying to set me up with this Brian, are you?" she asked.

"Hardly! He's a priest and he's nearly a hundred!"

"No!"

"Well, fifty anyway. Not about to break his vows. Anyway, don't you *have* a fellow?"

"Not really," Lisa said, admitting it for the first time to herself.

"Of course you do," Katie said briskly. "Anyway, I'm glad you're free tonight—come around seven-thirty."

Lisa was free that night. She had been free the night before, and the night before that. It had been three days since Anton had gone to April's party. Lisa was waiting for him to contact her.

Waiting and waiting.

Brian Flynn turned out to be a very decent man and great company. He told them about his mother, who had dementia but seemed quite content and happy in whatever world she lived in. How his sister had married a man called Skunk, how his brother had left one wife and fled from one girlfriend.

He told them about a holy well that he didn't rate very highly and about the immigrant center where he worked now and how he had a lot of respect for the people there.

Occasionally, he asked Katie and Lisa about their family. They both made excuses to get onto other subjects, so he either gave up or realized this was not an area where they were comfortable.

Garry talked cheerfully about his parents and how his father had originally said that being a hairdresser was only a job for "nancy" boys, but had slightly softened in his view over the years.

He told them about the time he had gone to the zoo on his birthday when he was seven and his parents had told the elephant that he was the best boy in the country, and they told him that the elephant would never forget this because elephants don't forget. And to this day Garry always thought that the elephant remembered.

They smiled at the notion.

Lisa wondered why she had ever thought Garry plodding. He was just decent. And romantic too. He showed them pictures on his phone of Katie with her hair blowing as they went for a cruise on the Bosporus and another of her with minarets in the background. But he hardly saw anything except her face.

"Katie looks so happy," he said over and over.

"And do you have a young man of your own?" Brian Flynn asked Lisa unexpectedly.

"Sort of," Lisa answered him truthfully. "There is a man I fancy a lot, but I don't think he is as serious as I am about it."

"Oh, men are fools, believe me," Brian Flynn said with the voice of authority. "They have no idea what they want. They are much more simple than women think, but more confused as well."

"Did you ever love anyone? I mean before you joined up . . . ," Lisa asked.

"No, nor after either. I'd have been a useless husband anyway. By the time they end this celibacy thing for priests, I'll be too old to get involved with anyone and that's probably all for the best."

"Is it lonely?"

"No more than any other life," he said.

As Lisa walked home from Katie's house she took a detour that brought her past Anton's. There were lights on upstairs in the room he was going to have as his office. She yearned to go in, but was too afraid of what she might find. April with her legs stretched out on his desk, Miranda sitting on the floor and any number of others. She went home in the dark and let herself into the house where there were no lights and no hints as to whether anyone was at home or not.

Just silence.

Next morning, she got a text from Anton: WHERE ARE YOU? I AM LOST WITHOUT YOU TO ADVISE ME AND SET ME ON TARGET AGAIN. I'M LIKE A JELLYFISH WITH NO BACKBONE. WHERE DID YOU GO, LOVELY LISA? A TOTALLY ABANDONED ANTON

She forced herself to wait two hours before replying, then she wrote: I WENT NOWHERE. I AM ALWAYS HERE. LOVE LISA

Then he wrote: DINNER HERE? 8PM? DO SAY YES.

Again, she forced herself not to reply at once. It was so silly, all this game playing, yet it appeared to work. Eventually she texted: DINNER AT 8 SOUNDS LOVELY.

She made no offer to bring cheese or salmon or artichoke hearts. She couldn't afford them, for one thing, and for another he was inviting *her*—he must remember that.

He had, of course, expected she would bring something to eat. She realized that when he went to the freezer to thaw out some frozen Mexican dishes, but she sat and sipped her wine, smiling, and asked him all about the business. She didn't mention the reception that April had invited him to. She only asked had he made any new contacts to help him with the launch.

He seemed slightly distracted as he prepared the meal. He was his usual efficient self, expertly slicing avocado, deseeding chilies and squeezing limes over prawns as a starter, but his mind was somewhere else. Eventually he got around to what he wanted to say.

"Have I annoyed you, Lisa?" he asked.

"No, of course not."

"Are you sure?"

"Well, obviously I am. Why do you think you did?"

"I don't know. You're different. You don't call me. You didn't bring anything for dinner. I didn't know if you were trying to say something to me . . ."

"Like what?"

"Like you're pissed off with me or something?"

"But why should I be? You invited me to dinner and I'm here. I'm having a lovely time."

"Oh, good. It's just a feeling I had. . . ." He seemed totally satisfied.

"Fine. So that's out of the way," she said cheerfully.

"I mean I value you, Lisa. We're not joined at the hip or anything, but I really do appreciate all you've done to help me get started. . . ." He paused.

She looked at him expectantly, not helping him out.

"So, I suppose I was afraid that there had been a misunderstanding between us, you know."

"No, I don't know. What kind of a misunderstanding?"

"Well, that you might be reading more into it than there is."

"Into what, Anton? You're talking in code."

"Into . . . well, into our relationship," he said eventually.

She felt the ground slip away from her and had to struggle hard to sound normal.

"It's fine, isn't it?" Lisa said, hearing her own voice as if from very far away.

"Sure. It's just me being silly. I mean it's not a commitment or anything . . . exclusive like that."

"We sleep together," Lisa said bluntly.

"Yes, we have, of course, and will again, but I don't ask you about who you meet after the lectures at your college. . . ."

"No, of course not."

"And you don't ask me about where I go and who I meet. . . ."

"Not if you don't want me to."

"Oh, Lisa, don't take an attitude." He was definitely frowning now.

The food tasted like lumps of cardboard. Lisa could barely swallow it.

"Will I make you a margarita? You're only nibbling at your food." Anton feigned concern.

Lisa shook her head.

"So cheer up then, and let's talk about the launch. April has all her people working on it."

"So what's left to talk about, then?" She knew she sounded childish and mutinous but she couldn't help it.

"Oh, Lisa, don't turn into one of those whining women. *Please, Lisa . . .*"

"Does this relationship, as you call it, mean anything to you? Anything at all?"

"Of course it does. It's just that I've taken a huge risk, I'm scared shitless that I'm going to fall on my face in this new venture, juggling a dozen balls in the air, just ahead of the posse in terms of debt and I haven't the *time* to think of anything seriously yet like . . . you know . . . permanent things." He looked lost and confused.

She hesitated. "You're right. I'm just tired and intense because I'm doing too much. I think I *would* like a margarita. Will you put salt around the rim of the glass?"

He brightened up at once.

Maybe that priest who lived over Katie and Garry was right: men *were* simple. And to please them, you had to be equally simple in return. She beat down her feeling of panic and was rewarded with one of Anton's great smiles.

The evening classes were going well. Lisa was actually much more interested than she had expected to be. She *was* quick, she realized.

Noel told her that she was the first in the group to understand any concept. He felt slow and was tempted to give up, but life in his job was so dreary and dull and he had no qualifications; this would give him the confidence and clout he needed.

She learned about him during their coffee breaks. He said the classes and his AA meetings were his only social outings of the week.

He was a placid person and didn't ask many questions about Lisa's life. Because of this, she told him that her parents had always seemed to dislike each other greatly and that she couldn't understand why they stayed together.

"Probably for fear of finding a worse life," Noel said glumly, and Lisa agreed that this might well be true.

He asked her once did she have a fellow and she had replied truthfully that she loved someone but it was a bit problematical. He didn't want to be tied down so she didn't really know where she was.

"I expect it will sort itself out," Noel said, and somehow that was fairly comforting.

And Noel was right, in a way. It sort of sorted itself out.

Lisa never called around to Anton without letting him know she was on her way. She took an interest in all he was doing and made no more remarks about April's involvement in anything. Instead, she concentrated on making the cleverest and most eye-catching invitations to the pre-launch party.

There was no question of her getting anything new to wear. There wasn't any money to pay for an outfit. She confided this to Noel.

"Does it matter all that much?" he asked.

"It does a bit because if I thought I looked well I'd behave well, and I know this sounds silly, but a lot of the people who will be there sort of judge you by what you wear."

"They must be mad," Noel said. "How could they not take notice of you? You look amazing, with your height and your looks— that hair . . ."

Lisa looked at him sharply, but he was clearly speaking sincerely, not just trying to flatter her. "Some of them are mad, I'm sure, but I'm being very honest with you. It's a real pain that I can't get anything new."

"I don't like to suggest this but what about a thrift shop? My cousin sometimes works in one. She says she often gets designer clothes in there."

"Lead me to it," Lisa said with a faint feeling of hope.

Molly Carroll had the perfect dress for her. It was scarlet with a blue ribbon threaded around the hem. The colors of Anton's restaurant and the logo she had designed.

Molly said the dress could have been designed just for her. "I'm not very up-to-date in fashion," she said, "but you'll certainly stop them in their tracks in this one."

Lisa smiled with pleasure. It *did* look good.

Katie treated her to a wash and blow-dry and she set out for the party in high good spirits. April was there in a very official capacity, welcoming people in.

"Great dress," April said to Lisa.

"Thanks," Lisa said. "It's vintage," and went to find Anton.

"You look absolutely beautiful," he said when he caught sight of her.

"It's *your* night. How's it going?" Lisa asked.

"Well, I've been working for two days on all these canapés but you wouldn't think it was my night. April believes it's hers. She's insisting on being in every picture." Just then a photographer approached them.

"And who's this?" he asked, nodding at Lisa.

"My brilliant designer and stylist, Lisa Kelly," responded Anton instantly.

The photographer wrote it down, and out of the corner of her eye Lisa could see April's disapproval. She smiled all the more broadly.

"You're really gorgeous, you know." Anton was admiring Lisa openly. "And you wore my colors too."

She savored the praise. She knew there would be times when she would play this scene over and over again in her mind. But she mustn't dwell on herself and her dress.

Lisa blessed Noel and his cousin Emily's thrift shop. She had paid so little for this outfit and she was one of the most elegant women in the room. More photographers were approaching her. She must try to look as though she wanted to deflect attention from herself.

"There's a great crowd here," Lisa said. "Did all the people you wanted turn up?" Across the room she saw that April had a face like a sour lemon. "But I mustn't monopolize you," she added as she slipped away, knowing that he was looking after her as she went to mingle with the other guests.

Miranda was slightly drunk.

"I think it's game, set and match to you, Lisa," she said unsteadily.

"What do you mean?" Lisa asked innocently.

"Oh, I think you've knocked April into Also-Ran. . . ."

"What?"

"It's a saying, you know, in a horse race. There's the winner and there's Also-Ran, meaning the ones that didn't win."

"I know what it *means*," Lisa said, "but what do *you* mean?"

"I think you have the single, undivided attention of Anton Moran," Miranda said. It was a complicated phrase to finish and she sat down after the effort.

Lisa smiled. What should she do now? Try to outstay April or leave early? Hard though it was to do, she decided to leave early.

His disappointment was honey to her soul.

"You're never going? I thought you were going to sit down with me afterwards and have a real postmortem."

"Nonsense! You'll have lots of people. April, for example."

"Oh, God, no. Lisa, rescue me. She'll be talking of column inches of coverage and her biological clock."

Lisa laughed aloud. "No, Anton, of course she won't. See you soon. Call me and tell me how it all went." And she was gone.

There was a bus at the end of the lane and she ran to catch it. It was full of tired people going home late from work. She felt like a glorious butterfly in her smart dress and high heels, while they all looked drab and colorless. She had drunk two cocktails, the man she loved had told her that she was gorgeous and wanted her to stay.

It was only nine o'clock at night. She was a lucky, lucky girl. She must never forget this.

Chapter Five

For Stella Dixon the time just flew by: there was so much to see to every day. There was a lawyer to talk to, a nurse from the health authorities, another nurse—this time from the operating theater—who tried to explain the procedure (though Stella was having none of it; she was far too busy, she said). Once she got her anesthetic "that would be curtains" for her. While she was still here she had to try to deal with everything.

Her doctor, Declan Carroll, came in to see her regularly. She asked after his wife.

"Maybe the babies will get to know each other," Stella had said wistfully one day.

"Maybe. We'll have to work on it." He was a very pleasant young man.

"You mean *you* will have to work on it," she said with a smile that broke his heart.

For Noel there weren't enough hours in the day either. Anytime that he was not slaving in Hall's, going to twelve-step meetings or catching up on his studies, he spent surfing the net for advice on how to cope with a new baby. He had moved into his new place in Chestnut Court and was busy making preparations for her arrival.

He had AA meetings every day, since the thought that most

things could be sorted out by several pints and three whiskeys was always with him. He managed to stay away from the bar at his father's retirement party. There wasn't a dry eye in the place as they presented a watch to Charlie that he said he would wear every day.

Noel began to wonder how he had ever found time to drink.

"Maybe I'm nearly over it," he said hopefully to Malachy, whom he had met on his first visit and who was now his sponsor at AA.

"I don't want to be downbeat, but we all feel this in the early days," Malachy warned him.

"It's not really early days. I haven't had a drink for twenty-one days," Noel said proudly.

"Fair play to you, but I am four years dry and yet if something went seriously wrong in my life I know only too well where I would *want* to find a solution. It would solve everything for a couple of hours and then I'd have to start all over again . . . as hard as the first time, only worse. . . ."

For Brian Flynn the days flew by as well. He adapted perfectly to his new living quarters and began to think that he had always lived over a busy hair salon. Garry cut his hair for him and tamed the red-gray thatch into a reasonable shape. They said he was better than any security firm and that the fact that he lived there was a deterrent to intruders.

He left each morning for the immigrant center where he worked; as he passed through the salon he encountered many ladies in varying degrees of disarray and marveled to himself how they endured so much in the cause of beauty. He would greet them pleasantly, and Katie always introduced him as the Reverend Lodger Upstairs.

"You could hear confessions here, Brian, but I think you'd be electrified by what they'd tell you," Katie said cheerfully.

She had discovered that even in the middle of a recession, women were more anxious than ever to have their hair done. It kept them sane, somehow, and feeling in control.

.   .   .

For Lisa Kelly the time crawled by.

She was finding it difficult to get decisions made about her designs for Anton's restaurant, as a decision meant money being spent. Although the restaurant was open and full to bursting every night, there was still no verdict on whether to use her new logos and style on the tableware. Instead, she was concentrating on her course-work and giving Noel a hand.

Noel had undergone some amazing conversion; when Lisa heard about his plan to take on a baby, she thought it was a fantasy. She had felt sure he would never be able to cope with a job, a college course and a newborn: it was too much to ask from one person, especially someone who was weak and shy like Noel. However, she was beginning to change her mind.

Noel had surprised her, and in a way she almost envied him. He was so dedicated to all that he was doing. Everything was new for him. He had a whole new life ahead, while Lisa felt that it was for-ever more of the same. Of course it was all still theoretical; the baby wasn't even born yet. But he was preparing as much as he could to be a father. His notes always had lists scribbled in the margins: *nappy-rash cream, baby wipes,* they would say. *Four bottles, bottle brush, nip-ples, steriliser . . .*

Her parents were still living in their icy, uncaring way, sharing a roof but not a bedroom, not a dining table, not any leisure time. They had no interest in Lisa or her life, any more than they cared how Katie fared with Garry in the salon. It was just casual indiffer-ence, not amazing hostility, that existed between them as a couple. One had only to come into a room for the other to leave it.

Lisa had never been able to pin Anton down: there was always *this* conference and *that* sales meeting and *this* television appearance and *that* radio interview. She had never seen him alone. The pictures of her and Anton together had given way to shots of him with any number of beautiful girls; though she would have heard if he had any new real girlfriend. It would have been in the Sunday papers.

That was the way Anton attracted publicity—he gave free drinks to columnists and photographers and they always snapped him with several beautiful women and gave the impression that he was busy making up his mind among them all.

And it wasn't as if he had abandoned her or was ignoring her, Lisa reminded herself. A day didn't pass without a text message from Anton. Life was so busy, he would text. They had a rock band in last night, they were going to do a society wedding, a charity auction, a new tasting menu, a week of Breton specialties. Nowhere any mention of Lisa or her designs and plans.

Then, just as she was about to face the fact that he had left her, he wrote about this simply beautiful restaurant he had heard of in Honfleur, where the seafood was to die for. They *must* sneak away there for a weekend of self-indulgence soon. No date was fixed—just the word "soon," and when she was starting to think that it meant "never," he said that there was a trade fair next month in Paris that they could both go to and fish for ideas and *then* run off to Honfleur. They might even dream up a whole Normandy season for the restaurant while they were there.

It was an unsettling life, to say the least.

Lisa couldn't seem to get on with other work. She kept changing or improving the proposals she had done for Anton—ideas that had never been discussed or even acknowledged.

She was doing all right at school. Nothing like Noel, of course. *That* man was like something possessed. He said that he made do with four and a half hours' sleep. He laughed it off, saying that he would probably get less when the new baby arrived. He was so calm and accepting about it all.

"Did you love her, this Stella?" Lisa had asked.

"I think 'love' is too strong a word. I like her a lot," he replied, struggling to be honest.

"She must love you, then, to leave you in charge," Lisa said.

"No, I don't think she does. I think she trusts me. That's all."

"Well, that's a big part of life. If you trust someone, you're halfway there," Lisa said.

"Do you trust this Anton you talk about?"

"Not really," Lisa said, with a face that closed the door on any further conversation about the topic.

Noel shrugged. He was off anyway up to the hospital to visit Stella.

Three days later, Declan Carroll was in the delivery room holding Fiona's hand as she groaned and whimpered.

"Great, girl. Just three more. . . . Just three . . ."

"How do you know it's only three?" gasped Fiona, red-faced, her hair damp and stuck to her forehead.

"Trust me, I'm a doctor," Declan said.

"You're not a woman, though," Fiona said, teeth gritted and preparing for another push.

But he was right—there were only three more. Then the head of his son appeared and he began to cry with relief and happiness.

"He's here," he said, placing the baby in her arms. He took a photograph of them both and a nurse took a picture of all three of them.

"He'll hate this when he grows up," Fiona said, and John Patrick Carroll let out a wail in agreement.

"Only for a while and then he'll love it," said Declan, who had had his fair share of a mother who showed pictures of him to total strangers at the Laundromat where she worked.

He left the delivery ward of St. Brigid's and headed for oncology. He knew what time Stella was going down for surgery and he wanted to be there as moral support.

They were just putting her on the trolley.

"Declan!" she said, pleased.

"Had to come and wish you well," he said.

"You know Noel. And this is his cousin Emily." Stella was totally at ease, as if she were at a party instead of about to make the last journey of her life.

Declan knew Emily already, as she came regularly to the group practice where he worked. She filled in at the desk as a receptionist or made the coffee or cleaned the place. It was never defined exactly what she did except that everyone knew the place would close down without her. She also helped his mother in the Laundromat from time to time. No job seemed too menial for her, even though she had a degree in art history. He tried to think about her as they stood in a little tableau waiting for Stella to be wheeled to the operating theater. It helped to concentrate on the living rather than on Stella, who would not be in their number for much longer.

"Any news of *your* baby yet, Declan?" Stella asked.

Declan decided against telling her of his great happiness with his brand-new son. It would make things even worse for the woman who would never see her own child.

"No, not a sign," he lied.

"Remember they are to be friends," Stella urged him.

"Oh, that's a promise," said Declan.

Just at that moment the ward sister came in. She smiled when she saw Declan.

"Congratulations, Doctor, we hear you've had a beautiful baby boy!"

He looked like something trapped in the headlights of an approaching car. He could not deny his son, nor could he pretend to be surprised when it would be known that he was there for the birth.

He had to face it.

"Sorry, Stella. I didn't want to be gloating."

"No, you wouldn't ever do that," she said. "A boy! Imagine!"

"Yes, we didn't know. Not until he was born."

"And is he perfect?"

"Thank God."

And then she was wheeled out of the ward, leaving Noel, Emily and Declan behind.

Frances Stella Dixon Lynch was delivered by cesarean section on October 9 at seven p.m. She was tiny, but perfect. Ten tiny, perfect fingers, ten tiny, perfect toes and a shock of hair on her tiny, perfect head. She frowned at the world around her and wrinkled her tiny nose before opening her mouth and wailing as if it were already all too much.

Her mother died twenty minutes later.

The first person Noel telephoned was Malachy. "I can't live through this night without a drink," he told him. Malachy said he would come straight to the hospital. Noel was not to move until he arrived.

The women in the ward were full of sympathy. They arranged that he get tea and biscuits, which tasted like sawdust.

There was a small bundle of papers in an elastic band on her locker. The word NOEL was on the outside. He read them through with blurred eyes. One was an envelope with FRANKIE written on it. The others were factual: her instructions about the funeral, her wishes that Frankie be raised in the Roman Catholic faith for as long as it seemed sensible to her. And a note dated last night.

Noel, tell Frankie that I wasn't all bad and that once I knew she was on the way I did the very best for her. Tell her that I had courage at the end and I didn't cry my eyes out or anything. And tell her that if things had been different you and I would both have been there to look after her. Oh—and that I'll be looking out for her from up there. Who knows? Maybe I will.
Thanks again,
Stella

Noel looked down at the tiny baby with tears in his eyes. "Your mam didn't want to leave you, little one," he whispered. "She wanted to stay with you, but she had to go away. It's just you and me now. I don't know how we're going to do it, but we'll manage. We've got to look after each other." The baby looked at him solemnly as though concentrating on his words in order to commit them to memory.

·   ·   ·

Baby Frances was pronounced healthy. A collection of people came
to visit her as she lay there in her little crib. Noel, who took time off
from work, came every day. Moira Tierney, the social worker,
showed up at odd times, asking too many questions. Emily brought
Charles and Josie to see their grandchild, and they visibly melted at
the sight of the baby. They seemed to have completely forgotten
their earlier condemnation of sex without marriage, and Josie was
even seen to lift the child in her arms and pat the baby's back.

Lisa Kelly visited a couple of times, as did Malachy. Mr. Hall
came from Noel's workplace; even Old Man Casey came and said
that Noel was a sad loss to his bar. Young Dr. Declan Carroll came in
carrying his own son and introduced the babies formally to each
other.

Father Brian Flynn came in and brought Father Kevin Kenny
with him. Father Kenny, still on one crutch, was eager to take up his
role as hospital chaplain again. He seemed slightly put out that
Father Flynn had been so warmly accepted as his replacement.
Many people seemed to know him and called him Brian in what
Father Kenny thought of as a slightly overfamiliar way. He had obviously been involved in every stage of the unfortunate woman's
pregnancy and the birth of the motherless baby who lay there looking up at them. Father Kenny assumed that they were there to
arrange a baptism and started to clear his throat and talk about the
technicalities.

But no, Father Flynn had brushed that away swiftly. The baby's
grandparents were extraordinarily devout people and they would
discuss all that sort of thing at a later time.

Charles and Josie Lynch's neighbor Muttie Scarlet came to pay
his respects to the child. He was in the hospital anyway, he said, on
business, and he thought he would take advantage of the occasion to
visit the baby.

And eventually Noel was told that he could take his baby daughter home to his new apartment. It was a terrifying moment. Noel
realized that he was about to stop being a visitor and become

entirely responsible for this tiny human being. How was he going to remember all the things that needed to be done? Supposing he dropped her? Poisoned her? He couldn't do it, he couldn't be responsible for this baby, it was ludicrous to ask him. Stella had been mad, she was ill, she didn't know what she was doing. Someone else would have to take over, they'd have to find someone else to look after her baby—*her* baby, nothing to do with him at all. He had a sudden urge to flee, to run down the corridor and out into the street, and to keep on running until the hospital and Stella and Frankie and all of them were just a memory.

Just as his feet were starting to turn towards the doorway, the nurse arrived with Frankie, wrapped in a big pink shawl.

She looked up at him trustingly, and suddenly, from nowhere, Noel felt a wave of protectiveness almost overwhelm him. This poor, helpless baby had no one else in the world. Stella had trusted him with the most precious thing she ever had, the child she knew she wouldn't live to see. Nervously, almost shyly, he took the baby from the nurse.

"Little Frankie," he said to the tiny baby. "Let's go home."

Emily had said she would come to stay with him for a few days to tide him over the most frightening bits. There were three bedrooms in the apartment, two reasonably sized and one small one, which was to be Frankie's, so she would be perfectly comfortable. The visiting nurse came every couple of days but even so, there were so many questions.

Was that horrible-colored mess in the baby's nappy normal, or did she have something wrong with her? How could anyone so very small need to be changed ten times a day? Was that breathing normal? Did he dare go to sleep in case she stopped?

How on earth did anyone manage to get all those snaps on a baby's sleep suit in the right places? Was one blanket too much or too little? He knew she mustn't be allowed to get too cold, but the pamphlets were full of terrible warnings about the dangers of over-heating.

Bath times were a nightmare. He knew to test the temperature of the water with his elbow, but would a mother's elbow signal a different temperature from his? Emily needed to come to test the water as well.

She was kept busy: she would do the laundry and help him prepare the bottles and they could read the hospital notes and the baby books and consult the Internet together. They would take the baby's temperature and make sure they had supplies of nappies, wipes, newborn formula. So much of it and so expensive. How did anyone cope with all this?

How did anyone learn to identify what kind of crying meant hunger, discomfort or pain? To Noel all crying sounded the same: piercing, jagged, shrill, drilling through the deepest, most exhausted sleep. No one ever told you how tiring it was to be up three, four times every night, night after night. After three days he was near to weeping with fatigue; as he walked up and down with his daughter trying to burp her after her third feed of the night, he found himself stumbling against furniture, almost incapable of remaining upright.

Emily found him asleep in an armchair. "Don't forget you have to go to the center every week."

"They're not taking any chances with me," Noel said.

"It's the same for everyone. They call it the Mothers and Babies Group, but more and more it can be Fathers and Babies." Emily was practical.

"It's not just that they think I'm a bit of a risk—past history of drinking and all that?" Noel asked.

"No. Don't be paranoid. And aren't you a shining example of what people can achieve."

"I'm terrified, Emily."

"Of course you are. So am I, but we'll manage."

"You won't go back to America and leave me here all on my own. . . ."

"No plans to do that, but I think you should set up some kind of a system for yourself from the very start. Like going to your mother and father for lunch on a Sunday every week."

"I don't know . . . *Every* week?"

"Oh, at least, and in time you should offer to take Declan and Fiona's baby one evening a week to give them a night off. They'll do the same for you."

"You definitely sound as if you're going to jump ship and you're just building me up some support to keep me going," Noel said.

"Nonsense, Noel. But you have to learn to do it without me. You'll be on your own soon." Emily had no plans to go back to New York for a while, but she must be practical and get this show properly launched on the road.

Father Flynn found a gospel choir, which sang at the funeral Mass down at his church at the welcome center for immigrants. Twins called Maud and Simon, who seemed to be related to Muttie Scarlet, prepared a light lunch in the hall next door. There were no orations or speeches. Declan and Fiona sat next to Charles and Josie; Emily had the bag of baby essentials while Noel held Frankie wrapped in a warm blanket.

Father Flynn spoke simply and movingly about Stella's short and troubled life. She had died, he said, leaving behind a very precious legacy. Everyone who had come to know and care for Stella would support Noel as he provided a home for their little daughter. . . .

Katie was there with Garry and Lisa. She had only recently found out that Lisa was on the same course as Noel and had begun at the same time. They knew each other, had had coffee together once or twice; Lisa knew the story. Katie had hoped that Lisa would learn something from Noel—like that it was totally possible to get up and leave the safety of the family home. Home was not a healthy place to be, Katie thought, but there was no talking to Lisa, beautiful and restless as she had always been. Katie noticed that Lisa, for once, was not being distant and withdrawn as she so often was. Instead she was being helpful, offering to pass plates of food or pour coffee. She was talking to Noel in terms of practicalities.

"I'll help you whenever I can. If you have to miss any lectures I'll give you the notes," she offered.

"People are being very kind," Noel said. "Kinder than I ever expected."

"There's something about a baby," Lisa said.

"There is indeed. She's so very small. I don't know if I'll be able . . . I mean, I'm pretty clumsy."

"All new parents are clumsy," Lisa reassured him.

"That's the social worker over there. Moira," he said with a nod in her direction.

"She's got a very uptight little face," Lisa said.

"It's a very uptight job. She's always coming across losers like me."

"I don't think you're a loser—I think you're bloody heroic," Lisa said.

Moira Tierney had always wanted to be a social worker. When she was very young she had thought she might be a nun, but somehow that idea had changed over the years. Well, nuns had changed, for one thing. They didn't live in big, quiet convents chanting hymns at dawn and dusk anymore. There were no bells ringing and cloisters with shadows. Nuns, more or less, *were* social workers these days, without any of the lovely ritual and ceremony.

Moira was from the west of Ireland, but now she lived alone in a small apartment. When she first came to Dublin, she went home to see her parents every month. They sighed a lot because she hadn't married. They sighed over the fact that she was working among the poor and ruffians instead of bettering herself.

They sighed a great deal.

After her mother died, her visits became less frequent. Now she would go back just once or twice a year to the ramshackle farmhouse she had once called home.

She wished that her block of flats had a garden but the other residents had all voted for more car parking, so it was just yards of concrete outside. Still, democracy ruled, she thought, and made do with window boxes that were the envy of her neighbors. She liked her work, but it was rarely, if ever, straightforward.

Noel Lynch was someone who puzzled her. It appeared he had known nothing of the child he had fathered until a few short weeks before the baby arrived. He had lost touch with the mother. And then, suddenly, he had almost overnight changed his lifestyle totally, joined a twelve-step program, taken up lectures and approached his job in Hall's seriously. Any one of these things would have been life-changing, but to take them all on while looking after an infant seemed to be ludicrous.

Moira had read too many concerned and outraged articles about social workers who didn't do their jobs properly to feel any way at ease. She knew what they would write. They would say that all the signs were staring everyone in the face. This was a dangerous situation. What were the social workers *doing*? She didn't know why she was so certain about this, but it was a feeling that wouldn't go away. Every box had been ticked, all the relevant authorities had been contacted, yet she was completely convinced that there was something out of place here.

This Noel Lynch was an accident waiting to happen. A bomb about to explode.

Lisa Kelly was thinking about Noel at the same time.

She had said to Katie that if she were a betting woman she would give him one week before he went back on the drink and two weeks before he gave up his lectures. And as regards minding an infant—the social workers would be in before you could say "foster home!"

Just as well she hadn't found a betting shop.

Lisa had done a job for a garden center but her heart wasn't in it. All the time that she toyed with images of floral baskets, watering cans and sunflowers in full bloom she thought of Anton's restaurant.

She found herself drawing a bride throwing a bouquet—and then the thought came to her.

Anton could specialize in weddings.

Real society weddings. People would have to fight to get a date there. They had an underused courtyard where people often escaped for a furtive cigarette. It could be transformed into a permanent, mirror-lined marquee for weddings.

He didn't open for Saturday lunch so that was the time to do it; the guests would have to leave by six o'clock. There was a singing pub called Irish Eyes nearby and they could make an arrangement with the pub that there would be a welcoming pint or cocktail and the scene would move seamlessly onward. The bride's father would be relieved that he wasn't paying for champagne all night and the restaurant could get straight into "serving dinner" mode. There would be only fifty "Anton Brides" a year, so there would be huge competition to know who they would be.

It was too good an idea to keep to herself.

Anton had sounded fretful in his recent texts. Of course he couldn't fix a date for their trip to Normandy. Not now, not in the middle of a recession. Business was so up and down. No groups of estate agents and auctioneers celebrating another sale, like they had every day during the property boom. No leisurely business lunches. Times were tough.

So Lisa knew that he would love this idea. But when to tell him?

If only she had her own place. It would have been totally different: Anton could have popped around in the afternoon or the early evening. Or better, he could have come to visit late in the evening, when he could unwind and stay the night. When she did spend time with Anton it was always at a conference hotel or on a visit to a specialty restaurant where they would stay overnight at a nearby inn. This hope of Honfleur was what had kept her going for weeks and now it looked as if it wasn't definite, but when he saw all the work she had done on the concept of Anton Brides, he would pay attention. Yet again she would have rescued him and he would be so grateful.

She just couldn't wait any longer. She would tell him tonight. She would go to his restaurant tonight, straight after her lectures. She would go home and change first. She wanted to look her very best when she told him about this news that would turn his fortunes around and change their lives.

At home, Lisa went to her room and held two dresses up to the light, the first a black and red dress with black lace trimming, the other a light wool rose-colored dress with a wide belt. The black-and-red was sexy, the pink more elegant. The black-and-red was a little tarty but the pink would attract every stain going and would need to be dry-cleaned.

She had a quick shower and put on the black and red dress and a lot of makeup.

Teddy the maître d' was surprised to see her when she arrived at Anton's.

"You're a stranger round here, Lisa," he said with his professional smile.

"Too busy thinking up marvelous ideas for this place, that's why," she laughed. In her own ears her laughter sounded brittle and false; she didn't much care for Teddy. Tonight, though, she was going to establish her place in this restaurant. Anton would see how brilliant her scheme was; she wasn't even remotely nervous about meeting him and explaining her new plan.

"And are you dining here, Lisa?" Teddy was unfailingly polite but very focused. There was no room for vagueness in Teddy's life.

"Yes. I hoped you could squeeze me in. I need to talk to him about something."

"Alas, full tonight." Teddy smiled regretfully. "Not a table left in the place." They were having a special event, he explained, a four-for-the-price-of-two night in order to get the word out about Anton's. Of course it had been April's idea.

"The place is packed out tonight," Teddy said. "There's a wait list for cancellations."

This was not what she had come to hear. She had come here to give Anton news about how to change the downward spiral.

"But I really need to talk to him," she insisted. "I've got a great idea for bringing in new business. Look, Teddy," she continued, becoming aware that the shrillness in her voice was attracting attention, "he's really going to want to hear my ideas—he's going to be very angry if you don't let me see him."

"I'm sorry, Lisa," he said firmly. "That's just not going to be possible. You see how busy we are."

"I'll just go back into the kitchen and see what Anton has to say about that . . . ," Lisa began.

"I think not," said Teddy firmly, stepping smoothly to one side and gripping her elbow. "Why don't you telephone tomorrow and make an appointment? Or better still, make a reservation. We'd love to see you here again, and I will certainly tell Anton you called in." As he spoke, he was guiding her firmly towards the door.

Before she knew what had happened, Lisa found herself outside on the street, looking back at the diners, who were staring at her as if hypnotized.

She needed to get away quickly; turning on her heels, she fled as quickly as her too-tight skirt would allow her.

When she was able to draw breath, she pulled out her cell phone to call a taxi and found, to her annoyance, that she had let the battery run down. The night was going from bad to worse.

And then it started to rain.

The house was quiet when she let herself in but that didn't make it any different than usual. Here there was no conversation, unless Katie had come on one of her infrequent visits. Lisa hoped that no one was going to be there tonight. She was in luck. As she reached the bottom of the stairs, there was just silence about the house, as if it were holding its breath.

And that's when it happened. Lisa saw what the newspapers would have called "a partially clothed woman" come out of the bathroom at the top of the stairs holding a mobile phone to her ear. She had long, damp hair and was wearing a green satin slip and nothing much else by the look of her.

"Who are *you*?" Lisa asked in shock.

"I might ask you the same," the woman said. She didn't seem annoyed, put out or even embarrassed. "Are you here for him? I'm just ringing a taxi."

"Well, why are you ringing it here?" Lisa asked childishly. Who could she be? You often heard of burglars coming into a house and just brazening it out with the householders. Maybe she was part of a gang?

Then she heard her father's voice. "What is it, Bella? Who are you talking to?" And her father appeared at his bedroom door in a dressing gown. He looked shocked to see Lisa. "I didn't know *you* were at home," he said, nonplussed.

"Obviously," Lisa said, her hand shaking as she reached for the front door.

"Who *is* she?" the girl in the green satin slip asked.

"It doesn't matter," he said.

And Lisa realized that it didn't. It had never mattered to him who she was or Katie either.

"Well, who am I to say what you should do with your own money. . . ." The woman called Bella shrugged in her green satin underwear and went back into the bedroom.

Lisa and her father looked at each other for a long minute; then he followed Bella back into the bedroom as, unsteadily, Lisa left the house again.

Noel allowed himself to think that Stella would have been pleased with how he was coping with their daughter. He had been without an alcoholic drink for almost two months. He attended an AA meeting at least five times a week and telephoned his friend Malachy on the days he couldn't make it.

He had brought Frankie to Chestnut Court and was making a home for her. True, he was walking round like a zombie from tiredness, but he had kept her alive, and what's more, the visiting nurses seemed to think she was doing well. She slept in a small crib beside him and when she cried he woke and walked around the room with her. He sterilized all the bottles and nipples, made up her formula and changed her. He bathed her and burped her and rocked her to sleep.

He sang songs to her as he paced up and down the bedroom every night, every song he could think of, even if some of them were mad and inappropriate. "Sittin' on the Dock of the Bay" . . . "I Don't Like Mondays" . . . "Let Me Entertain You" . . . "Fairytale of New York" . . . Any snippet of any song he could remember. Why didn't he know the words to proper lullabies?

He had conducted three satisfactory meetings with the social worker Moira Tierney and five with Imelda, the visiting nurse.

His leave was over and he was about to go back to work at Hall's; he wasn't looking forward to it, but babies were expensive and he really needed the money. He would wait a while and then ask for a bit of a raise in salary. He was catching up with his lectures from the college—Lisa had been as good as her word—and was back on track again there.

He was tired all the time, but then so was every young mother whom he passed on the street or at the supermarket. He was certainly too tired to pause and wonder was he happy with it all himself. The little baby needed him and he would be there. That's all there was to it. And his life was certainly much better than it had been eight weeks ago.

He put his books away in the silent apartment. His cousin Emily was asleep in her room, little Frankie was sleeping in the crib beside his own bed. He looked out of his window in Chestnut Court. It was late, dark, drizzly and very quiet.

He saw a taxi draw up and a young woman get out. What strange lives people led! Then, two seconds later, he heard his doorbell ring.

Whoever it was was coming to see him—Noel Lynch—at this time of night!

"Lisa?!" Noel was puzzled to see her on the entry-phone screen at this time of night.

"Can I come in for a moment, Noel? I want to ask you something."

"Yes . . . well . . . I mean . . . the baby's asleep . . . but, sure, come in." He pressed the buzzer to release the door.

She looked very woebegone. "I don't suppose you have a drink? No, sorry, of course you don't. I'm sorry. Forgive me." She had forgotten with that casual, uncaring, shruggy attitude of someone who had never been addicted to drink.

Malachy had told Noel that it was this laid-back attitude that really got to him. His friends saying they could take it or leave it, bypassing the terrible urgency that the addicted felt all the time.

"I can offer tea or chocolate," he said, forcing back his annoyance. She didn't know. She would never know what it felt like. He would not lose his temper, but what was she doing here at this time of night?

"Tea would be lovely," she said.

He put on the kettle and waited.

"I can't go home, Noel."

"No?"

"No."

"So what do you want to do, Lisa?"

"Can I sleep on your sofa here, please? *Please*, Noel. Just for tonight. Tomorrow I'll sort something out."

"Did you have a row at home?"

"No."

"And what about your friend Anton, whom you talk so much about?"

"I've been there. He doesn't want to see me."

"And I'm your last hope—is that it?"

"That's it," she said bleakly.

"All right," he said.

"What?"

"I said all right. You can stay. I don't have any women's clothes to lend you. I can't give you my bed—Frankie's crib is in there and she's due a feed in a couple of hours. We'll all be up pretty early in the morning. It's no picnic being here."

"I'd be very grateful, Noel."

"Sure, then have your tea and go to bed. There's a folded blanket over there and use one of the cushions as a pillow."

"Do you not want to know what it is about?" she asked.

"No, Lisa, I don't. I haven't got the energy for it. Oh, and if you're up before I am, Emily, that's my cousin, will be getting Frankie ready to take her to the health center."

"Well, I'll sort of explain to her then."   ·

"No need."

"What a wonderful way to be," Lisa said in genuine admiration.

She didn't think she would sleep at all, but she did, stirring slightly a couple of times when she thought she heard a baby crying. Through a half-opened eye she saw Noel moving about with an infant in his arms. She didn't even have time to think about what kind of mind games Anton was playing with her or whether her father was even remotely embarrassed by the incident in their home. She was fast asleep again and didn't wake until she heard someone leave a mug of tea beside her.

Cousin Emily, of course. The wonder woman who had stepped in just when needed. She in turn didn't seem remotely surprised to see a woman in a black and red lace-trimmed dress waking up on the sofa.

"Do you have to be anywhere for work or anything?" the woman asked.

"No. No, I don't. I'll just wait until my parents have left home, then I'll go back and pick up my things and . . . find myself somewhere else to stay. I'm Lisa, by the way."

Emily looked at her.

"I know. We met at Stella's funeral. And I'm Emily. What time will your parents be gone?" she asked.

"By nine—on a normal morning, anyway."

"But this might not be a normal morning?" Emily guessed.

"No, it might not. You see . . ."

"Noel left half an hour ago. It's eight o'clock now. I have to go to the clinic with Frankie via the charity shop fairly soon . . . and I'm not quite sure what's the best thing to do."

"I'm a friend of Noel's, from college . . ." Lisa began.

"Oh, I know that too."

"So you wouldn't have to worry about leaving me here when you go out, but then you might not want to. . . ."

Emily shook her head as if to get rid of any evidence of such deep thinking on her part. "No, I was thinking of breakfast, actually. Noel made a banana sandwich for himself and then he'll have coffee on his way to work. I'm going to open up the thrift shop when I've given Frankie her bottle; I'll have some fruit and cereal there. I thought you might like to come with me. Would that suit?"

"That would be great, Emily. I'll just go and give myself a quick wash."

Lisa hopped up and ran to the bathroom. She looked quite terrible. All her makeup was smeared across her face. She looked like a tart down on her luck.

No wonder the woman didn't want to leave her in charge of the apartment. Nobody would let anyone who looked like Lisa did be in charge of anything at all. Maybe Lisa would be able to buy something at the thrift shop to take away the wild look of her. She cleaned her face and gave herself a splash wash, then put on over her dress a sweater Emily had given her.

Emily was ready to leave: she was dressed in a fitted green wool dress and she carried a huge tote bag. The baby in the pram was tiny—barely a month old—looking up trustfully at the two women.

Lisa felt a great wave of warmth towards the small, defenseless baby relying on what were after all two strangers, Emily and Lisa, to get her through this day. She wondered if anyone had looked out for her like this when she was tiny and defenseless. Possibly not, she thought bleakly.

It was the most unreal day Lisa had ever lived through. Emily asked nothing of Lisa's circumstances. Instead she talked admiringly of Noel and the great efforts he was making on every front. She told Lisa how she and Noel had known nothing about how to raise a child but between the Internet and the health clinics they were doing fine.

Emily found a dark-brown trouser suit in the thrift shop and asked Lisa to try it on. It fit her well enough.

"I have only forty euros to see me through today," Lisa said apologetically, "and I may need a taxi to take my things out of my parents' home."

"That's all right. You can pay for it by working, can't you?" Emily saw few problems.

"Working?" Lisa asked, bemused.

"Well, you could help me out today. For now, we need to feed Frankie and change her and take her to the clinic. Then you could come with me while I pop into the medical center and later we could walk down St. Jarlath's Crescent, where I look after the gardens, and you could walk the pram around if baby Frankie gets bored. That would be a good day's work and would well cover the cost of that trouser suit."

"But I have to collect my things," Lisa pleaded. "And find somewhere to live."

"We have all day to think about that," Emily said calmly.

And the day began.

Lisa had never met so many people in one working day. She, who worked alone at her desk tinkering with drawings and designs for Anton, often these days spent hours without talking to another human being. Emily Lynch lived a different life.

When Frankie was fed and changed, they moved to the health clinic, where Frankie was weighed and pronounced very satisfactory. There had been an appointment to see Moira, but when they arrived they heard that she had been called away on an emergency.

"That poor woman's life must be one long emergency." Emily was sympathetic instead of being annoyed that she had just made a totally unnecessary visit to the social worker's office. Then it was up to the doctors' practice, where Emily collected a sheaf of papers and spoke pleasantly to the doctors.

"This is Lisa. She's helping me today." They all nodded at her acceptingly. No other explanations. It was very restful indeed.

Frankie was a pretty baby, Lisa thought. Hard work, of course, but babies were, weren't they? Or at least they were supposed to be. She didn't suppose she or Katie had ever got half the attention this one was getting.

Emily had left a parcel for Dr. Hat, who was expected in shortly. He did a day's locum work at the doctor's offices each week. Emily had discovered that he couldn't cook and didn't seem anxious to learn, so she always left a portion of whatever she and Noel had cooked the night before. Today it was a smoked cod, egg and spinach pie, plus instructions on how to reheat it.

"Only meal that Hat eats in the week, apparently," Emily said disapprovingly.

"Hat?"

"Yes, that's his name."

"What's it short for?" Lisa was curious.

"Never asked. I think it's because he seems to wear a hat day and night," Emily said.

"Night?" Lisa asked, with a sort of a laugh.

"Well, I have no way of knowing that." Emily looked at her with interest and Lisa realized that this was the first time today she had allowed herself to relax enough to smile, let alone laugh. She had been like a clenched fist, unable to think about the only family she had known and the only man she had ever loved.

"Right. Where to now?" Lisa was determined to keep cheerful.

"The market and then St. Jarlath's Crescent. We'll give Frankie to her grandmother for a couple of hours, then I can make a start on this paperwork. I'll ask Dingo Duggan to drive you up to collect your things. He can use the thrift shop van."

"Hey, wait a minute, Emily, not so fast. I haven't found anywhere to go yet."

"Oh, you'll find somewhere." Emily was very confident of this. "You don't want to delay once you make a decision like this."

"But you don't know how bad things are," Lisa said.

"I do," Emily said.

"How do you know? I didn't even tell Noel."

"It must have been something very bad for you to come to Chestnut Court in the middle of the night," Emily said, and then seemed to lose interest in it. "Why don't we see if they have any chicken livers down in the market. We could get some mushrooms and rice. Tonight's one of Noel's lectures. He'll need a good meal to see him through. Well, of course, you know that, and you'll need all *your* papers and files and everything."

"Oh, no, I can't go tonight. The world is falling to bits on me. I have no time at all to go to classes!" Lisa cried.

"Always the very time we *must* go—when the world is falling to bits," Emily said, as if it were totally obvious. "Now, would you like a baked potato with cheese for lunch? I find it gives you lots of energy, and you'll need that over the next couple of days."

"Baked potato is just fine," Lisa gasped.

"Good. Then off we go. And after the market we'll go on garden patrol. Could you have a paper and pencil ready and write down what we need for the various gardens in St. Jarlath's Crescent?"

Lisa wondered what it would be like to have a life like this— where everyone sort of depended on you, but nobody actually loved you.

Dingo Duggan said that of course he'd drive Lisa to collect her things. Where would he bring them?

"We will be discussing that over lunch, Dingo," Emily explained. "We'll let you know when we see you."

Lisa was almost dizzy with the speed with which it was all happening. This small, busy woman with the frizzy hair had involved her effortlessly in a series of activities and at no stage had suggested she explain the situation at home and why she had to flee from it. Instead she had been to market and bargained at every stall. Emily seemed to know everyone. Then they had pushed the pram down St. Jarlath's Crescent, where Lisa made lists of plants needed, weeds dug up, paint required for touch-ups. Some gardens were expertly kept, some were neglected, but Emily's regular patrol gave the street a comfortable, established air of being well cared for. Lisa had only begun to take it all in when they arrived at Noel's family home. Again, Lisa marveled at Emily's speed.

The introductions to his parents were made briskly and briefly.

"Charles and Josie are very good people, Lisa. They do good works all day and are busy setting up a fund to have a statue erected to St. Jarlath. We won't detain them from their good work for too long. This is Lisa. She's a good friend of Noel's from his college lectures and has been a great help today in looking after Frankie. And here is your beautiful granddaughter, Josie. She has been longing to see you."

"Poor little thing." Josie took the baby in her arms and Charles beamed up from his unappetizing-looking sandwich.

In Emily's room on the ground floor a bottle of wine was produced.

"Normally I don't have a drink anywhere around Noel, but today is special," Emily explained. "We'll wait until you've collected your things and then we'll have lunch."

"Yes, you must be worn out." Lisa thought that Emily was referring to the hectic pace of the morning.

"Oh, no, that's nothing." Emily dismissed it. "I meant that today is a day of decision for all of us. A glass of wine might be badly needed."

At his restaurant, Anton was planning menus and talking about Lisa. "I'd better call her," he said gloomily.

"You'll know exactly what to say, Anton. You always do." Teddy was admiring and diplomatic.

"Not as easy as it sounds," said Anton, reaching for his phone.

Lisa's phone was switched off. He tried the number of the house where she lived with her parents. Her mother answered.

"No, we haven't seen her since yesterday." The voice was distant, not at all concerned. "She didn't come home last night. So . . ."

"So . . . what?" Anton was impatient with the woman.

"Well . . . nothing, really . . ." Her voice trailed away. "Lisa is, as you must know, an adult. It would be fruitless, to say the least, to worry about her. Shall I give her a message for you?" Lisa's mother had a voice that managed to be indifferent and courteous at the same time in a way that irritated him hugely.

"Don't bother!" he said and hung up.

Lisa's mother shrugged. She was about to go upstairs when her husband let himself in the front door.

"Has Lisa been talking to you?" he began.

"No, I haven't seen her. Why?"

"She will," he said.

"Will what?"

"Will talk to you. There was an incident last night. I didn't realize she was at home and I had a young woman with me."

"How lovely." His wife's scorn was written all over her face.

"She seemed upset."

"I can't imagine why."

"She doesn't have your sense of detachment—that's why."

"She hasn't gone for good. I see her door is open. She's left all her things here." Lisa's mother spoke as if she were talking about a casual acquaintance.

"Of course she hasn't gone for good. Where would she go?"

Lisa's mother shrugged her shoulders again. "She'll end up doing what she wants to do. Like everyone . . . ," she said and walked out the door that her husband had just come in.

.   .   .

"Where will we take your things?" Dingo asked Lisa.

"We're just going to leave them in the van, if that's all right?" Lisa said. She was feeling slightly dizzy from the many encounters that the morning had brought.

"Where are you going to live?" Dingo persisted.

"It hasn't been decided yet." Lisa knew that she sounded as if she were avoiding his questions, but she was actually telling the truth.

"So where do you plan to lay your head tonight, then?" Dingo was determined to get all the answers.

Lisa felt very weary indeed. "Why do they call you Dingo?" she asked in despair.

"Because I spent seven weeks in Australia," he said proudly.

"And why did you come back?" She *must* keep the conversation going about him and avoid cosmic questions about herself.

"Because I got lonely," Dingo said, as if this were the most natural thing in the world. "You will too, mark my words. When you're living with Josie and Charles and saying ten Rosaries a day, you'll look back on your own home and there'll be an ache in you."

"Living with Charles and Josie Lynch? No, that was never on the cards," Lisa said, horrified.

"Well, where am I to bring you when we've collected your things? Oh, look, here's your house."

"I'll be ten minutes, Dingo." She got out of the van.

"Emily said I was to go in with you and carry out your things."

"Does she think she runs the whole world?" Lisa grumbled.

"There's others who'd make a worse job of it," Dingo said cheerfully.

It didn't take Dingo long to pack the van. He already had a dress rail installed in there, so he just hung up Lisa's clothes on that. He had cardboard boxes in which he expertly packed her computer and files, and more boxes for her personal possessions. It wasn't much to show after a lifetime, Lisa thought.

The house was quiet, but she knew her father was at home. She had seen the curtain of his room shift slightly. He made no move to come out to stop her. No attempt to explain what she had seen last night. In a way she was relieved, yet it did show how little he cared about whether she stayed or left.

As she and Dingo got into the van, she saw the curtains move again. However much of a failure her own life had been, it was nothing compared to his and her mother's.

She wrote a note and left it on the hall table.

> *I am leaving the house key. You will realise now that I have left permanently. I wish you both well and certainly I wish you more happiness than you have now. I have not discussed my plans with Katie. I will wait until I am settled, then I will let you have a forwarding address.*
> *Lisa*

No love, no thanks, no explanation, no good-byes. She looked around the house as if she had never seen it before. She realized it was the way her mother looked at things.

Not long ago Katie had said Lisa was turning into her parents and that she should leave home as soon as possible. She longed to tell Katie that she had finally taken her advice but she would wait until she had found somewhere to stay. It would not be in St. Jarlath's Crescent with Charles and Josie, no matter what Dingo thought, and no matter how Emily might try to persuade her.

Back at the Lynches' house, Emily wanted to know how it had all gone. She was relieved that there had been no confrontation. She had feared that Lisa would say more than she meant to.

"I'm never going to say anything to them again," Lisa said.

"Never is a long time. Now let's get these potatoes into the microwave."

Lisa sat down weakly and watched Emily moving expertly around this little place, which she had made completely her home, and suddenly it was easy to talk, to explain the shock of seeing her father with a prostitute last night, the realization that Anton did not see her as the center of his life, the fact that she had no money, nowhere to live, no career to speak of. Lisa spoke on in measured tones. She did not allow herself to get upset. There was something about Emily that made confiding easy—she nodded and murmured agreement. She asked the right questions and avoided the awkward ones. Lisa had never been able to talk like this before. Eventually she came to a full stop.

"I'm so sorry, Emily. I've been going on about myself all afternoon. You must have plans of your own."

"I've telephoned Noel. He'll be here around five. I'll take Frankie back to Chestnut Court and Dingo can spring into action then."

Lisa looked at her blankly.

"What action exactly, Emily? I'm a bit confused here. Are you suggesting that I live with Charles and Josie, because I honestly don't think . . ."

"No, no, no. I'm going to live here again for a little bit, then who knows what will happen?" Emily looked as if it should have been obvious to anyone that this was going to happen.

"Yes, well . . . but, Emily, all my things are outside in Dingo's car. Where am I going to live?"

"I thought you could go to live with Noel in Chestnut Court," Emily said. "It would sort out everything. . . ."

Chapter Six

Moira Tierney was good at her job. She had a reputation for following up the smallest detail. With its faultless filing system, her office was a model for young social workers. Nobody ever heard Moira moan and groan about her caseload or the lack of backup services. It was a job and she did it.

Social work was never going to be nine-to-five; Moira expected to be called by problem families after working hours. In fact, this was often when she was most needed. She was never away from her cell phone, and her colleagues had become used to Moira getting up and leaving in the middle of a meeting because there was an emergency call. She was easy about it. It went with the territory.

Moira spent days and nights picking up the pieces for people where love had gone wrong: where marriages had broken down, where children were abandoned, where domestic violence was too regular. These had once been people filled with romance and hope, but Moira had not known them then. They wouldn't have been in her casebook. It didn't make her deliberately cynical about love and marriage; it was more a matter of time and opportunity.

At the end of a day Moira had little energy left to go to a night-club. Anyway, even if she had she might well have had to take a call while on the dance floor—a call meaning that she would have to go deal with somebody else's problems.

Yes, of course she would like to meet somebody. Who wouldn't?

She wasn't a beauty—a little squarish, with curly brown hair—but she wasn't ugly either. Much plainer women than Moira had found boyfriends, lovers, husbands. There must be someone out there, someone relaxed and calm and undemanding. Someone much more peaceful than those she had left behind her at home.

When Moira visited Liscuan, she took the Saturday train across the country and the bus to the end of their road. She spent most of her time there cleaning up the house and trying to find out what benefits her father could claim. She came back the following day.

Nothing ever changed; in all the years since she had left to study in Dublin, things had been like this. Nothing altered.

People didn't much like coming to the house anymore, and her father took to going to Mrs. Kennedy's house, where she would give him a meal in return for his cutting logs for her. Apparently Mr. Kennedy had gone to England looking for a job. He may or may not have found one, but he had never come back to report.

Moira's brother, Pat, was left to his own devices. He worked around the place, milking the two cows and feeding the hens. He went for a couple of pints in Liscuan village on a Saturday night, so Moira had very little conversation with him. It made her sad to see him dress himself up in a clean shirt and put on hair oil for his weekly outing. Any more than in her own, there was no sign of a love in Pat's life.

Pat said little about it all, just burned the bottom of one frying pan after another as he cooked bacon and eggs for supper every night. This cramped little farmhouse would never know the laughter of grandchildren.

It was lonely going home to Liscuan but Moira did it with a good grace. She could tell them nothing about her life in Dublin. They would be shocked if they knew she had dealt with an eleven-year-old girl constantly raped by her father and now pregnant, or a battered wife, or a drunken mother who locked her three children in a room while she went to the pub. Nothing like this happened in Liscuan, or so the Tierneys thought.

So Moira kept her thoughts to herself. This particular weekend she was glad of the time. She needed to think something through. Moira Tierney believed that you often had a nose for a situation that wasn't right, and this was your role in the whole thing. After all that, what those years of training and further years on the job taught you was to recognize when something wasn't right.

And Moira was worried about Frankie Lynch.

It seemed entirely wrong that Noel Lynch should be given custody of the child. Moira had read the file carefully. He hadn't even lived with Stella, the baby's mother. It was only when she was approaching her death and the baby's birth that she had got in touch with Noel.

It was all highly unsatisfactory.

Admittedly, Noel had managed to build up a support system that looked pretty good on paper. The place was clean and warm and adequately stocked with what was necessary for the baby. The sterilizing for bottles was set up, the baby bath in position. Moira couldn't fault any of that.

His cousin, a middle-aged, settled person called Emily, had stayed with him for a time, and she still took the baby with her wherever she went. And sometimes the baby stayed with a nurse who had a new baby of her own and was married to a doctor. Very safe environment. And there was an older couple called Signora and Aidan who already looked after their grandchild.

There were other people too. Noel's parents, who were religious maniacs and were busy drumming up a petition to erect a statue for some saint who died thousands of years ago; then there was a couple called Scarlet: Muttie and Lizzie and Simon and Maud—they were part of the team. And there was a retired doctor who seemed to be called Dr. Hat, of all things, who was supposed to be particularly soothing to infants, apparently. All reliable people, but still . . .

It was all too bitty, Moira thought: a flimsy daisy chain of people, like the cast of a musical. If one link blew away, everything could crash to the ground. But could she get anyone to support her instinct? Nobody at all. Her immediate superior, who was head of the team, said that she was fussing about nothing—everything seemed to be in place.

She had tried to enlist the American cousin on her side, but to no avail. Emily appeared to have a blind spot about Noel. She said he had made amazing strides in turning his life around so that he could look after his daughter. He was persevering at his job. He was even studying at night to improve his work chances. He had given up alcohol, which he found very hard to do, but he was resolute. It would be a poor reward for all this if the social workers were going to take his child away. He had promised the baby's mother that the child would not be raised in care.

"Care might be a lot better than he can offer," Moira had muttered.

"It might, but then again it might not." Emily was not to be convinced.

Moira had to hold back. But she was watching with very sharp eyes for anything to go out of step.

And now it had.

Noel had brought a woman in to live in the flat.

He had done up the spare room for her to sleep in.

She was young, this woman—young and restless. One of those tall, rangy women with hair down to her waist. She knew nothing about babies and seemed defensive and resentful when asked about any parenting skills.

"I'm not here permanently," she had said over and over. "I'm in a relationship elsewhere. With Anton Moran. The chef. Noel is just giving me somewhere to stay, and in return I'm helping him with Frankie." She shrugged as if it were simple and clear to the meanest intelligence.

Moira didn't like her at all. There were too many of these bimbos around the place, leggy, airheaded young women with nothing in their minds except clothes. You should *see* the dress that this Lisa had hanging on her wall! A red and blue designer outfit probably costing the earth.

Whatever doubts Moira had had about Noel's judgment, they had been increased a hundred-fold by the arrival of Lisa Kelly on the scene.

There were great plans afoot for a double christening. Frankie Lynch and Johnny Carroll, born the same day, minded by all the same people, were to be baptized together. No one but Emily saw the irony in their names. Frankie and Johnny were as famous as apple pie at home. She started to hum the familiar lyrics *"Frankie and Johnny were lovers . . ."* then shuddered when she remembered the line *"He was her man, he done her wrong."* Well, that wasn't going to happen with this Frankie and Johnny! She decided to keep it to herself, but she had to write to Betsy about it:

> Betsy, everyone here is so intent that the two babies should be best friends; I just hope that these namesakes never live up to the originals. And if I have anything to do with it, and I intend to, they won't. You should see them together in their carriages with all the love around them. It makes me feel so warm inside.

Moira was surprised to be invited. Noel had said that there would be a baptism in Father Flynn's church down by the Liffey, and a little reception in the hall afterwards. Moira was very welcome to join them.

She tried to put the right amount of gratitude onto her face. They didn't need to do this, but perhaps they were trying to underline the stability of their situation.

"What kind of christening gift would you like?" she said suddenly.

Noel looked at her in surprise.

"There's no question of that, Moira. Everyone is giving a card to both Frankie and Johnny; we're going to put them in albums for them with the photographs so that they will know what this day was like."

Moira felt very reproved and put down. "Oh, yes, of course, certainly," she said.

Noel couldn't help being pleased to see her wrong-footed for once. "I'm sure everyone will be delighted to see you there, Moira," he said with no conviction whatsoever.

There was a much larger congregation than Moira had expected at Father Flynn's church. How did they know all these people? Most of them must be friends of Dr. Carroll and his wife. Surely Noel Lynch wouldn't know half the church?

The two godmothers were there, Emily holding Frankie, and Fiona's friend Barbara, who was also a nurse in the heart clinic, carrying Johnny. The babies, freshly fed and changed, were beautifully behaved and for the most part slept through the ceremony. Father Flynn kept it brief and to the point. The water was poured over their little foreheads—that of course woke them up, but they were quickly soothed and calmed—vows were made for them by the godparents and they were now part of God's Church and His family. Father Flynn hoped that they would both find happiness and strength in this knowledge.

Nothing too pious, nothing that anyone could object to. The babies took it all in their stride. Then everyone moved to the hall next door, where there was a buffet and a huge cake with the names Frankie and Johnny iced on it.

Maud and Simon Mitchell were in charge of the catering, Moira remembered the names being listed among Noel's babysitters for Frankie. They seemed out of place in her vision of Frankie's life. But then, so did this whole christening party.

Moira stood on the outside watching the people mingle and talk and come up to gurgle at the babies. It was a pleasant gathering, certainly, but she didn't feel involved.

There was music in the background and Noel moved around easily, drinking orange juice and talking to everyone. Moira watched Lisa, who was there looking very glamorous, her honey-colored hair coiled up under a little red hat.

Maud noticed Moira standing alone and came over to her, offering her the serving tray. "Can I get you another piece of cake?" she offered.

"No, thank you. I'm Moira, Frankie's social worker," she said.

"Yes, I know you are. I'm Maud Mitchell, one of Frankie's babysitters. She's doing very well, isn't she?"

Moira leaped on this. "Didn't you expect her to do well?" she asked.

"Oh, no, the reverse. Noel has to be both mother and father to her, and he's doing a really great job."

More solidarity in the community, Moira thought. It was as if there were an army ranked against her. She could still see in her mind the newspaper headlines: SOCIAL SERVICES TO BLAME. THERE WERE MANY WARNINGS. EVERYTHING WAS IGNORED . . . "How exactly are you and your brother friends of Noel?" she asked.

"We live on the same street as he used to live, where his parents live now. But we're hoping to go to New Jersey soon—we have the offer of a job." Her face lit up.

"No work here?"

"Not for freelance caterers, no. People have less money these days, they're not giving big parties like they used to."

"And your parents—will they be sorry to see you go . . . ?"

"No, our parents sort of went ages ago, we live with Muttie and Lizzie Scarlet, and it will be hard saying good-bye to them. Honestly it's too long a story, and I'm meant to be collecting plates. That's Muttie over there, the one in the middle telling stories." She pointed out a small man with a wheeze that didn't deter any of his tales.

Why had he brought up these two young people? It was a mystery, and Moira hated a mystery.

·   ·   ·

At the weekly meeting, Moira's team leader asked for a report on any areas that were giving cause for alarm.

As she always did, she brought up the subject of Noel and his baby daughter. The team leader shuffled the papers in front of her.

"We have the nurse's report here. She says the child is fine."

"She sees only what she wants to see." Moira knew that she sounded petty and mulish.

"Well, the weight gain is normal, the hygiene is fine—he hasn't fallen down on anything so far."

"He's brought a flashy girl in to live there."

"We are not nuns, Moira. This isn't the nineteen fifties. It's no business of ours what he does in his private life as long as he looks after that child properly. His girlfriends are neither here nor there."

"But she says she's *not* a girlfriend, and that's what he says."

"Really, Moira, it's impossible to please you. If she *is* a girlfriend you're annoyed and if she's not you're even *more* annoyed. Would anything please you?"

"For that child to be put into care," Moira said.

"The mother was adamant and the father hasn't put a foot wrong. Next business."

Moira felt a dull, red flush rise around her neck. They thought she was obsessing about this. Oh, let them wait until something happened. The social workers were always blamed and they would be again.

But not Moira. She had made very sure of this.

The next morning, Moira decided to go and examine this St. Jarlath's Thrift Shop, where the baby spent a couple of hours a day.

The place was clean and well ventilated. No complaints there. Emily and a neighbor, Molly Carroll, were busy hanging up dresses that had just come in.

"Ah, Moira," Emily said, welcoming her. "Do you want a nice knitted suit? It would look very well on you. It's fully lined, see, with satin. Some lady said she was tired of looking at it in her wardrobe and sent it over this morning. It's a lovely heather color."

It was a nice suit, and ordinarily Moira might have been interested. But this was a work visit, not a social shopping outing.

"I really called to know whether you are satisfied with the situation in Chestnut Court, Ms. Lynch?"

"The situation?" Emily looked startled.

"The new 'tenant,' for want of a better word."

"Oh, Lisa! Yes, isn't it great? Noel would be quite lonely there on his own at night, and now they go over their college notes together and she wheels Frankie down here in the mornings. It's a huge help."

Moira was not convinced. "But her own relationship. She says she's involved with someone else?"

"Oh, yes, she's very keen on this young man who runs a restaurant."

"And where is this 'relationship' going?"

"Do you know, Moira, the French—who are very wise about love, cynical but wise—say, 'There is always one who kisses and one who turns the cheek to be kissed.' I think that's what we have here: Lisa kissing and Anton offering his cheek to be kissed."

This silenced Moira completely. How had this middle-aged American woman understood everything so quickly and so well? Moira wondered would she buy the heather knitted suit. But she didn't want them to think that somehow she was in their debt. She might ask a colleague to go in and buy it later.

There was a notice on the corridor wall just outside Moira's office. The heart clinic in St. Brigid's wanted the services of a social worker for a couple of weeks.

Dr. Clara Casey said they needed a report done that she could show to the hospital management to prove that the part-time help of a social worker might contribute to the well-being of the patients who attended the clinic. The staff, though eager and helpful, were not aware of all the benefits and entitlements that existed, nor did they have the expertise to advise patients about how best to get on with their lives.

Moira looked at it vaguely. It wasn't of any interest to her. It was just politics. Office politics. This woman, Dr. Casey, wanted to enlarge her empire, that's all. Moira couldn't have cared less.

She was surprised and very annoyed, therefore, when the team leader dropped in to see her about it. As usual, she admired the streamlined office and sighed, wishing that all the social workers could be equally organized.

"You see that job in St. Brigid's—it's only for two weeks. I'd like you to do it, Moira."

"It's not my kind of thing," Moira began.

"Oh, but it is! No one would do it better or more thoroughly. Clara Casey will be delighted with you."

"And my own caseload?"

"Will be divided between us all while you are away."

Moira didn't have to ask was it an order. She knew it was.

Moira had tidied up all the loose ends about Noel before her two weeks at St. Brigid's. But she had one more stop to make. She called on Declan Carroll, who opened the door with his own son in his arms.

"Come on in," he said. "The place is like a tenement. Fiona is going back to work tomorrow."

"And how will you cope?" Moira was interested.

"Oh, there's a baby mafia on this street, you know—we all keep an eye out for Frankie; well, they'll do the same for Johnny. My parents are dying to get their hands on him, turn him into a master butcher like my dad! Emily Lynch, Noel's parents, Muttie and Lizzie, the twins, Dr. Hat, Signora and Aidan. They're all there for the children. The list is as long as my arm."

"Your wife works in a heart clinic?" Moira had checked her notes.

"Yes, up in St. Brigid's."

"I'm going there for two weeks tomorrow, as it happens," Moira said glumly.

"Best place you'll ever work. There's a great atmosphere in the place," Declan Carroll said effortlessly, shifting the baby round in his arms.

"Do you think Noel is fit to raise a child?" Moira asked suddenly. If she had hoped to shock him into a direct answer, she had hoped in vain.

Declan looked at her, perplexed. "I beg your pardon?" he said slowly.

Nervously, she repeated the question.

"I can't believe that you are asking me to give you a value judgment about a neighbor."

"Well, you'd know the setup. I thought I'd ask you."

"I think it's best if I assume you didn't just say that."

Moira felt the slow, red flush come up her neck again. Why did she think that she was good at working with people? It was obvious that she alienated everyone everywhere she went.

"That social worker is a real pain in the arse," Declan said that evening.

"I suppose she's just doing her job," Fiona said.

"Yeah, but we all do our jobs without getting people's backs up," he grumbled.

"Mostly," Fiona said.

"What did she expect me to say? That Noel was a screaming alcoholic and the child should be taken away? The poor fellow is killing himself trying to make a life for Frankie."

"They're pretty black-and-white, social workers," Fiona said.

"Then they should join the world and be gray like the rest of us," Declan said.

"I love you, Declan Carroll!" Fiona said.

"And I you. I bet nobody loves Miss Prissy Moira, though."

"Declan! That's so unlike you. Maybe she has a steaming sex life that we know nothing about."

Moira had sent her colleague Dolores in to buy the knitted suit. Dolores was a foot smaller than Moira and two feet wider. Emily knew exactly what had happened.

"Wear it in happiness," she said to Dolores.

"Oh . . . um . . . thank you," said Dolores, who would never have got a job in the Secret Service.

Moira wore the heather-colored suit for her first day at the heart clinic. Clara Casey admired it at once.

"I love nice clothes. They are my little weakness. That's a great outfit."

"I'm not very interested in clothes myself." Moira wanted to establish her credentials as a hands-on worker. "I've seen too many people get distracted by them over the years."

"Quite." Clara was crisp in response and yet again Moira felt that she had somehow let herself down. That she had turned away the warmth of this heart specialist by a glib, smart remark. She wished, as she wished so many times, that she had paused to think before she spoke.

Was it too late to rescue things?

"Dr. Casey, I am anxious to do a good job here. Can you outline to me what you hope I will report to you?"

"Well, I am sure that you won't hand my own words back to me, Ms. Tierney. You don't seem that sort of person."

"Please call me Moira."

"Later, maybe. At the moment Ms. Tierney is fine. I have listed the areas where you can investigate. I do urge, however, some sensitivity when talking to both staff and patients. People are often tense when they are confronted with heart problems. We are heavily into the reassurance business and we emphasize the positive."

Not since she was a student had Moira received such an obvious ticking-off. She would love to be able to rewind the meeting to the moment where she had come in; at the point when Clara had admired her outfit, she would thank her enthusiastically—even show her the satin lining. Someday she would learn, but would it be too late?

The head of the team had not said she must stay away from her caseload. Moira went home by way of Chestnut Court. She rang Noel's doorbell. He let her in immediately.

They looked like a normal family. Lisa was giving the baby a bottle and Noel was making spaghetti Bolognese.

"I thought you were going to work somewhere else for two weeks?" Lisa said.

"I never take my eye off the ball," Moira said. She looked at Lisa, who was now holding the infant closely and supporting the baby's head as she had been taught to do. She was rocking to and fro and the baby slept peacefully. The girl had obviously bonded with this child. Moira could find nothing to criticize; on the contrary, there was something very safe and solid about it all. Anyone looking in might think they were a normal family instead of what they were: unpredictable.

"Must be dull for you here, Lisa," she said. "And I thought *you* had a relationship."

"He's away at the moment. Anton went to a trade fair," Lisa said cheerfully.

"Bit lonely for you, I imagine." Moira couldn't resist it.

"Not at all. It's a great chance for Noel and myself to catch up on our studies. Do you want a bowl of spaghetti, by the way?"

"No, thank you. It's very nice of you, but I have to get on."

"Plenty of it . . . ," Lisa said.

"No . . . thanks again." And she left.

Moira was going back to her own flat. Why had she not sat down and eaten a bowl of spaghetti? It smelled very good. She had hardly any food at home: a little cheese, a couple of rolls. It wasn't compromising her whole stance to have stayed and eaten some of their supper.

But as she walked home, Moira was glad she hadn't stayed. This was all going to end in tears, and when it did she didn't want to be anyone who had stayed and had dinner in their house.

As she walked along the canal, Moira saw a small man surrounded by dogs walking towards her. It was Noel's father, Charles Lynch, marching along with dogs of different sizes and shapes: a spaniel, a poodle and a miniature schnauzer trit-trotting on their leads on one side and a huge Great Dane padding along on the other. Two elderly Labradors, unleashed, circled the group, barking joyously. Charles Lynch should have looked ridiculous. Instead he looked blissfully happy. In fact, Charles took his dog walking very seriously. Clients paid good money to have their pets exercised, and he never shortchanged them.

He recognized the stony-faced social worker who had been dealing with his son and granddaughter.

"Miss Tierney," he said respectfully.

"Good evening, Mr. Lynch. Glad to see someone else apart from myself in this city is actually working."

"But what easy work I have compared to yours, Miss Tierney. These dogs are a delight. I have been minding them all day, and now I am taking them home to their owners—except Caesar, here, who lives with us now."

"There are two other dogs not on leads—whose are they?" Moira asked.

"Ah, those are just our local dogs, Hooves and Dimples, from St. Jarlath's Crescent. They came along for the fun of it." And he nodded in the direction of the old dogs that had just come along to share the excitement.

Moira wished that life was as simple for her. Charles Lynch didn't have to fear a series of articles in the newspapers saying that yet again the dog walkers had been found wanting and that all the signs had been there ready for anyone to see.

Next day, Moira began to understand the nature of her job. She was helped in this by Hilary, the office manager, and a Polish girl, Ania, who had recently had a miscarriage and had only just returned to work. She seemed devoted to the place and totally loyal to Clara Casey.

There was, apparently, a bad man called Frank Ennis who was on the hospital board and was the hospital manager, who tried to resist spending one cent on the heart clinic. He said there was absolutely no need for any social services whatsoever in the clinic.

"Why can't Clara Casey speak to him herself?" Moira asked.

"She can and does, but he's a very determined man."

"Suppose she just took him out to lunch one day?" Moira was anxious for this matter to be tied up so she could get back to her real work.

"Oh, she does much more than that," Ania explained. "She sleeps with him. But it's no use—he keeps his life in different compartments."

Hilary tried to gloss over what had been said. "Ania is just giving you the background," she said hastily.

"I'm sorry. I thought she was on our side." Ania was repentant.

"And I am, indeed," Moira said.

"Oh, that's all right then," Ania said happily.

The whole atmosphere in the clinic was a combination of professionalism and reassurance. Moira noticed that the patients all understood the functions of the various medications they received and they had little booklets where their weight and blood pressure were recorded at every visit. They were all very adept at entering information and retrieving it from the computer.

"You wouldn't *believe* the trouble we had getting a training course organized. Frank Ennis managed to make it sound like devil worship. Clara practically had to go to the United Nations to get the instructors in."

"He sounds like a dinosaur, this man," Moira said disapprovingly.

"That's what he is, all right," Hilary agreed.

"But you say that Dr. Casey sees him . . . um . . . socially?" Moira probed.

"No. Ania was saying that, not me—but indeed it is true. Clara has humanized him a lot but there's a long way to go still."

"Does Frank Ennis know that *I'm* here?"

"I don't think so, Moira. No point in troubling him, really, or adding to his worries."

"I like playing things by the book," Moira said primly.

"There are books and *books,*" Hilary said enigmatically.

"If I am to write a report, I'll need to know his side of things as well."

"Leave him until you've nearly finished," Hilary advised.

And as she so often did these days, Moira felt she wasn't handling things as well as she might have. It was as if Hilary and the clinic were drawing away from her. She had meant to be there as their savior but somehow playing it by the book had meant that she had stepped outside her brief and that they were all withdrawing their support and enthusiasm.

The story of her life.

Moira worked on diligently.

She saw that there was a case for having a social worker attend one day a week. She looked through her notes. There was Kitty Reilly, possibly in the early stages of dementia, conducting long conversations with saints. There was Judy, who definitely needed home help but had no idea where to turn to find it. There was Lar Kelly, who gave the appearance of being an extroverted, cheerful man but who was obviously as lonely as anything, which was why he kept dropping into the clinic "just to be sure," as he put it.

A social worker would be able to point Kitty Reilly in the direction of care a few days a week, find an aide for Judy and arrange for Lar to go to a social center for lunch and entertainment.

It was time to approach the great Frank Ennis.

She made an appointment to see him on her last day in the clinic. He was courteous and gracious—not at all the monster she had been told about.

"Ms. Tierney!" he said, with every sign of pleasure at meeting her.

"Moira," she corrected him.

"No, no, Clara says you are a 'Ms.' person for sure."

"Really? And did she say anything else about me?" Moira was incensed that Clara had somehow got in ahead of her.

"Yes. She said you were probably extremely good at your job, that you were high in practicality and doing things by the book and low in sentimentality. All the hallmarks of a good social worker, it would appear."

It didn't sound that way to Moira. It sounded as if Clara had said she was a hard-faced workaholic. Still, on with the job.

"Why do you think they *shouldn't* have the part-time services of a social worker?" she asked.

"Because Clara thinks the hospital is made of money and that there are unlimited funds that should be at her disposal."

"I thought you and she were good friends . . . ," Moira said.

"I like to think we are indeed friends, and more, but we will never see eye-to-eye about this bottomless-pit business," he said.

"You really do need someone part-time, you know," Moira said. "It would round it all off perfectly; then St. Brigid's can really be said to be looking after patients' welfare."

"All the social workers and people in pastoral care are run off their feet in the hospital already. They don't want to be sent over to that clinic, coping with imaginary problems from perfectly well people."

"Get someone new in for two or three days a week." Moira was firm.

"One day a week."

"One and a half," she bargained.

"Clara is right, Ms. Tierney: you have all the skills of a negotiator. A day and a half a week and not a minute more."

"I feel sure that will be fine, Mr. Ennis."

"And will you do it yourself, Ms. Tierney?"

Moira was horrified even at the thought of it. "Oh, no! No way, Mr. Ennis. I am a senior social worker. I have a serious caseload. I couldn't make the time."

"That's a pity. I thought you could be my friend in court: my eyes and ears, curb them from playing fast and loose with expenses and taxis." He seemed genuinely disappointed not to have her around the place, which was rare these days. Most people seemed to be veering away from her.

But of course it was totally impossible. She could barely keep up with her own work, let alone take on something new. And yet she would be sorry to leave the place.

Ania had brought in some shortbread for their afternoon tea to mark the fact that Moira was leaving. Clara joined them and made a little speech.

"We were lucky that they sent us Moira Tierney. She has done a superb report and has even braved the lion's den itself. Frank Ennis has just telephoned to say that the board have agreed to us having the services of a social worker for one and a half days a week."

"So you'll be coming back!" Ania seemed pleased.

"No, Ms. Tierney made it clear that she has much more important work to do elsewhere. We are very grateful to her for putting it on hold for the two weeks that she was here."

Frank Ennis had obviously briefed his girlfriend very adequately on the situation so far. Moira wished she had not stressed so heavily to Frank Ennis how important her own work was compared to the work here in the clinic. In ways, it would be pleasant to come here on a regular basis. Apart from Clara Casey, they were all welcoming and enthusiastic. And to be fair, Clara had been enthusiastic about the work Moira had done.

Hilary was always practical. "Maybe Ms. Tierney knows someone who might be suitable?" she said.

As if from miles away Moira heard her own voice saying, "I can easily reorganize my schedule, and if you thought I would be all right, then I would be honored to come here."

They all looked at Clara, who was silent for a moment. Then she said, "I feel that we would all love Moira to join us here, but she will have to sign in under the Official Secrets Act. Frank will expect her to be his eyes and ears, but Moira will know that this can never happen."

Moira smiled. "I get the message, Clara," she said.

And to her great surprise she got a round of applause.

The head of the social-work team was not impressed.

"I asked you to write a report, not to get yourself yet another job, Moira. You work too hard already. You should lighten up a little."

"I did there. I lightened up a lot. I know the setup in the clinic now. It makes sense that I do it rather than train someone in."

"Right. You know what you *can* do and what you *can't,* and no more behaving like some kind of private eye."

"I'm just watchful, that's all," Moira said.

She went to Chestnut Court with her briefcase and clipboard. Noel was out, but Lisa was there. Moira went through the routine that had been agreed upon.

"Who bathed her today?" she asked.

"I did," Lisa said proudly. "It's quite hard on your own—they get so slippery, but she enjoyed it and she clapped her hands a lot."

The baby was clean and dry and powdered. Nothing to complain about there.

"When is her next feed?" Moira asked.

"In an hour's time. I have the formula there and the bottles are sterilized."

Again, Moira could find no fault. She checked the number of nappies and whether the baby's clothes had been aired.

"Would you like a coffee?" Lisa suggested.

Last time Moira had been rather swift and ungracious, so she decided she would say yes.

"Or, actually, I'm exhausted. You don't have a proper drink or anything? I could do with a glass of wine."

Lisa looked at her with a very level glance.

"Oh, no, Moira. We don't have any alcohol here. As you know, Noel has had a problem with it in the past so there's nothing at all. You *must* know that—you were always asking about it before, hunting for bottles stacked away and everything."

Moira felt humbled. She had been so obvious. She was, indeed, like some kind of a private eye, except an inefficient one.

"I forgot," she lied.

"No, you didn't, but have a coffee anyway," Lisa said, getting up from a table covered with papers and drawings to go to the kitchen.

"Did I interrupt you?"

"No, I was glad of the interruption. I was getting stale."

"Where's Noel tonight?"

"I have no idea."

"Didn't he say?"

"No. We're not married or anything. I think he went back to his parents' house."

"And left you literally holding the baby?"

"He's given me a place to live. I'm very pleased to hold the baby for him. Very pleased indeed," Lisa said.

"And why exactly did you leave home?" Moira fell easily into interrogation mode.

"We've been over this a lot, Moira. I told you then and I tell you now, it was for personal reasons. I am not a runaway teenager. I am a quarter of a century old. I don't ask you why you left home, do I?"

"This is different . . . ," Moira began.

"It's not remotely different and honestly it's got nothing to do with the case. I know you have to look out for Frankie, and you do it very well, but I'm just the lodger helping out. My circumstances have nothing to do with anything." She went into the kitchen and banged around for a while.

Moira sought subjects that wouldn't cause any further controversy. They were hard to find.

"I met Fiona Carroll. You know . . . Johnny's mother."

"Oh, yes?" Lisa said.

"She said that you and Noel were doing a great job minding Frankie."

"Yes . . . well . . . good."

"Most impressed, she was."

"And were you surprised?" Lisa asked suddenly.

"No, of course not."

"Good, because I tell you I have *such* admiration for Noel. All this came out of a clear blue sky at him. He's been very strong. I wouldn't have anyone bad-mouthing him, not anyone at all." She looked like a tiger defending her cub.

Moira made a few bleating noises intended to suggest support and enthusiasm. She hoped she was giving the desired impression.

Her next visit was to a family where they were trying to make an elderly father a ward of the court. To Moira, Gerald, the old man, was perfectly sane. Lonely and frail, certainly, but mad? No.

His daughter and her husband were very anxious to have him defined as being incapable and sign his house over to them and then have him committed to a secure nursing home facility.

Moira was having none of it. Gerald wanted to stay in his home and she was his champion. She picked up a stray remark from the son-in-law, something that made her think that the man had gambling debts. It would suit him nicely if his father-in-law were put away. They might even sell the house and buy a smaller place.

It wouldn't happen on Moira's watch. Her clipboard was filled with notes for letters she would send to the relevant people. The son-in-law collapsed like a house of cards.

The old man looked at Moira affectionately.

"You're better than having a bodyguard," he said to her.

Moira was very proud of this. This was exactly what she saw herself as being. She patted the old man's hand.

"I'll get you a regular carer to come in and look after you. You can tell her if anyone steps out of line or anything. I'll liaise with your doctor also. Let me see . . . that's Dr. Carroll, isn't it?"

"It used to be Dr. Hat," Gerald said. "Dr. Carroll is a very nice lad, certainly, but he could be my grandson, if you see what I mean. Dr. Hat was nearer to my own generation."

"And where is he?" Moira asked.

"He comes in to their practice from time to time when they're short-staffed," the old man said sadly. "I always seem to miss him, though."

"I'll find him for you," Moira promised and went straightaway to the doctors' group practice at the end of St. Jarlath's Crescent.

Dr. Carroll was there and happy to talk about Gerald.

"I think he's totally on the ball and playing with the full deck."

"His family think otherwise." Moira was terse.

"Well, they would, wouldn't they? That son-in-law would do anything to get his hands on the family checkbook."

"That's my view too," Moira said. "Can I ask you—does Dr. Hat do house calls?"

"No, not really. He's retired, but he does the odd locum for us. Why do you ask?"

Moira chose her words carefully for once.

"He thinks very highly of you, Doctor. He said that several times, but I think he finds Dr. . . . er . . . Hat more in his age group."

"Lord, he must be fifteen years older than Hat!"

"Yes, but he's fifty years older than you, Doctor."

"Hat's a very decent man. He might well go round and see your Gerald as a social visit from time to time. I'll tell him."

"Could I tell him, do you think?" Moira had a history of people promising to do things that they fully intended to do but that never got done.

"Of course. I'll give you his address."

For Declan Carroll it was just one less thing to do. She was efficient, this Moira Tierney, and dedicated to her job. Such a pity that
she had taken so against poor Noel, who was breaking his back trying to keep the show on the road.

Dr. Hat was indeed wearing headgear: a smart navy cap with a peak.
He welcomed Moira in warmly and offered her a cup of hot chocolate.

"You don't know what I'm here about yet," she said cautiously.
Maybe he would find this intrusive. She didn't want to accept a hot
chocolate under false pretenses.

"Yes, I do. Declan called me so that I could be prepared."

"That was courteous of him," Moira said, though she would have
preferred to handle this on her own.

"I like Gerald. I have no problem going to see him. In fact, we
could play chess. I'd like that."

Moira's shoulders relaxed. She would have the hot chocolate now.
Sometimes things worked out well at work. Not always, but sometimes. Like now.

Just after she got back to her flat there was a phone call from home.
Her brother, Pat, never called her usually: she was alarmed. She
knew from experience that there was no point in hurrying him. He
would take his time. "It's Dad," he said eventually. "He's selling
everything—the house, the land, the livestock. He's moved out."

"Moved out where?"

"He's up with Mrs. Kennedy. He's not coming back."

"Well, can't you bring him back?"

"I did once and he wasn't best pleased," Pat said. "Couldn't you
do something, Moira?"

"God Almighty, Pat, I'm two hundred miles away. You and Da have
to sort this out between you. Go on up to Mrs. Kennedy. Find out
what he's up to. I'll come down next weekend and see what's going on."

"But," Pat asked, "what am I to do? I'll have nowhere to go."

"Why would he want to sell the farm?" Moira was impatient.

"You don't know the half of it," said Pat.

Moira sat in her chair for a while thinking about what to do. She knew how to run everyone else's lives but not her own. Eventually she pulled herself together and got on the phone. She had kept Mrs. Kennedy's number in her huge address book in case she ever needed to contact her father when he was chopping wood up there. She asked could she speak to her father and, to use Pat's phrase, he certainly was not best pleased with the call.

"Why are you bothering me here?" he asked querulously.

"I'll be down next weekend. I need to see you, Dad. We need to talk about all this. . . ." And she hung up before she could learn exactly how displeased her father was with this call.

Clara Casey turned out to be a friend rather than a foe. In fact, she even suggested that Moira come to lunch with her one day. This was not the norm at work. Her team leader would never have suggested a social lunch.

Moira was surprised, but very pleased. She was even more pleased when the restaurant turned out to be Quentins. Moira had thought they would go somewhere in the shopping precinct.

Clara was obviously known in the place. Moira had never been there before.

It was amazingly elegant, and Brenda Brennan, the proprietor, recommended the monkfish: it was beautifully prepared in a saffron sauce.

"I don't suppose this restaurant is feeling any bad effects of the recession," Clara said to Brenda.

"Don't you believe it. They're all drawing in their horns. Plus we have a rival now. Anton Moran is getting a lot of business for his place."

"I read about it in the papers. Is he good?" Clara asked.

"Very. Huge flair and a great manner."

"Do you know him?"

"Yes, he worked here once and came back to do the odd shift. A real heartbreaker—he has half the women in Dublin at his beck and call."

Moira was thoughtful. Surely this was the name of the young man whom Lisa Kelly had a relationship with? She had mentioned his name more than once. Moira smiled to herself. For once, it looked as if Lisa might not find the world going entirely her way.

Clara was easy company. She asked questions and was helpful about Moira's brother.

"You might want to stay there Monday morning and catch people at work," Clara said. "We can change your days around—no problem."

Moira wished they didn't have to go back to the clinic. It would have been lovely to have had a bottle of wine and a real conversation where Clara could tell her about the other people who worked in the clinic and maybe even about this friendship she had with Frank Ennis, which seemed entirely improbable. But it was an ordinary working day. They each had one drink, a mixture of wine and mineral water, and they didn't linger over the meal.

Moira had learned little about Clara, except that she was long divorced from her husband and she had two married daughters: one working on an ecology project in South America and the other running a big CD and DVD store. She had originally taken on the heart clinic for one year, but it was now her baby and she would let nobody, particularly anyone like Frank Ennis, take away one single vestige of its power or authority.

Clara was particularly sympathetic about Moira's mother having died. She said her own mother was straight out of hell, but she knew that this was not the case with everyone. Hilary, back at the clinic, had been heartbroken when her own mother had died.

Moira was to take the time she needed to sort out her family problems. It was as simple as that.

.   .   .

Of course it wasn't simple when she got back home to Liscuan. Moira had known that it wouldn't be. Pat had completely broken down. He hadn't milked the cows, he hadn't fed the hens, he babbled about his father's plan to sell the family home from under him and move in with Mrs. Kennedy. This did indeed appear to be the case.

Moira asked her father straight out. "Pat has probably got this all wrong, Da, but he thinks that you have plans to move in permanently with Mrs. Kennedy and sell this place."

"That's right," her father said. "I intend to go and live with Mrs. Kennedy."

"And what about Pat?"

"I'm selling up." He shrugged, gazing around at the shabby kitchen. "Look around you, Moira. I can't do it anymore. I've dealt with this all my life while you were having a fine time up in Dublin. I deserve a bit of happiness now."

With every single client in her caseload, Moira knew what to do. She had known how to set things in order for Kitty Reilly, Judy and Lar at the heart clinic. Why was her own situation so totally impossible?

She spent the Monday helping Pat to look for accommodation. Then she wished her father well with Mrs. Kennedy and took the train back to Dublin.

In Chestnut Court, Frankie was crying again. Noel was beginning to think that he would never know what the crying meant. Some nights she didn't sleep for more than ten minutes at a time. There was one level for food, but she'd just been fed and burped. Perhaps it was more wind. Carefully, he picked up his daughter and laid her against his shoulder, patting her back gently. She cried on. He sat down and laid her chest across his arm while he rubbed her little back to soothe her.

"Frankie, Frankie, please don't cry, little one, hush now, hush now . . ." Nothing. Noel was aware that his voice was sounding increasingly anxious as Frankie cried on piteously. Perhaps for a nappy that needed changing? Could it be a changing job?

He was right. The nappy was indeed damp. Carefully he placed the baby on a towel spread over the table where they changed her. As soon as he removed her wet nappy, the crying stopped and he was rewarded with a sunny smile and a coo.

"You, my pet," he said, smiling back at her, "are going to have to learn how to communicate. It's no good just wailing. I'm no good at understanding what you want."

Frankie blew bubbles and reached up towards the paper birds flying from the mobile above her head. As Noel stretched out his hand to reach for the cleaning wipes, to his horror she twisted away from him and began to slip off the table.

Quick as he was, he was not in time.

It felt as though everything were happening in slow motion as the baby began to fall from the table. As Noel froze in horror, she hit the chair beside, then fell to the floor. There was blood around her head as she started to scream.

"Frankie, *please, Frankie,*" he wept incoherently as he picked her up and clutched her to him. He couldn't tell if she was hurt or where she was hurt or how badly. Panic overwhelmed him. "No, please, *dear God, no,* don't take her away from me, make her be all right. Frankie, little Frankie, please, please . . ."

It was a few moments before he pulled himself together and called an ambulance.

Just as the train was pulling into Dublin, Moira got a text message on her cell phone.

There had been an accident. Frankie had cut her head. Noel had taken her to the A&E of St. Brigid's Hospital, and he thought he should let Moira know.

She took the bus straight from the railway station to St. Brigid's. She had *known* that this would happen, but she felt no satisfaction at being proved right. Just anger, a great anger that everyone else's bleeding-heart philosophy said that a drunk and a flighty young girl could be left responsible for raising a child.

It had been an accident waiting to happen.

She found a white-faced Noel at the hospital. He was almost babbling with relief.

"They say it's just a deep graze and she'll have a bruise. Thank God! There was so much blood I couldn't imagine what it was."

"How did it happen?" Moira's voice was like a knife cutting across his words.

"She rolled over when I was changing her and fell off the table," he said.

"You let her fall from the table?" Moira managed to sound taken aback and full of blame at the same time.

"She hit the chair. . . . It sort of broke her fall." Noel was aware of how desperate this sounded.

"This is intolerable, Noel."

"Don't I know that, Moira? I did the best I could. I called an ambulance straightaway and brought her here."

"Why didn't you get Dr. Carroll? He was nearer."

"I saw all the blood. I thought it was an emergency and that he'd probably have to send her here anyway."

"And where was your partner while all this was going on?"

"Partner?"

"Lisa Kelly."

"Oh, she had to go out. She wasn't there."

"And why did you let the child fall?"

"I didn't *let* her fall. She twisted away from me. I told you. . . ." Noel looked frightened and almost faint from the stress of it all.

"God, Noel, we're talking about a defenseless baby here."

"I know that. Why do you think I'm so worried?"

"So, what caused you to let her fall? That's what it was—*you* let her fall. Was your mind distracted?"

"No, no, it wasn't."

"Did you have a little drink, maybe?"

"*No,* I did *not* have a little drink or a big drink, though by God I could do with one now. It put the heart across me and of course I feel guilty but now I have you yapping at me as if I threw the child on the floor."

"I'm *not* suggesting that. I realize that it was an accident. I am just trying to work out how it happened."

"It won't happen again," Noel said.

"How do we know this?" Moira spoke gently, as if she were talking to someone of low intelligence.

"We know because we are going to move the table up against the wall," Noel said.

"And we didn't think of this sooner?"

"No, we didn't."

"Can I have a word with Lisa when we get back to Chestnut Court? I'd like to go over some of the routines with her once more."

"I told you, she's gone away."

"But she'll be back, won't she?"

"Not for a couple of days. Anton has been asked to take part in a celebrity chef thing in London and it's going to be televised. He's taking Lisa with him."

"Is this Anton happy about his girlfriend living with you, do you think, Noel?"

"I never thought about it one way or the other. It suits her. He knows we aren't a couple in *that* sense. Why do you ask?"

"It's my business to make sure Frankie grows up in a stable household," Moira said righteously.

"Yes, sure. Well, now that you're here, will you help me get her to the bus stop?"

"How do you mean?"

"You know, open doors for me and things. I didn't bring her pram, you see. I was afraid I wouldn't get it into the taxi."

Moira went ahead of him, opening doors and assisting him through the maze of corridors. He *did* seem concerned and worried about the child. Maybe this was the wake-up shock he needed. But she must be very firm with him. Moira had found over the years that firmness always paid off in the end.

Noel didn't want to let the baby out of his grasp. He lay back in his chair with Frankie clutched to his chest.

"You're going to be just fine, Frankie," he said over and over as he rocked her in his arms. If only he could have a drink to steady his nerves. He contemplated calling Malachy, but he was all right. The child was more important than the drink. He would manage.

"Here, Frankie, I'm going to stop talking to myself, I'm going to read you a story," he said. He put all the concentration in the world into reading her a story about a bird that had fallen out of its nest. It all ended very happily. It worked for Noel: it drove all thought of a large whiskey way out of his mind.

It worked for Frankie too, as she fell into a deep sleep.

Three days later Lisa Kelly phoned her.

"Oh, Moira, Noel asked me to call you. He said you want to go over some of Frankie's routines with me."

"Did you have a good time in London?" Moira asked.

"So-so. What routines did you want to discuss?"

"The usual: bath time, feeding, changing. You know she had an accident while you were away?"

"Yes. Poor Noel is like a hen on a hot griddle about it all. No harm done, I gather."

"Not this time, but it's not good for a baby to fall on its head."

"Well, I know that, but Declan has been round and he says she's fine."

Moira was pleased she had obviously scared Noel enough to make him aware of the gravity of it all.

"And did your friend do well in the celebrity chef thing?"

"No, not as well as he should have. But then I'm sure you read that in the papers."

"I thought I saw something, yes."

"It was all totally slanted the wrong way. You see, this woman

April turned up out of the blue there, talking about column inches and potential. She knows nothing really, except how to get her own name into the papers."

"Yes, I saw she was mentioned. I was a little surprised. Noel told me that *you* had gone to assist him, but it made it seem as if she did all the work."

"If drinking cocktails and handing people her business card is work then she did a lot of that, all right," Lisa said. Then she pulled herself together. "But about this routine you wanted?"

"I'll call round this evening," Moira said.

Not for the first time Lisa told Noel that Moira's social life must be the most empty and dull canvas in the whole world.

"Let's ask Emily to be here. She can take some of the heat away from us," Noel suggested.

"Good idea," Lisa agreed. "I was going to ask Katie to come to supper. The more lines of defense we can draw up, the easier it will be for us coping with Generalissimo Moira."

Moira was surprised to see the little flat full of people. She wished that she had not been wearing the heather-colored suit she had bought from St. Jarlath's Thrift Shop. Now they would know that she had sent her friend Dolores to make the purchase!

Noel showed her the new positioning of the table. He stood obediently while she measured the formula out, even though he had been doing these bottles perfectly for months. Frankie went off to sleep obediently like a textbook baby.

"Please join us for some supper *this* time, Moira," Lisa suggested. "I put two extra drumsticks in for you."

"No, really, thank you."

"Oh, do, for God's sake, Moira. Otherwise we'll all fight over the extra bits," Lisa's sister, Katie, said.

They sat down and Lisa produced a very tasty supper. Moira decided that for a brainless blonde she *did* have some skills. But then, of course, she was a chef's girlfriend.

Katie was practical and down-to-earth. She showed them pictures of her trip to Istanbul and talked affectionately of her husband, Garry.

Neither she nor Lisa talked about their home life. But then, to be fair, Moira told herself, she didn't talk about her home life much either.

Instead they talked about Noel and Lisa's lectures, and when Katie mentioned that Father Flynn was away visiting his mother in Rossmore, Noel mentioned that he'd first met the priest when he used to bring Stella cigarettes in hospital.

"Hardly a helpful thing to do under the circumstances." Moira was very disapproving.

"Stella's view was that it was already way too late and she just wanted to enjoy the last bit," Noel said.

"Why don't the clergy provide the priest with a place to live? They do have these flats, I believe. . . ." Moira needed to know the answer to everything.

"He doesn't want that. Says it's like living in a religious community and he's more of a lone bird, really."

"And why didn't you go and stay in Katie's flat, Lisa, rather than here?" Moira asked.

Lisa looked at her impatiently. "Are you *ever* off the job, Moira?" she asked, annoyed.

Emily stepped in to make peace. "Moira has all the best qualities of a social worker, Lisa. She is very interested in people." And then she turned to Moira. "Father Flynn was installed before Lisa needed to move. That's right, isn't it?" She looked around her good-naturedly.

"That's it." Lisa was brief.

"Exactly." Katie was even briefer.

It would have been churlish to ask any more, like why Lisa had needed to move, so very reluctantly Moira decided to leave it there. Instead she said that the chicken was delicious.

"Just olives, garlic and tomatoes," Lisa said, pleased. "I learned it from Emily, actually."

They *seemed* a normal enough group and there was no sign of alcohol anywhere during the meal. Moira sometimes wished she didn't have such a strong instinct for when things were going to go wrong. And she had felt this about Noel from the very beginning.

Anton's restaurant was advertising Saturday lunches. Moira decided to invite Dr. Casey, to return the hospitality at Quentins.

"There's no need, Moira," Clara had said.

"No, of course not, but I'd enjoy it. Please say yes."

It didn't suit Clara at all. Normally she had an easy lunch with Frank Ennis on a Saturday and then they went to the cinema or a matinee at the theater. Sometimes they went to an art exhibit. It had become a relaxed and undemanding routine. But what the hell, she could meet him later.

"That would be delightful, Moira," she said.

Moira booked the table. She would like to have that easy confidence that Clara had. She would like it if they knew her in Anton's and made a fuss of her, as had happened with Clara in Quentins. But that would never happen.

When she went to make the table reservation she was greeted by Anton himself. He was indeed very charming. Small and handsome in a boyish way, he pointed around the room.

"Where would you like to sit, Ms. Tierney? I'd love to give you the nicest table in the room," he said.

She pointed out a table.

"Excellent choice. You can see and be seen there. Are you inviting a friend?"

"Well, my boss, actually. She's a doctor in a heart clinic."

"Well, we'll make sure you both have a good time," he said.

Moira left feeling ten years younger and much more attractive. No wonder this girl Lisa was so besotted with the boy. Anton was truly something special.

. . .

And he had not forgotten that they were to be well looked after. As soon as she entered the restaurant, she was greeted as though she were a regular and valued customer.

"Ah, Ms. Tierney!" Teddy said, as she gave him her name. "Anton said to look out for you and to offer you and your guest a house cocktail."

"Lord, I don't think so," Clara said.

"Why not? It's free." Moira giggled.

And they sipped a colored glass of something that had fresh mint and ice and soda, some exotic liqueur and probably a triple serving of vodka.

"Thank God it's Saturday," Clara said. "Nobody could have gone back to work after one of these house cocktails."

It was a very pleasant lunch. Clara talked about her daughter Linda, who was very anxious to have a child and had been having fertility treatment for eighteen months without success.

"Any babies coming up for adoption in your line of business?" Clara asked.

Moira gave the question serious attention. "There might be," she said, "a little girl, a few months old now."

"Well, I mean is she available for adoption or not?" Clara was a cut-and-dried person.

"Not at the moment, but I don't think she's going to last long in the present setup," Moira explained.

"Why? Are they cruel to her?"

"No, not at all. They are just not able to manage properly."

"But do they love her? I mean they'll never give her up if they are mad about her."

"They might have no choice in it," Moira said.

"I won't tell Linda anything about it in case. No point in raising her hopes," Clara said.

"No. If and when it does come up, I'll let you know immediately."

Then they chatted about the various patients who came to the heart clinic. Moira asked about Clara's friend Frank Ennis and learned that he was a very decent man in most ways, but had a blind spot about saving St. Brigid's money.

Clara asked did Moira have anyone in her life and Moira said no because she had always been too busy. They touched briefly on Clara's ex-husband, Alan, who was the lowest of the low, and on Moira's father, now happily settled in with Mrs. Kennedy, who had asked only for one more crack at happiness and seemed to have found it.

Just as Moira was paying the bill, Anton came in accompanied by a very pretty girl who looked about twenty. He came over to their table.

"Ms. Tierney, I hope everything was all right for you?" he said.

"Lovely," Moira said. "This is Dr. Casey. . . . Clara, this is Anton Moran."

"It was all delicious," Clara said. "I will certainly tell people about it."

"That's what we need." Anton had an easy charm.

Moira looked at the young woman expectantly.

Eventually Anton broke and introduced her. "This is April Monaghan," he said.

"Oh, I read about you in the papers. You were in London recently," Moira said, gushing slightly.

"That's right," April agreed.

"It's just that I know a great friend of yours. A *great* friend, Lisa Kelly, and she was there too at the same time."

"Yeah, she was," April agreed.

Anton's smile never faltered.

"How exactly do you know Lisa, Ms. Tierney?"

"Through work. I'm a social worker," Moira said, surprised at herself for answering so readily.

"I thought social workers didn't discuss their cases in public." His smile was still there, but not in his eyes.

"No, no, Lisa isn't a client. I just know her sort of through something else. . . ." Moira was flustered now. She could sense Clara's disapproval. Why had she brought up this matter, anyway? It was in order to fill in the missing parts of the jigsaw in Chestnut Court. The unaccustomed house cocktail and the bottle of wine had loosened her tongue. Now she had somehow managed to spoil the whole day.

Everything settled into a routine at the heart clinic. Clara Casey seemed pleased by Moira's input and could not fault her in terms of diligence and following up everything that needed to be checked. But the warmth had gone. Moira did not feel as included as she had thought herself to be.

The others were all welcoming, but Clara seemed to have lost respect for her. Moira had seen some forms on Hilary's desk asking whether the part-time social worker was to be a permanent position. Clara had attached a note.

"Tell them not yet. Position is still under review."

So Clara Casey didn't really trust her just because of a stupid, tactless slip in the restaurant. Moira redoubled her efforts on all fronts.

She got Gerald full-time care in his home, to the great annoyance of his daughter and son-in-law. She had saved him from going to the old people's home, which he had dreaded, and he told everyone she was a knight in shining armor. She managed to get children of a drug addict mother fostered in a happy home where they had warmth and toys and regular meals for the first time in their lives. She found a teenage runaway sleeping rough under a bridge by the river and invited her home for soup and a good talking-to. The girl slept for seventeen hours on Moira's sofa and then went back like an obedient lamb to her family home.

She managed to frighten a couple who were signing on for unemployment benefits at the same time as making a very reasonable living from a sandwich bar and to terrify a factory owner who was paying much less than the minimum rate with threats of major publicity. She had even managed to get her brother, Pat, into not only sheltered housing but a sheltered workshop doing woodwork as well.

Her father had agreed to sell his house and divide the money among himself and his two children. Mrs. Kennedy had apparently thought this was highly satisfactory and was busy planning a new kitchen. So there were *some* areas of Moira's life that were a great success.

But not all. Maybe she was just too ambitious about her success rate.

Her father's house did not fetch a big price at the auction. It was a small holding and this was the wrong time to sell. But it did mean that she had the deposit for a house. She must look around for somewhere to live.

"Make sure you get a place with a small garden," Emily advised.

"Have it be somewhere near a tram or a bus," said Hilary, who managed the heart clinic with the same practical sense.

"Buy a dilapidated sort of house and do it up," said Johnny, who did the exercise routines at the heart clinic.

"Get a nice, modern place that isn't falling to bits," said Gerald, who seemed to have a new lease on life and whose brain cells seemed to be working at full power.

She called at Noel's family home in St. Jarlath's Crescent, as she did from time to time. It was easier than facing Noel and Lisa in Chestnut Court, where they both seemed very resentful of her role in anything. At least Emily and Noel's parents could have a civilized conversation.

"This is exactly the kind of street I would like to live in," Moira said. "Do you know of any houses coming up for sale in the area?"

Emily knew that Noel wouldn't like Moira, who was regarded as "the enemy," moving closer to him and being a neighbor of his parents.

"I've heard nothing of anyone moving," Emily said, and, as they did so often, Josie and Charles took their lead from her.

"It's nice to think that people would want to come to live here," Josie said, heading off down memory lane. "When Charles and I were young it was regarded as the last place on earth."

"Maybe Declan would know of someone thinking about moving . . . ," Emily said.

She knew very well that Declan and Fiona had no great love for Moira, and thought her unnecessarily interfering in Noel's efforts to make a reliable home for himself and Frankie. Even if Declan knew that half the street was for sale, he wouldn't give the news to Moira.

Moira asked politely about the campaign for the statue to St. Jarlath and Josie and Charles showed her some quotes they had from sculptors. Bronze was very expensive, but they hoped they might be able to afford it.

"Do you have a particular devotion to St. Jarlath, by any chance?" Josie was always hopeful of recruiting others to the cause.

"Admiration, certainly," Moira murmured, "but *devotion* might be putting it a bit strongly."

Emily hid her smile. When Moira was being diplomatic you could see she'd be good at her job. What a pity she couldn't see what huge strides Noel was making. Why did she have to behave like a policeman with him rather than an encourager and someone he could turn to if there were any problems? As usual, Emily wrote it all to her friend Betsy back in New York. Somehow, typing it on her laptop made it seem clearer.

Honestly, Bets, you just have to get yourself over here. When you and Eric get married, as you will, sooner rather than later, I hope, you will need a honeymoon. Find a good airfare and I'll find you somewhere to stay. But you have to meet this cast. Noel and his little girl. A changed man, he hasn't had a drink in months and he's working his butt off in this dreary company *and* he is keeping up with his lectures too.

He and a slightly kooky girl named Lisa live like an old married couple in their apartment, taking care of the child and studying for their diploma. There's no sex because she is involved with some society guy—a celebrity chef, no less! They are being stalked by this social worker, Moira. She *is* doing her job, but she sort of hides in their garden and pounces on them, hoping to catch them at something.

And the campaign for the statue is going great guns. We are thinking of having it cast in bronze at this stage. And the whole business of the thrift shop has given Josie a new lease on life. She works away there happily with Molly Carroll and me. A lovely fedora came in last week and Josie took it to this man Dr. Hat to add to his collection.

My uncle Charles has a very satisfactory dog-walking business now—even the hotel where he used to work has employed him to come and walk their customers' dogs.

He has even become a babysitter for his granddaughter on the evenings when Noel and Lisa go to their lectures.

When I'm not helping out at the doctors' clinic I'm busy doing gardens and window boxes—the whole crescent looks just great. We might even win a prize in a competition for Most Attractive Street. In fact, I'm so busy that I haven't read a book or been to a play. And as for an art exhibit—it's been months!

Tell me about yourself and life back there. I have forgotten I ever lived in New York!

Love,
Emily

She got a reply in minutes:

Emily,

You must be psychic.

Eric asked me to marry him last night. I said I would if, and only if, you came back to New York to be my maid of honor.

Considering our great age, I thought a small wedding would be best, but nobody said anything about keeping the honeymoon low-key.

Ireland, here we come!

Love,
Betsy

"I hear your aunt is going back to America for a vacation," Moira said to Noel.

"She's actually my cousin, but you're right—she *is* going to New York. How did you know?" Noel asked, surprised.

"Someone mentioned it," Moira, who made it her business to know everything, said vaguely.

"Yes, she's going to be in her friend's wedding," Noel said. "But then she's coming back again. My parents are very relieved, I tell you. They'd be lost without Emily."

"And you would too, Noel, wouldn't you?" Moira said.

"Well, I would miss her certainly, but as far as my mother is concerned, the thrift shop would close down without Emily, and my father thinks the world of her too."

"But surely you are the one she has helped most, Noel?" Moira was persistent.

"How do you mean?"

"Well, didn't she pay your tuition fees at the college? Get you this apartment, arrange a babysitting roster for you and probably a lot more. . . ."

There was a dull red flush on Noel's face and neck. He had never been so annoyed in his whole life. Had Emily blabbed to this awful woman? She had gone over to the enemy and told Moira all about things that were meant to be private between them. *Nobody* was ever going to know about the fees—that was their secret. He felt betrayed, like he had never felt before. There was no way he could know that Moira was only guessing.

She was looking at him politely, waiting for a reply, but he didn't trust himself to speak.

"You must have thought about who would take over her duties when she was away?"

"I thought maybe Dingo might help," Noel said eventually in a strangled voice.

"Dingo?" Moira said the name with distaste.

"You know, he does some deliveries to the thrift shop. Dingo Duggan."

"I don't know him, no."

"He only helps out the odd time when no one else is available."

"And you never thought to tell me about this Dingo Duggan?" Moira asked, horrified.

"Listen to me, Moira, you give me a pain right in the arse," Noel said suddenly.

"I beg your pardon?" She looked at him in disbelief.

"You heard me. I'm breaking my back to do this right. I'm nearly dead on my feet sometimes, but do you ever see any of this? Oh, no, it's constantly moving the goalposts and complaining and behaving like the secret police."

"Really, Noel. Control yourself."

"No, I will *not* control myself. You come here investigating me as if I were some sort of criminal. Repeating poor Dingo's name as if he were a mass murderer instead of a decent poor eejit, which is what he is."

"*A decent poor eejit.* I see." She started to write something down, but Noel pushed her clipboard away and it fell to the ground.

"And then you go and pry and question people. And try to get them to say bad things about me, pretending to look out for Frankie's good."

Moira remained very still during this outburst. Eventually she said, "I'll leave now, Noel, and come back tomorrow. You will hopefully have calmed down by then."

And she turned and left the apartment.

. . .

Noel sat and stared ahead of him. That woman was bound to bring in some reinforcements and get Frankie taken away from him. His eyes filled with tears. He and Lisa had been planning her first Christmas, but now Noel wasn't certain that Frankie would still be with them by next week.

Noel picked up his phone and called Dingo. "Mate, can you do me a great favor and come and hold the fort for a couple of hours?"

Dingo was always agreeable.

"Sure, Noel. Can I bring a DVD or is the child asleep?"

"She'll sleep through it if it's not too loud."

Noel waited until Dingo was installed. "I'm off now," he said briefly.

Dingo looked at him. "Are you okay, Noel? You look a bit, I don't know, a bit funny."

"I'm fine," Noel said.

"And will you have your phone on?"

"Maybe not, Dingo, but the emergency numbers are all in the kitchen, you know: Lisa, my parents, Emily, the hospital or anything. They're all there on the wall." And then he was gone. He took a bus to the other side of Dublin, and in the anonymity of a cavernous bar Noel Lynch drank pints for the first time in months.

They felt great . . . bloody great. . . .

Chapter Seven

It was Declan who had to pick up the pieces. Dingo phoned him a half an hour after midnight, sounding very upset.

"I'm sorry for waking you, Declan, but I didn't know what to do—she's roaring like a bull."

"Who is roaring like a bull?" Declan was struggling to wake up.

"Frankie. Can't you hear her?"

"Is she all right? When did you last feed her? Does she need changing?"

"I don't do changing and feeding. I was just holding the fort. That's what he asked me to do."

"And where is he? Where's Noel?"

"Well, I don't know, do I? Fine bloody fort-holding it turned out to be. I've been here six hours now!"

"His phone?"

"Turned off. God, Declan, what am I to do? She's bright red in the face."

"I'll be there in ten minutes," Declan said, getting out of bed.

"*No*, Declan, you don't have to go out. You're not on call!" Fiona protested.

"Noel's gone off somewhere," Declan told her. "He left the baby with Dingo. I have to go over there."

"God, Noel would never do that!" Fiona was shocked.

"I know, that's why I'm going over there."

"And where's Lisa?"

"Not there, obviously. Go back to sleep, Fiona. No use the whole family being unable to go to work tomorrow."

He was dressed and out of the house in minutes.

He was worried about Noel—very worried indeed.

"God bless you, Declan," Dingo said with huge relief when Declan came into Chestnut Court. He watched, mystified, as Declan expertly changed a nappy, washed and powdered the baby's bottom, made up the formula and heated the milk, all in seamless movements.

"I'd never be able to do that," Dingo said admiringly.

"Of course you would. You will when you have one of your own."

"I was going to leave it all to the woman, whoever she might be . . . ," Dingo admitted.

"I wouldn't rely on it, Dingo, me old mate. Not these days. It's shared everything, believe me. And quite right too."

Frankie was perfectly peaceful. All they had to do now was to find her father.

"He didn't say where he was going, but I sort of thought it was for an hour or two. I thought he was going home to his parents for something."

"Was he upset about anything before he went out?"

"I thought he was a bit distracted. He showed me all the numbers on the wall. . . ."

"As if he were planning to stay out, do you think?"

"God, I don't know, Declan. Maybe the poor lad was hit by a bus and we're all misjudging him. He could be in an A&E somewhere with his phone broken."

"He could." Declan didn't know why he felt so certain that Noel had gone back on the drink. The man had been heroic for months. *What* could have changed him? And, more important, how would they ever find him?

"Go home, Dingo," Declan sighed. "You've held the fort for long enough. I'll do it until Noel gets back."

"Should we ring anyone on this list, do you think?" Dingo didn't want to abandon everything.

"It's one in the morning. No point in worrying everyone."

"No, I suppose not." Dingo was still reluctant.

"I'll call you, Dingo, when he's found, and I'll tell him you didn't want to leave but I forced you to." He had hit the right note. Dingo hadn't wanted to leave his post without permission. Now he could go back home without guilt.

Declan sat down beside Frankie's crib. The baby slept on as peacefully as his own son slept back at home. But little Johnny Carroll had a much more secure future ahead of him than poor baby Frankie here. Declan sighed heavily as he settled himself into an armchair.

Where could Noel be until this hour?

Noel was asleep in a shed on the other side of Dublin.

He had no idea how he had got there. The last thing he could remember was some kind of argument in a bar and people refusing him further drink. He had left in annoyance and then found, to his rage, that he couldn't get back in again, and there were no other public houses in the area. He had walked for what seemed a very long time and then it got cold, so he decided to have a rest before he went home.

Home?

He would have to be careful letting himself in to 23 St. Jarlath's Crescent—then he remembered with a shock that he didn't live there anymore.

He lived in Chestnut Court with Frankie and Lisa.

He would have to be even more careful going back there. Lisa would be shocked at him and Frankie might even be frightened. But Lisa was away. He remembered that now. His heart gave a sudden jump. What about the baby? He would never have left Frankie alone in the apartment, would he?

No, of course he hadn't. He remembered Dingo had come in. Noel looked at his watch. That was hours ago. Hours. Was Dingo still there? He wouldn't have contacted Moira, would he? Oh, please, God, please, St. Jarlath, please, anyone up there, let Dingo not have rung Moira.

He felt physically ill at the thought and realized that he was indeed going to be sick. As a courtesy to whoever owned this garden shed, Noel went out to the road. Then his legs felt weak and wouldn't support him. He went back into the shed and passed out.

In spite of the discomfort, Declan slept for several hours in the chair. When the light came in the window he realized that Noel hadn't come home. He went to make himself a cup of tea and decide what to do. He rang Fiona.

"Is today one of Moira's days up in your clinic?"

"Yes, she'll be there for the morning. Are you coming home?"

"Not immediately. Remember, don't say a word to her about any of this. We'll try to cover for him, but she can't know. Not until we've found him."

"Where is he, Declan?" Fiona sounded frightened.

"Out on the tear somewhere, I imagine. . . ."

"Listen, Signora and Aidan will be here soon. They're collecting Johnny and will be going to pick up Frankie then and take them to their daughter's place. . . ."

"I'll wait until they're here. I'll have her ready for them."

"You really are a saint, Declan," Fiona said.

"What else can we do? And remember, Moira knows nothing."

"Not a word to the Kamp Kommandant," Fiona promised.

The clinic was in a state of fuss because Frank Ennis was paying one of his unexpected visits.

"You were out with him last night—did he not give you *any* idea he was coming in today?" Hilary asked Clara Casey.

"*Me?*" asked Clara in disbelief. "I'm the very last person on earth that he'd tell. He's always hoping to catch me out in something. It's driving him mad that he hasn't been able to do it so far."

"Look, he's talking to Moira very intently about something," Hilary whispered.

"Well, we marked her card for her about Frank," Clara said, "and if Ms. Tierney says a word out of order she's out of here."

"I'll get nearer and see what they're talking about," Hilary offered.

"Really, Hilary, I *am* surprised at you," Clara said in mock horror.

"You go away and I'll hover," said Hilary. "I'm a great hoverer. That's why I know so much."

Clara made for her desk, which was in the center of the clinic; there was a phone call from Declan.

"Don't say my name," he said immediately.

"Sure, right. What can I do for you?"

"Is Moira near you?"

"Quite, yes."

"Could you find out what she's doing after she leaves you today? I'll make myself clear. We share baby-minding arrangements with a friend and his baby. It's just that they're clients of Moira's and she's been a bit tough on him. He's gone off on a batter. I have to drag him back here and sort things out. We want to keep Moira out of the place until tomorrow, at any rate. If she discovers the setup, then things will really hit the fan."

"I see . . ."

"So, if there was any other direction you could head her towards . . . ?"

"Leave it with me," Clara said, "and cheer up—maybe your worst scenario won't turn out to be right."

"No, I'm afraid it's only too right. His AA buddy has just called in. He's getting him back here in about half an hour."

Hilary came over to Clara with a report.

"He's pumping her for information. Like 'Do you see any areas of conspicuous waste,' and 'Do the healthy cookery classes work or are they just a distraction.' You know, the usual kind of thing he goes on about."

"And what's she singing in response?"

"Nothing yet, but that may be because she's here under our eye. If he got her on his own, Lord knows what he'd get out of her."

"Be more confident, Hilary. We're not doing anything wrong here. But you've given me an idea."

Clara approached Frank Ennis and Moira.

"Seeing you two together reminded me that Moira hasn't seen the social-work setup in the main hospital. Frank, maybe you could introduce her to some of the team over there—today, possibly?"

"Oh, I have a lot of calls to make on my caseload."

Clara gave a tinkling laugh. "Oh, really, Moira, you're so much on top of everything, I imagine your caseload is run like clockwork."

Moira seemed pleased with the praise.

"You know the way it is. You've got to be watchful," she said.

"I agree," Frank boomed unexpectedly. "Everyone should be much more watchful than they are."

"I *was* hoping, Moira, that you could link up with the whole system, but of course if you feel it's too much for you . . . then . . ."

Clara had judged it exactly right. Moira made an arrangement to meet Frank at lunchtime.

Clara had managed to give Noel, Declan and the man from Alcoholics Anonymous a bit of a head start.

Aidan and Signora Dunne had arrived with little Johnny Carroll and taken Frankie with them. They would wheel the two baby buggies along the canal to Aidan's daughter's house. There Signora would look after all three children—their grandson, Joseph Edward, along with Frankie and Johnny, while Aidan gave private Latin lessons to students who hoped to go to university.

It was a peaceful and undemanding morning. If they had wondered what Dr. Carroll was doing in Noel Lynch's place and why there was no sign of a normally devoted father, they had said nothing. They minded their own business, the Dunnes. Declan was glad of them many times, but never more so than today. The fewer people who knew about this, the better.

Malachy arrived, more or less supporting Noel in the doorway. Noel was shaking and shivering. His clothes were filthy and stained. He seemed totally disoriented.

"Is he still drunk?" Declan asked Malachy.

"Hard to say. Possibly." Malachy was a man of few words.

"I'll turn on the shower. Can you get him into it?"

"Sure."

Malachy was as good as his word. He propelled Noel into the water, letting it get cooler all the time until it was almost cold. Meanwhile, Declan picked up all the dirty clothes and put them into the washing machine. He laid out clean clothes from Noel's room and made them all a pot of tea.

Noel's eyes were more focused now, but still he said nothing.

Malachy was not speaking either.

Declan poured another mug of tea and allowed the silence to become uncomfortable. He would *not* make things easy for Noel. The man would have to come up with something. Answers, or even questions.

Eventually Noel asked, "Where's Frankie?"

"With Aidan and Signora."

"And where's Dingo?"

"Gone to work," Declan said tersely. Noel was going to have to speak again.

"And did he phone *you*?" He nodded towards Declan.

"Yes, that's why I'm here," Declan said.

"And are you the only one he phoned?" Noel's voice was a whisper.

Declan shrugged. "I've no idea," he said. Let Noel sweat a bit. Let him think that Moira was on the case.

"Oh, my God . . . ," Noel said. His face had almost dissolved in grief.

Declan took pity on him. "Well, no one else turned up, so I suppose I was the only one," he said.

"I'm so sorry," Noel began.

"Why?" Declan cut across him.

"I can't remember. I really can't. I felt a bit uptight and I thought one or two drinks might help and wouldn't matter. I didn't know it was going to end like this. . . ."

Declan said nothing and Malachy was silent too. Noel couldn't bear it.

"Malachy, why didn't you stop me?" he asked.

"Because I was at home doing a jigsaw with my ten-year-old son. I didn't hear from you that you were going out—that's why." Malachy hadn't spoken such a long sentence before.

"But, Malachy, I thought you were meant to . . ."

"I am *meant* to come when there's a danger that you might be about to go back to drinking. I am *not* meant to be inspired by the Holy Ghost as to when you decide this kind of activity all on your own," Malachy said.

"I didn't know it was going to turn out like this," Noel said piteously.

"No, you thought it would be lovely and easy like the movies. And I bet you wondered what we were all doing at those meetings."

Noel's face showed that this is exactly what he had wondered.

Declan Carroll suddenly felt very tired. "Where do we go from here?" he asked both men.

"It's up to Noel," Malachy said.

"Why is it up to me?" Noel cried.

"If you want to try to kick it again, I'll try to help you. But it's going to be hell on earth."

"Of course I want to," Noel said.

"It's no use if you are just waiting for me to get out of your hair so that you can sneak off and stick your face into it again."

"I won't do that," Noel wailed. "From tomorrow on it will be back just the same as it was up to now."

"What do you mean *tomorrow*? What's wrong with *today*?" Malachy asked.

"Well, tomorrow, fresh start and everything."

"Today, fresh start and everything," Malachy said.

"But just a couple of vodkas to straighten me up and then we can start with a clean slate?" Noel was almost begging now.

"Grow up, Noel," Malachy said.

Declan spoke. "I can't let you look after our son anymore, Noel. Johnny won't come here again unless we know you're off the sauce," he said slowly and deliberately.

"Ah, Declan, don't hit me when I'm down. I wouldn't hurt a hair of that child's head." Noel had tears in his eyes.

"You left your own daughter with Dingo Duggan for hour after hour. No, Noel, I wouldn't risk it. And even if I did, Fiona wouldn't."

"Does she have to know?"

"I think so, yes." Declan hated doing it, but it was the truth. They couldn't trust Noel anymore. And if he felt like that, what would Moira feel?

It didn't bear thinking about.

"We have to tell Aidan and Signora," Declan said.

"Why?" Noel asked, worried. "I'm over it now. I hate them knowing I'm so weak."

"You're *not* weak, Noel—you're very strong. It's not easy for you doing what you do. I know. Believe me."

"No, I don't believe you, Declan. You were always a social drinker, a pint in the evening and no more. That's balance and moderation—two things I was never any good at."

"You took on more than most men would have done. I admire you a lot," Declan said simply.

"I don't admire myself. I disgust myself," Noel said.

"And what help will that be to Frankie as she grows up? Come on, Noel—it's her first Christmas coming up. The whole street is going to celebrate. You've got to get yourself into good form for it. No self-pity."

"But Signora and Aidan?"

"They know *something* is wrong. We mustn't play games with them. They can cope with it, Noel. They've coped with a lot in their lives."

"Anyone else I should tell?" Noel looked defensive and hurt by it all.

"Yes, Lisa, of course, and Emily." Declan was very definite.

"No, please. Please, not Emily."

"No need to tell your parents or my parents or anyone like that, but Emily and Lisa need to know."

"I thought it was over," Noel said sadly.

Declan forced himself to be cheerful. "It will be over soon and meanwhile the more help you can get, the better."

"Go back to the real world and heal the sick, Declan. Don't bother with me and my addictions."

"What could be more real than the man whose daughter is going to be best friends with our son—remember? We arranged it with Stella."

"Thank God she doesn't know how it all turned out," Noel said fervently.

"It turned out very well until now and it will again. Anyway, according to people like your parents and mine, Stella *does* know, and she understands it all perfectly."

"You don't believe any of that claptrap, Declan, do you?"

"Not exactly, but you know . . ." Declan ended it vaguely.

"No, I don't know, I don't know at all. But if I have to tell Aidan and Signora then I will. Is that okay?"

"Thanks, Noel."

Declan had, of course, already told Fiona all about Noel. She had been, as usual, practical and optimistic.

"He sounds shocked by what he did," she said.

"Yes, but I wish I knew *why* he did it," Declan said, worried.

"You said yourself he was in bad form."

"But he must have been in bad form a hundred times during the last few months and he never went out on the town. He loves that child. You should see him with her. He's as good as any mother."

"I know, I *have* seen him . . . everyone has. That child has a dozen families round here who'll all do a bit more at the moment."

"Noel's very sensitive about not letting people know, but he has to tell them. Until he does, don't say anything."

"Quiet as the grave," Fiona said.

Declan Carroll took his morning surgery. He had been two hours late, so Dr. Hat had been called in to help.

"Muttie Scarlet rang a couple of times. He said you'd have some results for him today."

"And I do," Declan said glumly.

"I thought you might." Dr. Hat was sympathetic.

"Isn't it a shit life, Hat?" Declan said.

"It is indeed, but I'm usually the one who says that and you always say it's not so bad."

"I'm not saying that today. I'm off out to Muttie's house. Can you stay a bit longer?"

"I'll stay as long as you like. They don't want me, though; they'll ask when the *real* doctor will be back," Dr. Hat said.

"I bet they do! They still ask me was I born when they got their first twinge of whatever they have and the answer is always that I wasn't."

"Ah, Declan, any news yet?" Muttie answered the door. He spoke in a low voice. He didn't want his wife, Lizzie, to hear the conversation.

"You know how they are," Declan said. "They're so laid-back up there in the hospital they give a new urgency to the word *mañana. . . .*"

"So?" Muttie asked.

"So I was wondering would we go and have a pint?" Declan said.

"I'll go and get Hooves," Muttie suggested.

"No, let's go to Casey's instead of Dad's and your pub—too many Associates there . . . we'd get nothing said."

Declan saw from Muttie's face that he realized immediately that the news wasn't good.

Old Man Casey served them and, since there was no response to his conversation about the weather, the neighborhood and the recession, he left them alone.

"Give it to me straight, Declan," Muttie said.

"It's only early days yet, Muttie."

"It's bad enough for a drink in the middle of the day, lad. Will you tell me or do I have to beat it out of you?"

"They saw a shadow on the X-ray; the scan showed a small tumor."

"Tumor?"

"You know . . . a lump. I've made an appointment for you with a specialist next month."

"Next *month*?"

"The sooner we deal with it, the better, Muttie."

"But how in the name of God did you get an appointment so soon? I thought there was a waiting list as long as your arm?"

"I went private," Declan said.

"But I'm a workingman, Declan, I can't afford these fancy fees. . . ."

"You won a fortune a few years back on some horse. You've got money in the bank—you *told* me."

"But that's for emergencies and rainy days. . . ."

"This is a rainy day, Muttie." Declan blew his nose very loudly. This was more than he could bear at the moment. He heard himself lying as he felt he had been lying all day.

"The thing is, Muttie, once this appointment is made you can't cancel it. You have to pay for it anyway."

"Isn't that disgraceful!" Muttie was outraged. "Aren't they very greedy, these people?"

"It's the system," Declan said wearily.

"It shouldn't be allowed." Muttie shook his head in disapproval.

"But you'll go, won't you? Tell me you'll go?"

"I'll go because you can't get me out of it. But it's very high-handed of you, Declan. But if he suggests some mad, expensive treatment, he's not getting another cent out of me!" Muttie vowed.

"No, it's just to know the treatment that he would advise. One visit . . ."

"All right then," Muttie grumbled.

"You never asked me one single thing about the whole business," Declan said. "I mean, there are a lot of options: chemotherapy, radiotherapy, surgery . . ."

Muttie looked at him with the air of a man who has seen it all and heard it all. "Won't I hear all about it from the fellow whose Rolls-Royce *I'm* paying for? No point in thinking about it until I have to. Okay?"

"Okay," agreed Declan, who was beginning to wonder would this day ever end.

By the time that Moira called at Chestnut Court, things had settled down a lot.

Noel had agreed not to drink today. Malachy had taken him to an AA meeting, where nobody had blamed him but everyone had congratulated him on turning up that day.

Halfway through the meeting, Noel remembered that he had not let them know in Hall's that he wouldn't be in today.

"Declan did that ages ago," Malachy said.

"What did he say?"

"That he was your doctor and you weren't able to go in. That he was telephoning from your flat."

"I wonder how Mr. Hall took that?" Noel was full of anxiety.

"Oh, Declan would have reassured him. You'd believe anything he said. Anyway, it was all true. You weren't able to go in and he *was* at your flat."

"He looked very put out about everything," Noel said. "I hope he won't turn against me."

"No, I think he was put out about something else." Malachy knew when there was a time to be very firm and a time to be more generous.

Moira viewed the presence of Malachy in the house with no great pleasure.

"Are you a babysitter?" she asked.

"No, Ms. Tierney, I am from Alcoholics Anonymous. That's how I know Noel."

"Oh, really . . ." Her eyes narrowed slightly. "Any reason for the visit?"

"We were at a meeting together up the road and I came back for some tea with Noel. That's permitted, isn't it?"

"Of course—you mustn't make me into some kind of a monster. I'm merely here for Frankie's sake. It's just that we had a full and frank exchange of views yesterday and I suppose, well, when I saw you here, I thought that you might . . . that Noel could possibly . . . that all was not well."

"And so now you are reassured?" Malachy asked silkily.

"Frankie will be coming back shortly. We want to get things ready for her . . . unless there's anything else?" Noel spoke politely.

Moira left.

Malachy turned to Noel. "One ball-breaker," he said, and for the first time that day Noel smiled.

Everyone had been planning a Christmas party for Frankie and Johnny. Balloons and paper decorations had been discussed at length and in detail. It was going to be held in Chestnut Court: the apartment block had a big communal room that could be rented for such occasions. Lisa and Noel had reserved it weeks back. Was it to go ahead or was Noel too frail to be part of it?

"We've got to go for it," Lisa encouraged him. "Otherwise when she looks back on her album she'll wonder why there was no celebration for her first Christmas."

"She won't be looking back on any album with us," Noel said grimly.

"What do you mean?"

"They'll take her from me, and rightly so. Who would leave a child with me?"

"Well, thank you very much from the rest of us who are doing our best to make a home for her," Lisa said tartly. "We are not going to give up so easily. Get her into the pram, Noel, and we'll head off and look at this room."

Just then the phone rang.

"Noel, it's Declan. Can we leave Johnny with you for an hour or so—it would be a great help." This was the first time since Noel's drinking incident that Johnny had been offered.

Noel knew it was a peace offering and an olive branch. But he also knew it was a vote of confidence. He stood a bit taller now.

"Sure, Declan, we'll take him off to see the room where he's having his first Christmas party," he said. And he felt that Declan was pleased too, glad to know the party was going ahead.

Having a party for the children three days before Christmas was a great opportunity for the families to get together. Most of them celebrated the actual day quietly, eating too much of their own turkeys and sitting with family in front of the television. But this was an excuse to get together and wear paper hats and pretend that it was all for the children, two small babies who would sleep through most of it.

Lisa was in charge of decorating the hall, and she did it in scarlet and silver. Emily helped her to drape huge red curtains borrowed from the church hall, Dingo Duggan had brought a van full of holly from what he described vaguely as the countryside, Aidan and Signora had decorated a tree that would be left in the big room over the Christmas season. They were going to bring their own grandson, Joseph Edward, to the party as a guest, and Thomas Muttance Feather, Muttie's grandson, was coming on the assurance that he wouldn't have to talk to babies or sit at a children's table.

Josie and Charles were wondering if a picture of St. Jarlath would be appropriate in the decorations, and tactfully, Lisa found a place for it. Somewhere it wouldn't look utterly ludicrous.

Simon and Maud had a job doing a house party, so they couldn't do the catering, but Emily had arranged a supper where all the women would bring a chicken or vegetable dish of some sort, and all the men would bring wine and beer or soft drinks and a dessert. The desserts had of course turned out to be an immense number of chocolate ones bought in supermarkets. They were arranged artistically on paper plates on a separate table to be wheeled in after the main course was finished.

Noel showed Frankie all the Christmas decorations and smiled at her adoringly as she squealed with pleasure and sucked her fingers. Dressed in a red Babygro and with a little red pixie hat keeping her head warm, she was passed around from one doting adult to another, and featured in a hundred photographs along with Johnny. Even Thomas was persuaded to join in and posed for pictures with the three youngsters and a plate of mince pies.

Father Flynn had brought a Czech trio to play. They had been lonely in Dublin and missed their homeland, so he arranged a number of outings like this, which they enjoyed doing while they got a good meal and their bus money, and an audience cheering them on.

They sang Christmas songs and carols in Czech and in English. And when it came to

Away in a manger
No crib for His bed
The little Lord Jesus
Laid down His sweet head

a hush fell on family and friends as they looked at the two sleeping babies. Then they all joined in the singing for the next bit:

The stars in the bright sky
Looked down where He lay
The little Lord Jesus
Asleep on the hay

and everyone in the room, believers or nonbelievers, felt some sense of Christmas that they had not felt before.

"You're very good giving Muttie a lift," Lizzie said when Declan called at the Scarlet house on a cold, gray January morning. "He hates going to the bank—it makes him feel uneasy. He's dressed himself up likes a dog's dinner, but he's been like a caged lion all morning."

"Oh, don't worry, Lizzie—I'm going there anyway and I'd enjoy the company."

Declan realized that Muttie had told Lizzie nothing whatsoever about his appointment with the specialist. He looked at Muttie, dressed in his best suit and tie, and couldn't help noticing how thin the older man had become. It was a wonder Lizzie hadn't seen it.

They drove in silence while Muttie drummed his fingers and Declan rehearsed what he was going to say when Dr. Harris delivered the news that was staring at Declan from X-rays, scans and reports. They called first at the bank, where Declan cashed a check just to prove that he had business there. Muttie withdrew 500 euros from his savings.

"Even Scrooge Harris can't charge that much," he said, nervously putting it in his wallet. Muttie Scarlet wasn't happy about carrying huge sums of money like this, but he was even less happy still about handing it over it to this greedy man.

As it turned out, Dr. Harris turned out to be a kindly man. He was more than pleased to have Declan join them for the consultation.

"If I start talking medical jargon, Dr. Carroll can turn it into ordinary English," he said with a smile.

"Declan is the first person who grew up on our street who became a professional man," Muttie said proudly.

"That so? I was the first in my family to get a degree too. I bet they have a great graduation picture of you at home." Dr. Harris seemed genuinely interested.

"It replaces the Sacred Heart lamp." Declan grinned.

"Right, Mr. Scarlet, let's not waste your time here while we go down memory lane." Dr. Harris came back to the main point. "You've been to St. Brigid's and they've given me a very clear picture of your lungs. There are no gray areas—it's black-and-white. You have a large and growing tumor in your left lung and secondary tumors in your liver."

Declan noted that there was a carafe of water on the desk and a glass. Dr. Harris poured one for Muttie, who was uncharacteristically silent.

"So, now, Mr. Scarlet, we have to see how best to manage this."

Muttie was still wordless.

"Will an operation be an option?" Declan asked.

"No, not at this stage. It's a choice between radiotherapy and chemotherapy at the moment and arranging palliative care at home or in a hospice."

"What's palliative care?" Muttie spoke for the first time.

"It's nurses who are trained to deal with diseases like yours. They are marvelous, very understanding people who know all about it."

"Have they got it themselves?" Muttie asked.

"No, but they have been well trained and they know a lot about it from nursing other people—what patients want and how to give you the best quality of life."

Muttie thought about this for a moment. "The quality of life I want is to live for a long, *long* time with Lizzie, to see all my children again, to see the twins well settled in a business or good jobs and to watch my grandson Thomas Muttance Feather grow up into a fine young man. I'd like to walk my dog, Hooves, for years to the pub, where I meet my Associates, and go to the races about three times a year. That would be a great quality of life."

Declan saw Dr. Harris remove his glasses for a moment and concentrate on cleaning them. When he trusted himself to speak again he said, "And you *will* be able to do a good deal of that for a time. So let's look forward to that."

"Not live for a long, long time, though?"

"Not for a long, long time, Mr. Scarlet, no. So the important thing is how we use what time is left."

"How long?"

"It's difficult to say exactly. . . ."

"*How long?*"

"Months. Six months? Maybe longer, if we're lucky. . . ."

"Well, thank you, Dr. Harris. I must say you've been very clear. Not worth hundreds of euros, but you were straight and you were kind as well. How much exactly do I owe you?" Muttie took his wallet from his pocket and laid it on the desk.

Dr. Harris didn't even look at it. "No, no, Mr. Scarlet, you were brought here by Dr. Carroll, a fellow doctor. There's a tradition that we never charge fellow doctors for a consultation."

"But there's nothing wrong with Declan," Muttie said, confused.

"You're his friend. He brought you here. He could have gone to other specialists. Please accept this for what it is, normal procedure, and put that away. I will write my report and recommendations to Dr. Carroll, who will look after you very well."

Dr. Harris saw them to the lift. Declan noticed him shake his head at the receptionist as she was about to present the bill and Declan breathed a little more easily. Now all he had to do was to keep Noel on the wagon and, more immediately, go home with Muttie and help him tell Lizzie.

Thank God Hat was able to keeps things going until he got back to his surgery.

· · ·

Fiona knew there was something wrong the moment he came in the door.

"Declan, you're white as a sheet! What happened? Was it Noel?"

"I love you, Fiona, and I love Johnny," he said, head in his hands.

"Ah, God, Declan, what *is* it?"

"It's Muttie."

"What's happened to him? Declan, tell me in the name of God. . . ."

"He has just a few months," Declan said.

"Never!" She was so shocked she had to sit down.

"Yes. I was at the specialist this morning with him."

"I thought you were taking him to the bank."

"I did, so that he could get the money for a specialist."

"Muttie went private? God, he *must* have been worried," Fiona said.

"I hijacked him into it, but the specialist waived the fee."

"Why on earth did he do that?"

"Because Muttie is Muttie," Declan said.

"He'll have to tell Lizzie," Fiona said.

"It's done. I was there." Declan looked stricken.

"And?"

"It was as bad as you'd think. Worse. Lizzie said she still had so many things to do with Muttie. She had been planning to take him to the Grand National in Liverpool. You know, Fiona, Muttie's never going to make it to Aintree."

And then he sobbed like a child.

Maud and Simon, who had grown up with Muttie and Lizzie and hardly remembered any former life, were heartbroken.

"It's not as if he were really old," Maud said.

"Sixty is meant to be only middle-aged nowadays," Simon agreed.

"Remember the cake we made for his birthday?"

" 'Sixty Glorious Years.' "

"We'll have to put off going to America," Maud said.

"We can't do that. What if they won't keep the job for us?" Simon was very anxious.

"There will be other jobs. Later, you know, afterwards." Maud didn't want them to go.

But Simon wasn't willing to let it go easily. "It's such a chance, Maud. He'd want us to have it. We'll be earning a big salary. We could send him money."

"When was Muttie ever interested in money?"

"I know . . . you're right. I was just trying to think of excuses, really," Simon admitted.

"So let's try to get shifts in good Dublin restaurants."

"They'd never take us on. We don't have enough experience."

"Oh, come on, Simon, don't be such a defeatist. We have terrific recommendations and references from all the people we did catering for. I bet they'll take us on."

"Where will we start?"

"I think we should invest a little money first, have dinner somewhere like Quentins, Colm's or Anton's. You know, top places. And we'd regard it as research, keep our eyes open and *then* go back and ask for a job."

"It seems a heartless sort of thing to be doing when poor Muttie is in such bad shape."

"It's better than going to the other side of the earth," Maud said.

They would start with Colm's up in Tara Road. They chose the cheapest items on the menu, but took notes on everything: the way the waiters served, how they offered the wine for tasting, the way the cheeses were brought to the table and how they were sliced according to the customers' wishes, with some advice from the waiter.

"We had better learn our cheeses before trying here," Maud whispered.

"That's the head guy there." Simon pointed out Colm, the owner.

He came to their table. "Nice to see a younger set coming in," he said, welcoming them.

"We're in the catering business ourselves," Maud said suddenly.

"Really?"

Simon was annoyed. They hadn't planned to blurt it out so quickly. Now they had exposed themselves as spies and not real diners.

"We have terrific recommendations and I was wondering if we could leave you our business card. Just in case you were short-staffed."

"Thank you. Of course I'll keep it. Here, are you any relation of Cathy Mitchell of Scarlet Feather?"

"Yes, she trained us," Maud said proudly.

"She was married to a cousin of ours, Neil Mitchell." Simon saw no need to explain the situation any further.

"Well, well, if Cathy trained you, you must be great! But I won't have anything just for the moment. My partner's daughter Annie—that's her over there—she's just started here, so we're fairly well covered at the moment. Still, I'll put your names in the book." Then he retired to the kitchen.

"He was nice," Maud whispered.

"Yeah, I hope he won't go checking up with Cathy on us just now. She's very upset about Muttie and it would look a bit heartless."

They decided on chemotherapy for Muttie, and by this stage everyone in St. Jarlath's Crescent knew about him and had a variety of cures. Josie and Charles Lynch said that in recognition for Muttie's interest in the campaign for his statue, St. Jarlath would put in a word for him. Dr. Hat said that he would be happy to drive Muttie to the pub any evening he wanted to go. Hat wouldn't stay, but he'd come back and pick him up later. Emily Lynch managed to distract Muttie by planting winter-color shrubs in his garden.

"But will I be still here to see them, Emily?" he asked one day.

"Oh, come on, Muttie. The great gardeners of history always knew that someone would see them. That's what it's all about."

"That makes sense," Muttie said, and put aside any thought of self-pity.

Declan's own parents saw that there was a half leg of lamb left over at the end of the day or four fillet steaks.

Cathy came by every day, often with something to eat.

"We made far too many of these little salmon tarts, Dad. Mam, you'd be helping me out if you were to take them."

Often she brought her son, Thomas, with her. He was a lively lad and kept Muttie well entertained.

In fact, it was all going better than Declan could have hoped. He had thought that the normally cheerful Muttie would fall into a serious depression. But it was far from being the case. Declan's father said that Muttie was still the life and soul up at the pub and he had the same number of pints as ever on the grounds that there wasn't much damage they could do to him now.

Declan wrote to the specialist, Dr. Harris.

> You were so kind and gracious when I brought Muttie Scarlet to a consultation. Your gesture about the fees was so appreciated that I thought you would like to know he is making very good progress, keeping his spirits up and generally living each day to the full.
>
> You and your positive attitude have contributed greatly to this, and I thank you most sincerely.
> Declan Carroll

Mr. Harris responded by return.

> Dr. Carroll,
> I was glad to hear from you. I have friends who run a general practice and they are looking for a new partner. They asked me could I recommend anyone and I immediately thought of you. It's in a very attractive part of Dublin and would come with

accommodation, which would be available for purchase, if required. I have attached some details for your interest.

These are very good, concerned people and just because their neighbourhood is affluent does not mean that their patients are rich people with hypochondria. They are sick and worried like people everywhere.

Let me know if it interests you, and send me your CV, and it can be arranged. Sooner rather than later, they tell me.

I will never forget your friend Muttie Scarlet. Only occasionally in life do you come across a genuinely good person like that. Someone with no disguises whatsoever.

I look forward to hearing from you.

Sincerely,

James Harris

Declan had to read the letter three times before it sank in. He was being offered a place in one of the most prestigious practices in the whole of Dublin. A house with a big garden and a posh school for Johnny. It was the kind of post he might have tried for in ten years' time. But *now*! Before he was thirty! It was too much to take onboard. Fiona had gone to work when the letter arrived so he couldn't share the news. Emily had come to pick up Johnny and wheel him up to Noel's to collect Frankie. Today the children were going to the thrift shop for the morning and back here to his parents' in the afternoon. The system ran like clockwork and Noel seemed to be back on track also.

Declan's surgery began at ten so he would have time to call in to Muttie and discuss the palliative-care nurse who was arriving for the first time today. Declan knew the nurse. She was an experienced, gentle woman called Jessica, trained in making the abnormal seem reasonable and quick to anticipate anything that might be needed.

"He's his own man, Jessica," Declan had warned her. "He might tell you there's nothing wrong with him at all."

"I know, Declan, relax. We'll get on fine together." And Declan knew that they would.

Moira was bustling down St. Jarlath's Crescent when Declan went out. She seemed surgically attached to her clipboard of notes. Declan had never seen her without them. He waved and kept walking, but she stopped him. She clearly had something on her mind.

"Where are you heading?" he asked easily.

"I heard there was a house for sale in this street," Moira said. "I've always wanted a little garden. Do you know anything about it? It's Number Twenty-two."

Declan thought quickly; it belonged to an old lady who was going into an old people's home, but it was exactly next door to Noel's parents. Noel would not welcome that.

"Might be in poor condition," Declan said. "She was a bit of a recluse."

"Well, that might make it cheaper," Moira said cheerfully. She looked nice when she smiled.

"Noel still okay?" she asked.

"Well, you actually see him more than I do, Moira," Declan said.

"Yes, well, it's my job. But he can be a little touchy at times, don't you find?"

"Touchy? No, I never found that."

"Just one day there recently, he actually pushed my notes out of my hands and shouted at me."

"What was all that about?"

"About someone called Dingo Duggan who had been appointed as an extra babysitter. I asked about him and Noel shouted at me that he was a *decent poor eejit* and used most abusive language. It was quite intolerable."

Declan looked at her steadily. So *that* was what had tilted Noel that night. He hardly trusted himself to speak.

"Is anything wrong, Declan?" she asked. "I get the feeling that I am not being told everything."

Declan swallowed. Soon he would be far away from Moira and

Noel and St. Jarlath's Crescent. He reminded himself he must not explode and leave behind him a trail of confusion and bad feeling.

"I'm sure you were able to handle it very well, Moira," he said insincerely. "You must be used to the ups and downs of clients, as we are with patients."

"It's good when you're told the full story," Moira said. "But at the moment I think something is being kept from me."

"Well, when you discover what it is, you'll let me know, won't you?" Declan managed to fix a smile on his face and moved on.

He called in at the Laundromat where his mother worked, and kissed his son, who was sitting with his friend Frankie. The children were both like advertisements for Bonny Babies; they seemed to be endlessly fascinated with their hands.

"Who is his daddy's little boy, then," Declan said.

His voice sounded different. Molly Carroll looked at her son, concerned.

"Did you come in for anything, Declan?" she asked.

"Just to say hello to my son and heir and to thank my saintly mother and my friend Emily for making life so easy for us both." He smiled. A real smile this time.

"Well, isn't it the least I could do?" Molly was pleased. "Haven't I got what every mother dreams of? Her son and now her grandson living at home! When I think of all the people who hardly ever see their grandchildren, I feel blessed every single day."

Not for much longer, Declan thought to himself grimly. He went on to see Muttie and Lizzie. They were having a good-natured argument about how to welcome Jessica, who was going to arrive on her first call that day.

"I've made some scones, but Muttie thinks she'd like a good dinner. What do you think, Declan?"

"I think the scones would be fine and you can suggest lunch to her another time," Declan said.

"Is she a married person or a single lady?" Muttie asked.

"She's a widow, as it happens. Her husband died about three years ago."

"The Lord have mercy on him—it must be very hard on her," said Lizzie, without any apparent acknowledgment that she too would soon be a widow.

"Yes, but Jessica has great heart. She puts everything into her family and her work."

"That's very wise," said Lizzie. "And I hope she had a great doctor at the time like we do." She looked at Declan fondly.

"You can say that again," said Muttie.

"Stop that, Muttie, you're making my head swell!" he said.

"It deserves to swell. I've told everyone about that Dr. Harris and how he wouldn't charge me because you were a professional colleague of his and I was your Associate."

Declan felt a slight stinging behind his eyes. By the time that Muttie died, Declan and Fiona would be in a totally different part of Dublin. Not only would Muttie and Lizzie have lost their trusted doctor, but his own parents would have lost their son and grandson.

Before he got to work, he met Josie and Charles Lynch.

"I believe the house next door to you is up for sale?" he said.

"Yes, the notice is going up tomorrow. How do you know already?"

"Moira," he said simply.

"Lord, that woman can hear the grass grow," Josie said.

"She's been round to the house checking that there are no dog hairs. What kind of a world does she live in thinking that dogs don't shed hairs?"

"She's thinking of buying the house," Declan said.

"*Never!*" Josie was shocked. "Lord, she'll be practically *living* in our house!"

Charles shook his head. "Noel won't like this . . . not one little bit."

"Well, we always have Declan to stand up to her for us all." Josie was good at looking on the bright side.

Not for long, Declan thought to himself.

In the surgery that morning all the patients seemed to need to tell him some story or recall some instance where he had helped them. If Declan were to believe a quarter of the praise he got that morning, he would have been a very vain man. He just wished they had not chosen today to tell him all this. Today, of all days, when he was just about to change his life and leave them all.

He booked a table at Anton's restaurant for dinner. He wanted to tell Fiona in good surroundings, not in the house they shared with his parents, where everything could be heard in some degree anyway.

"How did you hear of us, sir?" the maître d' asked.

Declan was about to say that Lisa Kelly talked of little else, but something made him keep this information to himself.

"We read about it in the papers," he said vaguely.

"I hope we will live up to your expectations, sir," said Teddy.

"Looking forward to it," said Declan.

It seemed a long day until Dingo would come to pick them up at seven.

A couple of weeks before, Dingo had been to a party in a Greek restaurant and danced unwisely on some broken plates. Declan had tweezed the worst bits out of the soles of Dingo's feet. Money had not changed hands. It didn't, usually, in Dingo's case, but an offer of four trips in his van was agreed to be a fair exchange. This meant they could have a bottle of champagne when he told Fiona the great news.

Just before he left the surgery, Noel came by.

"Just three minutes of your time, Declan, please."

"Sure, come on in."

"You're always so good-natured, Declan. Is it real or is it an act?"

"Sometimes it's an act, but sometimes, like now, it's real." Declan smiled encouragingly.

"I'll come straight to the point then. I'm a bit worried about Lisa. I don't know what to do. . . ."

"What's wrong?" Declan was gentle.

"She's lost complete touch with reality when it comes to this Anton. I mean, she doesn't know what's real and what's not. Listen, I should know. I know what denial is. She's right in the center of it."

"Is she drinking or anything?" Declan wondered whether Noel might have developed an alcoholic's sudden lack of tolerance for any kind of drinking.

"No, no, nothing like that, just an obsession. She's deluding herself all the time. There's no future there."

"It's tough, all right."

"She needs help, Declan. She's ruining her life. You're going to have to refer her to someone."

"I'm not her doctor and she hasn't *asked* anyone to refer her anywhere."

"Oh, you were never one to play it by the book, Declan. Get somebody . . . some sort of psychiatrist to throw an eye over her."

"I *can't*, Noel. It doesn't work that way. I can't go in off the side of the road and say: Lisa, Noel thinks you are heading in the wrong direction, so let's go and have a nice soothing visit to a shrink."

"It *should* be the way things work, and anyway, you'd know how to say it." Noel was pleading with him.

"But she hasn't done anything out of line. Your feelings about all this do you credit, but honestly there's no way that outside interference is going to help. Can't *you* get her to see sense? You live with her—you're flatmates."

"Sure, who would listen to a word I say?" Noel asked. "*You* always did, to give you your due. You used to make me feel I was a normal sort of a person and not a madman."

"And you *are*, Noel." Declan wondered was there anyone left who hadn't told him how important he was to them.

Fiona was in great form. She said she had starved herself at lunchtime. Barbara had wanted them to go for lunch together for a long chat about the complexity of men, but Fiona had said that she was going to Anton's that evening, so Barbara said there was no point in talking about the complexity of men to her anyway, that she had got a jewel of a husband and there weren't enough of them to go round.

She was all dressed up in her new outfit: a pink dress with a black jacket. Declan looked at her proudly as they were settled in at the restaurant. She looked so beautiful. She had a style equal to any of the other guests. He took her face in his hands and kissed her for a long time.

"Declan, really! What will people think?" she asked.

"They'll think we are alive and that we are happy," he said simply, and suddenly he made the second biggest decision of his life. The first had been to pursue Fiona to the end of the world. This one was different. It was about what he was not going to do.

He wouldn't tell her now about the letter from Dr. Harris. In fact, he might never tell her. It suddenly seemed so clear to him.

"I was thinking . . . I was wondering should we buy Number Twenty-two in the Crescent? It would be a home of our own, and we'd still be beside everyone."

Chapter Eight

"I have a bit of a problem," Frank Ennis said to Clara Casey as he picked her up at the heart clinic.

"Let me guess," she said, laughing. "We used one can of air freshener too many in the cloakroom last month?"

"No nothing like that," he said impatiently, as he negotiated the traffic.

"No, don't tell me. I'll work it out. It's the brass plates on the door. We got a new tin of brass-cleaning stuff and I forgot to ask you? That's it, isn't it?"

"Truly, Clara, I don't know why you persist in painting me as this penny-pinching sort of clerk instead of the hospital manager. My worry has nothing to do with you and your extraordinary and lavish expenditure on your clinic."

"On *our* clinic, Frank. It's part of St. Brigid's."

"I'd say it's an independent republic—always was from day one."

"How petty and childish of you," she said disapprovingly.

"Clara, are you wedded to this concert tonight?" he asked suddenly.

"Is anything wrong?" She looked at him sharply. Frank never canceled arrangements.

"No, nothing is *wrong,* exactly, but I do need to talk to you," he said.

"Will you promise that it's not about boxes of tissues and packets of paper clips and huge areas of wastefulness that are bleeding your hospital dry?" Clara asked.

He actually smiled. "No, nothing like that."

"All right, then. Sure, we'll cancel the concert. Will we go out to a meal somewhere?"

"Come home with me."

"We have to eat somewhere, Frank, and you don't cook."

"I asked a caterer to leave in a dinner for us," he said, embarrassed.

"You were so sure I'd say yes?"

"Well, in a lot of areas of life you are quite reasonable—normal, even." He was struggling to be fair.

"Caterers. I see . . ."

"Well, they're quite young. Semi-professional, I'd say. Haven't learned to charge fancy prices yet."

"Slave labor? Ripe for exploitation, yes?" Clara wondered.

"Oh, Clara, will you give over just for one night?" Frank Ennis begged.

Maud and Simon were in Frank's apartment. They had set a table and brought their own paper napkins and a rose.

"Is that over the top?" Simon worried.

"No, he's going to propose to her. I know he is," Maud said.

"Did he tell you?"

"Of course he didn't, but why else is he making a meal for a woman in his flat?" To Maud it was obvious.

They had laid out the smoked salmon with the avocado mousse and a little rosette carved from a Sicilian lemon. The chicken-and-mustard dish was in the oven. An apple tart and cream were on the sideboard.

"I hope to God she says yes," Simon said. "It's a heavy outlay for that man, all this food and the cost of us and everything."

"She must be fairly old. . . ." Maud was thoughtful. "I mean, Mr. Ennis is as old as the hills. It's amazing that he still has the energy to propose, let's not even mention anything else!"

"No, let's not," said Simon, with relief. They let themselves out of the house and posted the keys back through the door.

Clara had always thought Frank's apartment rather bleak and soulless. Tonight, though, it looked different. There was subdued lighting and a lovely dinner table prepared.

And she noticed the red rose. This wasn't Frank's speed. She wondered whether the young caterers had dreamed it up. Suddenly she felt a great thudlike shock. He couldn't possibly be about to propose to her. Could he?

Surely not. Frank and she had been very clear about where they were going, which was a commitment-free relationship. They were both able to go out with other people. Sometimes when they went away for a weekend, such as the time they had that holiday in the Scottish Highlands, they stayed in the same room and had what Clara might have described as a limited, but pleasant, sex life. That was if she were to tell anyone about it. But she told nobody. Not her great friend Hilary in the clinic, nor her oldest friend, Dervla.

Certainly not Clara's mother, who made occasional inquiries about her new escort. Not her daughters, who were inclined to think that their poor old mother was long past that sort of thing. Not her ex-husband, Alan, who was always hovering in the background, waiting for her to come running back to him.

No. Frank could not have got the wires so hopelessly crossed? Definitely not!

He went into his study and came out with some papers.

"This all looks very nice." Clara admired the place.

"Well, good. Good. And thank you for agreeing to change the plans so readily."

"Not at all. It must be important. . . ." Clare wondered what she would say if he really *had* lost the run of himself and proposed. It would obviously be no, but how to put it without hurting him or making him look ridiculous. That was the problem.

Frank poured her a glass of wine and then passed the papers over to her.

"This is my problem, Clara. I've had a letter from a boy in Australia. He says he's my son."

Simon and Maud had asked Muttie to test out a recipe they had for koulibiac for them that evening. In fact, they both knew the dish worked perfectly well. They just wanted to give themselves an excuse for going to the trouble for him and to give him a role to play. They showed Muttie carefully how they had folded the pastry leaves and prepared the cooked salmon, rice and hard-boiled eggs.

He watched with interest. "When I was young, if we ever got a bit of salmon we'd be so delighted that we'd never wrap it up in rice and eggs and all manner of things!" He shook his head in wonder.

"Ah, well, nowadays, Muttie, they like things complicated," Maud explained.

"Is that why you're always talking about making your own pasta instead of buying it in the shops like everyone else?"

"Not a bit," Simon butted in with a laugh. "She's interested in pasta because she's interested in Marco!"

"I hardly know him," said Maud unconvincingly.

"But you'd like to know him more," Simon responded definitely.

"Who's Marco, anyway?" asked Muttie.

"His father is Ennio Romano—you know, Ennio's restaurant, the place we were telling you about," Simon added.

"We were hoping to get work there," said Maud.

"Some of us were *praying* we get work there," Simon added, laughing at his sister's blushes.

Maud tried to look businesslike. "It's an Italian restaurant; it makes sense for us to know how to make our own pasta. And even if we don't get work there, it would be useful for our home catering. The clients would be very impressed."

"And thinking they're knocking people's eyes out with envy," Simon said.

"But what's the point of asking people to your house and then upsetting them?" For Muttie this was a real problem.

The twins sighed.

"I wonder, has he asked her yet?" Maud said.

"If he doesn't want his dinner burned to a crisp, I'd say he has."

"Who's this?" Muttie asked with interest.

"A desperately old man called Frank Ennis is proposing to some very old woman."

"Frank Ennis? Does he work up in St. Brigid's?"

"Yes, he does. Do you know him, Muttie?"

"Not personally, but I know all about him from Fiona. Apparently, he is their natural enemy in the clinic where she works. Declan knows him too. He says your man is not a bad old skin, just obsessed with work."

"That will all end if he marries the old lady," Simon said thoughtfully.

"It will change for the old lady too, remember," Maud reminded them.

"Has he paid you?" Muttie asked suddenly.

"Yes. He left an envelope for us," Simon confirmed.

"Good. That's fine, then. I hear from Fiona that he's a total Scrooge and won't pay his bills until the last moment."

"He did mention thirty days' grace," Simon said.

"You didn't tell me!" Maud said.

"I didn't need to. I said to him we operated a money-up-front, no-credit business. He totally understood."

Simon was immensely proud of his negotiating skills and his command of the language of commerce.

Clara Casey was looking at the letter that Frank had handed to her.

"Are you sure you want me to read it?" she asked. "He didn't write it to me. . . ."

"He didn't *know* about you," Frank explained.

"But the question is what does he know about *you*?" Clara asked gently.

"Read it, Clara."

So she began to read a letter from a young man:

> You will be surprised to hear from me. My name is Des Raven and I believe that I am actually your son. This will probably strike terror into your heart and you will expect someone searching for a fortune turning up on your doorstep. Let me say at once that this is not at all the case.
>
> I live very happily here in New South Wales, where I'm a teacher and—just to reassure you—where I will go on living!
>
> If my presence in Dublin will cause embarrassment to you and your family, I will quite understand. I just hoped it might be possible for us to meet at least once when I am in Ireland. My mother, Rita Raven, died last year. She got a heavy pneumonia and didn't have it properly treated.
>
> I have not lived at home for the past six years while I went to teachers' training college, but I always came home once a week and cooked her a meal. Sure, she put the washing through the machine for me, but she liked to do that. Truly she did.
>
> Funny thing, I never asked her any questions about where I came from and what kind of a guy was my father. I didn't ask because she didn't seem very easy about the whole thing. She would say she had been very young and very foolish at the time and hadn't it all worked out so well. She said she never regretted one day of having me, which was good. And Australia had been good to her. She arrived here pregnant and penniless when she had me and then she trained as a hotel receptionist.
>
> She had a couple of romances: one fellow lasted six years. I didn't much like him but he made her happy . . . and then I think something marginally more interesting for him turned up. She had a lot of good friends and kept in touch with her married sister, who lives in England. She was forty-two when she died,

*although she claimed to be thirty-nine and I'd say, all in all, she
had a good and happy life.*

*Of you, Frank Ennis, I know nothing except your name on my
birth certificate. I found you on the Internet and called the
hospital from here and asked were you still working there and they
said yes.*

So here goes with the letter!

*You only have my assurance that I will not make trouble for
you and your present wife and family. I also know that you didn't
know anything about where I lived. Mum was very adamant
about that. She told me that every single birthday so that I
wouldn't expect a gift.*

I truly hope that we will meet.

Until then . . .

Des Raven

Clara put the letter down and looked over at Frank. His eyes were
too bright and there was a tear on his face. She got up and went
across to him with her arms out.

"Isn't this *wonderful,* Frank!" she cried. "You've got a son! Isn't
that the best news in the world?"

"Well, yes, but we've got to be cautious," Frank began.

"What do we have to be cautious about? There was a woman
called Rita Raven, wasn't there?"

"Yes, but . . ."

"And she disappeared off the scene?"

"She went to some cousins in the U.S.A.," he said.

"Or to some non-cousins in Australia . . . ," Clara corrected him.

"But it will all have to be checked out . . . ," he began to bluster.

She deliberately misunderstood him. "Of course the airlines and
everything, but let him do that, Frank—the young are much better
at getting flights online than we are. The main thing is what time is
it in Australia? You can ring him straightaway." She busied herself
removing the plastic wrap from the smoked salmon.

He hadn't moved. He couldn't bring himself to tell her he had had the letter for two weeks and hadn't been able to decide what to do.

"Come on, Frank, it's surely morning there and if you leave it any longer he'll have gone out to school. Call him now, will you?"

"But we'll have to talk about it?"

"Like what do we have to talk about?"

"But don't you mind?"

"*Mind,* Frank? I'm delighted. The only thing I mind is you, after all these years, having to talk to an answering machine."

He looked at her, bewildered. There were so many things that he would never understand.

"How was Frank last night?" Hilary asked Clara the next day at the clinic. Only Hilary was ever given any information, and she was the only one who dared to ask.

"Amazing," Clara said and left it there.

"And did you enjoy the opera?" Hilary persisted.

"We didn't go. He arranged a catered meal in his apartment."

"My God, this sounds serious!" Hilary was delighted. She always said that they were made for each other. Something Clara continued to deny.

"Frank is as he always was and always will be: cautious and watchful, never spontaneous. Stop trying to matchmake, will you, Hilary?"

Frank had dithered so long last night that the telephone rang unanswered in Des Raven's home on the other side of the world. Frank had managed to miss talking to the son he hadn't known he had, just because he was anxious to talk it over and check it out. All this had led to nothing, but Clara told none of this to Hilary. It was still Frank's secret. She wasn't going to blurt it out.

"Where is Moira? Today's one of her days, isn't it?"

"She's just taken Kitty Reilly on a tour of residential homes. She has a checklist as long as her arm about what Kitty needs—you know, easy access to church, vegetarian food . . . that sort of thing." Hilary sounded half impressed, half annoyed.

"She's very thorough, I'll say that for her," Clara said grudgingly.

"I know what you mean. If she smiled more, maybe?" Hilary wondered. "Anyway, Linda rang you earlier. You were with somebody, so I took the call."

Hilary's son was married to Clara's daughter. The two women had schemed to introduce their children to each other and it had worked spectacularly well. Apart from not producing a grandchild. Despite a lot of intervention, there was no success. Both her son, Nick, and Clara's Linda were very despondent.

"She said no luck again."

"If she's so het up, she will *never* conceive. She has a list of three dozen people she phones every month. You, me and about thirty more."

"Clara!" Hilary was shocked. "She's your daughter and she thinks you are as excited as she is at the thought of you becoming a granny, and of me becoming one at the same time!"

"You're right—I'd forgotten. Pass me the phone." Hilary watched as Clara soothed Linda and patted her down.

Linda was obviously crying at the other end. Hilary moved away. She would have loved Nick and Linda to have given them good news. She could hear Clara saying, "Of *course* you're normal, Linda. Please stop crying, sweetheart. You'll have horrible, piggy, red eyes. I *know* you don't care, but you will later on when you're getting dressed to go out. . . . Well, to Hilary's, of course—that's where we're all going tonight. Don't even consider canceling, Linda. Hilary has bought *the* most gorgeous dessert."

"Oh, I have, have I?" Hilary said when Clara hung up.

"I had to say something. She was about to go home to a darkened room."

"All right, then. I had been going to serve cheese and grapes, but you've raised my game," Hilary said. "What did Frank Ennis serve last night as a dessert?"

"Apple tart," Clara said.

"Are you *sure* he didn't ask you some question? Something you've forgotten to tell me. . . ."

"Oh, shut up, Hilary. Look, here comes Moira. Let's pretend to be doing *some* work here."

Moira was triumphant. The fifth place they had looked at was perfect for Kitty Reilly—full of retired nuns and retired priests and a vegetarian option at every meal. All you could ask for, in fact.

"Lord, I hope I'll ask for a lot more than that when the time comes," Clara said piously.

"What would you like, exactly?" Moira asked.

An innocent enough question, but Moira's tone seemed to suggest that for Clara the time probably had come already.

"I don't know: a library, a casino, a gym, oh, and a grandchild!" Clara said. "What about you, Moira, when the time comes?"

"I'd like to be with friends. You know, people I have known for a long time so that we could do a lot of remembering together."

"And will you do that, do you think? Get a group of friends and set up your own place?" Clara was interested. She and her friend Dervla had often discussed doing just that.

"Probably not. I don't have many friends. I never had time to make friends along the way," Moira said unexpectedly.

Clara looked at her sharply. For a moment the veil had been lifted and she saw a very lonely woman indeed. Then the veil fell again and it was as before.

"Will you come round this evening and we'll call him? Earlier than we did last night . . ." Frank was full of plans.

"No, Frank, I can't tonight. Hilary's cooking dinner," Clara said.

"But you *have* to come!" He was outraged.

"I can't, Frank. I told you . . ."

"You're very doctrinaire," he said crossly.

"And so are you. If you had called immediately you would have caught him."

"Please, Clara."

"No. I'm not saying it again. Wait until the next night if you need me to be there and hold your hand for you." She hung up.

Frank sat listening to the empty line. What a fool he had been not to have telephoned the boy immediately! Clara was right. He *had* dithered, and the only result of his delay was the boy would think he was having a door closed in his face. Of course he remembered Rita Raven. Who wouldn't have remembered her? His mother and father had been most disapproving.

Rita was from entirely the wrong kind of family. The Ennises hadn't worked hard and risen to this degree of respectability just to be dragged down by their son. Frank Ennis had had parents who acted swiftly. Rita Raven had disappeared from everyone's life. Frank had thought of her from time to time slightly wistfully, and now she had died. So young. He still saw her as the pretty seventeen-year-old she had been then. Imagine, she had gone all the way to Australia and had her child without ever letting him know. He had had simply no idea of this.

If he had known, what would he have done? He was uneasy thinking about it. Back then, on the edge of a career, back then, in a more disapproving climate, he might not have acted well. His parents had been so hostile about his relationship with Rita and so open in their relief that she had left the country. They couldn't possibly have known more than they said, could they? His stomach churned at the possibility of it. But they *couldn't*. Not paid a sum of money to buy her off. That was impossible. They were careful with money. No, he mustn't go down that avenue of suspicion.

Damn Clara and her hen parties! He really needed to have her at his side.

Hilary served them an elegant meal. When she had gone to the gourmet shop to buy a deluxe dessert, she saw some unusual salads and bought those too.

The conversation was tense and stilted, as it always was on the days after Linda had discovered that, yet again, she wasn't pregnant. Clara and Hilary looked at each other. Years ago it had been so different. There were orphanages full of children yearning for happy homes. Today, there were allowances and grants for single mothers.

Clara wondered if Moira had any further news about the child she said would shortly be going into care. She'd said the little girl was a few months, exactly the same age as Declan and Fiona's baby. Lucky little girl if she got Linda and Nick as parents. No child would find a more welcoming home, not to mention two besotted grannies. She must ask Moira about it tomorrow.

Clara let her mind wander to Frank's apartment. She hoped he was being tactful and diplomatic with Des Raven. Had she stressed enough that he must *sound* delighted and welcoming? The first impression was crucial. This boy had waited for over a quarter of a century to talk to his father. Let Frank make it a good experience for him. *Please.*

Yet again the call went to the answering machine.

Frank was unreasonably annoyed. Did this guy spend *any* time at home? It must be about six-thirty in the morning. Where *was* he? Absently, later in the evening he dialed again, and to his surprise the phone was answered by a girl with what seemed a very strong Australian accent. Frank realized that Des Raven probably spoke like that too.

"I was looking for Des Raven . . . ," he began.

"You missed him, mate," she said cheerfully.

"And who am I talking to?" Frank asked.

"I'm Eva. I'm housesitting."

"And when will he be back?"

"Three months. I'm walking his dog and looking after his garden."

"Oh, and are you his girlfriend?"

"Who are *you*?" she asked with spirit.

"Sorry, I'm just a . . . friend . . . from Ireland."

"Well, he's on his way to you, then." Eva was pleased to have it all settled so easily. "Probably there now. No, wait, he's going to England first because that's where he lands. It's near you, right?"

"Yes, under an hour's plane journey." Frank felt the entire conversation was very unreal.

"Right, then, he knows where to find you?"

"He does?"

"Well, he left here with a briefcase full of papers and notes and letters. He showed a big batch to me. I think they were all from people he had written to who had written back."

"Yes, yes, indeed . . ." Frank was miserable.

"So, will I say who called him? I'm keeping a list beside the phone."

"Have many people called?" he asked out of interest.

"Nope, you're the first. What will I put down?"

"As you say, he'll be here in a day or two. . . ." Frank Ennis had no wish to muddy these waters any further.

He contemplated telling Clara, but she was at this confounded dinner and might not value an interruption about his private life. It was *impossible* to know how women would react to anything. Look at Rita Raven, heading to the ends of the earth to have a child by herself! Look at how childishly pleased Clara had been to hear that Frank had fathered a child outside marriage!

He thought morosely about the women after Rita and before Clara. A line, not a long line, but they all had one thing in common: they were incredibly hard to understand.

The boy would have to get in touch through the hospital. He didn't know Frank's home address. He wasn't going to blurt out the whole story to whoever he met first. Frank had no fears on that score. The boy, Des, as he must learn to think of him, had written that he understood the moral climate might not have changed or moved on in Ireland as much as it had in Australia. He wished Des had sent a picture of himself. Then he realized that the boy . . . all right, Des . . . didn't know what his father looked like either.

Quite possibly there was a picture of Frank from many years ago.

He hoped not. He hated being seen twenty-five years later, hair beginning to thin, stomach beginning to expand. What would Des Raven think of the father he had waited so long to meet? The days seemed to be crawling by.

When it happened it was curiously flat.

Miss Gorman, who had been hired by Frank ten years previously because she was not flighty, came in to see him. The years had resulted in Miss Gorman becoming even less flighty, if this was possible. She had a disapproval rating about almost everything. A man with an Australian accent had been on the phone wishing to talk to Mr. Ennis on a personal matter. He had been condemned because of his accent, his persistence and his defining anything to Miss Gorman as being personal. It was surprising, then, that Frank seemed to take it all so seriously.

"Where was he calling from?" he asked crisply.

"Somewhere in Dublin. He didn't really know *where* he was, Mr. Ennis." Miss Gorman's sniff was unmerciful.

"When he calls again, make sure that you put him right through."

"Well, I am sorry if I did the wrong thing, Mr. Ennis. It's just that you never *ever* talk to anyone you don't know."

"Miss Gorman, you didn't do the wrong thing. You are *incapable* of doing the wrong thing."

"I hope that I have been able to make this clear over the years." She was mollified and withdrew to await the call.

"I'm putting you through, Mr. Ennis," she said eventually.

"Thank you, Miss Gorman." He waited until she was off the line, then in a shaky voice he asked, "Des? Is that you?"

"So you *did* get my letter?" Very Australian but not very warm, not excited like his letter had been.

"Yes, I tried to call you but first it was the answering machine and then it was Eva. I talked to her and she told me that you had set out. I've been waiting for your call."

"I nearly didn't ring. . . ."

"Why was that? Was it nerves?" Frank asked.

"No, I thought why bother. You don't want to be involved with me. You've made that clear."

"That's *so* wrong," Frank cried out, stung by the unfairness of this. "I do indeed want to be involved with you. Why else would I have called you in Australia and talked to Eva?" He could almost hear the shrug of shoulders at the other end of the phone. "Why would I do that?"

Frank felt hollow. Somehow Clara had been right. He had paused when he should have gone enthusiastically forward. But that wasn't his nature. His nature was to examine everything minutely, and when he was sure, and not a moment before, then he would pronounce.

"You probably thought I was coming to claim my inheritance," Des said.

"It never crossed my mind. You said you wanted to get in touch. That's what I thought it was. I was as astonished as you. You know I only just heard of your existence, and I'm delighted!"

"Delighted?" Des sounded unconvinced.

"Yes, sure, I was delighted," Frank was stammering now. "Des, what *is* all this? You got in touch with me, I called you back. Will you come and have lunch with me today?"

"Where do you suggest?" Des asked.

Frank breathed out in relief. Then he realized he had to think quickly. Where to take the boy? "Depends what you'd like. . . . Quentins is very good and this new place, Anton's, is talked about a lot."

"Are these jacket-and-tie jobs?"

Frank realized that it had been years since he had gone anywhere that a jacket and tie was *not* necessary. There would be a lot of adapting ahead.

"Sort of traditional but not stuffy."

"I'll take that as a yes. Which place?"

"Anton's. I've never been there. Will we say one o'clock?"

"Why *don't* we say one o'clock?" Des sounded faintly mocking as if he were sending Frank up.

"I'll tell you how to get there . . . ," Frank began.

"I'll find it," Des said and hung up.

Frank buzzed through to Miss Gorman. Could she kindly find him the number for Anton's restaurant? No, he would make the reservation himself. Yes, he was quite sure. Perhaps she would cancel all appointments for the afternoon. She called back with the number and then added that she had spoken to Dr. Casey from the heart clinic, who said that there was no way the four p.m. meeting could be canceled. Too many people were setting too much store on the outcome. To have the meeting without Frank Ennis would be *Hamlet* without the prince. He would *have* to be back by four. What kind of a lunch would last three hours?

Chastened, Frank rang the restaurant.

"Can I speak to Anton Moran, please? . . . Mr. Moran? I have never begged before and I never will again, Mr. Moran, but today I arranged to meet for the first time a son I never knew I had and I picked your restaurant. Now I am hoping you will be able to find me a table. I don't know where to contact the young man . . . my son. . . . It will be such a messy start to our relationship if I have to tell him we couldn't get a booking."

The man at the other end was courteous. "This is far too important a matter to mess up," he said gracefully. "Of course you can have a table. Service today isn't full," he added, "but your story sounds so dramatic and so obviously true that I would have found a table for you even if I had to kneel down on all fours and pretend to be one."

Frank smiled, and suddenly he remembered Clara saying that he should be more immediate, more up-front with people. Nothing worked as well as the truth, she had advised him.

Another round to Clara. Was the woman going to be right about *everything?*

. . .

Frank was in the restaurant early. He looked around at the other diners, not a man without a collar, tie and smart jacket. *Why* had he chosen this place? But then again, if he had brought them to a burger place, it would hardly look festive. Or celebratory. It would look as if he were hiding this new member of his family. He watched the door and every time some man came in who might be about twenty-five his heart gave a lurch.

Then he saw him. He was so like Rita Raven that it almost hurt. Same little freckles on the nose, same thick, fair hair and same huge, dark eyes. Frank swallowed. The boy was talking to the maître d' at the door and making signs around his neck. Seamlessly, Teddy produced a necktie, and Des tied it quickly. Then Teddy was leading him over to the table.

"Your guest, Mr. Ennis," he said and slipped away.

Frank thought this man should have been an ambassador somewhere rather than working in what he realized was an outrageously expensive restaurant.

"Des!" he said and held out his hand.

The boy looked at him appraisingly.

"Well, well, well . . . ," he said. He ignored the hand that had been offered to him.

Frank wondered should he attempt the kind of bear hug men did nowadays.

He was bound to get it wrong, of course, and knock half the things off the table. And maybe the boy, used to more rugged Australian ways, might pull away, revolted.

"You found the place," Frank said foolishly.

He shrugged and looked so dismissive.

"I didn't know where you were, you see. Where you would be starting out from . . ." Frank's voice trailed away. This was going to be much harder than he had thought.

. . .

Near the kitchen door Teddy spoke to Anton.

"I've had Lisa on the phone."

"Not again," he sighed.

"She wants to come in for a meal sometime when we are not too busy."

"Try to head her off, will you, Teddy?"

"Not easy . . . ," Teddy said.

"Just buy me a week, then. Tell her Wednesday of next week."

"Lunch or dinner?"

"Oh, God, lunch."

"She has her eyes on dinner," Teddy said.

"An early-bird dinner, then." Anton was resigned.

"She does work her butt off for this place. I don't think we ever pay her anything."

"Nobody asked her to slave." Anton strained to hear what the newly united father and son were saying to each other. The conversation seemed to be limping along.

"Wouldn't families make you sick, Teddy?" Anton said unexpectedly.

Teddy paused before answering. Anton's family had not troubled him very much. Teddy didn't understand what was wrong with families from Anton's viewpoint, but he knew enough to agree with him.

"You're so right, Anton, but think of all the business we get out of the guilt that families create! Half the people here today are here from some kind of family guilt. Anniversaries, birthdays, engagements, graduations. We'd be bankrupt without it." Teddy always saw the bright side.

"Good man, Teddy." Anton was slightly distracted. That man, Mr. Ennis, was making heavy weather over his meeting with his son. Even from across the room you could cut the atmosphere with a knife.

Clara always said that when in doubt, you should speak your mind. Ask the question that is bothering you. Don't play games.

"What's wrong, Des? What has changed? In your letter you were eager to meet. . . . Why are you so different?"

"I didn't know the whole story. I didn't know what your family did."

"What did they do?" Frank cried.

"As if you didn't know."

"I don't know," Frank protested.

"You don't fool me. I've got documents, receipts, forms signed— I know the whole story now."

"You know more than I do," Frank said. "Who was writing these documents and filling in these forms?"

"My mother was a frightened girl of seventeen. Your father gave her a choice. She could leave Ireland forever and she would get a thousand pounds. One thousand pounds! That's how much my life was worth. A miserable grand. And for this she was to sign an undertaking that she would never approach the Ennis family claiming any responsibility for her pregnancy."

"This can't be true!" Frank's voice was weak with shock.

"Why did you think she had gone away?"

"Her mother told me she had gone to America to stay with cousins," Frank said.

"Yes, that's the story they all put out."

"But why shouldn't I have believed them?"

"Because you weren't a fool. If you played according to their rules you were in a win-win situation. Troublesome girl irritatingly pregnant, out of your hair, out of the country. Everything sorted. You leapt at the chance."

"No, I didn't. I didn't know there was anything *to* sort out. I never knew until I got your letter that I had a child."

"Try another story, Frank."

"Where did you hear all this about my parents asking Rita to sign documents?"

"From Nora. Her sister. My aunt Nora. I went to see her in London and she told me everything."

"She told you wrong, Des. Nothing like that ever happened."

"Give me credit for some brains. You're not going to admit it now if you didn't then."

"There was nothing to admit. You don't understand. All this came to me out of a clear blue sky."

"You never got in touch with her. You never wrote to her once."

"I wrote to her for three months every day. I put proper stamps for America on them, but got no reply."

"Didn't that ring any alarm bells?"

"No, it didn't. I asked her mother if she was forwarding the letters and her mother said she was."

"And eventually you gave up?"

"Well, I was getting no response. And her mother said . . ." He stopped as if remembering something.

"Yes?"

"She said I should leave Rita alone. That she had moved on in life. She said there had been a lot of fuss made, but the Ravens had done everything according to the letter of the law."

"And you didn't know what she meant?" Des was not convinced.

"I hadn't an idea what she meant, but now I see . . . no, it couldn't be . . ."

"What couldn't be?"

"My parents—if you had known them, Des! Sex was never mentioned in our house. They would be incapable of any discussion about paying Rita off."

"Did they like her?"

"Not particularly. They didn't like anyone who was distracting me from my studies and exams."

"And her folks, did they like you?"

"Not really, same sort of reasons. Rita was skipping her classes to be with me."

"They thought you were a pig," Des said.

"Surely not!" Frank was surprised at his calmness in the face of insult.

"That's what Nora says. She says you ruined everyone's life. You and your so-grand family. You broke them all up. Rita never came back from Australia because she had to swear not to. A perfectly decent family, minding its own business, ruined because of you and your snobbish family." He looked very upset and very angry.

Frank knew he had to walk carefully. This boy had been so excited and enthusiastic about meeting him; now he was hostile and barely able to sit at the same table as the father he had crossed the world to meet.

"Rita's sister in London—Nora, is it? She must be very upset."

"Which is more than you are," Des said mulishly.

"I *am* sorry. I tried to tell you that, but we got bogged down in a silly argument."

"Silly argument is what you call it? A row that destroyed my mother's family!"

"I didn't know *any* of it, Des. Not until I heard from you."

"Do you believe me?"

"I believe that's what Nora said to you, certainly."

"So you think *she* was lying?"

"No, I think she believes what she was told. My parents are dead now. Your mother is dead. We have no one to ask." He knew that he sounded weak and defeated.

But oddly Des Raven seemed to recognize the honesty in his tone. "You're right," he said, almost grudgingly. "It's up to us now."

Frank Ennis had seen the waiter hover near them and leave several times. Soon they must order.

"Would you like something to eat, Des? I ordered an Australian wine to make you feel at home."

"I'm sorry—I like to know who I am eating and drinking with." Des was taking no prisoners.

"Well, I don't know how well you'll get to know me. . . . They say that I'm difficult and that I make a mess of things," Frank said. "That's what I'm told, anyway."

"Who tells you that? Your wife?"

"No. I never married."

Des was surprised. "So no children, then?"

"Apart from you, no."

"I must have been a shock."

Frank paused. He must not say the wrong thing here. It was a time to be honest and speak from the heart. But how could he admit to this boy that his instincts and first reactions had been doubt and confusion and a wish to check it all out? He knew that if he were wholly truthful he could alienate Des Raven forever and lose the son he had only just met.

"It may sound cold to you, Des, but my first reaction was shock. I couldn't believe that I had a child—my own flesh and blood—without my having an idea about it. I am a tidy, meticulous sort of person. This was like having my whole neat world turned upside down. I had to think about it. That's what I do, Des, I think about things slowly and carefully."

"Really?" Des sounded slightly scornful.

"Yes, really. So when it had got clear in my mind, I called you."

"And what had you to get clear, exactly?"

"I had to get my head around the fact that I had fathered a son. And if you think that's something that can be accepted as natural and normal in two minutes then you are an amazing person. It takes someone like me a bit of time to get used to a new concept, and as soon as I did I called you and you had already gone."

"But you must have been afraid that people would find out." Des was still taunting him.

"No, I wasn't afraid of that. Not at all." He had to think what Clara might have said, and it came to him. "I was proud to have a son. I would want people to know."

"I don't think so. . . . Big Catholic hospital manager having illegitimate child. No, I can't see you wanting people to know."

"There is no such word, no concept of an illegitimate child nowadays. The law has changed and society has changed too. People are proud of their children, born in wedlock or outside." Frank spoke with spirit.

Des shook his head. "All very fine, very noble, but you haven't told anyone about me yet."

"You are *so* wrong, Des. I have indeed talked about you and said how excited I was to be going to meet you. . . ."

"*Who* did you tell? Not Miss Frosty in your office, that's for sure. Did you tell your mates at the golf club or the racetrack or wherever you go? Did you say, 'I have a boy too. I'm like you, a family man'? No way. You told nobody."

Frank sat there, miserable. If he started to tell him about Clara it made it all the more pitiable. There was only one person to whom he had told the secret. At that moment Anton Moran appeared at their side.

"Mr. Ennis," he said, as if Frank had been a regular customer since the place had opened.

"Ah, Mr. Moran." Frank had the feeling of being rescued. It was as if this man were throwing him some sort of a lifeline.

"Mr. Ennis, I was wondering would you and your son like to try our lobster? It is this morning's catch, done very simply, with butter and a couple of sauces on the side."

Anton looked from one to the other. A sudden silence had fallen between the two men. They were looking at each other, dumbfounded.

"I'm sorry," the younger man said.

"No, I'm sorry, Des," said Frank. "I'm sorry for all those years. . . ."

Anton murmured that he would come back in a few moments to take their order. He would never know what was going on there, but they seemed to have turned a corner. At least they were talking, and soon they were ordering food. He looked over again and they were raising a glass of Hunter Valley Chardonnay to each other. That was a relief. As soon as he had mentioned the boy being the man's son, Anton had felt a twinge of anxiety.

Possibly he had been indiscreet? But no, it seemed to be working fine. Anton breathed deeply and went back into the kitchen. Imagine—there were some people who believed that running a restaurant was all to do with serving food!

That was only a very small part of it, Anton thought.

Chapter Nine

Moira had an appointment with Frank Ennis. It was her quarterly report. She had to show the manager her case list and explain the work she had done that was costing the hospital a day and a half's wages.

Miss Gorman, his fearsome secretary, asked Moira to take a seat and wait. Today she was, if possible, more fearsome still.

"Is Mr. Ennis very busy?" Moira inquired politely.

"They never leave him alone, pulling him this way and that." Miss Gorman looked protective and angry. Maybe she fancied him and was annoyed that he had taken up with Dr. Casey.

"He always seems so much in control," Moira murmured.

"Oh, no, he's at their beck and call all day. It's totally disrupting his schedule."

"Who is doing this disrupting?" Moira was interested. She liked stories of confrontation.

Miss Gorman was vague. "Oh, people, you know. Fussing people saying it's a personal matter. It's so distracting for poor Mr. Ennis."

She *definitely* fancied him, Moira thought, sighing over the way people wasted their lives over love. Look at that Lisa Kelly, who thought she was the girlfriend of Anton Moran despite all the women that he paraded around the place. Look at that silly girl in her own social worker team who had refused promotion because her plodding boyfriend might have felt inadequate.

Look at poor Miss Gorman, sitting here fuming because these people, whoever they were, were actually daring to ring Frank Ennis saying that it was personal. She sighed again and settled down to wait.

Frank Ennis was much more cheerful than on earlier visits. He checked her figures and report carefully.

"You certainly seem to be taking a load off the main hospital . . . the *real* hospital," he said.

"I think you'll find that the heart clinic thinks of itself very much as the *real* hospital," Moira corrected him.

"Which is why I wouldn't use such an expression in front of them. Credit me with *some* intelligence, Ms. Tierney."

"It's very well run, I must say."

"Well, yes, they do deliver a service. I give them that much, but it's like a mothers' meeting in there—this one is having a baby, that one is getting engaged, the other one is getting married. It's like a gossip column in a cheap newspaper."

"I couldn't agree with you less." Moira was cold. "These are professional women; they know their subject and they do their job well. They reassure the patients and teach them to manage their own condition. I don't see that as being in *any* way like a gossip column or a mothers' meeting."

"But I thought I could talk to you about it. I thought you were my eyes and ears. My spy in there . . ."

"You suggested that, certainly, but I never accepted the role."

"That's true, you didn't. I suppose you've been sucked into it like everyone else."

"I doubt it, Mr. Ennis. I'm not easily sucked into things. Shall I leave this report with you?"

"Have I annoyed you in any way, Ms. Tierney?" Frank Ennis asked.

"No, not at all, Mr. Ennis. You have your job to do, I have mine.

It's a matter of mutual respect. Why do you think you might have annoyed me?"

"Because apparently that's what I *do*, Ms. Tierney, annoy people, *and* you look disapproving, as if you didn't like what you saw."

Several people had said that to Moira, but usually in the heat of the moment when they were objecting to something she had to do in the line of work. Nobody had ever said it in a matter-of-fact way and an even tone like Frank Ennis.

"It must be the way my face is set, Mr. Ennis. I assure you, I'm not disapproving of anything you do."

"Good, good." He seemed satisfied. "So you'll smile a bit from now on, will you?"

"I can't smile to order. It would only be a grimace," Moira said. "You know . . . twisting my features into a smile . . . it wouldn't be real or sincere."

Frank Ennis looked at her for a moment.

"You're quite right, Ms. Tierney, and I hope we will meet under some circumstances that do call for a real or sincere smile."

"I hope so," Moira said. She thought that he was looking at her with some sympathy and concern. Imagine, this man pitied *her*!

How ridiculous.

It was a long weekend and everyone was going somewhere.

Noel and his parents were taking baby Frankie to the country for two nights. They had booked a bed-and-breakfast place outside Rossmore. There was a statue of St. Ann and a holy well there; Josie and Charles were very interested in it. Noel said he would probably give the holy well a miss, but he would take the baby for walks in the wood for the fresh air. He had shown Moira the case he had packed for the journey. Everything was there.

Lisa was going to London. Anton was going to look at a few restaurants there and she was going to take notes. It would be wonderful. Moira had sniffed, but said nothing.

Frank Ennis said that he was going to take a bus tour. It would take in some of Ireland's greatest tourist attractions. It seemed a very unusual thing for him to do. He had someone he wanted to show Ireland to and this seemed to be the best way. It was certainly going to be interesting, he told Moira.

Emily said that she was going to see the west of Ireland for the first time. Dingo Duggan was going to drive the van, taking Emily and Declan's parents, Molly and Paddy Carroll. They would have a great time.

Simon and Maud were going with friends to North Wales. They were bringing sleeping bags and a sort of makeshift tent. They would take the boat to Holyhead and then might find a hostel, but if not, they could sleep anywhere with all their gear. There would be six of them altogether. It would be terrific fun.

Dr. Declan Carroll and his wife, Fiona, were taking Johnny to a seaside hotel. Fiona said that she was going to sleep until lunchtime both days. They had baby minders there to look after young children. It would be magical.

Dr. Hat was going to go fishing with three friends. It was an all-in weekend with no hidden extras. Dr. Hat said he was a poor old pensioner now and had to be careful with his money—Moira never knew whether he was joking or not. It certainly wasn't the time to bring out one of those rare smiles.

Most of her colleagues were going away or else they were having parties or doing their gardens.

Moira suddenly felt very much out of it, as if she were on the side of things looking on. Why wasn't she going somewhere, like sitting in Dingo's van heading west or going to see some statue in Rossmore or setting out for the lakes in the Midlands with Dr. Hat and his mates?

The answer was only too clear.

She had no real friends.

She had never needed them in life—the job was too absorbing—and to do it right you needed to be on duty all hours of the day.

Friends would find it very tedious to go out to supper with someone who might well have to disappear in the middle of the main course.

But it was lonely and restless to see everyone else with plans for the long weekend.

Moira announced that she was going home to Liscuan. She talked so little about her private life, people assumed that there must be a big family waiting for her.

"That will be nice for you, to go home and meet everyone," Ania said. "You will have a great welcome, yes?"

"That's right," Moira lied.

Ania lived in a world where everyone was good and happy. She was pregnant again and taking things easy. The doctor had said that she needed bed rest, and so she lay at home contemplating a great future with their child. This time it would happen, and if lying around in bed would ensure it, then Ania was willing to do it.

Once a week, Carl drove her in to the clinic so that she could see everyone and keep up to date on what was happening. She was pleased that Moira was going to the country place for the weekend. It might cheer her up. . . .

Moira looked out of the train as she crossed Ireland towards her home. She had packed her little case and had no idea where she would stay. Perhaps her father and Mrs. Kennedy might offer her a bed?

Mrs. Kennedy was fairly frosty when Moira telephoned to speak to her father. "He's having a lie-down. He always takes a siesta from five till six," she said, as if Moira should somehow have known this.

"I'm in the area," Moira said. "I was wondering if I could call in and see him?"

"Would that be before or after supper?" Mrs. Kennedy inquired.

Moira drew a deep breath.

"Or even *during* supper?" she suggested.

Mrs. Kennedy was more practical than welcoming. "We only have two lamb chops," she said.

"Oh, don't mind about me. I'm happy with vegetables," she said.

"Will you arrange that with your father when he wakes up? We don't know what he would want."

"Yes, I'll call again at six," Moira said through her teeth. She had eased her father's passage to live openly with Mrs. Kennedy and this was the thanks she got. Life was certainly unfair.

But then Moira knew that already from her work. Men laid off from work with no warning and poor compensation; women drawn into the drugs business because it's the only way to get a bit of ready money; girls running away from home and refusing to go back because what was there was somehow worse than sleeping under a bridge. Moira had seen babies born and go home from the hospital to totally unsatisfactory setups while hundreds of infertile couples ached to adopt them.

Moira sat in a café waiting for the time to pass until her father woke from his siesta. Siesta! There would have been little of that in the old days. Father would come in tired from his work on the farm. Sometimes Mother had cooked a meal—most times not. Moira and Pat used to peel the potatoes so that that much was done anyway. Pat was not considered a reliable farmhand, so Dad would ensure that all the hens had been returned to their coop. He would call out until the sheepdog came home. Then he would pat the dog's head. "Good man, Shep." Every dog they had over the years was called Shep.

Only then would he have his supper. Often he had had to get the supper ready—a big pot of potatoes and a couple of slices of ham, the potatoes often eaten straight from the saucepan and the salt spooned from the packet.

Life had changed for the better in her father's case. She should be glad that he had that wordless Mrs. Kennedy looking after him and cooking him a lamb chop of an evening. Why was the woman so unwelcoming? She had no fear of Moira and she should know that.

But then she had always been stern and forbidding. She seldom smiled.

With a shock she realized that this is what people actually said about *her.* Even Mr. Ennis had mentioned that Moira was very unsmiling and seemed highly disapproving of things.

When Moira rang back, her father sounded lively and happy. She knew that he spent a lot of time wood carving nowadays and had built an extra room for his work. He did most of the talking and finally said, "So are you coming for supper tonight?" as if there was never any question.

She took a bus out to Mrs. Kennedy's and knocked on the door timidly.

"Oh, Moira." Mrs. Kennedy showed just enough recognition and acknowledgment that she had arrived, but no real pleasure.

"I'm not disturbing you or my father?"

"No, please come in. Your father is freshening himself up for supper."

That was a personal first, Moira thought to herself. Her poor father would sit down for whatever meal there might be with muddy boots and a sweaty shirt, ready to spoon out the potatoes to Pat and herself and her mother, if she ever sat down. Things were very different now.

Moira saw a table set for three. There were folded table napkins and a small vase of flowers. There were gleaming saltcellars and shining glass. It was far from suppers like this that he had spent his former life.

"You have the house very nice." Moira looked around her as if she were a housing inspector looking for flaws or damp.

"Glad it passes the test," Mrs. Kennedy said.

Just then her father came out. Moira gasped—he looked ten years younger than the last time she had seen him. He wore a smart jacket and he had a collar and tie.

"You look the real part, Dad," she said admiringly. "Are you going out somewhere?"

"I'm having supper in my own home. Isn't that worth dressing up for?" he asked. Then, softening up a little, he said, "How are you, Moira? It's really good to see you."

"I'm fine, Dad."

"And where are you staying?"

So no bed here, Moira thought. She waved it away. "I'll find somewhere . . . don't worry about me." As if he worried! If he did, then he would ask his fancy woman to get a bed ready for her.

"That's grand, then. Come and sit down."

"Yes, indeed," Mrs. Kennedy said. "Have a glass of sherry with your father. I'll serve the meal in about ten minutes."

"Isn't she great?" Her father looked admiringly at the retreating Mrs. Kennedy.

"Great, altogether," Moira said unenthusiastically.

"Is there anything wrong, Moira?" He looked at her, concerned.

"No. Why? Should there be?"

"You look as if something's wrong."

Moira exploded. "God Almighty, Dad, I came across the country to see you. You never write . . . you never phone . . . and now you criticize the way I look!"

"I was just concerned for you, in case you'd lost your job or something," he said.

Moira looked at him. He meant it. She must have looked sad or angry or disapproving—all these things that people said.

"No, it's just it's the long weekend. I came back to see my family. Is that so very unusual? The train was full of people doing just that."

"I thought it was kind of sad for you: your home gone, sold to other people, Pat all tied up in his romance."

"Pat has a romance?"

"You haven't seen him yet, then?"

"No, I came straight here. Who is it? What's she like?"

"Remember the O'Learys who ran the garage?"

"Yes, but those girls are far too young. They'd only be fourteen or fifteen," Moira said, shocked.

"It's the mother. It's Mrs. O'Leary—Erin O'Leary."

"And what happened to Mr. O'Leary?" Moira couldn't take it in.

"Gone off somewhere, apparently."

"Merciful hour!" Moira said. It was an expression of her mother's. She hadn't said it in years.

"Well, exactly. You never know what's around the next corner," her father agreed.

He was in an awkward position, Moira realized. He couldn't really remonstrate with Pat for moving in with a married lady. Hadn't he done the very same thing himself? Mrs. Kennedy came in just then to ask would Moira like to freshen up before supper. Her father was nodding. Moira decided that she did want to freshen up. She took a clean blouse out of her suitcase and went to the bathroom.

It was an amazing room. The wallpaper had lots of blue mermaids and blue sea horses on it. There were blue and white china ornaments on the windowsill and a blue shell held the soap. A crinoline lady dressed in blue covered the next roll of lavatory paper in case people might know what it was and be affronted. There were blue gingham curtains on the window and a blue patterned shower curtain.

Moira washed her face and shoulders and under her arms. She put on her clean blouse and returned to the table.

"Lovely bathroom," she said to Mrs. Kennedy.

"We do our best," Mrs. Kennedy said, serving melon slices with a little cherry on top of each. Then she brought in the main course.

"Remember, vegetables are fine for me," Moira said.

Her father waved her protest aside. "I walked into town and got an extra lamb chop," he said.

Mrs. Kennedy looked as if Moira's father had given her a priceless jewel.

Moira showed huge gratitude. She didn't feel that she could easily discuss Pat's new situation, so she ate her supper mainly in silence. Her father and Mrs. Kennedy talked animatedly about this and that—his wood carving of an owl, a festival that was going to exhibit some local art. Mrs. Kennedy said that of course he should offer some of his work to be put on show. This was also news to Moira.

They spoke about Mrs. Kennedy's involvement in a local women's group. They all felt that farming was finished and that there was no living to be made from the land. A lot of them were training to go into the bed-and-breakfast business. Mrs. Kennedy was thinking she might join in. After all, they had three rooms more or less ready; all they'd need to buy was new beds. That would be six people, and they would make a tidy living.

Moira realized that she didn't know Mrs. Kennedy's first name.

If she had, she might say suddenly, "Maura" or "Janet"—or whatever she was called—"can I sleep the night in one of those three rooms, please?" But she had never known her name and Dad referred to her as "herself" and, when he was talking to her, as "dear" or "love." No help there.

When she had finished the meal, Moira stood up and picked up her suitcase.

"Well, that was all lovely, but if I am to find a place to stay, I'd better go now. The bus still goes by at half past the hour, right?"

"Leave it to the next half hour," her father said. "You'll easily get into Stella Maris. They'll give you a grand room."

"I was thinking of calling on Pat," Moira said.

"He won't be there. He'll be up at the garage. Leave him till the morning, I'd say."

"Right, I'll do that, but I'll go now, as I'm standing. Thank you again for the nice meal."

"You're very welcome," Mrs. Kennedy said.

"It's good to see you, Moira. Don't work too hard up there in Dublin."

"Do you know what kind of work I do, Dad?"

"Don't you work for the government in an office?"

"That's it, more or less," Moira said glumly.

She set out on the road. She wanted to go past her old home before the next bus came. She walked down the old familiar lane, a lane that her father must have walked many a time before he had officially left his home to live with Mrs. Kennedy. And why would he *not* want to live with her? A bright, clean house where he got a welcome and a warm meal and maybe a bit of a cuddle as well. Wasn't it much better than what he had had at home?

She arrived at her old house. Straightaway she could see that the new owners had given it a coat of paint; they had planted a garden. The stables, byres and outhouses had all been changed, cleaned and modernized, and this was where they made their cheese. They had a successful business, and it all centered around the house where Moira had grown up.

She went into the old farmyard and looked around her, bewildered. She must now see the house. If they came out, she would tell them that she had once lived here. She could see through the windows that there was a big fire in the grate and a table with a wine bottle and two glasses on it.

It made her very sad.

Why couldn't her parents have provided a home like this for Pat and herself? Why were there no social workers then who would have taken them away to be placed in better, happier homes?

Her mother and father were not functioning as parents over those years. Her mother was in deep need of help, and her father struggled ineffectually to cope. Moira and Pat should have grown up in a household where they could have known the language of childhood. A family where, if Pat ran round pretending to be a horse, they would have laughed with him and encouraged him and not cuffed him around the ears, as would have happened in this house.

Moira never had a doll of her own, not to mention a doll's house. There were no birthday celebrations that she could remember. She could never invite her school friends home, and that was how she had learned to be aloof. She had feared friendship and closeness as a child because sooner or later that friend would have expected to be invited to Moira's home and then the chaos would be revealed.

There were tears in her eyes as she saw what the house could have been like when she was young. It could have been a home.

Moira caught the bus to town and booked two nights at the

Stella Maris. The room was fine and the cost reasonable, but Moira burned with injustice. She had a father who had a home with spare bedrooms, and yet she was forced to pay for a bed and breakfast in her own hometown.

She would go to see how Pat was faring the next morning. It was ludicrous to think of him with Mrs. O'Leary—she was so much older. It was nonsense. Mr. O'Leary couldn't have left because of Pat.

She would find out tomorrow.

Next morning, she went to the garage. Pat was there on the fore-court, filling cars with petrol or diesel. He seemed genuinely pleased to see her.

"Have you got a car at long last, Moira?" he called.

"I have, but it's up in Dublin," she said.

"Well, we can't fill it up for you from here then." He laughed amiably. He was totally suited to this work, easygoing and natural with the customers, good-tempered and cheerful in what some might have found a tedious and repetitive job.

"I came to see *you*, actually, Pat. Do you have a break or anything coming up?"

"Sure, I can go anytime. I'll just tell Erin."

Moira followed him towards the pay desk and the new shop that had been built in a once-falling-down garage.

"Erin, my sister, Moira, is here. Okay if I take a break and go and have a coffee with her?"

"Oh, Pat, of course it is. Don't you work all the hours God sends? Go for as long as you like. How are you, Moira? Long time no see."

Moira looked at her. Erin O'Leary—about ten years older than Moira—a mother of two girls and wife of Harry, who was a traveler and often traveled rather longer and farther than his job required. He had now traveled out of the country, it was said at the Stella Maris, where Moira had brought up the subject at breakfast.

Erin was wearing a smart yellow shop coat with a navy trim. Her loose, rather floppy hair was tied back neatly with a navy and yellow ribbon. She was slim and fit and looked much younger than the forty-four or -five she must have been. She looked at Pat with undeniable affection.

"I hear you've been very good to my brother," Moira said.

"It's mutual, I tell you. I couldn't do half the work I do without him."

Pat had come back wearing his jacket and heard her say that. He was childishly pleased.

"I'm glad. He was a great brother," Moira said, trying to put a lot of sincerity into her voice. In fact, he had been a worry and given her huge concern over the years—but no point in sharing that with Mrs. O'Leary.

"I don't doubt it," Erin O'Leary said, putting her arm affectionately around Pat's shoulders.

"And is all this a permanent sort of thing?" Moira asked, trying desperately to smile at the same time so that they would realize it was a good-natured, cheery kind of inquiry.

"I certainly hope so," Erin said. "I'd be lost without Pat, and so would the girls."

"I'm not going anywhere," Pat said proudly.

Would she have encouraged this setup herself as a social worker? She might have examined Erin O'Leary's circumstances more carefully, checked that her husband would not return and evict Pat Tierney from his home and business. She would always have put the best needs of her client forward, but was there a possibility that by challenging the living arrangements at Mrs. O'Leary's, she might have deprived Pat of the loving home and workplace that he now seemed to have?

They went for coffee to a nearby place where everyone knew Pat. He was his own man, with plenty to say.

People asked him about Erin and he told them how she had made a cake with his name on it for his birthday last week and they had all given him a present. And Erin must have told some of the regular customers too, because there wasn't room on the mantelpiece for all his cards.

With a heart like stone, Moira remembered that she had not sent him a card.

She had, she said, been to see their father. "He seems happy with Mrs. Kennedy," she said grudgingly.

"Well, why wouldn't he be? Isn't Maureen the best in the world?"

"Maureen?" Moira was at a loss.

"Maureen Kennedy," he said, as if everyone knew her as that.

"And how did you find out her name?"

"I asked her," Pat said simply, looking at his watch.

"Are you anxious to be back there?" Moira asked him.

"Well, she's on her own—there's only a young girl in the shop and she's a bit of an eejit with the till."

Moira looked at him and bit her lip. She hoped that there were not tears in her eyes. Pat reached over and took her hand.

"I know, Moira, it's hard for you having no one of your own and seeing Dad all settled with Maureen and me with Erin, but it will happen, I'm sure."

She nodded wordlessly.

"Come back to the garage with me. Come in and talk to Erin."

"I will." Moira paid for their coffee and walked like an automaton back to the garage.

Erin was pleased to see them. "There was no hurry, Pat. You could have stayed longer."

"I didn't want to leave you on your own too long."

"Well, there, Moira! Isn't that music to the ears?" Pat had gone to put on his working gear again.

Moira looked at Erin. "It's great that he's here with you. He has had so little warmth and affection. He was never in a loving family. You won't . . . you wouldn't . . ."

Erin interrupted her. "He's found a loving family now and here he will stay. Rest assured of that."

"Thank you, I will," Moira said.

"And come back and see us again and when you do, stay in our house—don't be paying fancy prices up in Stella Maris."

"How did you know I was there?"

"One of my friends works there. She rang and told me you were asking questions about me. Harry's long gone, Moira. He's not coming back. Pat is staying. He is exactly what we all need. He's cheerful and happy and reliable and always there. I didn't have that before, and for me it's lovely too."

Moira gave her an awkward hug and went back to Stella Maris.

"I wonder if it will be an inconvenience if I cancel tonight's booking? I find I have to go back to Dublin on the afternoon train."

"No problem, Ms. Tierney. I'll just prepare your bill for one night. Will you be coming back to us again?"

Moira remembered that Erin had a friend here who reported things.

"Well, I may stay with Erin O'Leary next time. She very kindly invited me. I was so pleased."

"Very nice," the receptionist said. "Always nice to stay in a family home. . . ."

Moira looked out the window at the rain-covered countryside. Cows standing wet and bewildered, horses sheltering under trees, sheep oblivious to the weather, farmers in rain gear going along narrow lanes.

Most people on the train were going to Dublin for some outing or activity. Or else they were going back to a family. Moira was going home to an empty flat halfway through the long weekend. She could not bear to stay in the place where her brother and her father had found such happiness and where she had found nothing but resentment and sadness.

It was still early enough to go somewhere. But where? She was hungry, but she didn't feel like going to a café or a restaurant on her own. She went into a shop to buy a bar of chocolate.

"Gorgeous day, isn't it? The rain's gone," said a woman about her own age behind the counter.

"Yes, it is," Moira said, surprised she hadn't noticed that the weather had improved.

"I've only another hour here and then I'm off," the shop assistant confided. She had stringy hair and a big smile.

"And where will you go to?" Moira asked. She wasn't being polite; she was interested. Possibly this woman, like everyone else in the universe, had a huge, loving family dying for her shift to finish.

"I'll go out to the sea by train," she said. "Don't know where yet, but maybe Blackrock, Dun Laoghaire, Dalkey or even Bray. Anywhere I can walk beside the sea, have a bag of chips and an ice cream. Maybe I'll have a swim, maybe I'll meet a fellow. But I wouldn't be standing indoors here all day with the sun shining outside and everyone else free as a bird."

"And you'd do all this by yourself?" Moira was curious.

"Isn't that the best part? No one else to please, and all my options open."

Moira walked out thoughtfully. She had never taken the train out to the seaside. Not in all her years in Dublin. If work brought her that way, she would go. Not otherwise. She didn't know that people *did* that—just went out to the sea, like children in storybooks.

That's what she would do now. She would walk on beside the River Liffey until she caught the little train south. She would sit beside the sea, go for a paddle, maybe. It would calm her, soothe her. Oh, yes, there would certainly be crowds of people playing at Happy Families or Being in Love with each other, but maybe Moira would be like the woman in the shop who was aching to have the sunshine on her shoulders and arms and watch the sea lapping gently towards the shore.

That's what she would do. She would spend some of the long weekend by the sea.

Of course it wasn't magic.

And it didn't really work.

Moira did not become calm and mellow. The sun did shine on her arms and shoulders but there was a breeze coming in from the sea at the same time and it felt too chilly. There were too many people who had decided their families must go to the seaside.

Moira studied them.

In her whole childhood she never remembered once being brought to the seaside and yet it seemed that every child in Dublin had a God-given right to go to the seashore as soon as the sun came out. Her sense of resentment was enormous and she frowned with concentration as she sat silently amid all the families who were calling out to one another on the beach.

To her surprise, a big man with a red face and an open-necked red shirt stopped beside her.

"Moira Tierney as I live and breathe!"

She hadn't an idea who he was. "Um, hello," she said cautiously.

He sat down beside her.

"God, isn't this beautiful to be out in the open air? We're blessed to live in a capital city that's so near the sea," he said.

She still looked at him, confused.

"I'm Brian Flynn. We met when Stella was in hospital and then again at the funeral and the christening."

"Oh, *Father* Flynn. Yes, of course I remember. I just didn't recognize you in the . . . I mean without the . . ."

"A Roman collar wouldn't be very suitable for this weather." Brian Flynn was cheerful and dismissive. He was a man who rarely wore clerical garb at all, except when officiating at a ceremony.

"Did your parents take you to the sea when you were young?" Moira asked him unexpectedly.

"My father died when we were young, but my mother brought us for a week to the seaside every summer. We stayed in a guesthouse called St. Anthony's and we all had a bucket and spade. Yes, it was nice," he said.

"You were lucky," Moira said glumly.

"You didn't get to the sea when you were young?"

"No. We never got anywhere. We should never have been left in our home. We should have been placed somewhere . . . anywhere, really."

Brian Flynn saw where the conversation was leading. This woman seemed to have an obsession about taking children away from parents and into care. Or that's what Noel said, in any case. Noel was terrified of Moira, and Katie said that Lisa felt just the same way.

"Well, I suppose things have changed a bit . . . moved on," Brian Flynn said vaguely. He began to wish that he hadn't approached Moira but she had looked so lonely and out of place in her jacket and skirt, right in the middle of all the seaside people.

"Do you ever feel your work is hopeless, Father?"

"I wish you'd call me Brian. No, I don't feel it's hopeless. I think we get things wrong from time to time. I mean the Church does. It doesn't adapt properly. And I get things wrong myself, quite apart from the Church. I keep battering away to get people a Catholic wedding and, just when I succeed, it turns out that they got tired of waiting and got the job done in a register office and I'm left like a fool. But, to answer your question, no, I don't think it's all hopeless. I think we do *something* to help and I certainly see a lot that inspires me. I expect you do too?" He ended on a rising note, but if he was expecting some reciprocal statement of job satisfaction he was wrong.

"I don't think I do, Father Flynn, truly I don't. I have a caseload of unhappy people, most of them blaming their unhappiness on me."

"I'm sure that's not true." Brian Flynn wished himself a million miles from here.

"It *is* true, Father. I got a woman into exactly the kind of facility she was looking for—a place with vegetarian cookery and, if you'll excuse the expression, with religion seeping from the walls. It's coming down with saintliness, and she's still not happy."

"I expect she's old and frightened," Brian Flynn said.

"Yes, but she's only one of them. I have a very nice old man called Gerald. I kept him *out* of a home and stopped a lot of nonsense with his children, built up all the support systems for him, but now he says he's lonely all day. He'd like to go to a place where they play indoor bowls."

"He's probably old and frightened too," Brian Flynn suggested.

"But what about the ones who are *not* old? They don't want any help either. I have a thirteen-year-old girl who slept rough. I got her back to her family. There was a row over something—black lipstick and black nail polish, I think. Anyway, she's gone again. The Garda are looking for her. It needn't have got this far. All that talking, sitting under a bridge way into the night, and it meant nothing."

"You never know . . . ," Brian Flynn began again.

"Oh, but I *do* know. And I know how there's an army of people lined up against me over that unfortunate child who is being raised by an alcoholic. . . ."

Brian Flynn's voice was a lot more steely now.

"Noel adds up to much more than being just an alcoholic, Moira. He has turned his life around to make a home for that child."

"And that child will thank us all later for leaving her with a drunken, resentful father?"

"He loves his daughter very much. He's *not* a drunk. He's given it up." Brian Flynn was fiercely loyal.

"Are you telling me, hand on heart, that Noel never strayed, never went back on the drink since he got Frankie?"

Brian Flynn couldn't lie. "It was only the once and it didn't last long," he said. Immediately he realized that Moira hadn't known. He saw that in her face. As usual he had managed to make things worse. In future he would walk about with a paper bag over his head and slits cut for his eyes. He would talk to nobody. Ever again.

"I hope you don't think I'm rude, Moira, but I have to um . . . meet someone . . . um . . . farther along here . . ."

"No, of course." Moira realized that there was less warmth in his face now. But then that was often the case in her conversations.

Father Flynn had moved on. She felt conspicuous on this beach. It wasn't her place. Slowly Moira gathered her things together and headed towards the station, where a little train would take her back into the city.

Most people liked the train journey. Moira didn't even see the view from the window. She thought instead of how she had been duped. They had even told that priest, who had nothing to do with the setup. But they hadn't seen fit to tell the social worker assigned to the case.

Moira could not call to Chestnut Court armed with her new information, since she knew that Noel and his parents had taken the baby off to some small town that she had never heard of—a place with a magic statue, apparently. Or, to put it another way, Charlie and Josie would be investigating the statue. Noel could well have the child in some pub by now.

She would deal with Emily when she came back from her sojourn in the west with Dingo Duggan, with Lisa when she and Anton came back from London, and eventually she would deal with Noel, who had lied to her. There were so many places where she could put Frankie, where the child would grow up safely, with love all around her. Look at that couple—Clara Casey's daughter Linda and her husband, Nick, who was the son of Hilary in the heart clinic—they were just aching for a baby girl. Think of the stability of a home like that: two grandmothers to idolize the child and a big, extended family.

Moira sighed again. If only there had been a magical social worker who could have placed Pat and herself in a home like that. A place where they would have been loved, where there would have been children's books on a shelf, maybe a story read to them at night, people who would be interested in a child's homework, who would take her to the seaside on a hot day with a bucket and spade to make sandcastles.

Coming fresh as she did from visiting the wreckage that was her own childhood, Moira was now determined that she would ease Frankie Lynch's path into a secure home.

It would be the only thing that might make any sense of Moira's own loss—if she could make it right for someone else. All she had to do was to get through this endless weekend until all the cast eventually came back from their travels and reassembled and she could get things going.

Lisa was actually back in Dublin, even though Moira didn't know it. There had been some crossed wires in London. Lisa had thought that it was a matter of visiting restaurants and talking to various patrons. April had thought it was a PR exercise and had arranged several interviews for Anton.

"They don't have a bank holiday in England this weekend, so it will be work as usual," April had chirruped to them.

"Not much work at a weekend, though." Lisa had tried hard to be casual.

"No, but Monday is an ordinary day in London and we can rehearse on Sunday." April's face was glowing with achievement and success. It would have been churlish and petty for Lisa not to enthuse. So she had appeared delighted with it all; she decided to get out with her pride.

She had loads to see to back in Dublin, she said casually, and saw, to her pleasure, that Anton seemed genuinely sorry to see her go. And now she was back in Dublin with nothing to do and nobody to meet.

As she let herself in to Chestnut Court she thought she saw Moira in the courtyard talking to some of the neighbors. But it couldn't be. Noel and the baby were off in this place Rossmore; Moira, herself, was meant to have gone to the country to see her family. Lisa decided she was imagining things.

But she looked over the wall on the corridor leading to their apartment and saw that it was indeed Moira. She couldn't hear the conversation, but she didn't like the look of it. Moira knew nobody in this apartment block except them. She was here to spy.

Lisa turned and crossed the courtyard.

"Well, *hello,* Moira," she said, showing great surprise. The two middle-aged women whom Moira had been interrogating shuffled with embarrassment. Lisa knew them both by sight. She nodded at them briefly.

"Oh, Lisa . . . I thought you were away?"

"Well, yes, I was," Lisa agreed, "but I came back. And you? You were going away too?"

"I came back too," Moira said. "And did Noel and Frankie come back as well?"

"I don't think so. I haven't been in to the apartment yet. Why don't you come up and see with me?" The women neighbors were busy making their excuses and looking to escape.

"No, no, it wouldn't be appropriate," Moira said. "You've only just got back from London."

"Moira is our social worker," Lisa explained to the fast-retreating neighbors. "She's absolutely great. She drops in at the least expected times in case Noel and I are battering Frankie to death or starving her in a cage or something. So far she hasn't caught us out in anything, but of course time will tell."

"You completely misunderstand my role, Lisa. I am there for Frankie."

"We're all bloody there for Frankie," Lisa said, "which is something you'd realize if you saw us walking her up and down at night when she can't sleep. If you saw us changing her nappy, trying to spoon food into her when she keeps turning her head away."

"Exactly," Moira cried. "It's too hard for you both. It's my role to see whether she would be better placed with a more conventional family . . . people with the maturity to look after a child."

"But she's Noel's daughter!" Lisa said, unaware that the other women who had been about to leave were standing there, open-mouthed. "I thought you people were all meant to be keeping the family together and that sort of thing."

"Yes, but you are not family, Lisa. You're just a roommate, and Noel, as a father, is unreliable. We have to admit that."

"I do *not* have to admit that!" Lisa knew she looked like a fishwife with her hands on her hips, but really this was too much. She began to list all that Noel had done and was doing. Moira cut across her like a knife.

"Can we move somewhere that we can have more privacy, please?" She glared at the two neighbors, who were still hovering at the corner, and they vanished quickly.

"I don't want any more time with you," Lisa said. She knew she sounded pettish but she didn't care.

Moira was calm but furious at the same time. "In all this hymn of praise about Noel," she said, "you managed to forget that he went off the rails and was back on the drink. That was a situation where the baby was at risk and not one of you alerted me."

"It was over before it began," Lisa said. "No point in alerting you and starting World War Three!"

Moira looked at her steadily for a moment. "We are all on the same side," she said eventually.

"No, we're not," Lisa said. "You want to take Frankie away. We want to keep her. How's that the same side?"

"We all want what is *best* for her." Moira spoke as if to a slow learner.

"It's best for all of us if she stays with Noel, Moira." Lisa sounded weary suddenly. "She keeps him off the drink and keeps his head down at his studies so that he'll be a good, educated father for her when the time comes for her to know such things. And she keeps me sane too. I have a lot of worries and considerations in my life, but minding Frankie sort of grounds me. It gives it all some purpose, if you know what I mean."

Moira sighed. "I *do* know what you mean. You see, in a way, she does exactly the same for me. Minding Frankie is important to *me* too. I never had a chance as a child. I want her to have a start of some kind, not to get bogged down by a confused childhood like I did."

Lisa was stunned. Moira had never admitted anything personal before. "Don't talk to me about childhood! I bet mine could leave yours in the ha'penny place!" Lisa said in a chirpy voice. Moira didn't know what to say, then she surprised herself as much as she did Lisa.

"You don't feel like having supper tonight, do you? It's just that I'm a bit beaten. I was down in my old home and it was all a bit upsetting and there seems to be nobody in town . . ."

Lisa ignored the gracelessness of the invitation. She didn't want to go back to the flat alone. There was nothing in—well, there might be a tin of something in the kitchen cupboard or a pack of pasta in sauce in the freezer. But it would be lonely. It might be better to hear what Moira had to say, but would it only be more of the same?

"Will we agree that Frankie is not on the agenda?" Lisa asked.

"Frankie who?" Moira said, with a strange kind of lopsided look on her face. Lisa realized that it was meant to be a smile.

They chose to go to Ennio's trattoria. It was a family restaurant: Ennio himself cooked and greeted; his son waited on the tables. Ennio had lived in Dublin for rather more than twenty years and was married to an Irishwoman; he knew that having an Italian accent added to the atmosphere. Anton, on the other hand, had said to Lisa that Ennio was a fool of the first order and that he would never get anywhere. He never advertised, you never saw celebrities going in and out, he never got any reviews or press attention. It seemed like an act of independence to go there.

Moira had often passed the place and wondered who would pay seven euros for a spaghetti Bolognese when you could make it at home for three or four euros. For her it was an act of defiance to go there, defying her natural thrift and caution.

Ennio welcomed them with a delight that made it appear as if he had been waiting for their visit for weeks. He gave them huge red and white napkins, a drink on the house and the news that the cannelloni was like the food of angels—they would love it with an almighty love. He had opened his restaurant two decades ago and his simple, fresh food had proved instantly popular. Since then, word of mouth had kept the place full to bursting almost every night. Lisa thought to herself that Anton might be wrong about Ennio. The place was almost full already, everyone was happy, there were hardly any overheads. No client was attracted here by style or decor or lighting—nor, indeed, publicity interviews. Maybe Ennio was far from being a fool.

Moira was beginning to realize why people actually paid seven euros for a plate of pasta. They were paying for a bright, checked tablecloth, a warm welcome and the feeling of ease and relaxation. She could have put together a cannelloni dish, but it wouldn't be the same as this if eaten in her small, empty flat. It would not be the food of angels.

She relaxed for the first time in a long time and raised her glass. "Here's to us," she said. "We may have had a bad start, but, boy, we're survivors!"

"Here's to surviving," Lisa said. "Can I begin?"

"Let's order his cannelloni first and then you can begin," Moira agreed.

She was a good listener. Lisa had to hand her that. Moira listened well and remembered what you said and went back and asked relevant questions, like how old was Lisa when she realized that her parents disliked each other, and irrelevant questions, like did they ever take the girls to the seaside? She was sympathetic when she needed to be, shocked at the right times, curious about *why* Lisa's mother stayed in such a loveless home. She asked about Lisa's friends and seemed to understand exactly why she never had any.

How could anyone bring a friend home to a house like that?

And Lisa told her about working as a graphic designer for Kevin and how she met Anton and everything had changed. She had left the safe harbor of Kevin's office and set up on her own. No, she didn't really have any other clients, but Anton had needed her to give him that boost and he always said he would be lost without her. Even this time in London, this very morning, he had begged her not to leave, not to abandon him to April.

"Oh, April," Moira said, breezily, recalling her lunch with Clara at Anton's. "A very *vapid* sort of person."

"*Vapid!*" Lisa seized on the word with delight. "That's exactly what she is! Vapid!" She said it again with pleasure.

Moira gently moved the conversation away, towards Noel, in fact. "And wasn't it great that you found somewhere to stay so easily?" she hinted.

"Oh, yes, if it hadn't been for Noel, I don't know what I would have done that night, the night when I realized my father, my own father, in our own house . . ." She paused, upset at the memory.

"But Noel welcomed you?" Moira continued.

"Well, I suppose 'welcomed' might be putting it a bit strongly . . . but he gave me a place to stay, which, considering he hardly knew me, was very generous of him, and then we worked out with Emily that it might be best if I could stay; it would share the whole business of looking after Frankie and I could have a place to stay for free."

"Free? You mean Noel has to pay for you as well as all his other expenses?" Moira's eyes were beginning to glint. More and more information was coming her way without her even having to ask for it.

Lisa seemed to recognize that she had spoken too freely. "Well, not exactly *free*. I mean, we each contribute to the food. We have our own phones and we share the work with the baby." Lisa didn't say she was overdrawn on her bank account.

"But he could have let that room to a real tenant for real money."

"I doubt it," Lisa said, with spirit. "You wouldn't get anyone paying real money to live in a house with a baby. Believe me, Moira, it's like 'Macbeth shall sleep no more.' It can be total bedlam at three a.m. with the two of us trying to soothe her down."

Moira just nodded sympathetically. She was getting more and more ammunition by the second.

But, oddly, it did not delight her as much as she had once

thought it would. In a twisted way, she would prefer if these two awkward, lonely people—Lisa and Noel—should find happiness to beat their demons through this child. If it were Hollywood, they would also find great happiness in each other.

Lisa knew nothing of her thoughts.

"Now you," she said to Moira. "Tell me what was so terrible."

So Moira began. Every detail from the early days when she came home from school and there was nothing to eat, to her tired father coming in later and finding only a few potatoes peeled. She told it all without self-pity or complaint. Moira, who had kept her private life so very, very private for years, was able to speak to this girl because Lisa was even more damaged than she was.

She told the story right up to the present, when she had left Liscuan and come back because the sight of her father and brother having made something of the shambles of their lives was too much to bear.

Lisa listened and wished that someone—anyone—had ever said to Moira that there was a way of dealing with all this, that she should be glad for other people instead of appearing to triumph over their downfall. She might have to pretend at first, but soon it would become natural. Lisa had managed to make herself glad that Katie had a happy marriage and a successful career. She was pleased that Kevin's agency was doing well. Of course, when people were enemies like her father was, and April was, then it would be superhuman to wish them well. . . .

As Lisa's mind began to drift, she realized that the woman at the next table was beginning to choke seriously. A piece of amaretto had become lodged in her throat; the young waiter stared, goggle-eyed, as she changed from scarlet to white.

"What is it, Marco?" asked the young blond waitress—was that Maud Mitchell? What was she doing working here? Lisa wondered—who then, taking in the situation at a glance, called over her shoulder, "Simon, we need you here *now!*"

Immediately her brother arrived, and he too was dressed in a waiter's uniform.

"She's getting no air in . . . ," Maud said.

"It's a Heimlich . . . ," Simon agreed.

"Can you get her to cough once more?" asked Maud, in total control.

"She's trying to cough—something's stuck there. . . ." The woman's daughter was nearly hysterical at this point.

"Madam, I'm going to ask you to stand up now and then my brother is going to squeeze you very hard. Please stay calm, it's a perfectly normal maneuver," said Maud in a voice both firm and reassuring.

"We've been trained to do this," Simon confirmed. Standing behind the woman and putting his arms around the diner's diaphragm, he pushed hard inwards and upwards. The first time there was no response but the second time he squeezed her abdomen, a small piece of biscuit shot out of her mouth.

Instantly she was breathing again. Tears of gratitude followed, then sips of water and a demand to know the names of the young people who had saved her life.

Lisa had been mesmerized by the entire scene and suddenly realized she hadn't been listening to a word Moira had been saying for the last few minutes. The entire episode had happened so quickly it looked as though few other people had noticed anything amiss. Really, those twins were something else. Out of the corner of her eye, she saw the waiter they'd called Marco shake Simon enthusiastically by the hand and then give Maud a hug that looked more than just grateful. . . .

Lisa and Moira divided the bill and got up to leave, well pleased with their evening.

Ennio, in his carefully maintained broken English, wished them good-bye.

"Eet is always so good to meet the good friends who 'ave a happy dinner together," he said cheerfully, as he escorted them to the door. They were not good friends but he didn't know this. If they had been real friends, they would not have gone home with such unfinished business between them. Instead they just touched the levels of each other's loneliness but had made no effort each to find an escape route for the other or a bridge between them for the future. It was one night made less bleak by a series of circumstances and the warmth of Ennio's welcome, but it was no more than that.

It would have saddened him to know this as he locked the doors after them—they had been the last to leave. Ennio was a cheerful man. He would have much preferred to think he had been serving a pair of very good friends.

Chapter Ten

Emily had a wonderful weekend in the west with Paddy and Molly Carroll. Dingo Duggan had been an enthusiastic, if somewhat adventurous, driver. He seemed entirely unable and unwilling to read a map and waved away Emily's attempts to find roads with numbers on them.

"Nobody can understand those numbers, Emily," he had said firmly. "They'll do your head in. The main thing is to point west and head for the ocean." And they did indeed see beautiful places like the Sky Road, and drove through hills where big mountain goats came down and looked hopefully at the car and its occupants as if they were new playmates come to entertain them. They spent evenings in pubs singing songs, and they all said it had been one of the best outings they had ever taken.

Emily had told them about her plans to go to America for Betsy's wedding. The Carrolls thought this was marvelous: a late marriage, a chance for Emily to dress up and be part of the ceremony, two kindred souls finding each other.

Dingo Duggan was less sure. "At her age marriage might all be too much for her," he said helpfully.

Emily steered the conversation into safer channels.

"How exactly did you get your name, Dingo?" she inquired.

"Oh, it was that time I went to Australia to earn my fortune," Dingo said simply, as if it should have been evident to everyone, and it wasn't asked by one and all. Dingo's fortune, if represented by the very battered van he drove, did not seem to have been considerable, but Emily Lynch always saw the positive side of things.

"And was it a great experience?" she asked.

"It was, really. I often look back on it and think about all I saw: kangaroos and emus and wombats and gorgeous birds. I mean *real* birds with gorgeous feathers looking as if they had all escaped from a zoo, flying round the place picking at things. You never saw such a sight." He was settled happily, remembering it all with a beatific smile.

"How long did you stay there?" Emily was curious about the life he must have led thousands of miles away.

"Seven weeks." Dingo sighed with pleasure. "Seven beautiful weeks and I talked a lot about it, you see, when I got back, so they gave me the nickname Dingo. It's a kind of wild dog out there, you see. . . ."

"I see." Emily was stunned at the briefness of his visit. "And, er . . . why did you come back?"

"Oh, I had spent all my money by then and couldn't get a job . . . too many Irish illegals out there snapping them all up. So I thought, Head for home."

Emily had little time to speculate about Dingo's mind-set and how he seriously thought he was an expert on all things Australian after a visit of less than two months, ten years ago. She had a lot of e-mailing to cope with to and from New York.

Betsy was having pre-wedding nerves. She hadn't liked Eric's mother, she was disappointed with the gray silk outfit she had bought, her shoes were too tight, her brother was being stingy about the arrangements. She needed Emily badly.

Could Emily please come a few days earlier, she asked, or there might well be no wedding for her to attend. Emily soothed by e-mail, but also examined the possibility of getting an earlier flight. Noel helped her sort through the claims and offers of airlines, and they found one.

"I don't know why I am helping you to go back to America,"

Noel grumbled. "We're all going to miss you like mad, Emily. Lisa and I have been working out a schedule for Frankie and it's looking like a nightmare."

"You should involve Dr. Hat more," Emily said unexpectedly. "Frankie likes Dr. Hat, he's marvelous with her."

"Do I tell Moira?" Noel was fearful.

"Most certainly."

Emily was already busy e-mailing the good news to her friend Betsy; she would be there in three days. She would sort out the dull gray dress, the tight shoes, the miserly brother, Eric's difficult mother. All would be well.

"Moira will be worse than ever when you're gone," Noel said, full of foreboding.

"Just take Frankie to Hat's place in the afternoon. He plays chess online with a boy in Boston—some student, I gather. Hat gets great fun out of it. He even asked me if I could go to visit him when I was in the States and give the boy a chess set, but I told him that I'd never have time to get all that way in such a short time."

"Hat playing chess online! How did he ever learn how to use the computer?"

"I taught him," Emily said simply. "He taught me chess in exchange."

"I don't know the half of what's going on round here," Noel said.

"Don't be afraid of Moira. She's not the enemy, you know."

"She's so suspicious, Emily. When she comes into the flat she shakes a cushion suddenly in case she might find a bottle of whiskey hidden behind it and looks in the bread bin for no reason, just hoping to unearth a half a bottle of gin."

"I'll be back, Noel, and Frankie will have grown, so she'll need a couple of new dresses from New York. Just you wait until she's old enough for me to teach her painting. We can start booking the galleries for twenty years ahead because she'll be exhibiting all over the world."

"She might too." Noel's face lit up at the thought of his daughter being a famous artist. Maybe he'd take out his art supplies box from the closet. He had made sure before he moved it that there were no bottles hidden, but he hadn't had time to draw. Wouldn't it be a good influence on Frankie if he started drawing again?

"If she wants it enough it will happen." Emily nodded as if this were a certainty.

"What about you? What did you want for yourself, Emily?"

"I wanted to teach art and I got that and then eventually, when they thought I wasn't modern enough for them, I wanted to travel and I've started that. I like it very much."

"I hope you won't want to move on again from here," Noel said.

"I'll wait until Frankie's raised and you've found yourself a nice wife." She smiled at him.

"I'll hold you to that," Noel said.

He was very pleased. Emily didn't make promises lightly, but if she had to wait for him to find a nice wife . . . Emily might well be here forever!

They would all miss Emily. Down at the charity shop there was already confusion. Molly said that Emily was able to judge someone's size and taste the moment that she walked in the door. Remember that beautiful heather suit that Moira had bought and pretended she hadn't? People whose window boxes she had planted and tended were beginning to panic that their flowers would wilt during Emily's three-week absence.

Charles Lynch was wondering how he could keep his dog-walking business in credit. Emily was always finding him new clients and remembering to segregate dogs of different sexes in case they might do something to annoy their owners greatly. Emily did his books for him so that nobody from the income tax could say that he was anything other than meticulous.

At the doctors' practice they would miss her too. Nobody seemed to know exactly where to find this document or that. Emily was a reassuring presence. Everyone who worked there had her mobile number, but they had been told that she couldn't be called for three weeks. As Declan Carroll said, it was unnerving, just like going out on a high diving board, facing all this time without Emily.

Who else would know all the things that Emily knew? The best bus route to the hospital, the address of the chiropodist whom all the patients liked, the name of the pastoral care adviser in St. Brigid's?

"Perhaps you could get all this wedding business over within a week?" Declan suggested.

"Dream on, Declan. I don't want to 'get it over with.' I'm longing for it. I want it to go on for at least two months! My very best friend getting married to a man who has adored her for years! I have to sort out shoes that turned out to be too tight, brothers, mothers-in-law, a dress that turned out to be dull. I can't be dealing with you, Declan, and where you put your dry-cleaning ticket."

"I suppose we'll have to muddle through without you," Declan grumbled. "But don't stay away too long."

Lisa was just the same. "We can't phone you if Frankie starts to cough."

"Well, you don't normally," Emily said mildly.

"No, but we *feel* that we could," Lisa confessed. "Listen, while I have you, Emily, I may have slightly ballsed things up with Moira. We had a meal together and I sort of said or let drop that it was fairly exhausting cleaning Frankie, feeding her, burping her and taking her from place to place. I meant it to be a compliment to Noel, you know, and how well we are managing things, but it came out sounding like a whine or a moan, and of course Moira picked up on it and wondered were we capable of minding Frankie and all that, which was the *last* thing . . ."

"Don't worry about it," Emily advised. "I'll have a talk with Moira."

"I wish you'd stay and have a talk with her every day," Lisa grumbled.

"You can always e-mail me, but, for the Lord's sake, don't tell everyone else that."

"Just about Frankie," Lisa promised.

"That's a deal, then—just about Frankie," said Emily, knowing that no law was so strict that it couldn't be bent for an emergency.

Eventually Emily got away.

She could hardly believe that it was just a matter of months since she had arrived here knowing nobody and now she seemed to be making seismic gaps in their lives by leaving for three weeks. It was amazing how much she had been absorbed into this small community.

She hoped she wasn't going to speak with an Irish brogue when she got back to the United States. She hoped too that she wouldn't use any Irishisms such as saying "Jaysus!" like they did in Dublin with no apparent blasphemy or disrespect. It had startled her at first, but then it had become second nature.

As she got nearer to New York she became excited at all that lay ahead. She tried to force the Irish cast of characters away from the main stage of her mind. She had to concentrate on Eric's mother and Betsy's brother, but images kept coming back to her.

Noel and Lisa in Chestnut Court soothing the baby as they prepared for a college degree that might or might not be any help to either of them. Josie and Charles kneeling down saying the Rosary in their kitchen, remembering to add three Hail Marys for St. Jarlath and a reminder that the statue campaign was going well. Dr. Hat playing chess with the boy in Boston who had something wrong with his foot and was out of school for a week. Molly in the thrift shop wondering how much to charge for a pleated linen skirt that had never been worn. Paddy Carroll bringing round, big wrapped parcels that contained juicy bones for the dogs that passed through. Aidan and Signora singing Italian songs to three children: their own grandchild, as well as Frankie and little Johnny Carroll. She thought about Muttie, wheezing happily to his dog, Hooves, or solving the world's problems with his Associates. She thought about the decent priest Father Brian Flynn, and how he tried to hide his true feelings about the statue of a sixth-century saint being erected in a Dublin working-class street.

There were so many images that Emily dropped off to sleep thinking about them all. And there she was in Kennedy Airport, and, after collecting her luggage and clearing customs, she could see Eric and Betsy jumping up and down with excitement. They even had a banner. In uneven writing it said WELCOME HOME, EMILY! How very odd that it didn't seem like home anymore.

But home or not, it was wonderful.

Emily talked to Eric's mother in a woman-of-the-world manner. She managed to convey the impression that Eric was very near his sell-by date and that he was very, *very* lucky that Betsy had been persuaded to consider him. Betsy had, apparently, written over to Ireland that there were some "obstacles" in the way of the marriage. Emily couldn't think what they might be. She looked Eric's mother in the eye and asked if *she* knew of any. Betsy's future mother-in-law, who was just a bit of a fusspot, started to babble a bit. Emily felt the point had been made. Betsy needed huge enthusiasm and support for her big day; otherwise she might pull out at the last moment and poor Eric would be left bereft.

Emily sorted out the shoes simply by insisting Betsy buy a pair in the correct size; she sorted out the dull dress problem by taking the very plain gray dress to an accessories store and asking everyone's advice. Together, they chose a rose-pink-and-cream-colored stole, which transformed it.

She went to Betsy's brother and explained that since Betsy had waited this long to get married, it had better be a classy celebration; this way she managed to upgrade the menu considerably and arranged sparkling wine.

And, of course, the wedding was splendid. Emily was pleased to see her friend in comfortable shoes wearing a newly adorned dress. Betsy's brother had put on a very elegant spread, and her mother-in-law had been like charm personified.

Betsy cried with happiness; Eric cried and said that this was the best day of his whole life; Emily cried because it was all so marvelous; and the best man cried because his own marriage was on the rocks and he envied people just starting out.

When all the relations went home and the best man had gone to make one more ineffectual stab at repairing his own marriage, the bride and groom set off with the maid of honor for Chinatown and had a feast. There would be no honeymoon, but a holiday in Ireland would certainly be in the cards before the end of the year.

Emily told them about some of the people they would meet. Eric and Betsy said they could hardly wait. It all sounded so intriguing. They wanted to go right out to Kennedy Airport and fly to Ireland at once.

To: Emily
From: Lisa

I know we agreed only to e-mail about Frankie and there's no crisis—I just felt like talking to you. She is very well and sleeping much better.

Moira didn't seem to pick up on what I had said about Frankie being a lot of work, so with any luck that's all been forgotten.

Frankie seems to enjoy going to Dr. Hat. He sings little sea shanties to her. He got her some jars of apple puree and spoons them into her all the time—she can't get enough of them!

Maud and Marco from Ennio's restaurant are a definite number—they've been seen at the cinema together. Nice for Maud because things are sad in that house, but I think Simon is feeling a bit left out.

Noel went out on a date last week. I set him up with a friend of Katie's called Sophie, but it just didn't take. When he told her about

Frankie, she asked, "And when do you give her back to her mother?" Noel told her that Stella was dead and suddenly this girl Sophie wanted to be miles away. A man with a child! Beware! Beware!

Poor Muttie looks awful. Declan doesn't say anything, but I think it's not sounding too good.

Life is very good otherwise.

Everything going well. Anton's picture was in the paper today and April has blotted her copybook, I am delighted to say.

How was the wedding?

Love,
Lisa

There were a lot of questions when Emily read the e-mails to Betsy and Eric, so Emily explained who was who. Moira was considered the enemy and April was considered a love rival of Lisa's; the twins were teenagers in the catering business; Muttie was their grandfather or uncle or guardian, no one quite knew. And Anton? The nonavailable object of Lisa's adoration . . .

From: Emily
To: Lisa

Thanks for the news. The wedding was fabulous—will show you pictures.

What did April do? How did she make a mess of things?

Love,
Emily

To: Emily
From: Lisa

April told everyone that a group of food critics were coming to Anton's on Tuesday last, and amazingly they never turned up:

someone had told them it had been canceled. Anton was SO furious with her. He and I had a dinner together in the restaurant to cheer him up. . . .

Eric and Betsy, by now an established married couple, saw Emily off at the airport. They waved long after she had disappeared in the crush of people heading into Terminal 4. They would miss her, but they knew that soon she would be sitting on that Aer Lingus flight, resetting her mind and orienting herself towards Dublin again.

It sounded like an insane place and it had certainly changed Emily. Normally so reserved and quiet, she seemed to have been entirely seduced by a cast of characters who sounded as if they should be on an old Broadway variety show. . . .

Emily didn't sleep, like so many of the other passengers did. She sat making comparisons between this journey and the one she had made across the Atlantic when coming to Ireland for the very first time. Then she had been looking for roots, trying to work out what kind of life her father had lived back then in Dublin and how it had shaped him. She had learned next to nothing about this, but had become deeply involved in a series of dramas, ranging from helping to raise a motherless child who was living with a functioning alcoholic to working in a thrift shop trying to help her aunt to raise money to build a statue to an unknown saint who, if he had ever existed, had died back in the sixth century, to organizing a dog-walking business for her uncle.

It seemed quite mad, and yet she felt like she was going home.

It was early morning in Dublin when the transatlantic flights came in, and the crowds stood around the luggage carousels. Emily reached for her smart new suitcases—a gift from Eric to thank her for being maid of honor.

As they moved out through customs, she thought it would be nice if someone had come to meet her, but then who would have been able to?

Josie and Charles didn't have a car. Neither did Noel or Lisa. Dingo Duggan, with his van, would have been nice, but that was hardly likely. She would get the bus as before. Except this time she would know what she was getting into.

Just as she came out into the open air, she saw a familiar figure; Dr. Hat was standing there waving at her.

"I thought I'd come to meet you," he said, taking one of her cases.

In the midst of all the crowds of people embracing each other, Emily was thrilled to see him.

"I'm in the short-term car park," he said proudly and led the way. He must have gotten up very early to be there in time.

"It's so good to see you, Hat," she said as she settled into his small car.

"I brought you a flask of coffee and an egg sandwich. Is that as good as America?" he asked.

"Oh, Hat, how wonderful to be home!" Emily said.

"We were all afraid that you would stay out there and get married yourself." Hat seemed very relieved this was not the case.

"I wouldn't do that," Emily said, flattered that they had wanted her back here. "Now you can tell me all the news before I get back to St. Jarlath's Crescent."

"There's a lot of news," Hat said.

"We've a lot of time." Emily settled happily back in his car.

It was mixed news.

The bad news was that Muttie had got a great deal worse. His prognosis, though not discussed or admitted in public, was no more than a few months now. Lizzie seemed to find it difficult to take this onboard and was busy planning a trip to the sunshine. She was even urging the twins to speed up their plans to go to New Jersey—somewhere that she and Muttie could come and visit.

Simon and Maud realized that there would be no such journey; they were very down. Young Declan Carroll had been marvelous with them, giving them extra babysitting to keep their minds off things.

Hat's good news was that baby Frankie was going from strength to strength. Emily didn't dare to ask, but Hat knew what she wanted to know.

"And Noel has been a brick. Lisa has been away a bit, but he manages fine."

"Which means that you help him too." Emily looked at him gratefully.

"I love the child. She's no trouble." Hat negotiated the traffic.

"Any more news?" Emily inquired.

"Well, Molly Carroll said you wouldn't believe how many garments she got from some madwoman."

" 'Mad'? Angry or crazy? I never know which you mean."

"Oh, crazed is what she was. She discovered her husband had been buying clothes for another lady and she took them all and brought them to the thrift shop!" He seemed amused.

"But are we entitled to them? Were they the crazy lady's to give?"

"Apparently so. The husband was singing dumb over it all, saying that he had bought them for his wife, but they were entirely the wrong size and the wrong color! Amazing things, I heard, like black and red corsets!"

"Heavens! I can't wait to get back," Emily said.

"And you know the old lady who gave Charles the dog?"

"Mrs. Monty, yes? Don't tell me she took Caesar away. . . ."

"No. The poor lady died—rest in peace—but didn't she leave all her money to Charles!"

"Did she have any money?"

"We think, amazingly, that she did."

"Isn't that wonderful!" Emily cried.

"It is until you think how it's going to be spent," Dr. Hat said, drawing a halo around his head with his finger.

Charles and Josie were waiting for her at Number 23; they were fussing over Frankie, who had a bit of a cold and was very fretful, not her usual sunny self. Emily was delighted to see her and lifted her up to examine her. Immediately, the child stopped grizzling.

"She's definitely grown, so much in three weeks. Isn't she wonderful?" She gave the baby a hug and was rewarded with a very chatty babble. Emily realized how much she had missed her. This was the child none of them had expected or, to be honest, really wanted, at the start—and look at her now! She was the center of their world.

Dr. Hat had been invited in for a cup of tea and was enjoying a game of picking up Frankie's teddy bear in order for her to drop it again, and Molly Carroll stopped in to welcome Emily back. Noel rang from work to make sure she really *had* returned and hadn't decided to relocate to New York.

Frankie was fine, he said, a runny nose, but otherwise fine. The nurse had said she was thriving. Lisa was away again. She had missed three lectures now and it would be so hard for her to catch up. Oh, yes, he had plenty of help. There was this woman called Faith at his lectures who had five younger brothers at home and had no place to study, so she had come to help Noel three evenings a week.

Faith was delighted with Frankie. She had a lot of experience bringing up younger brothers herself but had never been close to a little girl.

The evening slipped into an easy routine: bath time, bottle, Frankie off to sleep, then revision papers and the Internet notes to help them study. Faith sympathized deeply with Noel having to work in a place like Hall's: she was in a fairly dead-end office job but had great hopes that the diploma they were working for would make a difference. People in her office respected such things greatly.

She was a cheerful and optimistic woman of twenty-nine; she had dark curly hair, green eyes, a mobile face and a wide smile and she loved walking. She showed Noel a great many places he had never known in his own city. She said she needed to walk a lot because it concentrated her mind. She had suffered a great blow: six years ago, her fiancé had been killed in a car accident just weeks before the wedding day. She had coped by walking alone and being very quiet, but recently she had felt the need to get involved with the world about her. That was one of the reasons she had joined the course at the college, and it was one of the reasons she had adapted so easily to Noel's demanding life.

She had bought a baby album for Frankie and put in little wisps of the child's hair, her first baby sock and dozens of photographs.

"Have you any pictures of Stella?" she asked Noel.

"No—none at all."

Faith didn't inquire further.

"I could do a drawing of her, maybe," he said after a while.

"That would be great. Frankie will love that when she gets older."

Noel looked at her gratefully. She was very good company to have around the place. Perhaps later he might try to sketch her face too.

Lisa and Anton were at a Celtic food celebration in Scotland. They were looking into the possibility of pairing with some similar-type Scottish restaurant where they could do a deal: anyone who spent over a certain sum in Anton's could get a voucher for half this amount in the Scottish restaurant and vice versa. It would work because it was tapping into an entirely new market, mainly American.

It was Lisa's idea. She had special cards printed to show how it would work. The Scottish restaurant's name was a blank at the moment until the deal was done.

Several times Lisa felt rather than saw Anton's glance of approval, but she knew better now than to look at him for praise. Instead, she concentrated entirely on getting the work done. There would be time later over meals together.

At one of the hotels they had visited the receptionist asked them if they'd like the honeymoon suite. Lisa deliberately said nothing. Anton asked, with apparent interest, if they looked like a honeymoon couple.

"Not really, but you *do* look happy," the girl said.

Lisa decided to let Anton speak again. "Well, we are, I hope. I mean, who wouldn't be happy in this lovely place and if there was a complimentary upgrade to the honeymoon suite, that would be the icing on the cake." He smiled his heartbreaking smile and Lisa noticed the receptionist join the long line of women who fancied Anton.

It was so cheering to be here with him and to know that April was out in the wilderness, not posturing and putting her small bottom in her skintight jeans on Anton's desk or the arm of his chair. April was miles and miles away. . . .

But then the trip was over and it was back to reality. Back to lectures in the college three nights a week, back to Frankie waking up all hours of the night, back to April, who was inching her way again into Anton's life.

Lisa noted that a lot of free events had been arranged in Anton's, occasions that would be written up in the papers, perhaps, but that did not put paying customers in seats, which was what they needed. She worried that too much was being spent on appearance rather than reality. The bottom line was the numbers of people you got in to pay for the meals and tell their friends, who would also come in and hand over money. Not just another charity press conference with minor celebrities who would be photographed for gossip columns. This was April's world.

Lisa was not so sure it was right. But when Lisa was alone with Anton, she kept quiet about her misgivings. Anton hated being nagged. To tell him he was high on publicity and low on paying punters could well have been considered nagging.

Lisa was not happy to be home.

Emily was walking towards Muttie and Lizzie's house when she saw Lisa, and she could judge Lisa's mood from a long way off. She wondered was it going to be her only role in life from now on cheering people up and stressing the positive.

"How are things, Lisa? Noel told me you've been on a great trip to Scotland," Emily said, without giving Lisa a chance to ask her about Betsy's wedding.

"It was magic, Emily. Were you ever somewhere and wished that it would never end?"

Emily thought for a moment. "Not really. I suppose there has been a day here and there that I never wanted to end. My friend Betsy's wedding day was one, and driving around Connemara was another. I suppose there were good days when I was teaching art too."

"I had days which were all like that in Scotland," Lisa said, her face radiant at the thought of it all.

"Great—you'll have the memory of that to keep you going when you get back to your studies." Emily knew she sounded brisk.

"Noel's been marvelous; he has all his notes photocopied for me and he's arranged for Molly Carroll to take Frankie for a walk in the park and he had to make sure that Bossy Boots knows all our plans. I'm just coming down here to make sure that Mrs. Carroll has cover for the thrift shop."

"You can't stand in the thrift shop all day—you have your studies to catch up on."

"I have some of my notes here. It won't be that busy," Lisa said.

"I'll look in after I've seen Muttie and Lizzie."

"Not much good news there," Lisa said, shaking her head. "Muttie's chemo has stopped and Lizzie keeps making impossible plans for the future. Hey, you have enough to do getting over jet lag and visiting Muttie. I'll survive in the thrift shop for a bit."

"We'll see," Emily said.

Muttie looked much frailer even after three weeks. His color was poor and his face seemed to have hollows in it; his clothes hung off him. His good humor was clearly not affected, though.

"Well . . . show us pictures of how the Americans do a wedding," he said, putting on his spectacles.

"It's not very typical," Emily explained. "Fairly mature bride and maid of honor, for one thing."

"The groom is no spring chicken either," Muttie agreed.

"Look at the lovely clothes!" Lizzie was delighted with it all. "And what are all these Chinese signs?"

"Oh, we went to Chinatown for dinner," Emily said. "Dozens of Chinese restaurants, Chinese shops and little pagodas and decorations everywhere."

"That's where we'll go when we go to New York later on in the year. Emily will mark our card."

"That's if I can ever get myself on the plane." Muttie shook his head. "I seem to have run out of puff, Emily. Hooves here wants me to take him up to have a drink with my Associates, but I find the walk exhausts me."

"Do you get to see them at all?" Emily knew how much Muttie loved talking horses to the men in the bar while Hooves sat with his head on Muttie's knee and his eyes full of adoration.

"Oh, Dr. Hat is very good. And sometimes young Declan Carroll gets a fierce thirst on him and he drives me up there for a few pints."

Emily knew very well that Declan would often pretend a fierce thirst and get himself a pint or two of lemonade shandy while he drove his elderly neighbor up to the pub.

"And how are all the family?" Emily inquired.

As she had expected, they all seemed to be making sudden visits to Ireland from Chicago. Muttie was shaking his head at the coincidence of it all.

"I don't know where they get the money, Emily, I really don't. I mean, there's a recession out in those places as well as here."

"And the twins? Busy as ever?"

"Oh, Maud and Simon are wonderful. There's less chat about their going to New Jersey, but then again Maud has an Italian boy-friend—a really polite, respectful young man called Marco. They're all setting up this phone for us where you can see the person at the other end. It's called Skype and this weekend we'll be calling my daughter Marian in Chicago and we'll see her and all her family. It doesn't sound right to me."

"Amazing thing, technology," Emily agreed.

"Yes, but it's almost going too quickly. Fancy our children getting on planes and coming from the ends of the earth over here to see us and then this magic phone. I don't understand it at all. . . ."

Emily went to the thrift shop and found the twins working there. Lisa was in a corner sighing over her notes. There were no customers.

"We don't all have to be here," Emily said, taking off her coat.

"Maud and I were just wondering . . ."

"We don't want to put anyone out . . ."

"It's just there's this Italian cookery demonstration . . ."

"At Ennio's restaurant on the quays . . ."

"And Maud fancies the son of the house there rotten . . ." Simon wanted everything to be clear.

"Not true. We've been out a few times . . ."

"But it's starting in half an hour, you see . . ."

"And if it was possible for us to work here some other time . . ."

Emily cut across this double act. "Go now. This minute," she said.

"If you're sure . . ."

"If it's not putting you out . . ."

"Is that the pasta house where I saw you?" Lisa asked suddenly.

"You were there with Moira. Traitor!" Maud took no prisoners.

"You saw her socially?" Simon sounded disgusted.

"It was different. She was lonely."

"I wonder why. . . ." Maud was unforgiving.

"Are you still here?" Emily asked, opening the door of the thrift shop. As they left, she turned to Lisa. "Go back to Chestnut Court and study properly, Lisa, and I'll do the pricing on the new clothes that have come in. Otherwise you and I will waste the morning and not a penny will be raised for St. Jarlath."

Lisa looked at her in surprise. "But you don't believe any of this St. Jarlath nonsense, do you, Emily?"

"I suppose we're just keeping our options open." Emily was slightly apologetic.

"But think about it, Emily. If there were a God, then I would be engaged to Anton, Stella wouldn't have died in childbirth and Frankie would have a mother. Noel would be recognized for what he could do at Hall's, Muttie wouldn't be dying of cancer, you would be running the world or the civil service or something, with a nice, undemanding husband to cook you a meal when you got home every night."

"What makes you think that's what I'd want a God to get for me?" Emily asked.

"What else would you want? Except to run things . . ."

"I'd want something totally different: a home of my own, the chance to take up painting to see if I was any good at it, a small office from which I could run Emily's Window Boxes . . . I don't want the undemanding husband or the great power of running the country. No way!"

"So you say." Lisa knew it all.

"Is it going to be as hard to get rid of you as the twins?" Emily asked.

"Right. I'm going. Thanks, Emily. You're amazing. If I'd just come back from America, I'd be on all fours rather than going straight in to work. I'm nearly a basket case and I was only in Scotland!"

"Well, you were probably much more active on your holiday than I was on mine," Emily said.

Rather than work out what Emily might have in mind, Lisa left. As she walked up the road she thought about Scotland. They had stayed in five different hotels and in every one of them Anton and she had made love. Twice in the place where they had the honeymoon suite. Why did Anton not miss this and want her to stay with him every night? He had kissed her good-bye when they got to Dublin Airport and said it had been great. Why did he use the past tense? It could all have continued when they were back home.

It was meant to continue.

He had said he loved her—four times he had said it—two of them were sort of jokey when she had got things right about various hotels and restaurants, but twice when they were making love. And so he must have meant it, because who would say something like that at such an intense time and not mean it?

In the thrift shop there was a beautiful green and black silk blouse. An "unwanted gift," said the lady who had brought in. It was still in its box with tissue paper. Emily hung it up on a clothes hanger and tried to price it.

When it was new it had probably cost a hundred euros, but nobody who came here would pay anything remotely like that. The lady who had donated it wouldn't be back to see how it was priced, but in any event Emily didn't want to price it too low. It was beautiful. If it were in her own size she would happily have paid fifty euros for it. She was still holding it when Moira came in.

"Just checking where Frankie is," she said abruptly.

"Good morning, Moira," Emily said, with pointed politeness. "Frankie has gone to the park with Mrs. Carroll, Dr. Declan's mother."

"Oh, I know Mrs. Carroll, yes. I was just making sure nobody had put Frankie in a 'File and Forget' file." Moira smiled to take the harm out of her words. It was not entirely successful.

Emily had a touch of frost in her voice. "That would never happen to Frankie Lynch."

"You mean well, certainly, Emily, but she's not *your* responsibility."

"She's family." Emily's eyes glinted. "She is the daughter of my first cousin. That makes her my first cousin once removed."

"Imagine!" Moira wasn't impressed.

"Can I do anything else for you, Moira?" Emily was managing to hold on to her manners, but only just.

"Well, I'm going out to the heart clinic and the woman who runs it is like a clotheshorse. She's interested in nothing but clothes."

"I believe she's a good heart specialist also," Emily said.

"Oh, yes, well, I'm sure she is, but she's always commenting on what you wear. . . . I was just wondering if you had anything . . . well, you know . . ."

"This is your lucky day. I have this beautiful green and black blouse. It would look so good with your black skirt there. Do try it on."

Moira looked very well in it. "How much?" she asked, in her usual charmless way.

"Would be over a hundred in the shops. I was going to put fifty on it, but you're a good customer, so shall we say forty-five?" It was more than Moira had intended to spend, but they agreed on forty-five and Moira headed off towards the heart clinic in her finery. The shabby gray blouse she had been wearing was wrapped up in the bottom of her briefcase.

As soon as she was gone, Emily telephoned Fiona at the clinic.

"I know this is a bit sneaky . . . ," she began.

"I *love* sneaky," said Fiona.

"Moira Tierney is on her way to you wearing a smashing new blouse she bought here. She may start to regret her buy and grizzle about the price, so build her up to the skies."

"Will do," Fiona said enthusiastically.

By the time Moira reached the clinic, there were quite a lot of people there. Frank Ennis had come in for one of his unexpected and disliked visits. They were having tea when he arrived.

"Oh, nice biscuits," he said, with a look of utter disapproval.

"Paid for by ourselves, Frank," Clara said cheerfully. "Every week someone gets to choose the biscuits and pay for them. Lord forbid that the whole of St. Brigid's would have to come to a halt because the heart clinic charged the central fund for biscuits. Do have another while you're here. . . ."

Moira came in just then.

"You bring a touch of class to this place," Frank Ennis said.

Barbara took offense. "She doesn't have to wear a uniform," she whispered to her friend Fiona, nodding her head at Moira. To her bewilderment, Fiona didn't seem to agree.

"That's a beautiful blouse, Moira." Fiona played her part perfectly.

Clara was looking at it too.

"You have a great eye for clothes, Moira. That's top-class silk."

In a million years Moira would never tell them where she'd bought it. She murmured a bit, refused tea and biscuits and went straight to her room. She had three new patients to see today.

The first man came into her small room. He was large, with a lined face and shaggy hair, and was fairly wordless. Moira flashed him one of her very brief smiles and took out a piece of paper.

"Well, now, Mr. . . . er . . . Kennedy. Your address first, please."

"St. Patrick's Hostel."

"Yes, I see you've been there since you left hospital. And before that . . . ?"

"In England."

"Addresses?"

"Ah, well, I was here and there, you know . . ."

Moira did know. Only too well. Irishmen who had lost years of their lives working on the buildings, using a different name every month, paying no tax, having no insurance, no record of years spent and wages passed over in cash in a pub of a Friday evening.

"Before that, then," she said wearily. One way or another, she needed some kind of paperwork for this man.

"Oh, long ago I lived in Liscuan," he said.

She looked up sharply. She had thought he looked somehow familiar.

It was Maureen Kennedy's long-gone husband. She was planning the future of the man whose wife now lived with her father.

Noel came back from Hall's tired.

He let himself in to Chestnut Court and found Lisa asleep at the kitchen table with his college notes all around her. He had been hoping that she might have made supper and even gone down to the Carrolls' to collect Frankie.

But what the hell, she was probably worn out after her time in Scotland and was sorry to be home. He would go to collect Frankie. He might even bring home fish and chips. Thank God there were no lectures tonight. He might even drop in to see Muttie. Poor guy was looking desperate these days. . . .

Muttie welcomed him with a big smile. It made his skull-like face look worse than ever.

"Lizzie, it's Noel. Have you a slice of cake for the lad?"

"No, thanks, Muttie. I'm collecting Frankie from Molly and Paddy. I only came to say hello. I have to get her home and put to bed."

Maud and Simon were there, blond heads bent over a computer.

"We've put Skype on for Muttie," Maud said proudly.

"So he can talk to people face-to-face," added Simon, equally pleased.

"Well, when the two of you get settled in New Jersey, I can talk to you every week!" Muttie was bright and cheerful about it.

"Yeah, but we're not going to New Jersey," Maud said.

"Too much to keep us here," Simon added darkly.

"The cookery demonstration in Ennio's restaurant was brilliant today," Maud said.

"He's a very nice lad, that Marco. You'd walk many a mile before you'd meet as nice a fellow," Muttie said. "Hurry up now, Simon, and find yourself a girl before it's too late for us all."

They looked at him sharply, but he didn't mean anything sinister.

"It's too early to settle down," Simon said carelessly.

"Who said anything about settling down?" Maud asked.

There was a knock on the door. It was a young man with black curly hair who came in carrying a huge saucepan of something bubbling in a tomato sauce.

"This is for the grandfather of lovely Maud," he said.

"Well, thank you, Marco," Muttie said, pleased. "Lizzie, come in and see what's arrived."

Lizzie came running in from the kitchen.

"Marco! Imagine, I was just about to get the supper."

"So that was good timing, then?" Marco beamed around the little group.

"Well, I have to go." Noel stood up. "I'm Noel, by the way. I'd love to join you, but I have to pick up my daughter. *Buon appetito.*"

Noel wished he could stay. It was heartening to see such happiness in a house that was about to go through so much sadness soon.

In Chestnut Court Lisa woke with a stiff neck. She saw Noel's coat hanging on the back of the door. He must have come in and left again. She should have made him some kind of supper or gone to pick Frankie up from Molly Carroll's. Too late now. He had scrawled a note saying he would come back with a fish supper. He was so kind. Wouldn't it have been so easy if only she could have loved Noel rather than Anton. But then life didn't work like that and maybe there would be even more obstacles in the way. She got up, stretched and set the table.

She would really love a glass of wine with the cod and French fries, but that was something that would never be brought into this house. She thought back to the lovely wine they had drunk in Scotland. She had paid for the meals on alternate nights, but she had maxed out on her credit cards and was seriously broke now. But Anton never realized that. She hoped things would change soon; she would have to get a job if Anton didn't make a commitment.

Noel would be home shortly and she mustn't be full of gloomy thoughts.

At 23 St. Jarlath's Crescent, Josie and Charles Lynch sat in stunned silence. They had just closed the door behind a very serious lawyer in a striped suit. He had come to tell them just how much they had inherited from the late Meriel Monty. When all the assets were liquidated, the estate would come, the lawyer said very slowly, to a total of approximately 289,000 euros.

Chapter Eleven

It was good that Eddie Kennedy didn't recognize her, Moira thought. This way she could continue to be professional.

The hostel where he was living was only a short-stay place; soon he would need something long-term. If things had been different, she might have inquired more about the setup in Liscuan, wondered whether he might even at this late stage be able to patch things up with his wife. After all, he didn't drink now. But the very thought of destroying the great content that her father had finally found late in a troubled life was one she could not bear to let into her mind.

Wherever Eddie Kennedy was to find his salvation, it must not be in Liscuan.

Moira sighed deeply and tried to remember what she would have done for this man if things had been different, if she hadn't known for certain that his long-abandoned wife was living with her own father. Wearily she continued with fruitless questions about any possible benefits that might be due to him after a lifetime of working in England. This man had never signed on anywhere or joined any system. It would be a progression of hostels from now on.

It would have been the same if he had come across any other social worker, wouldn't it? Maybe one of them would have made inquiries back in Liscuan. And if inquiries *had* been made? Perhaps Mrs. Kennedy and her father would have sung low, in which case there would have been nothing different to the way it was now. . . .

Yet Moira felt guilty. This man shouldn't have his options restricted just because his social worker wanted her own father to continue undisturbed in what should have been this man's home. Moira wished, not for the first time, that she had a friend, a soul mate whom she could discuss it with.

She remembered that meal with Lisa in Ennio's: it had been pleasant and it was surprisingly easy to talk to Lisa. But of course the girl would think she was quite insane if she were to suggest it.

Worse—both insane and pathetic.

Muttie told Lizzie that something was worrying him.

"Tell me, Muttie."

Lizzie had listened to Muttie for years. Listened to stories of horses that were going to win, backs that ached, beer that had been watered and, more recently, of some poor unfortunates he had met up with at the hospital. Muttie had discovered there was a desperate lot of illness about—you just didn't come across it when you were in the whole of your health.

She wondered what she would hear now.

"I'm worried that the twins are putting off their trip to America because of my having to have those treatments." He said it defiantly, as if waiting, hoping, for her to deny it.

If that was what he wanted, then that was what he got. Lizzie's face split in two with a great laugh.

"Well, if that's all that's bothering you, Muttie Scarlet, aren't you a lucky man? Have you eyes in your head at all? They didn't want to go because Maud is crazy about Mario. The *last* thing she wants to do is to go away and let some Dublin dolly get her claws into Mario. It has nothing to do with you whatsoever!"

He was vastly relieved. "I suppose I was making myself the big man," he said.

. . .

Noel Lynch and Lisa Kelly were shopping for fruit and vegetables in a market where Emily had pointed them. Moira had complained that they did very little home cooking and Frankie's diet might be lacking in all kinds of nutrients.

"She always moves the bloody goalposts," Lisa said in fury.

"Why are home purees better than the ones we buy?" Noel said crossly. "What *are* all these additives she talks about? And why do the makers put them in?"

"I bet they don't. It's just Moira making life more difficult. Right, show me the list Emily made. Apples, bananas. No honey—that can poison her. Vegetables, but no broccoli. We have stock, and it's low-salt and organic—I checked."

"Have we?" Noel was surprised. "What does it look like?"

"Like a sort of toffee wrapped up. We have it, Noel. Come on, let's pay for this lot and we'll go home and puree it and while it's cooking we'll go over the notes for that lecture we both missed. Thank God for Faith!"

"Yes, indeed."

Lisa looked at him sharply. It was obvious to everyone except Noel that Faith fancied him. Lisa didn't feel at all drawn to Noel except as a housemate and friend, but she didn't want the situation complicated.

In some strange, odd way Anton felt slightly more on his toes because Lisa lived with a man. It was more racy somehow. Once or twice Anton had asked if there was any frisson between the two of them. That was a very Anton type of word and he asked it casually, as if he didn't care very much anyway.

But that was his way. He wouldn't have asked if he hadn't cared.

Lisa was comfortable in Chestnut Court. Noel made sure she went to her lectures when she wasn't running off with Anton at a moment's notice. And even though she wouldn't admit it to anyone, she had become amazingly fond of that little girl. Life without Frankie was going to be hard when it happened. As soon as Anton realized that commitment did not mean a life sentence, it meant the opening of doors.

Emily Lynch was also in the vegetable market; she had promised Dr. Hat she would teach him how to make a vegetarian curry for his friend Michael, who was coming to visit.

"Could you not just . . . er . . . make it for me?" Dr. Hat begged.

"No way! I want you to be able to tell Michael how you made it." She was very firm.

"Emily, *please.* Cooking is women's business."

"Then why are the great chefs mainly male?" she asked mildly.

"Show-offs," said Dr. Hat mutinously. "It won't work, Emily. I'll burn everything."

"Don't be ridiculous—we'll have a great time chopping everything up; you'll be making this recipe every week."

"I doubt it," said Dr. Hat. "I seriously doubt it."

The whole encounter with Eddie Kennedy had made Moira restless. Her own small apartment felt like a prison, with the walls enclosing her more and more. Perhaps she was a kindred soul to him and would end up beached, with no friends, being looked after by some social worker who was still at school now.

It was her birthday on Friday. It was a sad person who had nobody to celebrate with. Nobody at all. Yet again her thoughts went back to that pleasant evening at Ennio's restaurant. She had felt normal for once.

What would Lisa say if Moira asked her to have a meal with her—except that she wasn't free? Nothing would be lost. She would go around to Chestnut Court now.

"God Almighty, it's Moira *again!*" Lisa said when she had put down the entry phone and buzzed her in.

"What can she want now?" Noel looked around the flat nervously in case there was something that could be discovered, something that would be a black mark against them. Frankie's clothes were drying on the radiators—but that was good, wasn't it? They were making sure that the little garments were properly aired.

He continued spooning the puree into Frankie, who enjoyed it mainly as a face-painting activity and something to rub into her hair.

Moira arrived in a gray pantsuit and sensible shoes. She looked businesslike, but then she was always businesslike.

Noel saw her properly for the first time. There was a sort of shield around her, as if it were keeping people away. She had good, clear skin. Her hair was curly in a color that suited her. It was just that it didn't add up to much.

"Will you have a cup of tea?" he asked her wearily.

Moira had taken in the domestic scene at a glance: the child was being well cared for. Anyone could see that. They had even listened to her about getting fresh vegetables and making purees.

She saw the books and note files out for their studies. These were her so-called hopeless clients, a family at risk, not fit to be minding Frankie, and yet they seemed to have got their act together much better than Moira had.

"I had a tiring day today," she said unexpectedly.

If the roof had blown off the apartment block, Noel and Lisa could not have been more surprised. Even Frankie looked up, startled, with her food-stained face.

Moira never complained about her workload. She was tireless in her efforts to impose some kind of order on a mad world. This was the very first time she had even given a hint that she might be human.

"What kind of things were most tiring?" Lisa asked politely.

"Frustration, mainly. I know this couple who are desperate for a baby. They would provide a great home, but can they get one? Oh, no, they can't. People can ignore babies, harm them, take drugs all round them, and that's perfectly fine as long as they are kept with the natural parent. We are meant to be proud of this because we have kept the family unit intact. . . ."

Noel found himself involuntarily holding Frankie closer to him.

"Not you, Noel," Moira said wearily. "You and Lisa are doing your best."

This was astounding praise. Lisa and Noel looked at each other in shock.

"I mean it's a hopeless situation, but at least you're keeping to the rules," Moira admitted grudgingly.

Noel and Lisa smiled at each other in relief.

"But the rest of it's exhausting and I ask myself, Is it getting anyone anywhere?"

Lisa wondered whether Moira might be having a nervous breakdown.

"It must be very stressful, your job. I suppose you have to try to compensate for it in your private life," Lisa babbled, in an attempt to restore normality.

"Yes, indeed, if all I had to think about was Hall's, I'd be locked up by now," Noel agreed. "If I didn't have Frankie to come home to, I'd be a right mess."

"I'm the same." Lisa thought of Anton's. "Honestly, the comings and goings, the highs and lows, the dramas. I'm glad I have another life outside it all."

Moira listened to all this without much sign of agreement or pleasure. Then she delivered the final shock.

"It was actually about my social life that I called," Moira said. "I'm going to be thirty-five on Friday and I was hoping, Lisa, you might join me for supper at Ennio's. . . ."

"Me? Friday? Oh, heavens. Well, thank you, Moira, thank you indeed. I'm free on Friday, aren't I, Noel?"

Was she looking at him beseechingly, begging him to find some kind of excuse? Or was she eager to go? Noel couldn't work it out. Honesty seemed safest.

"Friday is my day on—you're free Friday evening," he said.

Lisa's face showed nothing. "Well, that's very kind of you, Moira. Will there be many people there?"

"In Ennio's? I don't know. I suppose there will be a fair number."

"No, I mean to celebrate your birthday?"

"Oh, just the two of us," Moira said, and she gathered herself up and left.

Noel and Lisa didn't dare to speak until she had left the building.

"We should have said she didn't look thirty-five," Lisa said.

"What does she look?" Noel asked.

"She could be a hundred. She could be any age. Why did she ask me to dinner?"

"Maybe she fancies you," Noel said, and then, "Sorry, sorry. I'm just making a joke."

"Right, you can afford to make jokes. You're not the one having dinner with her on Friday."

"She may be going mad," Noel said thoughtfully.

Lisa had been wondering exactly the same thing.

"Why do you say that?"

"Well . . ." Noel spoke slowly and deliberately. "It's a very odd thing to do. No one normal would invite you to dinner. You of all people."

She looked up at him and saw he was smiling.

"Yes, you're right, Noel. The woman's lonely and she has no friends. That's all."

"I was wondering . . ." Noel paused. "I was thinking of inviting Faith to dinner. A proper dinner, not just a bowl of soup or something on toast. You know, to thank her for the notes and everything."

"Oh, yes?" Lisa said.

"I wonder, would Friday be a good night? You'll probably be out late, hitting the clubs with Moira. I'd feel safer having a meal here. It's such a temptation to order a bottle of wine or have a cocktail in a restaurant." Noel rarely spoke of his alcoholism at home. He went to meetings and there was no drink in the flat. It was unusual for him to bring the subject up.

He must be interested in Faith after all. Lisa's mind leapt ahead again. Suppose Faith really did move in with Noel? Where would that leave Lisa? But she mustn't start to fuss. That was her least attractive quality. Anton had told her when they were in Scotland that she was an absolute angel when she didn't fuss. And Noel deserved some happiness in his life.

"That's a great idea. I'll do a salad for you before I go out and maybe you could cook that chicken in ginger you do sometimes. It's very impressive. And we'll make sure to iron the tablecloth and napkins."

"It's only Faith. It's not a competition," Noel protested.

"But you want her to know you've gone to some trouble to entertain her, don't you?"

Noel realized with a shock that this was the first date he had planned in years.

"And in return you have to help me think of a present for Moira. Not too dear. I'm broke!"

"Ask Emily to look out for something from the thrift shop for you. She finds great things—new things, even."

"That's an idea." Lisa brightened. "Well, Frankie, social life around here is getting very lively. You're going to be hard pushed to keep up with us. . . ."

Frankie stretched her arms out to Lisa.

"*Mama,*" she said.

"Nearly there, Frankie, but it's Lee-Za, much posher." But from this child, "mama" was perfectly fine.

Faith was surprised and pleased to be invited.

"Will there be many people there?" she asked nervously.

"Just the two of us," Noel said. "Will that be all right?"

"Oh, fine!" Faith seemed very relieved. She smiled at him. "Thanks, Noel, I'm looking forward to dinner."

"Me too," said Noel. He wondered suddenly was she expecting that they would go to bed together. He realized he had never made love in his life while sober. He had heard some terrible stories on this topic at AA. It was apparently fraught with difficulties and had disastrous effects on performance. Many people had told his AA group that they had taken a quick shot of vodka just to see them right and were back on full-time drinking within a week.

But he would face that if and when it occurred. No point in destroying Wednesday thinking about Friday. This one-day-at-a-time thing really worked.

Friday eventually came.

Emily had found a small mother-of-pearl brooch as a gift for Lisa to give Moira. She even produced a little box and some black velvet. Moira couldn't help but like that.

Anton had laughed when Lisa had said she was going to Ennio's with Moira.

"That should be a bundle of fun," he had said dismissively.

"It will be fine," she said, suddenly feeling defensive.

"If you want cheapo pasta, a bottle of plonk and a couple of Italians bunching up their fingers to kiss them and say '*bella signora*'..."

"They're nice there." Why she was being protective towards this little trattoria, she didn't know.

"Yeah and we're nice in Anton's too, so why didn't you and the social worker choose us?"

"Be real, Anton. A Friday night! And anyway, it was her shout. She chose Ennio's."

He looked like a small boy who had been crossed. "I'd have given you early-bird rates all night."

"I know that, she didn't. See you."

"Are you coming round later? It's Teddy's birthday too and we're having a few drinks after closing time."

"Oh, no, we'll be hitting the clubs by then." She remembered Noel's expression. It was worth it to see the look of surprise and irritation on Anton's face.

. . .

Noel set the table at Chestnut Court. Lisa had left the salad in the fridge covered in cling wrap and his chicken-and-ginger dish was under foil and ready to put in the oven for twenty-five minutes. The potatoes were in a saucepan.

Frankie had been delivered to Declan and Fiona's: she was going to have a sleepover.

"Dada," she said as he waved her good-bye, and his heart turned over as it always did when she smiled at him. Now he was in the apartment waiting for a woman to come to supper, like someone normal would do.

Lisa had looked very well as she set out to the birthday celebration. It was so comforting to know that Anton was jealous, that he really thought she would go to a nightclub.

At Ennio's the host was waiting for them.

"*Che belle signore!*" he said, giving them each a small bunch of violets. Exactly as Anton had said he would. "Marco, *vieni qui, una tavola per queste due bellissime signore.*"

The son of the house bustled towards them and dusted chairs. Moira and Lisa thanked him profusely.

Lisa spotted that Maud was working there that night, and Marco saw Lisa recognize her.

"I think you know my friend and colleague Maud," he said proudly.

"Yes, indeed I do. Lovely girl," Lisa said. "And this is Moira Tierney, who chose the restaurant for her birthday celebration."

"Moira Tierney . . . ," Marco repeated the words fearfully. "Maud has mentioned your name to me." Written all over his face was the fact that the mention had perhaps not been the most cordial, but he struggled to remember his job of welcoming guests and handed them the menus.

They began choosing their food. If Moira said once that the markup on the food was enormous, she must have said it a dozen times.

"Imagine charging that for garlic bread!" she gasped, as if astonished.

"We don't have to have garlic bread," Lisa said.

"No, no, we'll have everything we want. It's a celebration," Moira said in a sepulchral voice.

"Indeed it is." Lisa was bright and positive. This looked like it would be a long night.

Emily went to Dr. Hat's house to check that he had his curry ready for his friend Michael. She wanted to show him that he should have a dish of sliced bananas and a little bowl of coconut as well.

To her surprise the table was set for three.

"Will his wife be with him?" Emily asked, surprised. Only Michael had been mentioned up to now.

"No, Michael never married. Another crusty old bachelor," Dr. Hat said.

"So who is the third person?"

"I was rather hoping that *you* would join us," he said hesitantly.

Paddy Carroll and his wife, Molly, were going to a butchers' dinner. It took place every year; the wives dressed up and it was held in a smart hotel. It was an occasion where Paddy Carroll had been known to over-imbibe, so Declan would drive them there and a taxi would be ordered to take them home.

Fiona waved them off as they left in a flurry, then she sat down with a big mug of tea to watch over the two little ones crawling around the floor before she had to settle them in their cribs. They were both a bit restless this evening and she was going to have to separate them if they were going to go to sleep. She was wondering if she might possibly be pregnant again. If she was, it would be great and Declan would be so pleased, but it would mean that they would have to stir themselves and make sure the house was ready for them to move into before the baby was born. They couldn't put Paddy and Molly through all that business of a crying baby again.

Finally, along with the second bottle of wine, Moira broached the subject of Eddie Kennedy. Lisa thought she understood the situation, but she didn't really see the problem.

"Of course you don't have to do anything for him," she said. "It was the luck of the draw that he got you as a social worker. You don't have to tell him about the cozy little homestead down there."

"But he bought that house before he got addled with drink. He's entitled to live there."

"Nonsense. He gave up all rights and entitlements when he went off to England. He chose to opt out of this life. He can't expect you to turf your father out and get his wife to take him back. She probably wouldn't want him anyway. . . ."

"But is he to die in a hostel because I don't want to disturb things?"

"He chose that route." Lisa was firm.

"If it was your father . . . ," Moira began.

"I hate my father. I wouldn't spit on him if he was on fire!"

"I feel guilty. I've always given my clients the best. I'm not doing this with Eddie Kennedy," Moira said bleakly.

"Suppose you made it up to him in other ways? You know, went to see him in the hostel, took him out for the odd afternoon."

Moira looked at her in disbelief. How could this be doing her duty? It would be crossing the thin line that divided professionalism from friendship. Entirely unsuitable.

Lisa shrugged. "Well, that's what I'd do, anyway." She caught Marco's eye, and in thirty seconds a little cake with one candle came from the kitchen. The waiters sang "Happy Birthday" and everyone in the restaurant clapped.

Moira was pink and flustered. She tried to cut the cake and all the filling oozed out of one side. Lisa took the knife from her.

"Happy birthday, Moira," she said, putting as much warmth into it as she could. To her amazement she saw the tears falling down Moira's face.

Thirty-five and this was probably the only birthday party she had ever had.

Up in Chestnut Court the dinner was going very well.

"Aren't you a dark horse, being able to cook like this!" Faith said appreciatively. She was easy to talk to—not garrulous, but she talked engagingly of her background.

She spoke briefly about the accident that had killed her fiancé, but she didn't dwell on it. Terrible things happened to a lot of people. They had to pick themselves up.

"Do you still love him?" Noel asked as he spooned out another helping of chicken.

"No. In fact I can barely remember him. And you, Noel, do you miss Frankie's mother a lot?" Faith asked.

"No, I'm a bit like you. I hardly remembered Stella, but then that was in my drinking days. I don't remember anything much from those times." He smiled nervously. "But I love to have Frankie around the place."

"Where is she now? I brought her a funny little book of animals. It's made of cloth, so it doesn't matter if she eats it!"

"Lisa dropped her in to Fiona and Declan's. Lisa's gone out to supper."

"With Anton?"

"No, with Moira, actually."

"A different kind of outing, certainly." Faith knew the cast of characters.

"You could say that." Noel beamed at her. This was all going so well.

. . .

Fiona had just brought Declan a mug of coffee when she heard running feet outside the door and there was Lizzie, disheveled and distraught.

"Can Declan come quickly? I'm so sorry to interrupt you, but Muttie's been sick and it's all blood!"

Declan was already out of his chair and grabbing his doctor's bag.

"I'll come in a minute—I'll have to sort out the kids," Fiona shouted.

"Fine." In seconds Declan was through the Scarlets' front door. Muttie was ashen-faced, and he had been vomiting into a bowl. Declan took in the scene at a glance. "A thing of nothing, Muttie. They'll have you as right as rain in the hospital."

"Couldn't you deal with it, Declan?"

"No, you need to be where they can take care of you properly."

"But it will take forever to get an ambulance," Muttie objected.

"We're going in my car. Get in there right now," Declan said firmly.

Lizzie wanted to go with them, but Declan persuaded her to wait for Fiona. He took her back inside the house and whispered that as the hospital might need to keep Muttie in overnight, the best thing was for her to go and pack a small bag for him. Fiona would bring Lizzie up to the hospital in a taxi when she was ready, and not to worry, he would make sure that Muttie was in safe hands. He knew that having something useful to do would calm her.

By now, Fiona had arrived and they quickly realized that they had to find somewhere for Johnny and Frankie to spend the evening and do it fast or there would be total confusion. Noel was having the first date of his life; his parents were away. Lisa had gone out with Moira—which at least would keep the social worker out of their hair; Emily would be the one to call on. Leaving Fiona to make the arrangements, Declan sped off with Muttie beside him, looking pale and frightened.

Emily had insisted that Dr. Hat serve the meal himself. After all, he had made it.

Michael proved to be a quiet, thoughtful man. He asked her gentle questions about her past life. It was as if he were checking her out for his old friend Hat. She hoped that she was giving a good account of herself. Hat was such a good and pleasant companion, she would hate to lose his friendship.

She was surprised when her phone rang in the pocket of her jacket as they were at the dining table. She wasn't expecting any calls.

"Emily, big crisis. Can you do baby patrol?" Fiona sounded frightened.

Emily didn't hesitate. "Certainly. I'm on my way!" She quickly excused herself and hastened down the road.

Outside the Carrolls' house all was confusion. Lizzie was there crying and clutching a small suitcase; Fiona was hovering between the Scarlets' front door and her own. Hooves was barking madly. Dimples was answering from the Carrolls' back garden. Declan had taken Muttie to hospital. The taxi was on its way for Fiona and Lizzie.

"I'm going up to the hospital with Lizzie to be with her while we wait for news of him," Fiona said as soon as Emily arrived.

"Can I move baby patrol up to Dr. Hat's house? I'm sort of in the middle of a meal there."

"Of course, Emily. I'm so sorry. I didn't mean to interrupt. . . ."

"No, it's fine, don't worry. Two old bachelors and myself. This will lower the age level greatly. Good luck—and let us know . . ."

"Right," Fiona said, as the taxi pulled up outside the house. She grabbed Lizzie and the suitcase and bundled her into the back of the car. "Emily, you are amazing. Key under the usual flowerpot."

"Go now," Emily ordered. She ran to the Carrolls' house and picked Johnny up out of his crib in the front room and fastened him into his buggy.

"We're going for a visit to Uncle Hat and Auntie Emily," she said. She pushed the baby buggy out the door, locked it behind her and then put the key carefully under the flowerpot.

Dr. Hat and Michael were suitably impressed with little Johnny. The boy, exhausted from the journey, fell asleep on Dr. Hat's sofa and was covered with a blanket. The meal continued seamlessly.

Hat admitted, when he produced dessert, that he had not made the meringues himself but had bought them in a local confectionery shop.

"I think he'd have gotten away with saying he made them himself, don't you, Michael?" said Emily.

Michael was flushed with wine and good humor. "I'd have believed anything Hat were to tell me tonight." He beamed at them. "Never saw such a change in a person. If that's what retirement did for you, Hat, then lead on, I say. And I do admire the way you all look after these children. It was never like that in our day—people were stressed and fussed and never believed that anyone else could look after a child for more than two minutes."

"Ah, they have it down to a fine art," Dr. Hat said proudly. "Whenever Johnny and Frankie need a minder, they're all here on tap."

"Frankie?" Michael asked.

"She's my cousin Noel's daughter. He's bringing her up as a single father and doing a great job of it too. Actually Noel has a date tonight. All of us chattering spinsters have great hopes for this girl Faith. He's entertaining her in his own apartment."

"And so Faith is meeting the baby tonight?" Michael asked.

"No, she knows the child already; she goes in to study there, you see. But the baby is out for the night to give them a bit of space, I think."

"So who's minding Frankie tonight?" Michael asked. His question was innocent—he was fascinated by this toy town atmosphere, with good Samaritans coming out of every house in the street.

Emily stopped to think.

"It can't be Lisa. She's going out with the dreaded Moira. The twins are out on the town. The Carrolls have gone to a butchers' dinner. Noel's parents, my uncle Charles and aunt Josie, are in the west . . . who *is* minding Frankie?" Emily felt the first constriction of alarm in her chest.

If Noel had been going to bring in someone from outside the circle he would have told them. Moira had been behaving like a Rottweiler at the thought of any new face on the horizon.

"If you'll excuse me, I'll call Noel," she said, "just to set my mind at rest."

"You'd interrupt the boy's first proper date with Faith?" Dr. Hat shook his head. "Think, Emily, she must be somewhere."

"I have run out of options, Hat—let me call Noel."

"I only want to say you'll be annoyed with yourself when it's all perfectly all right."

"No. I'll be able to sleep easy," she said.

"Noel, I'm so sorry," she began.

"Is anything wrong, Emily?" He was alert to her tone immediately.

"No, nothing. I was just checking something. Where is Frankie tonight?"

"Lisa took her down to Fiona and Declan's earlier. I'm having a friend to dinner."

"To the Carrolls' house?"

"Is everything all right, Emily?" he asked again.

"Everything's fine, Noel," she said and hung up immediately. "You two mind Johnny here. I must have left Frankie in the Carrolls' house. There was only one baby in the crib." She was out the door before they could ask any more.

Emily ran down St. Jarlath's Crescent at a greater speed than she had known to be possible. What had Fiona said? She hadn't said "babies." She had said "baby patrol." Her hand shook as she reached under the flowerpot for the key and opened the door.

"Frankie?" she called as she ran into the house.

There was no sound.

In the kitchen there was a second crib with some of Frankie's toys in it. Frankie's buggy was parked beside it. There was no sign of the child. The strength left Emily's legs, and she sat down on a kitchen chair to support herself.

Someone had let themselves in and taken Frankie.

How could this have happened?

Then the thought struck her.

Of course! Fiona had come back home to check on things. Yes, that must be it.

She ran to Muttie and Lizzie's house. It was dark and closed. She knew before she started hammering on the door that there was no one there. Now she was really frightened. Fingers starting to shake, she dialed Fiona's mobile number. As the number connected, she heard a phone start to ring from inside the Scarlet house. It was Fiona's ring tone—she recognized it. After a few seconds the ringing stopped and she heard the voice-mail message start.

Declan. She had to call Declan.

"Emily?" He answered straightaway. "Is everything all right? Is it the children?"

"Johnny's fine," she said straightaway. "He's asleep on Dr. Hat's sofa."

"And Frankie?" Declan suddenly sounded alarmed. "What about Frankie?"

But Emily had already started running.

Chapter Twelve

They tried to be methodical about it but panic overwhelmed them; the list was checked over and over. Signora and Aidan knew nothing about where Frankie was, but would join in any searches. No point in trying to contact Charles and Josie: they were miles away and couldn't do anything; they'd just go mad with worry. It would be ages before Paddy and Molly would be home from the butchers' dance. Paddy would be fueled with brandy and good cheer; Molly's shoes would be too tight. Who could have come into the Carrolls' house and spirited Frankie away? She couldn't have got out herself and Emily had been back into the house and searched the place from top to bottom. Anywhere, any small space a child might be able to crawl into—she must be here somewhere.

She wasn't.

Could somebody have been watching the house? It seemed less than possible and there was no sign of a break-in. There must be a rational explanation. Should the police be called?

Having left Faith in the flat to answer any calls and white-faced with anxiety, Noel ran in and out of all the houses in St. Jarlath's Crescent. Had anyone seen anything? Anything at all?

He had sent Lisa a text and asked her to call him from the ladies', out of Moira's earshot. Lisa was shocked at how frightened she felt when he told her the news. For the time being, she was *not* to come home. It didn't matter where she went, as long as she kept Moira occupied. She felt sure that Moira must be able to tell something was wrong; nailing a smile onto her face, she went back to the table.

Up at the hospital, Lizzie wandered up and down the corridors asking plaintively when she was going to be able to see how Muttie was getting on. Fiona persuaded her to come back into the waiting room and sit down. They would wait for Declan to come.

He arrived twenty minutes later. "Well, he's stable now but they're going to keep him in for a while." His voice was grim. "They've made him comfortable and he's sleeping," he said to Lizzie. "You'll probably not be able to speak to him until tomorrow but he should feel better after a good night's rest. We should all go home."

Lizzie was pleased with the news. "I'm glad he's getting a good rest. I'll leave his suitcase in for him for tomorrow."

"Do that, Lizzie," Fiona said, realizing that there was something Declan hadn't told her. Could this night get any worse?

It was a time of frantic comings and goings. Michael stayed with Johnny as Hat and Emily went through the whole thing over and over. At least a hundred times Emily must have said that she should never have gone along with the silly phrase "baby patrol." She should have asked what it meant and how many babies were involved.

Hat, in her defense, said that it was all Fiona's fault. Imagine having two babies in different rooms and not mentioning it! It was unheard-of.

Noel was almost out of his mind with grief and worry and rage— what were those idiotic women doing, risking his daughter's safety like that? How could they be so stupid as to abandon her in that house, leaving her prey to—who knew what? And as for him, it was all his own fault. Stella had trusted him with their daughter and he'd let her down, all because he'd wanted to spend some time with a woman. Now some monster, some pervert, had taken his little girl, and he might never see her again. He might never hold her in his arms and see her smile. He might never hear her voice calling him "Dada." If anyone had hurt her, if anyone had touched a hair of his Frankie's head . . . And in the middle of St. Jarlath's Crescent, Noel knelt down on the pavement and wept for his little girl.

Lisa managed to escape Moira on two occasions by going back to the ladies' room, but she couldn't go on doing this all night. She decided to persuade Moira to go to Teddy's birthday party at Anton's.

"But I won't know anyone," Moira had wailed.

"Neither will I. Most of them will be strangers to me, friends of silly April, but come on, Moira, it's free drink and it's your birthday too. Why not?" And as Moira agreed, Lisa dragged herself together. She wished that she was at home with Noel helping to coordinate the search. There *must* be an explanation. Lisa had heard very little except a trembling hysteria from Noel about what could have happened.

"Noel, don't hate me for saying this, but in the name of God, don't go back on the drink."

"No, Lisa, I won't." His voice was clipped.

"I know you're cross with me, but I *had* to say it."

"Yes, I realize you did."

"Go back to where we were before I said it. She's fine. There's been a misunderstanding. It will be sorted."

"Sure it will, Lisa," he said.

.   .   .

Sergeant Sean O'Meara had seen it all and done it all and, if he was honest, he would say that most of it was fairly depressing, but this occasion was just bizarre.

An extremely drunk man called Paddy Carroll was explaining over and over that he had been at a butchers' dinner and someone had spiked his drinks. He had started to behave foolishly and so he agreed that his wife should take him home in a taxi. The wife, a Mrs. Molly Carroll, said that she was not a serious partaker of alcohol herself and had been delighted when her husband agreed to come home with her, as her feet were killing her. But when they got home, they were bemused to find Frankie asleep in the crib and their own family—son, daughter-in-law and grandson—nowhere to be found.

They had tried to contact several people, but hadn't been able to speak to anyone who might know what was going on. They'd tried to find the child's father but had arrived at his apartment block not knowing which flat he lived in. What sort of people don't put their names on doorbells, asked Paddy Carroll, looking around him accusingly. What sort of people don't want people to know where they lived? So what were they to do?

"So, you want us to find this Noel Lynch. Is that it?" Sergeant O'Meara asked. "Had you ever thought of ringing him?" And he handed the phone to Paddy Carroll, who suddenly looked even more confused.

Faith was pacing up and down at Chestnut Court. She had a sheet of paper beside the phone and she perched nervously beside it, trying not to jump when it rang. Anyone who phoned in was asked for their telephone number, but she had little information to give out. Yes, Frankie was still missing; no, Noel wasn't there, he was out looking. No, they hadn't called the police yet, but the time was fast approaching when they would have to do so. They had agreed that if Frankie were not found within the hour, Faith would call the guards. There wasn't long to go.

Noel had phoned her eight times already, knowing as he did that she would call him the moment there was any news.

She checked her watch again. It was time. She had to call the police. Hand shaking, she reached for the phone, and as she did so, it rang. Her stomach lurched. Anxiously she answered.

At first, she thought it was a crank call. The man's voice on the other end of the phone sounded muffled, incoherent, angry, she thought at first, but soon she realized he might be drunk. No, Noel wasn't there, he was . . . No, he had been at home earlier in the evening but . . . No, his daughter was missing and the police were about to be called. . . .

"But that's what I'm telling you," the voice said. "I've got his daughter here. She's with us now. . . ." And suddenly Faith heard the unmistakable sound of Frankie crying.

"She's *found*, Noel! Not a hair of her head touched," she said. "She's great. She's asking for her daddy."

"Have you seen her? Is she there with you?"

"No. They brought her to the Garda station. It was the Carrolls. It was Paddy and Molly Carroll. It was *all* a misunderstanding. They were looking for *you*."

"What the hell did they mean by that? What do you mean, *looking for me*? We were in all night!" Noel was torn between overpowering relief and fury.

"No, it's all right—don't get angry. They got enough of a shock already."

"They got a shock! What about the rest of us? What happened?"

"They came home early from their do and they found her in the crib alone in the house. They must have arrived just after Fiona and Lizzie set off for the hospital. They called on all the neighbors, but there was no one around—Declan and Fiona were at the hospital with the Scarlets, Emily had been at Dr. Hat's but they didn't know that and, of course, Charles and Josie weren't there. They tried to call Fiona, but she'd left her phone at Lizzie's. Declan's phone was busy, so they came to Chestnut Court to see you. Only by the sound of it they'd got the wrong flat number and were pressing the wrong doorbell. By the time we knew Frankie was missing they were on their way to the Garda. They thought something was terribly wrong and quite rightly didn't want to put the child at further risk. But she's fine and we need to get over there to pick her up."

But Noel was still distraught. "Frankie's in a police station. What chance will I have of keeping her once bloody Moira gets to hear of this?"

"Don't worry—I'll call Lisa as soon as I put the phone down and let her know Frankie is found. Then I'll put together some things for Frankie—why don't you collect me here and we'll go up together? Let's get her home before Moira ever knows she was missing. . . ."

Sergeant O'Meara had no idea what they were all doing in a police station, and he wished someone, anyone, would shut the screaming child up. Mrs. Carroll kept bouncing the baby up and down, but the decibel level was getting higher. It was all starting to grate on him.

"Why *exactly* did you bring the child here? If you know who she is and all belonging to her?"

Paddy Carroll tried to explain. "It seemed like the right thing to do at the time. Be on the safe side," he said.

"The safe side of what?" Sergeant O'Meara asked, raising his voice above the din.

Paddy wished that his mind was less fuzzy and his speech more clear. "Could I have a cup of tea?" he asked plaintively.

"It's a pity you didn't think of having tea earlier in the evening," Mrs. Molly Carroll said sharply.

Sergeant O'Meara went to get tea, glad to get away from the screaming baby for a moment. "So this Noel Lynch is on his way here now," he said wearily, when he came back with the tea.

"There he is!" Paddy Carroll cried out, pointing at the glass door out in the front office. "There he is! Noel! Noel! Come in here! We've got Frankie for you!"

And Sergeant O'Meara rescued Paddy Carroll's teacup just before it pitched onto the child as Noel threw himself at his baby girl.

"Frankie! Are you all right?" he cried, his voice muffled with emotion. "Darling little Frankie. I'm so sorry, really I am. I'll never leave you again. . . ." Frantically, he checked that she was all right, uninjured in any way; then he wiped her face and her nose, and dried her eyes.

Behind him, meanwhile, stood a small, slim woman with green eyes and a big smile. She was carrying one of Frankie's coats and a woolly scarf; more important, she was carrying a jar of baby food, which she handed to Noel straightaway.

As Noel fed his daughter, almost magically, the crying stopped, the baby calmed down and peace was restored.

Sergeant O'Meara was profoundly grateful that the situation seemed to be sorting itself out.

More and more people were arriving: a stressed-out middle-aged woman with frizzy hair and an older man, wearing a hat like something from a black-and-white movie.

"Oh, Frankie! I'm so sorry . . ." The woman bent down to kiss the baby girl. "I didn't know you were there. I'll never forgive myself. *Never.*"

The man in the hat introduced himself as Dr. Hat; he looked like the only person with any degree of control. "If ever there was a case of all's well that ends well . . . it's here." He beamed at everyone. "And well done, Mr. and Mrs. Carroll. You did exactly the right thing in the circumstances. Noel, we'll all get out of here, don't you think, and leave Detective O'Meara to his business. No need to write a report at all—wouldn't you agree?"

The sergeant looked at Dr. Hat gratefully. The writing of a report about this was going to be Gothic. "If everyone's satisfied . . ." he began.

"I'm so sorry about this," Dr. Hat said to him quietly. "It's a terrible waste of your time, but I assure you that it was well meant. We're sorry to have disturbed you—but no harm done. . . ."

And as they all shuffled out of the police station, Sergeant O'Meara heard them saying to one another in tones of relief that Moira need never know a thing about any of it. He wondered vaguely who Moira might be, but it was late and he could now go home to his wife, Ita, who always had a hundred stories of her day's work on the wards in St. Brigid's. He would tell her this one, if he had the energy to unpick who was who.

Muttie was asleep when Lizzie arrived at his bedside. They told her that he would need a scan in the morning but that he was comfortable now; far better for her to be at home and get a good night's sleep. She left the suitcase for him beside his bed.

"Can I leave him a note?" she asked, fearful of strange places and unfamiliar surroundings. A nurse brought her pen and paper.

Lizzie pinned a note to the suitcase.

> *Muttie, my darling, I've gone home but I'll be back tomorrow. You're going to be fine. The next time we use this suitcase will be when we go to New York and have dinner in Chinatown.*
> *Love from Lizzie*

She felt better, she told Declan, now that she had written a letter.

Declan's relief at the safe return of Frankie was tempered by what he had just discovered: he had spoken to the medical team that had examined Muttie. The cancer had spread all over his body.

It would not be long now.

Lisa thought that the night would never end. Teddy's birthday party at Anton's was in full swing when they got there. They had just put on music and were beginning to dance. Straightaway she noticed April dancing around Anton.

"Hey, that's not dancing! That's lap dancing!" she called in a very loud voice. A few people laughed. Anton looked annoyed.

April went on weaving and squirming.

"Suit yourself," she said to Lisa. "You dance your way—I dance mine."

Lisa, her rage fueled by alcohol and jealousy, was about to engage in further conversation, but Moira interrupted quickly.

"I need a glass of water, Lisa. Can you come and get one with me?"

"You don't need water," Lisa said.

"Oh, but I do," Moira countered, pushing her towards the ladies' room. There she took a glass of water and offered it to Lisa.

"You're not expecting me to drink this, are you?"

"I think you should, then we'll go home."

Lisa was only just holding herself together. Moira must never know Frankie was missing.

"I'll think about it," she said.

Moira spoke firmly. "I think it would be wise. Yes, then I'll phone us a taxi."

"No, we can't go home. Wherever we go, we can't go home!" Lisa said in fright.

Moira asked mildly, "Well, where *do* you want to go, then?"

"I'll think," Lisa promised. Just then her own phone buzzed with a text message. Trembling, she read it.

ALL CLEAR. COME HOME ANYTIME. F SAFE AND SOUND.

"They *found* her!" Lisa cried.

"Who?" Moira paused in the middle of talking to the taxi firm.

Lisa stopped herself in time. "My friend Mary! She was lost and now she's found!" she shouted, with a very unfocused look on her face.

"But you were talking to her earlier, weren't you?" Moira was perplexed.

"Yes and she got lost. And then found since then," Lisa said foolishly.

Moira completed her call to the taxi and began to support Lisa towards the exit. On the way, they passed Teddy, the birthday boy, who whispered in Moira's ear.

"Well done. Anton will owe you for this. We have an unexploded bomb here," he said, nodding towards Lisa.

"Well, it's a pity he wasn't able to do something about it!" Moira retorted.

"Not his problem." Teddy shrugged.

"Good enough to sleep with, but not important enough to be nice to, right?"

"I just said he'd be grateful to you. She was about to make a scene."

Moira pushed past him, supporting Lisa into the taxi. Her dismal outlook on men seemed to have been confirmed tonight.

Lisa sang a little in the taxi. Sad songs about loss and infidelity, and then they were in Chestnut Court.

"Lisa's home, slightly the worse for wear," Moira said into the entry phone.

"Can you help her in, please, Moira?"

"Certainly."

Noel put Frankie down for the first time since she had been found. He realized he had been clinging to her since they came back to the flat.

Faith had washed the dishes and tidied up the place.

Moira brought Lisa in the door and settled her into a chair.

"Partly my fault. We had a lot of wine at Ennio's and then we went to this party at Anton's."

"Oh, I see," Noel said.

"You'll be fine, Lisa," Faith said, holding Lisa's trailing hand.

"Oh, Moira, I'm Faith, by the way. A friend of Noel and Lisa's from the college."

"How do you do?" Moira was gruff. She felt an unreasoning jealousy of Lisa. Nobody was blaming her for having become drunk. There was a household of people welcoming her. Even the child had stretched out her little arms towards Lisa as she lay slumped in her chair. If it had happened to Moira, she would have had to go home to an empty apartment. It seemed that almost everyone else in the world had sorted out his or her relationships while she, Moira, still was alone.

She left abruptly. Lisa let out a deep breath.

"I didn't tell her," she said.

"I know you didn't," Noel said.

"You did a great job," Faith said soothingly.

"Good. Glad it's sorted," Lisa said, her voice slurring. She began to slide off the chair, but they caught her before she reached the ground.

"When I think," she said intensely, "when I remember what I said to you, Noel, that it would be terrible if you were to fall into drink . . . and then I went and did it myself . . ."

"It doesn't matter, Lisa. You'll be fine tomorrow," Noel said. "And you did great work keeping Moira distracted. You did brilliantly."

"Why don't we give Lisa a hand to get into bed?" Faith made it all sound as if it had been a completely normal evening, what everyone did every night all over the place. . . .

When she got home, Lizzie was surprised to see so many people in her house. Her sister Geraldine was there, her daughter Cathy and Cathy's husband, Tom Feather. The twins and Marco were there, and there were constant phone calls coming in from Chicago and Australia. Everyone seemed to be making tea and Marco had provided a tray of cakes.

"Won't Muttie be disappointed to have missed all this," Lizzie said, and people looked away before she could see the pain in their faces.

Eventually they persuaded her to go to bed. The sitting room was still full of people. Cathy went upstairs with her mother and tried to reassure her.

"They're terrific in St. Brigid's, Mam—don't be worrying about him. Geraldine's just been saying how good they are. All the best consultants and everything. They'll have Da right in no time."

"I think he's very sick," Lizzie said.

"But he's in the right place," Cathy said for the twentieth time.

"He'd prefer to be in his own home," Lizzie said for the thirtieth time.

"And he will be, Mam, so you're to get to sleep so that you'll be up and ready for him when he *does* come home. You're asleep on your feet."

That worked. Lizzie made a slight movement towards the bed and Cathy had her nightdress ready. Her mother looked so small and frail; Cathy wondered would she be able to bear all that lay ahead.

Maud said that Marco had texted to say that he and Dingo Duggan would be available night and day with Dingo's van if anyone needed to be driven anywhere.

Marco had said, "I am so sorry about your grandfather. Please God, he will get better."

"Please God, indeed," Simon said, when Maud read him the text message.

"I think he just says that automatically."

"Like Lizzie says 'DV,' " Simon agreed.

"Yes. I remember Mother used to say that too, except that she started to say 'VD' instead," Maud said. "Dad would explain it over and over. DV meant *Deo volente*, God willing, but Mother always nodded and said 'VD.' " Simon and Maud talked very little about the parents who had abandoned them when they were young. This was their home. Muttie was the man they loved, rather than the elegant father who had gone away on his travels. Lizzie was the mother they never really had. Their own mother had always been frail, with a light grip on reality. If they had heard that either of their biological parents had died, there would be a minor sense of regret. The news about Muttie was as if somebody had stuck a knife right into their bodies.

. . .

Nurse Ita O'Meara looked down at the man in the bed. He was in very poor shape. All she could do for him was to keep him under observation and make him comfortable.

"What's your name?" he asked her.

"I'm Ita, Mr. Scarlet."

"Then I'm Muttie," he said.

"Well, Muttie, what can I do for you? A cup of tea?"

"Yes, I'd love some tea. Could you sit down and talk to me for a bit?"

"I could indeed, and would be glad to. We're not busy tonight."

"Ita, you see, you don't know me from a hole in the ground."

"That's true, but I'll get to know you," she reassured him.

"No, that's not what I meant. I *want* someone who doesn't know me."

"Oh, yes?"

"It's easier to talk to a stranger. Will you tell me—am I for the chop?"

Ita had been asked this question before. It was never easy to answer. "Well, you know your illness is serious and that we're at the stage where all we can do is make you comfortable. But you're not on the way out tonight."

"Good. But some night soon, do you think?"

"It won't be long, Muttie, but I'd say you've time to sort things out." Ita was reassuring. "Is there anyone you want me to call for you?"

"How do you know I want to sort things out?" he asked.

"Everyone does at night, especially their first night in hospital. They want to make speeches and talk to lawyers and they want to talk to all kinds of people. Then, when they're leaving here, they've forgotten it all."

Muttie's eyes beseeched her. "And do you think I'll get out of here?"

Ita looked him in the eye. "I tell you, as sure as I know my own name, you'll go home from here and then you'll forget all about us. You won't remember me and my cups of tea anymore."

"I will indeed remember you and how kind you are. I'll tell everyone about you. And you're right, I do want to make speeches and talk to lawyers and tell people things. I hope to do it all from home."

"Good man, yourself, Muttie," Ita said, as she took his empty teacup away. She knew he didn't have long, but she'd do her best to make his mind easy. She sighed. He was such a warm little man. Why was he being taken when so many grumpy and sour-faced people were left for years with nobody involved in their lives? It was beyond understanding. She and Sean sometimes said it was very hard to believe in a kind, all-knowing God when you saw the random way fate worked. A decent man with a huge family and group of friends was about to die.

Sean would have similar stories from being a policeman. A kid who had joined a gang and had been caught on his first outing, faced with a criminal record; a mother who had no access to money of any kind, shoplifting to get food for her baby and ending up in court.

Life was many things, but it certainly wasn't fair.

It was clear that Muttie wanted to go home, so they contacted the palliative-care team. Two nurses would visit him each day. After three days, Ita handed him over to a small crowd of people, all of them delighted to see him coming home. Two of Muttie's children, Mike and Marian, together with Marian's husband, Harry, had arrived from Chicago, which shocked him.

"You must be made of money that you fly all that way just to see me. Aren't I grand? I'm going home today and Ita's going to come to see me," Muttie added.

"Oh, trust him to find someone else the moment I leave him out of my sight!" Lizzie said, with a laugh of pride in the notion of Muttie the Lothario.

· · ·

Muttie's Associates from the pub were anxious to see him when he returned. Lizzie wanted to keep them at bay, but her daughter Cathy wasn't so sure.

"He relaxes when he's talking to them," Cathy said.

"But is it sensible to have six big men in the sitting room when he's so tired all the time?" Lizzie wasn't sure how much relaxation that would involve. Cathy knew that she was trying to restore order to the home; her brother and sister were, she knew, going to be staying for some time. They all realized their father only had a very short time to live.

Much as Lizzie and Cathy wanted to keep Muttie to themselves, with only the family around him, he did seem to blossom when friends, neighbors and Associates visited. He had always been a man who loved talking with others. None of that side of him had disappeared. It was only his little thin body that showed any sign of the disease that was killing him.

Hooves sat at his feet most of the day. He stopped eating and lay in his basket listlessly.

"Hooves and I," said Muttie, "we're not able to get up and about much at the moment. Maybe tomorrow . . ."

Cathy and Lizzie provided endless cups of tea as a file of people passed through each day. The Associates all came together in a group and the women would hear bursts of laughter as they planned a great new world—a world without the present government, the previous governments, the banks and the law.

The Associates were mild men who talked big, and Muttie had always been at their center. They were jovial and blustering when they were with him, but Cathy could see their faces fall when they were out of his presence.

"It won't be long now, God save us all," said one of them, a man not usually known to respect the Almighty and ask for divine help.

But mainly people came in one by one, monitored by Lizzie and Cathy. They were given fifteen minutes at the most. The kind Ita O'Meara came. She spoke about everything except illness. They talked horses and greyhounds. "Very sound woman," Muttie remarked approvingly when she left. And they came in their droves, first asking Lizzie what would be a good time. She kept a notebook on the hall table.

Fiona and Declan came and brought little Johnny with them. They told their secret to Muttie: that they were expecting another baby. He said it would remain a secret right up to the end of his life.

Dr. Hat came and brought some scones that he had made himself. Emily Lynch had been teaching him to cook, and it wasn't bad at all if you put your mind to it. Muttie promised that when he got stronger he would think about it.

Josie and Charles came and talked about how a devotion to St. Jarlath could help in almost any situation. Muttie thanked them and said he was as interested in St. Jarlath as the next man and that if ever he needed him he would certainly try to get in touch with the saint. However, fortunately, he was getting better now and would be back to full strength before long.

Like everyone else, Charles and Josie Lynch were mystified. They so wanted to talk to Muttie about their inheritance from Mrs. Monty and how it should be spent or invested. Up to now they hadn't told anyone how much money was involved, not even Noel. But it seemed insensitive to talk about such things to a man who was so near death. Could Muttie really not know that he was dying?

Molly and Paddy Carroll felt the same. "He's talking of going to New York in a couple of months' time." Molly was genuinely puzzled. "Muttie won't go as far as the River Liffey, for heaven's sake—doesn't he know that?"

It was a mystery.

Noel came and brought Frankie. As Frankie sat on Muttie's knee and offered him her sippy cup, Noel talked more openly than he did to anyone. He told Muttie about the terrible fright when Frankie had been lost and how he had felt a pain in his chest as bad as if someone had put a great spade into him and lifted out his insides.

"You've made a grand job of this little girl," Muttie said approvingly.

"I sometimes dream that she's not my little girl at all and that someone comes to take her away," Noel confessed.

"That will never happen, Noel."

"Wasn't I lucky that Stella contacted me? Suppose she hadn't— then Frankie would be growing up in a different place and she'd never know any of you."

"And wasn't she lucky that she got you, even though you work too hard," Muttie said begrudgingly.

"I have to work hard. I want to have some kind of a job that I'd be proud of by the time she's old enough to know what I'm doing."

"And you gave up the gargle for her. That wasn't easy."

"It's not too bad most of the time. I'm so busy, you see, but there are days when I could murder six pints. Those are bad days."

"What do you do?" Muttie wanted to know.

"I ring my buddy in AA, and he comes over or meets me for coffee."

"Marvelous bloody organization. Never needed them myself, fortunately, but they do the job." Muttie was full of approval.

"You're a great fellow, Muttie," Noel said unexpectedly.

"I'm not the worst," Muttie agreed, "but haven't I a great family around me. I'm luckier than anyone I ever heard of. There's nothing they wouldn't do for us, traveling like millionaires back from Chicago because I had a bit of a turn back there. And as for the twins . . . ! If I lived in a high-class hotel, I couldn't get better food served to me. They're always coming up with something new for me." Muttie's smile was broad at the thought of it all.

Noel held Frankie tight and she, with her interest in sharing the sippy cup now complete, returned her father's hug. Noel wondered why he dreamed that she would be taken away. She was his daughter. His flesh and blood.

Marco came to see Muttie. He was dressed in a collar and tie as if he were going somewhere very formal. Lizzie said that of course he must go in to see Muttie, but to go very gently. Hooves had died during the night, and even though they had tried to keep it from Muttie he had known there was something wrong. Eventually, they had had to tell him.

"Hooves was a great dog—we won't demean him by crying over him," he said.

"Right," Lizzie agreed. "I'll tell the others."

When Marco was ushered in he came and stood beside the bed.

"I am so sorry about your dog, Mr. Scarlet."

"I never thought he'd go before me, Marco. But it's all for the best—he'd have been very lonely without me."

"Mr. Scarlet, I know you're not well and it's probably the wrong time to ask you this, but there is a question I would love to ask you."

"And what would that be, Marco?" Muttie smiled at the boy. The good suit, the anxious face, the sweaty palms. It was written all over him what question he was going to ask.

"I would like to ask you to give me the honor of your granddaughter's hand in marriage," Marco said stiffly.

"You want to marry Maud? She's very young, Marco—she hasn't grown up properly and seen the world or anything."

"But *I* would show her the world, Mr. Scarlet. I would look after her so well, see that she wanted for nothing."

"I know you would, lad, and have you asked her yourself?"

"Not yet—it's important I ask the father or grandfather first."

"I'm not her grandfather—you know that."

"She thinks of you as her grandfather, she loves you as if you were."

Muttie blew his nose. "Well, that's good, because that's the way Lizzie and I feel about her and Simon. But how can Maud marry you if she's going to New Jersey with Simon?"

"She's not going now, they've put that off," Marco said.

"That's only because I have been sick. They'll go . . . you know . . . afterwards."

"You will be here for a long time, Mr. Scarlet."

"No, son, I won't, but I'm sure you and Maud have it all worked out between you."

"I couldn't tell her I wanted to marry her until I asked you first. . . ." The boy's handsome face was beseeching him to give his blessing.

"And would she work with you in your father's restaurant?"

"Yes, for the moment, if she liked to do that, then we would both like to open a restaurant of our own. It may be many years ahead but my father says he will give me some money. You must have no fears about her—she will be treasured by our family."

Muttie looked at him. "If Maud says she would like to marry you, then I would be delighted."

"Thank you, dear Mr. Scarlet," said Marco, hardly daring to believe his good luck.

Lisa came to see Muttie also.

"I don't know you well, Mr. Scarlet, but you're a great character. I heard you'd been ill and I was wondering if there was anything I could do for you?"

Muttie looked around to make sure there was no one in the room with them.

"If I gave you fifty euro, could you put it on the nose of Not the Villain for me?"

"Oh, Mr. Scarlet, really . . ."

"It's my money, Lisa. Can't you do that for me? You *did* say you wanted to help me."

"Sure. I'll do it. What odds do you expect?"

"Ten to one. Don't take less."

"But then you'd win five hundred," she said, stunned.

"And you will get an enabler's fee," Muttie said, laughing heartily as Lizzie bustled in to clear the teacups and arrange a little rest time before the next visitor.

. . .

Lisa didn't know where there were any local betting shops, but Dingo Duggan was able to come up with the name of a nearby place.

"I'll drive you there," he said helpfully.

Dingo rather fancied Lisa and he liked to be seen with a good-looking girl sitting up front in his van.

"Got a good tip, then?" he asked.

"Someone asked me to put fifty euro on a horse at ten to one."

"God, that must be a great horse," Dingo said wistfully. "Wouldn't it be wonderful if you were to drop the name to me. I mean it won't shorten the price or anything. I have only ten euro, but it would be great to have a hundred. Great altogether."

Lisa told him the name of the horse but warned him, "The source is not entirely reliable, Dingo. I'd hate to see you lose your money."

"Don't worry," Dingo reassured her. "I have a very sharp mind."

Lisa felt out of place in the betting shop, and the presence of Dingo made it worse.

"Where are you off to now?" Dingo asked when the transaction was over.

"I'm going to see Anton," Lisa said.

"I'll drive you there," Dingo offered.

"No, thank you—I need a walk to clear my head and I've got to get my hair done too."

These were perfectly ordinary things to do, but Dingo noticed that Lisa announced them as if they were matters of huge importance. He shrugged.

Women were very hard to understand.

Katie sighed when Lisa came in. Yet another demand for a quick fix. The salon was already full. Had she ever heard of the appointment system?

"I need something, Katie," Lisa said.

"It will be half an hour at least," Katie said.

"I'll wait." Lisa was unexpectedly calm and patient.

Katie glanced at her from time to time. Lisa had magazines in her lap, but she never looked at them. Her eyes and mind were far away.

Then Katie was ready. "Big date?" she asked.

"No. Big conversation, actually."

"With Anton?"

"Who else?"

"You'd want to be careful, Lisa." Katie was concerned.

"I've been careful for years and where has it got me?" Lisa looked, without pleasure, at her reflection in the mirror. Her pale face and wet hair showed up the dark circles under her eyes.

"We'll make you lovely," said Katie, who seemed to have read her thoughts.

"It would help if I looked a bit lovelier, all right." Lisa smiled very weakly. "Listen, I want you to cut it all off. I want very short hair, cropped short all over."

"You're out of your mind—you've always had long hair. Don't do anything reckless."

"I want it short, choppy, a really edgy style. Will you do it or do I have to go to a rival?"

"I'll do it, but you're going to wake up tomorrow and wish you hadn't done it."

"Not if you give me a good cut, I won't."

"But you said he liked you with long hair," Katie persisted.

"Then he'll have to like me with short hair," Lisa countered.

It was achieved in two hours: a full makeup, a manicure and a new hairdo. Lisa felt a lot better. She offered to pay, but Katie waved it away.

"Don't say anything to Anton in a temper. Say nothing that you don't want to stand over. Be very careful."

"Why are you telling me this? You don't like Anton. You don't think he's right for me," Lisa asked in confusion.

"I know. But you like him and I like you a lot, so I want you to be happy."

Lisa kissed her sister. It was a rare thing to happen.

Katie felt it was unreal. Lisa, always so prickly and distracted, had actually put her arms around her, hugged her and kissed her on the cheek.

What next?

Lisa walked purposefully towards Anton's. This was a good time to catch him. The afternoons were easier and less fussed. All she would have to do was get rid of Teddy and hunt April off the premises if she was there, then she would talk to Anton properly.

Teddy saw her coming in but didn't recognize her at first.

"Fasten your seat belt," he hissed at Anton.

"Oh, God, not today, not on top of everything else . . ." Anton groaned.

When Lisa came in, she looked well and she knew it. She walked confidently and had a big smile on her face. She knew they were looking at her, Anton and Teddy, registering shock at the difference in her. The short hair gave her confidence; it was much lighter than before, still golden and silky. She smiled from one to the other, turning her head so that they could get a good view of her and her changed look.

"Teddy, will you forgive me—I have to talk to Anton about something for a short while?" She spoke on a rising note as if she were asking a question to which there was only one answer.

Teddy looked at Anton, who shrugged. So then he left.

"Well, Lisa, what is it? You look terrific, by the way."

"Thank you so much, Anton. How terrific do I look?"

"Well, you look very different, shiny, sort of. Your hair is gone!"

"I had it cut this morning."

"So I see. Your beautiful long golden hair . . ." He sounded bemused.

"It just covered the floor of the salon. In the olden days they used to sell their hair for wigs—did you know that?"

"No, I didn't," Anton said weakly.

"Oh, they did. Anyway, there we are."

"I liked your hair—in fact, I *loved* your long hair," he said regretfully.

"Did you, Anton? You *loved* my long hair?"

"You look different now, changed somehow, still gorgeous but different somehow."

"Good, so you like what you see?"

"This is silly, Lisa. Of course I like it. I like you."

"That's it? You like me?"

"Is this Twenty Questions or what? Of course I like you. You're my friend."

"Friend—not *love?*"

"Oh, well, love. Whatever . . ." He was annoyed now already.

"Good, because I love you. A lot," she said agreeably.

"Aw, come on, Lisa. Are you drunk again?" he asked.

"No, Anton. Stone cold, and the one time I ever did get drunk, you weren't very kind to me. You more or less ordered Teddy to throw me out of here."

"You were making a fool of yourself. You should thank me."

"I don't see it that way."

"Well, I was the one who was sober on that occasion—believe me, you were better out of here before even more people saw you."

"What do you think of when you think of me? Do you love me a lot or only a little?"

"Lisa, these are only words. Will you stop this thirteen-year-old chat?"

"You say you love me when we make love."

"Everyone says that," Anton said defensively.

"I don't think so."

"Well, I don't know. I haven't conducted a survey on it." He was really annoyed now.

"Calm down, Anton."

"I'm totally calm . . ."

"It would make this discussion easier if you didn't fly into a temper. Just tell me how important I am in your life."

"I don't know . . . very important—you do all the designs; you have lots of good ideas; you're very glamorous and I fancy you a lot. Now will that do?"

"And do you see me as part of your future?" She was still unruffled.

There was a silence.

Lisa remembered Katie's advice not to be reckless, not to say anything she couldn't stand over. Maybe he would say no, that she wasn't part of the future for him. This would leave her like an empty, hollow shell, but she didn't think he would say it.

Anton looked uncomfortable. "Don't talk to me about the future. None of us knows where we will be in the great future."

"We're old enough to know," Lisa said.

"Do you know what Teddy and I were talking about now when you came in and turfed him out?"

"No. What?"

"The future of this restaurant. The takings are appalling, we're losing money hand over fist. The suppliers are beginning to scream. The bank isn't being helpful. Some days we're almost empty for lunch. Today we had only three tables. We'd be better giving everyone who booked fifty euro and telling them to go away. Tonight we will be only half full. Investors notice these things. It needs some kind of a lift. It's going stale. You want to talk about the future—I don't think there is one."

"Do you see *me* in your future?" Lisa asked again.

"Oh, God Almighty, Lisa, I do if you could come up with some ideas rather than bleating like a teenager. That is if we *have* a future here at all . . ."

"Ideas—is that what you want?" Her voice was now, if anything, dangerously composed.

Anton looked at her nervously. "You're a great ideas woman."

"Okay. Light lunches—low-calorie healthy lunches in one part of the dining room, where they can't see roast beef or tiramisu going past. And even that fool April could get you some publicity for this. Oh, and you could organize a weekly section on a radio show where people could send in their recipes for things that are under two hundred and fifty calories and you could judge them. Are those good ideas?"

"As usual, you're right on the button. Will we call in the others to discuss this?"

"And what ideas do you have about me?" she asked.

"Are you still on this thing?"

"Just tell me. Tell me now—answer me and I'll stop asking you," she promised.

"Okay. I admire you a lot. I'm your friend. . . ."

"And lover . . . ," she added.

"Well, yes, from time to time. I thought you felt the same about it all."

"Like what, exactly?"

"That it was something nice we shared—but not the meaning of life or anything. Not a steady road to the altar."

"So why did you continue to have me around?"

"As I've said, you're bright, very bright, you're lovely and you're fun. And also I think a little lonely."

As she heard the words, something changed in Lisa's head. It was like a car moving into another gear. It was almost as if she were coming out of a dream. She could take his indifference, his infidelity, his careless ways.

She could not take his pity.

"And you might be a little lonely too, Anton, when this place fails. When Teddy has bailed out and gone to another trendy place, when little Miss April has flown off to something that's successful. There's nowhere in her little life for failure. When people say, 'Anton? Isn't he the one who used to own some restaurant . . . popular for a while but it disappeared without trace,' you might well be lonely then too. So let's hope someone will take pity on you and you'll see how it feels."

"Lisa, please . . ."

"Good-bye, Anton."

"You'll come back when you're more yourself."

"I think not." She was still composed.

"Why are you so angry with me, Lisa?" His head was on one side—his persuasive position.

But it didn't change her mind. "I'm angry with myself, Anton. I had a perfectly good job and I left it because of you. I meant to get other clients, but there was always something to be done here. I'm broke to the world. I'm depending on a horse called Not the Villain to win a race today because if he does I get something called an enabling fee and I'll be able to buy my share of the groceries for the flat where I have a room."

"Not the Villain," Anton said slowly. "That's how I see myself—I didn't think you were serious. I really am actually like that horse you've put money on. I'm not the villain here, you know."

"I know. That's why I'm angry. I got it so wrong. . . ."

Teddy heard the door bang closed and came in.

"Okay?" he asked.

"Teddy, if this place looked seriously like going under, would you go somewhere else?"

"Little bitch—she told you," Teddy said.

"Told me what?"

"She must have seen me or heard somehow. I went to the new hotel on the river to know if there might be a vacancy and they said they'd see. This city is worse than a small village. Lisa must have heard it from them."

"No, she didn't even know about it." Anton suddenly felt very tired. There had been something very final about the way Lisa had left the restaurant. But it was all nonsense, wasn't it? She hadn't been serious about any of it. Probably some of her girlfriends were settling down and getting pregnant and she felt broody. And that idea about the light lunches wasn't a bad one at all. They could get little cards designed with some kind of logo on them. Lisa would be great at that when she stopped all this other nonsense. . . .

Lisa walked out of the restaurant jauntily, and as she moved through the crowded streets she was aware that people glanced at her with what she thought was admiration. She wouldn't think about what she had just said and done. She would compartmentalize things. Park this side of her life here and leave it until it was needed again. Concentrate on another side of life. This was a city full of promise, potential friends and even possible loves. She would tidy Anton away and hold her head high.

Then, quite unexpectedly, she met Emily, who was wheeling Frankie in her buggy.

"I'm getting her used to shopping—she's going to spend years of her life doing it so she might as well know what it's all about."

"Emily, you are funny. What have you bought today?"

"A bedspread, a teapot, a shower curtain. Really exciting things," Emily said.

Frankie gurgled happily.

"She sounds happy now, but you should have heard her half an hour ago. I wonder if she's starting to teethe, poor thing. She was red-faced and howling and her gums look a little swollen. We're in for a bumpy ride if that's it," Emily explained.

"Sure we are," said Lisa. "I think I'd better move out for the next few months!" and, with a smile and a hug for Frankie, she was gone.

When Emily and Frankie got back to Number 23 it was obvious that Josie had something important to say.

"Things aren't great down the road," she said, her face grim.

That could have meant almost anything. That the takings were down at the thrift shop or Dr. Hat had put out some washing that had blown away in the wind or that Fiona and Declan were moving house. Then, with a lurch, Emily realized that Josie might be talking about Muttie.

"It's not . . . ?"

"Yes. Things are much worse." Josie seemed unsure whether she should call on the household or not.

Emily thought not. They would only be in the way. Muttie and Lizzie would have lots of family already. Josie accepted this.

"I saw Father Brian going in there earlier," she said.

Frankie chuckled, reaching out for Emily to be picked up.

"Good girl." Both women spoke slightly distractedly, then each of them sighed.

Josie was wondering whether saying another Rosary would help. Emily was wondering what would be of most practical help. A big shepherd's pie, she thought, something they could keep warm in the oven or whenever anyone needed food. She would make one straightaway.

Muttie was annoyed that he felt so weak. Day and night seemed to merge, and there was always someone in the room, usually telling him to rest. Hadn't he been resting since he came back from that hospital?

There were so many things still to sort out. The lawyer would drive you insane with the way he talked, but he did seem clear about one thing. The tiny amount of money the Mitchell family had paid towards the upkeep of the twins years ago and that had stopped promptly on their seventeenth birthday had all been kept in a deposit account, and with it there was a percentage of Muttie's Great Win, the time he won a fortune and they all nearly went into heart failure.

The rest of the will was simple: everything to Lizzie and their children. But Muttie was very agitated in case the twins were not properly provided for.

"They will be well set up when they inherit all this," the lawyer said.

"Well, so should they be. You see, when they came to us they gave up any chance of being in society. They were born to be with classier people than us, you see. They must be compensated properly."

The lawyer turned away so that Muttie wouldn't see his face and watch him swallowing the lump in his throat.

Father Flynn came to see him.

"God, Muttie, and you grand and peaceful here compared to the world outside."

"Tell me all about what's going on outside." Muttie's curiosity was undimmed, despite his illness.

"Well, down at the center where I work, there's all hell to pay over a Muslim wedding. This couple want one and I directed them towards the mosque. Anyway, some of the family don't want to go to it and some do. I said we would do the catering—your grandchildren could cook for anyone—and then there's a wing that says the center is a Catholic place and run with money from the Church. I tell you, you'd be demented by it all, Muttie."

"I wouldn't mind being out in it for a bit, though." Muttie sounded wistful.

"Ah, you will, you will." Brian Flynn hoped that he sounded convincing.

"But if I don't see it all again and I'm for the high jump, do you really think there's anything, you know . . . up there?"

"I'm going to tell you the truth, Muttie. I don't know, but I think there is. That's the glue that has held me together for all these years. I will be one disappointed man if there isn't anything up there."

Muttie was perfectly pleased with this as an answer. "You couldn't say fairer than that," he said approvingly.

And as Brian Flynn left the house, he wondered had any other priest of God delivered such a banal and bland description of the faith to a dying man.

.   .   .

Lisa Kelly came to call again. The family weren't sure Muttie was up to seeing her.

"I have a secret I want to tell him," she said.

"Go in then with your secret—but only ten minutes," Lizzie said.

Lisa put on her biggest smile.

"I have five hundred euro for you, Muttie. Not the Villain won by three lengths."

"Lower your voice, Lisa. I don't want any of them knowing I'm gambling," he said.

"No, I told them I had a secret to discuss with you."

"They'll think we are having an affair," Muttie said, "but Lizzie would prefer that than the gambling."

"So where will I put the money, Muttie?"

"Back in your handbag. It was only the thrill of winning I wanted."

"But, Muttie, I can't take five hundred euro. I was hoping for an enabler's fee of about fifty, that's all."

"Spend it well, child," Muttie said, and then his head drooped back on the pillow and Lisa tiptoed out of the room.

Immediately, Maud went in to see him.

Muttie opened his eyes. "Do you love this Marco, Maud?" he asked.

"Very much. I know I haven't had a series of people to compare him to, like you should."

"Says who?" Muttie asked.

"Says everyone, but I don't care. I'll never meet anyone better than Marco. They couldn't exist."

He put out his hand and held hers. "Then hold on to him, Maud, and find a nice girl for Simon too. Maybe at the wedding."

Maud held the thin hand and sat with him as he fell asleep. Tears came to her eyes and trickled down, but she didn't raise a hand to brush them away. Sleep was good. Sleep was painless. Maud wanted Muttie to have as much of this as he could get.

Muttie's children knew it would be today or tomorrow. They kept their voices low as they moved around the house. They reminded one another of days in their childhood when Muttie and Lizzie had made a picnic with jam sandwiches and taken them on a train to the sea in Bray.

They remembered the time of a small win, which Muttie had spent on two roast chickens and plates full of chips. And how they had always been dressed up for First Communion and Confirmation like the other children, though this might have meant a lot of visiting the pawnshop. Muttie at weddings; the dog, Hooves; Muttie carrying the shopping for Lizzie.

They had to share all these thoughts when they were out of Lizzie's hearing. Lizzie still thought he was getting better.

Ita, the nurse, came that day with an herbal pillow for Muttie. She looked at him and he didn't recognize her.

"He'll go into a coma shortly," she said gently to Maud. "You might ask Dr. Carroll to look in, and the care nurses will do all that has to be done."

For the first time it hit Maud really hard. She cried on Simon's shoulder. Soon there would be no more Muttie, and her last conversation with him had been about Marco.

She remembered what Muttie had said when their beloved Hooves had died: "We all have to be strong in honor of Hooves. He wasn't the kind of spirit that people go bawling and crying about. In his honor, be strong."

And they were strong as they buried Hooves.

They would be strong for Muttie as well.

"It's going to be hardest knowing that he doesn't exist anymore," Simon said.

Brian Flynn was having a cup of tea with them. "There is a thought that if we remember someone, then we keep them alive," he said.

There was a silence. He wished he hadn't spoken.

But they were all nodding their heads.

If keeping people in your memory meant that they still lived, then Muttie would live forever.

Lizzie said she was going to go in and sit with him.

"He's in a very deep sleep, Mam," Cathy said.

"I know. It's a coma. The nurses said it would happen."

"Mam, it's just . . ."

"Cathy, I know it's the end. I know it's tonight. I just want to be alone with him for a little bit."

Cathy looked at her, openmouthed.

"I knew for ages, but I just didn't let myself believe it until today, so look at all the happy days I had when the rest of you were worrying yourselves sick. . . ."

Cathy brought her mother into the room, and the nurse left. She closed the door firmly.

Lizzie wanted to say good-bye.

"I don't know if you can hear me or not, Muttie," Lizzie said. "But I wanted to tell you that you were great fun. I've had a laugh or a dozen laughs every day since I met you and I've been cheerful and thought we were as good as anyone else. I used to think we were lower, somehow. You made me think that even if we were poor, we were fine. I hope you have a great time until . . . well, until I'm there too. I know you're half a pagan, Muttie, but you'll find out that it's all there—waiting for you. Now won't that be a surprise? I love you, Muttie, and we'll manage somehow, I promise you."

Then she kissed his forehead and called the family back in for a short visit.

.   .   .

Twenty minutes later the palliative-care nurse came out and asked if Dr. Declan Carroll was there.

Fiona phoned his mobile.

"I'll be there in fifteen minutes," he said, and somehow they sat there for a quarter of an hour until Declan arrived and went into the bedroom.

He came out quickly. "Muttie is at peace . . . at rest," he confirmed.

They cried in disbelief, holding on to one another.

Marco had arrived, and he was considered family for this. Some of Muttie's Associates, who seemed to fill the house with their presence, took out handkerchiefs and blew their noses very loudly.

And suddenly Lizzie, frail Lizzie, who had until today held on to the belief that she was going to go to Chinatown in New York with Muttie, took control.

"Simon, will you go and pull down all the blinds, please. The neighbors will know then. Maud, can you phone the undertaker. His number is beside the phone, and tell him that Muttie has gone. He'll know what to do. Marco, can you arrange some food for us. People will call and we must have something to give them. Geraldine, could you see how many cups, mugs and plates we have? And could you all stop crying. If Muttie knew you were crying he would deal with the lot of you."

Somehow they managed a few watery smiles.

Muttie's funeral had begun.

The whole of St. Jarlath's Crescent stood as a guard of honor when the coffin was carried down the road.

Lisa and Noel stood with Frankie in her carriage and they were joined by Faith, who had heard so much about this man, she felt part of it all. Emily stood beside her uncle and aunt with Dr. Hat and Dingo Duggan. Declan and Fiona, holding Johnny close to her, stood with Molly and Paddy. Friends and neighbors watched as

Simon and Marco carried the coffin. They walked in measured steps.

The Associates stood in a little line, still stunned that Muttie wasn't there, urging them all to have a pint and a look at the 3:30 at Wincanton.

Somewhere far away a church bell was ringing. It had nothing to do with them but it seemed as if it were ringing in sympathy. The curtains, blinds or shutters of every house in the street were closed. People placed flowers from their gardens on the coffin as it passed by.

Then there was a hearse and funeral cars waiting to take the funeral party to Father Brian Flynn's church in the immigrant center.

Muttie had left very definite instructions.

> *If I die, which is definitely on the cards, I want my funeral service to be done by Father Brian Flynn in his center, after a very brief sort of speech and one or two prayers. And then I'd like to give my bits to science in case they're any use to anyone and the rest cremated without fuss.*
> *Signed in the whole of my wits,*
> *Muttance Scarlet*

Marco worked in Muttie and Lizzie's kitchen, producing platters of antipasti and bowls of fresh pasta. Lizzie had said he was not to hold back. He had brought forks and plates from his father's restaurant.

Though Muttie had given Marco permission to ask Maud to marry him, he wouldn't—not until she had stopped crying for her grandfather. Then he would ask her. Properly. He wondered would he and Maud be as happy as Muttie and Lizzie. Was he enough for her—she was so bright and quick.

There was a picture of Muttie on the wall. He was smiling as usual. Marco could almost hear him saying, "Go on there, Marco Romano. You're as good as any of them and better than most."

. . .

It was true what they had been saying: if people remember you, then you're not dead. It was very comforting.

At the church, Father Flynn kept the ceremony very short. One Our Father, one Hail Mary and one Glory Be to the Father. A Moroccan boy played "Amazing Grace" on a clarinet. And a girl from Poland played "Hail, Queen of Heaven" on an accordion. Then it was over.

People stood around in the sunshine and talked about Muttie. Then they made way back to his home to say good-bye.

Properly.

Chapter Thirteen

Everyone in St. Jarlath's Crescent was the poorer after Muttie's death, and people tried to avoid looking at the lonely figure of Lizzie standing by her gate, as she always had. It was as if she were still waiting for him. Of course, everyone rallied round to make sure that she wasn't alone, but one by one her children went back to their lives in Chicago and Australia; Cathy went back to her catering company. The twins were busy working at Ennio's and deciding on their future.

Everyone was slowly getting back to life, but with the knowledge that Lizzie had no life to get on with.

One night she might be invited to Charles and Josie's, but her eyes were far away as they talked of the campaign for the statue. Sometimes she went to sit with Paddy and Molly Carroll for an evening, but there was a limit to what she could listen to about Molly's work at the thrift shop or Paddy's confrontations at the meat counter. She had no tales of her own to tell anymore.

Emily Lynch was sympathetic company; she would ask questions about Lizzie's childhood and her early working days. She took Lizzie back to a time before Muttie, to places where Muttie had never walked. But then she couldn't expect Emily to be there all the time. She seemed to be very friendly with Dr. Hat these days. Lizzie was glad for her but at the same time she mourned Muttie.

There were so many things she wanted to tell him. Every day she thought of something new: how Cathy's first husband, Neil, had come to the funeral and said that Muttie was a hero; how Father Flynn had blown his nose so much they thought he might have perforated an eardrum and how he had said the kindest things about Muttie and Lizzie's wonderful extended family.

Lizzie wanted to tell Muttie that Maud would be getting engaged to Marco and that Simon was happy about it and was still thinking of going to New Jersey. She wanted to discuss with him whether she would stay on in the house or get a smaller place. Everyone advised her that she must make no decisions for at least a year. She wondered would Muttie think that was wise.

Lizzie sighed a lot these days but she tried to smile at the same time. People had always found good humor and smiles in this house, and it must not change now. It was when she was left alone in their little house that the smiles faded and she grieved for Muttie. She often heard his voice coming from another room, just not quite loud enough for her to hear what he said. When she made tea in the morning, she automatically made a cup for him; she set a place for him at mealtimes, and the sadness of it filled her with desolation.

Her bed felt huge and empty now, and when she slept, she did so with her arm around a pillow. She dreamed of him almost every night, sometimes good dreams of happy days and joyful times; often they were terrible dreams of abandonment, loss and sorrow. She didn't know which was worse: every morning she woke afresh to the knowledge that he was gone and he would never come back. It would never be all right again.

Dr. Hat suggested to Emily that they go for a picnic, as the summer had finally arrived and the days were long and warm. Emily suggested Michael come with them, though for some reason Dr. Hat looked a bit odd when she raised it. She made formal egg sandwiches and filled two flasks with tea. She brought chocolate biscuits in a tin and they drove in Dr. Hat's car out to the Wicklow Mountains.

"It's amazing to have all these hills so close to the city," Emily said admiringly.

"Those aren't hills, they're mountains," Dr. Hat said reprovingly. "It's very important to know that."

"I'm sorry." Emily laughed. "But then what can you expect from a foreigner, an outsider."

"You're not an outsider. Your heart is here," Dr. Hat said, and he looked at her oddly again. "Or I very much hope it is."

Michael started to hum tunelessly to himself as he gazed out the window. Dr. Hat and Emily ignored him and raised their voices.

"Oh, Hat, you feel safe enough saying that to me in front of Michael as a sort of joke."

"I was never as serious in my life. I *do* hope your heart is in Ireland. I'd hate it if you went away."

"Why, exactly?"

"Because you are very interesting and you get things done. I was beginning to drift and you halted that. I'm more of a man since I met you."

Michael's humming got louder, as if he were trying to drown them out.

"You are?" shouted Emily. "Well, I feel more of a woman since I met you, so that has to be good somehow."

"I never married because I never met anyone who didn't bore me before. I'd like . . . I'd like you to . . ."

"To do what?" Emily asked. Michael's humming was now almost deafening.

"Oh, stop it, Michael," Emily begged. "Hat is trying to say something, that's all."

"He's said it," Michael said. "He's asked you to marry him. Now just say yes, will you."

Emily looked at Hat for some clarity. Hat drew the car to a slow stop and got out. He went around to the passenger side, opened Emily's door and knelt in the heather and gorse on the Wicklow Mountains.

"Emily, will you do me the great honor of becoming my wife?" he asked.

"Why didn't you ask me before?"

"I was so afraid you'd say no and that we'd lose the comfortable feeling of being friends. I was just afraid."

"Don't be afraid anymore." She touched him gently on the side of his face. "I'd love to marry you."

"Thanks be to God," said Michael. "We can have the picnic now!"

Emily and Dr. Hat decided that there was no reason for delay at their age; they would marry when Betsy and Eric were in Ireland. This way Betsy would get to be matron of honor and Michael would be best man. They could be married by Father Flynn in his church. The twins would do the catering and they could all go on honeymoon, with Dingo driving them, to the west.

Emily didn't want an engagement ring. She said she would prefer a nice solid-looking wedding ring and just that. Dr. Hat was almost skittish with good humor, and for the first time in his life he agreed to go to a tailor and have a made-to-measure suit. He would get a new hat to match it and promised to take it off in the church for the ceremony as long as it could be restored for the photographs.

Betsy was almost squeaking with excitement in her e-mails.

And he proposed to you in the car in front of this other man, Michael? This is amazing, Emily, even for you. And you're going to be living around the corner from your cousins!

But can I ask, why is he called Hat? Is it short for Hathaway or was there an Irish St. Hat?

Nothing would surprise me.

Love from your elderly matron-of-honor-to-be,
Betsy

Emily still managed all her various jobs: she tended window boxes, she did her stints in the surgery, she stood behind the counter in the thrift shop—which was where she found her wedding outfit. It arrived from a shop that was about to close down. There were a number of pieces that had been display items, and the owner said she would get nothing for them and it was better they went to some charity.

Emily was hanging them up carefully on a rail when she saw it. A silk dress with a navy and pale-blue flower pattern and a matching jacket in navy with a small trim of the dress material on the jacket collar. It was perfect: elegant and feminine and wedding-like.

Carefully, Emily put the sum of money she would have hoped to get for it into the till and brought it home straightaway.

Josie saw her coming through the house.

"The very woman," Josie said. "Will you have a cup of tea?"

"A quick one, then. I don't want to leave Molly too long on her own." Emily sat down.

"I'm a bit worried," Josie began.

"Tell me." Emily sighed.

"It's this money Mrs. Monty left to Charles."

"Yes, and you're giving it to the Statue Fund." Emily knew all this.

"It's just that we're worried about how much it is," Josie said, looking around her in a frightened way. "You see, it's not just thousands . . . it's hundreds of thousands."

Emily was stunned.

"That poor old lady had that kind of money! Who'd have thought it!" Emily said.

"Yes, and that's the problem."

"What's that, Josie?" Emily asked gently.

Josie was very perturbed. "It's too much to give to a statue, Emily. It's sort of different from what we had thought. We wanted a small statue, a community thing with everyone contributing. If we give this huge sum we could have a huge statue up straightaway but it's not quite the same. . . ."

"I see. . . ." Emily hardly dared to breathe.

"It's such a huge amount of money, you see, we wonder have we a duty to our granddaughter, for example. Should we leave a sum for her education or to give her a start in life? Or should we give something to Noel so that he has something to fall back on if times get bad? Could I retire properly and could Charles and I go to the Holy Land? All these things are possible, I know. Would St. Jarlath like that better than a statue? It's impossible to know."

Emily was thoughtful. What she said now was very important.

"Which feels right to you, Josie?"

"That's the trouble. They both seem to be the right way to go. You see, we were never rich people. Now that we are, thanks to Mrs. Monty, could we possibly have changed and become greedy like they say rich people do?"

"Oh, you and Charles would never go that way!"

"We might, Emily. I mean, here am I thinking of an expensive tour to the Holy Land. You see, I tell myself that maybe St. Jarlath would *prefer* us to spend the money doing good in other ways."

"Yes, that is certainly a possibility," Emily agreed.

"You see, if I could only get some kind of a sign as to what he wanted. . . ."

"What would God have wanted, I wonder?" Emily speculated. "Our Lord wasn't into big show and splendor. He was more into helping the poor."

"Of course, the poor can be helped by a statue reminding them of a great saint."

"Yes . . ."

"You're going off the idea of the statue, aren't you?" Josie said, tears not far from her eyes.

"No, I'm all in favor of the statue. You and Charles have been working on it for so long. It's a *great* idea, but I think it should be the smaller statue you originally thought of. Greatness isn't shown by size."

Josie was weakening. "We could give one big contribution to the fund and then invest the rest."

"From what you know about St. Jarlath, do you think he'd be happy with that?" Emily knew that Josie must be utterly convinced in her heart before she abandoned the cracked notion of spending all this money on a statue.

"I think he would," Josie said. "He was all for the good of the people and if we were to put a playground at the end of the crescent for the children, wouldn't that be in the spirit of it all?"

"And the statue?"

"We could have it *in* the playground. Call it all 'St. Jarlath's Garden for Children.' "

Emily smiled with relief. Her own view of God was of a vague, benevolent force that sometimes shaped people's lives and other times stayed out of it and let things happen. She and Hat argued about this. He said it was a manifestation of people's wishes for an afterlife and helped put more sense into the time we spent on earth. But today Emily's God had intervened. He had ensured that Charles and Josie would help their son and their granddaughter. They would build a playground to keep the children safe. They would go to see Jerusalem and, most merciful of all, it would be a small statue and not a monstrosity that would make people mock them.

This was coming at a very good time for Noel. His exams were soon and he had looked strained and overtired in the past few days.

"Once you and Charles have agreed, you should tell Noel," Emily suggested.

"We'll talk it over tonight. Charles is out walking dogs in the park."

"I have a lovely lamb stew for you," Emily said. She had actually cooked it for Hat and herself but this was more important. Josie must not be given *any* excuse to put off telling Charles about her decision. Josie was easily distracted by things like having to put a meal on the table.

Emily would make something else for herself and Hat.

.   .   .

They did their roster every Sunday night. A page was put up on the kitchen wall. You could easily read who was minding Frankie every hour of the day. Noel and Lisa each had a copy as well. Soon Frankie would be old enough to go to Miss Keane's day nursery: that would be three hours accounted for each day. Only the name of who was to collect her would be needed for the mornings.

Lisa would take her to Miss Keane's and a variety of helpers would pick her up. Lisa wasn't free at lunchtime. She had a job making sandwiches in a rather classy place on the other side of the city. It wasn't a skilled job, but she brought all the skills she had to it. It paid her share of the groceries, and little by little she told them her ideas.

A gorgonzola and date sandwich? The customers loved it, so she suggested little posters advertising the sandwich of the week, and when they said it would be too expensive to do them, she drew them herself. She even designed a logo for the sandwich bar.

"You're much too good to be here," said Hugh, the young owner.

"I'm too good for everywhere. Weren't you lucky to get me?"

"We were, actually. You're a mystery woman."

He smiled at her. Hugh was rich and confident and good-looking. He fancied her, but Lisa realized that she had got out of the way of looking at men properly.

She had forgotten how to flirt.

She did other things to keep busy.

She joined Emily in the window box patrol and learned a lot about plants as well as about the lives of the people in St. Jarlath's Crescent. Feeding plants and repotting—it was a different world, but she picked it up quickly. Emily said she was a natural. She could run her own plant nurseries.

"I used to be bright," Lisa said thoughtfully. "I was really good at school and then I got a great job in an agency . . . but it all drifted away . . ."

Emily knew when to leave a silence.

Lisa went on almost dreamily, "It was like driving into a fog, really, meeting Anton. I forgot the world outside."

"And is the world coming back to you yet?" Emily asked gently.

"Sort of peering through the foggy curtains."

"Are there things you meant to do before and didn't get to do?"

"Yes, a lot of things, and I'm going to do them. Starting with these exams."

"It will concentrate the mind," Emily agreed.

"Yes, and keep me away from Anton's . . . ," Lisa said ruefully.

She knew very clearly that if she went back to the restaurant they would all greet her warmly. Her absence would not need to be explained. They would assume she had just had a hissy fit and had now come to her senses. April would look put out and Anton would look at her lazily and say she was lovely and the days had been lonely and colorless since she had gone. On the surface nothing would have changed. Deep down, though, it was all changed. He didn't love her. She had just been available, that was all.

But as she had said to Emily, there were still a lot of things that had to be done about other aspects of her life. One of these was meeting her mother.

Since she had discovered that her father brought prostitutes home, Lisa's meetings with her mother had been sparse. They met for coffee every now and then and they had lunch before Christmas. A dutiful exchange of gifts was made and they both engaged in a polite fiction of a conversation.

Her mother had asked about Lisa's design work for Anton's.

Lisa had asked about Mother's garden and whether she had decided on having a greenhouse or not. They had both talked a lot about Katie's salon and how well it was doing. Then, with relief, they had parted.

Nothing dangerous had been said, no forbidden roads had been opened up.

But this was no way to live, Lisa told herself. She must urge Mother to do what she had done herself and cut free from the old bonds.

She telephoned her mother immediately.

"Lunch? What's the occasion?" her mother asked.

"There's no law that says we can only meet on special occasions," Lisa said. She could tell that her mother was confused.

"Let's go to Ennio's," she suggested, and before her mother could find a reason not to go, it was all settled. "Ennio's, tomorrow, one o'clock."

Di Kelly looked well as she came into the restaurant. She wore a red belted coat with a white polo-necked collar underneath. She must be fifty-three but she didn't look forty. Her hair showed that all that brushing had not been in vain, and all that walking had ensured that she was trim and fit.

She did not, however, look at ease.

"This is nice," Lisa said brightly. "How have you been keeping?"

"Oh, fine. And you?"

"Fine also."

"And have you any news for me?" her mother asked with an interested expression on her face.

"What kind of news, exactly?"

"Well, I wondered if you were going to tell me that you and this Anton were getting married or anything. You've had him out on approval for long enough." She gave a tinkling laugh, showing she was nervous.

"Married? To Anton? Lord, no! I wouldn't dream of it."

"Oh, sorry, I thought that that was what this was about. You were going to ask me to the wedding but not your father."

"No, nothing as dramatic as that," Lisa said.

"So why did you invite me, then?"

"Does there have to be a reason? You're my mother and I'm your daughter. That's reason enough for most people."

"But we aren't like most people," her mother said simply.

"Why did you stay with him?" Lisa had not intended to ask this as baldly as it came out.

"We all have choices to make. . . ." Her mother was vague.

"But you couldn't *choose* to live with him, not after you knew what he was doing." Lisa was full of disgust.

"Life's a compromise, Lisa. Sooner or later you'll understand that. I had options: leave him and be by myself in a flat or stay and live in a house I liked."

"But you can have no respect for him."

"I was never very interested in sex. He was. That's all. I didn't enjoy it. You saw we had two separate beds . . ."

"I also saw him bringing that woman into what was your bedroom," Lisa said.

"It was only a couple of times. He was very ashamed that you saw. Did you tell Katie?"

"Why does that matter?" Lisa asked.

"I just wondered. She hardly ever calls. He thinks it's because you told her. I said she had stopped calling a long time ago."

"And did it not upset you that both your daughters feel a million miles from you?"

"You are always very courteous—you've invited me to lunch to keep up the relationship."

"What relationship? Do you think my asking you did the clematis grow over the garage and you asking me whether Anton's is doing well is a relationship?"

Di shrugged. "It's as good as most."

"No, it's not. It's totally unnatural. I live with a little baby girl. She's not yet one and she is loved by so many people you wouldn't believe it. She will never be left alone, bewildered, like Katie and I were. It's natural for people to love children. You were both so cold. . . . I just hoped you'd tell me why."

Di was quite calm. "I didn't like your father very much, even before we were married, but I hated my job more and I had no money to spend on clothes, on going to the cinema, on anything. So I have a part-time job which I like and I thought it was a fair exchange for marrying him. I didn't realize the sex thing was going to be so important, but, well, if I didn't want it, then it was only fair to let him go out and get it."

"Or stay in and have it," Lisa interrupted.

"I told you that was only two or three times."

"How could you put up with it?"

"It was that or start out on my own again and, unlike you, I had no qualifications. I have a badly paid job in a dress shop. As it is, I have a nice house and food on the table."

"So you'd prefer to share a man that you admit you don't like very much with prostitutes?"

"I don't think of it that way. I think of it as cooking and cleaning a fine house. I have a garden which I love, I play bridge with friends and go to the cinema. It's a way of living."

"You've obviously thought it through," Lisa said, with some grudging acceptance.

"Yes I did. I didn't expect to tell you all this. Of course, I didn't expect you to ask." Her mother was self-possessed now and eating her veal Milanese with every appearance of enjoyment.

Maud was serving in the restaurant but realized that this was a very intense conversation, so she steered away from personal chat. She moved gracefully around the room and Lisa saw Marco looking at her approvingly as he poured the wine for customers. That was what love and marriage was about—not this hopeless, downbeat bargain that her parents had made. For the first time ever, Lisa felt a wave of sympathy wash over her.

For both of them.

Faith stayed in the flat several nights a week now. She was able to look after Frankie and put her to bed on the evenings that all three of them studied. It was a curious little family grouping, but it worked. Faith said she found working like this so much easier than doing it alone. Between them they went over the latest lecture and talked it out. They made notes on what to ask the lecturer next week and they revised for their exams in August. They all felt that it had been worth doing, and now that graduation was in sight they began to imagine how it would all work out for them when they had letters after their names.

Noel would immediately seek a better position at Hall's, and if it wasn't forthcoming then he would have the courage and qualifications to apply somewhere else. Faith would put herself forward as a manager in her office. She was doing that work in all but name and salary, so they would have to promote her.

Lisa? Well, Lisa was at a loss to know what her qualifications would lead to.

At one time she had hoped to be a partner in Anton's. But now? Well, she would have to return to the marketplace. It was humiliating, but she would have to contact Kevin, the boss she had left when she went to work with Anton. That was last year when she had been reasonably sane and good at her job. She picked up the phone with trepidation.

"Well, *hello!*" Kevin was entitled to be surprised and a bit mocking. For months now Lisa had avoided him if ever they turned up at the same function; he had not been a customer in Anton's. It was very hard to call him and tell him that she had failed.

He made it fairly easy.

"You're on the market again, I gather," he said.

"You can crow, Kevin. You were right. I should have listened. I should have thought it out."

"But you were in love, of course," Kevin said. There was only a mildly sardonic tone to his voice. He was entitled to have a lot more I-told-you-so.

"That was true, yes."

If he noticed the past tense he said nothing.

"So he didn't pay you in cash—I'm guessing. Did he repay you in love?"

"No, that's in pretty short supply these days."

"So you're looking for a job?"

"I was wondering if you knew of anything? Anything at all?"

"But this may just be a lovers' tiff. In a week's time you could well be back with him."

"That won't happen," Lisa said.

"Right now I can only offer you a junior place. Somewhere to settle for a while. I can't give you a top job. It wouldn't be fair on the others."

She was very humble now. "I'd be more grateful than I could tell you, Kevin."

"Not at all. Start Monday?"

"Can I make it the Monday after? I'm working in a sandwich bar and I'll have to give them notice . . . get someone else for them."

"My, my, Lisa, you *have* changed," Kevin said as he hung up.

Lisa went and told her boss immediately. "I'll find you another sandwich maker in a week," she promised.

"Hey, I want much more than that. I want a market adviser and a graphic designer as well." Hugh laughed.

"That may take longer, but anyway I wanted to tell you."

"I'm sorry to lose you. I had ferocious designs on you, actually. I was biding my time."

"Always a mistake," she said cheerfully. "Now, Hugh, if you are to have any business at all, put your mind on sandwiches—what about a mild tandoori chicken wrap? They'd love that."

"Let's go out in a blaze of glory for your last week."

Lisa made the spicy chicken sandwiches and in between times texted Maud and Simon to look for a replacement. One of their friends would be able to do it without any problem. They had found somebody in a couple of hours.

"Send her up to me and I'll train her in," Lisa suggested.

The girl was called Tracey. She was eager-looking but covered in tattoos.

Tactfully, Lisa offered her a shirt.

"We wear these here buttoned at the wrist," she said. "Hugo is very insistent about that."

"Bit of an old fuddy-duddy, is he?" Tracey asked.

"Bit of a young fuddy-duddy; definitely a looker," she said.

Tracey brightened. This job might have hidden benefits.

Lisa was amazed at how quickly she managed to adapt to a life that didn't center around Anton's. Not that she didn't miss it; several times a day she wondered what they might all be doing and whether Anton would use any more of her ideas to beat the downturn in business. But there was plenty to occupy her, and on most fronts it was going very well.

Lizzie found the days endless. The savage, raw pain of grief was now giving way to a gnawing ache, and the void in her life was threatening to consume her.

"I'm thinking of getting a little job," she confided to the twins.

"What work would you do, Lizzie?" Simon asked.

"Anything, really. I used to clean houses."

"You'd be too tired for that nowadays," Simon said practically.

"You could work at managing something, Lizzie," Maud suggested.

"Oh, I don't think so. I'd be afraid of the responsibility."

"Would you like to work in Marco's restaurant? Well, his father's restaurant. They're looking for someone to come in part-time to supervise sending the laundry out and take in the cheese delivery and to sort yesterday's tips out from the credit card receipts. You could do that, couldn't you?"

"Well, I might be able to, but Ennio would never give me a big responsible job like that," Lizzie said anxiously.

"Of course he would," Simon said loyally.

"You're family, Lizzie," said Maud, looking down with pleasure at her engagement ring.

Ania's baby was due in a couple of months and there was great excitement in the heart clinic, mainly because Ania's period of bed rest was over and she was back at work, but under constant supervision.

"I feel much safer here," she said piteously, so they let her stay, even though everyone jumped when she took a deep breath or reached up to take a file out of a cabinet.

Clara Casey said that Ania had been so upset by her miscarriage that they must all be on hand to help her the moment there was the remotest sign of the baby. Clara knew the girl was apprehensive— far from home, from her mother and sisters. Her husband, Carl, was, if possible, even more excited than Ania. He took to hanging around the clinic himself in case there should be any news.

Clara was very tolerant. "Oh, work round him," she told the others. "The poor boy is distracted in case anything goes wrong this time."

Clara herself was fairly distracted by matters on the home front: Frank Ennis and his son. The relationship had been prickly from the start, and hadn't improved much during the boy's visit. Des had gone back to Australia and they kept in touch from time to time. Not often enough for Frank, who put great effort into writing weekly e-mails to the boy.

"You'd think he'd do more than send a postcard of the Barrier Reef," Frank grumbled.

"Look, be grateful for what you get. My daughter Adi only sends a card too. I don't know where she is and what she's doing. It's just the way things are."

Then came the word they had not expected.

I find myself thinking a lot about Ireland these days. I know I was rough on you and didn't really believe you when you said you didn't know what your family had done, but it took time to get my head around it all. Perhaps we should have another go. I was thinking of spending a year there, if that wouldn't put you out. I've been in negotiations about jobs and apparently my degree and diploma would be recognised there.

You must tell me if this is something you would be happy with

*and I would find myself an apartment, rather than crowd you
out. Who knows, during my year there we might try the father-son
thing and see how it goes. In any case, I'd like to meet Clara and
even my nearly stepsisters?*

They were both silent when they read the letter. It was the first
time Des Raven had shown any sign of wanting a father-son relationship. And also the first time that he had any thought of meeting
Clara. . . .

The results of the examinations had been posted on the college
notice board. Noel and Faith and Lisa had all done well and the
diploma would be theirs. They celebrated with giant ice creams at
the café beside the college and planned their outfits for graduation
day. They would be wearing black gowns and there would be pale-
blue hoods.

"Hoods?" Noel asked, horrified.

"That's just what they call them—they're just the bits that go
over our shoulders, to mark us out as different, not engineers or
draftsmen or anything." Lisa knew it all.

"I'm going to wear a yellow dress I have already—you won't see
much of it under the gown. I'll spend the money on good shoes,"
Faith said.

"I'm going to get a red dress and borrow Katie's new shoes." Lisa
had it sorted as well. "Now, Noel, what about you?"

"Why this emphasis on shoes?" Noel asked.

"Because everyone sees them when you go up on the stage for
your parchment."

"If I polished up these ones?" He looked down dubiously at his
feet. The girls shook their heads. New shoes were called for.

"I'll get you a pale-blue tie from one of my brothers," Faith
promised.

"And I'll iron your good shirt—any money there is, spend it on
shoes," Lisa commanded.

"It's a lot of fuss about nothing," Noel grumbled.

"Nights of lectures, hours of study—and you call it nothing!" Lisa was outraged.

"And what about the photos to show Frankie?" Faith asked.

"I'll get the damn shoes!" Noel promised.

The day of the graduation in September was very bright and sunny. That was a relief: there would be no umbrellas or people squinting into the rain. Frankie was excited to see them all dressing up.

She crawled around the floor, getting under everyone's feet and mumbled a lot to herself about it—words that didn't make much sense until they identified "Frankie too."

"Of *course* you're going too, darling." Faith lifted her up in the air. "*And* I have a lovely little blue dress for you to wear. It will match your daddy's tie and you'll be the most beautiful little girl in the whole world!"

Noel looked very well. He was much admired by the women, who dusted flecks off his shoulders and examined his new shoes with cries of approval. Then Emily arrived to take Frankie in the buggy wearing her new dress, and they all set out for the college.

Frankie behaved perfectly during the ceremony. Better by far than other babies, who cried or struggled at crucial times during the graduation. Noel gazed at her with pride. She was indeed the most beautiful little girl in the whole world! He had done all this for her—yes, for himself too, but all this work had been worth it for the chance to make a life for her.

The new graduates filed onto the stage and the audience raked through the ranks until they found their own. The graduates also searched the audience. Noel saw Emily holding Frankie and he smiled with pleasure and pride.

Lisa saw her mother and sister both dressed up to honor the day; she saw Garry there and all their friends.

Then she saw Anton.

He looked lost, as if he didn't belong there. She remembered writing down this date in his diary months back. It didn't mean anything to her that he was there and it had all been her own fault. Anton had never loved her. It had all been in her mind.

The president spoke warmly about the graduates.

"They had to give up a lot of social life to do this course. They missed television and cinemas and theaters. They want to thank you, their families and their friends, for supporting them on this undertaking. Each and every graduate here today has gone on a journey. They are different people to the people who started out with a leap of faith. They have much more than just mere letters after their names. They have the satisfaction of having set out to do something and seen it through.

"I salute them all on your behalf."

There was tumultuous applause at this, and the new graduates all beamed from the stage. Then the presentation began . . .

They had planned a special lunch in Ennio's together with Noel, his family, Emily and Hat, Declan, Fiona and the Carroll parents. Faith would bring her father and three of her five brothers. Lizzie was working there as a supervisor, and she had reserved a big table for them; Ennio would give them a special price; the twins and Marco would be serving. Lizzie would even sit down and join them for the meal.

Lizzie had found the job a great help. For whole sections of the day she didn't stop and think of Muttie with that sad, empty look that broke her neighbors' hearts. Here it was too busy, too frenetic. There was too much shouting to leave any time to go over all she had lost. Ennio was always there with a coffee or a word of encouragement. She met new people, people who had never known Muttie. It wasn't really any easier, but it was less raw. Lizzie would admit that much, and the twins were there for her every step of the way. Lizzie was a religious person. She thanked God every morning and every night for having arranged things so that Maud and Simon came to live with them.

Ennio had said they should have a banner over the table—

FELICITAZIONI—TANTI AUGURI—FAITH LISA NOEL: that would be alphabetical order, so nobody could be offended.

"What does it mean?" Faith asked.

"Congratulations, best wishes," Marco said excitedly.

They were a mixed group, including the two babies, but they all got along very well and there was no pause in the conversation. More and more food and wine kept coming to the table. And finally a great cake arrived, iced in the shape of a mortarboard and scroll.

People at other tables gathered round to see it.

"It was iced by Maud," Marco said proudly.

"And everyone else." Maud tried to shrug it off.

"But mainly by Maud," Marco insisted.

And then there was sparkling wine for the toast and a glass of elderflower cordial for Noel. The health of the three successful scholars was drunk to and they were cheered to the echo.

To everyone's surprise, Noel stood up.

"I think that, as the president said earlier, we owe a huge debt of gratitude to our families and friends and that we three should raise a toast to you also. Without you all, we wouldn't have been able to do all this and have this great graduation day and feast. To our families and friends," he said.

Lisa and Faith stood up and all three repeated the toast:

"To our families and friends."

Chapter Fourteen

Ania's baby was almost born in the heart clinic—not quite, but almost. It was too soon.

Her waters broke during one of the healthy cookery demonstrations and they got her into the maternity wing of St. Brigid's in the shortest possible time. Later that night the news went around: a baby boy, born prematurely and taken into the special-care baby unit. Everyone was concerned for Carl and Ania: it was going to be a traumatic time for both parents. They had been so anxious throughout the pregnancy, and the worrying wasn't over yet. They were staying with the tiny baby by his incubator; Carl would come down to the clinic later and tell them what was happening.

Clara Casey called her ex-husband and asked him to drop by her house.

"Don't like the sound of this," Alan said.

"Haven't I done everything you ever asked me: had two babies for you, left you free to follow your heart? I gave you a divorce when you wanted it. I never asked you for a penny."

"You got my house," Alan said.

"No. If you remember, the house was paid for by a deposit from my mother and every month by a mortgage which *I* earned. It was always my house, so we won't go down that road again."

"What do you want to talk about if I come over?" He sounded sulky now.

"Various things . . . the future . . . the girls . . ."

"The girls!" Alan snorted. "Adi's off in Peru doing God knows what . . ."

"Ecuador, as it happens."

"Same difference. And as for Linda, she won't speak to me if I do get in touch."

"That's because when she told you that she and Nick were going to adopt, you said that you personally would never raise another man's son yourself. That was helpful. . . ."

"You're hard to please, Clara. If I *am* honest it's wrong, if I'm not honest, it's wrong."

"See you tomorrow," Clara said and hung up.

He looked older and shabbier than before. A succession of new ladies later, he was now temporarily without a partner. Alan, who always prided himself on having women iron his shirts, looked vaguely down at heel.

"You look wonderful," he said, as he said to almost every woman almost all the time. Clara ignored him.

"Coffee?" she suggested.

"Or something stronger even?" he asked.

"No, you can't handle drink like you used to. You start crawling over me when you've had a couple of glasses of wine, and I certainly don't want that."

"You liked it well enough once," he muttered.

"Yes, that's true, but in those days I believed everything you said."

"Don't nag, Clara."

"No, of course not. I'm just showing you some courtesy here. Frank is going to be moving in here next week."

"But you can't let him!" He was shocked.

"Well, I have every intention of doing so. I just thought you should hear it from me, that's all."

"But, Clara, you're much too old for this," he said.

"Imagine, you were once considered quite charming and dashing," Clara said.

Emily had the spare room in Dr. Hat's house beautifully decorated, and she planned a series of outings to entertain Betsy and Eric. She had this ludicrous wish that they should love Ireland like she did. She hoped that it wouldn't rain, that the streets would be free of litter, that the price of everything would not be too high.

Emily and Hat were at the airport long before the plane arrived.

"It only seems the other day since you came out to meet *me* here," Emily said, "and you brought me a picnic in the car."

"I had begun to fancy you seriously then, but I was terrified you'd say it was all nonsense."

"I'd never have said that." She looked at him very fondly.

"I hope your friend won't think I'm too old and dull for you," he said anxiously.

"You're my Hat. My choice. The only person I ever even contemplated marrying," she said firmly. And that was that.

Betsy was bemused by the size of the airport and the frantic activity all around. She had thought the plane would land in a field of cows or sheep. This was a huge, sprawling place like an airport back home. She couldn't believe the traffic, the highways and the huge buildings.

"You never told me how developed it all is. I thought it was a succession of little cottages where you knew everyone who moves," she said, laughing. In minutes it was as if they had never been parted.

Eric and Dr. Hat exchanged relieved glances. It was all going to be fine.

Emily was going to be given away by her uncle Charles.

Charles and Josie had finally come to the conclusion that a children's playground and a *small* statue of St. Jarlath would fit the bill. They had been to see a lawyer and settled a sum for Noel and one for Frankie. They had even arranged for Emily to have a substantial sum as a wedding gift so that she wouldn't start her married life with no money of her own. It wasn't a dowry, of course, and Charles said that so often that Emily began to wonder.

Noel knew nothing about his inheritance. Charles and Josie had been waiting to talk to him on his own. There was always someone with him—Lisa or Faith or Declan Carroll. They could hardly remember the days before Frankie was born, when Noel was a man always by himself. Now the two of them were always the center of a group of people.

Finally they found him alone.

"Will you sit down, Noel? We have something to tell you," Charles said.

"I don't like the sound of this." Noel looked from one to the other anxiously.

"No, you are going to like what your father has to say," Josie said with a rare smile.

Noel hoped they hadn't seen a vision or anything, that St. Jarlath hadn't appeared in the kitchen asking them to build a cathedral. They had seemed so normal recently, it would be a pity if they had had a setback.

"It's about your future, Noel. You know that Mrs. Monty, may God be good to her, has left us a sum of money. We want to share this with you."

"Ah, no, Dad, thank you but that's for you and Mam. You did the dog minding—I wouldn't want to take any of it."

"But you don't know how much she left," Charles said.

"Is there enough to take you to Rome? Or even Jerusalem? That's wonderful news!"

"There's much more than that—you wouldn't believe it."

"But it's yours, Dad."

"We've made arrangements for an educational policy for Frankie, so that she'll never lack for a good school. And there'll be a lump sum for yourself, maybe the deposit on a house so you'd have your own place and not have to rent."

"But this is ridiculous, Dad. It would cost a fortune."

"She left us a fortune. And after a lot of thought we are spending it on a children's garden with a small statue, and on our own flesh and blood."

Noel looked at them wordlessly. They had sorted out everything that was worrying him. He would be able to have a proper home for Frankie and maybe, if she'd have him, for Faith. Frankie would get a top-class education. Noel would have his rainy-day security.

All because his father had been kind to Caesar, a little King Charles spaniel with soppy brown eyes.

Wasn't life totally extraordinary?

On the morning of the wedding, before they set out for the church, Charles made a little speech to Emily.

"By rights it should have been my brother doing this but I hope I'll do you credit."

"Charles, if it were up to my father, he wouldn't have turned up, or if he had, he would have been drunk. I much prefer having you."

Father Flynn married them. Emily could have filled the church five times over, but they wanted only a small gathering, so twenty of them stood in the sunlight as they made their vows. Then they went to Holly's Hotel in County Wicklow and back home to St. Jarlath's Crescent. Then the honeymoon continued for the two couples; Dingo Duggan got new tires to make sure that they got to the west and back.

They stayed in farmhouses and walked along shell-covered shores with purple-blue mountains as a backdrop. And if you were to ask anyone who they were and what they were doing, a hundred guesses would never have said that they were two middle-aged couples on honeymoon. They all seemed too settled and happy for that.

Two days after Emily's wedding, Father Flynn heard from the nursing home in Rossmore that his mother was dying. He got down there quickly and held her hand. His mother's mind was far from clear but he felt that by being there he might be of some comfort. When his mother spoke it was of people long dead, and of incidents in her childhood. Suddenly, however, she came back to the present day.

"Whatever happened to Brian?" she asked him.

"I'm right here."

"I had a son called Brian," she continued, as though she hadn't heard him. "I don't know what happened to him. I think he joined a circus. He left town and no one ever heard of him again. . . ."

When Mrs. Flynn died almost the whole of Rossmore turned out for the funeral. At the nursing home, the staff had gathered together the old lady's belongings and gave them to the priest. They included some old diaries and a few pieces of jewelry no one had ever seen her wear.

Brian looked through them as he came back in the train. The jewelry had been given to her by her husband, the diary told, but they had not been given in love but out of guilt. Brian read with pain and embarrassment that his father had not been a faithful man and he had thought he could buy his wife's forgiveness with a necklace and various brooches. Brian decided to give the jewelry to his sister Judy with no mention of its history.

He looked up the date of his own ordination to the priesthood in the battered diary. His mother had written:

This is simply the best day of my life.

It somehow made up for her thinking he had joined a circus.

·   ·   ·

Ania's family were on their way from Poland to be with her as she and Carl watched over baby Robert. He was so tiny, they could have held him in the palms of their hands; instead he was lying in an incubator attached to monitors and with tubes in and out of his tiny body. Ania watched carefully as the breathing monitor showed how Robert was having difficulty breathing on his own and how the machine was breathing for him. She was able to hold his tiny hand through the holes in the incubator. He looked so small, so vulnerable, so unprepared for the world.

Back at home, they had a nursery prepared, waiting for them to come home as a new family. The room was full of gifts given to them by friends and well-wishers. There were baby clothes and toys and all the equipment for a newborn child. Carl silently wondered if baby Robert would ever get to use it.

On the third day, Ania was able to hold her baby in her arms. Unable to speak for the emotion, her face was wet with tears of hope and joy as she held him, so tiny, so fragile.

"*Maly cud*," she whispered to him. "Little miracle."

The honeymoon had been a resounding success. Emily and Betsy were like girls, chattering and laughing. Hat and Eric found a great common interest in bird-watching and wrote notes each evening. Dingo met a Galway girl with black hair and blue eyes and was very smitten. The sun shone on the newlyweds and the nights were full of stars.

It was over too soon for everyone.

"I wonder if there's any news when we get back? I wonder how Ania's baby is doing. I do hope he's going to be all right," Emily said as they drew closer to Dublin.

"You're really part of the place now," Betsy said.

"Yes, isn't it odd? I never had a real conversation in my life with my father about Ireland or about anything else, but I do feel that I have come home."

Hat heard her say this and smiled to himself. It was even more than he had hoped.

When they did get back they heard the astounding news that Frank Ennis had moved in with the elegant Clara Casey, who ran the heart clinic, and, wait for it . . . he had a son. Frank Ennis had a son called Des Raven, who lived in Australia and was coming to Ireland.

Fiona could talk of nothing else. It had completely wiped her own pregnancy off the list of topics. Clara *living with* Frank Ennis— didn't people do extraordinary things. And Frank had a *son* she hadn't met yet. Imagine.

Their first chance to celebrate properly as a family came when Adi came back from Ecuador with her boyfriend, Gerry. Des had wanted to go back to Anton's. "It will be like starting over," he had said. This time, there was no need to plead for a table, even though they were nine: Clara, Frank and Des; then Adi and Gerry; Linda came with Nick. Hilary from the clinic and Clara's best friend, Dervla, made up the party.

The restaurant was half empty and there seemed to be an air of confusion about the place. The menu was more limited than before and Anton himself was working in and out of the kitchen. He said that his number one, Teddy, had gone, as he needed new pastures. No, he had no idea where he went. Des Raven was very courteous to his new almost-stepsisters. He talked to Adi about teaching; he spoke to Linda about some friends of his who had adopted a Chinese baby; he talked easily of his life in Australia.

Clara asked Anton's advice about what they should eat.

"There's a very good steak and kidney pie," he suggested.

"That's the men sorted, but what about the rest of us?" she asked. She noticed he was tired and strained. It couldn't be easy running a restaurant that looked as though it might be on the way down.

"Small, elegant portions of steak and kidney pie?" he suggested with a winning smile.

Clara stopped feeling sorry for him. With a smile like that he would get by. He was a survivor.

Frank Ennis, in his new suit, was in charge of the table. He poured wine readily and urged people to have oysters as the optional extra.

"I talk about my son a lot," he said proudly to Des.

"Good. Do you talk about Clara a lot?" he asked.

"With respect and awe," Frank said.

"Good," intervened Clara, "because she wants to tell you that her clinic needs some serious extra funding. . . ."

"Out of the question."

"The blood tests take too long from the main hospital. We need our own lab."

"I'll get your blood tests fast-tracked," Frank Ennis promised.

"You have six weeks for us to see a real difference; otherwise the fight is on," Clara said. "He is amazingly generous in real life," she whispered to Dervla. "It's just in the hospital that his rotten-to-the-core meanness shows."

"He's delighted with you," Dervla said. "He has said 'My Clara' thirty times during this meal alone."

"Well, I'm keeping my name, my job, my clinic and my house, so I'm doing very well out of it," Clara said.

"Go on out of that, playing the tough bird—you're just as soppy as he is. You're delighted at this playing-house thing. I'm happy for you, Clara, and I hope that you'll be very happy together."

"I will." Clara had it all planned out. Minimal disturbance to their two lives. They were both people who were set in their ways.

Lisa was surprised when Kevin asked her out to lunch.

She was in a junior position in the studio. She didn't expect her boss to single her out. In Quentins she was even more surprised that he ordered a bottle of wine. Kevin was usually a one-vodka person. This looked like something serious. She hoped he wasn't going to sack her. But surely he wouldn't take her out to lunch to give her the push?

"Stop frowning, Lisa. We're going to have a long lunch," Kevin said.

"What is it? Don't keep me in suspense."

"Two things, really. Did Anton pay you anything? Anything at all?"

"Oh, why are you dragging this up? I told you it was my fault. I went in there with my eyes open."

"No, you didn't. Your eyes were closed in mad, passionate love, and fair play to you, you're not bitter, but I really need to know."

"No, he paid me nothing, but I was part of the place, part of the dream. I was doing it for *us,* not for him. That's what I thought, anyway. Don't make me go on repeating all this. I *know* what I did for months . . . it doesn't make it any easier having to talk about that."

"It's just that he's going into receivership today and I wanted to make sure you got your claim in. You are a serious victim here. You worked for him without being paid, for God's sake. You are a major creditor."

"I haven't a notion of asking him for anything. I'm sorry it didn't work for him. I'm not going to add to his worries."

"It's just business, Lisa. He'll understand. People have got to be paid. It will be automatic. They'll sell his assets—I don't know what he owns and what is mortgaged or leased, but people have to be paid, you amongst them."

"No, Kevin, thanks all the same."

"You love clothes, Lisa. You should get yourself a stunning wardrobe."

"I'm not smart enough for your office? Is that it?" She was hurt, but she made it sound like a joke.

"No, you're too smart. Much too smart. I can't keep you. I have a friend in London. He's looking for someone bright. I told him about you. He'll pay your fare to London. Overnight in a fancy hotel, and you don't want to know the salary he's offering!"

"You really *are* getting rid of me and you're pretending it's a promotion," she said bleakly.

"*Never* have I been so misjudged! I'd prefer you to stay and in a year or two I could promote you, but this job is too good to ignore and I thought that anyway it might be easier for you."

"Easier?"

"Well, you know, there'll be a lot of talk about Anton's. Speculation, newspaper stuff."

"Yes, I suppose there will. Poor Anton."

"Oh, God, don't tell me you're going back to him."

"No, there's nothing to go back to. There never was."

"Ah, now, Lisa, I'm sure he *did* love you in his own way."

She shook her head. "But in ways you're right. I couldn't bear to be in Dublin while all the vultures were picking over the place."

"You'll go for the interview?" He was pleased.

"I'll go," Lisa promised.

Simon said it was time they talked about New Jersey. The amazing inheritance they had got from Muttie meant that Maud and Marco could put a deposit on their own restaurant and Simon could go to New Jersey and eventually have a place of his own.

"I'll miss you," Maud said.

"You won't notice I'm gone," he assured her.

"Who'll finish my sentences?"

"You'll have Marco trained in no time."

"You'll fall in love and live out there."

"I doubt it, but I'll be home often to see Lizzie and you and Marco." Maud noticed he didn't include their parents. Father was on his travels and Mother had only the vaguest idea of who they were.

As if he read her mind, Simon said, "Weren't we so lucky that Muttie and Lizzie took us in? We could have ended up anywhere."

Maud gave him a hug. "Those American girls don't know what's coming their way," she said.

.   .   .

It was a day of many changes.

Declan and Fiona and Johnny moved house. It was only next door but it was still a huge move. They arranged that Paddy and Molly Carroll should be part of it all so that they would realize how nothing had really changed. They would be next door; when Johnny was old enough to walk he would know two homes as his own. And as for the new baby? That would be born into a two-house family.

The house had been painted in a cheery primrose color that brought sunshine into every room. They would think about proper color schemes later, but the most important thing was to make it bright and welcoming. Johnny's room was ready and waiting for his crib. Declan and Fiona would have room for their books and music.

They would have their own kitchen at last.

The time with Molly and Paddy Carroll had been happy, but it couldn't go on forever. They had both looked forward to and dreaded the day when they would have to move to somewhere with more space: this had been an ideal solution.

They walked the few steps between the houses carrying possessions and stopping for a pot of tea in one house or the other so that it underlined how much together they were still going to be. Dimples came in and walked around the new house and seemed to approve. Emily had brought window boxes already planted as a housewarming gift.

Dr. Hat and Emily decided to open a garden store. There was still plenty of room beside the thrift shop. Now that so many residents of St. Jarlath's Crescent had begun to take an interest in beautifying their gardens, there was no end of demand for bedding plants and ornamental shrubs. They went up and measured it. It was now no longer a wish, but a reality; they would do it together, and it would be yet one more thing they could share.

. . .

In the disturbed world of Anton's restaurant the staff were making their plans. They would not open next week. Everyone knew this. April sat around the place with her notebook, suggesting places for Anton to do interviews on the difficulties of running a business during a recession. Anton felt unsettled. He wasn't listening. He wondered what Lisa would be saying.

It was the day that Linda and Nick decided to stop talking about adopting a baby and do something about it.

For Noel it was a good day also.

Mr. Hall had said that there was a more senior position in the company that had been vacant for some time. He now wanted to offer it to Noel.

"I have been impressed by you, Noel. I don't mind saying that you did much better than I would have thought at one stage. I always hoped you'd have it in you to make something of yourself, though I confess I had my doubts about you for a while."

"I had my doubts about myself," Noel had said with a smile.

"There's always some turning point for a man. What do you think yours was?" Mr. Hall had seemed genuinely interested.

"Becoming a father," Noel had said without having to stop and think for a second.

And now he was at home with Frankie helping her take her first independent steps. There were just the two of them. She still liked the comfort of something to hold on to, and every now and then she suddenly sat down with a surprised look on her face. She had been making great efforts to tear up the cloth books that Faith had given her, but they were proving very resistant. She was frowning with concentration.

"I love you, Frankie," Noel said to her.

"Dada," she said.

"I really do love you. I was afraid I wouldn't be good enough for you but we're not making a bad fist of it, are we?"

"Fst," Frankie said, delighted with the noise of the word.

"Say 'love,' Frankie. Say, 'I love you, Dada.' "

She looked up at him. "Love Dada," she said, as clear as a bell.

And to his surprise he felt the tears on his face. He wished not for the first time that there really was a God and a heaven because it would be really great if Stella could somehow see this and know that it was all working out like she had hoped.

Chapter Fifteen

Noel and Lisa planned a first birthday party for Frankie. There would be an ice cream cake and paper hats; Mr. Gallagher from Number 37 could do magic tricks and said he'd come along and entertain the children.

Naturally, Moira got to hear of it.

"You're having all these people in this small flat?" she asked doubtfully.

"I know—won't it be wonderful?" Lisa deliberately misunderstood her.

"You should do more for yourself, Lisa. You're bright, sharp, you could have a career and a proper place to live."

"This *is* a proper place to live." Noel was at the washing machine in the kitchen so didn't hear.

"No, it's not. You should have your own apartment. You'll need one soon anyway, if Noel's romance continues," Moira said, practical as always.

"But meanwhile I'm very happy here."

"We have to stir ourselves from our comfort zones. What are you doing here with a man who is bringing up some child that may or may not be his own?"

"Of course Frankie's his own!" Lisa was shocked.

"Well, that's as may be. She was very unreliable, the mother, you know. I met her in hospital. A very wild sort of person. She could have named anyone as the father."

"Well, really, Moira, I never heard anything so ridiculous," Lisa said, blazing suddenly at the mean-spirited pettiness of Moira's attitude. Wasn't life the luck of the draw? They could have got a very nice social worker like that woman Dolores who came to Katie to get her hair done at the salon. *She* would have been delighted with the way Frankie had turned out and would rejoice at such a successful outcome. But no, they were stuck with Moira. Thank God Noel had been in the kitchen while stupid, negative Moira was talking. It was just a miracle that he hadn't heard.

Noel had, of course, heard every word and he was holding on by a thread.

What a sour, mean cow Moira was, and he had just begun to see some good in her. Not now. Not ever again after such a statement. He managed to shout out a cheerful good-bye as he heard the door. He wouldn't think about it. It was nonsense. He would think about the party instead. About Frankie, his little girl. That woman's remarks had no power to hurt him. He would rise above it.

First he must pretend to Lisa that he hadn't heard. That was important.

Moira walked briskly along the road away from Chestnut Court. She was sorry she had spoken to Lisa like that. It was unprofessional. It wasn't like her. She had been thrown by Lisa's apparent freedom to get on with it and then, of course, she had her own worries about her father and Maureen Kennedy. Still and all, it was no reason to run off at the mouth about Noel. Mercifully, he was in the kitchen at the washing machine and didn't hear. Lisa was unlikely to bring the subject up.

Why did worries never come singly?

Moira's brother had written to say that their father and Mrs. Kennedy were getting married. Mr. Kennedy was now presumed dead after fifteen years' absence, with no contact being made and his name not found on any British register. They would marry in a month's time and a few people were being invited back to the house. Everyone was very pleased, her brother wrote.

Moira was sure they were, but then they didn't have to cope with the fact that Mr. Kennedy was alive and well, living in the hostel and on Moira's caseload.

"Father, it's Moira."

He sounded as surprised as if the prime minister of Australia had telephoned him.

"Moira!" was all he could say.

"I hear that you're getting married again. . . ." Moira came straight to the point.

"Yes, we hope to. Are you pleased for us?"

"Very, and is everyone okay with you getting married, what with . . ." She paused delicately.

"He's presumed dead," her father said in sepulchral way. "The state gives a declaration of death after seven years and he's been gone years longer than that."

"And . . . um . . . the Church?" Moira said.

"Oh, endless conversations with the parish priest, then they went to the archdiocese, but there's a thing called *presumptio mortis* and each case is argued on its merits, and since this boyo hasn't had an address or a record of any sort, there isn't any problem."

"And were you going to invite me?" It felt like probing a sore tooth. She hoped her father would say it was very small and, considering their age and circumstances, they had restricted the numbers.

"Oh, indeed. I'd be delighted if you were there. We both would be delighted."

"Thank you very much."

"Not at all. I'm glad you'll be there." He hung up without giving her the date, time or place but, after all, she could get those from her brother.

Frankie's birthday party was a triumph.

Frankie had a crown and so did Johnny, since it was his birthday too. Apart from the two birthday babies there were very few children coming to the party, but lots of grown-ups. Lizzie was helping with the jellies and Molly Carroll was in charge of the cocktail sausages. Frankie and Johnny were much too young to appreciate Mr. Gallagher's magic tricks but the grown-ups loved him and there were great sighs of amazement as he produced rabbits, colored scarves and gold coins from the air. The children loved the rabbits and searched fruitlessly in the magician's top hat to know where they had gone. Josie suggested a rabbit hutch in the new garden, and the idea was received with great enthusiasm.

Noel was glad the party went well. There were no tantrums among the children, no one was overtired. He had even arranged for wine and beer to be served to the adults. It hadn't bothered him in the least. Faith and Lisa cleared up and quietly put the unfinished bottles in Faith's bag.

But Noel's heart was heavy. Two chance remarks at the party had upset him more than he would have believed possible.

Dingo Duggan, who always said the wrong thing, commented that Frankie was far too good-looking to be a child of Noel's. Noel managed to smile and said that nature had a strange way in compensating for flaws.

Paddy Carroll said that Frankie was a beautiful child. She had very fine cheekbones and huge dark eyes.

"She's like her mother, then," Noel said, but his mind was far away. Stella had a vibrant, lively face, yes, but she didn't have fine cheekbones and huge dark eyes.

Neither did Noel.

Was it possible that Frankie was the child of someone else?

He sat very quietly when everyone had gone; eventually, Faith sat down beside him.

"Was it a strain having alcohol in the house, Noel?" Faith asked.

"No, I never thought about it. Why?"

"It's just you seem a bit down." She was sympathetic, and so he told her. He repeated the words that Moira had said: that he was naïve to believe he was Frankie's father.

Faith listened with tears in her eyes.

"I never heard anything so ridiculous. She's a sour, sad, bitter woman. You're never going to start giving any credence to anything she would say?"

"I don't know. It's possible."

"No, it's not possible! Why would she have chosen *you* unless you were the father?" Faith was outraged on his behalf.

"Stella more or less said that at the time," he said.

"Put it out of your head, Noel. You are the best father in the world and that Moira can't bring herself to accept this. That's all there is to it."

Noel smiled wanly.

"Here, I'll make us a mug of tea and we'll eat the leftovers," she said.

Moira went to visit Mr. Kennedy in the hostel to make sure he was getting all his entitlements. He had settled in well.

"Did you ever think of going back home to where you were from originally?" she asked him diffidently.

"Never. That part of life is over for me. As far as they're all concerned I'm dead. I'd prefer it that way," he said.

It made Moira feel a little bit, but not entirely, better. She was being unprofessional, and when all was said and done she had nothing left but her profession. Had she fallen down on that too?

She also regretted her outburst to Lisa when she questioned Noel's paternity of Frankie. It had been unforgivable. Fortunately, he hadn't heard it, or at any rate he was polite when she talked to him, which was the same thing.

Noel couldn't sleep, so he got up and went to the sitting room. He got a piece of paper and made a list of the reasons that he was obviously Frankie's father and another list of reasons that he might not be. As usual, he came to no conclusion. He loved that child so much—she must be his daughter.

And yet he couldn't sleep. There was only one thing to do.

He would get a DNA test.

He would arrange it the next day. He tore up the sheets of paper into tiny pieces.

That was all there was to it.

Noel didn't want to approach either Declan or Dr. Hat about the DNA test. He had asked at the AA meeting if anyone knew how it was done. He made it seem like a casual inquiry for a friend. As always, the assembly was able to find an answer. You went to a doctor, who took a swab of your cheek and sent it to a laboratory—couldn't be more simple.

Yes, all very well, but Noel didn't want Declan to know his doubts. He couldn't ask Hat either, since Hat was family now that he had married Emily. So it would have to be someone totally new.

He wondered what advice his cousin Emily would give him. She would say, "Be ruthlessly honest and do it quickly." There was no arguing with that.

He looked up a doctor on the other side of the city. It was a woman doctor, who was practical and to the point.

"It will cost you to have this test done. We have to pay the lab."

"Sure, I know that," Noel agreed.

"I mean, it's not just a whim or a silly row with your partner or anything?"

"It's nothing like that. I just need to know."

"And if it turns out that you are *not* the child's father?"

"I will make up my mind what to do then."

"You have to be prepared to hear something you don't want to hear," she persisted.

"I can't settle until I know," he said simply.

And after that it was straightforward. He brought Frankie in and swabs were taken. He would know for sure in three weeks.

Even though he had been told that it would take three weeks, Noel watched the post every day. The doctor had promised to let him have the results as soon as she got them. They had agreed that phones could be unreliable or too public.

Better to send it in a letter.

Noel examined every envelope that arrived, but there was nothing.

Lisa went to London and came back thrilled with a job offer.

He had never felt time moving so slowly. The days in Hall's were endless. His need for a drink after each day was so acute that he went to an AA meeting almost every evening. Why could it take so long to match up bits of tissue or whatever DNA was?

He would look at Frankie sometimes and feel covered in shame that he was doing this to her—that he wanted so much to know.

Noel had a long history of being in denial. When he was drinking, he denied the possibility that anyone would ever discover this at work. When he stopped drinking he banished all thoughts of comfortable bars from his head and memory. Mainly it worked for him, but not always.

It was the same now. He banished the possibility that Frankie might *not* be his child. He just would not think what he would do then. The fact that Stella might have lied to him or been mistaken and the heartbreaking possibility that Frankie might not be his little girl but somebody else's—it was too big to think about. It had to be left out of his conscious mind.

Once he knew one way or the other, it would be easier. This was the worst bit.

The letter arrived at Chestnut Court.

Lisa left it on the table as she went out; in the silent flat Noel poured himself another cup of tea. His hand was too shaky to pick up the envelope. The teapot had rattled alarmingly against the teacup. He was too weak to open it now. He had to get through this day without shaking like this. Perhaps he should put the letter away and open it tomorrow. He put it into a drawer. Thank God he had shaved already; he could never do it like this.

He dressed very slowly. He was pale and his eyes looked tired, but really and truly he might pass for a normal person, not someone with the most important secret of his life tidied away, unopened, in a drawer. A person who would give every single possession he had for a pint of beer accompanied by a large Irish whiskey.

How amazing that he looked perfectly normal. Now, looking at him, you might think he was a perfectly ordinary man.

Lisa was startled to find him there when she arrived back with Dingo Duggan and his van. She was going to take her possessions down to Katie and Garry's.

"Hey, I thought you'd be at work," she said.

Noel shook his head. "Day off," he muttered.

"Lucky old you. Where's Frankie? I thought you'd want to celebrate a day off with her."

"She went with Emily and Hat. No point in breaking the routine," he said flatly.

"You okay, Noel?"

"Sure I am. What are you doing?"

"Moving my stuff, trying to give you two lovebirds more room."

"You know you're not in the way—there's plenty of room for all of us."

"But I'll be going to London soon. I can't clutter your place up with all my boxes."

"I don't know what I'd have done without you, Lisa, I really don't."

"Wasn't it a great year!" Lisa agreed. "A year when you found Frankie and when I . . . well, when I let the scales fall from my eyes over so many things. Anton for one, my father for another . . ."

"You never said why you came here that night," Noel said.

"And you never asked, which made everything so restful. I'll miss Frankie, though, desperately. Faith is going to send me a photo of her every month so that I'll see her growing up."

"You'll forget all about us." He managed a smile.

"As if I would. This is the first proper home I ever had." She gave him a quick hug and went into her bedroom to check the boxes that were going to be driven over to her sister's.

"Give Katie my love," Noel said mechanically.

"I will. She's dying to tell me something—I know by her voice."

"It must be nice to have a sister," he said.

"It is. Maybe you and Faith could arrange a little sister for Frankie one day," she teased.

"Maybe." He didn't sound very confident about it.

Lisa was relieved to hear Dingo arriving to carry the boxes. Noel was definitely not himself today.

Katie did indeed want to tell Lisa something. It was that she was pregnant. She and Garry were overjoyed and they hoped Lisa would be pleased for them too.

Lisa said she was delighted. She hadn't known that this was in the plan at all, but Katie said it had been long hoped for.

"Two career people? Highfliers?" Lisa said, in mock wonder.

"Yes, but we wanted a baby to make it complete."

"I'll be a terrific aunt. I don't know anything about having a baby but I sure as anything know how to look after one."

"I wish you weren't going away," Katie said.

"I'll be back often," Lisa promised. "And this baby will grow up in a family that wants a baby—not like the way you and I grew up, Katie."

. . .

Emily and Hat were surrounded by seed catalogs, trying to decide from the huge amount on offer. Frankie sat with them and seemed to study the pictures of flowers as well.

"She's just no trouble," Emily said fondly.

"Pity we didn't meet earlier—we could well have had a few of those ourselves," Hat said wistfully.

"Oh, no, Hat, I have much more the personality of a grand-mother than a mother. I like a baby who goes home in the evening," she said.

"Is it dull for you here with me?" he asked suddenly.

"What do you mean?"

"Back in America you had a busy life, teaching, going to art exhibits, thousands of people around the place."

"Stop fishing for compliments, Hat. You know that I'm besotted with this place. And with you. And when we push this little pet back up to Chestnut Court I will make you the most wonderful cheese soufflé to prove it."

"Lord above, life doesn't get much better than this," Hat said with a sigh of pleasure.

The flat was very silent when Lisa and Dingo had departed with a chorus of good-byes.

Noel opened the drawer and took out the letter. Perhaps he should eat something to keep his strength up. He had eaten no breakfast. He made himself a tomato sandwich, carefully adding chopped onion and cutting off the crusts. It tasted like sawdust.

He pulled the envelope towards him.

When he saw it all confirmed that he was Frankie's father, then everything would be all right. Wouldn't it? This hollow, empty feel-ing would go and he would be normal again.

But suppose that . . . Noel would not allow himself to go down that road. Of course he was Frankie's father. And now that he had eaten his tasteless tomato sandwich, he was ready to open the envelope.

He took the letter from the drawer and slit it open with the knife he had used to make his sandwich. It was stilted and official, but it was clear and concise.

The DNA samples did not match.

A hot rage came over him. He could feel it burning around his neck and ears. He could feel a heavy lump in his stomach and a strange light-headedness around his eyes and forehead.

This could not be true.

Stella could not have told him a pack of lies and palmed off her child on him. Surely it was impossible that she had made all these arrangements and put his name on the birth certificate if she had not believed it was true.

Perhaps she had so many lovers she had no idea who might be Frankie's father.

She could have picked him because he was humble and would make no fuss.

Or possibly Frankie's real father was so unreliable or unavailable that he could not be contacted.

Bile rose in his throat.

He knew exactly what would make him feel better. He picked up his jacket and went out.

Moira was having a busy morning at the heart clinic. Once the word had got around that she was an expert on finding people entitlements, her caseload had increased. It was Moira's belief that if there were benefits there, then people should avail themselves of them. She would fill in the paperwork, arrange the carers, the allowances or the support needed.

Today Mr. Kennedy was coming to the clinic for his checkup; she would see him and make sure that he was being properly looked after. And unexpectedly Clara Casey had asked if Moira could spare her ten minutes on a personal matter.

Moira wondered what on earth it could be. The gossip around the clinic had said that Dr. Casey had moved Mr. Ennis into her home, but surely Clara didn't want to discuss anything quite as personal as that.

Just after midday, when Moira's stint ended officially, Clara slipped into her office.

"This is not on the clinic's time, Moira. It's a personal favor on my time and yours."

"Sure, go ahead," Moira said. A few months ago she might have said something sharper, something more official, but events had changed her.

"It's about my daughter Linda—she and her husband are very anxious to adopt a baby and they don't know how to set about it."

"What have they done so far?" Moira asked.

"Nothing much, except talk about it, but now they want to move forward."

"Fine—do you want me to talk to them sometime?"

"Linda is actually here today. She came to take me to lunch. Would that be too instant?"

"No, not at all. Do you want to stay for the conversation?"

"No, no—but I do appreciate this, Moira. I've realized over the last months you are amazingly thorough and tenacious. If anyone can help Linda and Nick, you can."

Moira couldn't remember why she had thought of Dr. Casey as aloof and superior. She watched as Clara ushered in her tall, handsome daughter.

"I'll leave you in good hands," Clara said, and mother and daughter hugged each other. Moira felt an absurd flush of pleasure all over her face and neck.

At lunch in the shopping precinct Linda was bubbling over with enthusiasm.

"I can't think why you didn't like that woman—she was *marvelous*. It's all very straightforward. You go to the health board and they refer you to the adoption section and fill in a lot of details, and they come for home assessment visits. She asked did we mind what nationality the child would be and I said of course not. It really looks as if it might happen."

"I'm so pleased, Linda." Clara spoke gently.

"So you and Frank had better polish up your babysitting skills," Linda said with unnaturally bright eyes.

Moira left the clinic in high good humor. For once it appeared her talents had been recognized. It was one of those rare occasions when people actually seemed pleased with the social worker.

She had warned Linda about delays and bureaucracy and said the most important thing was to be quietly persistent, keeping even-tempered no matter what the provocation. Linda had been delighted with her, and moreover, Linda's mother had given words of high praise.

This was a personal first.

Her steps took her past Chestnut Court, and she looked from habit at Noel and Lisa's flat. Noel would be at work, but maybe Lisa was there packing her belongings. She was heading off to London soon. Anyway, no point in going in there and talking to Lisa and being accused of spying or policing the situation. She didn't want to lose the good feeling that had come from the clinic, so she passed by.

Emily got a phone call at lunchtime. It was Noel. His voice was unsteady. She thought he sounded drunk.

"Everything all right, Noel?" she asked anxiously, her heart lurching. He should have been there to pick up Frankie. What could have happened?

"Yes. Everything's fine." He spoke like a robot. "I'm at the zoo, actually."

"The zoo?" Emily was stunned. The zoo was miles away, on the other side of the city. She didn't know whether to be relieved or horrified. If Noel was there, then he was safe; but then he was wandering around looking at lions and aviaries and elephants rather than picking up his daughter.

"Yes. I haven't been here for ages. They've lots of new things."

"Yes, Noel, I'm sure they do."

"So I was wondering could you possibly keep Frankie for a while longer?"

"Of course," Emily agreed, worried. Was he drunk? His voice sounded stressed. What could have brought all this on? "And are you at the zoo on your own?"

"Yes, for the moment."

Noel had been over and over it in his mind. For a year he had been living a lie. Frankie was not his child. God knew whose child she was. He loved her like his own—of course he did. But he had thought she was his own child and had no one else to look after her. His name was on the birth certificate; he had loved her and looked after her and fed her and changed her. He had protected her, given her a life surrounded by people who loved her; he had made her his. Did he regret all this? She was a year old, her mother was dead— what sort of start in life would it be if he washed his hands of her now?

Could he bring up another man's child as his own? He didn't think so. She was someone else's child; someone else had fathered her and walked away, got away with it. Should he find out who it was? Would it be a wild-goose chase?

And what sort of man would he be if he ran away now? Could he abandon her when she needed him every bit as much as when she was that tiny, helpless baby he had brought home from the hospital? He pictured the flat that was their home: Frankie's toys on the floor, her clothes warming on the radiators, her photographs on the mantelpiece. Her favorite food in the kitchen, the baby lotions in the bathroom; he knew where she was every minute of the day. He remembered the horror of the night she'd been missing. Everyone had been out looking for her—so many people had been concerned for her safety. She was with Emily and Hat now, and when they went to the thrift shop, they'd take her with them. His own parents knew her as their grandchild. She knew everyone in the neighborhood; they were all part of her life, as she was part of theirs. Was he going to end all that?

But could he bring up another man's child?

He needed a drink. Just the one, so he could see his way clearly.

When Moira called at St. Jarlath's Thrift Shop and seemed surprised to see Frankie asleep there in her pram, Emily kept her worries to herself.

"What time is her father picking her up?" Moira asked. She didn't really want to know; it was just a stance—she always liked them to know that she was in control.

"He will be along later," Emily said with a confident smile. "Can I interest you in anything here, Moira? You have such good taste. There's a very attractive bag here—it's almost a cross between a bag and a briefcase. I think it's Moroccan; it's got lovely designs on it."

It was, as Emily said, very attractive, and would be perfect for Moira. She fingered it and wondered. But before she spent money on herself she must think of a present for her father and Mrs. Kennedy. Maybe Emily could help here too.

"I need a wedding present, something unopened, as it were. It's for a middle-aged couple in the country."

"Do they have their own house?" Emily inquired.

"Yes, well she has a house, and he's living there . . . I mean, going to live there."

"Is she a good cook?"

"Yes, she is, actually." Moira was surprised at the question.

"Then she won't need anything for the kitchen—she'll have all that under control. There's a very nice tablecloth, an unwanted gift, apparently. We could open it to make sure it's perfect, then seal it up again."

"Tablecloth?" Moira wasn't sure.

"Look at it—it's the best linen and has hand-painted flowers on it. I'd say she'd love it. Is she a close friend?"

"No," Moira said. Then she realized that it sounded a little bit bald. "I mean, she's going to marry my father," she explained.

"Oh, I'm sure your new stepmother would love this cloth," Emily said.

"Stepmother?" Moira tried the word on for size.

"Well, that's what she'll be, surely?"

"Yes, of course." Moira spoke hastily.

"I hope they'll be very happy," Emily said.

"I think they will. It's complicated, but they are well suited."

"Well, that's what it's all about."

"Yes, it is in a way. It's just that there's unfinished business, hard to explain but that's what it is."

"I suppose there always is," Emily said soothingly. She hadn't an idea what Moira was talking about.

Moira left with both the briefcase and the tablecloth; she was rapidly becoming one of the thrift shop's best customers.

There was something weighing heavily on her mind. Surely Mr. Kennedy had a right to know that his house existed in Liscuan, that his wife was taking another man in as her husband, and this man was the social worker's father. Moira knew that many would advise her to stay out of it. It would all have gone ahead without a problem if Moira hadn't come across Mr. Kennedy and settled him into long-term hostel care. But there was no denying it. She had met Mr. Kennedy and she could not let it go.

"Mr. Kennedy, you're all right?" They sat in the dayroom of the hostel.

"Miss Tierney. It's not your day today."

"I was in the area."

"I see."

"I was wondering, Mr. Kennedy, are you properly settled here?"

"You ask me that every week, Miss Tierney. It's okay—I've told you that."

"But do you think of your time in Liscuan?"

"No. I'm gone years from there."

"So you said, but would you like to be back there? Would you try again with your wife?"

"Isn't she a stranger to me now, after all these years?" he asked.

"But suppose she got married again? Presumed you were dead."

"More power to her if she did."

"You wouldn't mind?"

"I made my choice in life, which was to go off—she's free to make hers."

Moira looked at him. This was good—but she wasn't off the hook yet. She still knew what was going on. She had to tell him.

"Mr. Kennedy. There's something I have to tell you," she said.

"Don't worry about all that," he said.

"No, please, you must listen. You see, things aren't as simple as you think. Actually, there's a bit of a situation I have to tell you about."

"Miss Tierney, I know all that," he said.

She thought for a wild moment that maybe he did, but realized that he couldn't possibly know anything of life in Liscuan. He had been an exile for years.

"No, wait, you must listen to me . . . ," she said.

"Don't I know it all—your father's moved into the house, and now he's going to marry Maureen. And why shouldn't they?"

"Because you are still her husband," Moira stammered.

"They think I'm dead, and I am as far as they are concerned."

"You've known all the time?" Moira was astounded.

"I knew you at once. I remember you well from back home—you haven't changed a bit. Tough, able to take things. You didn't have a great childhood."

This man, ending his days in a hostel, pitied her. Moira felt weak at the way the earth had tilted.

"You're very good to tell me, but honestly we should just leave things the way they are—that way there's the least damage."

"But . . ."

"But nothing. Leave it happen, let them get married. Don't mention me."

"How did you know?" Her voice was almost a whisper.

"I did have a friend I stayed in touch with—he kept me posted."

"And is he there in Liscuan now, your friend?"

"No, he's dead, Moira. Only you and I know now."

Secrets were a great equalizer, Moira thought. He wasn't calling her Miss Tierney now.

Linda told her mother that Moira was as good as her word. She had made appointments here and introductions there, and the process was now under way. Nick and Linda said they would have been lost in a fog without her. She seemed to find no obstacles in her way. A perfect quality in a social worker.

"I can't understand why none of you like her," Linda said. "I've never met anyone as helpful in my life."

"She's fine at her work," Clara agreed. "But, God, I wouldn't like to go on a holiday with her. She manages to insult and upset everyone in some way."

Frank agreed with her. "She's a woman who never smiles," he said disapprovingly. "That's a character flaw in a person."

"She had the strength of character to refuse to be your spy when she came to the clinic," Clara said cheerfully. "That's another point in her favor."

"I think she must have misread the situation there. . . ." Frank didn't want to bring disharmony into their home.

. . .

It was nine o clock in the evening when Noel and Malachy turned up at Emily and Hat's house to collect Frankie.

Noel was pale but calm. Malachy looked very tired.

"I'm going to spend the night in Chestnut Court," Malachy said to Emily.

"That's great. Lisa's taken her things so it might be a bit lonely there otherwise," Emily said neutrally.

Frankie, who had been fast asleep, woke up and was delighted to be the center of attention.

"Dada!" she said to Noel.

"That's right," he said mechanically.

"I've been explaining to Frankie that her granny and granda are going to build a lovely, safe garden where she and all her friends can play."

"Great," said Malachy.

"Yes," said Noel.

"Your parents are going to have a sod-turning ceremony for the children's garden on Saturday. The work is going to start then."

"Sure," Noel said.

Wearily, Malachy got them on the road. Frankie was chattering away from her stroller. Words that were recognizable but not making any sense.

Noel was silent. He was there in body but not in spirit; surely people were able to guess something was different, something had changed. Frankie was just the same child she had been this morning but everything else had changed, and he hadn't yet had time to get accustomed to the idea.

Malachy slept on the sofa. During the night he heard Frankie start to cry and Noel get up to soothe the little girl and comfort her. The moonlight fell on Noel's face as he sat and held the child; Malachy could see there were tears on his cheeks.

Moira took the train to Liscuan. She was met at the station by Pat and Erin.

"Who's minding the store?" she asked.

"Plenty of help, good neighbors, all delighted that we're going to your father's wedding." Erin was dressed to the nines with a rose-and-cream-colored outfit, a big pink rose in her hair. Moira felt dowdy in her best suit. She looked at Erin's dainty, girlish handbag and wished she had not brought her own serious-looking briefcase. Still, too late to change now. They would need to hurry to be in time for the ceremony.

There were about fifty people waiting at the church.

"You mean all these people know that our father is getting married?" she asked Pat.

"Aren't they all so pleased for him?" Pat said. It was as simple as that.

And Moira prepared to sit through the whole ceremony, nuptial Mass and papal blessing knowing that she was the only person present who knew the whole story. When it came to the part where the priest asked was there any reason why these two persons should not marry, Moira sat dumb.

The presents were displayed in one of the reception rooms at the Stella Maris, and everyone seemed to think highly of the hand-painted tablecloth. Maureen Kennedy, now Maureen Tierney and her stepmother, drew Moira aside.

"That was really a most thoughtful gift, and I hope now that the situation has been regularized you will come sometime and stay under our roof and maybe we will eat dinner with this beautiful cloth on the table."

"That would be lovely," Moira breathed.

Faith had been away for three days, and when she came back she rushed in to pick up Frankie.

"Have I brought you the cutest little boots?" she said to the baby as she hugged her.

"The child has far too many clothes," Noel said.

"Ah, Noel, they're lovely little boots—look at them!"

"She'll have grown out of them in a month," he said.

The light had gone out of Faith's face. "Sorry—is something annoying you?"

"Just the way everyone piles clothes on her. That's all."

"I'm not everyone and I'm not piling clothes on her. She needs shoes to go to the opening of the site for the new garden on Saturday."

"Oh, God—I'd forgotten that."

"Better not let your parents know you did. It's the highlight of their year."

"Will there be lots of people there?" he asked.

"Noel, are you all right? You look different somehow, as if something fell on you."

"It did in a way," Noel said.

"Are you going to tell me?"

"No, not at the moment. Is that all right? I'm sorry for being so rude—they're adorable shoes; Frankie will be the last word on Saturday."

"Of course she will—now will I get us some supper?"

"You're a girl in a million, Faith."

"Oh, much more than that—one in a billion, I'd say," she said and went into the kitchen.

Noel forced himself into good humor. Frankie was unpacking the little pink boots from their box with huge concentration. Why couldn't she be his child? He sat in the kitchen and watched Faith move deftly around, getting together a supper in minutes, something that would have taken him forever.

"You love Frankie as much as if she were yours, don't you?" he said.

"Of course I do. Is this what's worrying you? She is mine in a way, since I mostly live with her and I help to look after her."

"But the fact that she's not yours doesn't make any difference?"

"What are you on about, Noel? I love the child. I'm mad about her—don't you know that?"

"Yes, but you've always known she wasn't yours," he said sadly.

"Oh, I know what this is all about—it's this ludicrous Moira who started this off in your head. It's like a wasp in your mind, Noel, buzzing at you. Chase it away. You're obviously her father; you're a great father."

"Suppose I had a DNA test and found she wasn't—what then?"

"You'd insult that beautiful child by having a DNA test? Noel, you're unhinged. And what would it matter what the test said, anyway?"

He could have told her there and then. Gone to the drawer and taken out the letter with the results. He could have said that he had done the test and the answer was that Frankie was not his. This was the only girl he had ever felt close enough to even consider marrying; should he share this huge secret with her?

Instead, he shrugged.

"You're probably right—only a very suspicious, untrusting person would go for that test."

"That's more like it, Noel," Faith said happily.

Noel sat for a long time at the table when Faith left. He had three envelopes in front of him: one contained the results of the DNA test, one had the letter that Stella had left for him before she died and one held the letter she had addressed to Frankie. Back in the frightening early days when fighting to keep away from drink on an hourly basis, he had often been tempted to open the letter to Frankie. In those days he was anxious to look for some reason to keep going, something that might give him strength. Today he wanted to read it in case Stella had told her daughter who her real father was.

Something stopped him, though, perhaps some sense of playing fair. Although, of course, that was nonsense. Stella certainly hadn't played fair. Still, if he hadn't opened it back then, he would not do it now.

What had Stella got from it all, anyway? A short, restless life, a lot of pain and fear, no family, no friends. She never got to see her baby or know the little arms around her neck. Noel had got all this and more. A year ago, what did Noel have going for him? Not much. A drunk in a dead-end job, without friends, without hope. It had all changed because of Frankie. How lonely and frightened Stella must have felt that last night.

He reached out and read the letter she had written to him in that ward. *"Tell Frankie that I wasn't all bad . . ."* she had said. *"Tell her that if things had been different you and I would both have been there to look after her . . ."*

Noel straightened his shoulders.

He was Frankie's father in every way that mattered. Perhaps Stella had made a genuine mistake? Who knew what happened in other people's lives? And suppose somehow Stella was looking out for Frankie from somewhere—she deserved to know better than that the baby had been abandoned at the age of twelve months. Noel had loved this child yesterday, he still loved her today. He would always love her. It was as simple as that.

He reached across the table and put the two letters from Stella into the drawer. The letter with the DNA results he tore into tiny pieces.

It was a fine day for the turning of the sod. Charles and Josie put their hands together on the shovel and dug into the ground of the small waste patch they had secured for the new garden. Everyone clapped and Father Flynn said his customary few words about the great results that came from a sense of community involvement and caring.

Some of Muttie's Associates had come to watch the ceremony, and one of them was heard to say he would much prefer a statue of Muttie and Hooves to be raised instead of some long-dead saint whom nobody knew anything about.

Lizzie was there, with her arm around Simon's shoulders. He was going to New Jersey next week but had promised to be back in three months to tell them all what it was like. Marco and Maud stood together; Marco had hopes of a spring wedding but Maud said she was in no hurry to marry.

"Your grandfather gave me his blessing to marry you," Marco whispered.

"Yes, but he didn't say in the blessing *when* you were to marry me," Maud said firmly.

Declan, Johnny and a visibly pregnant Fiona were there, with Declan's parents and Dimples, the big dog. Dimples had a love-hate relationship with Caesar, the tiny spaniel. It wasn't that he had anything against Caesar—it was just that he was too small to be a proper dog.

Emily and Hat were there, part of the scenery now. People hardly remembered a time when they were not together. Emily was noting everything to tell Betsy that night by e-mail. She would even send her a picture of it all. Betsy too had fallen under the spell of this little community and was always asking for details of this and that. She and Eric had every intention of coming back again next year and catching up where they had left off.

Emily thought back to the first day that she herself had arrived in this street and heard her uncle and aunt's plans to build a huge statue. How amazing that it had all turned out so differently and so well.

Noel, Faith and Frankie were there, Frankie showing everyone her new pink boots. People pointed out to Noel that one of the houses in the Crescent would shortly be for sale—maybe he and Faith could buy it. Then Frankie would be near her garden. It was a very tempting idea, they said.

And as they wound their way back to Emily and Hat's house, where tea and cakes were being served, Noel felt a weight lift from his shoulders. He passed the house where Paddy Carroll and his wife, Molly, had slaved to raise their son, a doctor, and then past Muttie and Lizzie's house, where those twins had found a better home than they could have dreamed of. He blinked a couple of times as he began to realize that a lot of things didn't matter anymore.

Frankie wanted to walk the length of the road, even though she wasn't really able to; Faith followed with the buggy but Frankie struggled hard, holding Noel's hand and calling out "Dada" a lot. Just as they got to Emily and Hat's place, her little legs began to buckle and Noel swung her up into his arms.

"Good girl, Daddy's good little girl," he said over and over. His chest was much less tight, the awful feeling of running down a long corridor gone. He put his other arm around Faith's shoulders and ushered his little family into the house to have tea.

My dear, dear Frankie, my lovely daughter,

I will never see you or know you, but I do love you so very much. I fought hard to live for you but it didn't work. I started too late, you see. If only I had known that I would have a little girl to live for . . . But it's all far too late for those kind of wishes now. Instead I wish you the very best that life can give you. I wish you courage—I have plenty of that. Too much, some might say! I hope that you will not be as foolhardy and as reckless as I was. Instead, may you have peace and the love of good people who will mind you and make you happy. Tonight I sit here in a ward where nobody can really sleep. It's my last night here, you see, and tomorrow is your first day here. I wish we had been able to meet.

But I know one thing. Noel will be a great father. He is very strong and he can't wait to meet you tomorrow. He has been preparing for weeks, getting things ready for you, learning how to hold you, to feed you, to change you. He will be a wonderful dad and I have this very clear feeling that you will be the light of his life.

So many people are waiting for you tomorrow. Don't be sad for me—you have managed to make sense of my life eventually!

Live well and happily, little Frankie. Laugh a lot and be full of trust, not suspicion.

Remember your mother loved you with all her heart.
—Stella

Acknowledgments

I would like to thank my editor, Carole Baron, and my agent, Chris Green, who have been hugely supportive and great friends to me during the writing of this book.

A NOTE ABOUT THE AUTHOR

Maeve Binchy is the author of numerous best-selling books, including her most recent novel, *Heart and Soul,* in addition to *Nights of Rain and Stars, Quentins, Scarlet Feather, Circle of Friends* and *Tara Road,* which was an Oprah's Book Club selection. She has written for *Gourmet; O, The Oprah Magazine; Modern Maturity* and *Good Housekeeping,* among other publications. She and her husband, Gordon Snell, live in Dalkey, Ireland.

A NOTE ON THE TYPE

This book was set in Adobe Garamond. Designed for the Adobe Corporation by Robert Slimbach, the fonts are based on types first cut by Claude Garamond (ca. 1480–1561). Garamond was a pupil of Geoffroy Tory and is believed to have followed the Venetian models, although he introduced a number of important differences, and it is to him that we owe the letter we now know as "old style." He gave to his letters a certain elegance and feeling of movement that won their creator an immediate reputation and the patronage of Francis I of France.

Composed by Creative Graphics, Allentown, Pennsylvania
Printed and bound by Berryville Graphics, Berryville, Virginia
Designed by Virginia Tan

ENDING POVERTY
IN AMERICA

ENDING POVERTY
IN AMERICA

HOW TO RESTORE THE
AMERICAN DREAM

Edited by
Senator John Edwards,
Marion Crain,
and Arne L. Kalleberg

Published in conjunction with the
Center on Poverty, Work and Opportunity
University of North Carolina at Chapel Hill

THE NEW PRESS

NEW YORK
LONDON

Compilation © 2007 by the University of North Carolina at Chapel Hill on behalf of the Center
on Poverty, Work and Opportunity
Individual essays © 2007 by each author
All rights reserved.
No part of this book may be reproduced, in any form, without written permission from the publisher.

Requests for permission to reproduce selections from this book should be mailed to:
Permissions Department, The New Press, 38 Greene Street, New York, NY 10013.

Published in the United States by The New Press, New York, 2007
Distributed by W.W. Norton & Company, Inc., New York

CIP data available.
978-1-59558-176-1 (hc.)

The New Press was established in 1990 as a not-for-profit alternative to the large, commercial publishing
houses currently dominating the book-publishing industry. The New Press operates in the public
interest rather than for private gain and is committed to publishing, in innovative ways, works
of educational, cultural, and community value that are often deemed insufficiently profitable.

www.thenewpress.com

Composition by Westchester Book Group
This book was set in Janson Text

Printed in the United States of America

2   4   6   8   10   9   7   5   3   1

Contents

Preface

The University of North Carolina (UNC) Center on Poverty, Work and Opportunity was established in February 2005 with the support of the Office of the Provost at UNC-Chapel Hill and the UNC School of Law. Its founder and Director, Senator John Edwards, selected the Center's staff: Marion Crain, Deputy Director and Paul Eaton Professor of Law; Laura Hogshead, Assistant Director; and Tracy Sheyda Brown, Administrative Assistant. The Office of the Provost appointed an Advisory Board composed of distinguished faculty from across the UNC-Chapel Hill campus. In December 2006, Senator Edwards completed his service as Director of the Center and Marion Crain was appointed Director. Based in the School of Law, the Center is a nonpartisan interdisciplinary academic center that brings together scholars, policymakers, lawyers, community leaders, and students to further research and policymaking on issues relating to poverty, work, and opportunity. The Center focuses on the centrality of work to economic survival and social and economic equality, and all of its programs and efforts are devoted to issues of the working poor. Its core mission is effectively captured in the Center's three-word title: poverty is the problem, work is the solution, and opportunity is what is faltering in the American system.

The Center's programming marries academic rigor with the valuable frontline experience of talented practitioners from nonprofit organizations around the nation. This book arose out of a desire to share the unique union of academic research and practical experience from which the Center has benefited during its first two years of operation. One of the first activities of the Center was to host a day-long Summit on Poverty, "New Frontiers in Poverty Research and Policy," wherein leading poverty scholars from across the country engaged in nonpartisan dialogue across disciplines and ideologies. The Summit's proceedings are published in the *Employee Rights and Employment Policy Journal* 10, no. 1 (Fall 2006): 1–204. The Center also sponsored its first large conference, "Challenging the Two Americas: New Policies to Fight Poverty," in March 2006. This book collects some of the best ideas born out of the Center's programming. We hope that the insights of the esteemed academics, practitioners, and thought leaders who joined in this collaborative venture will inform, challenge, and inspire the fight against poverty.

Acknowledgments

The Center on Poverty, Work and Opportunity is grateful to the University of North Carolina at Chapel Hill and the School of Law for founding and supporting the Center. We would also like to thank the following people, whose time, expertise, and dedication ensured that the important discussions and ideas from the Center's work would be shared with a large audience through this publication: Interim Dean Gail Agrawal, Dean John C. Boger, Tracy Sheyda Brown, Laura Hogshead, and Heather Hunt.

ENDING POVERTY
IN AMERICA

Introduction

Marion Crain and Arne L. Kalleberg

DEFINING POVERTY

What is poverty? Who are the poor? Statisticians and government define poverty according to income and wealth. In 2005, 37 million Americans—about one in eight people—lived below the income poverty level, defined as $19,874 for a family of four. Almost 13 million were children under 18. A disproportionate number are African American and Hispanic: about a quarter of African American families and about a fifth of Hispanic families are poor. The income gap between the rich and the poor is growing as well: in 2005 the top 20 percent of U.S. households received over half of all income, while the bottom 20 percent of households received only about 3 percent of total income.[1]

Wealth inequalities are also on the rise: in 2004 the top 1 percent of households by income held more than a third of all net worth and financial assets. Approximately 80 percent of stock is held by the top 10 percent of wealthy households; the poorest 40 percent of households own less than 1 percent of all stocks. Although homeownership rates are rising across the population, Hispanics and African Americans continue to lag behind whites: fewer than half of Hispanic and African American families owned homes, compared with almost three-quarters of white families.[2]

Over 46 million Americans (about 16 percent of the population) lacked health insurance coverage in 2005, and the number continues to rise. Of children under age 18, 8.3 million lacked health-care coverage (about 11 percent of this age group). African Americans and Hispanics constitute a disproportionate share of the uninsured. Most Americans obtain health insurance through employment, yet the percentage of employers that provide coverage is decreasing; less than 60 percent of Americans enjoyed employer-sponsored coverage in 2005. Over 27 million workers are employed with no health insurance. Most of the uninsured are concentrated at the bottom of the income distribution.[3]

But the poor are not statistics. They are human beings—our neighbors, our children, our fellow Americans. Poverty is not a "sustainable condition" that the more well-to-do have the luxury to turn away from. In the words of Barbara Ehrenreich, poverty in America is "a state of emergency."[4]

WHAT BECAME OF THE AMERICAN DREAM?

The statistics just outlined are alarming enough in their own right, but the greatest loss for all of us is confidence in the American Dream, defined as "having a good job, being able to retire in security, owning a home, having affordable health care, and a better future for [our] children."[5] A survey conducted in August 2006 found that 51 percent of the workers surveyed believed that their children would be worse off economically than the current generation. Indeed, only 38 percent believed that they themselves were better off financially than they had been four years previously, and 29 percent believed that their fortunes had declined.[6] Poverty thus represents a poverty of opportunity, as well as a poverty of circumstance. It eats away at what is most uniquely American: the American Dream.

WHAT CAUSES POVERTY? TWO STORIES

There are two general views about why some people are poor and others are economically secure. In the first story, people are poor because of their individual characteristics. Proponents of this view focus on the socioeconomic attributes and individual behavioral tendencies of the poor, emphasizing the "culture of poverty" that sets them apart from other Americans.[7] The poor have shortcomings such as inadequate education or skills, poor motivation to work and other negative attitudes or habits, or inability to form stable families. These attributes make it difficult for them to obtain and hold jobs that pay wages sufficient to meet their economic needs and those of their families. Compared with the nonpoor, those classified as poor are also disproportionately nonwhite and more likely to be immigrants, more likely to have relatively little education, and more likely to be in families that are headed by single women.[8]

A contrasting view sees poverty as a structural feature of a capitalistic economy that is rooted in the institutions of society. According to this story, attributing the causes of poverty to the characteristics of individuals is "blaming the victims" for their poverty and economic distress.[9] Poverty is not attributable to the deficiencies of individuals, but rather to social factors that are beyond their control; these social conditions are public issues, not personal troubles.[10] The structural factors that contribute to poverty and economic stress include the proliferation of low-wage, low-skilled jobs; poor schools and inadequate investment in training and skill formation; lack of access to higher education; residential segregation; discrimination in labor, credit, and housing markets; and so on.

The relative importance of these two explanations—inadequate individual human and social capital versus structural features, especially a lack of well-paying jobs—has been the subject of considerable debate among social scientists, politicians, business leaders, and others concerned about the problem of poverty and economic distress. Policy proposals aimed at alleviating the situation of the working poor are generally framed around one or the other of these two explanations for the causes of poverty. The first explanation suggests a need for programs that improve the skills, attitudes, and other attributes of the poor. By contrast, the second explanation points toward the need to create higher-paying jobs, remove barriers produced by discrimination, and enhance educational access for all.

As with most such debates, each of these views is partially correct and thus also partially wrong. Poverty and economic distress result from a complex interaction between the structure of society and the economy, on the one hand, and characteristics of the people who live and work in them, on the other. For example, lack of education and skills limits the opportunities people have for getting jobs that pay living wages. The existence and persistence of low-wage jobs, in turn, reduce the chances people have of obtaining jobs that pay living wages despite their educational attainments, and reduce their motivation for obtaining the skills necessary to qualify for high-paying jobs.

David Shipler describes vividly the complexity of the factors that are responsible for creating and maintaining poverty in America:

> [P]overty is a constellation of difficulties that magnify one another: not just low wages but also low education, not just dead-end jobs but also limited abilities, not just insufficient savings but also unwise spending, not just poor housing but also poor parenting, not just the lack of health insurance but also the lack of healthy households. . . . The troubles run strongly along both macro and micro levels, as systemic problems in the structure of political and economic power, and as individual problems in personal and family life.[11]

ANTIPOVERTY PUBLIC POLICY

The shifting conceptions of what constitutes poverty and who is poor or economically distressed have dictated historically the shape of antipoverty public policy. Early antipoverty programs divided the poor into two groups: the "deserving" poor and the "undeserving" poor. The fault line between the two was the reason for their inability to work. The "deserving" poor—those temporarily out of the waged labor force through the vicissitudes of labor-market shifts, age, injury, or disability—were the beneficiaries of an uncontested host of government programs aimed at providing a social safety net, including unemployment insurance, disability insurance, old-age insurance, and Medicare insurance.[12] By contrast, the "undeserving" poor, variously referred to as the "underclass" or the "welfare poor," were assumed to be unable to support themselves through work because of their personal or moral shortcomings. Disproportionately female, minority, and unemployed, the undeserving poor were seen as an "other" group—an anomaly amid prosperity. Their many interrelated problems, including dysfunctional family structures, low levels of education and literacy, substance abuse, criminal behavior, hypersegregation, and widespread unemployment, were regarded as qualitatively different from those of the working or middle classes. They were the recipients of income-based programs, including welfare, food stamps, and Medicaid insurance.

By the mid-1990s antipoverty policy had begun to emphasize minimizing the social and economic dependence of the poorest Americans upon government programs. The politics of welfare reform spawned legislation—the 1996 Temporary Assistance for Needy Families (TANF)—that pressed welfare recipients into the workforce and turned the administration of welfare programs over to the states. These programs, like the early years of the War on Poverty in the 1960s, emphasized "labor-supply" policies that involved direct interactions with the poor and were designed to help them move into the paid workforce or upgrade their skills and motivation to work through education and training programs.[13]

It soon became apparent, however, that paid labor-force participation was not necessarily an escape from poverty. Most of the poor in the United States live in working families.[14] One in four people who work full-time, year-round, still earn less than the amount of money needed to keep a family of four above the poverty threshold.[15] The labor-supply programs that accompanied the shift from welfare to work were not successful in alleviating poverty: The bulk of former welfare recipients moved into the ranks of the working poor, finding employment at low-wage jobs with few benefits.[16]

Poverty and economic insecurity were thus revealed as a continuum rather than a dichotomy, with the barriers between the underclass, the working class, and even the middle class far more permeable than was once believed. The working poor and the middle class found themselves facing variants of the same problems that plague the underclass: they work, but at jobs with too little wage income, too little job security, too few opportunities for advancement, and too few health insurance or retirement benefits. They depend upon poorly functioning public schools and inadequate child- and day-care systems, face soaring housing and transportation costs, and stagger under a rising debt load. They survive on the edge. The economic devastation in the wake of job loss, medical crises, the loss of one income from divorce, or natural disasters (such as Hurricane Katrina) can easily push them off their precarious perch.

In short, labor-supply programs have proved inadequate to address the phenomenon of a "working poor"; there remains a need for labor-demand policies that increase the quality of the jobs available.[17] Quoting Shipler again:

> There is no single variable that can be altered to help working people move away from the edge of poverty. Only where the full array of factors is attacked can America fulfill its promise. . . . Relief will come, if at all, in an amalgam that recognizes both the society's obligation through government and business, and the individual's obligation through labor and family—and the commitment of both society and individual through education.[18]

POLICIES TO RESTORE THE AMERICAN DREAM

Policies to restore the American Dream must accomplish several tasks. If economic insecurity exists along a continuum with highly permeable boundaries between the poor and the nonpoor, programs that further opportunity for all are crucial. Direct government assistance through income-based programs should be a strategy of last resort. Instead, we need to create jobs that pay living wages, and to prepare people for these jobs. In addition to policies targeted at the labor market and the workplace, we need policies that promote strong families and that strengthen our communities in both rural and urban areas. The government plays a central role in adopting these kinds of policies and encouraging employers to do so. Nevertheless, policies to help low-wage workers and families in economic distress would be more likely to be enacted if they were encouraged by strong unions.

In this book we reject the false choice between the competing explanations of "cultural poverty" and "structural poverty," recognizing that both have explanatory power. People fail to achieve the American Dream both because they do not have opportunities to obtain jobs that pay living wages and because they do not have the skills and abilities to take advantage of the economic opportunities generated by the economy when it is expanding. We adopt the broadest possible definition of poverty and emphasize proposals for policy reform that create opportunity not only by improving jobs, providing income supports, and encouraging savings, but also by strengthening the community and family institutions that mediate economic opportunity (schools, social supports for youth, community organizations, and family structure).

This book outlines a variety of policies that are likely to be effective in alleviating poverty and helping to restore the American Dream for millions of people. Given the urgency of these issues, we emphasize concrete solutions, not theoretical debates. The chapters are authored by eminent social scientists, but also by practitioners who have experience putting policy prescriptions into action.

Part One defines the "what and who" of poverty: the underclass, the working poor, and the middle class who stand on increasingly shaky ground. It describes the day-to-day experience of the poorest Americans, the growth of the working poor, and the disappearance of the middle class. Part Two outlines the "why" of poverty—the causes and forces that polarize income and wealth in America. Parts Three, Four, and Five address the "how," exploring potential levers for change and proposing concrete reform strategies in three core areas: the labor market and work supports, asset-building programs, and programs designed to build social capital by strengthening family and community. Many of these chapters also include sidebars that describe particular aspects of the policy reforms we discuss or outline how successful programs in each area function.

The concluding chapter, authored by Senator John Edwards, outlines a strategy to end poverty and to restore the American Dream. Drawing upon the chapters in this book, he connects the "what," "why," and "how" of poverty and economic distress. He suggests the contours of a new direction in poverty policy that offers a multipronged approach that addresses the many facets of this complex and persistent problem in American society.

NOTES

1. U.S. Bureau of the Census, Poverty Thresholds 2005, http://www.census.gov/hhes/www/poverty/threshld/thresh05.html. See also Michael B. Katz and Mark J. Stern, "Poverty: 1940s to Present," in *Poverty in the United States: An Encyclopedia of History, Politics, and Policy*, ed. Gwendolyn Mink and Alice O'Connor (Santa Barbara, CA: ABC-CLIO, 2004), 1:33–45 (defining poverty and describing major trends).

2. "Wealth Inequality Between Rich and Poor Is Growing, EPI Analysts Say in New Book," *Daily Labor Report* (BNA), no. 167, August 29, 2006, A-10.

3. "Census Bureau Says 46.6 Million Americans Lacked Health Insurance Coverage in 2005," *Daily Labor Report* (BNA), no. 168, August 30, 2006, D-15.

4. Barbara Ehrenreich, *Nickel and Dimed: On (Not) Getting By in America* (New York: Henry Holt, 2001), 214.

5. "'American Dream' Out of Reach for Most Workers, Survey Says," *Daily Labor Report* (BNA), no. 169, August 31, 2006, A-12. The survey results are available at http://www.changetowin .org/features/the-american-dream-survey.htm.

6. Ibid.

7. Alice O'Connor, *Poverty Knowledge: Social Science, Social Policy, and the Poor in Twentieth-Century U.S. History* (Princeton, NJ: Princeton University Press, 2001).

8. Lawrence Mishel, Jared Bernstein, and Sylvia Allegretto, *The State of Working America, 2004/2005* (Ithaca, NY: Cornell University Press, 2005: 340–43).

9. William Ryan, *Blaming the Victim* (New York: Vintage Books, 1976).

10. C. Wright Mills, *The Sociological Imagination* (New York: Oxford University Press, 1959).

11. David K. Shipler, *The Working Poor: Invisible in America* (New York: Knopf, 2004), 285.

12. Alice O'Connor, "Poverty Research," in *Poverty in the United States: An Encyclopedia of History, Politics, and Policy*, ed. Gwendolyn Mink and Alice O'Connor (Santa Barbara, CA: ABC-CLIO, 2004), 2:585–91.

13. Timothy J. Bartik, *Jobs for the Poor: Can Labor Demand Policies Help?* (New York: Russell Sage Foundation, 2001).

14. William P. Quigley, *Ending Poverty as We Know It: Guaranteeing a Right to a Job at a Living Wage* (Philadelphia: Temple University Press, 2003), 73.

15. Mishel, Bernstein, and Allegretto, *State of Working America, 2004/2005*.

16. Katz and Stern, "Poverty: 1940s to Present," 33, 45.

17. Bartik, *Jobs for the Poor*.

18. Shipler, *Working Poor*, 11, 300.

PART ONE

CONFRONTING POVERTY AND DECLINING OPPORTUNITY

Although the federal government defines poverty according to a set of income guidelines, the chapters in Part I make clear that poverty is far more complex; its tentacles touch all Americans. It is not a category, but a continuum of economic insecurity, a lack of opportunity, and this suggests that solutions to poverty must be crafted with an eye toward universality.

In "Connecting the Dots" David Shipler describes how poverty looks from the bottom. The whole of poverty is much larger than the sum of its parts, much more insidious than a low income. Poverty is also a lack of assets and a mountain of debt, compounded by hardships as varied as those who are caught in its clutches. Health problems, poor nutrition, lack of affordable housing, difficulties with accessing transportation, and substandard education intertwine in the lives of the poor. Simply put, poverty is the absence of choices, a moment-by-moment hand-to-mouth existence that defies planning and saving; poverty is expensive. Shipler's eloquent portrayal of the human face of poverty shows how the structural forces that shape poverty intertwine with the cultural forces that perpetuate it. Trying to address the many-headed hydra of poverty by cutting off only one of the heads is an incomplete solution; the hydra will simply grow another head. Shipler argues for gateways to multiple services to replace our existing system of separate silos and urges us to harness the best in ourselves to redress poverty.

In "Economic Mobility in the United States: How Much Is There and Why Does It Matter?" Jared Bernstein describes the permeability of the barriers between those traditionally described as poor, the working poor, and the increasingly insecure middle class. Tracking the economic progress of families across the life cycle, he shows how the gap between the richest and poorest Americans has widened at the same time that economic mobility has declined or stagnated in the United States, rendering attainment of the American Dream a myth for many families. Moreover, the legacy of poverty is so powerful that it would take a poor family of four almost 10 generations to achieve the income of a middle-class family: for the poorest Americans, class has become a form of caste. The story is worse for black families: downward mobility is increasing, and black individuals and families are more likely to stagnate in poverty or to fall into it. Bernstein attributes much of this to inherited wealth patterns and educational access and observes how the absence of social safety nets in the United States increases class-related disadvantage.

Elizabeth Warren details the growing instability of the middle class in "The Vanishing Middle Class." Without a strong middle class there is nothing for the poor to lift themselves toward. Although the median middle-class income has risen in dollars, the increase is almost entirely attributable to working mothers' entry into the labor force. Most middle-class families today bring home two paychecks; single-earner households have slipped down the class ladder. Even families with two labor-market participants are struggling, however, because fixed costs are rising. Warren documents the startling rise in expenditures on housing, medical insurance, transportation, child care, and taxes. She recommends innovation in credit rules to better protect the poor and the middle class from an aggressive and sometimes usurious credit marketplace.

1

Connecting the Dots

David K. Shipler

Since September 11, 2001, we have been told that if only we had connected the dots, we might have foiled the plot. To fight terrorism, it seems, we have to draw lines among scattered facts until a complete picture emerges.

The same is true of poverty. To understand it and to fight it, we have to connect the dots. The far-flung problems that burden an impoverished American—housing and health, transportation and debt—may seem unrelated to one another, but they are all part of a whole, and they interact in surprising ways. Each element of vulnerability is worsened by the entire whirlwind of hardship.

WHAT IS POVERTY?

The federal government defines poverty very simply. If you were a single parent with three children and earned $19,874 in 2005, you were poor.[1] If you earned a dollar more, you were not. Naturally, working families at the bottom know very well that getting out of poverty is more complicated than showing a passport and crossing a frontier.

Poverty is not just income, and using a year's income as the only index is like portraying a complex life with one still photograph. You may catch the essence, or you may miss the full ebb and flow of suffering and struggle. Poverty is not just income.

Poverty is also debt. The wealthiest 10 percent of the country's households had an average net worth in 2004 of $3.11 million, according to the Federal Reserve, up 6.1 percent from 2001. But the poorest 25 percent, whose assets equaled their debts in 2001, dropped to a net worth of minus $1,400 in 2004. In other words, they owed more than they owned.[2]

I met such a man while researching my book *The Working Poor: Invisible in America*.[3] His name was Willie Goodell. While he was unemployed and without medical insurance, he never saw a dentist, so whenever he got a cavity and a tooth ached, he went to an emergency room. If you show up with an emergency, hospitals are required by law to treat you, but they can also bill you, so Willie ran up $10,000 in debt that he could not pay. Even after he got a roofing job, whose wage put him above the poverty line, his credit report was so bad that he couldn't get a phone installed. Such is the way of debt, a burden of the past carrying a hard history into the present. It restricts the future by draining off options, stifling choice, and sapping a person's power.

Poverty is a sense of powerlessness, often a learned helplessness in which choices seem absent. Today's decisions appear deceptively small, without long-term consequences. The timeline of planning is relentlessly short, with little room for imagining that a deed done now will have benefit much later. A poor person on the edge of crisis is trapped in a perpetual moment of acute fragility.

Poverty is relative. A Vietnamese farmer who owns a water buffalo to plow his few acres of rice paddy is not poor in Vietnam. But a Mexican farmworker paid by the bucket of cucumbers he harvests, and crammed with five other men into the concrete cell of a miserable barrack in eastern North Carolina, is poor in America.

The working poor stand on the margins of an affluent society looking in, unable to enjoy the comfort to which they contribute. The single parent with three children, working a full 40 hours a week for 52 weeks a year, must earn $9.55 an hour to stay at the poverty line.[4] This does not happen in many low-skilled jobs, no matter how essential to the economy they are. And so the man who washes cars does not own one. The assistant teacher cannot afford to put her own two children in the day-care center where she works. The woman who files canceled checks in the back room of a bank has a balance in her own checking account of $2.02.

The working poor harvest sweet potatoes in time for Thanksgiving. They cut trees in time for Christmas. The fruits of their labor are in our lives every day, yet we rarely see them. Even when we encounter them face-to-face stocking shelves in Wal-Mart or checking us out at the supermarket, we do not see them as whole people, and we surely do not see them as poor. They are hidden in plain sight, to borrow a phrase from Edgar Allan Poe.

The reason for their invisibility is that they wear their jobs like camouflage, blending into the American Dream, the American Myth, which holds that anyone who works hard can prosper. It is such an important myth in defining what we imagine to be our reality that Richard Wright called it "the truth of the power of the wish."

THE AMERICAN MYTH AND ANTIMYTH

A society's myths are often valuable, as is this one about the American Dream. It is useful because it sets a high standard, a lofty goal to which we aspire. And the gap between the goal and the reality is a gap that most Americans yearn to close. That is a noble yearning.

The myth has a judgmental side, however, for if it is true that anyone who works hard can prosper in America, then it must also be true that anyone who does not prosper does not work hard. So this myth is a coin with two sides: one an ideal, one a condemnation.

Alongside the myth stands the antimyth, which holds societal institutions, not individuals, responsible for poverty. The failures of public schools, private enterprise, and government programs line up to thwart even the most persistent ambitions of those who begin life as poor. So holds the antimyth.

The myth and the antimyth parallel the conservative Republican and the liberal Democratic sides of the debate over poverty. This is a sterile game of blame. Conservatives tend to see individuals and families as responsible for their own predicaments; liberals often fault the private sector and government alone.

But real people do not fit comfortably into such neat boxes. I've had trouble finding poor folks whose own behavior has not contributed something to their hardships: having babies out of wedlock, dropping out of school, doing drugs, showing up late to work or not at all. Yet it is also difficult to find behavior that has not somehow been inherited from the legacy of being badly parented, badly schooled, badly housed in neighborhoods where the horizon of possibility is so near at hand that it blinds people to their own potential for imagination.

Conservatives have their pieces of the jigsaw puzzle, the internal individual and family dysfunctions, and liberals have theirs, the external failed institutions. Imagine if, in this age of political stalemate between the extremes, conservatives who care and liberals who dare to listen would each bring their pieces of the puzzle to the table and assemble them all together. Then they would have a full picture of the problems of poverty. You cannot solve a problem without defining it, and if you don't allow yourself a complete definition, you will never approach a thorough solution. Connect the dots.

In the 1950s anthropologist Oscar Lewis popularized the term "culture of poverty," which has since been twisted into an epithet used by the Right to absolve the society of responsibility for the poor.[5] But I don't think that poverty is a culture. It is not an array of rituals, mores, and values passed down from generation to generation. It is, rather, an ecological system of interactions among individuals and families, on the one hand, and on the other, the environment of neighborhoods, housing, schools, government programs, and the private economy. Altering this ecology of poverty is not easy, but it is also not impossible.

THE ECOLOGY OF POVERTY

When asthma attacks brought an eight-year-old boy repeatedly to the pediatrics department of the Boston Medical Center, doctors prescribed the usual steroid inhalers, but they doubted that the treatment would work, for they knew from the mother that her apartment had a leaky pipe and wall-to-wall carpeting, perfect for mold and dust mites, features of poor housing that studies show can trigger asthma attacks. And in this case the boy was missing so much school that he was falling behind; the mother was missing so much work that she risked being fired.

A nurse wrote a letter to the landlord asking that the carpeting be torn up and the pipe be repaired. There was no reply. So a lawyer at the pediatrics department called the owner twice, and presto! The pipe was fixed and the carpet removed. The boy improved, and the mother saved her job.

The Boston Medical Center now has five full-time attorneys in its pediatrics department. As doctors have learned that lawyers can help treat disease caused or worsened by conditions of poverty, the idea has caught on, and nearly 40 clinics in the country now use attorneys.

Housing is a key link in the chain reaction of hardships that afflict poor families. Lisa Brooks, who was a single mother when I met her, lived through a domino effect of startling difficulties, one after another, that began with the interaction between her bad housing and her son's asthma.

She was just 24, but she wore weariness on her face as if every year of her young life had been multiplied by her ordeals. Paid $8.21 an hour as a caretaker in a group home for mentally ill adults, she was covered by medical insurance. But she couldn't afford to save anything; every dime that came in went out. When she had to move into a drafty wooden house, her son's asthma grew worse.

Twice, when he couldn't breathe, he had to be rushed by ambulance to the hospital. For reasons that Lisa was never able to unravel, her insurance paid for the emergency room but not the ambulance charges, which amounted to $240 one time and $250 the next. Lisa could not pay them either, not all at once, so they went on her credit report.

With that bad credit rating, she was denied a mortgage to improve her housing by purchasing a mobile home. When her old car died (she needed one to get to work), and a dealership ran a credit check, it came up so negative that the salesman said that he couldn't offer her a car loan. So she ended up at a sleazy used-car lot that didn't check her credit but charged her 15.747 percent interest on a loan. A low wage thus led to a bad house, to a sick child, to a poor credit rating, to a car loan with exorbitant interest. Connect the dots.

Housing, then, is more than a place to live. In a perverse way, it can also contribute to malnutrition. Many low-wage working families without government subsidies—no public housing, no Section 8 vouchers that help pay private landlords—have to spend as much as 50 to 75 percent of their incomes on rent. In a tight, high-rent housing market there is no way families can economize to squeeze that part of their budget. They have to pay the rent, they have to make the car payment, they have to pay for auto insurance, electricity, telephone. These bills come due relentlessly, and the penalties for deferring them are unacceptable.

The part of the budget that can be squeezed is for food. If you spend time in malnutrition clinics, as I have, and you talk to parents who bring in their underweight, developmentally delayed children for treatment, you will quickly discover that virtually all of them are struggling on the private housing market, without subsidies. They are skimping on food because they don't have enough cash, the food stamps they may get are inadequate, and they are not earning enough in wages to sustain their children adequately.

There are other reasons for malnutrition, including the junk-food inventories of stores in poor neighborhoods, inadequate knowledge of what foods are nutritious, allergies that cannot be avoided because parents cannot stock and test a variety of foods, or work schedules that shuttle children among multiple caregivers who don't monitor a toddler's intake. High rents loom especially large, however: a 2005 study of nearly 12,000 low-income households in six cities found an increased incidence of underweight children in families without housing subsidies.[6]

Malnutrition that occurs in the last trimester of pregnancy or the first two or three years of childhood can cause lifelong cognitive impairment. Longitudinal studies have found that even if children get proper nutrition later, the early deficit does lasting damage. That, in turn, affects school performance and life opportunities. Older children who go to school hungry do not do well either. "Learning is discretionary," says Dr. Deborah Frank, head of the Boston Medical Center's malnutrition clinic, "after you're well-fed, warm, secure."[7]

I asked youngsters in inner-city schools what percentage of the time they did not understand what the teacher was saying. Their answers were shocking: 25, 50 percent. I wondered how those children could bear spending hours every day, days every week, weeks and weeks every year sitting in class-rooms where half of what was said was not getting through. There would be no pleasure in learning, no joy of discovery or mastery, no sense of compe-tence. Who would stay in school after years of such an experience? Is the high dropout rate any great surprise?

There are many reasons that children drop out besides cognitive impair-ment and malnutrition. But it is important to see the interactions and to rec-ognize that as the federal government plans to reduce housing subsidies even further, malnutrition and school performance are bound to worsen. Connect the dots.

PERSONAL AND FAMILY PROBLEMS

Internal obstacles often seem insurmountable to folks in poverty, and chief among them is a corrosive sense of incapacity. If you have failed in school, failed in relationships, and failed in job after job, you don't suddenly expect to succeed.

One evening, at a halfway house for recovering drug addicts within sight of the Capitol in Washington, D.C., a group of men talked among themselves about their search for jobs. They were tough. They had survived the crack wars in Washington. Many had lived on the streets. A few had been in prison. Yet the emotion they talked about feeling as they looked for work was fear. They were afraid to apply. They were afraid of being asked about their police records. They were afraid of being rejected. And a couple even said that they were afraid of being accepted into jobs they did not think they could do.

At a couple of Los Angeles housing projects that had job-placement pro-grams, I asked staff members what obstacles faced the residents. All put "fear" near the top of the list. People in the projects wanted to work, but they wanted jobs with the Housing Authority inside the projects. They were afraid to go out into the larger working world whose customs and procedures they did not know. The projects were centers of gang and drug activity (I was advised not to interview there after dark), but that is where residents felt most comfortable.

The best job-training programs aim to repair these internal disabilities. At one center I met a woman then living in a homeless shelter, who asked that I call her "Peaches." She had been terribly abused as a child in a foster home, had bounced from one violent man to another, and thought so little of her-self that when she had to steal food to survive, she said, she never thought to take anything good like a steak. She figured she was worth nothing more than a package of bologna.

Many of the trainees in the center, run by a Washington, D.C., Catholic organization called So Others Might Eat, arrived barely able to conduct a conversation.[8] They looked at the floor; they mumbled. But over several months remarkable transformations took place. The training was calibrated to give each person at least a small success every day, to treat the full range of handicaps, to teach not only the hard skills of reading, math, and computer mastery, but also the soft skills of self-esteem, personal interaction, anger management, and work ethics. Slowly, slowly, the eyes came up off the floor, the voices gained clarity, and most people began to believe in themselves. They often ended up with respectable jobs that had potential for advancement.

Some hard-nosed employers and politicians scoff at the touchy-feely notion that self-esteem needs to be cultivated, but I believe that it has an impact on job performance. After hearing employers complain repeatedly about low-wage workers not showing up on time, not showing up at all, and not calling when they were out sick, I put the problem to Ann Brash, a brilliant woman who grew up in the middle class and fell into poverty after a divorce. Ann had an unusual perspective on the syndrome of destitution, and she had a perceptive observation on this point. "People who don't call when they can't come to work probably don't think they're important enough to matter," she said.

Among the most severe disabilities mentioned by women I interviewed were the results of sexual abuse. The question that usually triggered the stories was a simple request to tell me about their childhoods. More often than not, they said that they had been abused by their fathers, their stepfathers, their mothers' boyfriends, or the older siblings in a foster home. Sometimes the accounts would come in the first interview, sometimes not until the second, third, or fourth. To these women, the experience of abuse seemed a central explanation for the kind of life in which they now found themselves.

They distrusted men—no surprise there. They could not form lasting emotional attachments. They were alone, usually with children, single wage earners at low pay. If two people in their households had been earning $6.00 or $7.00 an hour, they wouldn't be getting rich, but they would be getting along. With only one person bringing in that kind of wage, however, they were consigned to poverty.

They also felt powerless and vulnerable, having often been left unprotected by their mothers, and that sense of helplessness eroded their capacity to see and make choices, even in adulthood. Some suffered from paralyzing depression. Some displayed the attributes of post-traumatic stress disorder, with its dissociative reactions and emotional cutoffs—defense mechanisms that made them inadequate parents.

I would never argue that low-income families experience a higher incidence of sexual abuse than the middle class or the affluent. No reliable data I have seen provide a clear correlation between the affliction and socioeconomic status, and I suspect that the sexual abuse of children is a secret pandemic that crosses class lines. But it is safe to say that the poor are especially fragile victims. Someone who cannot afford professional therapy has lower odds of healing. Some people manage to heal without counseling, and others who receive counseling do not recover. But if you are sophisticated enough to know how to get the services, and if you have the money to buy them, you have at least a fighting chance of obtaining assistance that can be decisive.

GATEWAYS TO REDUCING POVERTY

We know more than we think we do about poverty's causes and solutions. Specialists and experts in various parts of our society now understand the interactions between environmental assaults and certain diseases, between early nurturing and babies' brain development, between a woman's childhood abuse and her later parenting, between the lack of self-esteem and the lack of employability, between the high cost of housing and the high price paid for malnutrition and cognitive impairment.

Those who work with the poor, including teachers and social workers, probation officers and job trainers, recognize that people who come to an agency with one problem invariably suffer from an array of problems. Yet few agencies are equipped to tackle any issue other than the one presented. Teachers who take granola bars to school to toss to pupils with the glazed look of hunger in their eyes know that hungry children cannot concentrate and cannot learn. Yet most schools offer teachers no tools to help families get food stamps or housing subsidies or other benefits to which they may be entitled. Probation officers who see the violent homes and low job skills of those they supervise know that their parolees will be back in prison without a systemic change in their lives. Yet most jurisdictions provide officers with little or no capacity to get their charges into services and programs that could help them and perhaps save them.

If schools, probation departments, job-training centers, medical clinics, and other institutions were broadened into gateways through which needy families could pass into multiple services for their multiple problems, a great deal of good could be done. Here and there, this happens in fragmented forms, mostly in private, nonprofit agencies. But the approach needs to be widespread. Then, teachers could do more than gripe among themselves about kids not learning, trainers could do more than instruct in hard skills, and doctors could do more than dispense medication vainly against the onslaught of disease-producing poverty.

Would this cost money? Yes, but some of the expense would ultimately be saved. The more we invest in children, the less we will have to invest later in prisons. The more we invest in health insurance and preventive care, the more productive our workforce will be. The lower the dropout rate from high school, the lower the associated costs in later life, and these savings can be substantial: compared with a high-school graduate, a dropout earns an average of $260,000 less and pays $60,000 less in taxes over a lifetime, according to researchers Henry Levin and Nigel Holmes. In total, dropouts are responsible for annual losses of $50 billion in taxes and reductions of $192 billion in the gross domestic product, $1.4 billion in additional law-enforcement costs due to their higher crime rates, and $7.9 billion to $10.8 billion in payments for welfare and other government benefits.[9] I am waiting impatiently for business leaders to realize this and to tell their Republican allies, especially, that the system needs help.

In an age of wealth disparity and ostentatious greed, when our political leaders tell us that we should strive to keep as much money as possible in our own pockets, it is important to remember the strong currents of generosity that run through America. Remember the outpouring of help after the Asian tsunami. Remember the money and shelter given to the dispossessed after Hurricane Katrina. And across the country I have asked audiences of all kinds—students and professors, lawyers and judges, doctors and business executives, social workers and many others—how many would be willing to pay higher taxes to help address the problems of poverty. Nearly all raise their hands.

Now, these are biased samples: people willing to come out and listen to a speech on poverty. But then I ask how many have told elected officials that they'd like to see more taxes for this purpose. Hardly any hands go up. That is a gap that needs to be closed. Let's not underestimate ourselves.

When I first met Tom and Kara King, they were both unemployed, and Kara had been diagnosed with cancer. She had just been told that she needed a bone marrow transplant, and so they took what little cash they had scraped together and treated themselves and their children to dinner out at a truck stop.

They laughed and talked, and when it came time to pay the bill, the waitress told them it had already been paid by a man at the bar. They were taken aback and a bit offended, especially Kara, who hated to be pitied. I always thought that she had an internal balance sheet: anything nice that anybody did for her would go on the debit side, and she'd have to do some favor in return to balance it off. So Kara fumed all the way home in the car, and when she got to the house she called the diner and asked the waitress for the man's name. He was still there, and the waitress handed him the phone. He was a truck driver just passing through, he explained, and had never heard a family discuss problems that openly. "I counted," he told her. "Your children said they loved you twenty times."

I think that there are a lot of Americans like that truck driver.

NOTES

1. U.S. Bureau of the Census, Poverty Thresholds 2005, http://www.census.gov/hhes/www/poverty/threshld/thresh05.html.

2. Federal Reserve Board of Governors, *Recent Changes in U.S. Family Finances: Evidence from the 2001 and 2004 Surveys of Consumer Finances* (Washington, DC: Board of Governors of the Federal Reserve System, 2006), 8, http://www.federalreserve.gov/pubs/bulletin/2006/financesurvey.pdf.

3. David K. Shipler, *The Working Poor: Invisible in America* (New York: Knopf, 2004).

4. U.S. Bureau of the Census, Poverty Thresholds 2005, http://www.census.gov/hhes/www/poverty/threshld/thresh05.html.

5. Oscar Lewis, *Five Families: Mexican Case Studies in the Culture of Poverty* (New York: Basic Books, 1959).

6. Alan Meyers et al., "Subsidized Housing and Children's Nutritional Status: Data from a Multistate Surveillance Study," *Archives of Pediatrics and Adolescent Medicine* 159 (June 2005): 551–56.

7. Deborah Frank, interview with author.

8. The organization's web site is http://www.some.org/.

9. Henry Levin and Nigel Holmes, "America's Learning Deficit," *New York Times*, November 7, 2005.

Economic Mobility in the United States: How Much Is There and Why Does It Matter?

Jared Bernstein

The historically high degree of income or wealth concentration in America in recent years has been amply documented. The Congressional Budget Office (CBO) produces especially comprehensive household data by income class, including the value of capital gains, an important dimension of inequality omitted from census analysis. These data, presented in Figure 2.1, show that between the business-cycle peaks of 1979 and 2000, the real income of the bottom fifth of households grew 6 percent, that of the middle fifth grew 12 percent, and that of the top fifth grew 70 percent. The household income of the top 1 percent grew 184 percent over these years.[1]

Such data compare two snapshots of the income distribution at two points in time. These kinds of comparisons inform us of the changes in real income levels for different income classes of households. They tell us, for example, how low-income households have fared relative to middle- and higher-income households; they reveal how economic growth was distributed among different income groups. They do not, however, compare the income trajectories of the same people or families over time.

To take another common example, living-standard analysts often examine the inflation-adjusted level of the median income at two points in time and discuss these results in terms of how "middle-income families" are faring. These are clearly not, however, the same families. That is, the family in the middle of the income scale today may be at the 70th percentile 10 years later.

The analysis in this chapter is not of snapshots, but of "movies," as it were, tracking the economic progress of the same families, or parents and

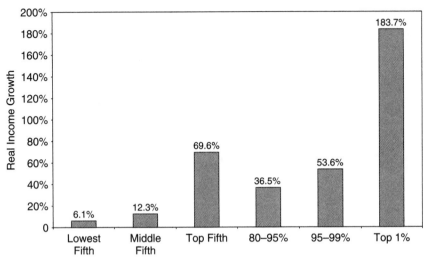

Figure 2.1 The Growth of Income Inequality, 1979–2000
   Source: Congressional Budget Office, *Effective Federal Tax Rates, 1979–2003* (Washington, DC: CBO, December 2005), Table 1-C.

their children, across the life cycle. That is, I examine income, wealth, and other aspects of living standards through a lens of income mobility. I first clarify the importance of studying two kinds of income mobility: intragenerational and intergenerational mobility. I then present data on these two types of mobility. Next I examine the role of wealth and education in generating intergenerational mobility, as well as how the United States compares with other countries in intergenerational mobility. I finally summarize the results on mobility and indicate some of their implications.

STUDYING INCOME MOBILITY

Why is the distinction between snapshots and longitudinal analysis important? One principal reason has to do with how the rate of mobility has changed over time. Here the critical question is: has the rate of economic mobility increased enough to offset the increase in inequality? The answer is "no," but before I examine the evidence, it will be helpful to "unpack" this pointed, if seemingly obscure, question.

Imagine a hotel whose 10 floors improve in quality as you go up the elevator. The poor reside on the bottom floor, the wealthy in the penthouse. The same families live in this hotel, and over time some move up, others move down, and others stay put.

Now imagine that over the years the hotel changes in the following manner.

There are still 10 floors, but the quality of life in the penthouse has soared, while that of the bottom floors is largely unchanged. The distance between the floors, in terms of living standards, has greatly expanded. Compared with earlier years, those in the middle and lower floors are much further behind top-floor residents than used to be the case.

Comparing the two snapshots of the old, more equal hotel and the newer one would reveal this increase in inequality, much like the one shown in the previous figure. But suppose that the likelihood of moving up the floors had increased. That is, suppose that a family from the bottom floor now had a much better chance of making it into the penthouse. This change would represent an increase in mobility, and if it were large enough, it could potentially offset the increase in inequality. True, the floors are further apart in terms of living standards, and we might bemoan this increase in inequality, but if the rate of mobility accelerated enough to give folks a better chance of climbing the ladder, that might mitigate our concern.

As noted, the research on this question has been quite clear on this point: the rate of mobility has not increased. A number of studies suggest that the rate has decreased, though others maintain that it remains essentially unchanged. In other words, people are much further from each other across the economic spectrum and are no more likely to span the increased distances.

Thus far, my discussion has focused on intragenerational mobility: the economic mobility of families as they age. If families move between the floors of the hotels a lot over the span of their lifetimes, this would imply a high level of intragenerational mobility. Conversely, if families tend to stay on or near the floor on which they started, this implies less such mobility.

A related part of the analysis examines the extent to which children's fortunes differ from that of their parents. This refers to the role of intergenerational mobility: the degree to which a child's position in the economy is determined by that of his or her parents. Surely, if class barriers are such that children's economic fates are largely determined by their family's position in the income scale, then the likelihood that, for example, a poor child will be a middle-class adult is diminished.

In fact, there are significant positive correlations between parents and their children, implying that income mobility is at least somewhat restricted because one generation's position in the income scale is partially dependent on its parents' position. One recent study finds the correlation between parents and children to be 0.6.[2] One way to view the significance of this finding is to note that it implies that it would take a poor family of four with two children approximately 9 to 10 generations—over 200 years—to achieve the income of the middle-income four-person family. Were that correlation only half that size, meaning that income differences were half as persistent across generations, it would take 4 to 5 generations for the poor family to catch up.

These two concepts—intra- and intergenerational mobility—both shed light on the fluidity, or lack thereof, of class in America. The evidence presented here shows some degree of mobility: families do change hotel floors, and the correlation between parents and children is far from one. Yet two important points emerge. First, there is not as much mobility as American mythology might lead one to expect. Most families end up at or near the same relative income position in which they start, and, as noted, when it comes to parent/children income correlations, the apple does not fall very far from the tree. Second, the rate of mobility has not increased and may have fallen. The United States is a more unequal society, yet Americans have not become more mobile.

INTRAGENERATIONAL FAMILY INCOME MOBILITY

Table 2.1 presents three "transition matrices" for three time periods, essentially the 1970s, 1980s, and 1990s. Across the columns for each row in the table, the numbers reveal the percentage of persons who either stayed in the same fifth or moved to a higher or lower one. For example, the first entry in the top panel shows that just under half—49.4 percent—of families in the bottom fifth in 1969 were also in the bottom fifth in 1979. The family income data are adjusted for family size. (Size adjustments divide family income by the poverty threshold for families of the relevant size, and then these values are ranked by the bottom fifth.) About the same share—49.1 percent—started and ended the 1970s in the richest fifth. The percentages of "stayers" (those who did not move out of the fifth they started in) are shown in bold.[3]

Note that large transitions are uncommon. In each of the periods covered, the share of families moving from the poorest to the richest fifth never exceeds 4.3 percent. Conversely, the share moving from the top fifth to the bottom fifth never exceeds 5 percent. Those transitions that do occur are most likely to be a move up or down to the neighboring fifth. For example, in both the 1970s and the 1980s about 25 percent began and remained in the middle fifth. But close to 50 percent of those who started in the middle ended up in either the second or fourth quintile (for example, summing the relevant percentages in the 1980s table gives 47.9 percent—23.3 percent plus 24.6 percent).

Comparing mobility rates across the decades answers the question of how these rates have changed over time. In the 1990s the entries on the diagonal, that is, the "stayers," are larger than in either of the other two decades. For example, 36.3 percent started and ended in the second fifth in the 1990s, compared with 27.8 percent in the 1970s and 31.5 percent in the 1980s. In

Table 2.1
Family Income Mobility over Three Decades

Quintile in 1969	Quintile in 1979				
	First	Second	Third	Fourth	Fifth
First	**49.4**	24.5	13.8	9.1	3.3
Second	23.2	**27.8**	25.2	16.2	7.7
Third	10.2	23.4	**24.8**	23	18.7
Fourth	9.9	15	24.1	**27.4**	23.7
Fifth	5	9	13.2	23.7	**49.1**

Quintile in 1979	Quintile in 1989				
	First	Second	Third	Fourth	Fifth
First	**50.4**	24.1	15	7.4	3.2
Second	21.3	**31.5**	23.8	15.8	7.6
Third	12.1	23.3	**25**	24.6	15
Fourth	6.8	16.1	24.3	**27.6**	25.3
Fifth	4.2	5.4	13.4	26.1	**50.9**

Quintile in 1989	Quintile in 1998				
	First	Second	Third	Fourth	Fifth
First	**53.3**	23.6	12.4	6.4	4.3
Second	25.7	**36.3**	22.6	11	4.3
Third	10.9	20.7	**28.3**	27.5	12.6
Fourth	6.5	12.9	23.7	**31.1**	25.8
Fifth	3	5.7	14.9	23.2	**53.2**

Source: Katherine Bradbury and Jane Katz, "Women's Labor Market Involvement and Family Income Mobility When Marriages End," *Federal Reserve Bank of Boston New England Economic Review* Q4 (2002).

terms of upward mobility, whereas 12.4 percent moved from the poorest fifth to the fourth or fifth highest in the 1970s, in the 1980s and 1990s that share was 10.6 percent and 10.7 percent. Finally, the share of families staying in the top fifth grew consistently over the decade, implying diminished mobility over time.

Combining all family types masks important differences in mobility by race. Economist Tom Hertz analyzes the extent of upward and downward mobility by white and African American families.[4] The data in Table 2.2 reveal far less upward mobility—and more downward mobility—among black families relative to whites. The data give the percentage of families by race who moved between the bottom and top 25 percent of the income scale between 1968 and 1998 (income data are again adjusted for family size). The share of upwardly mobile families—those moving from the bottom quartile

Table 2.2

Income Mobility for White and African American Families, Percentage Moving
from the Bottom 25% to the Top 25% and Vice Versa Between 1968 and 1998

	Bottom to Top Quartile	Top to Bottom Quartile
All	7.30%	9.20%
White	10.20%	9.00%
African American	4.20%	18.50%
African American/White difference	-6.00%	9.50%

Source: Tom Hertz, "Rags, Riches, and Race: The Intergenerational Economic Mobility of Black and White Families in the United States," in *Unequal Chances: Family Background and Economic Success*, ed. Samuel Bowles, Herbert Gintis, and Melissa Osborne Groves (New York: Russell Sage Foundation; Princeton: Princeton University Press, 2005), Table 9.

to the top—was 7.3 percent, slightly lower than the share moving the other direction (9.2 percent). But this overall measure is quite different by race. For white families, 10.2 percent were upwardly mobile, compared with 4.2 percent for black families, a statistically significant difference. Note also that far more black families than whites were likely to fall from the top 25 percent to the bottom quartile, 18.5 percent compared with 9 percent (though given the small sample size of black families in the top 25 percent, the difference does not reach statistical significance).

Table 2.3 adds a few new dimensions to the analysis. Shifting from families, the table tracks individuals by age, following young persons from childhood until early adulthood. The values in the table show the likelihood that low-income teenagers will become low-, middle-, or high-income adults. In addition, the table compares two cohorts, permitting me to revisit the question of whether the rate of mobility has changed.[5]

Two important findings can be seen in these data. First, about half of white teenagers and three-quarters of black young adults ended up at or near the income fifth where they started, that is, the poorest fifth. Looking at the most recent cohort, 54.3 percent of white children starting in the first fifth ended up in either the first or second fifth; the comparable share for African Americans was 73.4 percent. Compared with white children, more than twice the share of poor black children remained in the bottom fifth, regardless of cohort. On the other end of the income scale, only a small share of poor African American teenagers made it to the top fifth in early adulthood—2.3 percent—compared with 8 percent for whites.

Second, reflecting the findings from Table 2.1, the latter cohort was less likely to experience upward mobility, especially African Americans. Whereas 55.4 percent of black teenagers from the earlier cohort remained in the first quintile by young adulthood, for the later cohort, the share was 61.2 percent.

Table 2.3
Income Mobility of Young Adults, by Cohort and Race

Income Fifth at Age 24–26	At Age 15–17			
	White		African American	
	Born 1952–59	Born 1962–69	Born 1952–59	Born 1962–69
Lowest fifth	22.0%	26.7%	55.4%	61.2%
Second fifth	26.1%	27.6%	22.1%	12.2%
Middle fifth	21.1%	18.4%	8.3%	19.6%
Fourth fifth	17.5%	19.3%	10.0%	4.7%
Top fifth	13.2%	8.0%	4.2%	2.3%
Total	100.0%	100.0%	100.0%	100.0%

Source: Mary Corcoran and Jordan Matsudaira, "Is It Getting Harder to Get Ahead? Economic Attainment in Early Adulthood for Two Cohorts," in *On the Frontier of Adulthood: Theory, Research, and Public Policy,* ed. Richard A. Settersten Jr., Frank F. Furstenberg Jr., and Ruben G. Rumbaut (Chicago: University of Chicago Press, 2005).

Across the white cohorts, the increase was smaller: from 22 percent to 26.7 percent. In other words, there is a conspicuous absence of evidence that increased mobility offset growing inequality.

These mobility studies show that while some degree of family income mobility certainly exists in America, it has not accelerated in such a way as to offset the increase in income inequality shown in Figure 2.1. To the contrary, it appears to have diminished somewhat over the 1990s. In addition, what mobility does exist varies significantly by race, as white families are more than twice as likely as black families to be upwardly mobile.

INTERGENERATIONAL MOBILITY

This section looks at just how far the apple falls from the tree by tracking the correlations between parents' economic status and that of their children. If one's position in the earnings, income, or wealth distribution is largely a function of birth, this implies a more rigid society where even those with prodigious talents will be held back by entrenched class barriers. Conversely, a society with a high level of intergenerational mobility, implying little correlation between parents' position and that of their children, is one with more fluidity between classes. There is solid evidence of considerable persistence, and some evidence that these correlations have grown larger over time.

What drives these correlations? Certainly unequal educational opportunities and historical discrimination play a role. In fact, the transmission of these variables across generations appears to be correlated as well, such that opportunities for advancement are limited for those with fewer economic resources. For example, children from wealthy families have much greater access to top-tier universities than children from low-income families, even once we control for innate skills. Though the data on the persistence of wealth across generations are less rich, such data also suggest that this is an important channel that restricts the mobility of the "have-nots."

Economists measure the extent of intergenerational mobility by a statistic called the intergenerational elasticity (which is similar to a correlation) in income, earnings, or wealth between parents and children. For example, one recent study finds the correlation between the incomes of parents and those of their sons and daughters to be 0.49 and 0.46, respectively.[6] That is, a 1 percent increase in parents' income translates into a .5 percent increase in the child's income.

Is this a high, medium, or low level of income persistence? Certainly a correlation of about half belies any notion of a totally fluid society with no class barriers. Yet without various benchmarks against which to judge these correlations, it is difficult to know what to make of their magnitude. The next figure provides this context by showing how the correlation for sons translates into future earnings mobility.

Figure 2.2 shows where sons of low-income (10th percentile) fathers would be expected to end up in the earnings scale on the basis of their fathers' position. The figure shows that while income mobility certainly exists, the apple does not end up very far from the tree. Sons of low-earning fathers have slightly less than a 60 percent chance of reaching above the 20th percentile

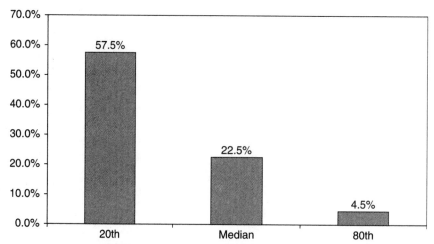

Figure 2.2 Likelihood That Low-Income Son Ends Up Above Various Percentiles
   Source: Gary Solon, unpublished data provided to author.

by adulthood, about a 20 percent chance of surpassing the median, and a very slight chance—4.5 percent—of ending up above the 80th percentile. A son whose father earns about $16,000 a year has only a 5 percent chance of earning over $55,000 per year.

How stable are these values over time? Has the degree of mobility between generations increased or fallen in recent years?

One long-term analysis that tracked the extent of intergenerational mobility since 1940 found that, in fact, the rate of mobility has declined significantly in recent decades. As shown in Figure 2.3, the correlation between the earnings of sons and the income of their families was flat or falling from 1950 to 1980 and then climbed through 2000.[7] This implies a trend toward diminished mobility (the relationship between mobility and the intergenerational correlation is inverse—higher correlations mean greater income persistence across generations and thus less mobility). Note that this trend occurred over the very post-1970s period when cross-sectional inequality was increasing. Thus, instead of faster mobility that might have offset the rise in inequality, the opposite trend occurred.

There is disagreement among mobility experts regarding the conclusion reached by the authors of the previous figure, however. Gary Solon, a premier expert in this field, has not found evidence of any trend in intergenerational mobility in his work. Even so, this finding confirms that there has been no increase in mobility that might have offset the clear increases in inequality.

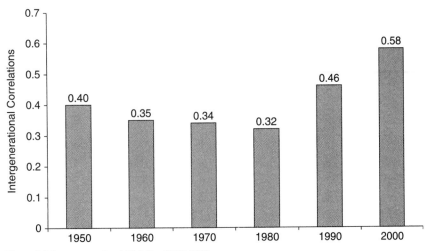

Figure 2.3 Intergenerational Mobility, 1950–2000
    Source: Daniel Aaronson and Bhashkar Mazumder, "Intergenerational Economic Mobility in the U.S., 1940 to 2000" (Federal Reserve Bank of Chicago WP 2005-12, 2005).

THE ROLES OF WEALTH AND EDUCATION IN
INTERGENERATIONAL MOBILITY

Mobility analysts have investigated the mechanisms that influence the degree of mobility across generations. Two such mechanisms are education and wealth. Since education is correlated with income, if children of highly educated parents have a better chance of achieving high levels of education themselves, this will lead to greater persistence of income positions across generations. Similarly, wealth might be expected to be positively correlated across generations, because wealthy parents make bequests to their children. Compared with children who do not benefit from these bequests, children of the wealthy have an asset source that potentially generates income growth over their lives. Kerwin Charles and Erik Hurst show, for example, that 65 percent of children with parents in the least wealthy fifth ended up in the bottom 40 percent of the wealth scale.[8]

With regard to education, researchers have found that about 40 percent of the extent of a person's educational attainment is determined by that of his on her parents. One way in which this process is reinforced is through the diminished access to top-tier schools for children with lower incomes. Figure 2.4 compares the family income of children in the entering classes at top-tier[9] universities versus community colleges.[10] Over 70 percent of those in the top tier come from families with the highest incomes, while 3 percent and 6 percent of the entering class come from the lowest and second-lowest income

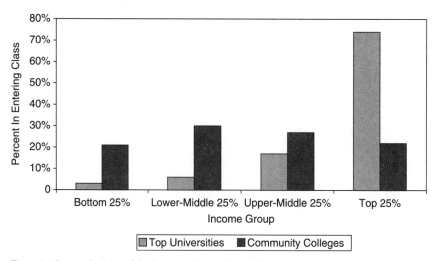

Figure 2.4 Income Position of the Entering Class at Top Colleges and Community Colleges
   Source: Anthony P. Carnevale and Stephen I. Rose, "Socioeconomic Status, Race/Ethnicity, and Selective College Admissions" (Century Foundation Paper, 2003).

groups, respectively, that is, the bottom 50 percent of families. At community colleges, however, the distribution is much more uniform.

Still, one might argue that the findings in Figure 2.4 simply represent a meritocracy at work, because those from high-income families have, perhaps through their privileged positions, acquired the intellectual tools to succeed at the top schools. Figure 2.5 belies this argument. The figure shows that even once academic ability is controlled, it remains the case that the higher-income children are more likely to complete college. Each set of bars shows the probability of completing college for children based on income and their math test scores in eighth grade. For example, the first set of bars, for the students with the lowest test scores, shows that 3 percent of students with both low scores and low incomes completed college, while 30 percent of low-scoring children from high-income families managed to complete college.[11]

The fact that each set of bars has an upward gradient is evidence against a completely meritocratic system. The pattern implies that at every level of test scores, higher income led to higher completion rates. The third set of bars, for example, shows that even among the highest-scoring students in eighth grade, only 29 percent of those from low-income families finished college, compared with 74 percent of those from the wealthiest families.

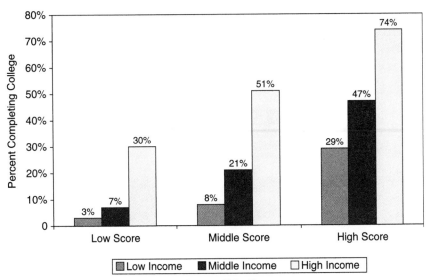

Figure 2.5 College Completion by Income Status and Test Scores
Source: Mary Ann Fox, Brooke A. Connelly, and Thomas D. Snyder, "Youth Indicators 2005: Trends in the Well-Being of American Youth" (U.S. Department of Education, National Center for Education Statistics, 2005), Table 21, http://nces.ed.gov/pubs2005/2005050.pdf.

INTERGENERATIONAL MOBILITY FROM AN
INTERNATIONAL PERSPECTIVE

A deeply embedded piece of U.S. social mythology is the Horatio Alger story: the notion that anyone who is willing and able can "pull themselves up by their bootstraps" and can achieve significant upward mobility. What is more, conventional wisdom holds that there are many more Algers in the United States than in Europe or Scandinavia. The idea behind such thinking is that there is a trade-off between unregulated markets and mobility. Since our economic model hews much more closely to the fundamentals of market capitalism—lower tax base, fewer regulations, less union coverage, no universal health care, and a much less comprehensive social contract—there should be greater mobility here.

However, as shown in Figure 2.6, this is not the case, because the correlations between fathers' and sons' earnings are lower in all the comparison countries except the United Kingdom. The Scandinavian countries in the figure, Finland and Sweden, both have significantly lower correlations (and therefore, higher rates of mobility) than the United States, as does Canada.[12]

These differences mean that poor families in the United States, for example, have a lesser chance of exiting their low-income status than similarly placed families in other countries. Figure 2.7 shows the probability that sons and daughters with fathers whose earnings placed them in the bottom fifth will themselves end up with low earnings.[13] For sons, the chance of having the same low earnings as their fathers is at or below 30 percent in each country except the United States, with lower probabilities in the Scandinavian

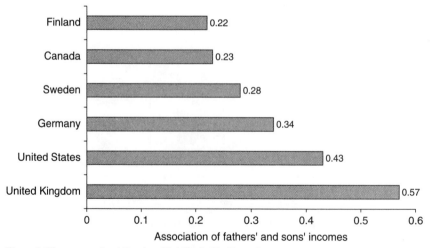

Figure 2.6 Intergenerational Earnings Mobility in Six Countries
   Source: Gary Solon, "Cross-Country Differences in Intergenerational Earnings Mobility," *Journal of Economic Perspectives* 16, no. 3 (2002): 59–66.

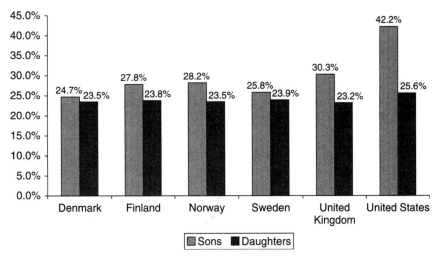

Figure 2.7 Intergenerational Mobility: Percentage of Sons and Daughters in Lowest Fifth, Given Fathers in Lowest Fifth

Source: Markus Jäntti et al., "American Exceptionalism in a New Light: A Comparison of Intergenerational Earnings Mobility in the Nordic Countries, the United Kingdom and the United States" (Discussion Paper no. 2006: 1938, Institute for the Study of Labor, 2006).

countries. The least mobility is for sons in the United States, who face a 42 percent chance of remaining low earners. Daughters have greater earnings mobility, though here too the United States is the least mobile country in Figure 2.7.

Since these figures are derived before taxes and transfers, they reflect greater mobility generated by market outcomes in these countries. That is, they do not directly reflect the more extensive social safety nets in countries other than the United States. However, it may well be the case that these safety nets serve to diminish class barriers that loom large in the United States. Programs such as universal health care (which exists in all the other countries in Figure 2.7) and greater child-care subsidies for working parents (in Scandinavian countries) may free up some of the less advantaged members of these societies to better reach their economic potential than is possible in the United States.

CONCLUSION

It is widely acknowledged that income inequality has increased sharply over time, because income growth at the top of the income scale has far surpassed that of middle- and low-income families. That analysis, however, depended on snapshots of the U.S. income distribution in different periods. These developments have legitimately prompted concern among those of us concerned about diminished equity in the U.S. economy. Yet a counterargument maintains that while the United States may be more unequal "in the cross section," Americans are more likely to vault across the income distribution, offsetting this increased inequality.

The data presented in this chapter belie this claim. Some of the findings, such as those in Table 2.1 or Figure 2.3, show that Americans have become less mobile over time; others suggest little change. None shows greater mobility.

I find that income, wealth, and opportunity are significantly correlated across generations. A son of a low-income father has only a small chance of achieving very high earnings in his adulthood. Almost two-thirds of children of low-wealth parents (those in the first wealth quintile) will themselves have wealth levels that place them in the bottom 40 percent.

One of the most surprising findings of this research is that the United States has less mobility than other advanced economies, even including those of Scandinavia. Certainly these results belie a simplistic story of a favorable trade-off between less regulation and social protection and greater mobility. These other countries manage to provide far more extensive safety nets, yet families there appear to face fewer class barriers.

Finding ways to diminish these barriers should be a primary concern of public policy. Clearly, access to higher education is important, but this cannot be the sole solution. Such access increased significantly over this period, yet Americans arguably became more immobile. Other measures are necessary, including programs that help build wealth for those with few assets, and significant improvement in the quality of jobs and career trajectories to those starting out in the workforce.

NOTES

The author thanks Bhashkar Mazumder and Gary Solon for providing data. Rob Gray provided excellent research assistance. Any mistakes are my own.

1. Congressional Budget Office, *Effective Federal Tax Rates, 1979–2003* (Washington, DC: CBO, December 2005).

2. Bhashkar Mazumder, "Fortunate Sons: New Estimates of Intergenerational Mobility in the United States Using Social Security Earnings Data," *Review of Economics and Statistics* 87, no. 2 (2005): 235–55.

3. Katherine Bradbury and Jane Katz, "Women's Labor Market Involvement and Family Income Mobility When Marriages End," *Federal Reserve Bank of Boston New England Economic Review* Q4 (2002): 41–74.

4. Tom Hertz, "Rags, Riches, and Race: The Intergenerational Economic Mobility of Black and White Families in the United States," in *Unequal Chances: Family Background and Economic Success*, ed. Samuel Bowles, Herbert Gintis, and Melissa Osborne Groves (New York: Russell Sage Foundation; Princeton: Princeton University Press, 2005).

5. Mary Corcoran and Jordan Matsudaira, "Is It Getting Harder to Get Ahead? Economic Attainment in Early Adulthood for Two Cohorts," in *On the Frontier of Adulthood: Theory, Research, and Public Policy*, ed. Richard A. Settersten Jr., Frank F. Furstenberg Jr., and Ruben G. Rumbaut (Chicago: University of Chicago Press, 2005).

6. Chul-In Lee and Gary Solon, "Trends in Intergenerational Income Mobility" (NBER Working Paper 12007, Washington, DC, 2005), available online at http://www.nber.org/papers/w12007.

7. Daniel Aaronson and Bhashkar Mazumder, "Intergenerational Economic Mobility in the U.S., 1940 to 2000" (Federal Reserve Bank of Chicago WP 2005-12, 2005).

8. Kerwin Charles and Erik Hurst, "The Correlation of Wealth Across Generations," *Journal of Political Economy* 111, no. 6 (December 2003): 1155.

9. "Top tier" is defined by (*a*) the grades of entering students (grade point average of B or better and at least 1240 on the SAT) and (*b*) colleges that accept less than 50 percent of their applicants.

10. Anthony P. Carnevale and Stephen J. Rose, "Socioeconomic Status, Race/Ethnicity, and Selective College Admissions" (Century Foundation Paper, 2003).

11. Mary Ann Fox, Brooke A. Connolly, and Thomas D. Snyder, "Youth Indicators 2005: Trends in the Well-Being of American Youth" (U.S. Department of Education, National Center for Education Statistics, 2005), Table 21, http://nces.ed.gov/pubs2005/2005050.pdf.

12. Gary Solon, "Cross-Country Differences in Intergenerational Earnings Mobility," *Journal of Economic Perspectives* 16, no. 3 (2002): 59–66.

13. Markus Jäntti et al., "American Exceptionalism in a New Light: A Comparison of Intergenerational Earnings Mobility in the Nordic Countries, the United Kingdom and the United States" (Discussion Paper no. 2006:1938, Institute for the Study of Labor, 2006).

3

The Vanishing Middle Class

Elizabeth Warren

A strong middle class is the best ally of the poor.

The issues of poverty are typically framed around the poor themselves—the causes of their problems and the help they need. But lifting the poor out of poverty means finding a place for them in the middle.

A middle class that is rich with opportunity opens the paths out of poverty. A middle class that is financially strong can support the programs needed to give the poor a helping hand. A middle class that is prosperous provides the model for how education and hard work pay off. And a middle class that is secure provides the kind of political stability that wards off xenophobia and embraces the pluralism that is critical for the economic and social integration of the poor into mainstream America.

The best ally of the poor is a strong middle class, but America's middle class is under attack economically. Multiple forces are pushing those families closer to the financial brink. What is bad for the middle class is ultimately disastrous for the poor.

MAKING IT TO THE MIDDLE

What is the middle class? Whatever it is, most Americans believe that they are in it. When asked in an open-ended question to identify their class membership, more than 91.6 percent of the adult population of the United States volunteer an identification with "working" or "middle" class.[1] Although there are people who call themselves upper class and others who call themselves lower class, these identifications are numerically somewhat rare.

Although the U.S. government has defined the poverty level, no government agency defines the middle class. One reason is that class status is not a function merely of money or other easily counted characteristics. The running joke of *The Beverly Hillbillies* was that money did not change the social class of the Clampetts. On the other side, people from "good families" who have fallen on hard times might be described as "high class," but their status is not a matter of current income.

Careful studies of the American population show that Americans determine class identification using many variables, including education, occupational status, cultural factors, lifestyle, beliefs and feelings, income, wealth, and more.[2] Political scientists Kenneth Dolbeare and Janette Hubbell assert, "Middle-class values are by definition those of the American mainstream."[3]

This discussion is concentrated on the economic median—the numerical middle—of America. Few families hit the dead center of the economic spectrum, but there is a large group that is roughly in the middle. Even if we cannot tell precisely where the middle shifts over to the lower class or the upper class, knowing what happens to the exact middle explains a lot about what happens to America's middle class.

HIGHER INCOMES, BUT AT A PRICE

Over the past generation new economic forces have reshaped the middle class. The most profound changes have taken place in family income.

As Figure 3.1 shows, today's median-earning family is making a lot more money than their parents did a generation ago. (Throughout this discussion all dollar figures will be adjusted for the effects of inflation.) Today the two-parent family right in the middle is earning about $66,000.[4]

But notice that there are two lines on Figure 3.1. The second line shows what has happened to the wages of a fully employed male over the same time period. The answer is that the typical man working full-time, after adjusting for inflation, earns about $800 less than his father earned in the early 1970s. After decades of rising incomes earlier in the twentieth century, about 30 years ago wages for middle-class men flat-lined.

How did family incomes rise? Mothers of minor children went back to work in record numbers. In the early 1970s the median family lived on one paycheck. Today the family in the middle brings home two paychecks.

The shift from one income to two has had seismic implications for families across America. It means that all the growth in family income came from adding a second earner. Among two-paycheck families median income is now

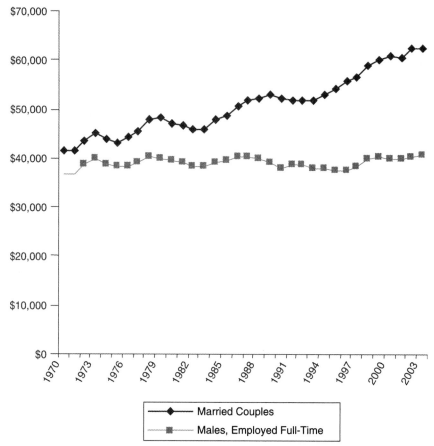

Figure 3.1 Median Income of Married Couples and Fully Employed Males, 1970–2004
  Source: U.S. Bureau of the Census.

$76,500, but the middle one-paycheck family now earns only $42,300.[5] This means that one-income households—whether they are couples where one works and one stays at home or households with only one parent—have fallen sharply behind. A generation ago a one-earner family was squarely in the middle, but now that average one-earner family has slipped down the economic ladder. Over the past generation critical economic divisions within the middle class have begun to emerge.

SAVINGS AND DEBT

While not every family brought home two paychecks, by the 2000s a substantial majority of families sent both parents into the workforce. For those families, it would seem that the economic picture would be rosy. Not so.

In the early 1970s the typical one-income family was putting away about 11 percent of its take-home pay in savings (Figure 3.2).[6] That family carried a mortgage, and it also carried credit cards and other revolving debt that, on average, equaled about 1.3 percent of its annual income.[7]

By 2004 that picture had shifted dramatically. The national savings rate dropped below zero.[8] Revolving debt—largely credit cards—ballooned, topping 12 percent of the average family's income.[9]

In a single generation the family had picked up a second earner, but it had spent every dollar of that second paycheck. Worse yet, it had also spent the money it once saved, and it had borrowed more besides. By the most obvious financial measures the middle-class American family has sunk financially.

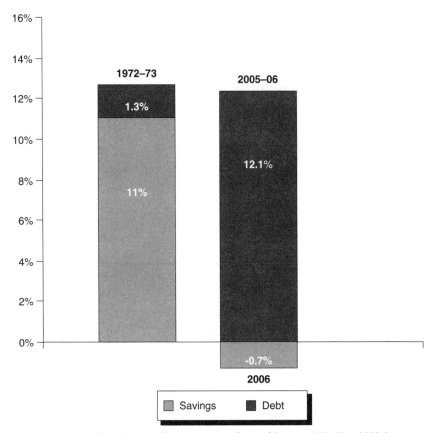

Figure 3.2 Savings and Revolving Debt as Percentage of Annual Income, 1972–73 to 2005–06
Sources: U.S. Census Bureau, Federal Reserve Bank.

OVERCONSUMPTION—THE STANDARD STORY

There is no shortage of experts who are willing to explain exactly where the money went. The story is all about overconsumption, about families spending their money on things they do not really need. Economist Juliet Schor blames "the new consumerism," complete with "designer clothes, a microwave, restaurant meals, home and automobile air conditioning, and, of course, Michael Jordan's ubiquitous athletic shoes, about which children and adults both display near-obsession."[10] Sociologist Robert Frank claims that America's newfound "luxury fever" forces middle-class families "to finance their consumption increases largely by reduced savings and increased debt."[11] John de Graaf and his co-authors claim that "urge to splurge" is an affliction affecting millions of Americans who simply have no willpower.[12] The distinction is critical: overconsumption is not about medical care or basic housing, and it is not about buying a few goodies with extra income. It is about going deep into debt to finance consumer purchases that sensible people could do without.

The beauty of the overconsumption story is that it squares neatly with many of our own intuitions. We see the malls packed with shoppers. We receive catalogs filled with outrageously expensive gadgets. We think of that overpriced summer dress that hangs in the back of the closet or those new soccer shoes gathering dust there. The conclusion seems indisputable: the "urge to splurge" is driving folks to spend, spend, spend like never before. But is it true? Deep in the recesses of federal archives is detailed information on Americans' spending patterns going back for more than a century. It is possible to analyze data about typical families from the early 1970s, carefully sorting spending categories and family size.[13] If today's families really are blowing their paychecks on designer clothes and restaurant meals, then the expenditure data should show that they are spending more on these frivolous items than their parents did a generation earlier. But the numbers point in a very different direction.

Start with clothing. Everyone talks about expensive sneakers, designer outfits, and the latest fashions. But how much more is today's typical family of four spending on clothing than the same family spent in the early 1970s? They are spending less, a whopping 32 percent less today than they spent a generation ago.[14] The differences have to do with how people dress (fewer suits and leather shoes, more T-shirts and shorts), where they shop (more discount stores), and where the clothes are manufactured (overseas). Compared with families a generation ago, today's median earners are downright thrifty.

How about food? People eat out now more than ever before, and bottled water turns something that was once free into a $2 purchase. So how much more is today's family of four spending on food (including eating out) than the same family in the early 1970s? Once again, they are spending less, about 18 percent less.[15] The reasons are that people eat differently (less meat, more pasta) and shop differently (big discount supercenters instead of corner grocery stores), and agribusiness has improved the efficiency of food production.

What about appliances? Families today have microwave ovens, espresso machines, and fancy washers and dryers. But those appliances are not putting a big dent in their pocketbooks. Today's family spends about 52 percent less each year on appliances than their counterparts of a generation ago.[16] Today's appliances are better made and last longer, and they cost less to buy.

Cars? Surely luxury vehicles are making a difference. Not for the median family. The per car cost of owning a car (purchase, repairs, insurance, gas) was on average about 24 percent lower in 2004 than in the early 1970s.[17]

That is not to say that middle-class families never fritter away any money. A generation ago no one had cable, big-screen televisions were a novelty reserved for the very rich, and DVD and TiVo were meaningless strings of letters. Families are spending about 23 percent more on electronics, an extra $225 annually. Computers add another $300 to the annual family budget.[18] But the extra money spent on cable, electronics, and computers is more than offset by families' savings on major appliances and household furnishings alone.

The same balancing act holds true in other areas. The average family spends more on airline travel than it did a generation ago, but it spends less on dry cleaning; more on telephone services, but less on tobacco; more on pets, but less on carpets.[19] And, when it is all added up, increases in one category are pretty much offset by decreases in another. In other words, there seems to be about as much frivolous spending today as there was a generation ago.

WHERE DID THE MONEY GO?

Consumer expenses are down, but the big fixed expenses are up—way up. Start at home. It is fun to think about McMansions, granite countertops, and media rooms. But today's median family buys a three-bedroom, one-bath home—statistically speaking, about 6.1 rooms altogether.[20] This is a little bigger than the 5.8 rooms the median family lived in during the early 1970s. But the price tag and the resulting mortgage payment are much bigger. In 2004 the median homeowner was forking over a mortgage payment that was 76 percent larger than a generation earlier.[21] The family's single biggest expense—the home mortgage—had ballooned from $485 a month to $854. (Remember that all the numbers have already been adjusted for inflation.)

Increases in the cost of health insurance have also hit families hard. Today's family spends 74 percent more on health insurance than its earlier counterparts—if it is lucky enough to get it at all.[22] Costs are so high that 48 million working-age Americans simply went without coverage in 2005.[23]

The per car cost of transportation is down, but the total number of cars is up. Today's family has two people in the workforce, and that means two cars to get to work. Besides, with more families living in the suburbs, even a one-earner family needs a second car for the stay-at-home parent to get to the grocery store and doctor appointments. Overall transportation costs for the family of four have increased by 52 percent.[24]

Another consequence of sending two people into the workforce is the need for child care. Because the median 1970s family had someone at home full-time, there were no child-care expenses for comparison. But today's family with one preschooler and one child in elementary school lays out an average of $1,048 a month for care for the children.[25]

Taxes also took a bigger bite from the two-income family of 2004. Because their second income is taxed on top of their first income, the average tax rate was 25 percent higher for a two-income family in 2004 than it was for a one-income family in 1972.[26]

The ups and downs in family spending over the past generation are summarized in Figure 3.3. Notice that the biggest items in the family budget—the mortgage, taxes, health insurance, child care—are on the up side. The down side—food, clothing, and appliances—represents relatively smaller purchases.

Also notice that the items that went down were more flexible, the sorts of things that families could spend a little less on one month and a little more the next. If someone lost a job or if the family got hit with a big medical bill, they might squeeze back on these expenses for a while. But the items that increased were all fixed. It is not possible to sell off a bedroom or skip the health insurance payment for a couple of months. If both parents are looking for work, child-care costs will go on even during a job search.

When it is all added up, the family at the beginning of the twenty-first century has a budget that looks very different from that of its early 1970s counterpart. As Figure 3.4 shows, there is more income, but the relationship between income and fixed expenses has altered dramatically.

The family of the 1970s had about half its income committed to big fixed expenses. Moreover, it had a stay-at-home parent, someone who could go to work to earn extra income if something went wrong. By contrast, the family of 2004 has already put everyone to work, so there is no extra income to draw on if trouble hits. Worse yet, even with two people in the workforce, after they pay their basic expenses, today's two-income family has less cash left over than its one-income parents had a generation ago.

NEW RISKS FOR THE MIDDLE CLASS

The numbers make it clear that the cost of being middle class is rising quickly—much more quickly than wages. Many families have tried to cope by sending both parents into the workforce. But that change has helped push up costs, and it has increased the risks these families face. They now have no backup worker. Instead, they now need both parents working full-time just to make the mortgage payment and keep the health insurance. And when they need twice as many paychecks to survive, they face twice the risk that someone will get laid off or become too sick to work—and that the whole house of cards will come tumbling down.

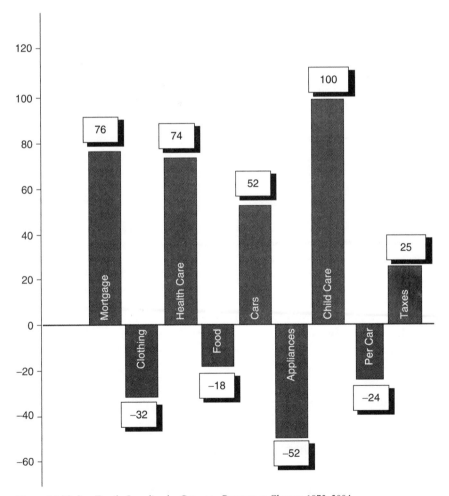

Figure 3.3 Median Family Spending by Category, Percentage Change, 1972–2004
    Source: Updated from sources cited in Elizabeth Warren and Amelia Warren Tyagi, *Why Middle-Class Mothers and Fathers Are Going Broke* (New York: Basic Books, 2003).

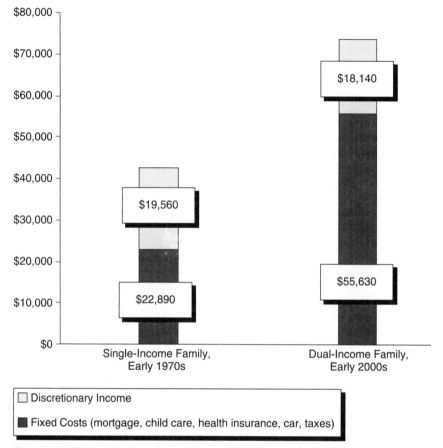

Figure 3.4 Fixed Costs as a Share of Family Income, 1972–2004

Source: Inflation adjusted. Updated from sources cited in Elizabeth Warren and Amelia Warren Tyagi, *The Two-Income Trap: Why Middle-Class Mothers and Fathers Are Going Broke* (New York: Basic Books, 2003).

The new two-income family faces other risks as well. In the 1970s, when a child was ill or grandma broke her hip, there was a parent at home full-time to deal with the needed care, to administer medications, and to drive to doctors' appointments. But someone in the family with no parent at home must take off work whenever anyone else in the family has a serious problem. As a result, problems that were once part of the ordinary bumps of life today have serious income consequences.

New risks keep multiplying. A trip to the emergency room can cost $10,000. The cost of sending a child to college is rising rapidly, while a family's ability to save continues to fall. Retirement presents another risk as generous pensions disappear and even the Social Security backup system looks shaky.

Some will read these data and conclude that one parent should just stay home. Whatever the advantages and disadvantages of that idea from a social perspective, for median earners, it is clearly a losing proposition from an economic perspective. Go back to Figure 3.1 and look at what a fully employed male can earn (and remember that a fully employed female will earn even less). Then look at the big, fixed expenses. Sure, the family can save on child care, and taxes will be lower, but the house payment and the health insurance stay the same, and car expenses are unlikely to drop much. That leaves the median one-income family with a 71 percent drop in discretionary income compared with a one-income family a generation ago. In other words, the two-income family can barely afford the basics, and the median one-income family is simply out of luck.

What do these data say to one-parent families? These families get the worst of both worlds. They have no partner to provide child care every day and no backup earner when something goes wrong. In those ways they look like the typical two-income family—except that they do not have that second income either. A typical one-parent household cannot cover even the basic expenses that would put that family squarely in the middle of American economic life.

It is no surprise that an increasing number of middle-class families have turned to bankruptcy. From 1980 until federal law was changed in 2005, the number of households filing for bankruptcy quadrupled.[27] By 2004 more children were living through their parents' bankruptcy than through divorce.[28] In fact, households with children were about three times more likely to file for bankruptcy than their childless counterparts. What were the main reasons cited for these bankruptcies? About 90 percent of the families cited some combination of job loss, medical problems, and family breakup.[29]

SOLUTIONS

The pressures on the middle class have come from many sources, which is both the good news and the bad news. It is bad in the sense that no single silver bullet will fix everything. But it is good in the sense that many different approaches can make things better—much better—for families across the economic spectrum.

Credit rules offer one option for innovation, providing better protection for the poor and the middle class at the same time. Americans are drowning in debt. Their difficulties are compounded by substantial changes in the credit market that have made debt instruments far riskier for consumers than they were a generation ago. The effective deregulation of interest rates, coupled with innovations in credit charges (e.g., teaser rates, negative amortization, increased use of fees, cross-default clauses, penalty interest rates), has turned ordinary purchases into complex financial undertakings.

In the mid-1980s the typical credit-card contract was about a page long; today it is more than 30 pages, often of dense legalese that even a lawyer cannot understand.[30] Small loans that seem safe in the beginning are repeatedly rolled over in the payday loan industry, making the average effective interest rate more than 400 percent.[31] Credit reports, the foundation of the modern credit system, have errors of 50 points or more in 31 percent of all files, and consumers have little help when they try to straighten out the tangle.[32]

Aggressive marketing, almost nonexistent in the early 1970s, now shapes many consumer choices. Six billion credit-card applications were mailed out in 2005, in addition to on-campus, phone, flyer, in-store, and all sorts of other marketing. Aggressive lenders who line up at the front gates of military installations now have the Department of Defense concerned about combat readiness and the stability of military families. The DoD explained how credit marketing works near military bases:

> Predatory lenders seek out young and financially inexperienced borrowers who have bank accounts and steady jobs, but also have little in savings, flawed credit or have hit their credit limit. . . . Most of the predatory business models take advantage of borrowers' inability to pay the loan in full when due and encourage extensions through refinancing and loan flipping.[33]

Consumer capacity—measured by both available time and expertise—has not expanded to meet the demands of a far more dangerous and aggressive credit marketplace.

The rules governing borrowing and lending have a long history, dating back to English rules imported to the colonies in the 1600s. Even the Bible has injunctions against usurious money lending, and the Koran forbids charging any interest at all. Since the founding of the Republic, the states have regulated interest, with detailed laws on usury (the maximum interest rate that a lender can charge on a loan) and other credit regulations. While the states still play some role, particularly in the regulation of real estate transactions, their primary tool—interest-rate regulation—has been effectively ended by federal legislation.[34] Currently any lender that gets a federal bank charter can locate its operations in a state with very high usury rates (e.g., South Dakota or Delaware) and then export those interest rates to customers located all over the country. Even in states that cap interest rates at 18 percent, a credit card from a bank that set up its operations in South Dakota can charge 39 percent. Local state laws suffer from another problem: as credit markets have gone national, a plethora of state regulations drives up costs while creating a patchwork of regulation that is neither effective nor well considered.

The Department of Defense is so worried about the effects of out-of-control lenders that it has asked Congress to impose a national usury ceiling to apply to protect military families.[35] This would be a good first start, but why not give all Americans the same protection? Moreover, is it clear that direct usury regulation, as opposed to several other ways to deal with credit, is the best approach?

I propose that Congress establish a Financial Product Safety Commission (FPSC) on the model of the Consumer Product Safety Commission. This agency would be charged with responsibility to establish guidelines for consumer disclosure, to collect and report data about the uses of different financial products, to review new financial products for safety and to require modification of dangerous products before they can be marketed to the public, and to establish guidelines and monitor creditor behavior to protect consumer information and prevent identity theft. In effect, the Financial Product Safety Commission would evaluate credit products to eliminate the hidden tricks and traps and slipshod practices that make some credit products far more dangerous than others. No customer should be forced to read the fine print in more than 30 pages of legalese in credit-card contracts to determine whether the company claims that it will raise its interest rate by more than 20 points if the customer gets into a dispute with another creditor. Data privacy should not be governed by hidden terms in contracts, and identity theft should be the responsibility of the company that let the data slip rather than the victim who tries to clean up the mess.

With an FPSC, consumer credit companies would be free to innovate, but such innovation should be within the boundaries of clearly disclosed terms and open competition—not hidden terms designed to mislead consumers. Those hidden terms not only disadvantage customers, they also disadvantage honest competitors who do not inflate their profits by using such tactics.

The consumer financial services industry has grown to $3 trillion in annual business. Credit issuers employ thousands of lawyers, marketing agencies, statisticians, and business strategists to help them increase profits. In a rapidly changing market, customers need someone on their side to help make certain that the financial products they buy meet minimum safety standards. The Financial Product Safety Commission would help level the playing field.

This is just one new idea for uniting the interests of the poor and the middle class, making millions of American families stronger financially. There are more. But the best ideas are those that are aimed at hardworking Americans everywhere, whether they are poor today or not. These are the ideas of opportunity and safety for all Americans who want to work hard and accomplish something important.

CONCLUSION

The strain on the middle class is growing, and more families are struggling just to make it from payday to payday. That leaves less room for families to move up from poverty. It also means that the middle class can offer the poor less help in their climb.

America was once a world of three economic groups that shaded each into the other—a bottom, a middle, and a top—and economic security was the birthright of the latter two. Today the lines dividing Americans are changing. No longer is the division on economic security between the poor and everyone else. The division is between those who are prospering and those who are struggling, and much of the middle class is now on the struggling side.

The solutions to poverty do not lie with programs aimed only toward the poor. The solutions lie with reuniting America, led by a strong middle class that looks forward to an even brighter future.

NOTES

1. General Social Survey, 1976–1996, Variable 185A CLASS, http://www.ssdc.ucsd.edu.

2. Mary R. Jackman and Robert W. Jackman, *Class Awareness in the United States* (Berkeley: University of California Press, 1983), 216–17 (reporting that only 4 percent of the population places itself in either the upper class or the lower class).

3. Kenneth M. Dolbeare and Janette Kay Hubbell, *U.S.A. 2012: After the Middle-Class Revolution* (Chatham, N.J.: Chatham House Publishers, 1996), 3.

4. U.S. Bureau of the Census, "2005 American Community Survey, S. 1901, Income in the Past 12 Months (in 2005 Inflation Adjusted Dollars)," http://factfinder.census.gov/servlet/STTable?_bm=y&-qr_name=ACS_2005_EST_G00_S1901&-geo_id=01000US&-context=st&-ds_name=ACS_2005_EST_G00_&-tree_id=305.

5. U.S. Bureau of the Census, *Historical Income Tables—Families*, Table F-13, http://www.census.gov/hhes/www/income/histinc/f13ar.html.

6. "Table 2, Personal Income and Its Disposition," http://www.bea.gov/bea/dn/nipaweb/TableView.asp#Mid (savings rates reported by quarter).

7. Computed from data on debt, both revolving and total, from the Federal Reserve (available at http://www.federalreserve.gov/releases/g19/hist/cc_hist_sa.html) and number of households and data on household income from the Bureau of the Census (available at http://factfinder.census.gov/servlet/ADPTable?_bm=y&-geo_id=01000US&-ds_name and http://factfinder.census.gov/servlet/STTable?_bm=y&-qr_name=ACS_2005_EST_G00).

8. The 2006 savings rate was –0.7 percent. Bureau of Economic Analysis, National Economic Accounts, Table 2.1, "Personal Income and Its Disposition," http://www.bea.gov/bea/dn/nipaweb/TableView.asp?SelectedTable=58&FirstYear=2004&LastYear=2006&Freq=Qtr.

9. See data cited in note 7.

10. Juliet B. Schor, *The Overspent American: Upscaling, Downshifting, and the New Consumer* (New York: Basic Books, 1998), 20, 11.

11. Robert H. Frank, *Luxury Fever: Why Money Fails to Satisfy in an Era of Excess* (New York: Free Press, 1999), 45.

12. John de Graaf, David Waan, and Thomas H. Naylor, *Affluenza: The All-Consuming Epidemic* (San Francisco: Berrett-Koehler, 2001), 13.

13. The Bureau of Labor Statistics maintains the Consumer Expenditure Survey (CES), a

periodic set of interviews and diary entries, to analyze the spending behavior of over 20,000 consumer units. Much of the analysis compares the results of the 1972–1973 CES with those of the 2004 CES. In some instances prepublished tables from the 1980 or the 2000 survey are used in order to use the most comparable data available. In both time periods the data used are for four-person families. Available online at www.bls.gov/cex/.

14. 1972–1973 CES, Table 5, "Selected Family Characteristics, Annual Expenditures, and Sources of Income Classified by Family Income Before Taxes for Four Person Families"; 2004 CES, Table 4, "Size of Consumer Unit: Average Annual Expenditures and Characteristics." See also Mark Lino, "USDA's Expenditures on Children by Families Project: Uses and Changes over Time," *Family Economics and Nutrition Review* 13, no. 1 (2001): 81–86.

15. 1972–1973 CES, Table 5; 2004 CES, Table 4. See also Eva Jacobs and Stephanie Shipps, "How Family Spending Has Changed in the U.S.," *Monthly Labor Review* 113 (March 1990): 20–27.

16. 1972–1973 CES, Table 5; 2004 CES, Table 4.

17. 1972–1973 CES, Table 5; 2004 CES, Table 4.

18. 1972–1973 CES, Table 5; 2004 CES, Table 1400. Electronics comparison includes expenditures on televisions, radios, musical instruments, and sound equipment. Computer calculation includes computer hardware and software.

19. For example, in 2000 the average family of four spent an extra $290 on telephone services. On the other hand, the average family spent nearly $200 less on floor coverings, $210 less on dry cleaning and laundry supplies, and $240 less on tobacco products and smoking supplies. 1972–1973 CES, Table 5; 2004 CES, Table 1400.

20. U.S. Bureau of the Census, *American Housing Survey, 1975: General Housing Characteristics*, Current Housing Reports, H-150-75A, Table A1; *American Housing Survey, 1997*, Current Housing Reports, H150/97 (October 2000), Table 3-3, "Size of Unit and Lot—Owner Occupied Units."

21. 1984 CES, Table 5; 2004 CES, Table 4.

22. 1972–1973 CES, Table 5; 2004 CES, Table 4.

23. Commonwealth Fund, "Gaps in Health Insurance: An All-American Problem" (2006).

24. Transportation costs, 1972 data: Bureau of Labor Statistics, *Consumer Expenditure Survey: Interview Survey*, 1972–73 (1997) Table 5, Selected Family Characteristics, Annual Expenditures, and Sources of Income Classified by Family Income Before Taxes for Four Person Families.

1985–2004 data: Bureau of Labour Statistics, Consumer Expenditure Survey, Customized Tables, Series CXUTR000405, Four Person in Consumer Unit, Transportation. Available at http://data.bls.gov/PDQ/outside.jsp?survey=cx.

To estimate 2006 numbers, I used the 2004 CES data as described above, inflated to 2006 dollars using the CPI seasonally adjusted average increase in transportation costs for all urban consumers.

Note: Includes all transportation costs, including privately owned vehicles, fuel, repairs, and public transportation.

25. Day-care costs are calculated from average child-care costs for mothers employed full-time with a child aged 5 to 14, and preschool costs are calculated from average child-care costs for mothers employed full-time with a child under 5. 2004 CES, Table 1A, "Consumer Price Index for All Consumers: U.S. City Average, by Expenditure Category and Commodity and Service Group," 1999 annual and 2004 annual. Preschool and day-care cost data were adjusted using the consumer price index for "Tuition and Childcare."

26. Claire M. Hintz, *The Tax Burden of the Median American Family*, Tax Foundation Special Report 96 (Washington, DC: Tax Foundation, March 2000), Table 1, "Taxes and the Median One-Income American Family." For more details on the complex tax calculations, see Elizabeth Warren and Amelia Warren Tyagi, *The Two-Income Trap: Why Middle-Class Mothers and Fathers Are Going Broke* (New York: Basic Books, 2003), chap. 2, pp. 206-7 n. 115.

27. Administrative Office of the United States Courts, Table F-2, 1980, 2004. In 1980, 287,570 households filed for bankruptcy. In 2004 that number had jumped to 1,563,145. Bankruptcy filing date are available at: http://www.abiworld.org/AM/Template.cfm?Section=Nonbusiness_Bankruptcy_Filings&Template=/TaggedPage/TaggedPageDisplay.cfm&TPLID=60&ContentID=34627.

28. Warren and Tyagi, *Two-Income Trap*, 13.

29. Ibid., 81.

30. Mitchell Pacelle, "Putting Pinch on Credit Card Users" *Wall Street Journal*, July 12, 2004.

31. Center for Responsible Lending, "Support SA 4331: Consumer Credit for Service Members," http://www.responsiblelending.org/policy/congress/page.jsp?itemID=29895875.

32. M.P. McQueen, "Credit Bureaus Create Single Rating: VantageScore to Streamline Process but Doesn't Improve Consumer Data Reliability," *Wall Street Journal Online*, March 15, 2006.

33. U.S. Department of Defense, "Report on Predatory Lending Practices Directed at Members of the Armed Forces and Their Dependents," (August 9, 2006), 4.

34. For more details on the history of credit deregulation, see Warren and Tyagi, *Two-Income Trap*, 123–62.

35. U.S. Department of Defense, "Report on Predatory Lending Practices Directed at Members of the Armed Forces and Their Dependents," 6–9.

PART TWO

THE FORCES UNDERMINING
THE AMERICAN DREAM

A variety of social and economic forces have combined to increase the ranks of the working poor and to swell the numbers of people in the middle class who are in economic distress. A greater understanding of these influences is necessary in order to propose effective policy recommendations. The four chapters in this part provide an overview of some of the basic forces that are undermining the American Dream.

Richard Freeman, in "The Great Doubling: The Challenge of the New Global Labor Market," underscores the role of globalization in generating economic distress. He notes that the size of the global labor market doubled in the 1990s with the entry of China, India, and the countries of the former Soviet Union. This "great doubling" expanded considerably the supply of low-wage workers in the world economy, fueled the trend toward outsourcing of high-wage jobs, and put downward pressure on wages in the United States. The creation of a global labor market makes it imperative for the United States to invest in education to keep up with the investments made by China and India, and to provide protections for those people left behind by economic growth.

Jacob Hacker, in "The Risky Outlook for Middle-Class America," describes the rising insecurity in jobs and greater instability in earnings. These reflect the defining feature of the contemporary economy: a "great risk shift" or massive transfer of economic risk from government and private sectors to American families. The shift in risk was fueled by economic restructuring over the past several decades, accompanied by the ideological view that individuals should be the sole guardians of their economic future. Hacker suggests that we need an "insurance and opportunity society" that provides a social safety net (including health insurance and retirement benefits that are portable from one employer to another) to help protect Americans from insecurity and the fear of economic loss.

In "Single Mothers, Fragile Families" Sara McLanahan explains that there has been an increase in single-mother families and in fragile families (unmarried parents raising a child together) in the United States, especially among women with low education. Families headed by single mothers and unmarried parents are more likely to be poor and to suffer a host of other negative consequences. McLanahan evaluates several possible solutions, including strategies to help parents become more responsible for their children and to increase parents' income. She argues that policies inhibiting the formation of fragile families may be more effective than those that try to keep them together after they are formed.

William Julius Wilson, in "A New Agenda for America's Ghetto Poor," maintains that joblessness is the main cause of concentrated urban poverty, especially in poor inner-city black neighborhoods. This "new urban poverty" results from the forces of globalization and other trends that have led to an exodus of middle-income families from inner cities and left behind few employment opportunities. Wilson insists that solutions must focus on fiscal, monetary, and trade policies that will stimulate the economy for all, rather than be targeted at particular race groups. At the same time, he emphasizes the need to ensure that the benefits of economic growth are widely shared through policies that combat racial discrimination in employment, revitalize poor urban neighborhoods, and provide job-training and education programs.

The Great Doubling:
The Challenge of the New Global
Labor Market

Richard B. Freeman

Before the collapse of Soviet Communism, China's movement toward market capitalism, and India's decision to undertake market reforms and enter the global trading system, the global economy encompassed roughly half of the world's population—the advanced Organization for Economic Cooperation and Development (OECD) countries, Latin America and the Caribbean, Africa, and some parts of Asia. Workers in the United States and other higher-income countries and in market-oriented developing countries such as Mexico did not face competition from low-wage Chinese or Indian workers or from workers in the Soviet empire. Then, almost all at once in the 1990s, China, India, and the former Soviet bloc joined the global economy, and the entire world came together into a single economic world based on capitalism and markets.

This change greatly increased the size of the global labor pool from approximately 1.46 billion workers to 2.93 billion workers (Figure 4.1). Since twice 1.46 billion is 2.92 billion, I have called this "the great doubling."[1] In this chapter I argue that the doubling of the global workforce presents the U.S. economy with its greatest challenge since the Great Depression. If the United States adjusts well, the benefits of having virtually all of humanity on the same economic page will improve living standards for all Americans. If the country does not adjust well, the next several decades will exacerbate economic divisions in the United States and risk turning much of the country against globalization.

The promise is that as the world economy grows rapidly, so too will the U.S. economy, giving opportunity for shared prosperity for all. The danger is

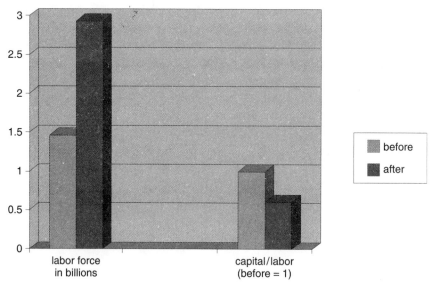

Figure 4.1 Workers in the Global Labor Force and the Global Capital/Labor Ratio, 2000, Before and After China, India, and the Former Soviet Bloc Joined the Global Economy

Source: Employment from ILO data, http://laborsta.ilo.org, 2000. Capital/labor ratio, calculated from Penn World tables as described in Richard Freeman, Usery Lecture, 2005, scaled so "before" is 1.00. "Before" is the workforce or capital/labor ratio that would have existed in the global capitalist system in 2000 if China, India, and the former Soviet bloc had remained outside the global economy. "After" is the workforce or capital/labor ratio in the capitalist global economy with the addition of the workers and capital from China, India, and the former Soviet bloc.

that as many firms invest in low-wage labor overseas, low-wage Americans will lose ground in the economy, as they have in the past two to three decades. Many will be unable to afford the health-care plans their firms offer, and many will find themselves in firms with no coverage. Fewer will have private retirement plans. The sentiments against globalization revealed in the NAFTA debate in the 1990s and in the debates over ways to deal with illegal immigrants in the early 2000s could combine to lead many Americans to blame the global economy for their woes. But it will not be globalization that is at fault, but the failure of the nation to choose policies that distribute the benefits of the global economy widely.

THE CAPITAL/LABOR BALANCE

What impact might the doubling of the global workforce have on workers? To answer this question, imagine what would happen if through some cloning experiment a mad economist doubled the size of the U.S. workforce. Twice as many workers would seek employment from the same businesses.

You do not need an economics Ph.D. to see that this would be good for employers but terrible for workers. Wages would fall. Unemployment would rise. But if the nation's capital stock doubled at the same time, demand for labor would rise commensurately, and workers would maintain their economic position. In the simplest economic analysis, the impact of China, India, and the former Soviet bloc joining the global economy depends on how their entry affects the ratio of capital to labor in the world. This in turn depends on how much capital they brought with them when they entered the global system. Over the long run it depends on their rates of savings and future capital formation.

Using data from the Penn World tables on yearly investments by nearly every country in the world, I have estimated the level of capital stock country by country and added the estimated stocks into a measure of the global capital stock. My estimates indicate that as of 2001 the doubling of the global workforce reduced the ratio of capital to labor in the world economy to 61 percent of what it would have been before China, India, and the former Soviet bloc joined the world economy.[2] The reason the global capital/labor ratio fell greatly was that the new entrants to the global economy did not bring much capital with them. India had little capital because it was one of the poorest countries in the world. China was also very poor and destroyed capital during the Maoist period. The Soviet empire was wealthier than China or India but invested disproportionately in military goods and heavy industry, much of which was outmoded or so polluting as to be worthless.

The immediate impact of the advent of China, India, and the former Soviet bloc to the world economy was thus to reduce greatly the ratio of capital to labor. This has shifted the global balance of power to capital. With the new supply of low-wage labor, firms can move facilities to lower-wage settings or threaten to do so if workers in existing facilities do not grant concessions in wages or work conditions favorable to the firm. Retailers can import products made by low-wage workers or subcontract production to lower-cost locales. In 2004 the Labor and Worklife Program at Harvard Law school[3] held a conference on the impact of the end of the Multi Fiber Arrangement that gave quotas to different developing countries for selling apparel in the United States and other advanced countries.[4] Union leaders representing apparel workers in Central America told the conference that firms were ordering workers to work extra hours without any increase in earnings under the threat of moving to China.[5] With wages in Central America three to four times those in China, the threat was a valid one. But the Chinese researcher at the meeting noted that the shift of apparel jobs to China was helping workers much poorer than those in Central America and thus was reducing world inequality and poverty.

In the long run China, India, and the former Soviet bloc will save and invest and contribute to the growth of the world capital stock. The World Bank estimates that China's savings rate is on the order of 40 percent to 50 percent, higher than the savings rate in most other countries, which will help increase global capital rapidly.[6] Though China is much poorer than the United States, it saves about as much as the United States because its savings rate far exceeds the U.S. savings rate. Still, it will take about three decades to restore the global capital/labor ratio to what it had been before China, India, and the former Soviet bloc entered the world economy and even longer to bring it to where it might have been absent their entry. For the foreseeable future the United States and other countries will have to adjust to a relative shortfall of capital per worker and to the power this gives to firms in bargaining with workers. This will affect workers in different parts of the world differently.

EFFECT ON WORKERS

The flow of capital to China and India to employ their low-wage workers will increase wages in those countries. Indeed, as their rates of economic growth have zoomed, real earnings have risen. In China the real earnings of urban workers more than doubled between 1990 and 2002. Poverty fell sharply despite a huge rise in inequality in China. Real wages in India also rose rapidly.

But workers in many of the developing countries in Latin America, Africa, and Asia did not fare well. Employment in Latin America, South Africa, and parts of Asia shifted from the formal sectors associated with economic advancement to informal sectors, where work is precarious, wages and productivity low, and occupational risks and hazards great. The entry of China and India to the world economy turned many developing countries from the low-wage competitors of advanced countries to the high-wage competitors of China and India. Countries such as Peru, El Salvador, Mexico, and South Africa can no longer develop by producing generic low-wage goods and services for the global marketplace that the Washington Consensus model of development envisaged that they would do.[7] The backlash against the orthodox World Bank/International Monetary Fund (IMF) form of globalization in Latin America reflects this failure.

The doubling of the global workforce challenges worker well-being in the United States and other advanced countries. First, it creates downward pressures on the employment and earnings of less skilled workers through trade and immigration. The traditional answer to this pressure is that the advanced countries should invest more in educating their workers. During the early 1990s debate in the United States over the impact of the NAFTA treaty with Mexico, proponents of the treaty argued that because U.S. workers were more skilled than Mexican workers and thus more capable of producing high-tech goods, the United States would gain high-skilled jobs from increased trade with Mexico while losing low-wage, less skilled jobs. Less skilled U.S. workers would benefit from trade if they made greater investments in human capital and became more skilled.

The argument that the United States will gain skilled jobs while losing less skilled jobs would seem to apply even more strongly to China and India. The average worker in China and India has lower skills than the average Mexican worker. From this perspective Chinese and Indian workers are complements rather than substitutes for American workers. Their joining the global labor pool reduces the prices of the manufacturing goods the United States buys and raises demand and prices for the high-tech goods and services the United States sells, which benefits educated labor. Lower prices for shoes, T-shirts, and plastic toys and higher prices for semiconductors and business consulting and finance would be in the interest of all U.S. workers save perhaps for the last shoemaker or seamstress.

But these analyses ignore the second challenge that the advent of the highly populous low-wage countries to the global economy poses for the United States and other developed countries. This is that these countries are becoming competitive in technologically advanced activities. The model that economists use to analyze trading patterns between advanced countries and developing countries assumes that the advanced countries have highly educated workers who enable them to monopolize cutting-edge innovative sectors, while the developing countries lack the technology and skilled workforce to produce anything beyond lower-tech products. In this model American workers benefit from the monopoly the United States has in the newest high-tech innovations. The greater the rate of technological advance and the slower the spread of new technology to low-wage countries, the higher paid are U.S. workers compared with workers in the developing countries.

But in such a model the spread of higher education and modern technology to low-wage countries can reduce advanced countries' comparative advantage in high-tech products and adversely affect workers in the advanced countries. In 2004, when many engineers and computer specialists were troubled by the offshoring of skilled work, Paul Samuelson reminded economists that a country with a comparative advantage in a sector can suffer economic loss when another country competes successfully in that sector.[8] The new competitor increases supplies, and this reduces the price of those goods on world markets and the income of the original exporter. Workers have to shift to less desirable sectors—those with lower chance for productivity growth, with fewer good jobs, and so on. Some trade specialists reacted negatively to Samuelson's reminder. What he said was well known to them but irrelevant. In the real world it would never happen.

Samuelson is right, and his critics are wrong. The assumption that only advanced countries have the educated workforce necessary for innovation and production of high-tech products is no longer true. Countries around the world have invested in higher education, and the number of college and university students and graduates outside the United States has grown hugely. In 1970 approximately 30 percent of university enrollments worldwide were in the United States; in 2000 approximately 14 percent of university enrollments worldwide were in the United States. Similarly, at the Ph.D. level the U.S. share of doctorates produced around the world has fallen from about 50 percent in the early 1970s to a projected level of 15 percent in 2010.[9] Some of the growth of higher education overseas is due to European countries rebuilding their university systems after World War II, and some is due to Japan and Korea investing in university education. By 2005 several EU countries and Korea were sending a larger proportion of their young citizens to university than the United States. But much is due to the growth of university education in developing countries, whose students made up nearly two-thirds of university enrollees in 2000. China has been in the forefront of this. Between 1999 and 2005 China increased the number of persons graduating with bachelor's degrees fivefold to four million persons.

At the same time, low-income countries have increased their presence in the most technically advanced areas. China has moved rapidly up the technological ladder, expanded its high-tech exports, and achieved a significant position in research in what many believe will be the next big industrial technology—nanotechnology. China's share of scientific research papers has increased greatly. India has achieved a strong position in information technology and attracts major research and development (R&D) investments, particularly in Bangalore. China and India have increasing footprints in high tech because as large populous countries, they can produce as many highly educated scientists and engineers as advanced countries, or more, even though the bulk of their workforce is less skilled. Indeed, by 2010 China will graduate more Ph.D.'s in science and engineering than the United States. The quality of university education is higher in the United States than in China, but China will improve quality over time. India has produced many computer programmers and engineers. And Indonesia, Brazil, Peru, and Poland—name the country—more than doubled their university enrollments in the 1980s and 1990s.

Multinational firms have responded to the increased supply of highly educated workers by "global sourcing" for workers. This means looking for the best candidates in the world and locating facilities, including high-tech R&D and production, where the supply of candidates is sufficient to get the work done at the lowest cost. Over 750 multinational firms have set up R&D facilities in China. Offshoring computer programming or moving call centers to lower-wage countries is the natural economic response to the availability of educated labor in those countries. I have called the process of moving up the technological ladder by educating large numbers of students in science and engineering "human resource leapfrogging" since it uses human resources to leapfrog comparative advantage from low-tech to high-tech sectors.[10] The combination of low wages and highly educated workers in large populous countries makes them formidable competitors for an advanced country.

The bottom line is that the spread of modern technology and education to China and India will undo some of the U.S. monopoly in high-tech innovation and production and place competitive pressures on U.S. workers. Eventually the wages of workers in China and India will approach those in the United States, as have the wages of European, Japanese, and to some extent Korean workers, but that is a long way off.

Finally, the development of computers and the Internet enhances the potential for firms to move work to low-cost operations. Business experts report that if work is digital—which covers about 10 percent of employment in the United States—it can and eventually will be offshored to low-wage highly educated workers in developing countries. The most powerful statement by a business group on this issue was given in 2005 by the Institute of Directors in the United Kingdom:

> The availability of high-speed, low-cost communications, coupled with the rise in high-level skills in developing countries meant off shoring has become an attractive option outside the manufacturing industry. Britain has seen call centres and IT support move away from Britain, but now creative services such as design and advertising work are being outsourced. There is more to come. In theory, anything that does not demand physical contact with a customer can be outsourced to anywhere on the globe. For many UK businesses this presents new opportunities, for others it represents a serious threat. But welcome it or fear it, it is happening anyway, and we had better get used to it.[11]

TRANSITION TO A TRULY GLOBAL LABOR MARKET

By bringing modern technology and business practices to most of humanity, the triumph of global capitalism has the potential for creating the first truly global labor market. Barring social, economic, or environmental disasters, technological advances should accelerate, permitting huge increases in the income of the world and eventually rough income parity among nations that will "make poverty history." But even under the most optimistic scenario it will take decades for the global economy to absorb the huge workforces of China, India, and potentially other successful developing countries. After

World War II it took 30 or so years for Western Europe and Japan to reach rough parity with the United States. It took Korea about 50 years to move from being one of the poorest economies in the world to the second rung of advanced economies. If the Chinese economy keeps growing rapidly and wages double every decade, as in the 1990s, Chinese wages would approach levels that the United States has today in about 30 years, and would approach parity with the United States about two decades later. India will take longer to reach U.S. levels. This period of transition to a truly global labor market presents both new opportunities and serious threats to worker well-being in the United States and other advanced countries.

How American workers fare in the transition will depend on a race between labor-market factors that improve living standards and factors that reduce those standards. On the improvement side are the likely higher rates of productivity due to more highly educated workers advancing science and technology and the lower prices of goods made by low-wage workers overseas. On the reduction side are the labor-market pressures from those workers and the worsening of terms of trade and loss of comparative advantage in the high-tech industries that offer the greatest prospects for productivity advances and the most desirable jobs. Which factors will win the race depends in part on the economic and labor-market policies that countries, the international community, unions, and firms choose to guide the transition. I can envisage a good transition scenario and a bad transition scenario.

In the good transition India, China, and other low-wage countries rapidly close the gap with the United States and other advanced countries in the wages paid their workers, as well as in their technological competence. Their scientists, engineers, and entrepreneurs develop and produce new and better products for the global economy. This reduces costs of production so that prices of goods fall, which improves living standards. The United States and other advanced countries retain comparative advantage in enough leading sectors or niches of sectors to remain hubs in the global development of technology. The world savings rate rises so that the global capital/labor ratio increases rapidly. As U.S. GDP grows, the country distributes some of the growth in the form of increased social services and social infrastructure—national health insurance, for instance—or through earned income tax credits so that living standards rise even for workers whose wages are constrained by low-wage competitors during the transition.

In the bad transition China and India develop enclave economies in which only their modern-sector workers benefit from economic growth while the rural poor remain low paid and a sufficient threat to the urban workers that wages grow slowly. The global capital stock grows slowly as Americans maintain high consumption and low savings. At one point citizens in the United

States begin to blame globalization for economic problems and try to abort the transition and introduce trade barriers and limit the transfer of technology. To add to the nightmare, huge within-country inequalities in China, India, and other countries produce social disorder that creates chaos or gets suppressed by a global "superelite" who use their wealth and power to control a mass of struggling poor. The bad scenario resembles some recalcitrant Marxist's vision of global capitalism.

The challenge to the United States is to develop business, labor, and government policies to assure that the country and the world make a good transition. What might this entail?

First, this requires that the United States invest in science and technology and keep attracting the best and brightest scientists, engineers, and others from the rest of the world. The United States leads in science, technology, and higher education in part because it attracts huge numbers of highly educated immigrants. In the 1990s dot.com and high-tech booms in the United States increased employment of scientists and engineers greatly without increasing the number of citizens graduating in science and engineering and without raising the pay of scientists and engineers relative to that of other professions. It did this by greatly increasing the share of foreign-born workers in the science and engineering workforce. Sixty percent of the growth of Ph.D. scientists and engineers consisted of foreign-born persons, with the largest numbers coming from China and India. In 2000 over half of employed doctorate scientists and engineers aged less than 45 were foreign born. Many of the foreign born were United States educated, but most of those with bachelor's degrees were educated overseas. The country needs to maintain itself as an attractive open society to keep a large flow of highly educated immigrants.

From the perspective of U.S. university graduates, however, the immigration of large numbers of highly educated workers and global sourcing of jobs to low-wage countries threatens economic prospects. It gainsays the notion that skilled Americans need not worry about competition from workers overseas. If you study or work in science and engineering, where knowledge is universal, you should worry. Your job may not go to Bombay or Beijing, but you will be competing with persons from those countries and other low-wage countries. For the United States to maintain its global lead in science and technology, it has to encourage American citizens to go on in these fields, as well as attract foreign talent. This requires more spending on basic research and development, allocating a larger share of research grants to young researchers as opposed to senior researchers, and giving more and higher-valued scholarships and fellowships. The United States needs to educate citizens with skills that differ sufficiently from those being produced in huge numbers overseas and to equip U.S. workers with complementary physical and social overhead capital.

For less skilled and lower-paid Americans, there is a need to restructure the labor market for their services so they do not fall further behind the rest of the country. Some of the policies that can help workers through this period are "tried and true": a strengthening of rights at work that would allow them to gain a share of the profits of firms in nontraded-goods markets through shared capitalist arrangements; trade unions; higher minimum wages, which can raise wages at the bottom of the job market with little cost of employment; expansion of the Earned Income Tax Credit (EITC), which will improve incomes and living standards without raising the cost of labor; and provision of social services such as health insurance that makes them less costly to hire. Given the doubling of the global labor force, these workers will need greater social support to advance in the economy than in years past.

With productivity and GDP rising, the country will have the resources to raise social safety nets and supplement earnings so that work will be attractive even for those who face low-wage competition from overseas. Ideally the competitive market would improve the well-being of all Americans without any policy interventions, but to the extent that globalization or any other factor prevents some groups from benefiting from economic growth, the country will need to buttress the living standards of those groups.

CONCLUSION

The world has entered a long and epochal transition toward a single global economy and labor market. There is much for the United States to welcome in the new economic world, but also much for the United States to fear. The country needs to develop new creative economic policies to assure that workers fare well during this transition and that the next several decades do not repeat the experience of the past 20 or 30 years in which nearly all the American productivity advance ended up in the pockets of the highest-paid persons and very little in the pockets of normal workers. National policies toward education, worker rights, taxation, and investment in social overhead capital can help the economy make the adjustments to assure that all will benefit.

NOTES

1. Richard Freeman, "The Great Doubling: America in the New Global Economy" (Usery Lecture, Georgia State University, April 8, 2005); Richard Freeman, "What Really Ails Europe (and America): The Doubling of the Global Workforce," *Globalist*, June 3, 2005, http://www.theglobalist.com/StoryId.aspx?StoryId=4542.

2. Freeman, "Great Doubling."

3. Harvard Law School, "Labor and Worklife Program," http://www.law.harvard.edu/programs/1wp/.

4. Wikipedia, "Multi Fibre Arrangement," http://en.wikipedia.org/wiki/Bra_wars.

5. Harvard Law School, Labor and Worklife Program, "The Ending of Global Textile Quotas: Understanding the New Shape of the World Economy" (briefing book available from Labor and Worklife Program, May 23–24, 2005).

6. World Bank, "World Development Indicators," Table 4.9, http://devdata.worldbank.org/wdi2005/Section4.htm.

7. For discussions of the Washington Consensus, see http://en.wikipedia.org/wiki/Washington_Consensus.

8. Paul A. Samuelson, "Where Ricardo and Mill Rebut and Confirm Arguments of Mainstream Economists Supporting Globalization," *Journal of Economic Perspectives* 18 (2004): 135–46.

9. Richard Freeman, "Does Globalization of the Scientific/Engineering Workforce Threaten US Economic Leadership?" *Innovation Policy and the Economy* 6 (2006): 123–58.

10. Ibid., 142–45.

11. Institute of Directors, "Offshoring Is Here to Stay," January 23, 2006, http://www.politics.co.uk/issueoftheday/institute-directors-offshoring-here-stay-$370499$367012.htm.

The Risky Outlook for Middle-Class America

Jacob S. Hacker

We have heard a great deal about rising inequality in the United States—the growing gap between the rungs of our economic ladder. Yet, to most Americans, inequality is far less tangible and worrisome than a trend we have heard much less about: rising insecurity, or the growing risk of slipping from the ladder itself.

Consider some of the alarming facts. As Elizabeth Warren shows in her chapter in this book, personal bankruptcy has gone from a rare occurrence to a routine one, with the number of households filing for bankruptcy quadrupling between 1980 and 2005. The bankrupt are pretty much like other Americans before they file: slightly better educated, more likely to be married and parents, roughly as likely to have had a good job, and modestly less likely to own a home.[1] They are not the persistently poor; they are refugees of the middle class, frequently wondering how they fell so far so fast.

Americans are also losing their homes at record rates. Since the early 1970s there has been a fivefold increase in the share of households that fall into foreclosure—a process that begins when homeowners default on their mortgages and can end with homes being auctioned to the highest bidder in local courthouses.[2] David Lamberger, a Detroiter who has worked in the auto industry most of his life, can testify to just how wrenching a process it is. When David lost his job at an auto parts maker, he declared bankruptcy to delay foreclosure on the modest home he shares with his wife and four children. But the money he makes working at a used-car lot has not been sufficient to keep them afloat, and now he may lose the family home.[3] For David and scores of other homeowners, the American Dream has mutated into what former U.S. Comptroller of the Currency Julie L. Williams calls "the American nightmare."[4]

Middle-class jobs are also less secure. The proportion of workers formally out of work at any point in time has remained low, but the share of workers who lose a job through no fault of their own every three years has actually been rising and is now roughly as high as it was during the recession of the early 1980s, the worst economic downturn since the Great Depression.[5] No less important, these job losses come with growing risks. Workers now invest more in education to earn a middle-class living, and yet in today's postindustrial economy these costly investments are no guarantee of a high, stable, or upward-sloping path. For displaced workers, the prospect of gaining new jobs with relatively similar pay and benefits has fallen, and the ranks of the long-term unemployed and "shadow unemployed" (workers who have given up looking for jobs altogether) have grown.[6] Increasing numbers of Americans find themselves in situations like that of Teresa Geerling, who in 2003 saw her relatively well-paying job for American Airlines eliminated. Though she was lucky enough to find a new job—a night shift at a local hospital—she now must pay $200 a month if she wants insurance coverage, a significant dip into her much-reduced earnings. And unlike her old job, her new one does not offer a guaranteed pension. Her husband's job is also in doubt, and they now think that they may not be able to hold on to their home.[7]

As Teresa's story suggests, workplace benefits are not what they used to be. The number of Americans who lack health coverage altogether has increased with little interruption over the last 25 years as corporations have cut back on insurance for employees and their dependents. Over a two-year period more than 80 million adults and children—one out of three nonelderly Americans, 85 percent of them working or the children of working parents—spend some time without the protection against ruinous health costs that insurance offers.[8]

At the same time, companies have raced away from the promise of guaranteed retirement benefits. Twenty-five years ago 83 percent of medium and large firms offered traditional "defined-benefit" pensions that provided a fixed benefit for life. Today the share is below a third.[9] Instead, companies that offer pensions provide "defined-contribution" plans such as the 401(k), in which returns are neither predictable nor assured.

Perhaps most alarming of all, as I show in this chapter, American family incomes are on a frightening roller coaster, rising and falling much more sharply from year to year than they did a generation ago. Indeed, the instability of families' incomes has risen substantially faster than the inequality of families' incomes. In other words, while the gaps between the rungs on the ladder of our economy have increased, what has increased even more quickly is how far people fall when they lose their footing. As David Lamberger, the Michigan man who is in the process of losing his house, describes his own bouncy ride, "There have been years I made $80,000, and there have been years I made $28,000. . . . Sometimes we're able to pay bills and get by, but then stuff from the slow times never goes away. You can't catch up, and it comes back to haunt you."[10]

We have heard about many of these trends in isolation. But there has been a curious silence about what they add up to: a massive transfer of economic risk from broad structures of insurance, both corporate and governmental, onto the fragile balance sheets of American families. This transformation, which I call "the great risk shift," is the defining feature of the contemporary economy, as important as the shift from agriculture to industry a century ago.[11] It has fundamentally reshaped Americans' relationships to their government, their employers, and each other, transforming the economic circumstances of American families—from the bottom of the ladder to its highest rungs.

One point must be understood from the outset: the great risk shift is not a natural occurrence, a financial hurricane beyond human control. Sweeping changes in the global and domestic economy have helped propel it. Yet America's leaders could have responded to these forces by reinforcing the floodwalls that protect families from economic risk. Instead, in the name of personal responsibility, many of these leaders are tearing the floodwalls down. Proponents of these changes speak of a nirvana of individual economic management—a society of empowered "owners," in which Americans are free to choose. What these advocates are helping create, however, is very different: a harsh new world of economic insecurity, in which far too many Americans are free to lose.

The forgotten alternative to this go-it-alone worldview is what I call a "security and opportunity society." A security and opportunity society is based on a simple but powerful notion: we are most capable of fully participating in our economy, most capable of taking risks and looking toward our future, when we have a basic foundation of financial security. Economic security is not opposed to economic opportunity; it is its cornerstone. And restoring a measure of economic security in the United States today is the key to transforming the nation's great wealth and productivity into an engine for broad-based prosperity and opportunity in an ever more uncertain economic world.

AMERICA'S HIDDEN INSECURITY

To see the great risk shift, we need to look at the economy the way that people actually live it—as a moving picture, rather than an isolated snapshot. We need to survey the same people over many years, following them even as they experience death, birth, marriage, and all the other events, good and bad, that mark the passage from childhood into old age. These kinds of surveys are called "panel surveys," and compared with the usual approach—contacting a different random group for each survey—they are exceedingly difficult to carry out. Given this, it is perhaps understandable that no official statistic tries to assess directly the dynamics of family income. Curious citizens who spend a few hours on the websites of the Commerce Department or Census Bureau will come away with a wealth of snapshots of the financial health of American families. But they will search fruitlessly for even the most basic information about how the economic status of American families changes over time, much less about what causes these shifts.

The answers can be found in the Panel Study of Income Dynamics (PSID), a nationally representative survey that has been tracking thousands of families from year to year since the late 1960s. Nearly 40 years into its operation, the survey has included over 65,000 people, some of whom have been answering questions for their entire adult lives, others of whom have been in the survey since their birth. As a result, the PSID is uniquely well suited for examining how and why incomes rise and fall over time.

What becomes immediately clear is that family incomes rise and fall a lot—far more than one would suspect just from looking at income-distribution figures. To take just one simple measure, displayed in Figure 5.1, during a recent 10-year period (1993–2002) Americans aged 25 to 61 have roughly a quarter the income in the year they are poorest, on average, that they have in the year they are richest. This striking disparity, it turns out, is a dramatic increase from even the relatively recent past: in the 1970s the low was only about 43 percent of the high.

These up-and-down swings are missed when we use annual snapshots to look at the distribution of American family income. There are not just the well-off and the poorly off. There are Americans who are doing well one year and poorly the next, and vice versa. In fact, a surprisingly big chunk of the income inequality that we see across families at any point in time—perhaps as much as half—is due to transitory shifts of family income, rather than to permanent differences across families.

This is a point that free-market conservatives love. Sure, inequality is growing, they say, but mobility is alive and well, making any comparison of income groups misleading. But this conclusion is as wrongheaded as the image of a frozen class structure that is sometimes taken from income-distribution statistics. Upward mobility is real, but it is usually not dramatic. And, as Jared Bernstein reports in his chapter in this volume, the evidence suggests it has not increased in the era of rising inequality.[12]

There is an even more glaring oversight of paeans to social mobility: what

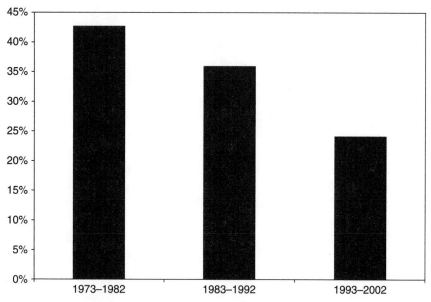

Figure 5.1 The Declining Average Ratio of Low to High Family Incomes
  Source: Panel Study of Income Dynamics; analysis follows household heads, with top and bottom 1 percent of observations trimmed.

goes up also goes down, and both research and common sense suggest that downward mobility is far more painful than upward mobility is pleasurable. In fact, in the 1970s psychologists Daniel Kahneman and Amos Tversky gave a name to this bias: "loss aversion."[13] Most people, it turns out, are not just highly risk averse—they prefer a bird in the hand to even a very good chance of two in the bush. They are also far more cautious when it comes to bad outcomes than when it comes to good outcomes of exactly the same magnitude. The search for economic security is, in large part, a reflection of a basic human desire for protection against losing what one already has.

This desire is surprisingly strong. Americans are famously opportunity loving, but when asked in 2005 whether they were "more concerned with the opportunity to make money in the future, or the stability of knowing that your present sources of income are protected," 62 percent favored stability and just 29 percent favored opportunity.[14] Americans like to gamble, but not, it seems, when their long-term security is on the line.

THE ECONOMIC ROLLER COASTER

Judged on these terms, what my evidence shows is troubling, to say the least. When I started out, I expected to see a modest rise in instability. But I was positively thunderstruck by what I found: instability of family incomes had skyrocketed. At its peak in the mid-1990s, instability of pretax family incomes was roughly five times as great as it was in the early 1970s. And although it dropped during the boom of the late 1990s, it never fell below its starting level, and it shot up in recent years (my data end in 2002) to three times the level of the early 1970s.[15]

But isn't this just a problem of the less educated, the workers who have fallen furthest behind in our economy? The answer is no. Volatility is indeed higher for less educated Americans than for more educated Americans. (It is also higher for blacks and Hispanics than for whites, and for women than for men.) Yet, surprisingly, volatility has risen by roughly the same amount across all these groups over the last generation. During the 1980s people with less formal education experienced a large rise in volatility, while those with more formal education saw a modest rise. During the 1990s, however, the situation was reversed: educated workers saw the instability of their income rise more, and by the end of the decade, as Figure 5.2 shows, the instability of their income had increased by nearly as much from the 1970s baseline. Increasingly, more educated workers are riding the economic roller coaster once reserved for the working poor.

Roller coasters go up and down. Yet when most of us contemplate the financial risks in our lives, we do not worry about the upward trips. We think

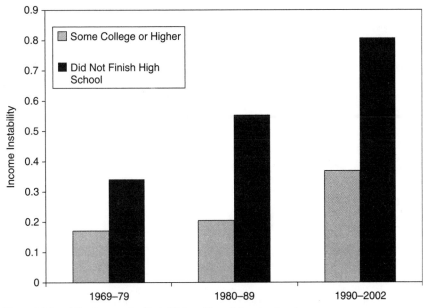

Figure 5.2 Instability Increased at Both High and Low Education Levels
Source: Panel Study of Income Dynamics; Cross-National Equivalent File, Cornell University.

about drops, and understandably so: we are loss averse, in major part, because losing what we have can require wrenching adjustments in our lives. Indeed, when losses are catastrophic, people have to confront what anthropologist Katherine Newman calls "falling from grace"—to contend "not only with financial hardship, but also with the psychological, social, and practical consequences" of losing our proper place.[16]

We can get a better sense of these "falls from grace" by looking specifically at drops in family income. About half of all families in the PSID experience a drop in real income over a two-year period, and the number has remained fairly steady. Yet families that experience an income drop fall much further today than they used to: in the 1970s the typical income loss was around 25 percent of prior income; by the late 1990s it was around 40 percent. And remember that this is the median drop: half of families whose incomes dropped experienced even larger declines.

Figure 5.3 uses somewhat fancier statistics to show the rising probability of experiencing a 50 percent or greater family income drop. The chance was around 7 percent in the 1970s. It has increased dramatically since, and although, like income volatility, it fell in the strong economy of the 1990s, it has recently spiked. There is nothing extraordinary about "falling from grace."

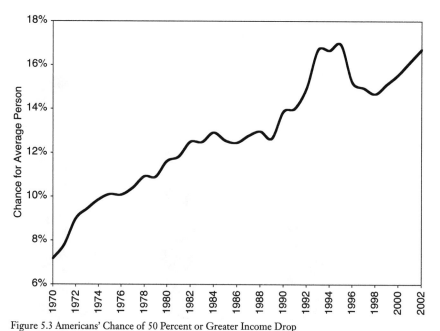

Figure 5.3 Americans' Chance of 50 Percent or Greater Income Drop
  Source: Panel Study of Income Dynamics; Cross-National Equivalent File, Cornell University.
  Note: Results are from a logistic regression predicting drops in family-size-adjusted family income among individuals aged 25–61.

You can be perfectly average—with an average income, an average-sized family, an average likelihood of losing your job or becoming disabled—and you are still two and one-half times as likely to see your income plummet as an average person was 30 years ago.

The most dramatic consequence of "falling from grace" is, of course, poverty—subsistence at a level below the federal poverty line. According to sociologists Daniel Sandoval, Thomas Hirscehl, and Mark Rank, the chance of spending at least a year in poverty has increased substantially since the late 1960s, even for workers in their peak earning years. People who were in their 40s in the 1970s had around a 13 percent chance of experiencing at least a year in poverty during their 40s. By the 1990s people in their 40s had more than a 36 percent chance of ending up in poverty.[17]

These numbers illuminate the hidden side of America's economic success story: the growing insecurity faced by ordinary workers and their families. And unlike other measures, these statistics are as direct and comprehensive as they come. Rates of bankruptcy or home foreclosure might go up because financial meltdowns have lost their stigma or because people are making foolish economic choices. But nobody files for a major income drop or spends his or her way into a highly unstable income. Income instability is the DNA of economic insecurity, its basic building block.

Income instability is the building block of insecurity, but it is not the whole. Indeed, as dramatic and troubling as the trends we have examined are, they vastly understate the true depth of the problem. For while income instability powerfully captures the risks faced by Americans today, insecurity is also driven by the rising threat to family finances posed by budget-busting expenses such as catastrophic medical costs, as well as by the massively increased risk that retirement has come to represent, as ever more of the responsibility of planning for the postwork years shifts onto Americans and their families. When we take in this larger picture, we see an economy not merely changed by degrees, but fundamentally transformed—from an all-in-the-same-boat world of shared risk toward a go-it-alone world of personal responsibility.

UNDOING THE GREAT RISK SHIFT

The great risk shift is not just an economic change. It is also an ideological change. For decades Americans and their leaders were committed to a powerful set of ideals that combined a commitment to economic security with a faith in economic opportunity. Animating this vision was a conviction that a strong economy and society hinged on basic financial security, on the guarantee that those who worked hard and did right by their families had a true safety net when disaster struck. Social Security, Medicare, private health insurance, traditional guaranteed pensions—all sent the same reassuring message: Someone is watching out for you when things go bad.

Today the dominant message is starkly different: You are on your own. Private employment-based health plans and pensions have eroded or been radically transformed to shift more and more risk onto workers' shoulders. Government programs of economic security have been cut, restructured, or simply allowed to grow ever more threadbare. Millions of Americans lack health insurance. Millions more lack guaranteed retirement benefits. Our jobs and our families are less and less financially secure.

Yet what do our political leaders tell us? They tell us that we need to take "ownership" of our economic future, giving up the security of insurance in favor of individualized private accounts that leave us at the mercy of market instabilities precisely when we most need stability.[18] They tell us that millions of middle-class Americans with children and homes who are declaring bankruptcy or losing their houses are failing to take "personal responsibility" for their lives.[19] They tell us that the economy is "strong and getting stronger" when for most of us it has only grown more uncertain and insecure.[20] Or they suggest, with a fatalism that scarcely befits a nation built on optimism and hope, that there is nothing that can be done. Our economy is insecure. Deal with it.

It is indeed time to deal with it. But the solution is not to shift more and more risk onto Americans' already-burdened shoulders. There can be no turning back the clock on many of the changes that have swept through the American economy and American society. Yet accepting these changes does not mean accepting the new insecurity, much less accepting the assumptions that lie behind the current assault on insurance. Americans will need to do much to secure themselves in the new world of work and family. But they should be able to do it in a context in which government and employers act as a help, not a hindrance. And they should be protected by an improved safety net that fills the most glaring gaps in present protections, providing all Americans with the basic financial security they need to reach for the future—as workers, as parents, and as citizens.

Make no mistake, however: this strengthened safety net will have to be different from the one that was constructed during the Great Depression and in the years after World War II. Our eroding framework of social protection is overwhelmingly focused on the aged, even though young adults and families with children face the greatest economic strains today. It emphasizes short-term exits from the workforce, even though long-term job losses and the displacement and obsolescence of skills have become more severe. It embodies, in places, the antiquated notion that family strains can be dealt with by a second earner—usually a woman—who can easily leave the workforce when there is a need for a parent at home. Above all, it is based on the idea that job-based private insurance can easily fill the gaps left by public programs, when it is ever more clear that it cannot.

Americans require a new framework of social insurance that revitalizes the best elements of the present system while replacing those parts that work least effectively with stronger alternatives geared toward today's economy and society. This new framework should include basic health coverage that moves with workers from job to job, enhanced protections against employment loss (and the wage and benefit cuts that come with it), and an improved framework for retirement savings. It should also include a new flexible program of social insurance that I call Universal Insurance—a stop-loss income-protection program that insures workers against very large drops in their income due to unemployment, disability, ill health, or the death of a breadwinner, as well as against catastrophic medical costs. For a surprisingly modest cost, Universal Insurance could help keep more than three million Americans a year from falling into poverty and cut in half the chance that Americans experience a drop in their income of 50 percent or greater.[21] In doing so, it would help provide all Americans with the basic economic security they need to reach for and achieve the American Dream.

Such a security and opportunity society will not be costless, though its long-term rewards will vastly exceed its short-term costs. It will not be uncontroversial, though it can and should rest on sensible ideas from a wide range of thinkers and leaders. And it will not be easy to achieve, though it can and must be sought. What it will do is restore a simple promise to the heart of the American experience: if you work hard and do right by your families, you should not live in constant fear of economic loss. You should not feel, as Teresa Geerling and David Lamberger and many others do, that a single bad step means slipping from the ladder of advancement for good. The American Dream is about security and opportunity alike, and rebuilding it for the millions of middle-class families whose anxieties and struggles are reflected in the statistics showcased in this chapter will require providing security and opportunity alike.

NOTES

1. Elizabeth Warren, "Financial Collapse and Class Status: Who Goes Bankrupt?" *Osgoode Hall Law Journal* 41, no. 1 (2003): 115–47.

2. Calculated from Peter J. Elmer and Steven A. Seelig, "The Rising Long-Term Trend of Single-Family Mortgage Foreclosure Rates" (Federal Deposit Insurance Corporation Working Paper 98-2, n.d.), available online at http://www.fdic.gov/bank/analytical/working/98-2.pdf.

3. Suzette Hackney, "Families Fight for Their Homes," *Detroit Free Press*, October 15, 2005.

4. Joe Baker, "Foreclosures Chilling Many US Housing Markets," *Rock River Times*, March 22–28, 2006, available online at http://www.rockrivertimes.com/index.pl?cmd=viewstory&id=12746&cat=2.

5. Henry Farber, "What Do We Know About Job Loss in the United States?" *Federal Reserve Bank of Chicago* 2Q (January 2005): 13–28.

6. Ibid.; Katharine Bradbury, "Additional Slack in the Economy: The Poor Recovery in Labor Force Participation During This Business Cycle" (Brief no. 05-2, Federal Reserve Bank of Boston Series, Boston, 2005); Andrew Stettner and Sylvia A. Allegretto, "The Rising Stakes of Job Loss: Stubborn Long-Term Joblessness amid Falling Unemployment Rates" (EPI & NELP Briefing Paper 162, Economic Policy Institute, Washington, DC, May 2005), available online at http://www.epinet.org/content.cfm/bp162.

7. Jonathan Krim and Griff Witte, "Average-Wage Earners Fall Behind—New Job Market Makes More Demands but Fewer Promises," *Washington Post*, December 31, 2004, available online at http://washingtonpost.com/wp-dyn/articles/A37628-2004Dec30.html.

8. Families USA Foundation, *One in Three: Non-elderly Americans Without Health Insurance, 2002–2003* (Washington, DC: Families USA Foundation, 2004), available online at http://www.familiesusa.org/issues/uninsured/about-the-uninsured/.

9. John H. Langbein, "Understanding the Death of the Private Pension Plan in the United States" (unpublished manuscript, Yale Law School, April 2006).

10. Hackney, "Families Fight for Their Homes."

11. Jacob S. Hacker, *The Great Risk Shift: The Assault on American Jobs, Families, Health Care, and Retirement—And How You Can Fight Back* (New York: Oxford University Press, 2006).

12. See also "Ever Higher Society, Ever Harder to Ascend." *Economist*, December 29, 2004, available online at http://www.economist.com/world/na/displayStory.cfm?story_id=3518560.

13. Daniel Kahneman and Amos Tversky, "Prospect Theory: An Analysis of Decisions Under Risk," *Econometrica* 47, no. 2 (1979): 263–92.

14. George Washington University Battleground 2006 Survey, March 2005. Results available at http://www.tarrance.com/pdfs/Democrat-analysis-BG27.pdf.

15. For a description of the model used to calculate over-time income variance, see Robert A. Moffitt and Peter Gottschalk, "Trends in the Transitory Variance of Earnings in the United States," *Economic Journal* 112 (March 2002): 68–73. Data on taxes and government benefits are from the Cross-National Equivalent File, Cornell University, available online at http://www.human.cornell.edu/che/PAM/Research/Centers-Programs/German-Panel/Cross-National-Equivalent-File_CNEF.cfm. Further information is available in Hacker, *Great Risk Shift*.

16. Katherine S. Newman, *Falling from Grace: The Experience of Downward Mobility in the American Middle Class* (New York: Free Press, 1988), 8.

17. Daniel Sandoval, Thomas A. Hirschl, and Mark R. Rank, "The Increase of Poverty Risk and Income Insecurity in the U.S. Since the 1970's" (paper presented at the American Sociological Association Annual Meeting, San Francisco, CA, August 14–17, 2004).

18. David Boaz, "Defining an Ownership Society," Cato Institute, available online at http://www.cato.org/special/ownership_society/boaz.html.

19. White House Press Release, "President Signs Bankruptcy Abuse Prevention, Consumer Protection Act," April 20, 2005, available online at http://www.whitehouse.gov/news/releases/2005/04/20050420-5.html.

20. President George W. Bush, radio address, March 27, 2004, available online at http://www.whitehouse.gov/news/releases/2004/03/20040327.html.

21. Jacob S. Hacker, "Universal Insurance: Enhancing Economic Security to Promote Opportunity" (Hamilton Project Discussion Paper, Brookings Institution, Washington, DC, September 2006), available online at www.brookings.edu/views/papers/200609hacker.pdf.

6

Single Mothers, Fragile Families

Sara McLanahan

During the latter part of the twentieth century major changes occurred in people's behavior that affected family formation, including delays in marriage and increases in cohabitation, divorce, and nonmarital childbearing. These changes have dramatically altered the types of families in which American children are being raised. Whereas in 1950 the vast majority of children were raised by two biological parents who were married when their child was born and who stayed married while he or she grew up, today more than half of all children are being raised in a variety of new family forms, including single-mother families, stepparent families, and fragile families, defined as unmarried parents raising a child together.

These new family forms are less stable than the more traditional families headed by two married biological parents. They also are associated with a host of negative outcomes for adults and children. Most important, perhaps, the changes in family formation have affected different groups of women differently. For one group of women—those with a college degree—the changes have meant greater economic independence and more satisfactory unions. The children in these families are doing well. For another group of women—those with less education—the changes have meant greater economic insecurity and more complex family structures. The children in these families are not doing as well.

Although nearly all researchers agree about the connection between non-traditional family structures and poor outcomes for adults and children, they do not agree about the causes of family change or the mechanisms that lead to poor outcomes. On the one hand, conservatives argue that the decline in marriage is driven by changes in social norms and values that have emphasized individual fulfillment and undermined family commitments. Others blame the welfare system for undermining the family. According to this view, poor child outcomes result from a lack of parental commitment and poor parenting. Liberals, in contrast, argue that family instability is caused by changes in the economy and the decline in wages among low-skilled men. For them, poor child outcomes are the consequence of low incomes and poverty.

Government has always provided support to poor single mothers and their children, although the level and type of support have varied over time.[1] Whereas in the past single-mother families were formed primarily by the death of the father, today they are increasingly formed by divorce and nonmarital childbearing. In the vast majority of cases the fathers of the children in single-mother families are alive and have some contact with their child. The challenge facing policymakers in the future is to strengthen the relationships between mothers and fathers and between fathers and children so that children grow up with the support of two biological parents.

In this chapter I begin by describing the demographic trends that have given rise to the recent changes in family structure and showing how women from different education strata have been differentially affected by these trends. Next I examine the causes and consequences of the trends as viewed by both conservatives and liberals. Finally I discuss what, if anything, government might do to strengthen fragile families.

TRENDS

Changes in family formation during the latter half of the twentieth century were driven by several demographic trends, including trends in marriage, cohabitation, divorce, and nonmarital childbearing.

As shown in Figure 6.1, the marriage rate—the number of marriages per thousand unmarried women—declined sharply after 1970 and has continued downward up to the present. The decline in marriage is reflected in the rising age at first marriage. After dropping for the first half of the twentieth century, the median age at first marriage reversed its trend after 1960. In 1960 the median age at first marriage was 20.3 for women and 22.8 for men; by 2000 it was 25.1 and 26.8, respectively. Note that in 1950 the age at first marriage was the lowest it had been since 1900, and thus the increase that began after 1960 was starting from a very low base. Nevertheless, by the turn of the twenty-first century the age at first marriage was higher than it had been at the turn of the twentieth century. While for most people the rising age at first marriage represents a postponement rather than a forgoing of marriage,

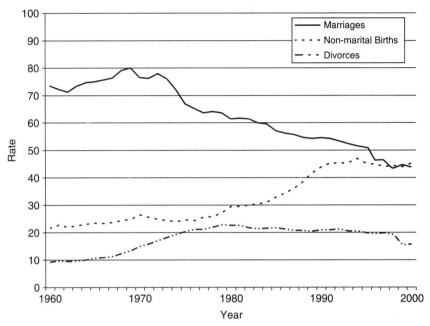

Figure 6.1 Trends in Marriage, Divorce, and Nonmarital Children

Source: Marriage and divorce rates for 1960–1990 come from *National Vital Statistics Reports*, 43, no. 9(S), 1995; marriage and divorce rates for 1991 to 1995 come from U.S. Bureau of the Census, *Statistical Abstract of the United States*, Table 156, 1998. Marriage and divorce rates for 1996–2000 come from the author's tabulations. The number of marriages and divorces come from the U.S. Bureau of the Census, *Statistical Abstract of the United States*, no. 83, 2003, with the exception of the number of divorces from 1999–2000, which are calculated from the provisional tables on marriages and divorces, National Center for Health Statistics, 46M6 Table 3-12, 1998–2000. The number of single and married females ages 15–44 from 1996–2000 comes from the U.S. Bureau of the Census, *Current Population Survey Reports*, Table MS-1, 2006. Nonmarital birth rates for 1960–2000 come from *National Vital Statistics Reports*, 48, no. 16, 2000.

for others it represents a more permanent change. The retreat from marriage has been especially dramatic for blacks. Demographers estimate that 46 percent of African American women born during the early 1960s will never marry.[2]

Along with the delay in marriage came an increase in cohabitation among unmarried couples. Our official statistics are much less reliable for cohabitation, as compared with marriage, since cohabiting relationships require no legal record. Nevertheless, there is very good evidence that cohabitation increased markedly during the 1980s and 1990s. According to demographers, the proportion of all women who ever cohabited grew from nearly 33 percent in 1987 to 45 percent in 1995, an increase of nearly 50 percent in less than 10 years.[3]

As marriage declined and cohabitation became more common, rates of nonmarital childbearing also increased, growing from 22 per 1,000 unmarried women in 1960 to 45 per 1,000 women in 2000. The increase in nonmarital childbearing led to dramatic changes in another statistic, the proportion of all children born outside marriage. In 1960, 5 percent of all births were to unmarried mothers; in 2000, over one in three births occurred outside marriage. The increase was even more dramatic among nonwhites, from 22 percent of all births in 1960 to 57 percent in 2000. Finally, divorce rates, which had been rising throughout most of the twentieth century, accelerated sharply during the 1960s and 1970s, leveled off at very high levels after 1980, and declined in the late 1990s.

Rather than affecting all women equally, the trends described here led to very different career and family trajectories for different groups of women.[4] For one group—those who were able to pursue higher education—the delay in marriage provided an opportunity to invest in human capital and gain economic independence. Having delayed motherhood until after marriage (the average age at first birth is 33, and 98 percent give birth within marriage), these women are using their economic independence to make good matches in the marriage market and to establish and maintain stable households. These mothers and children have also benefited from the increase in father involvement that has been occurring among married men.

For the other group of women—those who were unwilling or unable to invest in higher education—the delay in marriage and increase in cohabitation have led to a different trajectory. Rather than investing in human capital, these women have continued to have children as they did in the 1950s, although at somewhat older ages (23 for women without a high-school diploma and 26 for those with a diploma), but now they are having children outside marriage (70 percent for women with only a high-school diploma), whereas before, nearly all their children were born within marriage. Finally, their relationships with the fathers of the children born outside marriage are very fragile, and more than half have ended by the time the child is 5 years old. Once the relationship with the father is over, some of these mothers become single mothers and raise their child alone; others form new partnerships and have children with their new partners. Over time the combination of short-term partnerships and continuing fertility leads to increasingly complex family arrangements, with minimal contributions from nonresident fathers.

Figure 6.2, which shows the prevalence of single motherhood by education categories, illustrates the importance of education in shaping women's trajectories. The education difference in the prevalence of single mothers was present in 1960, but it was very small, ranging from less than 5 percent among women in the highest education group (top quartile) to 15 percent among women in the lowest group (bottom quartile). By 2000 the prevalence of single motherhood was much higher and the education gap was larger, ranging from less than 10 percent among women in the highest education group to over 40 percent among women in the lowest education group. Despite recent media

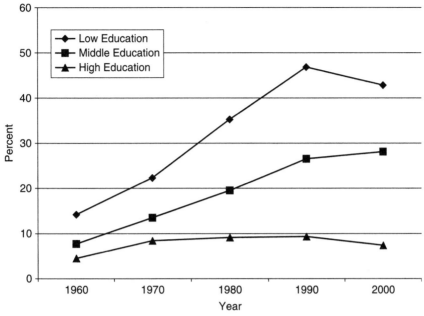

Figure 6.2 Trends in Single Motherhood, 1960–2000
  Source: Sara McLanahan, *Demography*, 2004, p. 619.

anecdotes to the contrary, this figure highlights the fact that single motherhood continues to be rare among highly educated women.

CONSEQUENCES AND CAUSES

But why should we care about the changes in family formation? Doesn't
growing diversity indicate more freedom and more choices for Americans? If
the trends described here were just a matter of growing diversity in family
forms, there would be little reason for concern except perhaps among those
who place a high value on tradition for its own sake. In fact, however, a large
body of research indicates that the new family forms are associated with negative outcomes for men, women, and children. Families headed by single
mothers are much more likely to be poor than families headed by two parents. In 2004 the poverty rate was 28.4 percent for single-mother families,
compared with 5.5 percent for two-parent families. Part of the gap, of course,
is due to differences in the types of people who become single parents versus
those who marry and stay married. As shown earlier, single motherhood is
much more common among women with only a high-school degree or less.
Thus many of the women who become single mothers would have been poor
even if they had married and stayed married. Nevertheless, divorce and single

motherhood increase the chances of poverty, even among women with low education.[5] Part of this is due to the fact that co-resident parents benefit from economies of scale. Another part is due to the fact that women typically earn less than men. Still another is due to the fact that many nonresident fathers do not pay child support.

In addition to poverty and economic hardship, single motherhood is associated with a host of other negative outcomes for adults, as well as children. In her 1995 presidential address to the Population Association of America, Linda Waite noted that a large body of research shows that married adults live longer and have fewer health problems than single adults. Married men have higher wage rates and lower rates of excessive drinking than their divorced or widowed counterparts. As for risk-taking behavior in general, both divorced and widowed men and women are more likely to engage in fights, dangerous activities, drinking and driving, and substance abuse than married men and women.[6] While some of these negative health behaviors may be associated with the stress of ending a marriage (or a spouse's death), Waite found that others arise from not being married. In a marriage a spouse may mitigate stress and encourage more healthful living either directly, by actively discouraging risky behavior, or indirectly, by conferring responsibility and purpose on the husband or wife's life. Married people also report more frequent and emotionally satisfying sex with a primary partner than single people. Most of the benefits associated with marriage do not extend to cohabiting relationships: the two exceptions are the gain in men's wages and improved sexual relations. Cohabiting unions may provide fewer benefits than marital unions because they are not expected to last as long. Not expecting any long-term benefits, cohabiting couples may be less willing than married couples to invest in one another and in their union. Thus cohabiting unions generate fewer public goods, including health and general well-being.

Finally, an extensive body of research shows that children who grow up with two biological parents do better than children who grow up with only one biological parent.[7] The latter are at risk of experiencing a variety of problems during childhood and adolescence. Girls who grow up apart from their biological fathers are more likely to become teen mothers and unmarried mothers, and boys who grow up apart from their fathers are more likely to become involved in delinquent activities and to have trouble holding a steady job. The problems extend into adulthood, with children from one-parent families showing higher rates of mental health problems and divorce.

Part of the negative association between living with a single mother and poor child outcomes is due to economic insecurity and poverty. As shown earlier, single-mother families are much more likely to be poor than two-parent families, and we know that poverty has negative effects on child development.[8] But economic hardship is not the only factor behind the poor child outcomes that are associated with divorce and single motherhood. We know, for example, that children who live in stepparent families exhibit some of the same behavioral problems as children who live in single-mother families. Many researchers believe that family instability—which is much more common in nontraditional families—is just as harmful to children as the absence of a parent.[9]

While most researchers agree that children who grow up apart from one of their biological parents are disadvantaged in a number of ways, they disagree about the cause of family disruption. Liberals, such as William Julius Wilson, argue that the changes in family life that occurred during the latter half of the twentieth century were driven by changes in the economy.[10] According to this argument, the demand for low-skilled workers declined sharply during the 1970s and 1980s, leading to rising unemployment and declines in wages. The loss of "good jobs" led to a sharp decline in the pool of "marriageable men" and eventually to a decline in marriage and an increase in nonmarital childbearing. For Wilson and other liberals, the changes in family structure are simply reflections of more fundamental changes in the economy.

In contrast, conservatives, such as James Q. Wilson, argue that the changes in the family that occurred after 1960 were driven by changes in social norms and values. According to this argument, the 1960s represented a major cultural shift in American values, with individual freedom and self-realization replacing traditional values such as family commitment and self-sacrifice.[11] The birth-control pill and the sexual revolution played a major role in this transformation, making it possible for young people to cohabit outside marriage and ending the stigma associated with nonmarital childbearing. Charles Murray, another leading conservative, offers a different explanation. He argues that the changes in family formation during the past several decades are due to overly generous welfare programs that have made single motherhood more attractive to low-income couples than marriage.[12]

Not only do liberals and conservatives disagree about the underlying causes of family change, they also disagree about why children raised by single mothers do worse than children raised by two married parents. Liberals emphasize the poor economic conditions that go with single motherhood; conservatives emphasize lower parental commitment and poor parenting.

Recent evidence from a large study of unmarried parents suggests that both economic factors and values play an important role in accounting for the lower rates of marriage among less educated adults, but not in the way most people think they do. According to data from the Fragile Families and Child Wellbeing Study, unmarried parents place a high value on marriage and view divorce as a serious failure.[13] At the same time, they face serious economic (and social-psychological) barriers to maintaining stable relationships.

Over 45 percent of unmarried mothers (and 40 percent of fathers) have less than a high-school degree (the numbers are 18 and 20 percent for married mothers and fathers, respectively). The average earnings of unmarried fathers are half as high as those of married fathers ($20,000 versus $40,000), even through they work nearly as many weeks a year (40 versus 44). Unmarried fathers have more mental health problems than married fathers, including depression (11 versus 8 percent), heavy drinking (30 versus 27 percent), and drug problems (8 versus 2 percent), and they are seven times as likely as married fathers to have been incarcerated (35 percent versus 5 percent).[14] With inadequate resources and fear of a divorce, these parents respond to their situation by setting very high standards for the level of economic success they must achieve before they marry. One young Hispanic father in his 20s put it this way: "I want to be secure. . . . I don't want to get married and be like, we have no money or nothing. . . . I want to get my little house in Long Island, you know, white-picket fence, and two-car garage, me hitting the garbage cans when I pull up in the driveway. You know . . . stuff like you see on TV."[15]

Since very few unmarried parents are able to meet these high expectations, most relationships do not last very long, and mothers continue to search for a better mate even as they are raising children from a previous union. This argument implies that during a period of rising divorce and declining earnings—which is what we have had during the past three decades—the high value placed on marriage may itself become a serious barrier to marriage.

SOLUTIONS

So what can be done to increase the proportion of children growing up in stable, two-parent families? Before attempting to answer this question, it is worth noting that the trends in marriage, divorce, and nonmarital childbearing are occurring in all Western industrialized countries, and governments' ability to reverse these trends may be quite limited.[16] That said, the United States stands out in terms of its high rates of divorce and its high proportion of children born to lone mothers (Figures 6.1 and 6.2). The question is: are U.S. policies exacerbating these broader trends, and can we be smarter in how we deal with the changes?

Conservatives argue that the welfare system discourages marriage by reducing the economic costs of single motherhood and by allowing fathers to shirk their parental responsibilities. Following this idea, for the past three decades states and the federal government have been experimenting with a variety of policies aimed at reforming the welfare system and making parents more responsible for their children. Cash benefits have declined since the mid-1970s, child-support enforcement has increased sharply, and, most recently, work requirements and time limits for welfare recipients have been implemented. Although there is some evidence that tougher welfare and child-support policies reduce nonmarital childbearing and single motherhood, the overall effects have been small.[17]

Liberals argue that low-income parents are reluctant to marry because men do not have steady jobs and/or because parents' joint income is too low and insecure. These ideas, which imply that increasing parents' income would lead to more stable unions, have also been tested during the past two decades by states such as Minnesota and Connecticut, which used welfare reform as an opportunity to increase family income, and by nonwelfare experiments, such as Wisconsin's New Hope and Canada's Self Sufficiency Program, which explicitly raised the incomes of single mothers.[18] In addition, the strong labor market in the 1990s, which reduced unemployment and raised the wages of low-skilled men and women, provides a "natural experiment" for testing how increasing income and employment would affect marriage. Again, while there is evidence that some of these programs reduced divorce or increased marriage among certain groups in certain regions, the overall effect has been small. In short, neither conservative nor liberal strategies have had a large impact on the trend in family formation.

The Bush administration is now supporting a new type of intervention that seeks to improve the communication and relationship skills of low-income parents. Such programs have been shown to be effective for middle-class parents,[19] and it is possible that they may help low-income parents as well. These programs are innovative in several respects and have attracted some bipartisan support. First, and most importantly, perhaps, the programs target couples rather than single mothers and thus acknowledge the fact that many single-mother families include a living father who is part of the family. For this reason they appeal to advocates for low-income fathers who have been seeking a greater role for biological fathers in the lives of their children. These advocates note that even if the romantic relationship between the parents ends, the programs are likely to improve parents' ability to cooperate and co-parent their child. Second, while the primary focus of the new programs is on relationship skills, they also screen parents for other problems and attempt to provide appropriate services if needed, including mental health treatment and employment services. Third, the programs target new parents around the time of their child's birth—the "magic moment." Data from the Fragile Families and Child Wellbeing Study indicate that many unmarried parents have "high hopes" for a future together and are motivated to make their relationship work. The marriage programs are responsive to these hopes and aspirations. Moreover, parents may be more willing to take advantage of other services (job training, mental health) when they are offered in the context of strengthening their new families. At present we have no idea if these programs will work, but fortunately, the Department of Health and Human Services is funding a large-scale, random-assignment evaluation of several model programs, and thus, like the welfare-reform policies before them, we will learn whether the programs are successful and for which groups.

Finally, it may be easier to prevent the formation of fragile families than to keep parents together after such a family is formed. A report by the Institute of Medicine finds that over two-thirds of births to unmarried mothers are "unplanned" or "unwanted."[20] Reducing such pregnancies would go a long way toward preventing the formation of single-mother families and fragile families. Doing this would require making sure that all women have access to effective contraception. It also would require providing young women with opportunities to increase their education and find good jobs. A large proportion of unmarried women become pregnant not because they lack access to contraception but because they do not use contraception consistently. These women are not "planning" to have a child, but neither are they sufficiently motivated to avoid a pregnancy. Education is highly correlated with nonmarital childbearing. Over 80 percent of women who gave birth outside marriage in large U.S. cities in 2000 had a high-school degree or less, and fewer than 20 percent had ever attended college.[21] Moving more women from the "high-school-only" category to the "some-college" category would increase the rewards of work and provide an incentive for young women to delay childbearing and avoid unplanned births. Many of these issues are discussed by Carol Cassell in Chapter 16 in this volume.

In sum, dealing with the family changes brought about by the trends in marriage, divorce, and nonmarital childbearing is a daunting task that requires accepting the fact that the trends are widespread and may be hard to reverse, acknowledging the failure of old strategies, and rethinking our policies toward low-income single mothers to include fathers and fragile families.

NOTES

I am grateful to Kevin Bradway, and Meridel Bulle, and Regina Leidy for research assistance and to the National Institute of Child Health and Development for support, Grant R01 HD036916.

1. Irwin Garfinkel and Sara McLanahan, *Single Mothers and Their Children: A New American Dilemma* (Washington, DC: Urban Institute Press, 1986).

2. Joshua R. Goldstein and Catherine T. Kenney, "Marriage Delayed or Marriage Foregone? New Cohort Forecasts of First Marriage for U.S. Women," *American Sociological Review* 66 (2001): 506–19.

3. Larry Bumpass and Hsien-Hen Lu, "Trends in Cohabitation and Implications for Children's Family Contexts in the United States," *Population Studies* 54 (2000): 29–41.

4. Sara McLanahan, "Diverging Destinies: How Children Are Faring Under the Second Demographic Transition," *Demography* 41 (2004): 619.

5. Karen C. Holden and Pamela J. Smock, "The Economic Costs of Marital Dissolution: Why Do Women Bear a Disproportionate Cost?" *Annual Review of Sociology* 17 (1991): 51–78.

6. Linda Waite, "Does Marriage Matter?" *Demography* 32, no. 4 (1995): 483–507.

7. Sara McLanahan and Gary Sandefur, *Growing Up with a Single Parent* (Cambridge, MA: Harvard University Press, 1994).

8. Greg Duncan and Jeanne Brooks-Gunn, eds., *Consequences of Growing Up Poor* (New York: Russell Sage Foundation, 1997).

9. Michael Rutter, "Stress, Coping, and Development: Some Issues and Some Questions," in *Stress, Coping, and Development in Children*, ed. N. Garmezy and M. Rutter (New York: McGraw-Hill, 1983), 1–42.

10. William Julius Wilson, *The Truly Disadvantaged: The Inner City, the Underclass, and Public Policy* (Chicago: University of Chicago Press, 1987).

11. James Q. Wilson, *The Marriage Problem: How Our Culture Has Weakened Families* (New York: HarperCollins, 2002).

12. Charles Murray, *Losing Ground* (New York: Basic Books, 1984).

13. Christina M. Gibson-Davis, Kathryn Edin, and Sara McLanahan, "High Hopes but Even Higher Expectations: The Retreat from Marriage Among Low-Income Couples," *Journal of Marriage and the Family* 67, no. 5 (2005): 1301–12. Also see Kathryn Edin and Maria Kefalas, *Promises I Can Keep* (Berkeley: University of California Press, 2005).

14. Sara McLanahan, "Fragile Families and the Marriage Agenda," in *Fragile Families and the Marriage Agenda*, ed. Lori Kowaleski-Jones and Nicholas Wolfinger (New York: Springer Science and Business Media, 2006).

15. Ibid., n. 14.

16. Kathleen Kiernan, "Unmarried Cohabitation and Parenthood: Here to Stay? European Perspectives," in *The Future of the Family*, ed. Daniel P. Moynihan, Timothy M. Smeeding, and Lee Rainwater (New York: Russell Sage Foundation, 2004), 66–95.

17. Robert Moffitt, "The Effect of Welfare on Marriage and Fertility," in *Welfare, the Family, and Reproductive Behavior*, ed. John Haaga and Robert A. Moffitt (Washington, DC: National Academy Press, 1998), 50–97; Anne Case, "The Effects of Stronger Child Support Enforcement on Nonmarital Fertility," in *Fathers Under Fire: The Revolution in Child Support Enforcement*, ed. Irwin Garfinkel, Sara McLanahan, Daniel Meyer, and Judith Seltzer (New York: Russell Sage Foundation, 1998), 191–215; Anna Aizer and Sara McLanahan, "The Impact of Child Support on Fertility, Parental Investments and Child Health and Well-Being," *Journal of Human Resources* 41, no. 1 (2006): 28–45.

18. Lisa Gennetian and Virginia Knox, "Staying Single: The Effects of Welfare Reform Policies on Marriage and Cohabitation" (Working Paper, MDRC, 2003); Kristen Harknett and Lisa A. Gennetian, "How an Earnings Supplement Can Affect Union Formation Among Low-Income Single Mothers,"*Demography* 40, no. 3 (2003): 451–78; Greg Duncan, Aletha Huston, and Thomas Weisner, *Higher Ground: New Hope for the Working Poor and Their Children* (New York: Russell Sage Foundation, 2007).

19. Philip Cowan, D. Powell, and Carolyn Cowan, "Parenting Interventions: A Family Systems Perspective," in *Handbook of Child Psychology*, vol. 4, ed. W. Damon (New York: J. Wiley, 1998).

20. Sarah S. Brown and Leon Eisenberg, eds., *The Best Intentions: Unintended Pregnancy and the Well-Being of Children and Families* (Washington, DC: National Academy Press, 1995).

21. Data from the Fragile Families and Child Wellbeing Study. This study was designed and conducted by researchers at Princeton and Columbia Universities. The data are available to the public at www.fragilefamilies.princeton.edu.

A New Agenda for America's Ghetto Poor

William Julius Wilson

Social scientists have rightly devoted considerable attention to concentrated poverty because it magnifies the problems associated with poverty in general: joblessness, crime, delinquency, drug trafficking, family breakups, and poor "social outcomes" such as school performance. Also, neighborhoods of highly concentrated poverty are seen as dangerous, and therefore they become isolated, socially and economically, as people go out of their way to avoid them.[1]

In this chapter I provide a framework for understanding the emergence and persistence of concentrated urban poverty. I pay particular attention to poor inner-city black neighborhoods, neighborhoods with the highest levels of concentrated poverty. I conclude this chapter by suggesting a new agenda for America's ghetto poor, based on the analysis I put forth in the following sections.

THE FORMATION OF CONCENTRATED INNER-CITY POVERTY

Before the 1970s African American families faced extremely strong barriers when they considered moving into white neighborhoods. Not only did many experience overt discrimination in the housing market, but some were recipients of violent attacks. Although fair-housing audits continue to reveal the existence of discrimination in the housing market, fair-housing legislation, including the Fair Housing Amendments Act of 1988, reduced the strength of these barriers. And middle-income African Americans increased their efforts to move from concentrated black poverty areas to more desirable neighborhoods in the metropolitan area, including white neighborhoods.

If whites had not moved out of these neighborhoods after significant black penetration, the proportion of working- and middle-class blacks residing in white neighborhoods would have significantly increased over the years. Also, a number of mixed-income areas adjacent to the highly concentrated black poverty areas experienced a significant out-migration of higher-income groups. Many of these neighborhoods were formerly white. The whites departed first, followed by middle-income blacks, leaving behind depopulated areas featuring higher concentrations of poverty and greater social and economic disadvantage.[2]

This pattern represents an important change in the formation of neighborhoods. In the earlier years communities undergoing racial change from white to black tended to experience an increase in population density as a result of the black migration from the South. Because of the housing demand, particularly in the late stages of the succession from white to black, homes and apartments in these neighborhoods were often subdivided into smaller units.[3]

However, 1970 marked the end of the great migration wave of blacks from the South to northern urban areas, and two developments affected the course of population movement to the inner cities after 1970. Improvements in transportation made it easier for workers to live outside the central city, and industries in the inner city gradually shifted to the suburbs. Because of the suburbanization of employment and improvement in transportation, inner-city manufacturing jobs were no longer a strong factor pulling migrants to central cities.[4] So with the decline of industrial employment in the inner city and the corresponding end of southern black migration to northern cities, poor black neighborhoods have changed from densely packed areas of recently arrived immigrants to communities gradually abandoned by the working and middle classes.[5]

HURRICANE KATRINA AND THE INCREASED PUBLIC AWARENESS OF GHETTO POVERTY

Until the Hurricane Katrina disaster in 2005 these areas had not been a part of our collective consciousness in the last few decades for several reasons, including scant media attention to the problem of concentrated urban poverty, little or no discussion of the problem by political leaders, and the fact that the residents in these isolated enclaves have been rather quiet in recent years; that is, unlike in the 1960s, they had not drawn attention to themselves through riots and other manifestations of dissatisfaction or discontent.

In revealing concentrated poverty in New Orleans, Katrina refocused our attention on these poor urban neighborhoods. As highlighted in numerous media reports, most of the families in the inner city of New Orleans were trapped there after Katrina because they did not have access to automobiles and other means of transportation. This problem is not unique to New Orleans. For example, research conducted in the Chicago inner-city ghetto areas revealed that only 19 percent of the residents have access to an automobile.[6] Yet some people argued that Katrina demonstrated the fallacy of relying on the government for protection rather than promoting self-reliance and individual responsibility. However, it is unfair and indeed unwarranted to blame people with limited resources for being trapped in their neighborhood and vulnerable to natural disasters.

A person in these segregated and highly concentrated poverty areas could be very self-reliant and responsible, working every day and barely making ends meet, but yet not be in a position to buy and maintain an automobile or accumulate sufficient funds to quickly relocate his or her family to other areas. People who are trapped in these poor ghetto neighborhoods not only include those on public assistance, but the working poor, many of whom have never been on welfare.

One of the legacies of segregation and discrimination is a disproportionate number of low-skilled people of color in highly concentrated poverty areas confronting complex and multifaceted problems. However, in addressing these problems it would be helpful if we could overcome the widely held view that the high poverty and jobless rates in the inner city are due to the shortcomings of the people who live there.

If television cameras had focused on the ghetto in New Orleans, or on any inner-city ghetto in our cities, before Katrina, I believe that the initial reaction to descriptions of poverty and poverty concentration would have been quite different. There would have been far less sympathy. The prevailing view would have been that these people are poor and jobless because of their own shortcomings or inadequacies. In other words, only a few sociologists and other thoughtful observers would have reflected on the larger forces in society that have adversely affected the inner-city poor, including segregation and discrimination, changes in the economy, and failing public schools.

However, since Katrina was clearly a natural disaster that was beyond the control of the inner-city poor, Americans were much more sympathetic and much more willing to consider the effects of racial isolation and chronic subordination. It is important to take advantage of this emotion and foster a greater awareness of the nature of the problems confronting the inner city and how they can be addressed.

THE IMPACT OF COMPLEX GLOBAL CHANGES

As discussed earlier, since the decline of industrial employment in the inner city and the corresponding end of southern black migration to northern cities, poor African American urban neighborhoods have changed from densely packed areas of recently arrived immigrants to communities gradually abandoned by the nonpoor. This pattern has occurred in many cities across the country, but it is most evident in the older central cities of the Midwest and Northeast, where depopulated poverty areas have experienced even greater problems.

Older urban areas were once the hubs of economic growth and activity and major destinations for people in search of economic opportunity. However, the economies of many of these cities have since been eroded by complex economic transformations and shifting patterns in metropolitan development, changes that have accelerated neighborhood decline and widened gaps in race and income between cities and suburbs.[7]

Since the mid-twentieth century the mode of production in the United States has shifted dramatically from a mass-production system featuring manufacturing to one increasingly fueled by finance, services, and technology. This shift has accompanied the technological revolution, which has transformed traditional industries and brought about changes that range from streamlined information technology to biomedical engineering.[8]

In other words, today's close interaction between technology and international competition has eroded the basic institutions of the mass-production system. In the last several decades almost all the improvements in productivity have been associated with technology and human capital, thereby drastically reducing the importance of physical capital.[9] With the increased internationalization of economic activity, firms have spread their operations around the world, often relocating their production facilities to developing nations that have considerably lower labor costs.[10]

These global economic transformations have adversely affected the competitive environment of many cities. For example, the cities of Cleveland, Detroit, Philadelphia, Baltimore, and Pittsburgh perform poorly on an important traditional measure of economic performance, employment growth. While national employment increased by 25 percent between 1991 and 2001, job growth in these older central cities either declined or did not exceed 3 percent.[11]

With the decline in manufacturing employment in many of the nation's central cities, most of the jobs for lower-skilled workers are now in retail and service industries. Whereas jobs in manufacturing industries were unionized and relatively stable and carried higher wages, those for workers with low to modest levels of education in the retail and service industries provide lower wages, tend to be unstable, and lack the benefits and worker protections typically offered through unionization. Workers who are relegated to low-wage service and retail industries experience hardships as they struggle to make ends meet. In addition, the local economy also suffers when residents have fewer dollars to spend in their neighborhoods.[12]

Beginning in the mid-1970s, the employment balance between central cities and suburbs shifted markedly to the suburbs. Manufacturing is now over 70 percent suburban; wholesale and retail trade is just under 70 percent. Since 1980 over two-thirds of employment growth has occurred outside the central city.[13]

The suburbs of many central cities, developed originally as bedroom localities for commuters to the central business district, have become employment centers in themselves. For example, in Detroit, Philadelphia, and Baltimore, less than 20 percent of the jobs are now located within three miles of the downtown central business district.[14]

Accompanying the rise of suburban and exurban economies has been a change in commuting patterns. Increasingly workers completely bypass the central city by commuting from one suburb to another. "In the Cleveland region, for example, less than one-third of workers commute to a job in the central city and over half of the commutes in the region (55 percent) begin and end in the suburbs."[15]

THE NEW URBAN POVERTY

Sprawl and economic stagnation aggravate the decline in the competitive position of many central cities, reducing residents' access to meaningful economic opportunities and resulting in significant neighborhood decline. Two of the most visible indicators of neighborhood decline are abandoned buildings and vacant lots. For example, there are 60,000 abandoned and vacant properties in Philadelphia, 40,000 in Detroit, and 26,000 in Baltimore.[16] Concentrated in inner-city neighborhoods, these properties have lost population following the cessation of migration from the South to the urban North, the out-migration of nonpoor families, and the relocation of manufacturing industries.[17]

Sprawl and economic stagnation not only fuel physical decline, they also isolate disadvantaged residents of the city from meaningful access to social and economic opportunities. With the departure of higher-income families, the least upwardly mobile in society—mainly low-income people of color—are stuck in neighborhoods with high concentrations of poverty and deteriorated physical conditions. These neighborhoods offer few jobs and typically lack basic services and amenities, such as good schools, banks, grocery stores, retail establishments, parks, and quality transit.[18]

Unlike previous years, labor markets today are mainly regional, and long commutes in automobiles are common. Most ghetto residents cannot afford an automobile and therefore have to rely on public transit systems that make the connection between inner-city neighborhoods and suburban job locations difficult and time consuming.[19]

To make matters worse, many inner-city residents lack information or knowledge about suburban job opportunities. In segregated inner-city ghettos the breakdown of the informal job information network aggravates the problems of job spatial mismatch.[20] Many central cities feature a severe spatial mismatch between inner-city residents and suburban jobs. For example, in Cleveland, although entry-level workers are concentrated in inner-city neighborhoods, 80 percent of the entry-level jobs are located in the suburbs.[21] The lack of feasible transportation options exacerbates this mismatch. In addition to the challenges in learning about and reaching jobs, there is persistent racial discrimination in hiring practices.[22]

All these factors contribute to what I have called the "new urban poverty." By the new urban poverty I mean poor, segregated neighborhoods in which substantial percentages of individual adults are either unemployed or have dropped out or never been a part of the labor force. This jobless poverty today stands in sharp contrast to previous periods when the working poor predominated. For example, as I pointed out in my book *When Work Disappears*, in 1950 a substantial portion of the inner-city adult population was poor, but they were working. Urban poverty was quite extensive, but people held jobs. This situation is therefore quite different from the high levels of joblessness in poor urban black neighborhoods today.[23]

When I speak of "joblessness," I am not solely referring to official unemployment. The unemployment rate represents only the percentage of workers in the official labor force—that is, those who are actively looking for work. Therefore, I use the term "joblessness" to refer not only to those who are actively looking for work, but also to those who are outside or have dropped out of the labor market, including millions of adult males who are not recorded in the labor-market statistics.

These uncounted males in the labor market are disproportionately represented in poor inner-city neighborhoods. In the last three decades low-skilled African American males have encountered increasing difficulty in gaining access to jobs, even menial jobs. The ranks of idle inner-city men have swelled since the early 1970s and include a growing proportion of adult males who routinely work in and tolerate low-wage jobs when they are available.

The impact of this joblessness is reflected in real earnings; by "real earnings" I mean earnings adjusted to take account of inflation. For example, between 2000 and 2004 the average real annual earnings of black males aged 24 who were in the bottom quarter of the earnings distribution (that is, the

25th percentile) were only $1,078, compared with $9,623 for their Hispanic male counterparts and $9,843 for comparable white males.[24] Although the earnings of Hispanic and white males at the 25th percentile were also somewhat depressed, they were far higher than the earnings of comparable black males.

For purposes of comparison, if you move to the 75th percentile of the earnings distribution, the average annual earnings for black males aged 24 during this period were $22,000, compared with earnings of $22,800 and $30,000, respectively, for Hispanic and white males. So we can see that the really significant discrepancy is for those at the 25th percentile.

The incredibly low annual average earnings for black males at the 25th percentile of the earnings distribution from 2000 to 2004 reflect the fact that many of them were jobless during this period, including those who had completely given up looking for work, and therefore had virtually no official income. And, as stated previously, these men are heavily concentrated in poor inner-city neighborhoods. Accordingly, I maintain that any program designed to address the problems of concentrated poverty will have to face the challenge of poor black male joblessness. The two are inextricably connected.

COMBATING CONCENTRATED URBAN POVERTY

In the preceding analysis I have attempted to show the intricate connection of concentrated poverty to the broader changes in our society, including the internationalization of economic activity, changes that have fundamentally altered the demographic, economic, and social profile of our many central cities. I think that it is important to understand the impact of the broader systemic changes in addressing problems of concentrated poverty so that we can appreciate the challenges that confront us.

The most important step is to ameliorate the problem that feeds concentrated poverty, and that is closely related to national and international changes in the economy, namely, inner-city joblessness. The ideal solution would be economic policies that produce tight labor markets.

The benefits of a strong economy, particularly a sustained tight labor market, for low-skilled workers should be emphasized in economic policy discussions. Unlike the situation for workers in a tight labor market, in a slack labor market—a labor market with high unemployment—employers are, and indeed can afford to be, more selective in recruiting and in granting promotions. They overemphasize job prerequisites and exaggerate the value of experience. In such an economic climate disadvantaged minorities, especially those with low levels of literacy, suffer disproportionately, and employer discrimination rises.

In a tight labor market, on the other hand, job vacancies are numerous, unemployment is of short duration, and wages are higher. Moreover, in a tight labor market the labor force expands because increased job opportunities not only reduce unemployment, but also draw into the labor force those workers who, in periods when the labor market is slack, respond to fading job prospects by dropping out of the labor force altogether. Thus in a tight labor market the status of all workers—including disadvantaged minorities—improves because of lower unemployment and higher wages.[25]

The impact of tight labor markets on concentrated poverty can be seen in the developments during the prosperous decade of the 1990s. A report for the Brookings Institution by a University of Texas social scientist, Paul Jargowsky, revealed that the number of people residing in high-poverty neighborhoods decreased by 24 percent, or 2.5 million people, from 1990 to 2000. Moreover, the number of such neighborhoods—the study defined them as census tracts with at least 40 percent of residents below the poverty level—around the country declined by more than a quarter.[26]

In 1990 almost a third of blacks lived in such neighborhoods; the 2000 figure was 19 percent. Yet despite this significant improvement, African Americans still have the highest rates of concentrated poverty. In part, the state of inner-city ghettos is a legacy of historic racial subjugation. Concentrated-poverty neighborhoods are the most visible and disturbing displays of racial and income segregation. And it is true that racial discrimination and segregation continue to play a role in limiting the progress of many African Americans.

However, neither the spectacular rise in black concentrated poverty from 1970 to 1990 nor the dramatic decline from 1990 to 2000 can be explained mainly in terms of race. Rather, these shifts demonstrate that the fate of African Americans and other racial groups is inextricably connected with changes across the modern economy.

Jargowsky's data bear this out. The declines in concentrated poverty in the 1990s occurred not just in a few cities but across the country. Los Angeles and Washington, D.C., were two of the few central cities that experienced a rise in concentrated poverty during the 1990s. Jargowsky advanced three arguments to account for the divergent trend in Los Angeles: (1) the destructive riot after the Rodney King verdict in 1992; (2) the city experienced a significant immigration of Latinos from Mexico and other Central and South American countries, and many of them reside in the high-poverty neighborhoods; and (3) "the recession in the early 1990s was particularly severe in Southern California, and the economic recovery there was not as rapid as in other parts of California."[27]

In Washington, D.C., the devastating fiscal crisis from the early to the mid-1990s resulted in drastic reductions in public services and an erosion of public confidence in the District's government. This development contributed to "a rapid out-migration of moderate- and middle-income black families, particularly into suburban Maryland counties to the east of the central city. The poor were left behind in economically isolated neighborhoods with increasing poverty rates."[28]

Virtually all racial and ethnic groups recorded improvements. The number of whites living in these neighborhoods declined by 29 percent (from 2.7 million people to 1.9 million), and the number of blacks decreased by 36 percent (from 4.8 million to 3.1 million). Latinos were the major exception to this pattern because their numbers in high-poverty areas increased slightly during the 1990s, by 1.6 percent. However, this finding should be placed in context because the number of Latinos overall increased dramatically in the 1990s, by 57.9 percent, compared with 16.2 percent growth for African Americans and only 3.4 percent for whites.[29] For all races, the greatest improvements against poverty concentration were in the South and Midwest, the smallest in the Northeast, mirroring wider economic trends.[30]

Thus the notable reduction in the number of high-poverty neighborhoods and the substantial decrease in the population of such neighborhoods may simply be blips of boom times rather than permanent trends. Data on concentrated poverty are provided only by the decennial census; however, unemployment and individual poverty rates have increased since 1999, and there is every reason to assume that concentrated poverty rates are on the rise again as well.

Nonetheless, there is a tendency among scholars, black leaders, and policymakers to view the economic problems in the African American community, including the growth of concentrated poverty, separately from national and international trends affecting all American families and neighborhoods. One reason may be a desire for tidy solutions. However, if the economic problems of the black community are defined exclusively in terms of race, they can be isolated and seen as requiring only race-specific solutions, as proposed by the political Left, or narrow political solutions with subtle racial connotations (such as welfare reform), as trumpeted by the Right.

A look at the long-term statistics shows that neither welfare reform nor race-based programs seem to have had much to do with changes in poverty concentration. The sharp rise in concentrated poverty occurred during a period of rising income inequality for all Americans that began in the early 1970s. This was a period of decline in inflation-adjusted average incomes among the poor and of growing economic segregation caused by the exodus of middle-income families from inner cities. What had been mixed-income neighborhoods were rapidly transformed into areas of high poverty.

More than 30 years ago African American economist Vivian Henderson pointed out that "the economic future of blacks in the United States is bound up with that of the rest of the nation."[31] So, just as blacks suffered greatly during the decades of growing separation between haves and have-nots, they benefited considerably from the incredible economic boom in the last half of the 1990s, which not only substantially reduced unemployment, including black unemployment, but sharply increased the earnings of all low-wage workers as well. Undoubtedly, if the robust economy could have been extended for several more years, rather than coming to an abrupt halt in 2001, concentrated poverty in inner cities would have declined even more.

The lesson for those committed to fighting inequality, especially those involved in multiracial coalition politics, is to fashion a new agenda that pays more scrutiny to fiscal, monetary, and trade policies that may have long-term consequences for the national and regional economies, as seen in future earnings, jobs, and concentrated poverty. This new agenda would therefore reflect an awareness and appreciation of the devastating effects of recent systemic changes on poor urban populations and neighborhoods.

However, this new agenda would also include an even more dedicated focus on the traditional efforts to fight poverty to ensure that the benefits from an economic upturn are widely shared among the poor and that they become less vulnerable to downward swings in the economy. I refer especially to combating racial discrimination in employment, which is especially devastating during slack labor markets; the revitalization of poor urban neighborhoods, including the elimination of abandoned buildings and vacant lots, to make them more attractive for economic investment that would help improve the quality of life and create jobs in the neighborhood; promoting job-training programs to enhance employment opportunities for ghetto residents; improving public education to prepare inner-city youngsters for higher-paying and stable jobs in the new economy; and strengthening unions to provide the higher wages, worker protections, and benefits typically absent from low-skilled jobs in retail and service industries.

In short, this new agenda would reflect a multipronged approach that attacks inner-city poverty on various levels, an approach that recognizes the complex array of factors that have contributed to the crystallization of concentrated urban poverty and limited the life chances of many inner-city residents.

NOTES

1. Paul Jargowsky, "Ghetto Poverty Among Blacks in the 1980s," *Journal of Policy Analysis and Management* 13 (1994): 288–310.

2. William Julius Wilson, *The Truly Disadvantaged: The Inner City, the Underclass, and Public Policy* (Chicago: University of Chicago Press, 1987); William Julius Wilson, *When Work Disappears: The World of the New Urban Poor* (New York: Knopf, 1996); and Lincoln Quillian, "Migration Patterns and the Growth of High-Poverty Neighborhoods, 1970–1990," *American Journal of Sociology* 105, no. 1 (1999): 1–37.

3. Quillian, "Migration Patterns."

4. Ibid.

5. Wilson, *Truly Disadvantaged*; Wilson, *When Work Disappears*; Quillian, "Migration Patterns."

6. Wilson, *When Work Disappears*.

7. Radhika K. Fox and Sarah Treuhaft, "Shared Prosperity, Stronger Regions: An Agenda for Rebuilding America's Older Core Cities" (Report prepared for PolicyLink, Oakland, CA, 2006).

8. Bill Joy, "Why the Future Doesn't Need Us," *Wired*, April 2000, 238–62; Fox and Treuhaft, "Shared Prosperity, Stronger Regions."

9. Wilson, *When Work Disappears*.

10. Fox and Treuhaft, "Shared Prosperity, Stronger Regions."

11. Ibid.

12. Ibid.; Wilson, *When Work Disappears*.

13. U.S. Department of Housing and Urban Development, *The State of the Cities* (Washington, DC: Government Printing Office, 1999).

14. Fox and Treuhaft, "Shared Prosperity, Stronger Regions."

15. Ibid., 32.

16. Ibid., 34.

17. Wilson, *Truly Disadvantaged*; Wilson, *When Work Disappears*.

18. Wilson, *Truly Disadvantaged*; Wilson, *When Work Disappears*; Fox and Treuhaft, "Shared Prosperity, Stronger Regions."

19. Wilson, *When Work Disappears*.

20. Ibid.

21. Fox and Treuhaft, "Shared Prosperity, Stronger Regions."

22. See, for example, Wilson, *When Work Disappears*; and Joleen Kirschenman and Kathryn Neckerman, " 'We'd Love to Hire Them, But . . .': The Meaning of Race for Employers," in *The Urban Underclass*, ed. Christopher Jencks and Paul E. Peterson (Washington, DC: Brookings Institution, 1991), 203–34.

23. Wilson, *When Work Disappears*.

24. The figures in this paragraph were calculated from data provided by economist David Ellwood of Harvard University, based on his analysis of data from the U.S. Department of Labor.

25. James Tobin, "On Improving the Economic Status of the Negro," *Daedalus* 94 (1965): 878–98.

26. Paul Jargowsky, *Stunning Progress, Hidden Problems: The Dramatic Decline of Concentrated Poverty in the 1990s* (Washington, DC: Brookings Institution, 2003).

27. Ibid.

28. Ibid., 9.

29. Ibid., 4.

30. Ibid.

31. Vivian Henderson, "Race, Economics, and Public Policy," *Crisis* 83 (April 1975): 50–54.

PART THREE

SPURRING BETTER JOBS AND CREATING HIGHER INCOMES

A multipronged approach is needed to address the problems of poverty and economic distress that we have described in the first two parts. An important set of such policies focuses on work. The authors of the three chapters and two insets in this part suggest a variety of strategies for creating better jobs and higher incomes for the working poor and the struggling middle class.

Katherine S. Newman, in "Up and Out: When the Working Poor Are Poor No More," draws upon insights she gleaned from her study of upward mobility among a sample of blacks and Latinos in Harlem, New York; she found that a substantial number of people in her study were able to work their way up from entry-level jobs to obtain higher-paying jobs. Newman argues for policies that are likely to help people exit poverty, such as increasing access to opportunities for higher education (helping people overcome financial barriers to higher education by extending Pell grants and by Lifetime Learning Credits); extending health and medical care; providing child-care assistance; and helping poor families get access to the benefits to which they are entitled. In addition, the poor would benefit greatly if their tax burdens were relieved, such as through breaks on sales taxes and the extension of the Earned Income Tax Credit (EITC). John Karl Scholz, in an inset to this chapter, describes the EITC's mechanics and benefits in more detail. He explains how the appeal of the EITC is due to its targeting low- and moderate-income working taxpayers, its beneficial labor-market effects that increase the incentive to work, and its administrative efficiencies.

In "Making Work Pay," Beth Shulman maintains that we can make low-wage service jobs the "good jobs" of the twenty-first century. These jobs are central to the economy and are unlikely to be sent overseas. Shulman argues that we first need to raise the minimum wage and index it to inflation. The minimum wage should be considered only as a floor, however: it is not sufficient to pull working people out of poverty. Employers should also be encouraged to take the "high road" toward competitiveness by paying their workers a living wage. This underscores the importance of guaranteeing workers the ability to choose to form a union, which provides them with a voice.

Harry J. Holzer, in "Education and Training for Less Affluent Americans in the New Economy," identifies numerous education and training strategies that are likely to help less affluent Americans succeed at work. He suggests three main strategies. First, he would expand early skill building for youth through preschool and primary-school programs, promote high-school completion through career academies and other "schools within a school" and college attendance through greater financial aid, and improve access to the labor market for those not attending college (such as via the Job Corps). Second, he recommends providing new opportunities for training and advancement among the working adult poor by means of labor-market intermediaries. In an inset to this chapter, David Spickard describes the origin and success of one such labor-market intermediary, Jobs for Life. This program is based in churches, prisons, rescue missions, homeless shelters, and community nonprofits in 22 states and provides job training and support to unemployed and underemployed individuals. Finally, Holzer calls for expanded protections against risks of job loss and displacement for all Americans, such as unemployment insurance and health insurance.

Up and Out:
When the Working Poor Are Poor
No More

Katherine S. Newman

The prosperity of the late 1990s shifted the economic landscape nationwide. True, the benefits of this expansion accrued disproportionately to those at the top, but the poorest among us caught the rising tide as well:

> The wages of America's worst-paid workers rose faster than prices for the first time in a generation. Real hourly wage rates among the bottom 20 percent of workers rose about 11 percent between 1995 and 2000. Mean family income among single mothers in the bottom half of the earnings distribution for all single mothers grew 16 percent during this period.[1]

What did these historic trends mean for the nation's working poor? Did the opportunities that opened up in the late 1990s permit them to move up and out of low-wage jobs and secure a place in the working or middle class? To answer these questions, I discuss the experience of Harlem's low-wage workforce between 1993 and 2001, looking first at their work experience, education, and wages. Then I consider how the experience of these Harlem workers compares with that of those just like them across the nation. Finally, I offer suggestions on the kinds of policies that would help sustain the remarkable progress the working poor made across the nation during those prosperous times.

THE WORKING POOR IN THE INNER CITY

If ever there was an acid test of the fate of the working poor, it was central Harlem in the early 1990s. In 1993 poverty rates in this segregated black community exceeded 40 percent, unemployment ran at 18 percent, and over 30 percent of the households were on public assistance. Yet as the end of the decade neared, the economy picked up dramatically: labor markets tightened as unemployment plummeted; growth accelerated while inflation remained low; and businesses began to experience labor shortages.

What did these trends mean for Harlem's working poor? I followed a sample of 200 Black and Latino fast-food workers and 100 people who applied and were rejected from those jobs, starting in 1993, with follow-ups at four- and eight-year intervals.[2] The news was encouraging: 73 percent were employed at the first follow-up. They had also completed more schooling and training. In 1993 only 42 percent of my sample had high-school diplomas, and a meager 9 percent had some college behind them. Four years later, in 1997, they looked much better: 78 percent had finished high school or received a GED, and 29 percent had some college education.

In 1993 the median wage of these workers was $4.25 an hour (1993 dollars). Four years later the median wage of those people who were working had increased substantially to $7.49 an hour (again in 1993 dollars). Among a randomly selected subsample of those who were employed in 2002, the median hourly wage was $11.64 (1993 dollars as well).[3] Only a few workers were stuck in jobs paying the minimum wage or anything close to it. Most have jobs that pay above 200 percent of this threshold, and more than 20 percent have risen above 300 percent of the minimum wage. This trajectory reflects improvement in the labor market in the 1990s, the increase in the federal minimum wage in 1997 (to $5.15 per hour), and the benefits of steady work experience and additional education.

Were these wages enough for the families who depended on them to cover their expenses? Fifteen percent of people in my sample were in a family whose income fell below the federal poverty line. Almost all of those who are still poor are out of the labor force. Those who are working have climbed above the poverty line through a combination of their own earnings and the wages of others in their households. Of course, in an expensive city such as New York, the poverty line is well below what is required for a family to be self-sufficient. Even at 200 percent of the poverty line, families face material hardship.

THE NATIONAL EXPERIENCE

Harlem is a special place in many ways; among other things, it is embedded in a city where the rich are richer and the poor are poorer than in any other American city. In the early 1990s it was virtually all-black. These special characteristics prompt the question: was the mobility experience of the working poor in Harlem common or unusual? It turns out that the Harlem workers did better than the national average, but the national experience points in the same direction. A significant proportion of low-wage workers graduate from minimum-wage jobs and move up into higher-income groups. Nationwide, 11 percent of black and Hispanic men living in poor urban households who worked in the food industry became "high flyers": they saw wage gains greater than $5 an hour over the same years in which I followed the Harlem fast-food workers, and 13 percent of women followed suit.

The food service industry is notorious for its low wages, particularly for those in nonmanagerial jobs. When we look at hourly workers from poor households who are employed in other industries, we see even stronger positive trends. Men's wages increased from an average $6.65 to $7.99. Women's wages climbed from $5.75 to $7.10. Similarly, the proportion of people who became "high flyers," that is, who saw an increase in real wages of more than $5 an hour in four years, jumped up to 19 percent for men and 16 percent for women when we look at all races across all industries, inside and outside metropolitan areas.[4]

While there is good news in this story, there is also bad news. Nationwide, about 40 percent of the workers in the food service industry saw wage losses over time. And many moved ahead, but not by enough to qualify them as high flyers. Nonetheless, a significant proportion saw real improvements in their wages, and the jobs they landed as they moved through the labor market got better. They earned more and had more responsibility.

POLICIES THAT MATTER

What kinds of policies make a difference in increasing the number of poor workers who can become high flyers? A healthy economy certainly helps. Tight labor markets lead employers to search harder among the applicants who approach them, and they often choose people they might have otherwise bypassed. Hence young black men, who are always at the bottom of the queue, have fared much better when labor markets tighten. Employers are more likely to give them a chance. When workers are in short supply, firms ask their existing employees to put in more hours, which increases their take-home pay. But we would not want to bank everything on good times; alas, they come around too rarely. Moreover, upward mobility occurs even in slack labor markets. What, then, would make a difference?

Higher Education

On average, high earnings go to those who complete college, and poverty awaits high-school dropouts. That message has clearly gotten through to most people in the United States, which is why we have seen the rates of high-school graduation climb higher and higher, even among poor minorities. Although serious problems remain for Hispanics at the high-school level, the real action now lies in access to college. Even without a degree, every semester spent in college improves the prospects of workers in the labor market.

Financial barriers prevent many qualified students from moving into higher education, and they multiply in the case of single parents and adult learners more generally. Our traditional financial aid system does not work particularly well for these working parents. The Higher Education Act was authorized by Congress in order to increase access to college, but it did not focus much attention or provide much money for working adults with dependent children, even though *"non-traditional* students—that is, students older than 24 years or enrolled on a part-time basis—are the majority of all students (an estimated 53% in 1999)."[5]

More than $9 billion a year flows from the Pell Grants program to students to support tuition and education-related expenses. Although adults with jobs and families are technically eligible for these funds, they often cannot qualify because the program is largely for "regular students" who are making "satisfactory progress." The Annie E. Casey Foundation advocates expanding the program overall and extending its largesse to students who are enrolled in short-term, nondegree programs to build their skills, rather than the current recipients who must be enrolled in formal degree or certificate programs.[6] If satisfactory progress meant "adults who take one or two classes at a time and often take time away from school," as well as young students who are in the classroom full-time, we would see more adult students improving their skills.

The Lifetime Learning Tax Credit was supposed to address the needs of adult learners. Authorized in 1997, this credit was a brainchild of Robert Reich, the secretary of labor in the Clinton administration. Reich recognized that increased turmoil in the labor market was disrupting the long-term affiliation of workers (both white collar and blue collar) with a single employer. He wanted to make it easier for adult workers to retrain, and this tax credit was an important policy instrument for achieving that end. Yet low-wage workers who owe little in income taxes to begin with have not been able to benefit from it because they do not owe enough taxes to need a credit and do not have the extra money to pay for courses up front, which is necessary to qualify for the credit. If the lifetime learning credit was refundable, meaning that those who have satisfied their tax obligations already would receive a cash payment, it would reach more nontraditional students.[7]

Increasing access to higher education for welfare recipients is critical to pushing them out of poverty. The Maine Parents as Scholars program makes it possible for welfare recipients to complete two- or four-year degrees. "Graduates increased their hourly median wages from $8.00 before college to $11.71 immediately after college—a 46 percent increase."[8] CalWORKs, the welfare program for the state of California, found even larger upticks in earnings for its recipients who attended college, even for those who did not have a high-school diploma or a GED beforehand. "Those who obtained an associate degree dramatically increased their earnings (from about $4,000 annually before college to nearly $20,000 two years after graduating) and those in vocational fields saw even larger increases."[9]

The Center on Budget and Policy Priorities (CBPP) has given some thought to how community college programs supported by the states could be tailored to benefit the working poor. CBPP points to some key design features that need to be taken into account if the payoff is going to be significant:[10]

- "The longer the program, the greater the economic payoff.... Vocational certificate programs needed to be at least ... 10 courses in length to yield earnings that topped $15,000 by the second year out of school.... Better paying health professions required longer support."
- "New services, such as child care, work study, service coordination, and job development and placement programs ... [are] often a key factor" in making community college programs work for welfare recipients. Work-study positions are particularly important, not only for the income they generate, but for the experience they provide, "especially when located off campus with private employers."
- "Anticipate realistic time frames for completion of credits." Community college students, who are often working while going to school (even if they are not parents), generally need more than three years to complete an associate's degree. Low-income parents, particularly those who need remedial education, may need longer.

California permits welfare recipients to satisfy their work requirements for up to 24 months by enrolling in community college. As of 2002, 28 percent of the adults on the Temporary Assistance for Needy Families (TANF) rolls were taking at least one course, and most of them worked while going to school as well. Twenty-two other states let their public assistance clients enroll in school and count their efforts toward the "work participation rate" that the federal government requires states to show. These policies pay off in higher earnings over the life course and should be expanded as much as possible.

Taxes, Taxes, Taxes

Working poor families have benefited immensely from the introduction in 1997 of the Earned Income Tax Credit (see inset). Only 17 states have followed the federal lead in establishing earned income tax credits of their own, and among them, only 13 declare it refundable. The other four reduce the recipient's tax burden to zero, so they do not owe state income tax. It would be a boon to the working poor if the other 33 states would follow suit and at least relieve their low-income citizens of tax burdens. Rewarding them through state checks would be even better, for this means money in the pocket.

Perhaps we should count our blessings, though, because "nearly half of the states impose income taxes on families with incomes below the poverty line."[11] Southern states are particularly aggressive about taxing their poorest residents, and the politics of doing otherwise are fraught. In 2003 the Republican governor of Alabama, Bob Riley, asked his constituents to vote for a modest tax increase on higher-income residents in order to increase support for the state's poorly funded public education system and eliminate the income tax for those below the poverty line. His bold proposal—to raise the amount a family of four could earn before it was taxed to $17,000, and to $20,000 after four years—was resoundingly defeated.[12] Hence an Alabama family of four with annual earnings of more than $4,600 still owes income tax, which makes them even poorer than their incomes suggest.

Income taxes are not the only instrument for collecting revenue that is hard on low-income families. State sales taxes—particularly on things such as cigarettes or gasoline—make up one-third of most state revenues. In 2002 sales and excise taxes alone took up 7.8 percent of the income of the bottom 20 percent of taxpayers.[13]

What could be done to relieve these burdens on low-income taxpayers? Some states have established "no-tax floors," meaning that families who earn below a set amount of money do not owe tax at all. After all other taxes are factored in, families below the floor can write "zero" across the "tax due" line of their state income tax forms, and those just above gradually lose the break. CBPP recommends additional measures that would make a difference, including the following:

- Creating sales tax rebates for families below the poverty line
- Adjusting tax credits so that they are conditioned on family size
- Adjusting the income level that qualifies families for credits annually so that inflation does not push them above the eligibility line

All these measures would have the effect of relieving low-income families of tax burdens and therefore permitting them to keep more of their resources.

THE EARNED INCOME TAX CREDIT

John Karl Scholz

The problems facing workers with low levels of human capital in the United States are severe. The Earned Income Tax Credit (EITC) is designed to increase the attractiveness of paid employment for low-skilled individuals, particularly those with children. In 2006 taxpayers with two or more children who filed for the EITC got a payment equal to 40 percent of earnings up to $11,340. Taxpayers with two or more children and earnings between $11,340 and $14,810 received the maximum credit of $4,536.[1] The credit was reduced by 21.06 percent of earnings between $14,810 and $36,348. The EITC is refundable: the Treasury pays it regardless of whether the taxpayer has any other tax liability. In 2003 the credit cost $38.7 billion. Seventeen states and the District of Columbia also have state EITCs.

The appeal of the credit arises from its targeting and antipoverty effectiveness, its behavioral effects, and the ability of tax authorities to administer the credit.

Only low- and moderate-income working taxpayers are eligible for the credit. Its effectiveness would be limited if eligible taxpayers did not file tax returns to claim it. Participation rates among eligible taxpayers appear high, however. Though the best available evidence is somewhat dated, between 64 and 87 percent of EITC-eligible families received the credit in 1990 and 1996.[2] The credit is also well targeted. More than 60 percent of the EITC goes to families with market incomes below the poverty line. It removed 1.6 million to 5.7 million persons from poverty annually between 2001 and 2003.[3]

The EITC has beneficial labor-market effects.[4] By increasing after-tax earnings, the credit provides unambiguously positive employment incentives for those entirely out of the labor market. Numerous studies have shown that these incentives increase employment.

For many taxpayers already in the labor market, the EITC provides incentives for individuals to work fewer hours. The credit's actual effect on hours (in contrast to employment), however, is likely to be small. The majority of EITC recipients pay a third party to prepare their tax returns, and it is difficult to infer the implicit tax rates embodied in the credit from the look-up table that accompanies the EITC instructions. Hence the precise relationship between the EITC and hours worked is likely to be poorly understood by most taxpayers.

Compared with alternative, more bureaucratic delivery mechanisms, the

EITC is inexpensive to administer. Because it does not have a program-specific administrative structure to assess eligibility, it will have higher noncompliance than income-transfer programs. The most recent study of EITC errors examined returns filed in 2000 (for tax year 1999) and found that of the $31.3 billion claimed in EITC, between $8.5 and $9.9 billion, or 27.0 to 31.7 percent of the total, exceeded the amount for which taxpayers were eligible.[5] EITC noncompliance appears to be the single most important threat to the credit's political viability.

Given its targeting, employment incentives, and administrative advantages, further modifications and expansions of the EITC may be an important component of a reform agenda to better assist low-income working families.

NOTES

1. The maximum credit for families with one child is $2,747, and the credit is phased in at a 34 percent rate. The maximum credit for childless workers is $412, and the credit is phased in at a 7.65 percent rate.

2. John Karl Scholz, "The Earned Income Tax Credit: Participation, Compliance, and Anti-poverty Effectiveness," *National Tax Journal*, 87, no. 1 (March 1994): 59–81; Internal Revenue Service, "Participation in the Earned Income Tax Credit Program for Tax Year 1996" (Fiscal Year 2001 Research Project 12.26 of the Internal Revenue Service, prepared by SB/SE Research, Fort Lauderdale/Greensboro, January 31, 2002), available online at http://www.taxpolicycenter.org/TaxFacts/papers/irs_eitc.pdf.

3. These are the author's calculations from the 2001 panel of the Survey of Income and Program Participation. The HHS poverty guidelines for 2006 are $9,800 for a one-person family, $13,200 for two-person families, $16,600 for three-person families, and $20,000 for four-person families.

4. Joseph V. Hotz, Charles Mullin, and John Karl Scholz, "Examining the Effect of the Earned Income Tax Credit on the Labor Market Participation of Families on Welfare" (unpublished manuscript, UCLA and University of Wisconsin, 2005), available online at http://www.ssc.wisc.edu/~scholz/Research/EITC_Draft.pdf; Joseph V. Hotz and John Karl Scholz, "The Earned Income Tax Credit," in *Means-Tested Transfer Programs in the United States*, ed. Robert Moffitt (Chicago: University of Chicago Press and NBER, 2003), 141–97; Steve Holt, "The Earned Income Tax Credit at Age 30: What We Know," (Brookings Institution, 2006), available online at http://www.brookings.edu/metro/pubs/20060209_Holt.htm.

5. Internal Revenue Service, *Compliance Estimates for Earned Income Tax Credit Claimed on 1999 Returns* (Washington, DC: IRS, February, 2002); Janet Holtzblatt and Janet McCubbin, "Issues Affecting Low-Income Filers," in *The Crisis in Tax Administration*, ed. Henry Aaron and Joel Slemrod (Washington, DC: Brookings Institution Press, 2004), 148–88.

In the case of cash rebates, these ideas are even more progressive, for they transfer funds to the working poor that are above and beyond their earnings.

Doctor, Doctor

America has been awash in the politics of health-care reform for many years now, spurred on by the skyrocketing cost of medical care, out-of-control insurance rates (for consumers and physicians), and the ever-growing population of uninsured Americans, many of them workers and their children. This is one policy front where a lot has been accomplished already, particularly in extending insurance coverage to children in poor and near-poor households.

Yet we have not matched our concern for uninsured children with attention to the health-care needs of their parents. Delivering health insurance through employers often leaves workers in jobs that pay only modest salaries in limbo. Their firms may not offer health insurance, or they may provide it at an exorbitant cost to employees. Only 16 states cover parents applying for Medicaid up to the poverty line. Families who are just above the poverty line are generally disqualified, which is absurd, given how low the poverty line is and how far short it falls from covering the real cost of living in a city such as Los Angeles or New York.

Until we secure a better system for everyone, we need to think about incremental changes that will help low-wage workers access health care. Even if we did not care about their physical well-being—which we should—just keeping adult workers on the job requires that we face the issue of the uninsured. Holding down the expense of emergency treatment, which is where you end up if you do not have preventive care, is another worthy goal. What, then, can be done?

One possibility is to extend the state child health insurance programs or Medicaid eligibility to parents above the current income limits. Is this going to bankrupt states that are already reeling under budget cuts and wrangling with the federal government over who should pay for what? It is not cheap, for sure. And demands to increase the generosity of Medicaid will generate howls from the federal government, which is driving in the opposite direction: cutting reimbursements, starving states that then turn around and cut the poor from the rolls, or shaving physician fees to the point where doctors refuse to serve uninsured patients.

The political conflict is reaching a boiling point. Nonetheless, many states have taken action that will help. Twenty-one of them have eliminated the Medicaid assets test so that families do not have to lose their cars, houses, or modest savings accounts before getting health care. Seven states—Arizona, California, Connecticut, Illinois, Maine, Ohio, and Rhode Island—and the District of Columbia have extended Medicaid to parents. They range from staunchly Republican to hard-core Democratic states, suggesting that it is possible to do more in many political climes.

Even with the best of health care, children get sick. Who is going to take care of them when that happens? The Family and Medical Leave Act was a first step in making it possible for parents to attend to children and elders who need their help. Hard as it was to pass this federal legislation, all that it accomplished was to protect the jobs of those who make use of it. It exempted millions of small businesses and provided no income replacement for anyone. Most families cannot go without the income that the working members of their households earn. California was the first state to address this problem in a fashion that genuinely deals with the burdens illness imposes. In 2002 Governor Gray Davis signed a bill that provides up to six weeks of partial pay "for eligible employees who need time off from work to bond with a new child or care for a seriously ill family member." The program, funded entirely by a payroll tax on employees, builds on California's existing State Disability Insurance system, and virtually all private-sector employees are included.[14]

What About the Children?

Middle-class mothers have a hard time finding comprehensive, affordable child care. Working poor families and those who have pulled themselves out of poverty but fall short of affluence face even more difficulty, particularly if they cannot turn to relatives for help, as many families are forced to do. In California, where the state's budget was hammered by the energy crisis that brought Governor Arnold Schwarzenegger into office, nearly 280,000 children are on waiting lists for day care.[15] In New York City about 11,000 low-income families are lining up for nonexistent spaces, a consequence of "relatively slow growth in the number of available . . . slots, combined with a huge increase in demand as nearly a million women left welfare rolls in the city since 1996."[16]

Nationwide, only 14 percent of the children who are technically eligible for federal assistance with child-care costs actually received it in 2001.[17] The population served is declining in size because the states have lowered income eligibility limits, frozen waiting lists, cut provider payments, and increased the amount families are expected to pay above the level of their grants. Yet the provision of reasonably priced child care is essential to keeping parents in the labor force. We need to increase the number of children who have subsidized child care by increasing the supply of places, lowering the threshold of eligibility, increasing the funds directed at providers (so they can afford to accept more children and provide them with quality care), and reducing the co-payments for families.

The most enlightened child-care policies are those that move young children into enriched early childhood development to improve cognitive skills and increase school readiness. Economist Robert Lynch points to the smart investment that high-quality early childhood programs represent in improved academic performance, lifetime earnings, and decreased rates of criminal conduct for poor children who participate in these programs. "Within 45 years," he writes, "the increase in earnings due to [early childhood development] investments would likely boost the GDP by nearly one-half of 1%, or $107 billion (in 2004 dollars)."[18] We now have several decades' worth of experience with Head Start, the ambitious federal initiative to boost the cultural capital of poor children, and it largely bears these findings out. Indeed, Lynch forecasts that benefits would outweigh costs by $31 billion by the year 2030 if we implemented a universal program of early childhood development today.

Fortunately, some states have moved ahead with ambitious plans for early childhood education. Georgia, Oklahoma, and New Jersey all provide prekindergarten classes as part of the public school system for most, if not all, four-year-olds. In December 2004 the Florida legislature voted to provide universal prekindergarten instruction to all four-year-olds in the state.[19] Several months later New Mexico's legislators approved a prekindergarten pilot program for four-year-olds in high-poverty areas.[20]

These are important steps to address the long-term educational needs of the country's youngest citizens and to put them on a footing that will help them avoid poverty in the first place. At the same time, these policies address a critical child-care need for parents. We could do even more if the 45 percent of American kindergarteners who are currently in half-day programs were provided full-day instruction.

One-Stop Shopping

Some of our best policy ideas have been put in place, but are not reaching the people they were designed to help. Only half the working families who should be getting food stamps actually claim them. Only one-quarter of the workers who are entitled to claim the EITC benefit do so.[21] According to the Kaiser Commission on Medicaid and the Uninsured, 40 percent of families whose children were eligible for Medicaid but not enrolled did not realize their children were qualified.[22] Minorities, especially low-income Hispanics, are less likely than virtually any other eligible group to know about the EITC.[23] Poor education, lack of access to information, language barriers, and the sheer complexity of navigating the bureaucracies involved in dispensing benefits help explain why many people who should be assisted by these programs are not.

SeedCo, a nonprofit organization in New York City, has some innovative ideas on how to make it easier for low-income families to claim benefits they are legally entitled to, such as the EITC, housing vouchers, or child-care subsidies. It has developed a Web-based tool that permits case managers to process client data so that in one fell swoop they can determine a family's eligibility for virtually all benefits and complete their enrollment. Replacing the cumbersome and time-consuming tradition of traipsing from one office to another, only to be told a document is missing—come back again in three weeks—would be a blessing for millions of poor families.

Investment in the health, education, and training of the working poor will pay off handsomely in higher earnings, greater productivity, and more prosperous neighborhoods. If the actual experience of the late 1990s and the early years of the twenty-first century offers any lessons, it is that millions of poor Americans were ready to jump at the opportunities that opened up to them when the economy improved. Capitalizing on their drive to improve their own lives, we will see a national payoff if we meet their energy with a national investment in their human capital.

NOTES

This chapter is adapted from *Chutes and Ladders: Navigating the Low-Wage Labor Market* by Katherine S. Newman, ©2006 by the Russell Sage Foundation. Adapted and reprinted by permission of Harvard University Press.

1. Scott Winship and Christopher Jencks, "Understanding Welfare Reform," *Harvard Magazine* 107, no. 2 (November–December 2004): 97.

2. Details on the sample and the methods and more data on the outcomes can be found in Katherine S. Newman, *Chutes and Ladders: Navigating the Low-Wage Labor Market* (New York: Russell Sage Foundation; Cambridge, MA: Harvard University Press, 2006), pp. 291–93.

3. For details, see Newman, *Chutes and Ladders*, Appendix A.

4. Ibid, chap. 5.

5. Almanac of Policy Issues, "Higher Education Act: Reauthorization Status and Issues," adapted from an article by James B. Stedman, Congressional Research Service (October 9, 2002), available online at www.policyalmanac.org/education/archive/crs_higher_education.shtml, cited in Wendy Fleischer, "Education Policy and the AECF Jobs Initiative" (Policy Brief no. 3, Annie E. Casey Foundation Jobs Initiative, 2003), 4.

6. For more on this idea, see Fleischer, "Education Policy and the AECF Jobs Initiative," 8.

7. Ibid.

8. Liz McNichol and John Springer, "State Policies to Assist Working-Poor Families" (Center on Budget and Policy Priorities, December 2004), 35, available online at http://www.cbpp.org/12-10-04sfp.pdf.

9. Ibid.

10. Ibid., 36.

11. Ibid., 9.

12. Larry Copeland, "Alabama Governor's Tax-Increase Plan Is a Switch with High Stakes," *USA Today*, September 5, 2003, 3A; Tom Baxter, "Alabama Looks at Budget Cuts," *Atlanta Journal-Constitution*, September 11, 2003, 6A; and Adam Cohen, "Editorial Observer: What Alabama's Low-Tax Mania Can Teach the Rest of the Country," *New York Times*, October 20, 2003, 16.

13. McNichol and Springer, "State Policies to Assist Working-Poor Families," 11.

14. Ruth Milkman and Eileen Appelbaum. "Paid Family Leave in California," *State of California Labor* 4 (2004): 45–67.

15. Ibid., 27.

16. Leslie Kaufman, "City Officials Call Budget 'a Disaster' for Day Care," *New York Times*, March 16, 2005, B5.

17. Jennifer Mezey, Mark Greenberg, and Rachel Schumacher, "The Vast Majority of Federally-Eligible Children Did Not Receive Child Care Assistance in FY 2000" (Center for Law and Social Policy, October 2, 2002), available online at http://www.clasp.org/publications/1in7sum.pdf, cited in McNichol and Springer, "State Policies to Assist Working-Poor Families," 27.

18. Quoted on the Economic Policy Institute website at http://www.epinet.org/content.cfm/books_exceptional_returns. See also Robert G. Lynch, *Exceptional Returns: Economic, Fiscal, and Social Benefits of Investment in Early Childhood Development* (Washington, DC: Economic Policy Institute, 2004).

19. David Lawrence Jr., "Pre-K Education: Legislature's Action Is an 'Honorable Start,'" *Miami Herald*, December 17, 2004, available online at http://www.ffcd.org/news/floridaPrek.html.

20. Deborah Baker and Barry Massey, "Senate Approves Pre-K as Adjournment Nears," Associated Press, March 19, 2005.

21. McNichol and Springer, "State Policies to Assist Working-Poor Families," 49.

22. Ibid.

23. Katherine Ross Phillips, "Who Knows About the Earned Income Tax Credit?" (Urban Institute Policy Brief no. B-27, January 2001), available online at http://newfederalism.urban.org/html/series_b/b27/b27.html, cited in Alan Berube and Benjamin Forman, "A Local Ladder for the Working Poor: The Impact of the Earned Income Tax Credit in U.S. Metropolitan Areas" (Brookings Institution Center on Urban and Metropolitan Policy EITC Series, September 2001), 2, available online at http://www.brookings.edu/dybdocroot/es/urban/eitc/eitcnational.pdf.

Making Work Pay

Beth Shulman

Americans share a tacit understanding—a belief, a promise—that everyone who works hard will be able to provide for themselves and their families. But for more than 30 million Americans in low-wage jobs, that promise has been broken. One in four workers does not make enough to secure the basic necessities of life.[1]

How do we fulfill the promise that honest labor will ensure a decent life? How do we create family-sustaining jobs? How do we make work pay? The American economy today looks more and more like an hourglass, with most of the jobs created in the last two decades clustered at the high and low ends of the income scale. At the high end are managerial and professional jobs that require at least a four-year college degree. At the low end are jobs such as home health aides, janitors, security guards, hotel workers, nursing-home workers, and food workers that pay little more than the minimum wage.

In the middle, and now conspicuous by their absence, used to be millions of manufacturing and technical jobs that practically guaranteed a hardworking American a good wage, decent health insurance, vacation time, and even a pension. The U.S. Congressional Budget Office estimates that the manufacturing sector alone has lost more than three million jobs between July 2000 and January 2004.[2]

A critical fact is that there is nothing inherent in putting together cars or handling molten steel that made these jobs "good." In fact, at one time these jobs were hazardous, low-wage jobs that provided few benefits. But they became the good jobs of the twentieth century because we as Americans made them that way. Through unionization and social legislation we pressured companies to provide good salaries and benefits to workers in the manufacturing industries.

In exactly the same way, nothing is inherently bad about the job of a childcare worker, nursing-home aide, security guard, emergency medical technician, janitor, or hotel worker. It is time we discarded the notion that something intrinsic in a particular job chains it forever to low pay and miserable conditions. It is not what one does on the job that determines whether it is a "good" or "bad" job. Employers make decisions about the working conditions of that job, and we as a nation can influence those decisions.

Today's low-wage service jobs can easily become the good jobs of the twenty-first century. The best part: these jobs cannot be shipped overseas. Unlike the task of putting a car or a computer together, these jobs must be done here in the United States where the consumers live. Workers living in China or Bangalore simply cannot be our security guards, nursing-home aides, or restaurant workers. And these jobs are continuing to grow. According to the Bureau of Labor Statistics, 5 out of every 10 new positions will be in these low-wage service jobs.[3]

Today the question is whether the people who protect our families, clean our office buildings, process our food, care for our children, and comfort our aged loved ones will have the resources to provide for their own families. A few simple steps could ensure that America's economic growth and profitability translate into a better life for all working Americans.

STEP 1: PROVIDE AN ADEQUATE MINIMUM WAGE
AND INDEX IT TO INFLATION

Modernizing the minimum wage is the first step toward ensuring that work provides the basics of a decent life. Our nation established a federal minimum wage in 1938 because we believed in the basic human dignity of work: no job should pay so little that it impoverishes Americans. But the fixed-level approach to the minimum wage fails dismally to keep up with the cost of living. The federal minimum wage has been frozen at $5.15 an hour since 1997, and its buying power in 2006 was at its lowest level since 1955.[4] As this volume goes to press, the Democratically-controlled 110th Congress is seeking to increase the minimum wage to $7.25 an hour.

One way to measure the worth of the minimum wage is against the average hourly wage. In the 1950s and 1960s the minimum wage averaged half of average hourly earnings. In 2006 the minimum was only 31 percent of average hourly earnings, its lowest level in more than 50 years.[5] That translated into barely more than $10,000 a year for full-time workers, around half the federal poverty level for a family of four.

Raising the minimum wage to what it would have been if it had merely kept up with inflation from its peak in purchasing power in 1968 (a little over $9.00 an hour according to the U.S. Bureau of Labor Statistics Inflation Calculator) and indexing it to the inflation rate to preserve those gains is a good first step to ensuring that work pays. The change would not bring minimum-wage workers into the middle class nor make up for the years of lost income, but it would at least bring them back to what they would have made had their wages kept up with inflation. It would also respond to the escalating costs of housing, health care, transportation, and college Americans are facing. And numerous studies have found that any change in the minimum wage has a ripple effect, helping workers who make more as well. Raising the wage floor would also help stop employers from restructuring jobs by cutting workers' wages and farming out the work to even lower-wage employers.[6]

Opponents of the minimum-wage increase argue that a raise will not lift the earnings of the lowest-wage workers because it is not well targeted to them. Yet the poorest 40 percent of households are those that reap the most gains from any wage increase, according to the Economic Policy Institute, and that includes seven million children under 12 who live in households with minimum-wage earners. And contrary to popular myth that most minimum-wage workers are teenagers, 80 percent of the recipients of a raise are adults. Women, who represent 60 percent of minimum-wage workers, would disproportionately benefit. Studies show that a raise in the minimum wage does in fact decrease poverty.[7]

Another canard against minimum-wage raises is that businesses will respond by slashing the number of jobs they offer. History does not bear this out. Recent studies by the Economic Policy Institute found no statistically significant job losses resulting from the last federal minimum-wage increase, in 1996–97. Other studies of the 1990–91 federal minimum-wage increase had similar findings, as did studies of various state minimum-wage increases.[8]

In fact, a study by the Fiscal Policy Institute found that in 12 states with minimum wages higher than the federal level of $5.15 an hour, employment rose more than in states where the federal level was standard. This finding held true for small businesses as well.[9] And why would it not? Workers' increased buying power leads to new purchases, which boost the entire economy—and that creates more jobs. It is a virtuous circle, one that helped power the American boom in the years after minimum wages and unionization first swept the U.S. manufacturing sector.

It is clear, in short, that raising the minimum wage has many economic benefits that reach beyond the workers who would directly benefit. Americans at the state level understand this. Frustrated by Congress's inability to move, 29 states, including more than half the national workforce, have increased their minimum-wage levels above the federal minimum through legislative action or state ballot initiatives. Many of these states also increase their wages to reflect inflation. And more states are expected to raise their minimum wage as well. This revolution is not surprising. Recent polling shows that 80 percent of Americans support an increase in the minimum wage.[10] Even Nevada and Florida, two states that went for George W. Bush in the 2000 election, voted to hike the state minimum wage past the federal level.

The minimum wage is not a liberal or conservative issue. It is a human issue. Modernizing it by restoring its value and indexing it is a crucial step in addressing the problem of inadequate wages and inadequate rewards for a hard day's work—but it is only the first step.

STEP 2: REWARD BUSINESSES THAT TAKE
THE HIGH ROAD

Living-wage ordinances provide incentives for employers to provide good jobs. A living-wage ordinance applies to entities that do business with or get benefits from a city, state, or the federal government in the form of subsidies, contracts, or tax abatements or in other ways. It requires such companies to provide a certain living wage and certain basic benefits to their workers. The premise is that corporations that receive taxpayers' dollars should not be using that money to impoverish those taxpayers.

To date there are more than 130 living-wage ordinances around the United States. The first was enacted in Baltimore in 1994. All the laws differ in what employers must provide, but the common element is a requirement for a wage level that allows workers to provide the basics of a decent life for themselves and their families. Some ordinances also require that employers provide health benefits or stay neutral in union organizing campaigns. Behind all of them is a commitment to creating family-sustaining jobs.

The concept of a living wage is different from that of the minimum wage. A minimum wage is a floor beyond which our society believes an employer should not go. A living wage considers what it really takes to make a family self-sufficient—that is, to obtain the basic necessities without government assistance. A living-wage calculation also considers the relative prices in particular geographic areas.

Although the official poverty line is supposed to define an adequate income, many leading scholars agree that the current measure is wholly inadequate and outdated.[11] The official poverty measure assumes erroneously, for example, that food costs about one-third of a family's budget and that everything else takes up the remainder. Calculators therefore merely multiply the price of a "typical" family food basket by three and call the result the official poverty line. Today, however, food costs less than 20 percent of an average household's budget. Housing, health care, and work expenses such as child care and transportation are usually a family's biggest costs. The official poverty line is therefore considered to be only about 60 percent of what it really takes to make ends meet.

The impact of the living-wage movement goes beyond the number of ordinances that have been enacted. Mostly local, they cover a relatively small number of people working at businesses that have certain kinds of contracts with local governments. Yet the concept of requiring companies to pay a living wage and provide basic benefits if they do business with the government has widened.

It is used in economic development at both the state and local levels. In 2003 Good Jobs First, a national policy resource center for corporate and government accountability in economic development, found that at least 89 jurisdictions, including 43 states, 41 cities, and 5 counties, had attached job-quality standards to at least one development subsidy. Since that time the number has significantly increased.[12] More recently the community benefits movement has been reframing the debate on economic development, creating agreements not only on minimum job standards but on housing and neighborhood services for public-private development projects.[13]

Cities are starting to require certain kinds of businesses to pay a living wage if they want to do business in their city. In Emeryville, outside San Francisco, a local law requires hotels to pay workers overall wages of $11 per hour. Through this growing push for living-wage provisions, the notion of a living wage has begun to take hold as an important goal in our society. The more it is used, the more it will begin to set norms about acceptable pay for workers in a given area. If it were used more widely throughout government, the concept could have a significant impact on overall wage levels and other elements of decent jobs.

One result would be to change the strategies many companies use to maximize profits. Corporations can become profitable in many ways. Some choose to pay low wages, provide few benefits, and invest little in their workers. Others choose a high-road model that aims to reduce employee turnover and increase productivity by paying a living wage, providing basic benefits, and investing in workers through education and training programs and other incentives. Living-wage ordinances would stimulate employers to choose the high-road model of doing business, conditioning receipt of taxpayer dollars on providing good jobs. This strategy would effectively close off the low-road option.

But why should society close off the low-road option? The best reason, aside from the damage it inflicts on workers and their families, is the enormous social costs the approach imposes on the rest of us—the hidden taxpayer costs. When companies pay low wages and provide few benefits, taxpayers must pick up the costs of feeding and caring for people who cannot manage for themselves—through government programs such as food stamps, Medicaid, housing subsidies, and children's health programs. Wal-Mart is the classic example of an employer whose "low-road" approach benefits the company to the detriment of the taxpayer. For example, because its wages are so low and its health insurance is so costly, more Wal-Mart workers take part in Georgia's Child Health Program than those of any other employer.

Living-wage ordinances could counteract the current harmful trend of a "race to the bottom," where local jurisdictions try to attract employers by offering larger subsidies than their neighbors. The more widespread living-wage ordinances are, the less able businesses will be to shop around for the cheapest workforce. Living-wage ordinances are one tool to ensure that economic development policies create good jobs.

Critics of living-wage ordinances have only one argument, and it is a false one: they assert that government should not intervene in the free marketplace. But governments intervene in the market all the time, primarily to help businesses—through such measures as crop and export subsidies, tax breaks, special exemptions, regulatory changes, and earmarked government projects. Living-wage laws merely set some socially important conditions for receiving those benefits, conditions that help the entire community by providing good jobs.

STEP 3: CLEAR THE WAY FOR WORKERS TO UNIONIZE

So how can we enact adequate minimum-wage and living-wage laws and ensure that employers adequately reward workers? One answer is to facilitate unionization. It has often been said that the best antipoverty program is a strong union. At the height of union representation in the mid-twentieth century, when 35 percent of the American labor force was organized, wages rose significantly nationwide. Millions of people moved into the middle class, creating what would be the most equal distribution of income this country has ever seen. Union contracts provided health-care coverage, paid vacations, and pension benefits to millions, and union political clout helped win passage of Social Security, Medicare, and Medicaid—the country's social safety net.

Today, however, with union representation down to 7.8 percent of the private-sector economy, America suffers from the greatest income inequality since the Gilded Age.[14] Amid increased worker productivity and skyrocketing corporate profits, ordinary Americans' wages have stagnated, not even keeping pace with inflation. Employers continue to shift more and more of the daily risks of working life onto their employees, so that more and more working families must rely on unstable jobs without health insurance, retirement security, or paid time off. Working conditions have deteriorated, so that many jobholders must work off the clock, in unsafe conditions, or under enormous stress.

Can unions do anything about this situation? Should we care that union representation is so low? The answer is most definitely yes.

No one can deny that unions have increased the paychecks of the workers who are organized under a collective bargaining agreement. According to the Economic Policy Institute, unions raise the wages of unionized workers by roughly 20 percent over those of their nonunionized counterparts. In traditionally low-wage service jobs such as hotel maintenance, nursing-home care, home health care, security services, and manual labor, unionized workers make 27 percent more. Because unions have a greater impact on low- and middle-income jobs than on high-wage positions, they reduce wage inequality.[15]

But wages are not the only difference. Fully 86 percent of union workers are covered by health benefits through their employer, according to the Employee Benefit Research Institute, compared with 59 percent of nonunion workers.[16] Unionized workers are also 54 percent more likely to have employer-provided pension plans, and they receive 26 percent more vacation time.[17]

Unions also bring workers a voice and basic dignity on their jobs. As a nonunion Alabama nursing-home worker stated, "You tell the supervisors that a resident in the nursing home isn't breathing right and they don't do anything. They have a suggestion box. But they never take your advice. I have suggestions regarding the residents because I'm with them all the time, but they never listen. That's why I want a union."

Where unions are active, they have clout, even in the service sector. Security guards are a good example. In Los Angeles a group of security guards earned $6.75 an hour before they were organized by the Service Employees International Union (SEIU). Now they earn $11.20 an hour. They have affordable health benefits, paid sick days, paid vacation and holidays, a pension plan, and a process to address unfair treatment at work. Their nonunion counterparts in the same city doing the same job get $8.50 per hour, with none of the benefits the union jobs now provide.[18]

The same is true elsewhere: when the workers get a union, the job begins to change into a good job. Take janitors. In unionized Philadelphia workplaces, for example, a maintenance worker makes $13.31 an hour, with full family health-care coverage. The same worker doing the same job at a union-free Houston site would make $5.30 an hour with no family health care. The only difference is that the job in Philadelphia is covered by a union contract and the one in Houston is not.

When unions have a presence in an industry, they set norms that put pressure on nonunion employers in that industry to improve their wages and benefits. Again in Los Angeles, after those security guards were unionized at several companies, nonunion employers raised their wages from $7.64 to $8.50 an hour in order to compete for workers and to stave off the unions. Nonunion workers benefit from strong unions that can set a pay and benefit standard. A high-school graduate whose workplace is not unionized, for example, but whose industry is 25 percent unionized is paid 5 percent more than similar workers in less unionized industries.

Unfortunately, the reverse is also true. As Wharton School of Business professor Peter Cappelli observes, "As the threat of union organizing declines, non-union companies are increasingly abandoning those [union] practices, in a kind of reverse spillover."[19] In the supermarket industry, for example, competition from the nonunion behemoth Wal-Mart has pushed down wages and benefits from unionized grocery operators that had previously provided good jobs. Such stores in Los Angeles recently demanded and won wage and benefit concessions from their unions, arguing that the cuts were necessary if they were to stay in business against Wal-Mart and its lower costs.

The most important role of unions may lie in bringing a human voice to the political debate about the future of our society. The union voice considers how working families can pay the rent, obtain health care, get time off to be together, send their children to college, and have a secure retirement. Individual voices alone simply cannot penetrate the constant bottom-line focus of multinational corporations and their executives' purchasing power in the political arena.

Unions historically led the fight for the average American. Remember the bumper sticker "Unions—the folks who brought you the weekend"? As columnist David Broder aptly stated, "When labor lobbied powerfully on Capitol Hill, it did not confine itself to bread-and-butter issues for its own members. It was at the forefront of battles for aid to education, civil rights, housing programs and a host of other social causes important to the whole community. And because it was muscular, it was heard and heeded."[20] It is no coincidence, then, that the decline of the labor movement has been accompanied by rising inequality, a dramatic decline in the value of the minimum wage, bankruptcy reform that chiefly hurt ordinary Americans, and tax cuts for the wealthy, while at the same time social programs that help ordinary Americans come under the knife.

So why aren't more workers organizing in American workplaces? Polls show that they would like to: 53 million Americans said in a recent Peter D. Hart Research Associates poll that they would support having a union at their job site if they were given the chance.[21] That is the problem: they are not getting that chance.

The National Labor Relations Act guarantees workers the right to form and join unions for the purpose of collective bargaining. Yet today's workers have virtually lost the right to organize. Virulent antilabor campaigns are common when workers attempt to organize, and current labor laws are both weak and poorly enforced. They do very little to deter illegal anti-union behavior, and complaints to the National Labor Relations Board (NLRB) often take years to resolve.

In a return to the bad old days, American workers who try to organize unions face employer harassment, intimidation, or worse. According to a 2000 Human Rights Watch report, "Workers who try to form and join trade unions to bargain with their employers are spied on, harassed, pressured, threatened, suspended, fired, deported, or otherwise victimized in reprisal for their exercise of the right to freedom of association."[22]

These acts of illegal employer intimidation have accelerated in recent years. In the 1950s the annual number of workers who suffered reprisals for trying to organize a union was in the hundreds. By 1990 it had climbed to 20,000. That horrific number continues to grow. The Center for Urban Economic Development found in a 2005 study that when faced with organizing drives, 30 percent of employers fire pro-union workers, 49 percent threaten to close a worksite if the union prevails, and 51 percent coerce workers into opposing unions with bribery or favoritism.[23]

It is not simply being fired that intimidates workers. Employers' raw power over their labor force can mean grueling shift changes, demotions, transfers, new responsibilities without adequate training, and other measures that make organizers' jobs unendurable. These union-busting tactics have gone virtually unpunished and unchecked by the NLRB, further jeopardizing workers' rights to form unions and collectively bargain.

As we move into the twenty-first century, which is already roiling with enormous change and turbulence, unions are more important than ever in bringing working families the decent treatment and respect they deserve. The vibrancy of the labor movement matters to all of us. It is the individuals who come together in unions and raise their voices loud enough to be heard who remind us of the needs and hopes of ordinary hardworking Americans. But instead of making it easy for employees anywhere to organize a union and exercise their right of freedom of association, we have made it perilous.

America needs to reform its labor laws to make it very costly for corporations to take the low road of violating their workers' human rights to organize a union. And then we must enforce those laws and treat those abusive companies as lawbreakers, for that is what they are. If we want to create family-sustaining jobs and improve wages, benefits, and working conditions for everyday Americans, workers must have a free and unfettered choice to form and join a union in an environment that is free of any kind of employer intimidation.

CONCLUSION

Every day in America, low-wage workers make our lives possible through their labor as security guards and teaching assistants, nursing-home aides and hospital workers, janitors and hotel workers, child-care workers and retail clerks. Yet we have turned these hardworking men and women and their families into the new poor. It is a blight on our democracy and our understanding of fair play that in such a prosperous country hardworking Americans cannot make ends meet no matter how hard they work.

It also has social costs. We all pay when wages do not support families. Taxpayers pay when they have to pick up the bill for employers whose wages do not cover housing, health care, or food. Communities pay as their tax base dwindles and the social ills of deprivation spread through their towns. Society pays as we become more economically polarized. As human beings, we all pay when we turn our backs on our fellow Americans who are working just as hard as we are but still cannot provide for their families.

It is clear that companies can remain competitive in the global economy by paying a living wage and providing basic benefits. But Americans should not leave it up to corporations to make the decision about how their workers are treated. That is our role as a society. It is up to us to ensure that work pays. We can make choices that ensure that work provides the basics of a decent life and that hardworking men and women and their families have a shot at the American Dream. All we have to do is act.

NOTES

1. Lawrence Mishel, Jared Bernstein, and Heather Boushey, *The State of Working America, 2002–2003* (Ithaca, NY: Cornell University Press, 2003), 134.

2. U.S. Congressional Budget Office, "What Accounts for the Decline in Manufacturing," February 18, 2004, Issue Brief.

3. Daniel E. Hecker, "Occupational Employment Projections to 2010," *Monthly Labor Review* 12, no. 11 (November 2001): 57–84.

4. Jared Bernstein and Isaac Shapiro, "Buying Power of Minimum Wage at 51-Year Low" (Economic Policy Institute and Center on Budget and Policy Priorities, June 20, 2006).

5. Ibid.

6. Eileen Appelbaum, Annette Bernhardt, and Richard J. Murnane, eds., *Low-Wage America: How Employers Are Reshaping Opportunity in the Workplace* (New York: Russell Sage Foundation, 2003), 23.

7. John Addison and McKinley Blackburn, "Minimum Wages and Poverty," *Industrial and Labor Relations Review* 52, no. 3 (April 1999): 393–409; Isabel Sawhill and Adam Thomas, "A Hand Up for the Bottom Third" (Brookings Institution, 2001).

8. See also David Card and Alan Krueger, "Minimum Wages and Employment: A Case Study of the Fast-Food Industry in New Jersey and Pennsylvania," *American Economic Review* 84, no. 4 (December 2000): 1397–1420; David Card, "Do Minimum Wages Reduce Employment? A Case Study of California, 1987–89," *Industrial and Labor Relations Review* 46, no. 1 (October 1992); David Card and Alan Krueger, "A Reanalysis of the Effect of the New Jersey Minimum

Wage Increase on the Fast-Food Industry with Representative Payroll Data" (WP 393, Princeton University, January 1998); Sawhill and Thomas, "A Hand Up for the Bottom Third."

9. Fiscal Policy Institute, "States with Minimum Wages Above the Federal Level Have Had Faster Small Business and Retail Job Growth" (March 30, 2006).

10. Pew Research Center, http://pewresearch.org.

11. Constance F. Citro and Robert T. Michael, eds., *Measuring Poverty: A New Approach* (Washington, DC: National Academy Press, 1995); Heather Boushey, Chauna Brocht, Bethney Gundersen, and Jared Bernstein, *Hardships in America: The Real Story of Working Families* (Washington, DC: Economic Policy Institute, 2001).

12. Anna Purinton, Nasreen Jilani, Kristen Arant, and Kate Davis, "The Policy Shift to Good Jobs: Cities, States and Counties Attaching Job Quality Standards to Development Subsidies" (Good Jobs First, November 2003).

13. Julian Gross, Greg LeRoy, and Madeline Janis-Aparicio, "Community Benefits Agreements: Making Development Projects Accountable" (Good Jobs First and the California Partnership for Working Families, 2005).

14. Bureau of Labor Statistics, "Union Members Summary," January 20, 2006.

15. Lawrence Mishel with Matthew Walters, "How Unions Help All Workers" (Briefing Paper, Economic Policy Institute, August 2003).

16. "Union Status and Employment Based Health Benefits," *Economic Benefits Research Institute Notes* 26, no. 5 (May 2005): 427.

17. Mishel with Walters, "How Unions Help All Workers."

18. Service Employees International Union Research Office.

19. Peter Cappelli et al., *Change at Work* (New York: Oxford University Press, 1997), 62.

20. David Broder, "The Price of Labor's Decline," *Washington Post*, September 9, 2004.

21. Peter D. Hart Research Associates, "The Silent War: The Assault on Workers' Freedom to Choose a Union and Bargain Collectively in the United States" (Study No. 7518, Issue Brief, AFL-CIO, September 2005).

22. Lance Compa, *Unfair Advantage: Workers' Freedom of Association in the United States Under International Human Rights Standards* (New York: Human Rights Watch, 2000).

23. Chirag Mehta and Nik Theodore, "Undermining the Right to Organize: Employer Behavior During Union Representation Campaigns" (Center for Urban Economic Development, University of Illinois, December 2005).

Education and Training for Less Affluent Americans in the New Economy

Harry J. Holzer

WHAT IS THE PROBLEM?

The American economy has changed quite dramatically over the past few decades and will continue to evolve in the years to come. New technologies and continuing globalization—including the growing offshoring of service jobs—will create a labor market in which higher education and a range of skills (including literacy and numeracy, problem-solving abilities, and communication) are even more heavily rewarded than they are now, and where inequality between more and less educated workers continues to grow.

Workers at all levels of education will also face greater risks of unemployment and earnings declines from more frequent job loss, as jobs become less permanent and American workers are more easily replaced by machines and foreign workers. At the same time, the retirements of baby boomers from the labor force (and their replacement by less educated immigrants) will create challenges for at least some employers—especially in particular sectors and geographic locations—to find semiskilled and highly-skilled workers for available jobs.[1]

But while the economy places ever-greater premiums on education, opportunities to develop skills and credentials in our society grow more unequal. The sons and daughters of more affluent families in the United States have always been able to obtain more education than those of middle- and lower-income families, but the gaps in college attendance and especially college completion between these groups have grown wider in the past few decades.[2]

While college remains out of reach for the children of most less-affluent families, just graduating from high school remains a challenge for many as well. Recent data suggest that as many as 30 percent of all ninth graders fail to graduate from high school on time (within four years), and that among minorities the rate is nearly one-half. Though there is some controversy about the exact numbers, there is little doubt that dropping out of high school remains a disturbingly common outcome for many of our youth.[3] And among some groups of high-school dropouts, especially young black men, a failure to earn a high-school diploma almost guarantees a future of low employment, unwed fatherhood of children, crime, and incarceration.[4]

Serious economic challenges are also faced by our working poor adult population. Millions of families have the equivalent of at least one full-time worker but have incomes at or near the poverty line. The "working poor" not only have low incomes and few benefits, but fairly low advancement prospects as well.[5]

Given this range of challenges, what kinds of education and training policies should the United States pursue in the coming years? Will any set of education policies alone be sufficient to restore widely shared prosperity to American workers, or will we need to supplement these approaches with other labor-market policies that encourage higher-wage job creation and provide additional supports for working families?

In my view, our education and training policies should aim for the following: (1) higher rates of early skill building, high-school completion, and college attendance for our youth, along with improved access to the labor market for those who do not pursue college diplomas; (2) new opportunities for training and advancement for our working adult poor; and (3) expanded protections against the risks of job loss and displacement for all Americans. And we will need to supplement these approaches with efforts to encourage higher-wage job formation and provide additional public benefits to the working poor.

IMPROVING EDUCATIONAL OUTCOMES FOR YOUTH

Efforts to improve the education and skills of low-income youth must start early in life, because large gaps in cognitive skills between lower-income or minority students and others develop even before they reach kindergarten.[6] Universal prekindergarten programs are one method that several states have already chosen to expand early school readiness, and limited evidence from Oklahoma suggests that these can be cost-effective ways of improving early skill formation. More intensive and higher-quality early childhood programs hold great promise as well for young disadvantaged children.[7]

Reforms in the K–8 schools include the high-stakes testing approaches already implemented in the No Child Left Behind legislation and other proposals that usually stress expanded school choice (including vouchers to private schools), greater funding for public schools, or changes in school governance. These proposals continue to be debated, while the research evidence continues to grow.[8] At a minimum, the need to recruit and retain higher-quality teachers into lower-income school districts and to support the development of their instructional abilities while rewarding their success is well established.[9]

Our need to reduce dropout rates and increase student achievement in high schools is also now widely accepted. But some proposals for high-school reform (such as a recent one by the National Governors Association) focus almost exclusively on college-preparatory work and high-stakes testing. Some such proposals might actually raise high-school dropout rates and will do little to motivate many of our youth who see little relevance of what they learn in high school to their later lives.[10]

In my view, all American high schools should offer a wide range of pathways to success, either directly through higher education or through the labor market or both. These should include high-quality options in career and technical education (CTE) that combine strong academic instruction with occupational training and early labor-market experience.

The clearest example we have of high-quality CTE is the career academy. These "schools within a school" generate small learning environments within larger high schools where students combine academic coursework with instruction targeted toward a particular sector of the economy, such as financial services or health care. Students also have the opportunity for summer and term-time employment in these sectors.

Recent evaluations of career academies by Manpower Demonstration Research Corporation (MDRC) showed large improvements in earnings (about 18 percent) for at-risk young men as much as four years after graduation from high school.[11] Other models that mix academics and work experience for youth, such as apprenticeships, are promising as well, as are a wider range of high-school reforms that reduce school sizes and provide strong instructional support for students.[12]

Does CTE "track" lower-income and minority students into noncollege paths that generate lower earnings over the long run? In the MDRC evaluation students in the career academies did not go to college or other postsecondary institutions at a lower rate than those in the control group, even though they gained higher earnings when they worked. Thus high-quality CTE can open new doors to labor-market success for lower-income students without closing any that lead to higher education.

The retirements of the baby boomers also generate opportunities for greater cooperation between high schools or technical/community colleges and local employers. Many kinds of jobs that pay reasonably high wages to workers without four-year college degrees—in construction, health care, elder care, wholesale and retail trade, and the like—cannot be outsourced and often cannot be filled with less educated immigrant labor. With some modest financial support and technical assistance from the U.S. Department of Labor, apprenticeships and internships could be expanded on a greater scale for disadvantaged American youth that would improve their access to higher-paying jobs and careers.

But how can we also improve the access of our lower-income young people to two-year and four-year colleges? For decades we have used public subsidies to keep tuition rates low at state universities and community colleges. But rising costs and competing pressures on state budgets from Medicaid and other expenditures have made this much more difficult, so tuition levels at public (as well as private) colleges will continue growing rapidly, making college even less affordable for lower- and middle-income students.[13]

Are there other ways to target more aid directly to the students who need it the most? The obvious mechanism is to provide expanded support through the Pell Grant program, which provides scholarship support for low-income youth and adults who attend college. Over the past few decades the maximum Pell grants available have failed to keep pace with rising tuition costs; and certain categories of students, such as those attending less than half-time and those with felony drug convictions, are excluded from eligibility altogether.

Also, recent research suggests that Pell grants have not increased college attendance among low-income youth, though they have apparently been somewhat more successful at improving college attendance among low-income adults. Increasing the generosity of these grants and widening eligibility for them might make them more useful to many youth, and making them less complicated and easier to obtain might help as well.[14]

There are other approaches to financial aid for college students. State-level "merit scholarship" programs, in which students who achieve and maintain a certain grade-point average in college get very substantial reductions in their tuitions, have expanded in recent years. Recent evidence from Georgia, Arkansas, and other states that have used this approach suggests that these programs do raise both college attendance and completion, particularly among minorities and women.[15] Perhaps these programs could be structured in ways that provide even more generous support for students from lower-income than middle- or upper-income families.

Other efforts to make college more accessible to lower-income youth might include giving some weight to low family income in college admissions decisions, improving the counseling low-income students obtain about colleges, and a variety of other supports and services to improve their rates of college attendance and completion.[16] Of course, any success we have in improving academic preparation in the K–12 years for minorities and lower-income students would help a great deal as well.

Finally, what can we do for high-risk youth who are failing in high schools and perhaps have already dropped out? We can expand access to a set of programs such as the Job Corps and the Youth Service and Conservation Corps that combine work experience, training, and life-skills/values development for these youth. These programs have fairly strong track records in the evaluation literature and deserve greater support. Newer approaches, such as the National Guard's ChalleNGe program, need further study but are also quite promising.[17]

We need to expand positive youth development efforts that reach at-risk young people during their adolescence. For example, the Harlem Children's Zone, developed by Geoffrey Canada, is an impressive private effort that reaches many hundreds of young people early and stays with them through their teen years. Efforts such as Big Brothers/Big Sisters have also been rigorously evaluated and show positive effects on young people.

We should continue experimenting with alternative public high schools that create specialized learning environments for returning youth who have already dropped out of mainstream schools.[18] And we need to create local youth "systems" that keep track of our youth in disadvantaged neighborhoods, rationalize the fragmented services available to them, and refer them to what is available. A first attempt to do this nationally was the Youth Opportunities program, developed by the Department of Labor in 2000 (and eliminated in 2003). These efforts need to be continued and expanded at the local level, with restored federal support.[19]

LOW-INCOME ADULTS: BETTER TRAINING AND JOBS

Among less educated and low-wage adults, advancement out of poverty-level earnings over many years occurs in just a modest fraction of cases (roughly 20 percent or fewer).[20] This usually occurs when these workers are able to move from lower- to higher-wage jobs and employers. Indeed, the same worker often earns more when she or he can obtain employment in a higher-wage sector (such as construction, durable manufacturing, wholesale trade, and certain services), with a larger or unionized employer (such as a hospital rather than a nursing home), and especially with an employer that provides more training and greater opportunities for advancement. Even within fairly narrowly defined industries and locations, employers often choose whether to compete on the basis of low wages and costs or higher productivity, and workers clearly gain in the case of the latter.[21]

Of course, the higher-productivity employers also seek evidence of higher basic skills or skill-building potential among the workers whom they hire. To obtain these skills, some adults will need to obtain training at a local community college or proprietary school, either in general skills or those more specific to the relevant occupation or industry. "Bridge" programs at community colleges are often used to provide some remedial efforts to the least skilled so they can take more demanding courses needed for specific occupations.

In general, training for low-income workers is most successful at improving subsequent earnings when it generates a meaningful credential (such as a community college certificate or degree) and when it matches the needs of employers in the local labor market.[22] But low-income adults often find it very difficult to juggle the pressures of work and schooling and are reluctant to undertake the latter if it is not directly tied to specific opportunities for advancement in the former.

What they need in many cases are the services of a labor-market intermediary—a third party that can help link them to both the employers and training providers and help them obtain the financial and other supports they need in the process. Some intermediaries, such as private "temp" agencies, do little more than provide job placements to their clients, though some also provide some general training and assistance with transportation and child care. Even these modest efforts seem to link workers with better jobs than they could obtain on their own, at least in the short run.[23] But other intermediaries (including faith-based organizations such as Jobs for Life [see inset]) also work more proactively with employers to help them develop career ladders and other human resource policies that better reward skill acquisition among their workers. Links between employers and community colleges or other training providers are developed as well.

Some of these efforts focus on specific sectors of the local economy (and are often referred to as sectoral programs); some of the best-known efforts have focused on the nursing-home and elder-care industries. There have also been broader citywide efforts in San Antonio (Quest), Cleveland (WireNet), and San Jose (the Center for Employment and Training [CET]) and statewide efforts in Wisconsin (Regional Training Partnership), Kentucky (Career Pathways), and elsewhere. The evaluation evidence on these programs to date, while not always rigorous, has been mostly positive.[24]

These approaches thus combine skill acquisition for workers with the creation of better job opportunities. Can the public sector play a greater role in supporting these efforts and bringing them to greater scale? One approach is to provide tax credits for firms that generate training and advancement

JOBS FOR LIFE

David Spickard

In 1996 a simple conversation birthed a profound movement of people and resources to combat joblessness and poverty in our country. During a casual lunch in Raleigh, North Carolina, Chris Mangum, head of a heavy highway construction company, mentioned to his friend, Rev. Donald McCoy, pastor of Pleasant Hill United Church of Christ, "I've got a lot of good trucks sitting idle at my business, I just can't find drivers."

Pastor McCoy quickly replied, "That's interesting, in my congregation, I have many good people who are idle because they just can't find jobs."

At that moment, Jobs for Life (JfL) was born.

Mangum and Pastor McCoy realized that each had a resource the other needed. Mangum had jobs; Pastor McCoy had people. From there, they found others with the same needs and built a strategy in which churches and community organizations are training and mentoring individuals who struggle to find and keep a job, providing a quality workforce to meet the pressing employment needs of businesses across the country.

Today Jobs for Life enables individual churches and organizations to become Jobs for Life sites, fully equipped to provide job training and support to unemployed and underemployed individuals. According to the Urban Institute, as of 2001, only 1 percent of churches in all of America did any outreach related to employment.[1]

As a result, Jobs for Life is mobilizing an underused resource in the fight against poverty and unemployment—members and volunteers of churches and community organizations on every street corner in America who need a proven strategy and tools to equip men and women who need employment.

Through JfL's training class, JfL sites build two foundational elements in people's lives that are critical to their long-term success. First, the training addresses the root causes of their problems. Based on timeless biblical principles, JfL's training focuses the students on their motivations to work, uncovers their gifts, skills, and talents, and helps them develop life skills such as responsibility, perseverance, integrity, and excellence that are critical for their success at work and in life.

Second, JfL sites connect individuals to a community of support—committed people who offer a network of friendships that supply not only emotional and physical help but also access to a wealth of resources and opportunities. Every

Jobs for Life student has a champion—a mentor or a team of mentors—who builds a relationship with the student, providing long-term support and encouragement and helping students overcome any barrier that inhibits their success.

By December 2006 Jobs for Life sites were located in churches, prisons and reentry programs, rescue missions, homeless shelters, and community nonprofits in 40 cities and 22 states. Surveys of JfL sites have shown that one full year after program completion, between 70 and 80 percent of those who commit to follow the Jobs for Life way are still employed, with stable, growing lives.

For more information, visit Jobs for Life's website at www.jobsforlife.com.

NOTE

1. Avis C. Vidal, *Faith-Based Organizations in Community Development* (Washington, DC: Urban Institute, 2001).

opportunities to their less educated incumbent workers. Evidence suggests that state programs of this type have been successful at raising worker productivity and firm performance, as well as worker earnings.[25]

More broadly, states and local workforce investment boards (WIBs) could use their federal funds to experiment with and evaluate these kinds of efforts, especially with more encouragement and assistance from the U.S. Department of Labor. However, training funds provided through the Workforce Investment Act (WIA) have been declining in recent years, while the need for more worker skills and training has grown.[26] Greater funding of training through WIA should therefore be provided, and efforts should be made to redirect some of that funding into greater support for local efforts to build more effective sectoral pathways for less skilled workers.[27]

Also, it is important to remember that many of our poorest adults are not yet job-ready and need more intensive forms of assistance before they can reenter the world of work and retain the jobs they receive. Workers with physical or mental health problems and disabilities, substance abuse problems, or criminal records often face multiple barriers to employment, as well as disincentives to work. For these hard-to-employ individuals, a wider set of supports and services is needed, perhaps including publicly funded transitional jobs for limited periods of time. For the large numbers of adult men with criminal records and child-support orders on which they have fallen behind, some additional fatherhood services and enhanced work incentives are particularly important.[28]

EASING THE RISKS OF DISPLACEMENT

Recent evidence suggests that workers at all levels of skill now face greater risks than in earlier times of losing their jobs as employers constantly seek to develop new ways of raising productivity and cutting costs.[29] Attempts to block these adjustments are likely to impede efficiency and productivity growth. But the workers who lose their jobs suffer lengthy periods of unemployment and permanent earnings losses when these adjustments occur, thus bearing the high costs of the broader economic gains we all enjoy.

In such an economic environment many adults may want to reenroll in colleges or technical schools, at least on a part-time basis, to retrain for new careers. Financial support for these efforts can be increased through a variety of mechanisms, such as the existing Lifetime Learning Tax Credit (for college tuition payments among adults), training funds for displaced workers through WIA,[30] and tax credits and exemptions for employer-provided training (through Section 127 of the Internal Revenue Service code). Helping colleges and universities make their course offerings more flexible and more accessible to working adults through more modular classes (especially on evenings and weekends) and more "distance learning" over the Internet would be useful as well.

Can we do more to cushion the blows that displaced workers experience and to help get them back on their feet? Making unemployment insurance last beyond its usual six-month duration or having it replace more than half of the typical worker's lost earnings might accomplish this, but at the cost of encouraging laid-off workers to take longer spells of unemployment. Instead, some economists have recently begun arguing for wage insurance for these workers.[31] Under these schemes, if displaced workers accept new jobs at lower wages than they previously earned, the federal government would make up half of the lost earnings for a substantial period of time (up to two years). This would encourage quicker job recovery among these workers while helping cushion the blows they experience from lost earnings.

In addition to lost earnings, one of the great fears of workers who lose their jobs is that they will lose health insurance for themselves and their families. Ultimately the United States will likely have to shift away from a system based primarily on employer-provided insurance, given its costs to employers and its unequal coverage across workers.[32] A new system of universal coverage that requires all individuals to be enrolled but that also provides a range of subsidies based on income levels for insurance premiums will likely take its place. Indeed, the state of Massachusetts has already embarked on such a path. Efforts to contain the growth of health costs may also be essential for the financial stability of these efforts.

CONCLUSION

The proposals advanced here lay out a fairly comprehensive set of policies that would increase the skills and education of our youth, improve the earnings potential of working poor adults, and protect all workers from the growing risks and costs of job loss. We do not necessarily have all the answers as to exactly what is cost-effective, so continued experimentation and evaluation are necessary. But in the meantime we can move ahead in many areas where the research evidence is fairly clear.

Given the budgetary pressures that the federal government will no doubt face in the coming years—especially as baby boomers retire and begin to draw on Social Security and Medicare—are these efforts affordable? In many cases investments in improved education and health for our workers would reduce the enormous costs to our society and to our public coffers associated with unemployment, crime and incarceration, and poor worker health. They would partially, though probably not entirely, pay for themselves.

But any realistic look at future federal budgets also suggests that dramatic expansions of public expenditures are unlikely, and that any efforts undertaken need to leverage state/local and especially private funds. This is yet another reason that our labor-market efforts need to actively engage employers and leverage the investments they can make in worker quality to meet their own business needs. No doubt some employers will prefer to look to China and India (or to immigrants domestically) for their future labor services, but others will have difficulty meeting their needs in these ways. Wherever possible, helping them meet their workforce needs in ways that generate more productive workers in better-paying jobs would be beneficial for all involved.

But it is also clear that improving the incomes of lower earners might require that we go beyond the realms of education and training. Efforts to directly raise wages through higher minimum wages and expanded collective bargaining make sense (as Beth Shulman argues in Chapter 9 in this volume). But the forces of technological change and growing globalization will give many employers other options and will likely continue to put downward pressure on wages, thus making it difficult to coerce or cajole many employers into paying higher wages and benefits. Accordingly, public supports for working families—through expanded subsidies for things such as parental leave, savings accounts, and the like—will need to grow. These supports must be part and parcel of any attempts to improve the living standards of American workers in the coming decades.

NOTES

1. Aspen Institute, *Grow Faster Together or Grow Slowly Apart* (Washington, DC: Aspen Institute, Domestic Study Group, 2002).

2. Sarah Turner, "Higher Education: Policies Generating the 21st Century Workforce," in *Reshaping Workforce Policies for a Changing Economy*, ed. H. Holzer and D. Nightingale (Washington, DC: Urban Institute Press, 2007).

3. Christopher Swanson, "Who Graduates? Who Doesn't? A Statistical Portrait of Public High School Education, Class of 2001" (Education Policy Center, Urban Institute, 2004); Lawrence Mishel and Roy Joydeep, *Rethinking High School Graduation Rates and Trends* (Washington, DC: Economic Policy Institute, 2006).

4. Harry Holzer et al., "Declining Employment Among Young Black Men: The Role of Incarceration and Child Support," *Journal of Policy Analysis and Management* 25, no. 2 (2005): 329–50.

5. Gregory Acs and Pamela Loprest, "Who Are Low-Income Working Families?" (Urban Institute, 2005); Fredrik Andersson et al., *Moving Up or Moving On: Who Advances in the Low-Wage Labor Market?* (New York: Russell Sage Foundation, 2005).

6. Roland Fryer and Steven Levitt, "The Black-White Test Score Gap in the First Two Years of School," *Review of Economics and Statistics* 86, no. 2 (2004): 1447–64.

7. William Gormley and Ted Gayer, "Promoting School Readiness in Oklahoma," *Journal of Human Resources* 40, no. 3 (2005): 533–58; Katherine Magnuson and Jane Waldfogel, "Early Childhood Care and Education: Effects on Ethnic and Racial Gaps in School Readiness," in "School Readiness: Closing Racial and Ethnic Gaps," special issue, *Future of Children* 15, no. 1 (2006): 169–96.

8. Alan Krueger, "Inequality: Too Much of a Good Thing," in *Inequality in America: What Role for Human Capital Policy?* J. Heckman and A. Krueger (Cambridge, MA: MIT Press, 2003), 1–72; Pedro Carneiro and James Heckman, "Human Capital Policies," ibid.; John Chubb and Tom Loveless, eds., *Bridging the Achievement Gap* (Washington, DC: Brookings Institution Press, 2002); Cecilia Rouse, "What Do We Know About School Choice?" (unpublished paper, Princeton University, 2006).

9. Robert Gordon et al., "Identifying Effective Teachers Using Performance on the Job" (Hamilton Project White Paper, Brookings Institution, Washington, DC, 2006).

10. National Governors Association, *An Action Agenda for Improving America's High Schools* (Washington, DC: National Governors Association, 2005); John Bridgeland, John J. Ditulio Jr., and Karen Burke Morison, *The Silent Epidemic: Perspectives of High School Dropouts* (Washington, DC: Bill and Melinda Gates Foundation, 2006).

11. James Kemple, *Career Academies: Impacts on Labor Market Outcomes and Educational Attainment* (New York: MDRC, 2004).

12. Richard Kazis, *Remaking Career and Technical Education for the 21st Century: What Role for High School Programs?* (Boston: Jobs for the Future, 2005); Robert Lerman, "Career-Focused Education and Training for Youth," in *Reshaping Workforce Policies for a Changing Economy*, ed. H. Holzer and D. Nightingale (Washington, DC: Urban Institute Press, 2006); Janet Quint, *Meeting Five Critical Challenges of High School Reform* (New York: MDRC, 2007).

13. David Ellwood and Thomas Kane, "Who Is Getting a College Education? The Growing Gaps in College Enrollment," in *Securing the Future*, ed. Sheldon Danziger and Jane Waldfogel (New York: Russell Sage Foundation, 2000), 289–324.

14. Turner, "Higher Education."

15. Susan Dynarski, "Building the Stock of College-Educated Labor" (Working Paper, National Bureau of Economic Research, 2005).

16. William Bowen et al., *Equity and Excellence in American Higher Education* (Charlottesville: University of Virginia Press, 2004); Anthony Carnevale and Stephen Rose, "Socioeconomic Status, Race/Ethnicity, and Selective College Admissions" (Century Foundation Paper, 2003); Thomas Brock and Allen LeBlanc, *Promoting Student Success in Community College and Beyond* (New York: MDRC, 2005).

17. Joann Jasztrab et al., *Youth Corps: Promising Strategies for Young People and Their Communities* (Cambridge, MA: Abt Associates, 1997); Peter Schochet, Joann Jastrzab, Julie Masker, John Blomquist, and Larry Orr, *Does Job Corps Work?* (Washington, DC: Mathematica Policy Research, 2006).

18. Nancy Martin and Samuel Halperin, *Whatever It Takes: How 12 Communities Are Reconnecting Out-of-School Youth* (Washington, DC: American Youth Policy Forum, 2006).

19. Linda Harris, *Learning from the Youth Opportunities Experience: Building Delivery Capacity in Distressed Communities* (Washington, DC: Center for Law and Social Policy, 2006).

20. Andersson et al., *Moving Up or Moving On.*

21. Eileen Appelbaum et al., eds., *Low-Wage America* (New York: Russell Sage Foundation, 2003).

22. Harry Holzer and Karin Martinson, *Can We Improve Job Retention and Advancement for Low-Income Parents?* Washington, DC: Urban Institute, 2005.

23. David Autor, "Why Do Temporary Help Firms Provide Free General Skills Training?" *Quarterly Journal of Economics* 116, no. 4 (2001): 1409–48; Andersson et al., *Moving Up or Moving On*; Julia Lane et al., "Pathways to Work for Low-Income Workers: The Effect of Work in the Temporary Help Industry," *Journal of Policy Analysis and Management* 22, no. 4 (2003): 581–98; David Autor and Susan Houseman, "Do Temporary Help Jobs Improve Labor Market Outcomes for Less-Skilled Workers? Evidence from Random Assignment" (Working Paper, National Bureau of Economic Research 2005).

24. Paul Osterman, "Employment and Training Policies: New Directions for Less-Skilled Adults," in *Reshaping Workforce Policies for a Changing Economy*, ed. H. Holzer and D. Nightingale (Washington, DC: Urban Institute Press, 2007).

25. Harry Holzer et al., "Are Training Subsidies for Firms Effective? The Michigan Experience," *Industrial and Labor Relations Review* 46, no. 4 (1993): 625–36; Amanda Ahlstrand et al., *Workplace Education for Low-Wage Workers* (Kalamazoo, MI: W.E. Upjohn Institute for Employment Research, 2003).

26. Harry Holzer and Margy Waller, "The Workforce Investment Act: Reauthorization to Address the Skills Gap" (Center for Urban and Metropolitan Affairs, Brookings Institution, Washington, DC, 2003).

27. Osterman, "Employment and Training Policies."

28. Dan Bloom and David Butler, "Overcoming Employment Barriers: Strategies to Help the Hard to Employ," in *Reshaping Workforce Policies for a Changing Economy*, ed. H. Holzer and D. Nightingale (Washington, DC: Urban Institute Press, 2007); Peter Edelman et al., *Reconnecting Disadvantaged Young Men* (Washington, DC: Urban Institute Press, 2006).

29. Henry Farber, "What Do We Know About Job Loss in the U.S.? Evidence from the Displaced Worker Survey" (Working Paper, National Bureau of Economic Research, 2005); Louis Uchitelle, *The Disposable American: Layoffs and Their Consequences* (New York: Knopf, 2006).

30. Louis Jacobson et al., "Should We Teach Old Dogs New Tricks?: The Impact of Community College Retraining on Older Displaced Workers" (WP 2003-25, Federal Reserve Bank of Chicago, 2003).

31. Gary Burtless, "Income Supports for Workers and Their Families: Earnings Supplements and Health Insurance," in *Reshaping Workforce Policies for a Changing Economy*, ed. H. Holzer and D. Nightingale (Washington, DC: Urban Institute Press, 2007).

32. Ibid.

PART FOUR

SHARING THE PROSPERITY THROUGH ASSET BUILDING

Poverty is more than insufficient income; it is also the lack of those household assets—savings, retirement accounts, stocks, home equity—that cushion the impact of emergencies, pave the way to a better life, and allow wealth to pass to the next generation. Yet the significance of these assets was long ignored in crafting solutions to poverty. Recently, however, some policymakers have embraced asset development as an important tool to combat poverty and to close the widening chasm between rich and poor.

Asset-fostering policies take various forms, but a few recurring themes emerge. First, these policies require a fundamental reformulation of how government redistributes wealth and to whom. A key question is whether such policies should be universal in application or targeted toward particular populations. Second, asset-based strategies to reduce poverty are eminently flexible and have a multitude of applications. Third, asset promotion is only one piece in a much larger poverty puzzle.

In "Reducing Wealth Disparities Through Asset Ownership" Melvin Oliver and Thomas Shapiro argue that four centuries of discriminatory governmental practices have yielded a legacy of low homeownership rates for minorities and gaps in access to affordable credit and banking systems. At the same time, asset-based policy in the tax code and elsewhere fosters asset acquisition by the middle class and the wealthy. They conclude that only a wholesale policy assault—including individual asset-based policies targeted toward the poor, programs that support regional equity, and progressive taxation—can reduce the racial wealth gap. In an inset to this chapter Michael

Barr suggests legislation that would establish tax credits for banks that offer low-cost accounts with debit cards. This would allow more people to access essential financial services and build assets.

In "Assets for All: Toward Universal, Progressive, Lifelong Accounts" Michael Sherraden describes the largely untapped potential of restricted-use savings plans, known as Individual Development Accounts (IDAs), to promote asset building. Small, short-term demonstrations targeted toward the poor show that IDA ownership confers a broad range of socioeconomic and personal benefits. Sherraden contends that IDAs cannot remain a limited, narrowly targeted program, but should encompass all Americans throughout their lives. In an inset to this chapter Peter Orszag outlines a mechanism to incentivize savings for retirement: 401(k) plans featuring automatic enrollment and contribution. He suggests expanding the number of these 401(k)s and creating automatic Individual Retirement Accounts (IRAs) for workers whose employers do not offer retirement plans.

Michael Stegman's chapter, "An Affordable Homeownership Strategy That Promotes Savings Rather Than Risk," observes that home equity is the largest source of wealth for many people, especially minorities and the poor. Stegman cautions that an emphasis on "no-down-payment" loans will lead to higher incidences of default and foreclosure. Instead, he proposes a one-two punch combining federally subsidized savings plans that help low-income households make a down payment with advances in the secondary market that make it easier for lenders to extend loans to low-income borrowers. In an inset to this chapter Martin Eakes supplies a dynamic illustration of a successful secondary-market program. An innovative partnership between Self-Help, a community development lender in North Carolina, and large banks showcases how new concepts can address old problems.

The Honorable Jack F. Kemp, in "The Role of the Entrepreneur in Combating Poverty," emphasizes the role of small business and entrepreneurship in fighting poverty. He points to the necessity of giving people access to capital and ownership of assets. Kemp identifies a variety of policies that are likely to help lift people out of poverty, including eliminating redlining and other barriers that prevent entrepreneurs and small businesses from acquiring the necessary capital; offering microfinancing; eliminating welfare rules that discourage people from working and saving; creating enterprise (or empowerment) zones that provide entrepreneurs with tax incentives and needed capital; and creating opportunities for homeownership and affordable housing.

Reducing Wealth Disparities Through Asset Ownership

Melvin L. Oliver and Thomas M. Shapiro

Until a few years ago most people thought that assets and income were essentially mirror images of one another.[1] The new understanding is that assets are conceptually distinct from income, and more important, assets play a unique role in poverty reduction. Assets are those resources that families and individuals use to strategize and navigate social mobility. They are the lumpy money needed to purchase an education, buy a home, and start a business. Income affords a level of consumption, a standard of living, while assets enable one to plan for and take advantage of opportunities. Income helps one get along; assets help one get ahead. Those truly interested in poverty reduction have to figure out how to increase the assets of the poor so they can truly take advantage of opportunities throughout their life course.

Asset inequality in America has been growing by leaps and bounds during the last 20 years. Today the net worth of the average American household (the value of all assets less any debts) is $59,706. However, many Americans own few assets. African Americans, for example, own only seven cents for every dollar of net worth that white Americans own; for Hispanics the figure is only slightly higher, nine cents for every dollar. The difference is starker for net financial assets, the liquid or cash assets available to a family. About one-quarter of all black and Hispanic families own no financial assets, compared with 6 percent of all white families.[2] This is magnified when one looks at the material context of the households in which children grow up. Nearly 9 out of 10 black households with children have financial assets that could not cushion three months of poverty-level resources. White children fare poorly on this indicator as well, with 45 percent of white households in a similar position.[3] This is the precarious position of millions of American households, especially those who are not only asset poor but also income poor.

For African Americans the issue of asset inequality is not only a marker of current economic hardship, but also the result of historically based policies and actions that have denied them the opportunity to develop and grow assets at the same rate as other American racial and ethnic groups. Racialized state policy, for example, has structured the opportunities that African Americans have had to acquire land, build community, and generate wealth.[4]

Slavery, the dominant state policy in reference to blacks for three hundred years, denied African Americans the opportunity to own property and to develop wealth. Considered legally the property of slaveholders, they were unable to enter into legal contracts to buy land, own a business, and develop wealth assets. Whites, even the most economically deprived, were, in contrast, "economic free agents" able to use the economic system in ways that enabled them to develop assets and wealth that could be passed down from generation to generation.

A major state policy that enabled millions of Americans to begin to accumulate wealth resources was the homestead laws that opened up the East and Southeast during colonial times and the West during the nineteenth century. These vast giveaways of land from public to private interests created vastly different opportunities for black and white settlers. While many whites were able to gain an economic foothold by moving to and working land in Indian country, blacks for the most part were denied that opportunity. As black homesteaders in California found, their claims were not legally enforceable. Thus the largest transfer of public lands into private hands was essentially a racialized transaction that left African Americans largely excluded.

Probably the largest set of state policies adversely affecting black wealth was, ironically, the reforms that grew out of the New Deal. For example, while Social Security is today one of the most progressive benefit programs, it did not begin that way. Initially the Social Security Act of 1935 excluded most African Americans and Latinos by exempting agricultural and domestic workers from coverage, along with other marginalized low-wage workers. Earning insufficient wages, African American workers were twice as likely as whites not to be covered by Social Security insurance. Likewise, the Supplementary Social Security Act laid the foundation for the basic program for mothers raising their children alone, Aid to Families with Dependent Children (AFDC), which for generations has restricted the ability of women who accepted their small cash transfers to develop assets. These asset tests led to a situation where AFDC recipients, particularly African American recipients, were subject to a state-sponsored policy to encourage and maintain asset poverty.

The major New Deal policy that has affected African American wealth was housing policy. While the New Deal creation of low-interest, long-term mortgages backed by the federal government was a major success story for most Americans, it did much to institutionalize vast differences in the net worth of the average black and the average white family. Policies discouraged loans to central cities and favored new construction and suburban locations. Furthermore, a formal and uniform system of appraisal was instituted that systematically denied loans to communities that were in the midst of racial transition, all-black, or "undesirable" and promoted and legitimated restrictive covenants that enabled homeowners to keep their communities all-white. Locked out of these homeownership opportunities, generations of African Americans were unable to pass down the massive home equity generated by this initial entry into the housing market.

This chapter analyzes the kinds of policies and institutional arenas that must be targeted in order to reduce the vast racial wealth disparities between blacks and whites. It focuses on four broad sets of policies: (1) homeownership, new mortgages, and credit markets; (2) individual asset policy; (3) regional equity; and (4) progressive taxation. These policies are important ways to close the racial wealth gap and to challenge the deeply embedded structures that create and maintain economic disadvantage and poverty in American society.

HOMEOWNERSHIP, NEW MORTGAGES, AND CREDIT MARKETS

Housing appreciation represents by far the largest reservoir of family financial wealth. As homes typically increase in value over time, homeownership has anchored the wealth-accumulation opportunities of most American families. Indeed, about two-thirds of the financial wealth of America's middle class is in home equity, not savings accounts, stocks, bonds, or businesses. To benefit from rising home equity, families must own homes, and the location of homes is key to housing appreciation. Homeownership rates have been rising, with more families able to afford down payments and closing costs, partly because of a massive extension of credit and new mortgage instruments to working, lower-income, and minority families previously shut out of home mortgage markets. Homeownership reached a historic high in 2004 when 69 percent of American families owned homes.[5]

Home equity plays an even greater role in the wealth portfolios of African American families, even though homeownership rates still lag 26 percentage points behind those of whites. Between 1996 and 2002 the typical African American homeowner saw his or her home increase $6,000 in value.[6] Yet home equity is fundamentally racialized, tracking residential segregation by holding appreciation rates down in minority and even in diverse neighborhoods, in effect creating a segregation tax that holds down wealth accumulation in highly segregated neighborhoods. For example, the typical home owned by whites increased $28,000 more than a similar home owned by blacks.[7] Residential segregation creates wealth for most homeowners but widens the racial wealth gap in the process.

For poor people, a comprehensive and progressive housing policy includes a spectrum of renting to owning that supports family stability, asset accumulation, and asset preservation. Homeownership is vital because of the use value of homes and because homeowners are more likely to become stakeholders and involved in improving their community.

In the mid-1990s much policy attention focused on access to credit. Subprime lending is a major new mortgage loan product essential to pushing homeownership rates to record levels by providing opportunities to prospective homebuyers with blemished credit histories or with high debt levels. Subprime loans increased 15-fold between 1994 and 2004, reflecting their meteoric rise as a share of the mortgage market; they represented less than 4 percent in 1995 and about 17 percent in 2004.[8] While this brought homeownership to millions of families, it came at a large price: higher interest rates, higher processing and closing fees, and often terms with prepayment penalties, balloon payments, and adjustable interest rates.

Given the cooling of the economy for most middle-class families after the late 1990s, and given that subprime lending terms often place Americans at greater risk for losing their homes, the ability of homeowners to pay mortgages in a timely fashion has become a private and public issue. Subprime loans with prepayment penalties face 20 percent greater odds of entering foreclosure than loans without such terms. Those with balloon payments face a 46 percent greater probability of entering foreclosure than those without such terms. Other terms also make these types of loans far riskier and families more likely to lose their homes. One in five of all first-lien subprime refinance loans originated in 1999 had entered foreclosure before 2004.[9] Although foreclosure rates are rising rapidly but are still in the low single digits, foreclosures are spatially concentrated; falling behind and losing one's home hits hardest in the most vulnerable neighborhoods. In Los Angeles, for example, between 2001 and 2004 over 14,000 families lost their homes. Furthermore, predominantly minority communities experienced foreclosure rates

12 times higher than more demographically balanced communities.[10] Los Angeles is part of an emerging national pattern.

Race and place play significant parts in this rapidly unfolding foreclosure drama. Whereas a little more than a decade ago blacks faced formidable obstacles to access to credit, now the policy issue concerns a new form of, and crisis resulting from, lending discrimination. Recent data indicate that blacks are three times as likely to confront riskier subprime lending terms. Much of the explanation for this is racial. When white and black testers with similar demographics and economic profiles applied for mortgages, the testing revealed a 45 percent rate of disparate treatment based on race.[11] Foreclosure, transparency, fair lending, and federal regulatory responsibility are central to policy debates regarding community building and closing the racial wealth gap.

The change in the financial landscape extends to how families make ends meet. Increasing numbers of African American and Hispanic families also are gaining access to credit via credit cards. Elizabeth Warren (see Chapter 3) provides a fuller discussion of issues around credit and debt. By 2001, 60 percent of African American families owned a credit card, compared with 45 percent just nine years earlier. However, this new access to consumer credit came under terms highly favorable to lenders, and debt became rampant, ensnaring millions of families in a debt trap. Among credit-card holders, nearly one in five African Americans earning under $50,000 spends at least 40 percent of his or her income paying debt service.[12] Even though black families carry smaller monthly credit-card balances than whites, a higher percentage of their financial resources go to paying off credit-card debt. Some might contend that this reflects conspicuous consumption, but it does not—spiraling health-care costs coupled with lower employer benefits for health care, rising housing costs, stagnating earnings, and increased employment instability are the main sources of credit-card debt.

Most Americans are connected to formal credit and banking systems, though about 8.4 million families lack a basic connection such as a checking account. Unbanked and underbanked poor families pay more for everyday financial services taken for granted by everybody else. In turn, they often are subjected to abusive practices. Simply cashing a payroll check at a check-cashing outlet or payday storefront costs a low-income worker approximately $250 annually. They also turn to tax-preparation services and costly refund loans, and they are without regular means to save. Establishing credit and short-term loans are especially expensive.[13] Finally, payday lending sets a vicious trap, because 9 of 10 payday loans go to repeat borrowers to help pay off the last high-interest, short-term loan, ensnaring about 5 million borrowers each year.[14]

BANKING THE POOR: OVERCOMING THE FINANCIAL SERVICES MISMATCH

Michael S. Barr

Low-income households often lack access to bank accounts and face high costs for transacting basic financial services through check cashers and other alternative financial service providers. Twenty-two percent of low- and moderate-income American households do not have a checking or savings account. Many other "underbanked" families have bank accounts but still rely on high-cost financial services.

These households find it more difficult to save and plan financially for the future. Living paycheck to paycheck leaves them vulnerable to medical or job emergencies that may endanger their financial stability, and lack of longer-term savings undermines their ability to improve skills, purchase a home, or send their children to college. High-cost financial services and inadequate access to bank accounts may undermine widely shared societal goals of reducing poverty, moving families from welfare to work, and rewarding work through the Earned Income Tax Credit.

The basic problem is our financial services mismatch: the mainstream financial system is not well designed to serve low- and moderate-income households. Traditional checking accounts often carry high account fees, high minimum balances, and high overdraft or insufficient-fund fees. Paper checks are held for a relatively long time before deposits are cleared. And millions of households who have had problems managing their accounts in the past are stuck in Chexsystem, a private clearinghouse used by most banks to block such individuals from opening new accounts.

The costs of financial exclusion are great. It is inefficient for the national economy. It is costly for low-income households. And it promotes dissaving rather than saving.

We need to shift our focus away from checking accounts and toward debit-card-based products and services that are lower cost and lower risk. Taking the paper check out of the equation and moving to direct deposit, ATM and point-of-sale withdrawals, and automatic money orders would lower costs and drive the risk of overdraft way down.

Congress should encourage the private sector to offer low-cost, electronically based bank account products with a new tax credit. The tax credit would be based on performance. Financial institutions could receive a tax credit equal to a fixed amount per account opened. Additionally, the credit could include a dollar-for-dollar incentive for banks to match the monthly savings contributions of low-income account holders, up to a fixed amount. Bank accounts with debit-card access, but no checks, could provide a means for lower-income households to receive their pay through direct deposit, pay their bills automatically, and set up regular savings plans as a cushion against emergencies.

It is time to transform financial services for the poor. Bank account ownership contributes to optimal income-redistribution policies because it increases the take-home pay of the low-wage working poor. Better access to financial services is critical for low-income persons seeking to enter the economic mainstream.[1]

NOTE

1. For further background, see Michael S. Barr, "Banking the Poor," *Yale Journal on Regulation* 21, no. 1 (2004): 121–237.

INDIVIDUAL ASSET POLICY

Individual asset policy is an important policy arena for reducing racial wealth disparities. For generations certain policies in the United States have helped provide resources to support the aspiring middle class and well-to-do Americans build assets. As we discussed, the array of homestead acts greatly facilitated the building of America's middle class. Land-grant colleges, Veterans Administration benefits, the GI Bill of Rights, and mortgage interest deductions also provide important asset-building foundations. It is hard to imagine that many Americans would have been able to plan for the future, buy homes, prepare for retirement, send their children to college, and weather unexpected financial storms without access to these important asset-building resources. The magnitude of direct and indirect governmental resources devoted to these resources is startling. Through the tax code that allows individuals and families lower rates or to exclude taxable earnings, the taxpayers financed $335 billion worth of asset policies for the nonpoor in fiscal year 2003, most of which accrued to wealthy families.[15]

The kind of individual asset-based social policy that will affect racial wealth disparities must be directed to poor individuals and families to help them build assets, just as the government subsidized the movement of the World War II generation into the middle class and homeownership and helped the well-off consolidate their wealth.[16] The major policy tool to accomplish this has revolved around various configurations of individual development accounts (IDAs).

Asset-based social policy attempts to facilitate savings and the accumulation of financial assets for low-income families and the poor who are usually excluded from traditional asset-building opportunities. Although asset-based social policy is still in its infancy, it has become a widely discussed policy tool and has a fairly impressive set of achievements. Michael Sherraden, the major architect of IDAs, discusses this policy in Chapter 12.

The concept of IDAs has increasingly morphed into a comprehensive set of supports to asset building over the life course. Children's Savings Accounts, for example, would enable youth to enter young adulthood with a sizable asset that they can use for education or homeownership, while traditional IDAs would help families hoping to pay for a home or their children's higher education, and retirement accounts would enable seniors to have greater independence and control over their financial life in their twilight years. (President Clinton proposed Universal Savings Accounts in his 1999 State of the Union address.)

Supporters insist that all these accounts must be universal yet progressive. Universality enables the program to create broad-scale social support that a poverty-focused program would have difficulty garnering. Including progressivity in the design of these programs would enable them to provide significantly more resources to the poor. For example, matches would be provided for contributions by low-income households. This would enable them to generate greater rates of savings and asset accumulation than those without matches. To the degree that African Americans and Latinos are disproportionately consigned to the lower classes, they would theoretically be eligible to build assets at a faster rate and thus reduce, but certainly not close, the racial wealth gap. These mechanisms have demonstrated significant potential to begin the process of asset building that can launch families on the road to economic success and stability, even if by themselves IDAs may not reduce wealth inequality.

While these policies are gaining legitimacy and policy traction in a short period, they face innumerable obstacles. So far, these programs have been implemented on a small scale, in terms of hundreds or thousands of participants. To make a difference, they must be implemented on a large scale, with millions of participants. However, these programs require significant funding that is unlikely in the current budget context. For example, a Children's Savings Account that would provide every child with a $1,000 account at birth and create the opportunity for the accumulation of up to $18,000 by age 18 would cost approximately $30 billion a year. Moreover, there is no definable political constituency that has made individual asset building a prime focus of its energies.

REGIONAL EQUITY

Racial segregation has traditionally been a limiting factor in the ability of African Americans to grow wealth. Segregation imposes a further "tax" on minorities—particularly African Americans—that is driven by underfunded communities, poor schools, and economic isolation (see Angela Glover Blackwell's discussion in Chapter 19).

Individual communities cannot reduce racial inequalities alone. The region should be the focus of action, the only entity with sufficient economic resources and political power to address these tough problems. As john powell puts it, "The community's work is on target, but the dynamics of inequality are region-sized."[17]

Regional solutions would directly attack racial segregation, isolation from jobs, and poor schools. If inner-city communities increase the economic and racial diversity of their communities, create economic opportunities for low-income residents to connect to the job-rich suburbs, and create a functioning and attractive public school system, the value of housing assets would likely increase, helping reduce the insidious processes that thwart the development of wealth among black inner-city households.

Some regional strategies that have been successful include inclusive zoning to increase the supply of affordable housing across a metropolitan region; transportation policies that connect isolated inner-city communities with job-rich suburbs and exurbs; and innovative approaches to educational equity that break down racially isolated schools, enable equal funding across regions or districts, and promote small schools that are anchored in neighborhoods. These are among the menu of regional strategies that could help stop the continued devaluation of the assets of many African Americans.

PROGRESSIVE TAXATION AND ASSET BUILDING

How are we going to pay for great ideas of asset building and bring them to scale, especially considering all the pressing issues and big-ticket items facing our nation, such as health care, the minimum wage, housing, or education? Rather than thinking about this question in terms of contending worthy needs jockeying for pieces of the pie, a brief examination of asset building in America's history and current social investments is instructive. This perspective allows for broader horizons for asset policy and opportunities to strengthen coalition building rather than promoting turf battles or fighting about what need or crisis deserves most attention.

In the United States one major avenue of social mobility and economic success has been policies and practices that provide resources to middle-class and well-to-do Americans to build assets. At critical times these structured opportunities served as indispensable springboards for mass mobility. Various policies have greatly facilitated building America's middle class, especially in acquiring homes, property, and businesses, sending young adults and veterans to college, planning for their future, and building a financial assets foundation: homestead acts, land-grant colleges, Veterans Administration benefits, the GI Bill of Rights, mortgage interest tax deductions, and others. However, if one examined only direct government expenditures, the social investments that enabled middle-class success would be hidden.

Similar policies abound today, etched in the tax code, largely out of view of public understanding and awareness. For example, the national social investment in housing is not primarily targeted at affordable housing or concerned with housing for low-income families; instead, the greater social investment is aimed at subsidizing homeownership through mortgage interest tax deductions, which highly favor families at upper-income levels. In other areas, too, the great magnitude of government assistance for asset acquisition and growth benefits those who already own property or businesses and/or those at the highest income levels. As previously noted, in aggregate, the public funded $335 billion worth of asset policies for the nonpoor in 2003, using conservative estimates. This wealth budget dwarfs direct government expenditures that encourage asset building for most American families. CFED's[18] analysis highlights how our nation invests $1 in direct expenditures for asset development at the same time it invests $642 to encourage and reward asset building through the tax code. Federal policies exacerbate wealth inequality and help widen the racial wealth gap by their top-heavy and lopsided distribution scheme.

The news has not improved over the past couple of years, as CFED's preliminary analysis for 2006 demonstrates that the wealth budget has risen to about $362 billion and the distribution has gotten more lopsided and top heavy. Families with incomes over $1 million, roughly 1 percent of the population, received 45 percent of the wealth budget benefits. Those in the top fifth (income of over $80,000) of the income distribution took in about 88 percent of these benefits.

The budget that builds wealth needs to become a contested terrain, not the entitled province of the well-to-do. Good asset-building lessons, best practices, and effective social investment cases can be drawn from how the wealth budget has operated in the American experience. The absolutely vital focal point needs to be how to spread effective asset-building incentives to families that are struggling or just making ends meet, as well as to groups that have been systematically excluded from these opportunities in the past. A modest goal might be to increase the percentage share of the benefits accruing to 60 percent of families from the current meager 3 percent to 10 percent in the next decade. Capping the home mortgage interest deduction and limiting it to primary residence is a worthy reform. Allowing a flat deduction for families who cannot or do not itemize deductions is another among a host of reforms to more equitably distribute asset-building opportunities written into the tax code.

This broader context of spreading asset-building opportunities to broad sectors of the population, that is, democratization of the wealth budget, provides a different sense of how government invests in individuals, families, businesses, and communities. Fairness in distribution of tax benefits is an anchoring theme for progressive taxation, in addition to the traditional concern of who is taxed at what rate. Taxing corporate profits, capital gains, investment earnings, dividends, and other ways that money expands itself over taxing work and earning itself provides a principal direction for progressive tax policy.

Many resources already exist, and this section identified deep sources of resources to pay for big-ticket asset-generating initiatives such as Children's Saving Aaccounts or first-time homeownership accounts. Other areas can be targeted for reform. An obvious candidate is to reform the estate tax in a way that simultaneously is fairer (thresholds and exemptions) and engages public support and that links it to providing opportunities to new generations of Americans.[19] Most relevant are reforms structured around reasonable exemptions grounded in a philosophy that passing along great advantages and wealth runs against the deep American spirit of fairness, equality, new starts, and opportunity. Equal opportunity and a level playing field for all cannot thrive side by side with great inherited wealth.

CONCLUSION

The racial asset gap threatens to permanently consign large portions of the African American population and other racial minorities to lives with restricted opportunities. In a society that is increasingly privatizing citizenship by making access to good education and health care more and more a function of wealth, these racial disparities in asset holdings mean less opportunity for social mobility and secure lives than ever before. The proposals just discussed will in no way equalize asset holdings, but they will lessen the gap in significant ways. These proposals will help better connect African Americans and the poor to the mainstream credit system and markets and enable the poor to save and accumulate assets that they can use to purchase a home, pursue education, or start a business; connect them to their regional economies so that they have access to jobs, quality education, and racially and economically diverse communities; and enable the federal government to invest not only in the asset-building opportunity of the rich and well-off, but also of the poor and least advantaged. These proposals place closing the racial wealth gap at the forefront of the civil rights agenda of the twenty-first century.

NOTES

1. With the publication of *Assets and the Poor* by Michael Sherraden (Armonk, NY: M.E. Sharpe, 1991), *Black Wealth/White Wealth: A New Perspective on Racial Inequality* (New York: Routledge, 1995, 2006) by Melvin Oliver and Thomas Shapiro, and *Being Black, Living in the Red* by Dalton Conley (Berkeley: University of California Press, 1999), the notion that assets and wealth are important and independent elements of economic status was firmly established.

2. Rakesh Kochhar, "The Wealth of Hispanic Households, 1996 to 2002" (Pew Hispanic Center, 2004).

3. Thomas Shapiro, *The Hidden Cost of Being African American* (New York: Oxford University Press, 2004), 36–41.

4. Oliver and Shapiro, *Black Wealth/White Wealth*.

5. Joint Center for Housing Studies of Harvard University, *State of the Nation's Housing 2004* (Cambridge, MA: Harvard University, 2004).

6. Kochhar, "Wealth of Hispanic Households."

7. Shapiro, *Hidden Cost of Being African American*.

8. Joint Center for Housing Studies of Harvard University, *State of the Nation's Housing*.

9. Roberto Querica et al., "The Impact of Predatory Loan Terms on Subprime Foreclosures" (Center for Community Capitalism, 2005).

10. Mark Duda and William Apgar, "Mortgage Foreclosure Trends in Los Angeles: Patterns and Policy Issues" (report prepared for Los Angeles Neighborhood Housing Services, 2004).

11. National Community Reinvestment Coalition, "Pre-approvals and Pricing Disparities in the Mortgage Marketplace" (June 2005).

12. Javier Silva, "A House of Cards: Financing the American Dream" (Demos, January 9, 2005); Tamara Draut and Javier Silva, "Borrowing to Make Ends Meet: The Growth of Credit Card Debt in the 90s" (Demos, 2003).

13. Michael Barr, "Banking the Poor," *Yale Journal on Regulation* 21 (Winter 2004): 121–237.

14. Keith Erns et al., "Quantifying the Economic Cost of Predatory Payday Lending: A Report from the Center for Responsible Lending" (Center for Responsible Lending, February 24, 2004).

15. Center for Enterprise Development, "Hidden in Plain Sight" (2004); Christopher Howard, *The Hidden Welfare State* (Princeton: Princeton University Press, 1997).

16. Trina Williams Shanks, "The Homestead Act: A Major Asset-Building Policy in American History," in Michael Sherraden and Lisa Morris, *Inclusion in the American Dream* (New York: Oxford University Press, 2006).

17. john powell, "Racism and Metropolitan Dynamics: The Civil Rights Challenge of the 21st Century" (briefing paper prepared for the Ford Foundation, Institute on Race and Poverty, August 2002), 5.

18. CFED was formerly known as the Corporation for Enterprise Development.

19. Oliver and Shapiro, *Black Wealth/White Wealth*, Tenth Anniversary Edition (New York: Routledge, 2006); William Gates, Sr. and Chuck Collins, *Wealth and Our Commonwealth: Why America Should Tax Accumulated Fortunes* (Boston: Beacon Press, 2002).

Assets for All:
Toward Universal, Progressive,
Lifelong Accounts

Michael Sherraden

Over the past two decades I have been thinking about asset accumulation as a key for development of all families, rich and poor alike. In 1991 I proposed asset-building accounts called Individual Development Accounts (IDAs), above and beyond the current Social Security system. IDAs would include everyone, provide greater support for the poor, begin as early as birth, and be used for key development and social protection goals across the lifespan such as education, homeownership, business capitalization, and retirement security in later life. IDAs have instead been implemented in the form of a short-term "demonstration" program targeted toward the poor. We have learned a great deal in this demonstration process, but it is time now to return to the larger vision, which can be described simply as assets for all.[1]

HISTORY AND CONTEXT

We have emerged from the twentieth century with welfare states that were designed for an industrial era. The original idea was that if families were not earning wages in industrial labor markets, then social policy would support them during any period of unemployment, disability, or retirement, or if a wage earner died, his children would be protected. This notion of income support when not employed is the basic idea of social policy as we came to understand it in the twentieth century. This is a very large and important idea. Even in the United States, which does not have the most generous set of social policies, income support (mostly in cash and health care) is about half of the federal budget. In a fiscal sense, modern states are, first and foremost, income-transfer mechanisms.

This simple income-support idea is outdated. The relatively low-skilled, long-term, and stable jobs of the industrial era are increasingly rare. Enhanced knowledge and skills are required for employment today, and employment transitions are more and more necessary. Continual retraining or gaining new skills throughout life will be required for most workers. With these changes in labor markets, and many other social and economic changes, the income-support theme of industrial-era social policy is no longer fully adequate. As a result, there is considerable political pressure on current policies.

Mostly this is discussed in ideological or political terms, but the basic issue is not ideological. Economies are changing, and many existing social policies do not fit the modern context. Related to this is a near revolution in the way social policies are being delivered. This is most evident in retirement policies. Many countries are moving toward individual account systems. In these social policies people are holding their own resources and are more in control of their "social welfare."

Examples of U.S. asset-based policies include homeownership tax benefits; investment tax benefits; defined-contribution retirement accounts with tax benefits at the workplace, such as 401(k)s and 403(b)s (named after sections of the Internal Revenue Code); and defined-contribution accounts away from the workplace, such as Individual Retirement Accounts (IRAs) and Roth IRAs. Other asset accounts with tax benefits include Individual Training Accounts, Educational Savings Accounts, State College Savings (529) plans, and Medical Savings Accounts. These asset-based policies in the United States are growing rapidly. Individual account policies have all appeared since 1970, and more variations appear all the time.

The problem is that these new policies are leaving a lot of people behind. Defined-contribution systems are serving the top of the income distribution and leaving people out at the bottom. One of the reasons for this is that these new policy systems are very much tied to income—the more income you have, the more money will go into these accounts, and public subsidies for these accounts, which operate through tax benefits, are tied to income in a regressive way. The larger your income, the greater your tax subsidy. The United States spends over $300 billion annually in tax expenditures for asset building, and over 90 percent of this goes to households with incomes over $50,000 per year.[2] If there is a "nanny state," asset building is taking care only of people at the top—and spending far more on this than on all the "welfare" programs for the poor combined.

Why does that matter? Other than the fact that large numbers of people have meager resources and little social protection, why should we care? We should care for several reasons. One is that asset accumulation and investment are the way that households develop. Families need to save in order to acquire an education, buy a house, own a small business, or make other investments that will improve their circumstances. This is the way in which families enhance their well-being over time and across generations—one generation accumulates assets and passes this wealth to the next generation.

Indeed, Americans have always known this. Property ownership is a fundamental American value. It goes back all the way to Thomas Jefferson, who believed that small property ownership was the bedrock of the democracy.

What we did with social policies for the poor, in the welfare-state era, was to forget that asset accumulation is essential to family development. Worse, we set up barriers to this accumulation. If you received a means-tested income benefit, you were actually not permitted to accumulate more than minimal savings and assets, or you lost eligibility for your benefit. This is the most counterproductive policy idea imaginable. This dual policy on asset building—subsidies for asset building at the top and penalties at the bottom—is not merely unfair, it is unproductive. Current policy is standing in the way of people reaching their potential, which means that they also undercontribute to the economy and society.

THE MEANING OF ASSET-BASED POLICY

The term "assets" has many potential meanings. These include financial wealth, tangible property, human capital, social capital, political participation and influence, cultural capital, and natural resources. Although all of these meanings have value, I focus on meanings of assets that have direct relevance for public policy.

Public policy cannot do all things well. Policy is most successful in simple, large-scale tasks. More complex and particular tasks are often better left to communities and families. When one considers asset building in the context of public policy, it is wise to focus on building financial wealth for the purpose of household social and economic development. This is something that public policy can do simply and effectively, with measurable outcomes.

Income (as a proxy for consumption) has been the standard definition of poverty in social policy. To be sure, income and consumption are essential, but they do not improve long-term conditions. Development of families and communities—that is, reaching potential—occurs through asset accumulation and investment.[3]

Today there is increasing questioning of income as the sole definition of poverty and well-being. Amartya Sen and others are looking toward capabilities. Asset-based policy can be seen as part of this larger discussion. Asset holding is one measure of long-term capabilities.[4] As public policy, asset building is a form of "social investment."[5] Asset-based policy would shift social policy from an almost exclusive focus on maintenance toward a focus on development of individuals, families, and communities. In this sense, asset-based policy is an explicit complement to income-based policy.

This is not to say that there is no role for social insurance. Indeed, the right idea is to balance asset-based policy with social insurance, supplemented by means-tested assistance where necessary. As I have testified before the President's Commission to Strengthen Social Security, if there are to be individual accounts, these should be above and beyond the existing Social Security system.[6]

The goal of asset-based policy should be inclusion. By inclusion I mean that policy should bring everyone into asset-based policy; make asset-based policy lifelong and flexible; provide at least equal public subsidies for the poor in dollar terms; and achieve adequate levels of asset accumulation, given the purposes of the policy.

POLICY PROGRESS

My first insight for this thinking came during my discussions with "welfare" mothers during the 1980s. These women said that they could not "get anywhere" because they could not accumulate resources for long-term goals such as better housing, education, or starting a small business.

These discussions led to my proposal for IDAs, and since that time there has been modest policy progress in the United States. There were increases in welfare asset limits in nearly all states during the 1990s. IDAs were included as a state option in the 1996 Welfare Reform Act. The federal Assets for Independence Act, the first public IDA demonstration, became law in 1998. Other legislation to extend IDAs is before the U.S. Congress.[7] Over 40 states have adopted some type of IDA policy.[8] All of this signals a change in thinking, but not yet a major change in policy. Most IDA programs in the United States are very small.

Perhaps the most important contribution to date is that saving and asset accumulation by the poor, which was seldom discussed 15 years ago, is today a mainstream idea in the United States with bipartisan support. Both Republicans and Democrats use the language of "asset building," "asset-based policy," "stakeholding," and "ownership society." The policy environment is bubbling with variations on this theme. Innovations are being proposed for universal 401(k)s and savings accounts for all children.

Research on IDAs at the Center for Social Development at Washington

University in St. Louis (CSD) has had some impact on policy development elsewhere, including the Saving Gateway and Child Trust Fund in the United Kingdom,[9] Family Development Accounts in Taipei,[10] IDAs and the Learn$ave demonstration in Canada,[11] and matched savings programs for the poor in Australia, Uganda, Peru, China, and elsewhere. Indonesia and South Korea have proposed, but not yet funded, legislation for IDA demonstrations.

THEORY, EVIDENCE, AND POLICY DIRECTIONS

Two basic ideas underlie this research. The first is that saving and asset accumulation are shaped by policy and program features, not merely individual preferences. CSD's research on IDAs has identified the following factors that may affect saving and asset accumulation: access, expectations, information, incentives, facilitation, restrictions, and security.[12] These constructs appear to be useful in explaining saving outcomes, and they have direct relevance for policy. For example, the monthly saving target (expectation) is associated with a 40- to 50-cent increase in average saving for every dollar the target is increased—a huge effect. Financial education (information) up to about 10 hours is associated with increased saving performance, but after 10 hours there appears to be no effect. Because financial education is expensive, this is important to know. Increasing the savings match (incentive) keeps people saving in the IDA program, but among the "savers" does not increase amounts saved. This result is very similar to findings in research on 401(k)s. Direct deposit (facilitation) also keeps people saving but among "savers" does not increase amounts saved.[13] These findings have direct policy implications for savings targets, financial education, match rates, and direct deposit.[14]

Another important research result is that IDA participants see the program as an opportunity (access) that they would not otherwise have, because few are offered retirement plans at work. In a focus group one potential IDA participant said, "I get it. This is like a 401(k), only for us." We find that IDA participants like the fact that their matched savings account is "off limits" and can be used only for specific purposes (restrictions), even though this is contrary to mainstream economic theory, which assumes that people prefer as much choice as possible.[15] These and other results from IDA research have direct relevance for savings policy, program, and product design.

The second idea is that assets have multiple positive effects beyond deferred consumption. To take one example, homeownership not only creates financial equity in housing, but also more stable and committed citizens. Theory regarding effects of asset holding, when specified and supported by evidence, has the potential to provide a solid rationale for inclusive asset-based policy.

The possible effects of asset holding may be to improve household stability, create orientation toward the future, stimulate enhancement of assets, enable focus and specialization, provide a foundation for risk taking, increase personal efficacy, increase social connectedness and influence, increase political participation, and enhance the well-being of offspring.[16] A broad range of research in economics, sociology, political science, anthropology, and social work provides evidence generally in support of these propositions.[17]

In a study of "the asset effect" using the longitudinal National Child Development Study in the United Kingdom, researchers found that holding assets at age 23 is associated with later positive outcomes such as better labor-market experience, marriages, health, health behaviors, and political interest. This generally supports the "multiple positive effects" perspective on asset holding. These researchers also find that the presence of an asset appears to matter more than the monetary value of the asset. This latter finding raises theoretical, measurement, and policy issues that are important. For example, if the presence of a housing asset matters most, then policy should encourage homeownership as early in adult life as possible.[18]

Looking at the impact of wealth on child developmental outcomes, another study found that parental wealth is positively associated with cognitive development, physical health, and socioemotional behavior of children. This supports the proposition that assets lead to improved well-being of offspring above and beyond economic well-being. The study finds that the effects occur even among very income-poor families, and that wealth seems to be a better predictor of well-being as children grow older (while income is a better predictor when they are younger). This last finding suggests that "asset effects" are a long-term phenomenon, perhaps not easily measured in the short term.[19]

In a study of assets, expectations, and educational performance, researchers reported that low-income single mothers' assets are positively associated with children's educational attainment. These results occur in part because of the educational expectations of the mother: assets are associated with higher educational expectations, which are in turn associated with higher educational attainment. This study supports a cognitive theory of "asset effects," wherein assets may change thinking, which in turn may change behavioral outcomes. Also, although income is associated with educational achievement when assets are not considered, it becomes nonsignificant when assets are included. This finding suggests that much prior research on effects of economic resources on well-being may be underspecified when assets are not included in the regression models.[20]

Among examples from applied research on IDAs, results of the American Dream Demonstration (ADD) have been illuminating.[21] One of the most important findings in ADD is that, controlling for many other individual and program variables, income was only weakly associated with saving outcomes; that is, the poorest participants saved about as much as those who were not as poor, and saved a higher proportion of their income.[22] This finding suggests that saving by the very poor should not be dismissed in public policy.

Additionally, in-depth interviews with IDA participants and controls revealed that IDA participants could "see more clearly" and "better visualize a future" than they could before IDAs. IDA programs are said to "create goals and purpose" and provide a "way to reach goals."[23] These findings also support the cognitive approach to understanding "asset effects" described earlier.

Experimental results from ADD indicate that IDA participants increased their rate of homeownership and total assets compared with a randomly assigned control group. Positive effects appear to be stronger for African Americans, perhaps because past discrimination in homeownership has led to greater demand.[24] These results may suggest that IDAs can move people into asset holding, though effects on net worth are less clear.[25] Finally, ongoing CSD research suggests that IDA participants experience positive social outcomes in marriage and household relationships.

This body of research is contributing to a change in thinking about poverty and policy. The idea of inclusive asset building is now common in U.S. policy discussions. This is apparent in proposals for expanded IDAs and many other ideas and proposals for asset building. While we are far short of a large, inclusive policy, this discussion is not speculative. For example, President Clinton proposed Universal Savings Accounts (USAs) in 1999 and again in 2000:

> Tens of millions of Americans live from paycheck to paycheck. As hard as they work, they still don't have the opportunity to save. Too few can make use of IRAs and 401(k) plans. We should do more to help all working families save and accumulate wealth. That's the idea behind the Individual Development Accounts, the IDAs. We ask you to take that idea to a new level, with new retirement savings accounts that enable every low- and moderate-income family in America to save for retirement, a first home, a medical emergency, or a college education. We propose to match their contributions, however small, dollar for dollar, every year they save.[26]

The USA proposal is like a 401(k) for all workers, with deposits and matching funds for those with lowest incomes. Current proposals for automatic 401(k)s and IRAs by Peter Orszag and others (see inset) follow in this policy tradition.

MAKING SAVING EASIER:
THE AUTOMATIC 401(K) AND
AUTOMATIC INDIVIDUAL
RETIREMENT ACCOUNT (IRA)

Peter Orszag

To help workers save for retirement, the government provides incentives for individuals to invest in 401(k) plans at the workplace and IRAs held at financial institutions. These 401(k)s and IRAs are not only retirement accounts, they are also key asset-building tools, since they can be tapped for various preretirement needs.

Unfortunately, few moderate- and low-income households utilize 401(k)s and IRAs. According to data from the Federal Reserve's Survey of Consumer Finances, half of all households headed by adults aged 55 to 59 had $15,000 or less in an employer-based 401(k)-type plan or tax-preferred savings plan account.[1] In 2004 less than 2.1 percent of households with cash income below $40,000 a year contributed to an IRA.[2] Automatic 401(k)s and automatic IRAs would make these accounts more effective for most households.

With the typical 401(k)-type plan, workers must choose whether to participate, how much to contribute, which of the investment vehicles offered by the employer to select, and when to pull the funds out of the plan and in what form. Many people shy away from these difficult decisions and do not participate. Those who do participate often make poor choices.

The automatic 401(k) recognizes the power of inertia in human behavior and enlists it to promote rather than hinder saving. Under an automatic 401(k), each of the key events in the process—enrollment, escalation, investment, and rollover—occurs without requiring worker decision making, thus removing a significant barrier to participation. Workers who prefer to control their own accounts can choose to opt out of the automatic design.

The automatic 401(k) has proved remarkably effective. Participation rates for newly hired moderate-income workers jump from under 15 percent to 80 percent when automatic enrollment is introduced.[3] Yet the majority of 401(k) plans still lack this feature. The 2006 Pension Protection Act clears the way for more companies to adopt the automatic 401(k) approach by removing legal barriers that had previously dampened interest in them.[4] With these concerns alleviated, companies are free to make the switch to an automatic 401(k); John Edwards and Jack Kemp have launched an effort to encourage them to do so.

Automatic IRAs are the second way to make saving easier. Since only about half of the workforce (and even less of the low-income workforce) is offered a 401(k) each year, automatic IRAs give workers an alternative to employer-based plans. As with the 401(k), the automatic nature of the IRA applies at each relevant step—enrollment, escalation, and investment; workers can choose to override the IRA defaults at any stage. The automatic IRA could also receive part of a household's tax refund each year. The IRS refund is the largest single payment that many households receive all year. The more than $200 billion issued annually in individual income tax refunds presents a unique opportunity to increase personal saving.[5]

Both the United Kingdom and New Zealand are rapidly moving to universal automatic retirement savings accounts.[6] The United States should also. Moderate- and low-income households would benefit substantially.

NOTES

1. Peter R. Orszag, J. Mark Iwry, and William G. Gale, eds., *Aging Gracefully: Ideas to Improve Retirement Security in America* (Century Foundation and Retirement Security Project, 2006).

2. Esther Duflo et al., "Saving Incentives for Low- and Middle-Income Families: Evidence from a Field Experiment with H&R Block," available online at http://www.brook.edu/views/papers/20050509galeorszag.htm.

3. Brigitte Madrian and Dennis Shea, "The Power of Suggestion: Inertia in 401(k) Participation and Savings Behavior," *Quarterly Journal of Economics* 116, no. 4 (November 2001), 1149–87.

4. For a scorecard on the automatic 401(k) aspects of the legislation, see "Analysis of the Pension Protection Act of 2006, Increasing Participation Through the Automatic 401(k) and Saver's Credit," http://www.retirementsecurityproject.org/img/File/RSP_Scorecard.Final.final-1.pdf?PHPSESSID=52405ba9a3ed01e8fe5a40f453cf9ed8.

5. For tax year 2003, the IRS issued $220 billion in refunds. See "IRS Tax Stats at a Glance," http://www.irs.gov/taxstats/article/0,,id=102886,00.html.

6. J. Mark Iwry, "Automating Saving: Making Retirement Saving Easier in the US, the UK, and New Zealand" (Policy Brief No. 2006-2, Retirement Security Project, June 2006).

THE POTENTIAL OF CHILDREN'S
DEVELOPMENT ACCOUNTS

A key to asset accumulation is time. Asset-building policy makes the most sense across a lifetime, beginning with children.[27] In this regard, the visionary and bipartisan ASPIRE Act, which would create a savings account for every newborn in the United States, was introduced in Congress in 2004 and is under consideration.[28]

A similar discussion of asset-based policy began in the United Kingdom in 2000.[29] In April 2001 Prime Minister Tony Blair proposed a Child Trust

Fund for all children in the United Kingdom, with progressive funding. He also proposed a demonstration of a Saving Gateway, with matched saving for the poor.[30] In April 2003 Blair announced that he would go forward with the Child Trust Fund. Beginning in April 2005, each newborn child, retrospective to children born from September 2002, is given an account. The children receive an initial deposit of at least 250 pounds, with children in the bottom third of family income receiving 500 pounds. Additional government deposits are not yet specified.[31] The Child Trust Fund provides universal and progressive contributions to the child's account.

Universal and progressive accounts for all children at birth have been proposed in the United States by several policy scholars.[32] Children's Development Accounts (CDAs) may be a promising pathway to inclusive asset building in the United States, one of the few economically advanced nations without a children's allowance (monthly cash payment to all families with children). The average children's allowance in Western Europe is 1.8 percent of GDP. For ideological and political reasons the United States is unlikely to adopt a children's allowance; however, a CDA is ideologically and politically much more feasible. Even 0.1 percent of U.S. GDP would be enough for a $2,500 start-in-life account for every newborn.[33]

The Ford Foundation and several other foundations are now in the process of demonstrating and testing an inclusive CDA in the form of the Saving for Education, Entrepreneurship, and Downpayment (SEED) initiative. SEED is a demonstration and research partnership among CFED,[34] CSD, the New America Foundation, the Institute for Financial Security of the Aspen Institute, and others. The goal of SEED is to model, test, and inform a universal CDA policy for the United States.[35]

The potential of CDAs as a long-term pathway to inclusive asset building may be great. First, lifetime accumulation and compounded earnings will lead to greater asset accumulation. Second, it is likely that having an account from birth will create positive psychological and behavioral effects for both parents and children. Third, there are very important reasons to save for education and homeownership, in addition to retirement; education and homeowning are ultimately retirement strategies as well. Finally, newborns are in some ways more politically appealing than adults. Investing in children can be a bipartisan effort, even in these very partisan times (as evidenced by the strong bipartisan support for the ASPIRE Act).

TOWARD INCLUSION

The greatest challenge in asset-based policy is inclusion. Creating an inclusive asset-based policy will require visionary leadership, raising asset building to the level of a long-term national project. This project would be, in the most basic sense, creation of a universal system of accounts, an infrastructure to promote asset accumulation. This is perhaps analogous to creation of a national system of highways to promote transportation. Once the infrastructure is in place, development will occur.[36] Political leaders and planners must understand asset building in these expansive terms. Once established, such a policy would likely generate strong political support, as the Central Provident Fund has in Singapore,[37] and as is likely to happen with the Child Trust Fund in the United Kingdom.

Asset accounts are ideally suited to the twenty-first century economy because of their greater individual control, choice, and portability. The continuing development of information-age financial services will be critical to asset-based policy by increasing feasibility and reducing risks.

If saving and asset building are to be inclusive, the policy must be in the form of a savings plan, such as a 401(k) or 403(b) plan, the Federal Thrift Savings Plan, or a College Savings (529) plan. Such plans are in fact how most Americans are able to save.

Savings plans (contractual savings) have important features that lend themselves to inclusion. These features are centralized and efficient accounting, outreach and education, a limited number of low-cost investment options, low initial and ongoing deposit requirements, automatic deposits, and opportunities to establish other practices and "defaults" that increase saving performance. These include automatic enrollment, savings match, match cap (amount of savings that can be matched), a default low-cost fund, and automatic increases in savings deposits with pay raises. During the payout period a required minimum annuitization may be desirable for income protection.[38] For these reasons the ASPIRE Act calls for a plan structure something like the Federal Thrift Savings Plan.

At the Center for Social Development we think that there is also potential in using College Savings (529) plans as a platform for inclusion in asset building, especially for Children's Development Accounts. To be sure, some state 529 plans are undesirable because of high fees and high investment costs. But other state 529 plans keep costs low, have very low deposit requirements, provide outreach to state residents, and match savings for the poorest savers. These state plans, or something like them, have the potential to be a platform for inclusive CDAs.[39]

CONCLUSION

The considerable policy advantages of asset building are that it is simple and clear, is easy to communicate, has widespread appeal and acceptance, and is flexible and adaptable; outcomes are relatively easy to measure; and multiple positive outcomes are likely.

The basic principles for an inclusive asset-based policy are that it should be universal (bring everyone into asset-based policy), fair (at least the same subsidies for the poor),[40] lifelong (birth to death and flexible across the life course), and adequate (sufficient assets for family security and development).

If properly designed as an inclusive and low-cost savings plan, an asset-based policy would be a large-scale public good. All citizens could benefit. The policy could drive asset accumulation in households, spur economic development, and create more engaged citizens for many decades into the future. This is not far-fetched. A transition to asset-based policy is already under way and will likely continue. The major challenge is to have the vision and commitment to include everyone and the policy wisdom to use a savings plan to do so.

NOTES

1. This chapter is adapted in part from the following: Michael Sherraden, "Inclusion in Asset Building," Testimony at Hearing on Building Assets for Low-Income Families, Subcommittee on Social Security and Family Policy, Finance Committee, U.S. Senate, April 28, 2005; "Assets, Poverty, and Public Policy," (speech at Sydney Institute, Australia, 2005); interview on "Ownership Society," *Weekend Edition* with Scott Simon, NPR News, February 5, 2005.

2. Michael Sherraden, *Assets and the Poor: A New American Welfare Policy* (Armonk, NY: M.E. Sharpe, 1991); Christopher Howard, *The Hidden Welfare State: Tax Expenditures and Social Policy in the United States* (Princeton: Princeton University Press, 1997); Laurence Seidman, "Assets and the Tax Code," in *Assets for the Poor: The Benefits of Spreading Asset Ownership*, ed. Thomas M. Shapiro and Edward N. Wolff (New York: Russell Sage Foundation, 2001), 324–56; Corporation for Enterprise Development, *Hidden in Plain Sight: A Look at the $335 Billion Federal Asset-Building Budget* (Washington, DC: Corporation for Enterprise Development, 2004).

3. Sherraden, *Assets and the Poor.*

4. Amartya Sen, "Capability and Well-Being," in *The Quality of Life*, ed. Martha Nussbaum and Amartya Sen (Oxford: Clarendon Press, 1993); Amartya Sen, *Development as Freedom* (New York: Knopf, 1999).

5. Sherraden, *Assets and the Poor;* James Midgley, "Growth, Redistribution, and Welfare: Toward Social Investment," *Social Service Review* 73, no. 1 (1999): 3–21, available online at www.journals.uchicago.edu/SSR/v73nltoc.html.

6. Michael Sherraden, "Assets and the Poor: Implications for Individual Accounts and Social Security," invited testimony, President's Commission to Strengthen Social Security, October 18, 2001.

7. Ray Boshara, "Federal Policy and Asset Building," *Social Development Issues* 25, nos. 1 & 2 (2003): 130–41; Reid Cramer, Leslie Parrish, and Ray Boshara, *Federal Assets Policy Report and Outlook* (Washington, DC: New America Foundation, 2005).

8. Karen Edwards and Leslie Marie Mason, "State Policy Trends for Individual Development Accounts in the United States, 1993–2003," *Social Development Issues* 25, nos. 1 & 2 (2003): 118–29.

9. H.M. Treasury, *Saving and Assets for All: The Modernisation of Britain's Tax and Benefit System, Number Eight* (London: H.M. Treasury, 2001); H.M. Treasury, *Details of the Child Trust Fund* (London: H.M. Treasury, 2003); Michael Sherraden, "Opportunity and Assets: The Role of the Child Trust Fund" (notes for seminar organized by Prime Minister Tony Blair, 10 Downing, and dinner speech with Chancellor of the Exchequer Gordon Brown, 11 Downing, London, September 19, 2002); Will Paxton, ed., *Equal Shares? Building a Progressive and Coherent Asset-Based*

Welfare Policy (London: Institute for Public Policy Research, 2003); Elaine Kempson, Stephen McKay, and Sharon Collard, *Evaluation of the CFLI and Saving Gateway Pilot Projects* (Bristol, UK: Personal Finance Research Centre, University of Bristol, 2003); Elaine Kempson, Stephen McKay, and Sharon Collard, *Incentives to Save: Encouraging Saving Among Low-Income Households* (Bristol, UK: Personal Finance Research Centre, University of Bristol, 2005).

10. Li-Chen Cheng, "Developing Family Development Accounts in Taipei: Policy Innovation from Income to Assets," *Social Development Issues* 25, nos. 1 & 2 (2003): 106–17.

11. Paul Kingwell, Michelle Dowie, Barbara Holler, and Lisa Jimenez, *Helping People Help Themselves: An Early Look at Learn$ave* (Ottawa, Canada: Social Research and Demonstration Corporation, 2004).

12. Sondra G. Beverly and Michael Sherraden, "Institutional Determinants of Saving: Implications for Low-Income Households and Public Policy," *Journal of Socio-economics* 28 (1999): 457–73; Michael Sherraden, Mark Schreiner, and Sondra Beverly, "Income, Institutions, and Saving Performance in Individual Development Accounts," *Economic Development Quarterly* 17, no. 1 (2003): 95–112; Michael Sherraden and Michael Barr, "Institutions and Inclusion in Saving Policy," in *Building Assets, Building Credit: Creating Wealth in Low-Income Communities*, ed. N. Retsinas and E. Belsky (Washington, DC: Brookings Institution Press, 2005).

13. Mark Schreiner, Margaret Clancy, and Michael Sherraden, *Saving Performance in the American Dream Demonstration* (research report, St. Louis: Center for Social Development, Washington University, 2002); Mark Schreiner and Michael Sherraden, *Can the Poor Save? Saving and Asset Building in Individual Development Accounts* (New York: Aldine de Gruyter, 2006).

14. These findings on IDAs are based on account-monitoring research in the American Dream Demonstration (ADD). ADD was implemented by the Corporation for Enterprise Development (now CFED). ADD research at CSD was funded by the Ford, Charles Stewart Mott, F.B. Heron, and MetLife foundations.

15. Margaret Sherraden et al., *Saving in Low-Income Households: Evidence from Interviews with Participants in the American Dream Demonstration* (research report, St. Louis: Center for Social Development, Washington University, 2005); Margaret Sherraden et al., "Short-term and Long-term Saving in Low-Income Households," *Journal of Income Distribution* 13, no. 3–4 (2006): 76–97.

16. Michael Sherraden, "Assets and the Poor: New American Welfare Policy."

17. For reviews, see Deborah Page-Adams and Michael Sherraden, "Asset Building as a Community Revitalization Strategy," *Social Work* 42, no. 5 (1997): 423–34; Edward Scanlon and Deborah Page-Adams, "Effects of Asset Holding on Neighborhoods, Families, and Children," in *Building Assets*, ed. R. Boshara (Washington, DC: Corporation for Enterprise Development, 2001), 25–49.

18. John B. Bynner and Will Paxton, *The Asset Effect* (London: Institute for Public Policy Research, 2001).

19. Trina R. Williams, "The Impact of Household Wealth and Poverty on Child Outcomes: Examining Asset Effects," Ph.D. diss., Washington University in St. Louis, 2003.

20. Min Zhan and Michael Sherraden, "Assets, Expectations, and Children's Educational Achievement in Single-Parent Households," *Social Service Review* 77, no. 2 (2003): 191–211.

21. The American Dream Demonstration (ADD) was the first major demonstration of IDAs. It took place at 14 IDA programs around the United States. ADD lasted from 1997 through 2001, with research continuing through 2005. ADD was organized by the Corporation for Enterprise Development (CFED) in Washington, DC, and research was designed by Center for Social Development.

22. Schreiner et al., *Saving Performance in the American Dream Demonstration.*

23. Margaret Sherraden et al., *Saving in Low-Income Households;* Margaret Sherraden et al. "Short-term and Long-term Saving in Low-Income Households."

24. Gregory Mills, Rhiannon Patterson, Larry Orr, and Donna DeMarco, *Evaluation of the American Dream Demonstration* (final evaluation report, Cambridge, MA: Abt Associates, 2004); M. Grinstein-Weiss and K. Wagner, "Using IDAs to Save for a Home: Are There Differences by Race?" (Working Paper 06-06, Center for Social Development, Washington University, St. Louis, 2006); Gregory Mills, William Gale, Rhiannon Patterson, and Emil Apostolov, "What

Do Individual Development Accounts Do? Evidence from a Controlled Experiment" (working paper, Brookings Institution, 2006).

25. Data irregularities have made it impossible to assess net worth at this stage. A fourth wave of ADD is being planned to shed more light on this.

26. President Bill Clinton, State of the Union Address, 2000.

27. Discussions of CDAs in the United States go back at least to the George H.W. Bush administration. Fred Goldberg, former IRS commissioner, was a proponent of CDAs in the Bush Senior administration, and at the request of the Bush White House, Michael Sherraden outlined a plan for a CDA with an initial deposit of $1,000 for all children in the United States.

28. An important background paper for what became the ASPIRE Act was written by Reid Cramer, *Accounts at Birth: Creating a National System of Savings and Asset Building with Children's Savings Accounts* (Washington, DC: New America Foundation, 2004). Ray Boshara and his team at the Asset Building Program at the New America Foundation have been very instrumental in organizing the introduction of the ASPIRE Act.

29. David Blunkett, "On Your Side: The New Welfare State as an Engine of Prosperity" (speech, Department of Education and Employment, London, June 7, 2000); Gavin Kelly and Rachel Lissauer, *Ownership for All* (London: Institute for Public Policy Research, 2000); David Nissan and Julie LeGrand, *A Capital Idea: Start-Up Grants for Young People*, Policy Report no. 49 (London: Fabian Society, 2000).

30. Tony Blair, "Savings and Assets for All" (speech, 10 Downing Street, London, April 26, 2001).

31. H.M. Treasury, *Details of the Child Trust Fund*.

32. Michael Sherraden, *Assets and the Poor: A New American Welfare Policy*; Duncan Lindsey, *The Welfare of Children* (New York: Oxford University Press, 1994); Ray Boshara and Michael Sherraden, "For Every Child, a Stake in America," *New York Times*, July 23, 2003; Cramer, *Accounts at Birth*; Fred Goldberg, "The Universal Piggy Bank: Designing and Implementing a System of Savings Accounts for Children," in *Inclusion in the American Dream: Assets, Poverty, and Public Policy*, ed. Michael Sherraden (New York: Oxford University Press. 2005).

33. Jami Curley and Michael Sherraden, "Policy Lessons from Children's Allowances for Children's Savings Accounts," *Child Welfare* 79, no. 6 (2000): 661–87.

34. CFED was formerly known as the Corporation for Enterprise Development.

35. I am particularly grateful to the Ford, Charles Stewart Mott, and MetLife foundations for funding SEED research so that we can learn as much as possible from this demonstration.

36. For this insight on universal asset accounts as a public infrastructure and public good, I am indebted to Fred Goldberg.

37. M. Sherraden, S. Nair, S. Vasoo, T.L. Ngiam, and M.S. Sherraden, "Social Policy Based on Assets: The Impact of Singapore's Central Provident Fund," *Asian Journal of Political Science* 3, no. 2 (1995): 112–33; S. Vasoo and J. Lee, "Singapore: Social Development, Housing, and the Central Provident Fund," *International Journal of Social Welfare* 10, no. 4 (2001): 276–83.

38. These plan features are expressions of institutional constructs for saving, discussed earlier.

39. For research and discussion, see M. Clancy, and M. Sherraden, *The Potential for Inclusion in 529 Savings Plans: Report of a Survey of States* (St. Louis: Center for Social Development, Washington University in St. Louis, 2003); M. Clancy, P. Orszag, and M. Sherraden, *College Savings Plans: A Platform for Inclusive Savings Policy?* (St. Louis: Center for Social Development, Washington University in St. Louis, 2004); M. Clancy, R. Cramer, and L. Parrish, *Section 529 Savings Plans, Access to Post-secondary Education, and Universal Asset Building* (Washington, DC: New American Foundation, 2005).

40. I prefer that asset-building policy be progressive, that is, greater subsidies for the poor, but I would settle for a policy that is at least fair, that is, equal subsidies for everyone in dollar terms. Today asset-based policy in the United States is a long way from fair. To take one example, some wealthy households get $20,000 or more in annual subsidy for homeownership (via the mortgage interest tax deduction), while most poor households get nothing. A fair homeownership policy would provide the same dollar amount to every household.

An Affordable Homeownership Strategy That Promotes Savings Rather Than Risk

Michael A. Stegman

With contemporary political discourse extremely polarized, policies that would expand homeownership opportunities are appealing because they are attractive to liberals and conservatives alike. They stimulate the economy, promote racial and ethnic unity, and enable more Americans to share in the risks and rewards of our unmatched system of market capitalism. Both the Clinton and Bush administrations embraced the goal of expanding home-ownership. Evidence of this proposition is that there is little practical difference in the Clinton administration's 1995 goal of achieving an all-time-high national homeownership rate by 2000 and President Bush's goal of increasing the number of minority homeowners by 5.5 million by 2010.[1] Because the white rate of homeownership is very high relative to minority homeownership rates, it is virtually impossible to raise the national homeownership rate without disproportionately increasing the number of minority homeowners.

Notwithstanding broad bipartisan agreement on the value of homeownership, significant debate remains on the most appropriate means of achieving this goal. One possibility is to reduce wealth constraints by eliminating down payments. Another way to increase affordability is with nontraditional mortgage products, such as interest-only loans or adjustable-rate mortgages that start with lower payments than a traditional mortgage and count either on a borrower's income rising over time to keep up with rising payment requirements or continued market appreciation of the home in order for the homeowner to accrue equity. For example, interest-only loans, on which no principal payments are made to pay down the mortgage debt, made up nearly one-third of mortgage originations during 2004 and 2005.[2] While these products address the right problems, they do so in the wrong ways for low- and moderate-income families.

While no-down-payment and other risky loans[3] make it easier to buy a home, they also drive up default rates, increase foreclosures, and possibly trigger neighborhood decline.[4] According to one estimate, of the 7.7 million households that took out adjustable-rate mortgages in 2004 and 2005 to buy or refinance, "up to 1 million could lose their homes through foreclosure over the next five years because they won't be able to afford their mortgage payments, and their homes will be worth less than they owe."[5]

A better way to deal with the wealth constraint is to help individual house-holds save for a modest down payment by promoting savings incentives as a part of homeownership policies. With research confirming that low- and moderate-income households positively respond to savings incentives the same way that higher-income households do, this policy reform should enable buyers to move into their homes with an equity stake from day one. Down-payment savings initiatives, financial literacy programs, and homeownership counseling target individual homebuyers, comprising the first part of a two-part homeownership strategy for the twenty-first century. The second part, which focuses on the market, builds upon recent advances to help lenders sell more affordable housing loans into the secondary market, which would gener-ate billions of dollars for new mortgage lending to underserved populations.

To better appreciate my strategy, it is important to understand recent changes in the demographics of homeownership, the resultant developments in affordable housing finance, and homeownership's role in democratizing capitalism and building household wealth, all of which I discuss here. I then examine past and current homeownership policies, including the two reform suggestions just mentioned.

RECENT HOMEOWNERSHIP GAINS

During the 1990s a perfect storm of favorable demographics, unparalleled economic growth, and low interest rates combined with an aggressively sup-portive public policy environment to propel national homeownership rates to record levels. Historically low interest rates sustained housing's bull market through the recession that ended in the fourth quarter of 2001, while rising home prices boosted consumer spending through the so-called wealth effect. But what is most notable about this housing boom is that it was led by gains in the affordable housing sector and among minorities, thanks in part to the widespread adoption of "affordable" mortgage products. These mortgages follow flexible underwriting guidelines that feature lower down payments, higher debt-burden limits, lower cash reserves, and nontraditional means of verifying creditworthiness. Flexible underwriting is important because it helps address barriers to homeownership among nontraditional borrowers.

From 1993 to 2003 home purchase loans grew almost six times faster to Hispanics than to whites, four times faster to Asians, and twice as fast to African Americans. At the same time, loans to low- and moderate-income (LMI) buyers doubled, while loans to higher-income borrowers rose by 88 percent. Importantly, conventional loans to LMI borrowers grew by 150 percent, compared with a 25 percent increase in government-guaranteed originations.[6] This means that these gains were driven much more by effective market demand than by federal subsidies.

Mortgage lending to underserved populations is on the rise because the changing demographics of the country and best business practices demand it. Minority homebuyers, once a submarket forged out of the fires of federal antiredlining mandates, are a critical component of the mortgage industry's core business. Redlining refers to a time "when it was not uncommon to walk into a bank that had maps with red lines on them indicating areas in which the bank would not lend, due either to the racial or economic make-up of the indicated community." This practice of redlining is what the Community Reinvestment Act (CRA) was intended to stop.[7] The minority share of the U.S. population, 26 percent in 2000, is estimated to reach 34 percent by 2020,[8] and 90 percent of the country's projected population growth through 2050 will consist of minorities. In short, the combination of public policies and business realities has fundamentally altered home lending practices for the better.

For the decade 1995–2005 minorities accounted for just under half of the 12.5 million new homeowners.[9] Despite impressive gains over the last decade—the percentage of black homeowners went from about 43 percent to more than 48 percent, and Hispanic homeowners from 42 percent to almost 50 percent—at the end of 2005 these groups still lagged behind white homeowners by nearly 25 percentage points.[10] Nevertheless, the 12 million African American and Hispanic households expected to enter the home purchasing market over the next five years will account for as much as 80 percent of all first-time homebuyers. Homeownership policies must recognize and build upon this new market-based reality.

THE IMPORTANCE OF HOME EQUITY IN HOUSEHOLD WEALTH

Homeownership is not just about building wealth. Surveys also find that families who own their homes tend to be more stable and satisfied with life.[11] Nevertheless, because of its significant potential to generate large returns on small amounts of invested capital, homeownership plays a powerful role in helping families secure their financial futures. Historically, Americans have always held an enormous amount of their collective wealth in their homes; in 2002 this was a staggering $7.6 trillion, which translates to an average equity per homeowner of $104,000.[12] However, since the high-tech meltdown in 2001, when stock portfolios lost $1.4 trillion in value, housing's relative importance in household portfolios has grown considerably. With housing outperforming the rest of the economy, home equity grew by more than $405 billion from 2001 to 2002. Among homeowners who also hold stock, 66 percent had more home equity than stock wealth in 2002, an increase of 5 percent from the previous year.[13] Moreover, the recent run-up in housing prices has pushed home equity levels even higher, to more than $11 trillion at the end of 2005.[14] While rising interest rates and excess inventories in the first three-quarters of 2006 have dampened price increases and in some of the hottest markets led to falling prices and reductions in home equity for some more recent buyers, at the end of this down part of the cycle, homeownership will likely retain its prominent role in household wealth portfolios.

Home equity has been especially important to those households at the bottom quintile by income. For homeowners in this group, the median net wealth in 2001 was $68,000, while that of similarly situated renters was only $500.[15] "Among these owners, home equity accounted for 80 percent of their net worth, compared with 48 percent for owners in the middle quintile and 26 percent for those in the highest quintile."[16] Home equity represented more than one-half of net wealth for moderate-income, African American, and Hispanic households.[17]

While the recent narrowing of the black-white wealth gap cannot be tied with statistical certainty exclusively to the recent rise in African American homeownership, the latter is without doubt a powerful factor. From 1989 to 2001 the ratio of median household wealth among African Americans compared with that of all U.S. households rose from about 9 percent to 22 percent, while the rate of homeownership among African Americans climbed from 42 percent to 48 percent over a roughly comparable period. In constant dollar terms, the median net wealth of the typical African American household rose from $2,500 in 1989 to $11,800 in 2004, an inflation-adjusted increase of 372 percent. By comparison, the median net wealth of the typical U.S. household rose by just 23 percent.[18]

Low-income homeownership policies are especially important in that research also suggests that, over time, nonhousing wealth accumulation is at best scant and, for minority families, often negative.[19] This proposition is confirmed in an early assessment of the wealth effects on lower-income participants in the Self-Help/Fannie Mae program described later in this chapter. Overall, Self-Help initiative homes bought between 1999 and 2003 enjoyed an average annual paper capital gain of 7.43 percent through the end of March 2006. This is slightly below the national house price appreciation index, which rose an average of 8.86 percent per year, but more than three times greater than the average annual rise in the Dow Jones Index (2.51 percent) and more than twice the average rate on a six-month CD (3.49 percent) over the same time period. As robust as these returns are, they pale in comparison with the returns that homeowners enjoyed on their original equity investments. For all owners, the average annual rate of return on initial equity was a whopping 65 percent, with black owners gaining 47 percent per year, Hispanics 73 percent, and whites 69 percent.[20]

INFUSING SAVINGS INCENTIVES INTO HOMEOWNERSHIP POLICIES

National policies should encourage greater household savings for macroeconomic and social purposes. Not only are our entrepreneurial economy and continued growth in productivity dependent upon a growing pool of national savings, but household savings are also a key to greater retirement security. Nevertheless, only about half of all private-sector wage and salary workers are covered by a pension plan, including just a fifth of workers in households with incomes below $20,000.[21] The reasons for savings incentives that target those near or at the bottom of the wealth and income scales are persuasive: one-third of all American households have zero or negative financial assets; nearly half of all children live in such households.[22]

Motivated by the adage that "income feeds the stomach while assets change the head," a growing number of social welfare academics and consumer advocates argue that finding ways to narrow the large and growing wealth disparity in the country is at least as important as, and perhaps even more important than, further narrowing the income gap. Where economists once argued that such inequality was the price of national economic progress, there is now evidence that social policies to lessen inequality are not necessarily inconsistent with economic policies to maximize growth.[23]

Because housing policies that increase homeownership also have the potential to both create and democratize wealth, it makes sense for the federal government to help low-wealth families save for a down-payment on a home. This is a much sounder idea than promoting no-down-payment loan programs, a favorite strategy of conservative administrations.[24] Such programs will lead to higher levels of failed homeowners because research confirms that borrowers who have none of their own money invested in their homes are more likely to default on their loans during challenging times.

A variety of tax credit measures have been introduced in Congress to stimulate the supply of affordable homes. Some would reward developers who agree to build affordable homes in underserved neighborhoods; others would reduce effective down-payment requirements to qualified buyers through a refundable tax credit; and still others would be used to capitalize deferred-payment second-mortgage loan pools.[25] While there are too many of these proposals to evaluate here, it should be noted that the full value of tax credits to developers is not always passed on to buyers, and such measures may also limit consumers' neighborhood choices. Policymakers should be mindful of the research that finds that the positive effects of homeownership on children are weakened in distressed neighborhoods, especially those that are residentially unstable and poor.[26]

In my opinion, a first-time homebuyer tax credit that would only be available to lower-income families in lower-income neighborhoods is neither sound public policy nor good community development policy. The forgone tax revenues that result from a tax credit program could be more productively invested in a down-payment savings initiative.

While I am not sure that tax credits are the best vehicle for capitalizing second-mortgage pools, in some very high-cost markets household savings, even with a government match, may not be sufficient to enable a working family to buy a home. In these cases a deferred-payment second mortgage in an amount equal to 10 to 20 percent of the home price may be necessary to make a starter home affordable. Sometimes referred to as a "silent second," a deferred-payment mortgage does not require monthly payments to be made, but is paid off in its entirety at the time that the home is either refinanced or sold. Many state and local agencies operate deferred-payment loan programs targeted to high-cost markets.

SPECIAL-PURPOSE SAVINGS INCENTIVES

Although none is at a scale to really matter, in the last 30 years the federal government has made at least four attempts to create special-purpose savings accounts to help low- and moderate-income households achieve homeownership. The first of these efforts came in the late 1960s. Under the Turnkey III public housing program, aspiring tenant-buyers could earn credit toward a down payment on a unit. This credit was based on the value of the labor, or "sweat equity," tenant-buyers contributed toward maintaining the units.[27]

The second effort, called the Family Self-Sufficiency (FSS) program, was developed in 1990 by the Department of Housing and Urban Development and has enabled more than 30,000 households to save for a down payment or other major expense.[28] In 1996 the Federal Housing Finance Board[29] began a program to encourage working families to save for a down payment and closing costs on a home. By amending the regulations for its Affordable Housing Program, the board permitted member banks to match each dollar of a first-time homebuyer's savings with up to $3 of Affordable Housing funds. The match generally was capped at $5,000 or $10,000 for a homebuyer living in public housing.[30] Several regional home loan banks have established pilot programs for their member thrifts, the most prominent being in the Seattle region. I mention these initiatives here to underscore the point that helping working families save for a home has significant precedent in federal policy. None of these initiatives, however, has achieved the visibility of Individual Development Accounts.

Since the concept was first developed by Michael Sherraden in 1991, Individual Development Account (IDA) programs have sprung up across the country with broad bipartisan support.[31] IDAs are matched, dedicated savings accounts that can be used by eligible participants for purchasing a first home, paying for postsecondary education, or capitalizing a business. Two national pilots together have supported nearly five hundred IDA programs across the country and about 15,000 matched savings accounts.[32] Empirical assessments of these pilots have shown that contrary to conventional wisdom, poor people can and do save in response to positive incentives such as the opportunity to have their deposits matched from outside sources.[33]

The proposed Savings for Working Families Act (SWFA) has the potential to institutionalize and dramatically expand public funding for IDA matches and operating funds by authorizing a national program of 900,000 Individual Development Accounts over a seven-year period (2007–14), with up to $500 in matching funds and up to $50 in administrative and financial literacy expenses per account per year.[34] As of September 2006, SWFA had yet to become law, due in large part to the philosophical opposition of House Republicans to using tax credits to help the poor build assets.[35]

All these proposals would work well in conjunction with local programs aimed at increasing the take-up rate among working poor families of the Earned Income Tax Credit. In 2005 alone, more than 21 million low-income working families received EITC refunds totaling $39 billion.[36] If just one-third of these tax refunds were channeled into homeownership savings accounts, even a low one-to-one match rate would generate $26 billion in down payments.

PUBLIC POLICY TO FOSTER GREATER SECURITIZATION OF AFFORDABLE MORTGAGE LOANS

In addition to proposals that encourage savings strategies for potential home-buyers, public policy should also look for ways to make loans for affordable housing more attractive to traditional lenders. Working families who manage to save a few thousand dollars of their hard-earned wages to put down on a house still need flexibly underwritten first-mortgage loans to buy a home, and they need a market that will support these flexible loans. This is why the second part of my two-part national homeownership strategy aims to expand the affordable lending capacity of thousands of conventional mortgage lenders.

As indicated earlier, the interaction of demographic and market forces with political and technological developments has put a premium on serving the homeownership needs of underserved populations. Over the last five years, 40 percent or more of all homes sold have been to low- and moderate-income persons, and the strength of this market is not likely to diminish in the coming years.[37] Notwithstanding strong demand, lenders would be reluctant to serve this market if it were not profitable to do so. The key is in this tension between a first-time homebuyer's need for a flexibly underwritten loan and the difficulty a lender faces in selling these flexible loans on the securitized secondary market.

The Community Reinvestment Act (CRA) presents an example of this tension. This act, enacted in 1977 in response to evidence that banks were refusing to lend in many inner-city urban areas, established that banks have "a continuing and affirmative obligation to help meet the credit needs of the local communities in which they are chartered to do business."[38] Since CRA's passage, it is estimated that covered lenders have made more than $1.7 trillion in CRA loan commitments to minority and lower-income neighborhoods.[39] Most CRA mortgage products feature the flexible underwriting necessary for low-income buyers, which makes these loans hard to pool into securities for sale in the secondary market without higher guarantee fees or credit enhancements such as private mortgage insurance, the cost of which frequently makes these transactions uneconomical for originating lenders and home seekers alike. Flexible underwriting also reduces liquidity and raises the overall risk profile of a lender's portfolios. Accordingly, when the volume of CRA mortgages lenders hold grows beyond a self-defined comfort level, they slow down their affordable mortgage lending.[40]

THE COMMUNITY ADVANTAGE SECONDARY MARKET
DEMONSTRATION PROGRAM (CAP)

The federal government can play a role in resolving the conflict just described. The government can leverage the expertise of CRA-covered institutions and other proven affordable housing lenders and can share in the increased risk assumed by lenders who are involved in affordable housing loans. By sharing the incrementally higher guarantee and credit enhancement fees, such a program would enable participating lenders to sell their affordable loan portfolios in the secondary market. This not only takes advantage of the market and reduces a lender's risk, it also frees up additional capital for new LMI lending.

One successful pilot that could be used to tailor such a national initiative is the Community Advantage Secondary Market Demonstration Program (CAP). Fannie Mae partnered with the Center for Community Self-Help, an innovative community development financial institution, on this effort to demonstrate that affordable housing loans made to low-income homebuyers can be profitable for lenders, as well as advantageous for the homebuyers themselves (see inset). Through CAP, Self-Help has pooled nearly 45,000 CRA loans to LMI families worth nearly $5 billion originated by more than 20 lenders across the country for sale to Fannie Mae.[41] These transactions freed up an equivalent amount of capital to enable participating lenders to originate new affordable housing loans. Though these loans could not readily be sold on the traditional secondary mortgage market, CAP set out to prove that lenders such as Fannie Mae could confidently serve this market, despite the higher risk involved in loans to low-income persons. The demonstration was implemented in 47 states and in the District of Columbia.

Assuming Self-Help's annual loss rate of less than 1 percent, a program that helps underwrite a portion of the transaction costs and perceived increased risk of CRA-backed mortgage securities would be more cost-effective than HUD's existing down-payment assistance program. It may be even more important during periods of rising interest rates, when originating lenders are less likely to be able to absorb the higher guarantee fees and still sell their portfolios without booking a loss. This is why pilots such as the CAP are important: they benchmark the risk profiles and market performance of loans to a low-income population in the expectation that over the long term many of these mortgage products will prove to perform sufficiently well to qualify for sale in the secondary market without any special credit enhancements. These pilot programs provide the evidence that traditional lenders need to participate in this non-traditional market. On a dollar-for-dollar basis, using scarce federal resources to expand and replicate the Self-Help/Fannie Mae partnership is a far more cost-effective way of expanding homeownership opportunities to lower-income households than either a similar-sized down-payment grant program or paying the insured losses that would result from a large-scale, government-insured zero-down-payment loan program.

MAKING HOMEOWNERSHIP A REALITY BY BELIEVING IN WORKING-CLASS FAMILIES

Martin Eakes

Self-Help, a North Carolina community development lender started in 1980, views homeownership as the single best way for working-class families to build wealth. The strong repayment history of our borrowers confirms our belief that low-wealth families are dependable borrowers who deserve a chance to own a home.

Self-Help's mission is to create wealth and ownership opportunities for minority, rural, and female-headed families. We started as a small-business lender but soon realized that home equity is often a business owner's primary source of capital. Further, 60 percent of African American and Latino family wealth is in home equity. The minority homeownership rate of 48 percent lags far behind the 73 percent homeownership rate for white families, and the corresponding equity gap has left a 10-to-1 wealth disparity between white families and families of color.

Clearly, in order to help families build wealth, we had to engage in home lending. In 1984 we started with loans mainly to African American single mothers then considered unbankable and now have made $200 million in home loans to 3,000 North Carolina families.

Realizing that our direct reach is limited, Self-Help started a secondary-market program in North Carolina to partner with large banks to provide more home loans to low-wealth borrowers. Assisted by the Ford Foundation, Fannie Mae, and conventional lenders, we took the secondary-market program national in 1998. To date we have provided financing of $4.5 billion to 45,000 low-income and minority families. Approximately 42 percent of the loans are to families of color, 39 percent to woman-headed households, and 18 percent to rural families. These families have an average income of 64 percent of area median income.

Our lending experience proves that low-income families are dependable borrowers who deserve a fair opportunity. These families have been able to pay back their loans. Our annual loan loss rate is well under 1 percent. And families also have created wealth through the program: a recent University of North Carolina study estimated a 30 percent appreciation by the end of 2005, which translates to $1.2 billion in home equity created to date.

Our lending also provides an alternative to high-cost subprime loans. Our loans have a standard 30-year amortizing fixed rate, the rates and fees are comparable with those of conventional loans, and foreclosure rates are 10 times lower than for subprime loans. We also work proactively to help families protect family wealth from predatory lenders and started the affiliated Center for Responsible Lending in 2001 (see www.responsiblelending .org).

Every hardworking American family should have an opportunity to own a modest home. In particular, America's low minority homeownership rate provides a window of opportunity for public policymakers. Self-Help believes that there should be a national goal of raising African American and Latino homeownership rates to the national average by 2020. Given the opportunity, we know that these borrowers will pay their mortgages. We believe that it is our collective responsibility to bring the American Dream of homeownership into reach for these families, and that our nation would be all the stronger for it.

CONCLUSION

Although owning a home is not a ticket to wealth, 59 present of renters rank buying a home among their top priorities in life.[42] And while history documents that not all homes increase in value, American adults believe by a four-to-one margin that buying a home is a safe investment compared with stocks.[43] I support current policy goals to increase homeownership, but I strongly oppose government initiatives such as zero-down-payment programs that by design will force one out of every six buyers into foreclosure or a forced sale to prevent one. Rather than continuing down the path toward the complete elimination of down payments or relying on the kinds of nontraditional mortgage products that are leading to a new wave of foreclosures, I urge the federal government to help families save for a modest down payment, and I have identified several ways this could be done. As illustrated earlier, there is no shortage of ideas of how savings and homeownership policies might be better coordinated. Given strong and enduring market fundamentals and secondary market innovations that have the potential to channel significantly more capital to affordable lending, the mortgage industry will respond to the upsurge in effective demand from households who come to the table with savings in hand, financially ready and able to become successful homeowners.

NOTES

1. Clinton goal at U.S. Department of Housing and Urban Development news release, "Celebrating National Homeownership Week," available online at http://www.metrokc.gov/exec/news/2000/0605001.htm; Bush goal at "In Focus: Homeownership," available online at http://www.whitehouse.gov/infocus/homeownership/.

2. Allen Fishbein and Patrick Woodall, "Exotic or Toxic? An Examination of the Non-traditional Mortgage Market for Consumers and Lenders" (Consumer Federation of America, May 2006), 4.

3. These include down-payment grants, seller-provided down-payment gifts combined with government-backed loans, and zero-down-payment mortgages. (I am treating these as three categories, not as two plus a definition.)

4. Brent Ambrose and Anthony B. Sanders, "High LTV Loans and Credit Risk," October 3, 2002, available online at SSRN: http://ssrn.com/abstract-355180; Sam R. Hakim and Mahmoud Haddad, "Borrower Attributes and the Risk of Default of Conventional Mortgages," *Atlantic Economic Journal* 27, no. 2 (June 1999): 212.

5. Noelle Knox, "Some Homeowners Struggle to Keep Up with Adjustable Rates," *USA Today*, April 3, 2006.

6. Loans to Hispanics rose 236 percent; to Asians, 163 percent; to blacks, 106 percent, and to whites, 44 percent. FFIEC [Federal Financial Institutions Examination Council] Reports—"Nationwide Summary Statistics for 2003 HMDA Data, Fact Sheet" (July 2004), available online at www.ffiec.gov/hmcrpr/hm_fs03.htm.

7. National Training and Information Center, History of CRA, available online at www.ntic-us.org/issues/cra/cra-history.htm.

8. Joint Center for Housing Studies of Harvard University, *The State of the Nation's Housing, 2004* (Cambridge, MA: Harvard University, 2004), 3.

9. Executive Summary: A Population Perspective of the United States, Population Resource Center, available online at www.prcdc.org/summaries/uspopperspect/uspopperspec.html.

10. Joint Center for Housing Studies, *The State of the Nation's Housing, 2006* (Cambridge, MA: Harvard University, 2006), Table A-5.

11. Fannie Mae, "The American Dream Commitment Expansion Plan: Expanding Access to Homeownership for Millions of First-Time Home Buyers" (2004), 2, available online at http://www.fanniemae.com/initiatives/pdf/adc/factsheet2004.pdf.

12. Ibid.

13. Center for Housing Studies of Harvard University, *The State of the Nation's Housing, 2003* (Cambridge, MA: Harvard University, 2003), 6.

14. Joint Center for Housing Studies, *State of the Nation's Housing, 2006*, 5.

15. Joint Center for Housing Studies, *State of the Nation's Housing, 2003*, 7.

16. Eric Belsky and Allegra Calder, *Credit Matters: Low-Income Asset Building Challenges in a Dual Financial Service System*, BABC 04-1 (Cambridge, MA: Joint Center for Housing Studies, Harvard University, 2004), 14.

17. Consumer Federation of America, "Study Concludes That Homeownership Is the Main Path to Wealth for Low Income and Minority Americans" (2003), 2, available online at http://www.consumerfed.org/americasaveshomeownership121603.pdf.

18. Economic Policy Institute, *The State of Working America*, chap. 5, "Wealth: Unrelenting Disparities," available online at www.stateofworkingamerica.org/swa06-ch05-wealth.pdf.

19. Tom Boehm and Allan Schlottmann, "Wealth Accumulation and Homeownership: Evidence for Low-Income Households" (Department of Housing and Urban Development, December 2004), available online at http://www.huduser.org/intercept.asp?loc=/Publications/pdf/WealthAccumulationAndHomeownership.pdf.

20. Michael A. Stegman, Allison Freeman, and Jong Gyu Paik, "Home Equity and Other Differences in the Wealth of Low- and Moderate-Income Homeowners: A Work in Progress" (Center for Community Capitalism, University of North Carolina at Chapel Hill, September 2006).

21. Eric M. Engen and William G. Gale, "The Effects of 401(k) Plans on Household Wealth: Differences Across Earnings Groups" (original draft, May 2, 2000; revised draft, August 2000), 2. Available online at http://papers.ssrn.com.sol3/papers.cfm? abstract_id-241237.

22. "Sense of Congress on the Assets for Independence Act," section 7 of House Report 105-565, *The Concurrent Resolution on the Budget for Fiscal Year 1999*, available online at http://thomas.loc.gov/cgi-bin/cpquery/?&db_id=cp105&r_n=hr565.105&sel=TOC_39375&.

23. Joseph E. Stiglitz and Jason Furman, "Economic Consequences of Income Inequality," *FOMC Alert* 2, no. 6 (September 29, 1998): 7. This paper was presented at the Federal Reserve Bank of Kansas City's Jackson Hole Symposium on August 29, 1998.

24. H.R. 3755, *Zero Downpayment Act of 2004*.

25. See, for example, S. 875, *Community Development Homeownership Tax Credit Act*, introduced April 10, 2002; H.R. 839, *Renewing the Dream Tax Credit Act*, introduced October 16, 2002; S. 198 and S. 602, *New Homestead Economic Opportunity Act*, introduced January 21, 2003; H.R. 1132, *Home at Last Tax Credit Act of 2003*, introduced March 6, 2002; and S. 1175, *First-Time Homebuyers' Tax Credit Act of 2003*, introduced June 3, 2003.

26. Joseph Harkness and Sandra J. Newman, "Homeownership for the Poor in Distressed Neighborhoods: Does This Make Sense?" *Housing Policy Debate* 13 (2002): 597.

27. Michael A. Stegman, *More Housing, More Fairly* (New York: Twentieth Century Fund Press, 1991), 46.

28. Letter from Robert W. Gray, Office of Policy Development and Research, U.S. Department of Housing and Urban Development, August 25, 1998.

29. This board is the safety and soundness regulator for the nation's savings associations.

30. Federal Home Loan Bank Seattle, "Home$tart Savings Programs: Home$tart, Home$tart Plus, and Home$tart Special Initiatives" (Policy CID-12, revised February 2004), available online at www.fhlbsea.com/FHLBSEA/main/communityinvestment3/content.cfm? pageid=251; Karen Edwards, "Individual Development Accounts: Creative Savings for Families and Communities" (Center for Social Development, 1997), 16.

31. Michael Sherraden, *Assets and the Poor: A New American Welfare Policy* (New York: M.E. Sharpe, 1991).

32. The two pilot programs are the American Dream Demonstration, funded by a group of private foundations, and the federal Assets for Independence demonstration, funded by Congress and administered by the U.S. Department of Health and Human Services. The Corporation for Enterprise Development tracks the number of IDA programs; information is available online at www.cfed.org/focus.m?parentid=2&siteid=374&id=382.

33. "Saving Performance in the American Dream Demonstration: A National Demonstration of Individual Development Accounts" (final report, Center for Social Development, Washington University, St. Louis, October 2002), iv, v.

34. SWFA was included in larger legislative bills such as the American Community Renewal/New Markets bill, which was signed into law without the IDA provision in 2000, and in the president's faith-based legislative proposal, the Charity, Aid, Recovery, and Empowerment Act, in both 2002 and 2003.

35. Corporation for Enterprise Development, *Assets: Update for Innovators*, no. 2 (2003): 3.

36. National Low Income Housing Coalition, "2006 Advocates' Guide to Housing and Community Development Policy: The Earned Income Tax Credit," available online at http://www.nlihc.org/advocates/eitc.htm.

37. U.S. Department of Housing and Urban Development, Summary: HUD's Proposed Housing Goal Rule—2004, 3. Available online at www.hudigov/offices/hsg/gse/summary.doc.

38. Susan White Haag, "Community Reinvestment and Cities: A Literature Review of CRA's Impact and Future" (Brookings Institution Center for Urban and Metropolitan Policy, March 2000).

39. California Reinvestment Coalition, "CRA Impacts," available online at www.calreinvest.org/policy/cra-impacts.

40. Forest Pafenberg, "The Single-Family Mortgage Industry in the Internet Era: Technology Developments and Market Structure" (Office of Federal Housing Enterprise Oversight,

January 2004), 1. Single-family mortgage-backed securities grew from less than $367 billion outstanding in 1981 to more than $3.3 trillion outstanding at the end of 2001, an 800 percent increase. Task Force on Mortgage-Backed Securities Disclosures, "Enhancing Disclosure in the Mortgage-Backed Securities Markets" (January 2003), 5, available online at www.ofheo.gov.

41. For a description of this pilot, see "Self-Help's Secondary Market Program," available online at www.self-help.org/secondarymarket/communityadvantage.asp.

42. Fannie Mae, "The American Dream Commitment Expansion Plan: Expanding Access to Homeownership for Millions of First-Time Home Buyers" 2, available online at http://www.fanniemae.com/initiatives/pdf/adc/factsheet2004.pdf.

43. Fannie Mae, "Understanding America's Homeownership Gap: 2003 Fannie Mae National Housing Survey" (2003), 4. Available online at www.fanniemae.com/global/pdf/media/survey/survey2003.pdf.

The Role of the Entrepreneur
in Combating Poverty

Secretary Jack F. Kemp

To ignore the potential contribution of private enterprise is to fight the war on poverty with a single platoon, while great armies are left to stand aside.
— SENATOR ROBERT F. KENNEDY

"It was the best of times, it was the worst of times." These memorable words of Charles Dickens echoed in everyone's mind at the 1984 Democratic Convention as Mario Cuomo of New York electrified the convention with his tale of America as two cities, one rich and one poor, permanently divided into two classes. Governor Cuomo discussed the cultural ramifications of the rich growing richer and the poor becoming poorer and concluded that "class conflict" was the only result, and the only solution was a redistribution of wealth.

Despite the power and poetry to this tale of two cities, and with all due respect to former Governor Cuomo, I believe that he misinterprets the highly controversial income gap in our nation. In my opinion, America is divided, but not into two cities; instead, I believe that America is divided de facto into two separate economies. There is one economy that works well and one that is inarguably flawed.

ONE NATION, TWO ECONOMIES

Our mainstream economy is primarily entrepreneurially capitalistic: it is market oriented and based on private property, ownership, and the rule of law. It rewards work, savings, investment, and productivity. Incentives abound for hard work and productive human economic and social behavior. It is this economy that dominates the American market and serves as an example to the world of democratic capitalism even though we can and must correct several flaws. Obviously we can and must do better, but this economy has been, and is now, a model for what Thomas Friedman called the "flattening out" of the world economy as outlined in his new book, *The World Is Flat*.[1]

The second economy functions in a fashion almost directly opposite to the mainstream capitalist economy. It predominates in the pockets of poverty throughout urban and rural America. Similar to a Third World socialist economy, this second economy, in effect, too often denies people an entry into the mainstream because of the huge barriers to productive human economic and social activities, along with a virtual absence of any link between human effort and reward. It perpetuates poverty, dependency, and welfare while discouraging employment and, in many cases, prevents access to capital, ownership, opportunity, and quality education. In other words, it is a recipe for poverty and despair.

The irony is that this second economy was created out of a desire to help the poor, alleviate suffering, and provide a social welfare safety net. However, the results were disastrous to the poor, because rather than a safety net, it became a swamp. Instead of independence, this welfare-based economy led to near-perpetual dependency. In an effort to minimize economic pain, it maximized bureaucracy, while the social and economic costs to our nation were enormous, not to mention the human disappointments, unfulfilled potential, and dashed dreams. The blame should not be on the poor, but on those who persist in perpetuating their powers over poor people.

In my time as secretary of HUD from 1989 to 1993 under President George H.W. Bush, I had numerous opportunities to see the effect of this second economy on people's lives. I visited pockets of poverty in ghettos and barrios throughout America. I saw this poverty firsthand and spoke personally with people living in the depths of poverty, despair, and, in some cases, near hopelessness. I met families torn apart by unemployment, poor housing, and drug-infested neighborhoods and talked to elderly Americans living in public housing who were literally prisoners in their own homes for fear of gangs and drug dealers. The grinding poverty and crippling despair from South Central and East Los Angeles to Harlem and the South Bronx, from Miami's Overtown and East St. Louis to East Palo Alto and many other areas of our country, highlight the abject failure of our nation's so-called war on poverty despite the noble intentions of many well-meaning people. It tore my heart out to think that this was happening in our nation, and I vowed to take part in a bipartisan effort to help create an urban American renaissance.

URBAN PROGRESSION

It is no accident that the roots of the words "civilization" and "city" have similar origins. Urban life traditionally was the fountainhead of movements for political, cultural, and economic development and human well-being. Our cities are home to millions of Americans, especially minorities and recently arrived immigrants. Traditionally, cities have been centers of educational opportunity and cultural diversity, helping those seeking social and economic opportunity to move into the mainstream of prosperity while becoming fully integrated into American society.

The post–World War II era's erosion of our urban economic base has eliminated many of those traditional assets and has weakened the city's ability to provide essential services to citizens most in need of them. Currently in our cities there are too few jobs available, too little investment, far too much poverty housing, and an educational system that all too often warehouses and baby-sits many of our young people.

As Adam Smith wrote 230 years ago in his magnum opus, *The Wealth of Nations*, the desire to improve one's life is a universal dream. It exists irrespective of color, condition, culture, or climate. It is what Professor Smith called "the fundamental aim of all people," everywhere. The problem with poverty in America is that self-improvement and ownership of assets are discouraged by regulatory and tax policies that literally trap people in impoverished areas. In all too many cases, the poverty that exists today is due in large part to government welfare coupled with regulatory and tax policies that punish work, savings, and investment and discourage home and asset ownership. As a result, the system ends up de facto redlining certain areas of our country, limiting people's access to capital, credit, mortgage loans, and well-paying jobs. Senator John Edwards and I agree that this is a moral and political disgrace to our twenty-first century America. While John and I may disagree on causes and solutions, we are both committed to raising the issue for national debate, dialogue, and discussion as a moral and political imperative.

THE ROLE OF REDLINING IN THE SECOND ECONOMY

In my years at HUD I found that access to capital is unusually restricted in impoverished areas. A few decades ago poverty areas were marked by red lines on bank maps. Bank statistics in impoverished neighborhoods reveal that although red lines are no longer actually drawn, redlining de facto still occurs. Banks, insurance companies, and other lending institutions are discouraged from investing capital in these so-called unstable neighborhoods. A recent report by the Federal Reserve found that minority Americans are more likely than whites to pay higher interest rates on mortgage loans, and in too many instances the lending industry is taking advantage of inexperienced borrowers.[2]

These obstacles prevent small businesses and entrepreneurs from receiving necessary start-up capital. And when workers and investors do not get access to capital, poverty is perpetuated, unemployment is extended, and people get trapped without any rungs of the economic ladder upon which to climb. While the cause of crime is multifaceted, there can be no disagreement as to how poverty and joblessness contribute to the crime statistics.

This wariness on the part of banks and other lenders is shared by people who consider developing businesses in urban areas. Open-ended environmental zoning and other regulations hold people associated with old industrial properties responsible for clean-up costs. These regulations force companies out of many urban areas and into the suburbs or beyond where they will not need to worry about being held accountable for the risks associated with urban economic development. It is, for instance, because of regulations such as this that in 1993 the *Cleveland Plain Dealer* decided to build its new production plant—with four-hundred jobs—in a Cleveland suburb instead of Cleveland proper. Similar stories abound. In 2004 Congressman Michael Turner from Ohio, the former mayor of Dayton, Ohio, authored the bipartisan Brownfields Reauthorization Act that aspired to create a federal urban redevelopment program where expenditures associated with the redevelopment and remediation of environmentally contaminated sites would receive income tax credits. The tax credits serve as incentives for cities and developers to restore contaminated sites into usable and profitable property.[3]

DISCOURAGED CAPITAL

Beyond government regulations, investors and entrepreneurs facing high tax rates are often discouraged from investing their surplus capital in urban areas because of poor education, high crime rates, and other risks. A failing education system means that many inner-city residents are unable to acquire the skills necessary to become valuable assets to the social and economic system. Crime drives out investment. Criminologist James K. Stewart identified a National Institute of Justice study that found that the fear of crime was a more important barrier to business investment than high labor costs or high taxes.[4] For example, in the early 1970s an East Brooklyn community in New York had about 200 businesses employing 3,000 people. Crime was on the rise, so stores began to leave or close. By 1979 the number of businesses had fallen to 45, with only 1,500 workers. These failures in urban communities, combined with zoning developmental regulations, pushed businesses into the suburbs and caused many of our cities to further decline.

Not only are small businesses discouraged in urban areas, but the urban residents are disheartened by government disincentives inherent in the current system. When people on welfare and unemployment take entry-level jobs to try to improve their lives, they lose their welfare benefits along with paying payroll and income taxes, thus decreasing their after-tax income. The startling fact in America today is that the highest marginal tax rates are being paid not by the rich, but by welfare mothers or unemployed fathers who take an entry-level job. According to a study done by Kathryn Edin and Christopher Jencks, a mother with two children who is employed at about $5 an hour would take home about 45 cents an hour less than if she were on welfare. She loses $4 a day after taking into account the loss of government benefits, taxes, and such work-related expenses as transportation and child care.[5]

Not only is labor discouraged, but so is saving. Grace Capetillo, a young welfare mother in Milwaukee, was charged with welfare fraud because of her attempts to save money. Capetillo, whose story appeared in the *Wall Street Journal* in the early 1990s, scrimped to save enough money to buy a washing machine and perhaps someday send her five-year-old to college. She managed to build a savings account of more than $3,000. But then the county Social Services Department took her to court, filing charges of fraud. The court fined her $15,000. Obviously Capetillo did not have $15,000, so the judge took her $3,000 savings and sentenced her to probation if she promised not to save. This is what many low-income families face in our welfare system. The message to Capetillo, and all those like her, was clear. Spend every cent you get, save nothing, and rely on government subsidies to pay for nearly everything while government bureaucrats control most, if not all, of your decisions.[6]

BIG SOLUTIONS FOR BIG PROBLEMS

Maimonides, the twelveth-century Talmudic philosopher, wrote that the highest form of charity is to enable someone not to have to rely on charity. In my opinion, to wage a real war on poverty, we should launch a twenty-first century Marshall Aid Plan in the cities of America to reform education, create job opportunities, and provide access to capital, credit, and ownership opportunities for low-income Americans. This twenty-first century plan must not be based on welfare and handouts, but on equal opportunities to get jobs, own homes, launch businesses, and move up the ladder we call the American Dream. But in reality, the American Dream is a universal dream from Asia to

Eastern Europe and from Latin America to Africa. I know because I have seen it firsthand all over the globe.

The first step in a twenty-first century Marshall Aid Plan is to create what I called enterprise zones (also known as empowerment zones). A real and effective enterprise zone would eliminate the capital gains tax in the newly green-lined zone areas, allow for expensing of all investment in plant machinery and technology, and eliminate payroll taxes for men and women who are first-time job holders up to 200 percent of the poverty line. The fundamental idea is that private enterprise, not government, is the main source of jobs and social development. Creating enterprise zones in low-income areas gives small-business entrepreneurs the necessary tax incentives and access to capital to invest in these zones and truly begin democratizing our capitalistic system.

I love the story of Governor Luis Muñoz Marín of Puerto Rico, who passed away in 1980. There were memorial remarks in the chamber of the House of Representatives. Muñoz Marín was a powerful and effective governor who identified with his hero, President Franklin Roosevelt. He was an intellectual socialist professor at San Juan University, yet he recognized when he was elected governor that dividing up a "loaf of bread" was not the best way to help people get bread because all they received was equal access to crumbs. Muñoz Marín understood the importance of government policies, public-private partnerships, and tax incentives to develop the Puerto Rican economy and create bakeries (the enterprises) that would feed more people and create jobs than just redistribution of income. In other words, he knew that you cannot create employees without first creating employers, that is, entrepreneurs.

He created what I would call the first enterprise zone. He called it "Operation Bootstrap." The governor knew that if he could get men and women to go into business building bakeries and creating jobs, they could produce more food, more bread, and feed more people. That is entrepreneurial enterprise at its most practical level, and, coupled with tax incentives for offshore U.S. companies, it worked to industrialize Puerto Rico. It was not perfect, but it was a good start.

I was one of the few Republicans to speak on behalf of Luis Muñoz Marín. I had read about him in Jude Wanninski's great book *The Way the World Works*, and I thought to myself, "Wouldn't it be great to have an Operation Bootstrap in Buffalo, or the South Bronx or South Central Los Angeles, or anywhere in America where people are really hurting for jobs and access to opportunity?" I believe that the purpose of good public policy is to use incentives and develop the public and private partnerships that would drive capital, jobs, and enterprise into areas that are starved for productive economic activities.

I have no doubt that inner-city entrepreneurs would respond to opportunities that offer real financial incentives to invest, take risks, and create jobs.

Take the example of New Jersey, which began its own enterprise zone program under then Governor Tom Kean. According to a 1990 study, its program in Camden, Newark, Trenton, Jersey City, Elizabeth, Orange, and other depressed communities created 9,193 jobs in one year. This program raised an estimated $1.90 to $5.20 of new tax revenue for every dollar of tax incentives it provided, and in doing so it improved these communities.[7] This is proof of the supply-side revenue gains from marginal rate reductions. Giving people, including those in the inner city and the rural poor, the opportunity to succeed and make the most of their God-given talents is what the American Dream is all about, and that is what enterprise zones are designed to achieve. These zones are working in the Middle East in places such as Dubai and in Africa, Hong Kong, and Shenzhen and Pudong, China, as well as in the maquiladoras along the border of Mexico and San Diego, California.

We also need to develop a strategy for microfinancing, which would give low-income people access to credit and capital to start investing and take the steps needed for economic and social stability. Microfinance is the jump-start many people need to begin the process of meeting their most basic human needs. We need to start green-lining those redlined areas so that people can access credit, and therefore capital.

Thirty-five years ago Al Whittaker, former president of Bristol Myers International, had a dream. He looked at the crisis of chronic poverty in the developing world and saw the two essential ingredients necessary for lifting millions of American men and women out of poverty: credit and entrepreneurship. By providing credit in the form of a small loan at fair-market value to poor, jobless people who had no collateral to borrow money from a conventional bank, Whittaker pioneered the way for microfinance.

Whittaker learned that small loans, sometimes as little as $50, in the hands of a low-income entrepreneur can transform the lives of individuals, families, and entire communities. Opportunity International, Whittaker's Christian ecumenical humanitarian organization, provides loans and job training directly to the poor at the grassroots level. The loans are then paid back to grow new businesses or expand existing ones. It is not about a "handout," it is about showing people how to work their way out of chronic poverty. In 2005 Opportunity International provided 536,033 loans that totaled $127.2 million for 397,489 clients.[8] Notions that the poor are not creditworthy are shattered by the success of this program. When people are given access to credit and capital, capitalism can be democratized.

After providing the necessary financial incentives for small businesses to grow, we need to cut bureaucratic red tape that makes development in urban areas difficult. We need to look at the legal barriers to production and commerce. Local impact (development) fees, application processing costs, building codes, zoning and land-use restrictions, and nongrowth policies greatly increase construction costs. Instead of creating regulations that make it more difficult for companies to build in urban areas, companies need to be offered incentives for investing in cities.

We need to get rid of disincentives for labor through continued welfare reform. We must develop a tax reform system that rewards labor, savings, and capital formation. A sure way to harm the economy and slow growth is through the capital gains tax. The capital gains tax is not a tax on the rich, who are already rich; the capital gains tax is a tax on the poor and the workers who want to get rich. You cannot get rich on wages. The only way to create wealth is to work, save, invest, make a profit, and reinvest.

The welfare system should stop penalizing the poor who take jobs, allow for savings and accumulation of capital, stop subsidizing family breakup, and reward families that stay together. We cannot allow another Grace Capetillo to learn that saving for one's future is illegal and imprudent. Instead, we need to encourage self-improvement because in doing so we encourage community and economic improvement. There should be no tax on the earnings of entry-level jobholders up to 190 to 200 percent of poverty level. We should expand the Earned Income Tax Credit immediately.

Finally, we need to provide homeownership opportunities and affordable housing to the most impoverished in society, who often become trapped in public housing. We need to reform the Section 8 voucher program so that vouchers can be used as down payments on homes, not just for subsidized rentals. We need to encourage more organizations like Habitat for Humanity to build up the type of housing people can own and thus improve their investment in communities. Through public-private partnerships with organizations such as Freddie Mac, Fannie Mae, the Federal Home Loan Bank, and others, we need to continue to dedicate a percentage of their profits to help develop affordable housing and encourage homeownership programs to get people on the path out of poverty in urban and rural communities. Property and homeownership affect people in profound ways that create the foundation from which they can go on to realize their full human potential.

Cochran Gardens, a public housing community in St. Louis, once was a picture of decay, drug wars, and crime. It was slated to be blown up in 1974, but under the inspired leadership of resident-manager Bertha Gilkey, the residents took control from the city-run public housing bureaucracy in 1976 and reclaimed their community, making it into a showplace of dignity, hope, and secure living. Now residents run a child-care center, a transportation system to get workers back and forth to jobs, job training, and drug prevention programs.

In 1862, when Abraham Lincoln signed the Homestead Act, he made a bold decision that empowered thousands upon thousands of immigrant Americans. Under that act, if you moved west to states such as Illinois, Indiana, Minnesota, Ohio, or Wisconsin, among others, you could receive 160 acres of land free and clear with title if you lived on it for five years and worked to improve it. Guess what? You do not need to tell people to improve that which they own. As soon as they own something, the improvement begins. I have seen this firsthand as a board member of Habitat for Humanity for over a decade. You touch that responsive chord in people's hearts and minds. It is through this type of homesteading that the problems of urban America can be gradually dealt with and resolved and its condition improved.

CONCLUSION: ACCESS TO OPPORTUNITY IS EVERYTHING

By giving people access to capital and allowing people to take ownership of assets, entrepreneurship is encouraged, and the cycle of poverty can be broken. Through eliminating America's second economy and tapping into the economic forces of a more democratic capitalism, we begin to develop the formula for ending chronic poverty in America. All persons should have the opportunity to go as high as their merit, ability, determination, and the quality of their performance can carry them.

Attacking the rich and class warfare are not in the interests of the poor. Allowing the poor to become rich, or at least richer, is what I have found to be the most attractive political and economic model for the war on poverty. Lincoln said, "I don't believe in laws to prevent a man from getting rich, I want every man to get rich. I want that man to be able to earn, save, and some day hire others to work for him, that's the true American System!" Lincoln's definition of entrepreneurial capitalism is the best I have ever heard (though I always add "woman" to any great nineteenth-century truism).

I believe that a bipartisan consensus could be reached in America on a twenty-first century war on poverty that takes the best of the "center left" and the best of the "center right" along with making the reforms necessary to achieve the American Dream for all our people. There are many other ideas as well that can be explored, discussed, and debated, but I remain an optimist about improving the human condition, expanding our democratic ideals, and making a partnership with private enterprise a reality in what must be an all-out war against poverty.

NOTES

Special thanks to J.T. Taylor, Rudy Barry, and Janet Olawsky for their contributions to this chapter.

1. Thomas L. Friedman, *The World Is Flat: A Brief History of the Twenty-First Century* (New York: Farrar, Straus and Giroux, 2005).

2. Robert B. Avery, Glenn B. Canner, and Robert E. Cook, "New Information Reported Under HMDA and Its Application for Fair Lending Enforcement," *Federal Reserve Bulletin*, 2005, 344–94.

3. "Dayton Congressman Turner Honored by APA as Legislator of the Year" (news release, American Planning Association, February 28, 2005), http://www.planning.org/newsreleases/2005/ftp02280501.htm.

4. James K. Stewart, "The Urban Strangler: How Crime Causes Poverty in the Inner City," *Policy Review* 37 (1986): 8.

5. Kathryn Edin and Christopher Jencks, "Reforming Welfare," in *Rethinking Social Policy: Race, Poverty, and the Underclass* (Cambridge, MA: Harvard University Press, 1992).

6. Robert L. Rose, "For Welfare Parents, Scrimping Is Legal, but Saving Is Out," *Wall Street Journal*, 1990.

7. Marilyn Rubin, "Urban Enterprise Zones: Do They Work? Evidence from New Jersey," *Public Budgeting and Finance* 10 (December 1990): 3–17.

8. Opportunity International, "2005 Highlights" (2005), http://www.opportunity.org/atf/cf/%7B4FDDA71B-2D42-4FAE-84B0-75A6C2E25802%7D/2005_HIGHLIGHTS.PDF.

PART FIVE

STRENGTHENING FAMILY AND COMMUNITY

The final series of chapters on antipoverty reform focuses on the network of human institutions that provide the foundation for hope and optimism: families, schools, and communities.

In "Why We Should Be Concerned About Young, Less Educated, Black Men," Ronald Mincy and Hillard Pouncy focus on a group that was largely overlooked during the era of welfare reform: young, less educated African American men. They explain that neither universal policies designed to enhance economic prosperity nor targeted antipoverty programs have significantly affected the high rates of unemployment, incarceration, and out-of-wedlock parenthood that prevail in this group. These problems amount to a crisis that we ignore at our peril. Mincy and Pouncy outline policies aimed at improving education and job training, promoting family self-sufficiency, and reforming the criminal justice system. Their guiding principles include addressing multiple generations, promoting work and responsibility in achievable ways, and dedicating sustained and substantial funding.

In "A Hopeful Future: The Pathway to Helping Teens Avoid Pregnancy and Too-Soon Parenthood," Carol Mendez Cassell examines the links between poverty and teen parenthood. Although teen pregnancy rates have declined dramatically over the last decade, they remain startlingly high relative to those in other industrialized nations and are directly responsible for much child poverty. Cassell argues that teen pregnancy is partly a symptom of larger socioeconomic evils, including substandard schools, high crime rates, unsafe housing and home environments, and limited employment options.

Without appealing options for the future, teens may feel ambivalence toward pregnancy, viewing parenthood as the most available marker of success. Cassell recommends a comprehensive approach, including sexuality education advocating abstinence or the use of contraceptives and support from families, schools, and communities to create a future filled with promise.

In "Public Schools: Building Capacity for Hope and Opportunity" Dennis Orthner explains the need for top-flight public elementary and secondary schools to prepare students to compete in the globalized labor market. He emphasizes the significance of strong foundational skills for a workforce that will navigate multiple occupational transitions in response to shifting labor market opportunities. Yet high school graduation rates in many states are still abysmally low, especially for minority students, and those students who do graduate are less proficient in math and science than their peers in other countries. Orthner argues that schools should function as agents of opportunity for students by emphasizing high standards, engaging students by teaching relevance of the material in the context of their lives, and promoting supportive teacher-student-parent relationships. In an inset to this chapter, Hugh Price underscores the importance of the need to engage families, churches, and community groups in education reform. The burden of educating children cannot be borne solely by our public schools.

In "Top-Down Meets Bottom-Up: Local Job Creation in Rural America," Anita Brown-Graham calls our attention to the persistence of extreme poverty in many of the nation's rural counties. Successful development for the poorest rural areas will require both bottom-up community development emphasizing initiatives designed by residents that capitalize on the natural or cultural assets of the area, and top-down economic development that brings business to the area, creates jobs, and promotes entrepreneurship. In an inset to this chapter, Ruston Seaman and Michael Ferber outline an example of one such successful program in rural West Virginia. World Vision Appalachia adopts an asset-focused approach that builds upon existing human capacities and forges connections between people through a community time bank.

In the final chapter in this part, "Fighting Poverty with Equitable Development," Angela Glover Blackwell explains that antipoverty strategies that are not guided by equitable principles risk replicating poverty in new forms, particularly for minority communities. She urges economic development that promotes equal access to opportunity, including efforts to connect people to jobs through affordable transit, zoning reform designed to increase housing affordability and create economically integrated neighborhoods, and attention to meaningful community participation in the reform process.

Why We Should Be Concerned About Young, Less Educated, Black Men

Ronald B. Mincy and Hillard Pouncy

A *New York Times* front-page article on March 20, 2006, raised public awareness of the challenges faced by young black males. It reported that the share of such men without jobs had "climbed relentlessly" so that by 2004, 72 percent of black male high-school dropouts aged 20 to 30 were jobless. In that same year only 34 percent of young white and 19 percent of young Hispanic dropouts were similarly jobless. By their mid-30s, 6 in 10 black men who had dropped out of school had spent time in prison. In urban neighborhoods more than half of all black men had not finished high school. Despite these low employment and education rates, some studies estimate that 25 percent of less educated black men are fathers, and only 13 percent are married.[1]

The *New York Times* article revived debates over causal explanations and sparked discussions on what to do in response. As Sara McLanahan notes in this volume, policymakers continue to debate whether cultural or structural causes lie at the root of persistent poverty. In the context of young, less educated black males, those who adopt cultural explanations point to the embrace of hip-hop culture, while those who focus on structural explanations point to a weak economy and flawed health, education, workforce development, and criminal justice systems. In addition, as William Julius Wilson notes in this volume, policymakers are torn between broad, universal policies such as growing the economy or Social Security and narrower, targeted efforts such as Temporary Assistance for Needy Families (TANF) or other specific programs. As we discuss in this chapter, young, black, less educated men occupy a unique policy niche. Neither universal nor targeted efforts will help them if those efforts are conducted as they have been in the past.

Significant gains for young black males have not been forthcoming from programs that produce statistically proven results for women, adults, and other important subgroups such as high-school dropouts, disadvantaged workers, disconnected and out-of-school youth, and the children of welfare recipients.[2] Even more distressingly, providers who develop pilot programs that demonstrate success for generic populations have no incentive to continue modifying programs or operations in order to secure favorable outcomes for young black males. As a result, organizations that have the capacity to secure public support for programs that work for disadvantaged youth and young adults neglect less educated black males.

Targeted policies that focus successfully on problems of special significance to young black males, for example, responsible fatherhood or prison reentry, also have difficulties. Since policymakers have only recently begun to focus on these problems, the programs that provide these services have had to operate with limited federal funding. These grassroots organizations typically serve clients with volunteer staff and limited resources. Data collection and other activities needed to build capacity are luxuries their organizations cannot afford. Without descriptions of their service models, documentation of program costs and outcomes, adequate facilities to operate program services, and trained or experienced staff, program expansion is difficult, even if they gain local or national publicity. It is little wonder that few grassroots organizations are able to build the capacity they need to compete successfully for funding through generic funding streams.

Policymaking for young black males must encourage organizations with proven strategies for generic populations to continue to tweak their programs so that they work for young black males. And policymakers must help organizations with targeted programs develop and evaluate their programs and build the capacity to compete for government funding. The cooperation of private donors who have played critical roles at the early stages of mature generic policies—welfare reform, domestic violence, and youth development, for example—will be critical.

Since the publication of the article in the *New York Times*, the plight of young black men has attracted much attention at think tanks and universities and in the media. We hope that this increased public awareness has enduring results. It was in the spirit of furthering this discussion and helping secure positive, lasting outcomes that we wrote this chapter. First, we review policymaking in four specific areas that illustrate why the problems of young black males escape both the universal and targeted policy options tried to date. In each area we outline approaches for which there is evidence of promise. We then outline five policy steps that we believe will create a framework for success.

FOUR SPECIFIC POLICY AREAS

Education

Elsewhere in this volume Dennis Orthner outlines a series of education reforms that, like most discussions of school reform, assume that the performance of black boys will improve as a result of efforts directed at the entire student body. However, we call special attention to the educational needs of black boys because traditionally they receive less support from teachers and school administrators than other students (even black girls).[3] In addition, they adapt to the risks posed by their schools and neighborhoods in ways that are more likely to be interpreted as behavioral problems by teachers and school administrators.[4] Finally, parents often cannot marshal the resources needed to protect or buffer their boys from the more daunting obstacles posed by their teachers, school administrators, schools, and neighborhoods.[5]

In the early 1990s, after the publication of an influential study of the crisis conditions facing young black men,[6] several strategies for reengineering schools were attempted. These included mentoring programs, youth development efforts, and single-sex schools. However, few mentoring and youth development efforts targeting young black males have been sustained or have gone to scale, and proposals for single-sex schools encountered strong opposition from women's groups and civil libertarians. Moreover, the best evaluations of single-sex schools find little evidence of positive effects on academic achievement, except for disadvantaged students.[7] Comparative studies also reach mixed conclusions about the effectiveness of single-sex schools.[8] We should carefully evaluate a new round of single gender schools, e.g., Eagle Academy, the first publicly-funded all boys academy to open in thirty years, and allow them to run long enough to glean the important lessons.

A key feature of the school reengineering plans proposed by more recent studies is the reduction of the adverse effects that teacher perceptions, arbitrary disciplinary practices, and other cultural and environmental factors have on the academic achievement and graduation rate of black boys.[9] The New Schools movement reforms discussed by Orthner in this volume are one approach that appears promising. Another approach involves career academies, a high-quality variant of career and technical education (see Harry Holzer's chapter in this volume). A rigorous evaluation shows positive effects of career academies on graduation rates, academic achievement, and postsecondary employment and earnings for young men.[10] Such findings are in marked contrast to the findings of most programs that serve disadvantaged youth.

Other suggestions for improving black male academic achievement involve after-school youth development programs operated by traditional youth-serving organizations, which also provide tutoring.[11] One such program serving the children of welfare recipients was found to be effective for black girls, but not for black boys.[12] Therefore, additional work may be required to make these programs appealing and effective for young black males. Finally, Call Me MISTER, a program that provides male African American college students with tuition assistance and academic support in exchange for a period of service as full-time teachers, appears promising. However, no formal evaluation of the effects of this program on the achievement and graduation rates of black boys in the elementary and middle schools that employ such teachers has yet been conducted.

Job Training

Elsewhere in this volume Holzer discusses general education and training policies for the less affluent. Here we briefly discuss the specific job-training needs of less educated black males and how the capacities of targeted training programs should be expanded to better serve them.

The 1962 Manpower Development and Training Act (MDTA) began as a program for skilled workers temporarily unemployed in the 1961 recession. By 1964 it and most subsequent job-training programs were treated as antipoverty tools. Most have failed young, less educated, black males because they did not achieve significant employment or earnings gains. Job Corps succeeded, but only served a small fraction of these men because it was grossly underfunded.[13] For example, the Job Training and Partnership Act of 1982, which became the largest single source of job-training assistance until its repeal in 1998, disproportionately targeted women because it defined disadvantaged persons as welfare recipients and only secondarily included youth living in a welfare household. It was so severely underfunded that it served less than 1 percent of those eligible.[14]

Nevertheless, since the 1990s an entire job-training industry catering to the disadvantaged has developed with positive results and the potential to be adapted to the needs of young black men. This industry has been most successful at understanding and implementing a key lesson of welfare-based job-training policy—many participants have more trouble in their lives than a stand-alone job program can correct. In response, the field recognizes three segments or client pools: the hardest to serve, or those not ready to work; the job-ready but hard to serve; and the working poor who may have already graduated from a job-training program and are seeking to increase their wages, presumably without going to college.[15]

Within each of these segments several outstanding programs have emerged, including AmericaWorks, the Center for Employment Training, and STRIVE (Support and Training Result in Valuable Employees). *Sixty Minutes*, CBS's national newsmagazine, has twice aired reports on the last group, a nonprofit started in New York City that, in addition to teaching traditional job skills and facilitating job placement, excels at imparting soft skills to clients who have not learned to "code-switch."[16]

In research and evaluation, analysts reached two conclusions. First, soft skills and soft-skills training are critical in the current job market generally and especially in connecting the disadvantaged to long-term employment.[17] Second, a key barrier is figuring out how to replicate successful prototypes such as STRIVE.[18]

Unfortunately, the Workforce Investment Act's (WIA) spending formulas and program guidelines have reduced the percentage of funds going into the program's training component, the part that supports these promising programs (see Figure 15.1). In 1998 the training component accounted for 88 percent of the Job Training Partnership Act budget. In 2001 the training component totaled 44 percent of the WIA budget. Restoring these training funds is the single most critical reform needed in job-training policy.

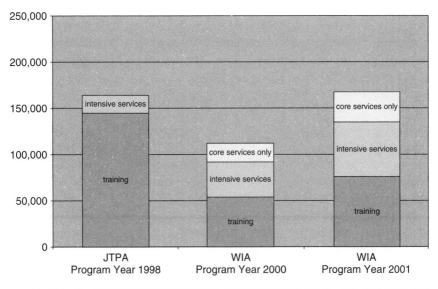

	JTPA Program Year 1998	WIA Program Year 2000	WIA Program Year 2001
Total Exiters	163,223	112,151	172,366
Core Services Only		20,300	36,918
Intensive Services	18,091	37,884	59,485
Training	145,132	53,967	75,963

Figure 15.1 Adult Exiters and Trainees

Source: U.S. Department of Labor, Employment and Training Administration (Training and Employment Notice No. 5-03), September 2003.

Family Self-Sufficiency

Both Holzer and McLanahan in this volume suggest expanding services for noncustodial parents to improve family self-sufficiency and increase incomes of low-skilled workers. Twenty-five percent of young, less educated men are noncustodial parents, and the figure is certainly higher for those who are black.[19] Expanding services for noncustodial parents is a critical way to increase access of young, less educated, black men to job opportunities, case management, and other services they need to overcome employment barriers.

Recent research points to positive and negative trends for black noncustodial parents and their encounters with the child-support enforcement system. Two positive trends are that paternity establishment rates have skyrocketed, and—at least for children born two years after welfare reform—the racial gap in paternity and child-support orders has disappeared. On the other hand, black children are less likely to receive the child-support payments they are due, especially because their unmarried fathers have lower levels of education, employment, and earnings and are less likely to have stable employment than white unmarried fathers.[20] Also, child-support orders are set so high that they lower compliance rates for many low-income men.[21]

Increased paternity establishment and child-support orders among minorities mean that the child-support enforcement system now has authority over more less educated black men than ever before. When low-income noncustodial parents are obligated to pay child support, guidelines usually require them to pay a much higher proportion of their income than higher-income noncustodial parents. As a result, fathers with annual earnings below $20,000 are responsible for a disproportionate share of the nation's accumulated child-support debt.[22] Studies find that high child-support debt levels create a work disincentive. This disincentive was partly responsible for the low employment rates observed for these men in the 1990s.[23]

Although the child-support enforcement system deepens the poverty of low-income noncustodial parents, the system can also help them. Lowering the required payments so that orders better reflect their ability to pay would give them more income to meet daily expenses, increase compliance, and avoid arrearages.[24] But while reducing child-support payments may help low-income noncustodial parents, it hurts low-income children. One way around this problem is providing noncustodial parents with earnings supplements parallel to the Earned Income Tax Credit, which was expanded to supplement the earnings of mothers leaving welfare. New York is the first state to provide such an earnings subsidy for noncustodial parents. Legislation pending in the Senate (S. 3267) would provide a similar subsidy to noncustodial parents in other states as well. Both the New York law and the Senate EITC proposal condition receipt of the EITC on payment of current child support; therefore, they benefit children by providing fathers with incentives to work and pay.

These efforts move in the right direction, but they may not go far enough. As William Julius Wilson points out in this volume, the inability to maintain employment throughout the year is one of the primary reasons that the annual earnings of black men are very low. Thus states should condition earnings subsidies to noncustodial parents upon proof of payment of their child-support obligations during each month of the last previous year in which they were employed. This would provide a work incentive while acknowledging that unemployment is a major reason for child-support noncompliance in this population.

In addition, states should reduce or eliminate penalties and interest charges associated with child-support debts that accrue during the period when a noncustodial parent is unable to find work. Moreover, states should consider reducing arrearages previously accumulated by a noncustodial parent for each month that he makes a timely child-support payment. Such debt-leveraging strategies are being tested in Colorado, Maryland, and Massachusetts.[25] If the experience of these states shows that providing low-income fathers with a second chance increases their employment and child-support payments, other states should adopt debt-leveraging strategies of their own.

There are a few other steps related to family self-sufficiency that could be taken to help young, less educated, black men, but these steps involve more than money. First, all child support collected from noncustodial parents should be passed on to custodial families formerly on welfare.[26] More states would do this now if they did not have to pay the federal government a portion of what they collect from noncustodial parents. Although the Deficit Reduction Act (DRA) makes some progress in this area, Congress should pass legislation that allows the full distribution of child-support collections to current and former TANF recipients. Passing all child-support payments on to families would enable fathers to play a larger role in improving family self-sufficiency. Second, the small federal program that helps parents resolve visitation and access disputes should be expanded, because it results in higher child-support payments.[27] Third, in addition to funding relationship-skills training for unwed parents interested in forming healthy marriages, as DRA does, such funding should also be available to improve co-parenting relationships for those unwed parents who do not wish to marry. By facilitating visitation, these two steps may also reduce behavior problems among young boys (and girls), according to the findings of a recent study.[28] At the time of birth of their new child, 35 percent of new unmarried mothers and fathers already have previous children with other partners.[29] Therefore, a final step would involve services to prevent repeat unwed conceptions among unmarried fathers in the same way that such services have been provided to unmarried mothers.

Crime

Beginning in the 1970s with policy initiatives that declared rehabilitation a dead letter and replaced it with the certainty of punishment, black males have been the unique "beneficiaries" of the last quarter century's prison boom. A recent study determined that incarceration rates for black men aged 18 to 65 rose from under 5 percent in 1980 to over 8 percent by 2000 (see Figure 15.2).[30] Incarceration rates for white males rose from .35 percent to less than 1 percent by 2000 and from 2 percent to less than 4 percent for Hispanics. Incarceration rates for young black males without a high-school education rose from under 10 percent in 1980 to 30 percent by 2000. For the other two groups, rates rose from under 2 percent to 5 percent for white men without a high-school education and from 5 percent to 10 percent for Hispanics.

Ex-offenders have lower wages, annual earnings, and marriage rates than men who have never been incarcerated, and these effects are especially pronounced for black men.[31] What could be done to reverse the toll of imprisonment on young black males? If the aforementioned policy changes were made in education, employment, and family self-sufficiency, fewer young black males would commit crimes. This would help somewhat, but reducing the crime rate alone is not sufficient. Despite declining crime rates during the 1990s, incarceration rates for young black males continued to grow.[32]

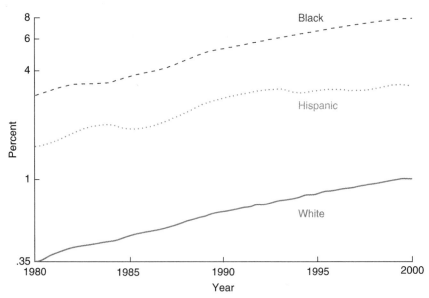

Figure 15.2 Incarceration Rates for All Men Aged 18 to 65 by Race, 1980–2000

Source: Meredith Kleykamp, Jake Rosenfeld, and Bruce Western, "Crime, Punishment, and American Inequality" (New York: Russel Sage Foundation, 2003).

Since more recent studies have overturned earlier social science research suggesting that rehabilitation does not work, perhaps more convicted criminals could be diverted from prison sentences.[33] Unfortunately, policymakers who champion diversion become politically vulnerable to the charge of being soft on crime.[34] For this reason, policymakers have addressed the issue through policies that facilitate reentry of ex-offenders into their communities and reduce recidivism. Opportunities for further reforms in this area could be identified by examining promising reentry initiatives that target ex-offenders with substance abuse problems[35] and mental illnesses,[36] those offered by faith- and community-based organizations,[37] and those that place ex-offenders in industries or occupations with high wages or high wage growth.[38]

FIVE GUIDELINES FOR MOVING AHEAD

Changing the four identified policy streams so that they support effective programs for young black males is the most important set of actions we can undertake now. However, it took several decades before we saw real signs of progress on teenage pregnancy and welfare reform. This suggests that progress for young black males may take some time as well. We outline here five principles that we believe should guide policy reform over the long haul.

Multigenerational Perspective

Our nation's approach for black males must be multigenerational. We should reject our past practice of choosing one age group over another in an attempt to identify the most advantageous point in the life cycle to intervene.[39] Instead, wherever possible, we should integrate policies and programs targeting young black boys with those targeting young black men. For example, McLanahan in this volume highlights both responsible fatherhood and healthy marriage policies that help young, unmarried fathers pay their child support and form healthy marital or co-parenting relationships with the mothers of their children. Further, we favor helping such parents become advocates of the reforms needed to change the learning environments in their sons' schools. Another approach would adapt intergenerational literacy programs, such as Even Start, to work with fathers, whether they are custodial parents or not.[40]

Responsible Reforms

We should ensure that our efforts to help young black males are not misinterpreted in ways that will sacrifice public confidence. One way to do this is to condition the supports we provide to young black males on their meeting basic, widely accepted requirements of citizenship. For example, the reforms we recommend in employment policy are meant to ensure that young black males work. Reforms in family self-sufficiency help ensure that young black males are responsible for their own children. Even the reforms in criminal justice policy are meant to ensure that ex-offenders return to their communities of origin as good citizens who respect the lives and property of their neighbors.

Reasonable Policies

Policies must also be reasonable. The requirements of citizenship must be achievable, given the current circumstances of young black males. Policy reforms must provide reasonable types and amounts of support, commensurate with those provided to other vulnerable populations. For example, although we described one of the goals of welfare reform as "family self-sufficiency," many former welfare recipients continue to receive food stamps, earnings subsidies, child-care assistance, and child health insurance. They work, but they are not self-sufficient.[41] Yet most policymakers and the public still view welfare reform as a resounding success. By contrast, child-support reforms required less educated men to meet their child-support obligations without enabling them to do so. We are beginning to recognize their mounting arrears as evidence that the policy is failing, underscoring the fact that the policy was the result of unreasonable expectations.

Patience

We have made substantial progress on other problems after decades of failure. Those efforts had the benefit of long and consistent public interest, although there were ebbs and flows. For example, welfare-to-work was first proposed in the 1967 amendments to the Social Security Act.[42] After 40 years of trial and error—including incentives, education and life-skills training, and job-search programs—work requirements, work supports, and a strong economy produced a decline in the welfare rolls and increased employment among young, less educated women, with the most dramatic changes occurring among black women.[43]

This longevity and consistency fostered a field of experts and practitioners whose knowledge about policies and programs improved from one episode to another. Young practitioners who began their careers working in entry-level positions were able to find employment in the same or related fields over time, thanks to sustained funding. The expertise they developed prepared them to hold positions of leadership later on. By contrast, public interest in the challenges facing young black males has been short-lived and episodic. Few practitioners remain in the field more than five years, and organizations continuously enter and exit. In order to produce experienced practitioners working in seasoned organizations dedicated to advancing the interests of young black males, more consistent funding is needed in this area as well.

Big Bucks

The last point raises the final principle in the framework, namely, the scale of the effort. Again, welfare reform provides a helpful benchmark. For work supports alone, Congress allocated $50 billion per year, most of which was spent on the EITC. In other words, Congress was willing to spend big bucks to assist welfare recipients to transition to work. Besides these expenditures, President Clinton used the bully pulpit to encourage the private sector to participate in the effort. This was only the most visible of efforts made by thousands of public servants to use their skills and energies to achieve this important public policy goal.

To be sure, young, less educated, black women were not the only recipients of these benefits and efforts. However, for decades they were the primary image of welfare dependency for most Americans, and the growth of nonmarital births among black women preceded trends now found among young women more generally. In the same way, the disconnection of young black males from the larger society is the worst and most visible indicator of the disconnections we are beginning to observe among other boys and less educated young men. It will probably take substantial spending, operating through both generic and targeted funding streams, to reconnect them all. Having identified reasonable standards of citizenship that we want these boys and young men to meet, how much are we prepared to commit to enable them to do so?

POLICYMAKING AT THE INTERSECTION OF RACE, GENDER, AND POVERTY

At the intersection of race, gender, and poverty, young, less educated, black males have been left behind. Newspapers routinely chart their worsening unemployment, crime, education, and family-formation problems—as we have done here. And, as we also note, few policies meant to help them have worked.

Young, less educated, black males belong to a disadvantaged race; we imagine that most Americans would be surprised to learn that among their peers, they are the disadvantaged gender. In popular culture, artists, authors, and filmmakers who speak in their name present them in images, attire, and story lines that belie that reality.

We have suggested ways in which policymakers can make the generic, universal policies discussed elsewhere in this volume more successful in addressing the needs of young black males. We have also suggested how the capacities of promising programs that successfully target services to young males can be increased.

NOTES

1. Ronald B. Mincy, ed., *Black Males Left Behind* (Washington, DC: Urban Institute Press, 2006), 5.

2. Gary Orfield, ed., *Dropouts in America: Confronting the Graduation Rate Crisis* (Cambridge, MA: Harvard Education Press, 2004); Andrew Hahn, Tom Leavitt, and Paul Aaron, *Evaluation of the Quantum Opportunities Program* (Waltham, MA: Heller Graduate School, Center for Human Resources, Brandeis University, 1994); Jeffrey R. Kling, Jeffrey B. Liebman, and Lawrence F. Katz, "Experimental Analysis of Neighborhood Effects" (Working Paper 11577, National Bureau of Economic Research, 2005).

3. Ronald F. Ferguson, "Teachers' Perceptions and Expectations and the Black-White Test Score Gap," *Urban Education* 38 (2003): 460–507; Margaret B. Spencer, "Old Issues and New Theorizing About African American Youth: A Phenomenological Variant of Ecological Systems Theory," in *African-American Youth: Their Social and Economic Status in the United States*, ed. Ronald L. Taylor (Westport, CT: Praeger, 1995); Margaret B. Spencer, "Social and Cultural Influences on School Adjustment: The Application of an Identity-Focused Cultural Ecological Perspective," *Educational Psychologist* 34 (1999): 43–57.

4. Dena P. Swanson, Michael Cunningham, and Margaret B. Spencer, "Black Males' Structural Conditions, Achievement Patterns, Normative Needs, and Opportunities," *Urban Education* 38, no. 5 (2003): 608–33; Margaret B. Spencer, Suzanne G. Fegley, Vinay Harpalani, and Gregory Seaton, "Understanding Hypermasculinity in Context: A Theory-Driven Analysis of Urban Adolescent Males' Coping Responses," *Research in Human Development* 1, no. 4 (2004): 229–57; Ann A. Ferguson, *Bad Boys: Public Schools in the Making of Black Masculinity* (Ann Arbor: University of Michigan Press, 2000).

5. Ferguson, *Bad Boys*.

6. Jewelle T. Gibbs, *Young, Black, and Male in America: An Endangered Species* (Dover, MA: Auburn House, 1988).

7. Terri Thompson and Charles Ungerleider, "Single Sex Schooling Final Report" (University of British Columbia, Canadian Centre for Knowledge Mobilisation, Vancouver, 2004).

8. Ronnie Hopkins, *Educating Black Males: Critical Lessons in Schooling, Community, and Power* (Albany: State University of New York Press, 1997).

9. Ronald F. Ferguson, "Spreading the Paradigm of a Master Teacher: The Great Expectations Initiative in Oklahoma" (Working Paper of the Taubman Center for State and Local Government, Harvard University, John F. Kennedy School of Government, 1993); Swanson, et al., "Black Males' Structural Conditions"; Spencer, "Social and Cultural Influences on School Adjustment."

10. James Kemple and J. Scott-Clayton, *Career Academies: Impacts on Labor Market Outcomes and Educational Attainment* (New York: Manpower Demonstration Research Corporation, 2004).

11. Olatokunbo S. Fashola, "Developing the Talents of African American Male Students During the Nonschool Hours," *Urban Education* 38, no. 4 (2003): 398–430.

12. Hahn et al., *Evaluation of the Quantum Opportunities Program*.

13. R.J. Lalonde, "The Promise of Public Sector–Sponsored Training Programs," *Journal of Economic Perspectives* 9, no. 2 (1995): 149–68.

14. Andrew Sum and Neal Fogg, "Trends in Funding for Youth Employment and Training Programs: Real Dollar Obligations for U.S. Department of Labor Employment and Training Programs

for Youth, 1979–1997" (paper prepared for the Sar Levitan Center on Social Policy Studies, Johns Hopkins University, Baltimore, 1997).

15. Hillard Pouncy, "New Directions in Job Training Strategies for the Disadvantaged," in *Securing the Future: Investing in Children from Birth to College*, ed. Sheldon Danziger and Jane Waldfogel (New York: Russell Sage Foundation, 2000).

16. Elijah Anderson, *Code of the Street: Decency, Violence, and the Moral Life of the Inner City* (New York: W.W. Norton, 1999).

17. Peter Cappelli, "Rethinking the 'Skills Gap,'" *California Management Review* 37, no. 4 (1995): 108–24; Phillip Moss and Chris Tilly, "Soft Skills and Race: An Investigation of Black Men's Employment Problems" (Working Paper, Russell Sage Foundation, 1995).

18. Pouncy, "New Directions in Job Training Strategies for the Disadvantaged."

19. D. S. Nightingale and E. Sorensen, "The Availability and Use of Workforce Development Programs Among Less-Educated Youth," in *Black Males Left Behind*, ed. Ronald B. Mincy (Washington, DC: Urban Institute Press, 2006).

20. Ronald B. Mincy, Lenna Nepomnyaschy, and Jean Brooks-Gunn, "Non-resident Father Involvement and Child Well-Being" (paper presented at the Annual Research Conference Association for Public Policy and Management, 2005).

21. Chien-Chung Huang, Ronald B. Mincy, and Irwin Garfinkel, "Child Support Obligations of Low-Income Fathers: Unbearable Burden vs. Children's Well-Being," *Journal of Marriage and the Family* 67, no. 5 (2005): 1275–86.

22. Elaine Sorensen, "Understanding Child Support Arrears" (paper presented at the Administration for Children and Families' 9th Annual Welfare Research and Evaluation Conference, Alexandria, VA, 2006).

23. Harry Holzer, Paul Offner, and Elaine Sorensen, "Declining Employment Among Young Black Less-Educated Men: The Role of Incarceration and Child Support," *Journal of Policy Analysis and Management* 24, no. 2 (2005): 329–50.

24. Vicki Turetsky, "Realistic Child Support Policies for Low-Income Fathers" (Center for Law and Social Policy, 2000).

25. Sorensen, "Understanding Child Support Arrears."

26. Turetsky, "Realistic Child Support Policies for Low-Income Fathers."

27. Department of Health and Human Services, *Effectiveness of Access and Visitation Grant Programs* (Washington, DC: Office of the Inspector General, 2002).

28. Mincy, Nepomnyaschy, and Brooks-Gunn, "Non-resident Father Involvement and Child Well-Being."

29. Ronald B. Mincy, "Who Should Marry Whom? Multiple Partner Fertility Among New Parents" (paper presented at the Annual Meeting of the Association for Public Policy and Management, Washington, DC, 2001).

30. Bruce Western, Meredith Kleykamp, and Jake Rosenfeld, "Did Falling Wages and Employment Increase U.S. Imprisonment?" *Social Forces* 84 (2006): 2291–2312.

31. Bruce Western, *Punishment and Inequality in America* (New York: Russell Sage, 2006).

32. Harry Holzer, Steven Raphael, and Michael Stoll, "How Do Crime and Incarceration Affect the Employment Prospects of Less Educated Black Men?" in *Black Males Left Behind*, ed. Ronald B. Mincy.

33. Francis Cullen, "The Twelve People Who Saved Rehabilitation: How the Science of Criminology Made a Difference," *Criminology* 43, no. 1 (2005): 1–42.

34. Jeffrey A. Butts and Adele V. Harrell, "Delinquents or Criminals? Policy Options for Young Offenders" (Urban Institute, 1998).

35. Tiffany Bergin, "Treating Trenton's Ex-Offenders: How Two-Pronged Drug Treatment Programs Can Reduce Recidivism, Repair Communities, and Save Tax Dollars" (Woodrow Wilson School of Public and International Affairs, Princeton University, 2006).

36. André Veiga, "Reducing Recidivism and Costs of Ex-Offenders with Mental Illness in Trenton, New Jersey" (Woodrow Wilson School of Public and International Affairs, Princeton University, 2006).

37. Jeremy Travis, *But They All Come Back: Facing the Challenges of Prisoner Reentry* (Washington,

DC: Urban Institute Press, 2005); Joshua Good and Pamela Sherrid, *When the Gates Open: Ready4Work—A National Response to the Prisoner Reentry Crisis* (Philadelphia: Public/Private Ventures, 2005).

38. Andrew De Mello, "Dynamic Rates of Recidivism: Effectiveness of High-Wage Vocational Employment Programs" (Woodrow Wilson School of Public and International Affairs, Princeton University, 2006).

39. Ronald B. Mincy, ed., *Nurturing Young Black Males* (Washington, DC: Urban Institute Press, 1994).

40. Robert G. St. Pierre, Anne E. Ricciuti, and Tracy Rim Izius, "Effects of a Family Literacy Program on Low-Literate Children and Their Parents: Findings from an Evaluation of the Even Start Family Literacy Program," *Developmental Psychology* 41, no. 6 (2005): 953–70.

41. Nancy E. Reichman, Julien O. Teitler, Irwin Garfinkel, and Sara McLanahan, "The Role of Welfare in New Parents' Lives" (paper presented at the Annual Meeting of the Association for Public Policy Analysis and Management, Washington, DC, 2001).

42. Gilbert Steiner, *The State of Welfare* (Washington, DC: Brookings Institution, 1971).

43. Rebecca Blank and Jonah Gelbach, "Are Less Educated Women Crowding Less Educated Men out of the Labor Market?" in *Black Males Left Behind*, ed. Ronald B. Mincy.

16

A Hopeful Future:
The Pathway to Helping Teens Avoid Pregnancy and Too-Soon Parenthood

Carol Mendez Cassell

THE LINK BETWEEN POVERTY, TEEN PREGNANCY, AND TEEN PARENTHOOD

Although it is difficult to untangle the intricate web of economic, cultural, and family forces that influence the life course of an adolescent, it is abundantly clear that poverty is the single biggest determinant of pregnancy among teens. Poverty is a cause, as well as a consequence, of teen pregnancy: there is a direct link between parenthood that occurs too early and the staggering number of young teenage mothers and children living in poverty.[1] This chapter examines the causes and effects of poverty and pregnancy among teens, reviews effective strategies aimed at motivating young people to avoid pregnancy, and offers recommendations on challenging, but essential, teen pregnancy prevention initiatives.

There is good news about our nationwide progress in the prevention of teen pregnancy. Over the past decade teen pregnancy rates have declined by 36 percent, showing that it is possible to make a dent in this seemingly impenetrable problem.[2] The two dynamics most often cited for the decline are that teens are delaying having sex, and sexually active teens are using more effective contraceptives.[3] The decline in teen pregnancy and the subsequent decrease in the teen birthrate between 1995 and 2002 are directly responsible for the 26 percent decrease in the number of children under age six living in poverty.[4]

Despite our significant progress in reducing teen pregnancy, there is also some dismaying news: our teen pregnancy numbers are alarming. One out of three teenaged American girls—close to 850,000—still gets pregnant each year.[5] Our teen pregnancy rates remain in starkly unfavorable contrast to those in other industrialized nations. Even though American adolescent patterns of sexual activity are not very different compared with those of adolescents in other countries, they use contraception less consistently and effectively. As a result, our rates of teen pregnancy are higher than those of Great Britain, France, or Spain and continue to pose major public health and socioeconomic problems with lasting repercussions for the teenage mothers and fathers, their children and families, and our communities and schools.[6]

Who Are the Teen Girls Behind the Statistics?

Teen (aged 15–19) pregnancy rates have declined across all groups: 34 percent for non-Hispanic whites and 19 percent among Hispanics, but the steepest decline, about 40 percent, has been among African Americans.[7] Still, there remains a great disparity in pregnancy rates among racial and ethnic groups, with teen birthrates disproportionately high among African American and Latino youth compared with other groups. In fact, 58 percent of African American girls and 50 percent of Latinas get pregnant at least once as a teen, compared with 34 percent of all teenage girls in the United States.[8]

Young women who come from advantaged families have lower pregnancy rates than young poor women; they rarely become teen mothers because they generally have abortions or, to a lesser degree, choose adoption. Conversely, more than 80 percent of teens aged 15–19 who give birth are from poor or low-income families, and most choose to raise their children.[9]

What About the Boys and Young Men?

It takes two to tango, and teen girls who become pregnant each year do not do it alone. However, we know little about the males involved. We do know that the majority of males who impregnate teen girls are over 19 years of age.[10] We also know that like teen mothers, most males who father children by teen girls are from poor, single-parent households, live in low-income neighborhoods, and drop out of high school. These young men are more likely to be unemployed or have low earnings, which means that even if they want to do right by their children, they are unable to fulfill their child-support obligations.[11] Jeffery Johnson, a professor at Eastern Oregon University, observes that they are "under-educated, unemployed and make so little money that they are themselves eligible for food stamps. These men aren't deadbeat dads. They are dead broke dads."[12]

WHY WE CANNOT BE COMPLACENT ABOUT
TEEN PREGNANCY: THE PLIGHT OF THE
CHILDREN OF CHILDREN

Teen pregnancy affects not just individual teenagers but all Americans. While most pregnant teens are 18 or 19 years old, approximately 40 percent are 17 or younger. Given that adolescence is a developmental phase of maturation, teen pregnancy is risky business, especially for those under age 17. It puts a psychological and physical strain on the health of the pregnant teenager and, at the very least, limits her life options.[13] Further, because a pregnant teen is less likely to graduate from high school than her peers, there is a great societal cost for caring for these young women and their children. Many poor young women are not poor because they have a child; they were already poor, and having a baby made their situation worse. More than 75 percent of teenage mothers receive public assistance within five years of delivering their first child.[14]

But the most heartrending and compelling reason to be concerned about teen pregnancy is that it casts a long shadow over the lives of the nearly half a million children born each year to poor teenage mothers—young women who are more like children themselves than adults.[15] As researcher Rebecca Maynard poignantly observed, "The odds are stacked against the offspring of adolescent mothers from the moment they enter the world."[16] Caught in the crosshairs of having a mother who in all likelihood is not developmentally capable or economically prepared to be a responsible parent and a father who often is not involved, these children suffer higher incidences of neglect and abuse, have chronic health problems, tend to drop out of school, are more likely to engage in problem behaviors, and often become teen parents themselves.[17]

The bottom line is that preventing teen pregnancy is a powerful investment in reducing poverty and improving the quality of life for millions of families. It is easier and more effective to help young people avoid pregnancy in the first place than to cope with the many negative social, educational, and economic consequences that condemn unmarried teenage girls and their children to the quagmire of poverty.

OVERCOMING BARRIERS TO REDUCING
TEEN PREGNANCY

Beyond poverty, it is impossible to single out any one social/political/familial barrier that impedes further progress to reduce teen pregnancy. We can, however, identify several factors that lead teens to make poor choices and become pregnant. While the precise contribution of any one factor is impossible to determine, a reasonable conclusion is that each plays a role. Outlined here is a brief overview of critical barriers and suggestions for strategies to overcome them.

The Street Where They Live

Teen pregnancy and too-soon parenthood are symptoms of larger social and economic predicaments of frayed communities and fractured families. Teens most at risk for pregnancy often live in neighborhoods that are plagued by problems including severe poverty, substandard schools, high crime rates, domestic and gang violence, and very visible drug abuse and dealing.[18] Without the tools of good schools, safe housing, and employment options, impoverished communities cannot hold out the promise of a better life to teens who postpone pregnancy and childbearing. Indeed, a lack of social and economic opportunities, rather than ethnicity, most accurately predicts high-risk sexual behavior and teen pregnancy.[19]

Given the diversity of these troubled communities, program planners need to develop a broad spectrum of community-based programs that are relevant to poor and high-risk teenagers regardless of the harsh circumstances of their lives. Effective interventions need to be built on the foundation of research indicating that young people who experience success, who are hopeful about their futures, and who are supported by their communities will postpone pregnancy.[20]

Teens' Conflicting Attitudes and Behaviors Toward Sex

Although the proportion of teens who have ever had sex has declined to 47 percent, about 25 percent of teens have had sex before the age of 16. By the age of 19, close to 70 percent of females and 65 percent of males have had sex.[21] Moreover, today's teens move from a kiss to sex in fast-forward mode: almost 33 percent of teens report that they had sex in the same month their relationship began; another 35 percent reported that they had sex within the first three months of dating.[22]

Our culture's conflicting attitudes and norms about sex often cloud a young person's understanding of what it means to be sexually responsible and weaken their capacity to make rational, healthy decisions about sex.[23] Teens grow up surrounded by a plethora of negative, mixed, and misleading messages about sex, delivered by their friends, on neighborhood streets, by the media in all forms, on the Internet, and even from their cell phones. A very high percentage (85 percent) of teens believe that sex should only occur in a long-term, committed relationship and that people should be married before having children. Yet at the same time, they say that it is acceptable to have sex with someone for whom they have strong affection and to live with someone outside marriage, and that a couple should not get married because of a pregnancy.[24] Teens also exhibit mixed feelings and behavior regarding contraception. Although they agree that sexually active teens should use contraceptives, 37 percent of sexually active high-school students said that they had not used protection the last time they had sex.[25]

To cut through the clutter of mixed messages, program designers and policymakers need to support intervention strategies and media efforts that provide clear messages that teens benefit from making good choices about relationships and avoiding risky sexual behavior. Studies have consistently shown that teaching responsible sexual behavior is not equivalent to promoting or encouraging sexual activity.[26] It does, in fact, empower young people to take more responsible actions to avoid pregnancy.

Teens' Ambivalence Toward Pregnancy and Parenthood

Although some teenage pregnancies occur despite the use of contraception, many are the result of ambivalence about getting pregnant and having a child. Teens' conflicting emotions make it difficult for them to make a clear-cut decision one way or the other: to abstain from sex or, if they have sex, to use contraception. As a result, a vast majority of teen pregnancies—approximately 80 percent—are unintended.[27] Although most pregnant teenagers say that they did not seek pregnancy or "intend" to get pregnant, most did not actively take actions to prevent pregnancy. They tend to blame the pregnancy on "bad luck" or "being swept away" or "something that just happened."[28]

As baffling as this may be to adults, teen pregnancy is not always unplanned, and a child is not necessarily unwanted.[29] Some disadvantaged teens may view pregnancy and motherhood positively, despite the fact that they may have witnessed their own mothers or sisters struggling with the grim reality of being a single mother. They may see pregnancy and childbirth as the ticket to achieving adult status: it is often the most available marker of success and social power in the face of otherwise limited opportunities.[30] Because it is very difficult to go against the cultural grain, girls growing up in poor families with a history of single teen mothers need to possess not just average, but above-average psychological resources and strengths to avoid pregnancy.

Intervention programs need to focus efforts on empowering young women to take a stronger, more self-protective and unequivocal stance to avoid pregnancy. They can also craft interventions that help both young teen girls and boys avoid risky sexual behavior by deciding not to have sex or to use effective contraception.

Teens' Lack of School Success

There are common roots and consequences between youth who drop out of school and youth who are most at risk of becoming a school-age parent. Students with low academic ability, who do not engage in school activities, and who have parents who are not supportive of their school experiences are twice as likely to become parents by their senior year as those students with high academic ability and solid parental support. Specifically, teen girls in the bottom 20 percent of basic reading and math skills are more likely to become pregnant and become mothers over a two-year high-school period than those in the top 20 percent.[31]

Although it is common wisdom that the primary reason girls drop out of school is because they are pregnant, that is not always the case. About 28 percent of teens leave school before they get pregnant. Those that are in school when they get pregnant drop out at a staggering rate, about 30 percent, and are not likely to return.[32] Complicating this serious problem is that close to 25 percent of teen mothers have a second child within two years.[33] A young mother may be able to finish school and obtain an entry-level job if she has one child, but these tasks become considerably more difficult if she has another.

Programs that offer after-school mentoring and tutoring to help young students gain the necessary skills to graduate from high school or get a GED have a dramatic impact on reducing dropout rates and pregnancy.[34] Educational and social services need to be provided for pregnant and parenting teens to improve the outcomes of teenage parenting. Programs that include both in-school classwork and case management, such as GRADS, which focuses on having teen parents graduate from high school or obtain a GED degree, have proven to be effective in helping teen mothers avoid a subsequent pregnancy and find employment.[35]

Nonvoluntary Sex: Sexual Abuse and Rape

Although the evidence is still accumulating, those experienced in working with sexual abuse and rape and those experienced in working with pregnant teens are well aware of the connection between sexual abuse in childhood and pregnancy in adolescence. For many teenage girls, sex is nonconsensual. Because this issue is so repulsive, our society often denies that it exists. Nevertheless, a study conducted by An Ounce of Prevention found that 60 percent of teens who experienced a first pregnancy by age 16 reported that their pregnancy was the result of being forced into sex; they were victims of incest, molestation, or rape.[36]

To address these tragic experiences, teen pregnancy prevention programs must incorporate training and services that recognize, counsel, and treat adolescents who are victims of sexual or physical abuse, and incorporate sexual abuse recovery into their programs.

The Abstinence Wars: While the Adults Argue, Teens Are Getting Pregnant

In many communities Americans have gone to battle over a topic that has erupted off and on again for years: what is the appropriate sexuality education curriculum to be taught to students in public schools? In one camp are the advocates for teaching abstinence-only-until-marriage (AOUM) education, which excludes contraceptive information. In the other camp are advocates for comprehensive sexuality education, often referred to as "abstinence-plus," an approach that teaches abstinence from sex (usually until the completion of high school) within health education programs that also provide contraceptive information. The debate is fueled by the federal government's greatly expanded support for AOUM despite evaluations that report that over the long term students who took virginity pledges as part of the AOUM programs were just as likely to get pregnant and contract sexually transmitted diseases as nonpledgers.[37]

The result of the conflict is a stalemate that impedes any progress in successful pregnancy prevention programs. In an effort to break that deadlock, the Society for Adolescent Medicine (SAM) announced support for a comprehensive approach to sexual risk reduction that includes abstinence, as well as correct and consistent use of condoms and contraceptives among teens who choose to be sexually active.[38] This last point is especially relevant. Although there has been a decline in sexual experience among teens, studies have found that the "use of contraceptives remains the most critical factor mediating the risk of pregnancy among sexually active teenagers."[39]

Exclusively promoting abstinence until marriage as the solution to the problem of teen pregnancy is inevitably an ineffective use of limited resources. Accordingly, policymakers should adopt SAM's recommendations and put an end to the "abstinence wars." Moreover, polls show strong public support for adopting comprehensive sexuality education (abstinence-plus) in public schools.[40]

SUCCESSFUL STRATEGIES FOR PREVENTION: APPLYING WHAT WE HAVE LEARNED

The interwoven problems of poverty and teen pregnancy can be so overwhelming that it is easy to overlook an encouraging fact of life: a majority of teenagers avoid pregnancy because they act responsibly. Continuing to make progress in preventing teen pregnancy means applying what we have learned so far about what motivates teenagers—especially those living in poverty—to avoid pregnancy. This section highlights the key elements of effective programs based on research and the experiences of those who work on the front lines of pregnancy prevention in schools and communities around the country.

Guiding Principles

Most successful programs are based upon two fundamental principles:

1. *Teens need a map and caring adults to guide them through the challenging maze of adolescence.* Because many teens from poor families do not believe that they have educational or career opportunities, becoming pregnant may not represent forfeited opportunities, as it would for a middle-class teen. Teens from disadvantaged backgrounds often feel that they have nothing to lose by becoming a parent; no doors will close because they believe from the outset that no doors are open to them. To motivate these teens to avoid pregnancy, it is not enough just to teach abstinence or to make contraception widely available. Programs need to engage young people in safe, structured, fun, and enriching activities that build self-worth and self-confidence—not just keep them out of trouble. This means having low-fee or no-fee activities, including sports, music, dance, and the arts; after-school programs such as tutoring and field trips; and community volunteer opportunities (for example, being a part of a neighborhood rebuilding project).[41] The key to teen participation is to have a diversity of teens involved in all phases of the program from planning to evaluation.

2. *Parents and "parents plus" need to be actively engaged in the planning and implementation of programs.* While parents cannot ultimately determine their teens' decisions about sex, young people with close family ties are less likely to be involved with a pregnancy. For most parents, it comes as a surprise that teens say that parents influence their decisions about sex more than friends do. Parents tend to underestimate their own influence and overestimate the influence of peers and the media.[42]

To help parents and teens build a deeper bond, successful programs conduct family-teen communication workshops/training to encourage family closeness.[43] But given the layers of problems that exist in many poor households, a focus on parents as the primary resource to help teenagers avoid pregnancy is too narrow. Some parents are simply not parental enough. Family- and child-oriented initiatives can widen the pool of caring adults available to mentor and guide young people by recruiting "parents plus"— extended family and close family friends, church and community members, and concerned neighbors. It truly does take a village to raise a child.[44]

Common Attributes of Successful Initiatives

No single strategy works for all youth, but prevention efforts that work to make a difference in preventing teen pregnancy share common attributes. They all deliver a clear message—not having sex is the safest choice, but if you choose to be sexually active, use contraceptives consistently and carefully. They also provide information on contraception and promote avoiding risky sexual behaviors, tailor their programs to participants' age level, are culturally relevant, encourage teens to practice communication and negotiation skills, and involve family members in planning and support for the program.[45] Five different but successful efforts are discussed here.

Safer Choices is a high-school curriculum of 20 sessions, evenly divided over two years and designed for use with grades 9 through 12. The program emphasizes delaying sexual initiation for teens who have not had sex and increasing condom use among sexually active teens. It also provides teacher training, parent education, and school-community linkages. The program is effective in reducing unprotected sex among sexually active youth and is especially effective in delaying sex among Hispanic teens.[46]

The Teen Outreach Program (TOP) is a teen pregnancy and dropout prevention program involving weekly classroom sessions to integrate the development tasks of adolescents with lessons learned from community after-school service (working as a supervised volunteer in a community agency). The program is designed around the curriculum "Changing Scenes" to increase teens' life skills and help them avoid pregnancy. It has proved to be effective in preventing pregnancy and school failure and is most successful at reaching high-risk youth and youth who were teen parents before the program.[47]

The Teen Life Center is an intensive and long-running school-community partnership program located in rural South Carolina. It bombards boys and girls with sex-education classes, offers life-skills sessions to teach self-esteem and the confidence to say no to sex, and provides practical one-on-one counseling that takes place "as often as basketball or track practice." Evaluations find that it is effective in preventing pregnancies among hard-to-reach teens who live in rural poverty.[48]

California's Male Involvement Program (MIP) is an innovative and highly regarded statewide effort involving young men aged 12–24 who are at risk of early or repeat fatherhood in conducting local community-based educational programs to help males avoid premature fatherhood. It has been effective in reaching large numbers of young men, keeping them in the program, and reducing the pregnancy rate among the youth active in the program.[49]

Plain Talk is an urban neighborhood-based initiative aimed at helping parents and community leaders develop the skills and tools they need to communicate effectively with young people about reducing adolescent sexual risk-taking. The program has proved to be successful in engaging community members and creating consensus about intervention efforts.[50]

SUMMING UP: PREVENTION CREATES "A FUTURE NOT OF RISK, BUT OF PROMISE"

Preventing teen pregnancy is a complex issue that will not be solved with wishful thinking and simple solutions. Beyond the obvious observation that teens have to be more responsible about avoiding pregnancy, adults need to do more to help young women avoid too-early pregnancy and young men avoid premature fatherhood. The recent declines in teen pregnancy rates are encouraging, but there is no guarantee that this trend will continue without a commitment to significant pregnancy prevention interventions. It will take nationwide appreciation of the magnitude and consequences of teen pregnancy to continue making progress in prevention. Time and again we have underestimated the extent of the resources necessary to change the circumstances of youth who are growing up in poverty and to help them avoid becoming parents too soon.

Research shows that preventing teen pregnancy is a highly effective way to reduce poverty. At the same time, reducing poverty is likely to reduce teen pregnancy. When we fail to address the issues of poverty and its impact on teen pregnancy, we develop ineffectual and irrelevant initiatives for those youths who are most in need of intervention. In the words of former Surgeon General Everett Koop, successful programs offer young people "a future not of risk, but of promise."[51] Simply put, the most powerful incentive for a young woman to do well in school and avoid getting pregnant is for her to gaze into a crystal ball and see herself living in a better future.

Programs need to move beyond the "risk, fear, dire consequences of sex" mantra of teen pregnancy prevention messages and put resources into effective ways to help teens put first things first—finish school, obtain gainful employment, and preferably get married before they consider pregnancy and parenthood. As one older and wiser teen mother advised young teenage girls attending one of my workshops: "Don't be stupid. Protect yourself. Graduate. Have fun, be free."

Last, but not least, all of us—parents, national, state, and local community leaders, members of the faith community, legislators, researchers, and teen-friendly media—need to be more willing to state unflinchingly that teen pregnancy and teen motherhood are not in anyone's best interests. We must provide comprehensive sexuality education in schools, implement vibrant neighborhood youth programs, and ensure that all teens have access to affordable, confidential reproductive health care. Most of all, as a community of caring adults, we can open doors that seemed shut and guide teens along the pathway to success.

NOTES

1. Isabel Sawhill, "What Can Be Done to Reduce Teen Pregnancy and Out-of-Wedlock Births?" (Policy Brief no. 8, Brookings Institution, October 2001): 1–11.

2. J.C. Abma, J.C. Martinex, W.D. Mosher, and B.S. Dawson, "Teenagers in the United States: Sexual Activity, Contraceptive Use, and Childbearing, 2002," National Center for Health Statistics, *National Vital Statistics* 23 (2004); Tamarah Moss, "Adolescent Pregnancy and Childbearing in the United States," *Transitions* 15, no. 2 (2003): 1–2.

3. Sawhill, "What can be Done?"; Priscilla Pardini, "Let's Talk About Sex: I Choose the Baby," *Rethinking Schools Online*, July 2005, http://www.rethinkingschools.org/sex/baby/174 .shtml, 1–11.

4. House Committee on Ways and Means (Democrats), "Steep Decline in Teen Birth Rate Significantly Responsible for Reducing Poverty and Single-Parent Families" (issue brief, Washington, DC, 2004).

5. Susheela Singh and Jacquelyn Darroch, "Adolescent Pregnancy and Childbearing: Levels and Trends in Developing Countries," *Family Planning Perspectives* 32, no. 1 (2000): 14–23.

6. Ammie N. Feijoo, "Adolescent Sexual Health in Europe and the U.S.—What's the Difference?" *Transitions* 15, no. 2 (2003): 13–15.

7. Alan Guttmacher Institute, "U.S. Teenage Pregnancy Statistics: Overall Trends, Trends by Race and Ethnicity and State-by-State Information" (2004), available online at http://www.guttmacher.org/pubs/state_pregnancy_trends.pdf.

8. S. Ventura, S. Curtin, and T. Mathews, "Variations in Teenage Birth Rates, 1991-1998: National and State Trends," *National Vital Statistics Reports* 48 (2000): 1–11.

9. Moss, "Adolescent Pregnancy and Childbearing in the United States."

10. Alan Guttmacher Institute, "U.S. Teenage Pregnancy Statistics"; William Marsiglio, Amy Ries, Freya Sonenstein, and Karen Troccoli, *It's a Guy Thing: Boys, Young Men, and Teen Pregnancy Prevention* (Washington, DC: National Campaign to Prevent Teen Pregnancy, 2006).

11. See Ronald B. Mincy and Hillard Pouncy, "Why We Should Be Concerned About Young, Less Educated, Black Men," in this volume; Marsiglio et al., *It's a Guy Thing*.

12. Wade Horn, *Father Facts* (Washington, DC: National Fatherhood Initiative, 2002), 2.

13. Carol Cassell, "Let It Shine: Promoting School Success and Life Aspirations to Prevent School Age Parenthood," *SIECUS Report* 30, no. 3 (February–March 2002): 6–12; Rebecca Levine Coley and P. Lindsay Chase-Lansdale, "Adolescent Pregnancy and Parenthood: Recent Evidence and Future Directions," *American Psychologist* 53 (February 1998): 152–64.

14. Sawsan As-Sanie, Angela Gantt, and Marjorie Rosenthal, "Pregnancy Prevention in Adolescents," *American Family Physician* 70, no. 8 (October 15, 2004): 1517–24.

15. Ibid.

16. Rebecca Maynard, ed., *Kids Having Kids: Economic Costs and Social Consequences of Teen Pregnancy* (Washington, DC: Urban Institute Press, 1997).

17. Cassell, "Let It Shine."

18. An insightful article about the influence of "place" is Wilhelmina Leigh, "Does Place Matter in the Reproductive Health Behaviors of Adolescents of Color?" *NOAPPP Network* 24, no. 4 (2003): 5–9.

19. Debra Kalmuss, Andrew Davidson, Alwyn Cohall, Danielle Laraque, and Carol Cassell, "Preventing Sexual Risk Behaviors: Linking Research and Program," *Perspectives in Sexual and Reproductive Health* 35, no. 2 (March–April 2003): 77–82.

20. Carol Cassell, John Santell, Brenda Colley Gilbert, Michael Dalmat, Jane Mezoff, and Mary Sehaven, "Mobilizing Communities: An Overview of the Community Coalition Partnership Programs for the Prevention of Teen Pregnancy," *Journal of Adolescent Health* 37 (2005): 3–10.

21. Elisabeth Terry-Humen, Jennifer Manlove, and Sarah Cottingham, "Trends and Recent Estimates: Sexuality Activity Among U.S. Teens" (Child Trends Research Brief, June 2006).

22. Barbara Dafoe Whitehead and Marline Pearson, *Making a Love Connection* (Washington, DC: National Campaign to Prevent Teen Pregnancy, 2006), 14.

23. Singh and Darroch, "Adolescent Pregnancy and Childbearing."

24. Whitehead and Pearson, *Making a Love Connetion*, 15.

25. Centers for Disease Control and Prevention, "Youth Risk Behavior Surveillance—United States, 2005," *Surveillance Summaries*, Morbidity and Mortality Weekly Report 55 (no. SS-5) (2006).

26. Douglas Kirby, *Emerging Answers: Research Findings on Programs to Reduce Teen Pregnancy* (Washington, DC: National Campaign to Prevent Teen Pregnancy, 2001).

27. Kalmuss et al., "Preventing Sexual Risk Behaviors."

28. Carol Cassell, "Reducing Ambivalence to Prevent Unintended Pregnancy," *Conversations in Counseling: Medical Economics* 6, no. 2 (May 2005): 13–16.

29. Kalmuss et al., "Preventing Sexual Risk Behaviors."

30. Arline Geronimus, "Damned If You Do: Culture, Identity, Privilege, and Teenage Childbearing in the United States," *Social Science and Medicine* 57 (2003): 881–93. Also see Kathryn Edin and Maria Kefalas, *Promises I Can Keep: Why Poor Women Put Motherhood Before Marriage* (Berkeley: University of California Press, 2005).

31. Cassell, "Let It Shine."

32. Jennifer Manlove, "The Influence of High School Dropout and School Disengagement on the Risk of School-Age Pregnancy," *Journal of Research on Adolescence* 8, no. 2 (1998): 197–220.

33. Ruth N. Turley, "Are Children of Young Mothers Disadvantaged Because of Their Mother's Age or Family Background?" *Child Development* 74, no. 2 (2003): 465–74; L.V. Klerman, B.A. Baker, and G.H. Howard, "Second Births Among Teenage Mothers: Program Results and Statistical Methods," *Journal of Adolescent Health* 32, no. 6 (2002): 452–55.

34. L.V. Klerman et al., "Second Births Among Teenage Mothers."

35. Claire Brindis and Susan Philliber, "Room to Grow: Improving Services for Pregnant and Parenting Teenagers in School Settings," *Education and Urban Society* 30, no. 2 (1998): 242–60.

36. Ounce of Prevention Fund, "Heart to Heart: An Innovative Approach to Preventing Child Sexual Abuse" (Study Report, Ounce of Prevention Fund, Washington, DC, 1995); Nancy Brown, Sandra Wilson, Ya-Min Kao, Verónica Luna, Elene S. Kuo, Claudette Rodriguez, and Philip W. Lavori, "Correlates of Sexual Abuse and Subsequent Risk Taking," *Hispanic Journal of Behavioral Sciences* 25, no. 3 (August 2003): 331–51.

37. John Santelli, Mary Ott, Maureen Lyon, Jennifer Rogers, Daniel Summers, and Rebecca Schleifer, "Abstinence and Abstinence-Only Education: A Review of U.S. Policies and Programs," *Journal of Adolescent Health* 38 (2006): 72–81.

38. Ibid.

39. John Santelli, Brian Morrow, John Anderson, and Laura Duberstein Linberg, "Contraceptive Use and Pregnancy Risk Among U.S. High School Students, 1991–2003," *Perspectives on Sexual and Reproductive Health* 38, no. 2 (2006): 106.

40. Linda Philips Lehrer, "More Evidence of Support for Comprehensive Sex Education," Planned Parenthood of New Mexico, *Sexuality Education Resource* 19 (January 2006): 1–2.

41. Robert Blum, Trisa Beuhring, and Peggy Mann Rinehart, *Protecting Teens: Beyond Race, Income and Family Structure* (Minneapolis: University of Minnesota, Center for Adolescent Health Press, 2000).

42. Bill Albert draws on material from two national surveys on parent influence in *Science Says: Parental Influence and Teen Pregnancy* (Washington, DC: National Campaign to Prevent Teen Pregnancy, February 2004).

43. Nicole Lezin, Lori Rolleri, Steve Bean, and Julie Taylor, *Parent-Child Connectedness: Implications for Research, Interventions, and Positive Impacts on Adolescent Health* (Santa Cruz, CA: ETR Associates, 2004).

44. Ibid. See also Betsy McKay, "Winning the Battle on Teen Pregnancy," *Wall Street Journal*, July 22–23, 2006, for "parents beyond parents" information.

45. Douglas Kirby, *Science Says: Characteristics of Effective Curriculum–Based Programs* (Washington, DC: National Campaign to Prevent Teen Pregnancy, September 2003).

46. Douglas Kirby and Karen Troccoli, *Progress Pending: How to Sustain and Extend Recent Reductions in Teen Pregnancy Rates* (Washington, DC: National Campaign to Prevent Teen Pregnancy, 2003), 13–22.

47. Ibid.

48. McKay, "Winning the Battle on Teen Pregnancy."

49. Hector Sanchez-Flores, "Young Male Involvement in Pregnancy Prevention and Parenting," *NOAPPP Network* (Fall 2003): 5–7.

50. Elaine Douglas, *Plain Talk: The Story of a Community-Based Strategy to Reduce Teen Pregnancy* (Baltimore: Population Services International, 1998).

51. Paul Burton, producer, *Listening to Teenagers* (New York: MacNeil/Lehrer Productions, 1990), film.

17

Public Schools: Building Capacity for Hope and Opportunity

Dennis K. Orthner

Our public elementary and secondary schools are critical to our nation's workforce development. Although private and parochial schools also help build the capacity of the next generation, 9 out of 10 children are in our public schools. The students in these schools must have the knowledge, skills, and confidence to contribute to the needs of our new and developing industries. If these schools fail, many of our youth and young adults will lose the opportunity to effectively compete for the careers of tomorrow, and some will also lose hope in a constructive future and turn to potentially destructive paths that can weaken our communities and society.

The competition for talent and skills is now worldwide, creating a global workforce that includes people from all nations. The student in an American high school today will compete for slots in colleges, entry-level jobs, and meaningful careers with teenage students now attending schools in China, Mexico, India, Finland, South Africa, and nearly every other country on our planet. These teens from other nations are also gaining admission to U.S. colleges and universities, coming here for basic work experiences, participating in industries that compete successfully for our outsourced jobs, and significantly improving their own quality of life, as well as that of their nations.

How well are our public schools doing in preparing the next generation for the jobs and careers of the future? What can America do to make them stronger and more capable of assuring success for their students? This chapter offers insights into the answers to these questions.

SCHOOLS AND WORKFORCE OPPORTUNITY

Public schools provide keys to the initial success or failure of our youth and young adults. The students in our public schools today are learning the basic concepts and skills that will be necessary for opportunities in higher education, career training, and workforce engagement. Fundamental knowledge of math and science, language arts, and social science is critical for the skills that our evolving industries require. Good schools offer a strong foundation in these subjects and provide students with the motivation and connections to build on this foundation in higher education or workforce training opportunities. And good schools give students hope and a vision for future opportunities and help students find direction in their lives.

But when these fundamental skills are poorly taught, inadequately understood, or otherwise not learned, our youth are handicapped in their ability to gain further education, training, or work opportunities. For some people, this can lead to poor work performance, frequent job turnover, and sometimes poverty, crime, and other challenges.[1] When these skills are weak for a sizable proportion of our youth, our nation fosters hopelessness and a broad underclass of people, and sometimes communities, who come to rely on public assistance and other means of ongoing support. This diverts valuable resources from productive ventures and weakens our ability to nurture the creative talent necessary to compete internationally for the jobs and industries of the future.

The quality of a person's education can also foster or limit short- and long-term choices and job opportunities. School dropouts or those with weak basic skills can find entry-level work or even technical training, but usually these efforts require some on-the-job skill building or remedial education that helps them catch up. Furthermore, we do not live in a static world in which the knowledge and skills activated in one's 20s can sustain a career into the 60s. All businesses and all industries, including farming and manufacturing today, are operating at high rates of change with increasing use of technology. Current skills and abilities, no matter what the field of work, will require continuous updating and exposure to the latest information and tools for each and every trade. More than ever before, this means that the foundation skills acquired in our primary and secondary schools will become fundamental for the many life-course transitions each person must make.

Our public education system is the foundation upon which our nation's opportunity structure is built. Just as in building a house, the bigger and stronger the foundation, the more can be built on top of it. A house with a larger and stronger foundation provides a base for more rooms, people, and activities. Likewise, a person with a stronger educational foundation has more room for other educational and career options, and the potential skill base upon which to consider evolving opportunities in the future. If the educational foundation is small and weak, however, then it is very difficult to build on top of it a robust and diverse opportunity structure. America's universities and community colleges try to help young adults compensate for weak educational foundations, but it is very difficult for most students to compensate for early school failures or having a weak knowledge base.

THE PERFORMANCE OF OUR PUBLIC SCHOOLS

So how are our public schools performing as they prepare the next generation of students for the opportunities and careers of the future? Here the data offer mixed results. There is some evidence that our students are performing well, but other data are quite worrisome. Overall, it would appear that the majority of U.S. students are graduating from high school, about half of these students are going on to college or a technical school, and most are making successful transitions into employment. These young adults are becoming the technically and socially competent people who help our nation compete on the global economic stage. These are also the young adults who are most likely to go on to pay taxes to support our nation's infrastructure, lead our nation's businesses and industries, and develop the new technologies and service industries upon which our nation depends.

But the picture is not entirely positive, and there are some problems that may create handicaps for our future. Recent data from the National Assessment of Educational Progress (NAEP) indicate that only about one-third of 4th-grade students are proficient in basic math and reading skills.[2] Among 8th graders very similar patterns were found, with less than one-third proficient in math and reading. The National Science Foundation (NSF) reports that by 12th grade dropouts have eliminated many students, yet only 16 percent of those remaining are proficient in math and 18 percent in science.[3] These scores do not build substantial confidence that the upcoming generation of youth is sufficiently prepared for the demanding knowledge requirements of our colleges or future employers.

A further key indicator of how well our public school students are performing can be seen in current high-school graduation rates. The Manhattan Institute measures the high-school graduation rate by the percentage of students who graduate compared with those who began 9th grade.[4] This is a better measure than the dropout rate, and only 70 percent of U.S. students who start 9th grade complete high school four years later. Although additional students eventually complete their graduation requirements or receive high-school equivalency by passing a GED exam, graduating in four years is the expectation for most parents and students and is a good indicator of educational progress.

One of the challenges of the current high-school graduation rate is the unevenness of this rate across states and across income and racial groups. Some states have graduation rates for their students approaching 90 percent. In other states only about half of their students graduate in the typical four-year period. The national high-school graduation rate for boys (65 percent) is considerably below that for girls (72 percent). The graduation rate is 78 percent for white students, compared with 72 percent for Asian students, 55 percent for African American students, and 53 percent for Hispanic students. When income of the parents is taken into account, the rates of high-school graduation are especially troubling for children from low-income families. Only about half of the students from low-income families graduate from high school, and graduation rates are even lower for African American and Hispanic boys.[5]

One hopeful trend for low-income students is indicated in a recent North Carolina study.[6] This study found that children from one-parent families had typically low high-school graduation rates, but when the mothers moved into the labor force and sustained steady employment, their children performed better in school and stayed in school at higher rates. In fact, the dropout rate for these students was 43 percent lower than for the students whose mothers were not working. These and other findings indicated that youth who see their parents working in their own jobs are encouraged to work harder on their schoolwork and stay in school to graduation.

The importance of a high-school diploma for later career opportunities and income cannot be denied. The U.S. Census Bureau finds that high-school graduates earn an average $27,280 per year, compared with $18,826 for nongraduates, a 45 percent improvement.[7] Of course, those going on for further education have significant economic advantages, with bachelor's degree holders averaging an annual income of $51,194 and advanced degree holders averaging $72,824.

FACTORS THAT PROMOTE STUDENT HOPE
AND OPPORTUNITY

The desire to transform schools into more effective agents of opportunity for their students is long-standing. School reform movements have been chronicled for as long as there have been public schools. Still, advocates of reform have found very few widespread efforts to reform public education that have had noteworthy success.[8] Small-scale efforts have sometimes produced meaningful results, but these have rarely been extended to statewide or national reforms. We have learned how to increase standardized test scores, but improving rates of high-school completion and postsecondary-school success have proven to be much more difficult. Major reports on the status of public education, such as the 1983 *A Nation at Risk* report by the U.S. Department of Education, appear every decade or so, but these are usually more summaries of failures than of successes. Commenting on the *Workforce 2000 Report* prepared in 1987, L.S. Johnson recently noted, "It was clear to many even then that the American educational system had to reconceptualize the way teaching and learning was being approached in schools if students were to be prepared for the new economy."[9]

Despite this pessimistic picture, much has been learned from recent small-scale school-based interventions and model testing that offer real hope for transforming public education. These new models and strategies are largely being summarized, supported, implemented, and tested through a variety of efforts. The Bill and Melinda Gates Foundation, for example, has many allies in the education, policy, and research communities and is stimulating major reforms at state and national levels. The umbrella for these reforms is conceptualized in a new definition of the "three Rs" of education: rigor, relevance, and relationships. There are additional components that should be added to these elements, but these three core elements appear to be necessary.

Rigor

Schools that graduate higher numbers of students appear to develop and engage students in courses and curricula that are challenging and build the competencies necessary to be a literate, participating member of our society. Courses that meet this standard of rigor prepare students for both college and careers and set high expectations for students, as well as creative demands on their teachers. Students in more rigorous schools are encouraged to take courses that stretch their knowledge and skills, not just meet the basic interests of the lowest common denominator of students in the class. An example of the value of rigor was found in the Breakthrough High School Project funded by the Gates Foundation.[10] This project identified common traits among high schools across the nation with at least 50 percent minority and 50 percent low-income students but with 90 percent or more of students graduating. One common theme at these schools was a "rigorous curriculum" that engaged students and pushed them into higher levels of learning. These schools had extensive tutoring and mentoring programs for students and teachers who were kept up-to-date on the latest information and instructional tools in their area of teaching. The bar for success was kept high for all students and all teachers.

These high standards for instruction and learning are not that common in public schools today. According to recent research by the National Center for

Public Policy and Higher Education, only half of our nation's high-school students take at least one upper-level mathematics course, and only one in four takes an upper-level science course.[11] But those states and schools with higher proportions of students taking more advanced courses also have higher graduation rates and more students going on to postsecondary education. One challenge states face in setting higher standards, however, is the lack of public support for the demands that rigor requires of students, and sometimes their parents. A recent survey of Ohio parents found that although most agreed that basic math skills (81 percent) and basic English skills (73 percent) should be required for graduation, fewer than half of these parents believed that advanced knowledge, such as in algebra, biology, or chemistry, should be required for graduation.[12] When this is coupled with demands by parents for less homework and more time for students to work, clearly many parents do not understand the needs of schools to enhance rigor and the needs of their children to commit to higher standards of achievement in more rigorous coursework.

To enhance rigor in public schools, it would appear that parents, teachers, and school administrators need to boost public understanding of the value of higher standards for school curricula. This will require more active campaigns to help parents and community groups see that higher standards in their schools will help students in the future (see inset box by Hugh Price for example). Parents and communities need to expect more from their schools and provide the resources necessary for schools to have the equipment and supplies that a more rigorous curriculum will require. This will also necessitate teacher education and teacher in-service training on how to include more demanding content in their classes, how to develop helpful homework assignments, how to engage tutors and parents in assisting students with learning, and at the same time how to develop an encouraging and enjoyable learning environment.

Relevance

Research has consistently demonstrated that students are more likely to learn content when it is offered in a meaningful context.[13] That is, students learn best when the teacher gives them an application of the content to current issues of the day or helps them see how this content can help them in future courses they will take or career decisions they will make. The successful Breakthrough high schools were distinguished by teachers who purposively connected student learning to future education and careers. Another high-school model called the Quantum Opportunity Program produced higher graduation rates by assuring that at-risk high-school students participated in developmental activities that promoted life skills and employment success.[14]

GETTING PARENTS AND COMMUNITY INTO THE SCHOOL REFORM ACT

Hugh B. Price

The campaign to improve public education should include a concerted effort to engage children, their families, and community groups. Many low-income parents work extremely hard these days. But they must not play hooky from their children's education. In my book titled *Achievement Matters*, I mentioned many practical things that parents and caregivers can do to help their children become good readers.[1] These include reading to their youngsters from the time they are infants and sharply limiting the amount of television they watch.

Churches and community groups should pitch in to create a culture of achievement that neutralizes peer pressure to lollygag in school. When I headed the National Urban League, we established a National Achievers Society that was modeled on a program that started in Florida. We inducted youngsters who had earned B averages or better into a community-based honor society. The ceremonies typically took place in black churches on Saturdays.

I vividly recall the ceremony that the local Urban League staged at Bayview Baptist Church in San Diego. Arrayed before us were 350 inductees, all of whom had earned B averages or better in school—and half of whom were boys. The church was packed with 1,000 well-wishers who cheered on the achievers. The local African American newspaper published their photos.

Not one of those inductees that day disparaged achievement as "acting white." They all eagerly stepped forward to be anointed as achievers and proudly wore the customized jackets available only to NAS members. Many whom I talked with there and in other ceremonies around the country in effect asked what took the grown-ups so long to celebrate them and provide the protective cover of a like-minded peer group.

Why stop there? How about local civic and community groups joining forces with the schools to stage an annual Achievement Day parade where every youngster who passes the state reading exam gets to march right through downtown, with their parents and teachers alongside them? If there can be St. Patrick's Day parades and ticker-tape parades for World Series champions, then surely cities can also stage Achievement Day parades for children who are getting the job done in school.

Volunteer organizations in the community can also promote academic achievement. For years I have been a member of a club composed of African American professional men, known as the Westchester Clubmen. In 1992 we launched an after-school program for black teenage boys who were struggling in school. Since our members are very busy with their careers, we wisely decided to put up the money for a program director and tutors to work four days a week after school with these young people. The program has succeeded in encouraging these youngsters to go on to postsecondary education and obtain high grades.

Education is a time-honored escape route from poverty. Yet the burden should not fall solely on educators. When it comes to equipping low-income and working-class youngsters for the journey to the mainstream, parents and community matter more than ever. The more motivated children are to learn, the easier it is for educators to empower them to achieve.

NOTE

1. Hugh B. Price, *Achievement Matters: Getting Your Child the Best Education Possible* (New York: Dafina Books, 2002).

The importance of school relevance is illustrated by a high-school dropout in the Ohio education study who stated, "If the school really cares about us and wants more kids graduating, they are going to have to give us something to look forward to."

Current policies, such as the federal No Child Left Behind effort, promote high standards for knowledge and the testing of knowledge, but knowledge attained for a test is not the same as knowledge retained for later use. This may explain why student test scores are increasing at the same time that there are high dropout rates. But building relevance into public school curricula requires innovations in teacher instruction and curriculum guidance. Studies show that students begin middle school believing that what they will learn will help them with future school, life, and career decisions, but that this belief declines with each additional year of schooling.[15]

To stop this critical decline in student engagement, schools must make student coursework challenging but also relevant. One strategy now being tested is called CareerStart.[16] This initiative provides 6th- through 8th-grade middle-school teachers in all core curricula with pre-prepared lessons, materials, and units that they can use to illustrate how the content in their class can apply to career and work situations in their own communities today and in the lives of their students tomorrow. Surveyed teachers overwhelmingly said that they wanted to include this kind of material in their classes, and surveyed 6th-grade students echoed that they hoped that their classrooms would help them understand the links between what they were learning and the world of work outside the classroom. This kind of program links rigor to relevance.

To a large extent, promoting school relevance will require teachers to learn new skills in how to illustrate their lessons with real-world examples and supportive classroom materials that help teachers and students see the applications of knowledge, as well as the content of the knowledge. Some of this is now being developed through videos or computer applications or new curricula and materials. But this will have to be encouraged and supported by school administrators, and these administrators need better ways of assessing student engagement and excitement for learning as a sign of student success, not just measures of short-term content learning through multiple-choice testing. Student engagement has several key indicators, including attendance at school, homework completion, behavioral indicators such as conduct problems, and eventually staying in or dropping out of school. These and other related measures may need just as much attention as test scores in the future.

Relationships

A school that creates an emotional and supportive connection between teachers, between teachers and students, and between the school and the community, especially parents, offers the third critical factor in school success. Research demonstrates that students perform better in their courses and are more likely to stay in school when they believe that the adults in their lives and their school genuinely care for them as persons and want to help them succeed.[17] When students consider themselves to be anonymous and view their teachers as detached, they are more likely to pull back psychologically from their classwork and then drop out of school when the opportunity arises.

There are many trends today that can make school relationships difficult, including larger class sizes, increasing school size, pressures for some students to work, and video games and other technologies that promote private space and independence. But schools can counter these trends by instituting strategies that promote more classroom interaction, personal time with teachers and mentors, parent and teacher meetings around positive learning issues, and constructive and engaging meetings among school staffs for joint planning and developing new creative strategies for student learning and engagement. At the high-school level these strategies are being implemented under various titles, including the New Schools movement. These "new schools" are designed to provide smaller schools or schools-within-a-school so that students come to know each other and their teachers much better. The new schools typically have no more than 400 students and often have a defined curriculum centered on a topic or career interest, such as international studies, business, technology, science, or the arts. Students in these schools have an adviser who provides ongoing counsel, teachers who often teach them multiple subjects, and a common cohort of fellow students who share similar interests and future education and career interests. Research indicates that these kinds of efforts lead to improvements in student engagement and high-school completion, especially among students from lower-income families.[18]

Shared Responsibility

There are other factors that also must be promoted if schools are to become the workforce capacity-building institutions that the public and the economy demand. One of these is for all schools and teachers, irrespective of their grade levels, to see themselves as contributing to the future of their students. Preparation for the workforce of tomorrow should not solely be left to high schools or to vocational-technical teachers and curricula. The foundation for basic workforce skills is laid in elementary schools, built on substantially in middle schools, and extended in high schools. When individual teachers limit their vision for their students to one grade or one class or one area of content, they severely restrict their students' visions for their own futures or force immature students to make connections on their own between their coursework and the education and career decisions that lie before them. Indeed, a recent report on U.S. economic growth strongly supports the contribution that education at all grade levels can have for future economic prospects, including even quality preschool education.[19]

Part of the shared responsibility within schools must come from building active learning cultures among all personnel in the schools. Schools should not just be places for students to learn; they must be places in which all staff members are actively engaged in the learning process. This is sometimes referred to as "continuous learning" or "organizational learning." Teachers cannot rely on outdated information in their classrooms, but teachers and school leaders do not always keep up with the latest information that is being gleaned by other teachers in their own schools or with the reams of new information being generated in their professions. Research has shown that organizational processes can be instituted in schools that promote staff learning, and that these processes in turn benefit students.[20] But teachers and administrators must be motivated to instill these processes into their schools and build a culture that supports learning among everyone in the school, including teachers, staff, and students.

A shared learning culture in the school can be fostered by creating learning teams in which parents, teachers, and administrators carefully and regularly examine options for improving each aspect of the school that contributes to the learning process. No stone can be protected from being turned over by these teams. The reward system in the school also has to support this process by encouraging innovations and allowing teachers to try new strategies, even if some of them do not work out as planned.[21] By creating a true learning culture, students are not the only "learners" in the school; every adult also benefits from participating in the learning process.

CONCLUSION

Public schools today have a growing responsibility to connect their students to future opportunities in the labor force of tomorrow. This will not be easy, given the challenges that teachers face in their own evolving areas of knowledge, that school leaders face with diminishing resources, that parents face as they are asked to connect their children to new educational priorities, or that students face in a world that focuses on the needs of the present rather than preparation for the future. But school reform is absolutely necessary. It cannot be on our wish list; it has to be on our must-do list. Other nations are reforming and strengthening their school systems, in part to catch up to where the United States has been but also to move ahead in the global race for high-quality industries and economic development. America risks falling further behind in this international race if it continues to allow its schools and students to lag behind the opportunities that are emerging. It also risks fostering a two-tiered society in which one tier has excellent schools and economic opportunities and another has poor schools, limited opportunities, and dysfunctional communities. None of these options should be acceptable in a society that truly hopes that its future lies in the prospects of the next generation.

NOTES

1. V. McLoyd, "Socioeconomic Disadvantage and Child Development," *American Psychologist* 53 (1998): 185–204.

2. Annie E. Casey Foundation, *Kids Count 2006 Data Book* (Baltimore: Casey Foundation, 2006).

3. National Science Foundation, "Student Learning in Mathematics and Science," in *Science and Engineering Indicators 2006* (Washington, DC: National Science Foundation, 2006).

4. J.P. Greene and M.A. Winters, "Leaving Boys Behind: Public High School Graduation Rates" (Civic Report no. 48, Manhattan Institute, New York, April 2006).

5. D.K. Orthner and K. Randolph, "Welfare Reform and High School Dropout Patterns for Children," *Children and Youth Services Review* 21 (1999): 785–804.

6. D.K. Orthner, P.G. Cook, R. Rose, and K. Randolph, "Welfare Reform, Poverty and Children's Performance in Schools: Challenges for the School Community," *Children and Schools* 24 (2002): 105–21.

7. U.S. Bureau of the Census, *School Enrollment—Social and Economic Characteristics of Students: October 2004* (Washington, DC: Department of Commerce, 2004).

8. L. Cuban, "Why Has Frequent High School Reform Since World War II Produced Disappointing Results Again, and Again, and Again?" in *Using Rigorous Evidence to Improve Policy and Practice* (New York: Manpower Demonstration Research Corporation, 2004).

9. L.S. Johnson, "The Relevance of School to Career: A Study in Student Awareness," *Journal of Career Development* 26 (2000): 264.

10. National Association of Secondary School Principals, *Breakthrough High Schools: You Can Do It, Too!* (Reston, VA: NASSP, 2006).

11. National Center for Public Policy and Higher Education, *Measuring Up 2002* (San Jose, CA: NCPPHE, 2002).

12. M. Ingwersen and C. Wick, *High-Quality High Schools: Preparing All Students for Success in Postsecondary Education, Careers and Citizenship* (Columbus, OH: State Board of Education, 2004).

13. G. Caine, R.W. Caine, and S. Crowell, *Mindshifts: A Brain-Based Process for Restructuring Schools and Renewing Education* (Tucson, AZ: Zephyr Press, 1994).

14. D. Stern, and J.Y. Wing, "Is There Solid Evidence of Positive Effects for High School Students?" in *Using Rigorous Evidence to Improve Policy and Practice* (New York: Manpower Demonstration Research Corporation, 2004).

15. Johnson, "Relevance of School to Career," 264.

16. D.K. Orthner, P. Akos, V. Cooley, and P. Charles, *CareerStart: A School and Career Engagement Strategy for Improving Education and Life Success in Middle Schools* (Chapel Hill, NC: Jordan Institute for Families, 2006).

17. T. Vander Ark, *Every Student a College Ready Graduate* (Seattle: Bill and Melinda Gates Foundation, 2005).

18. J. Quint, *Meeting Five Critical Challenges of High School Reform* (New York: Manpower Demonstration Research Corporation, 2006).

19. W.T. Dickens, I. Sawhill, and J. Tebbs, "The Effects of Investing in Early Education on Economic Growth" (Policy Brief 153, Brookings Institution, 2006).

20. D.K. Orthner, P. Cook, Y. Sabah, and J. Rosenfeld, "Organizational Learning: A Cross-National Pilot-Test of Effectiveness in Children's Services," *Evaluation and Program Planning* 29 (2006): 70–78.

21. P. Senge, et al., *Schools That Learn* (New York: Doubleday, 2000).

18

Top-Down Meets Bottom-Up: Local Job Creation in Rural America

Anita Brown-Graham

Rural America finds itself in the midst of an extraordinary episode of change. Profound advances in innovation and technology drive a dramatic and traumatic economic restructuring, bequeathing new prosperity to some places while seemingly dooming others to decades of economic displacement. For some rural communities, the restructuring has brought jobs, commercial services, population diversity, and a significant improvement in the quality of life for residents. These are the poster places for the much-heralded "rural turnaround" of the 1990s. Unfortunately, most rural places have fared less well. The highly promoted examples of turnaround economies cannot quell the disquieting facts that 340 of the nation's 386 "persistently poor" counties are rural or that nearly half of the poor who live in these rural counties are severely poor—that is, with incomes less than 50 percent of the official federal poverty threshold.[1] Nor can evidence of prosperous rural places dispel the nagging truths that roughly 6 of every 10 rural areas lag behind the national economy in terms of adding new jobs and that the gap in performance levels between rural and urban areas appears to be widening.[2]

In response to the stretching economic gaps between most rural and urban areas and the life realities that these differences represent, rural communities are scrambling to find effective development strategies that create jobs and alleviate poverty. Nearly every town and village, every county and countryside is hitching its future to the notion that it can compete in the new global economy. Four formidable realities about the global economy lie before them:

1. Increases in innovation are key to driving growth and prosperity in today's global economy. These innovations generate the productivity economists estimate accounts for half of U.S. gross domestic product growth over the past 50 years.[3]
2. Significant capital investments are required to put innovations to economic use.
3. Place matters in the global economy. Development efforts often rely upon and should seek, whenever possible, to protect natural assets.
4. Development is a "contact sport," best pursued through dense networks of personal contacts.

The question raised by this chapter is whether poor, rural areas can expect traditional local development strategies aimed at promoting economic growth to also address the issue of poverty alleviation. It first explores the development differences between rural and urban areas and those differences that distinguish the varying economic circumstances of rural areas. It then examines top-down economic development and bottom-up community development and suggests that effective rural development policies must continue to combine the strengths of each approach within a framework for observing the dual goals of economic growth and poverty alleviation. The chapter concludes by noting that the new economy matters to rural development prospects. Effective development will require an environment in which innovation is enabled, investments are available, preservation is valued and leveraged, and connections are embedded.

UNDER THE MAGNIFYING GLASS: THE RURAL/URBAN PARADOX

According to official U.S. Census Bureau definitions, rural areas comprise open country and settlements with fewer than 2,500 residents. These rural areas account for 80 percent of the nation's land area and 20 percent of the population. Urban areas comprise more densely settled areas. Although many cities, particularly inner cities, face significant development challenges of their own (see Chapter 19), the proximity of these distressed urban places to strong regional economic centers allows for a growing sense that the nation's economic future is tied to the promise of urban areas to drive innovation. As a result, the perceived divide between rural and more densely populated urban places continues to be magnified.

Although evidence of different levels of economic vitality is clear, the notion of "a rural/urban divide" has become a misleading metaphor that oversimplifies and even distorts the realities. To begin with, the debate on the rural/urban paradox is often imperceptive. It defies logic to suggest that rural places are disconnected from urban spaces or that the nation's economic prospects might be considered independently from the prospects of its rural places. To the contrary, the linkages and interactions between urban and rural areas are becoming ever more intensive. Many places are neither "urban" nor "rural"; they have features of both. Moreover, there are areas that are distinctly rural that are prospering in this new economy while others languish. Focusing solely on a rural/urban paradox, therefore, fails to tell the full tale of rural economic development prospects.

Admittedly, however, the four developmental challenges of innovation, investment, preservation, and connections are often manifested differently in rural areas. This creates important differences between rural and urban areas in aggregate comparative numbers. In particular, two indicators of economic performance are especially insightful when comparing rural and urban economic performance: income and employment.

First, rural incomes and wages lag far behind those in urban areas. In 2004 rural per capita income was 72 percent of urban income, and earnings per job were 66 percent of urban earnings. While not all high poverty rural areas can be characterized as experiencing persistent poverty, the severity of economic distress in persistent poverty areas is particularly telling. In "persistent-poverty" rural areas—those areas with poverty levels exceeding 20 percent for each of the last four decennial censuses—many households had incomes only moderately above the federal poverty threshold. In fact, just 48 percent of the population in persistent high-poverty rural counties lived in households with incomes at least double the poverty threshold.[4]

Second, the rural employment base is quite diverse, but it is less so and more reliant on old-economy activities such as farming, mining, and manufacturing than that of urban areas. For instance, 12 percent of the rural labor force was employed in manufacturing in 2003. That statistic reflected a drop from 17 percent in 2000, but it was still much higher than the 8.4 percent manufacturing employment figure in urban areas in 2003. Farming employs a lower percentage of the rural labor force (less than 6.5 percent), although the sector still dominates the economies of 403 rural counties.[5] Only 27 nonrural areas were classified as farming dependent. On the other hand, while urban areas have higher numbers of counties that are classified as service-sector dependent, rural employment in the service sector is definitely increasing. In 2003 the service sector accounted for 55 percent of jobs, up from 50 percent in 1992.[6] Many of those jobs were in the R and R of rural economies: recreation- and retirement-related fields.

KNOWING YOUR PLACE: RURAL VARIATIONS

Although a comparison between rural and urban areas reflects important trends, any meaningful examination of rural development prospects must acknowledge that "rural America is really a patchwork quilt of places and communities that are richly diverse."[7] Many rural communities continue to lose their historic job base of mining, farming, or low-wage manufacturing, but other rural communities face different challenges: rapid growth threatens to overwhelm traditional culture, and the benefits of an expanding economy fail to reach low-income residents. Others proudly proclaim that they face few consequential challenges in the economy. Many explanations for the variations among rural communities and means of categorization have been offered in the literature on rural America. This chapter focuses on two categories: new-economy winners and losers.

Some rural communities have transformed their economies with great dexterity and success amid the challenges presented by losses of factories and farms. These are the rural winners. They are mostly counties with economic bases in retirement and recreation, and those in close proximity to urban areas. In fact, recreation and retirement counties have consistently been the fastest-growing counties in rural America. Many have relied on agritourism, heritage tourism, and ecotourism; successful economic development strategies in areas in which the natural environment is perhaps the greatest distinguishing feature. Others have sought to recruit retirees. In 2003 the federal Economic Research Service (ERS) identified 440 rural retirement destinations in the United States. These were defined as areas in which the number of residents age 60 or older grew by over 15 percent due to in-migration. The ERS also identified 334 recreational counties on the basis of employment and earnings in recreational industries, concentrations of seasonal housing, and high expenditures on hotels and motels, together with contextual indicators of recreational activities.[8] Major concentrations of these counties exist in the mountain and coastal regions of the West, in the upper Great Lakes, in coastal and scenic areas of New England and upstate New York, in the foothills of the Appalachians and Ozarks, and in coastal regions from Virginia to Florida.[9]

For other rural areas, the challenge of creating and sustaining a vibrant economy seems insurmountable. These tend to be communities focused on farming and manufacturing and those more remote from urban areas. The often long-term economic and social distress of these communities is frequently characterized by high rates of joblessness, underemployment, school dropouts, poor health outcomes, and substandard housing, thereby causing them to be referred to as "the rural ghettos of America." It is here that the real challenge of rural development lies. For if "the rural ghetto . . . is allowed to continue and expand, [it] will be a powerful symbol of failure *in* America and *of* America."[10]

ECONOMIC DEVELOPMENT IN THE NEW ECONOMY: SAVIOR OR SAVAGE?

Obviously, rural development is not always aimed at poverty alleviation because not all rural areas are poor. However, in order to move areas that are in poverty to a state of prosperity, rural development must do more than raise the incomes of a few. It must affect the incomes of significant numbers of people, especially those who are in low-income households.

"Development" is a deceptively simple term for a remarkably diverse collection of strategies by which the public sector seeks to stimulate private sector investment. In rural development, the strategies have historically been divided into community development, and economic development. Of the two, community development has had the broader focus, encompassing social, economic, and physical environment initiatives that are designed and implemented by local people. These comprehensive initiatives embrace the value of community investment in and control over wealth creation. For example, a community development initiative might include the commercial revitalization of a blighted strip mall to include a business incubator to support the entrepreneurial activity of low-income individuals, an after-school program, and offices for a local community-based organization. These development efforts rely upon local investment in the assets of a particular place to develop the economic, physical, and social aspects of the community.

Economic development, by contrast, has been more focused on the intersection of public policy and private commerce for the purpose of creating jobs and businesses.[11] In the past, much rural economic development relied on exploitation of natural resources or recruitment of industry, often marketing cheap land and labor as community "assets." Today the myriad economic development strategies focus on how tax and other incentives can be used to recruit plants or other facilities of companies to a specific location, strengthen and expand existing businesses and industries, and promote entrepreneurship. Although local communities may well join state governments in offering incentives, the unique natural or cultural assets of the particular community tend to be less important than in community development. Moreover, the focus of economic development efforts is rarely on improving the ability of communities to increase local asset ownership, anchor jobs for lower-income persons, or improve the overall physical and social infrastructure of the community.

If traditional community development has been seen as "bottom-up," local economic development has been viewed as "top-down." Bottom-up

STRENGTHENING THE RURAL COMMUNITY

Ruston Seaman and Michael Ferber

In order to travel on the road out of poverty, an individual must possess the knowledge and confidence to navigate the passage and the belief that the journey's destination makes the trip worthwhile. After a combined 40 years of experience in rural West Virginia, we have come to believe that the most effective approaches mobilize communities to implement cooperatively strategies that create cultures of hope where personal worth and dignity are enriched while the relational fiber of associational life is enhanced. What an agency believes about poverty will determine the approach that agency takes toward its alleviation. When practitioners conceptualize poverty solely as a lack of resources, the interventions target symptoms rather than the capacities, abilities, and gifts of individuals. If agencies, governmental or otherwise, continually communicate to individuals that they are fundamentally deficient victims, incapable of taking charge of their lives or their community's future, these capacities will not be realized, and their need for assistance will continually grow.[1]

At World Vision Appalachia we take a transformational development approach to poverty, through which we help people move toward fullness of life with dignity, justice, and hope. We do not deny the power of structural economic forces, but as we approach the under-resourced, we do so with the perspective that those presently in poverty are fully capable human beings with much to offer. While we recognize the reality that some have differing capacities due to physical and/or mental challenges, we strongly believe that by discovering their own unique talents, all people can fulfill their Creator's intention. We believe that an effective intervention must address both the marred identity and vocational objectives[2] of those who struggle against a lack of resources.[3] With this approach, under-resourced individuals discover a personal purpose by employing their abilities and build social capital by enhancing the quality of life of others in their neighborhood and beyond.[4]

This asset-based approach is implemented through programs that emphasize education and youth development, health and safety, the provision of essential supplies, the connecting of community resources, and leadership development. For example, we host a community time bank through which members earn time dollars for helping other members or authorized organizations.[5] All hours, regardless of the type of service or level of skill involved, are valued equally. Time dollars transform interpersonal assistance from a one-way stream into a two-way symbiotic relationship, building personal worth and dignity while meeting material needs and decreasing isolation.[6] Every service act replicates and multiplies, generating a network of support that enhances trust while building community. In addition to time dollars, the time bank uses an incentive-based mechanism that encourages the distribution of goods to persons participating either as recipients or as providers in the program. Hence the time bank goes beyond traditional unilateral charity in an effort to address chronic, multigenerational poverty. The road out of rural poverty is paved with assets that already exist in communities through their creative energy and capacity to network and mobilize these assets.

NOTES

1. J. Kretzmann and J. McKnight, *Building Communities from the Inside Out: A Path Toward Finding and Mobilizing a Community's Assets* (Evanston, IL: Institute for Policy Research, 1993).

2. Bryant L. Myers, *Walking with the Poor: Principles and Practices of Transformational Development* (Maryknoll, NY: Orbis Books/World Vision, 1999).

3. Jayakumar Christian, *God of the Empty-Handed* (Monrovia, CA: MARC/World Vision, 1999).

4. Ram A. Cnnan, Stephanie C. Boddie, and Gaynor Yancey, "Bowling Alone but Serving Together," in *Religion as Social Capital*, ed. Corwin Smidt (Waco: Baylor University Press, 2003), 19–32.

5. Edgar Cahn, *No More Throw-away People* (Washington, DC: Essential Books, 2004).

6. Robert Putnam, *Bowling Alone: The Collapse and Revival of American Community* (New York: Simon and Schuster, 2000).

development relies on a diverse group of community stakeholders driving an agenda tailored to the specific community. Such development efforts are concerned with questions of who creates, leads, and implements development opportunities.[12] Like economic development, bottom-up development claims to create opportunities for jobs, income, wealth, and business growth.[13] However, unlike traditional economic development, community development combines community-building strategies with investments to create development outcomes. For example, community development corporations, which are not-for-profit community-based development organizations, do not pride themselves only on the number of affordable housing units they have constructed, small businesses they have supported, or commercial revitalization projects they have completed. They pride themselves on how many people participated in the development process and whether the resulting outcomes created wealth opportunities for those participants. Unfortunately, the down-side of community development's very focus on community building some-times makes it hard to tell whether it is primarily a process tool or one that is producing development outcomes. At a time when communities are suffering the effects of economic restructuring, economic outcomes are expected. There is little patience for process work that is seen as "predevelopment."

On the other hand, successful economic development policies or programs are usually measured only by the numbers of individual businesses or jobs cre-ated. These are important accomplishments but, without blind reliance on a trickle-down theory of economic benefit, neither measure captures either the creation of community wealth or the reduction of community poverty. More-over, the top-down nature of economic development means that beyond local government and business leaders, community residents are rarely involved in creating or leading traditional economic development projects.

Notably, the competing perspectives and points of emphasis between eco-nomic and community development render present local development poli-cies and programs a piecemeal set of myopic strategies incapable of adequately addressing poverty alleviation. Individually and collectively, these strategies lack the compelling narrative needed to focus development efforts on long-term prosperity for all areas. It is time for bottom-up to be combined with top-down development as a response to rural poverty.

MOVING BEYOND THE DIFFERENCES: PROMISING ECONOMIC DEVELOPMENT STRATEGIES FOR RURAL POVERTY ALLEVIATION

The diversity among high-poverty rural areas means that there is no single recipe for prosperity. However, certain facts remain constant across communi-ties. For these areas to compete in the new, global economy, their develop-ment strategies must explicitly promote both economic growth and poverty reduction in each of the following pillars: innovation, investments, connec-tions, and preservation. Those strategies must demand the outcomes of eco-nomic development—jobs, wealth, and prosperity—while building on the fundamental values of community development—development choices led by community residents that serve the needs of residents and promote economic opportunity, increase social equity, and nurture the natural environment.

Innovation (Talent and Technology)

New ideas—innovations—are the hallmark of the new knowledge-based economy. Therefore, on the most fundamental level, rural America's ability to share in a national and global economy depends on the ability of its workers and entrepreneurs to add value to that economy through their knowledge, creativity, and skills. This is true even of the poorest places.

In attempting to ensure the competitiveness of rural workers and entrepreneurs, local developers find themselves confronted with the competing circumstances of rural communities. They must seek to prepare communities for the growth of new-economy jobs while simultaneously strengthening the more traditional bases. For example, manufacturing-based economies can little afford to ignore their existing enterprises on the grounds that they will be unable to compete long term in a global market based on low-cost labor or in commodity products. To the contrary, developers must offer these manufacturers workers who can find ways to differentiate products through product design, production speed, logistics, the end-user experience, or superior marketing. For today's firms to survive, they will need supportive strategies that include a supply of highly trained workers.

Today's workforce development paradigm requires not only significant, but also continuous, human capital investments for a lifetime of learning (see also Chapter 10).[14] In representing the sum total of practical knowledge, acquired skills, and learned abilities of individuals, human capital also reflects the potential productivity of a community's residents. It includes both hard (technical) skills and soft (nontechnical) skills. Investments must be targeted to both hard and soft skill development.

Individuals who live in poverty may not be able to make the investments in human capital development necessary to enhance their skills. To break the cycle of individual and community poverty, communities must focus on building the organizational capacity of educational institutions to provide education, formal training, and opportunities for on-the-job training and facilitate family and nonfamily soft skill support. These strategies must target skill development, especially for those at the lowest rungs of the economic ladder, to growth sectors with promising career pathways. In addition to the economic benefits, human capital investments will yield social returns for a community. Investments will allow individual community members to apply particular aspects of their human capital to act as change agents, mobilize others, and catalyze action on important social challenges.

Human capital development must do more than create talent. It must also provide community residents with access to technology. Despite incredible growth in personal-computer ownership and Internet access in this country over the past 20 years, distinct disparities remain in technology literacy and access, especially in rural areas. This is unfortunate because access to new technologies, such as the computer and the Internet will be crucial to the economic success of American businesses, communities, and individuals. Increasingly, Americans are using these technologies to find jobs, contact colleagues, locate public information, take courses online, or otherwise prepare for the workplace of the twenty-first century. The competitive advantage (or lack thereof) of rural America will rest in the ability to drive innovations through talent and technology.

Capital Investments in People, Products, and Places

New ideas alone do not determine a community's economic success. Innovations must be put to use, and this step almost always requires capital investment. For a community to be competitive in the new economy, capital must exist for direct investment in the ideas of its innovators. Capital must also be available for investment in the community's supportive infrastructure, including educational institutions and physical capital (roads, water, sewer systems, and telecommunications).

There are two basic approaches to increasing access to capital: encouraging the existing private market to make financial capital available in these communities, and creating alternatives to the private market to serve the specific needs of community residents. The primary regulatory approach for increasing access to financial capital in underserved communities is implemented through the federal Community Reinvestment Act (CRA), which is discussed in detail in Chapter 13.

Unfortunately, even with "encouragement," private capital markets and traditional financial services often do not adequately meet the needs of low-income people, minorities, and small firms in distressed rural areas. The reasons for this are varied and include discrimination, suburbanization, and consolidation of the banking industry.[15] For example, as rural banks are merged into larger regional enterprises or acquired by statewide and national bank holding companies, there is often a reduction in lending to local businesses.[16] Other traditional sources of capital—especially traditional venture capital—significantly underserve rural areas, particularly poor areas. As a result, local developers must employ numerous tools that either provide better incentives for private financing or create new sources of capital outside the private market such as special savings accounts, tax credits, and public venture funds. Some of these mechanisms are also discussed in Chapter 13.

Preservation

Quality-of-life factors have become increasingly important in the process of stimulating private investment and creating jobs and wealth.[17] Simply put, place matters, and rural America has benefited as retirees and others move to rural areas to escape downsides of urban living. While conserving natural capital is of concern in both urban and rural places, it takes on additional significance for rural America, where "ecology of place" is often the basis of the economy.[18]

Development is consuming family farms at alarming rates in some areas; in others, family farms are being replaced by large-scale meat, poultry, and dairy processors that create jobs but generate enormous amounts of concentrated and sometimes hazardous wastes. In recreation communities, lakes, rivers, forests, and other wildlife habitats may face serious environmental concerns due to increased use. Critics of tying development to recreation opportunities argue that the strategy is not sustainable. They also argue that recreation communities, which averaged 24 percent employment growth during the 1990s, result in seasonal, unskilled, low-wage jobs that depress local wages and income, thereby increasing local rates of poverty. This critique is not supported by the existing data. Although variations exist based on the type of recreation involved, rural tourism and recreational development actually result in lower local poverty rates (13.2 percent versus 15.7 in other rural areas) and improvements in other social conditions, such as local educational attainment.[19]

However, the concern about environmental degradation has merit and reinforces the reality that local development efforts must protect the very assets that are leading to economic growth and poverty alleviation. Creative local development might involve investing in projects that preserve and connect natural areas such as greenways, waterways, wildlife habitats, parks, and open spaces in ways that support a community's quality of life.[20]

Connections (People, Institutions, and Places)

The physical and social isolation associated with rural poverty creates problems different from those in densely populated areas. Indeed, in comparing rural areas, it is clear that the more remote the rural area, the more challenging the economic prospects. Therefore, it is not surprising that poverty rates are highest in rural counties not adjacent to an urban county. Curiously, however, creating connections among people, institutions, and places is often not considered as an element of economic growth or poverty alleviation in rural areas. These relationships are, in fact, essential to both. Economic relationships are characterized by social and physical components.

First, social connection (or social capital) refers to relations among individuals, organizations, communities, and other social units that result in tangible economic benefits. People in communities endowed with a rich stock of social networks are in a stronger position to develop the capacity to address the problems of poverty, to rebuild their communities, and to achieve a measure of control over their lives.[21]

Within economies, social networks provide access to critical supports.

A young mother may depend on social relationships to find child care for her children while she works; an aspiring entrepreneur may rely on a relationship with a community development financial institution to secure a first loan; or a company may leverage a relationship with one of its suppliers to expand its business venture. All of these are economic uses of social networks. The geography of rural places provides unique challenges in creating and maintaining the types of dense social networks that might lead to such economic benefits. Thus the emphasis on social connections in poor rural places must be on linking disadvantaged people, businesses, and the institutions that serve them to wider regional economic networks and opportunities.[22] Community-based organizations could play a pivital role in connecting their existing constituencies to greater and more traditional economic development opportunities in innovation-based sectors. Rather than simply replicating market-based employment or entrepreneurial strategies, these organizations could serve to broker community investment and input in ways that yield economic outcomes intentionally targeted to alleviate poverty.

As a practical matter, rural connections must also be physical. If rural communities are to leverage their connections to their neighbors and the world, they must be connected by roads, rail, airports, and telecommunications. Rural areas in proximity to urban areas (metropolitan areas) and those in proximity to small towns (micropolitan areas) already experience greater growth, as a result of physical connections, than those in more remote areas. In fact, as a class, rural counties that adjoin urban areas experienced moderate growth between 1990 and 2000, while those not adjacent to urban areas experienced out-migration. These differential growth patterns suggest a need to find ways to reduce both the actual and perceived distance between more remote rural areas and more densely populated places. For too long some rural towns and counties have approached economic development as a zero-sum competition. In today's highly competitive global economy distressed communities will achieve more when they pool resources, identify common assets, and work together to develop the regional economy.

THE CHALLENGE: PUTTING IT ALL TOGETHER

Today a community's economic prospects depend on a flexible, well-trained workforce, access to technology and capital, cultural and natural amenities, and a strong civic infrastructure, including relationships that facilitate problem solving and collective action within the community and greater regions. Federal and state governments can facilitate the development of these fundamental pillars of development, but it is local creativity in marrying economic growth and poverty-alleviation strategies that will determine whether innovation, investment, preservation, and connections guide development possibilities toward new industries and markets, generate high-value, higher-paying jobs, and fuel more widely shared wealth creation and prosperity.

NOTES

I gratefully acknowledge the generous support of my colleagues William Lambe, Jonathan Morgan, and Jason Gray, who contributed thoughtful critique and useful resources to this work.

1. Calvin Beale and Robert M. Gibbs, "Severity and Concentration of Persistent High Poverty in Nonmetro Areas," *Amber Waves*, February 2006, available online at http://www.ers.usda.gov/Amberwaves/February06/DataFeature/.

2. Christian Ketels, "Competitiveness in Rural Regions" (Economic Development America, Summer 2004).

3. Council on Competitiveness, "Innovate America: Thriving in a World of Challenge and Change" (National Innovation Initiative Summit and Report, Washington, DC, 2004).

4. Beale and Gibbs, "Severity and Concentration of Persistent High Poverty in Nonmetro Areas."

5. Kenneth Johnson, "Demographic Trends in Rural and Small Town America" (Reports on Rural America 1, no. 1, Carsey Institute, University of New Hampshire, 2006).

6. Economic Research Service, "Measuring Rurality: 2004 County Typology Codes" (2004), http://www.ers/usda.gov/briefing/rurality/Typology/.

7. Don Macke, "Understanding Rural America" (Monograph 11, Center for Rural Entrepreneurship, June 2003).

8. Economic Research Service, "Measuring Rurality."

9. Johnson, "Demographic Trends in Rural and Small Town America."

10. Karl N. Stauber, "Why Invest in Rural America—And How? A Critical Public Policy Question for the 21st Century," in *Exploring Policy Options for a New Rural America* (Center for the Study of Rural America, Federal Reserve Bank of Kansas City, 2001), 11.

11. Jesse L. White Jr., "Economic Development in North Carolina: Moving Toward Innovation," *Popular Government* (Institute of Government, Chapel Hill, NC), Spring/Summer 2004, 5.

12. Pierre Clavel, Jesica Pitt, and Jordan Yin, "The Community Option in Urban Policy," *Urban Affairs Review* 32 (1997): 435–58.

13. Ron Shaffer, Steve Deller, and Dave Marcouiller, "Rethinking Economic Development," *Economic Development Quarterly* 20, no. 1 (2006): 59–74.

14. See Shari Garmise, *People and the Competitive Advantage of Place: Building a Workforce for the 21st Century* (Armonk, NY: M.E. Sharpe, 2006).

15. Lehn Benjamin, Julia Rubin, and Sean Zielenbach, "Community Development Financial Institutions: Current Issues and Future Prospects," *Journal of Urban Affairs* 26, no. 2 (2004): 177–78. See also Melvin Oliver and Thomas Shapiro, *Black Wealth/White Wealth* (New York: Routledge, 1995); Michael Stegman, *Savings for the Poor: The Hidden Benefits of Electronic Banking* (Washington, DC: Brookings Institution Press, 1999).

16. RUPRI Rural Finance Task Force. "The Adequacy of Rural Financial Markets: Rural Economic Development Impacts of Seven Key Policy Issues" (Rural Policy Research Institute, University of Missouri–Columbia, 1997), 97-1.

17. See Richard Florida, *The Rise of the Creative Class* (New York: Basic Books, 2002); David Salvensen and Henry Renski, *The Importance of Quality of Life in the Location Decisions of New Economy Firms* (Washington, DC: Economic Development Administration, 2002); Gary Paul Green, "Amenities and Community Economic Development: Strategies for Sustainability," *Journal of Regional Analysis and Policy* 31, no. 2 (2001): 61–76; Kilungu Nzaku and James O. Bukenya, "Examining the Relationship Between Quality of Life Amenities and Economic Development in the Southeast USA," *Review of Urban and Regional Development Studies* 17, no. 2

(2005): 89–103; John P. Blair, "Quality of Life and Economic Development Policy," *Economic Development Review* 16, no. 1 (1998): 50–54.

18. Timothy Beatley and Kristy Manning, *The Ecology of Place: Planning for Environment, Economy, and Community* (Washington, DC: Island Press, 1997).

19. Richard J. Reeder and Dennis M. Brown, *Recreation, Tourism, and Rural Well Being*, United States Department of Agriculture, Economic Research Service Report no. 7 (August 2005).

20. Mark Benedict and Edward McMahon, *Green Infrastructure: Smart Conservation for the 21st Century* (Washington, DC: Sprawl Watch Clearinghouse, 2001). See also Karen Williamson, *Growing with Green Infrastructure* (Doylestown, PA: Heritage Conservancy, 2003).

21. Mark R. Warren et al., "The Role of Social Capital in Combating Poverty," in *Social Capital and Poor Communities*, ed. Susan Saegert et al. (New York: Russell Sage Foundation, 2001), pp. 1–28.

22. William A. Galston and Karen J. Baehler, *Rural Development in the United States: Connecting Theory, Practice, and Possibilities* (Washington, DC: Island Press, 1995).

19

Fighting Poverty with Equitable Development

Angela Glover Blackwell

The more things change, the more they stay the same: the adage is playing out in metropolitan areas across the United States. Even as the old orthodoxies of cities and suburbs have dissolved, poverty—and the racial isolation that goes with it—has persisted through decades of social and demographic evolution and continues to plague far too many American communities today. Poverty was once a rural phenomenon, a function of geographic removal from urban centers of commerce. With mass post–World War II suburbanization, poverty became an inner-city pathology, fostered by structural and racial isolation from investment and employment.[1] Yet surprising reversals of fortune have occurred over the past 10 to 20 years. Crime rates dropped nationwide, the economy surged, young professionals and empty nesters rediscovered the benefits of urban living, and cities such as New York, San Francisco, Boston, and Washington, D.C., became coveted places in which to live and work—with soaring housing costs to match. At the same time, many "inner-ring" or "first-tier" suburbs—once symbols of prosperity and idyllic middle-class life—found themselves facing stereotypically urban problems of blight, unemployment, poverty, and crime as resources and sprawling, unchecked development leapfrogged from city to near suburb to ever more distant exurb.

The face of suburbia, too, is changing. Where urban exodus was historically labeled "white flight," minority residents are now contributing to population growth in inner and outer suburbs.[2] For example, the 2000 census revealed that Baltimore experienced "black flight" for the first time since the

Civil War era.[3] Immigrant enclaves, once attributes of cities such as New York and Los Angeles, have blossomed in suburbs; by the year 2000 more immigrants lived in suburbs than in cities.[4] With suburban migration, urban revitalization, and exurban sprawl, the region has emerged as the dominant economic engine in the United States. Each day millions of Americans crisscross from city to suburb, suburb to city, and suburb to suburb for work, school, shopping, or entertainment.

However, these changes have had little overall effect on poverty. Despite seismic metropolitan shifts, equity and opportunity remain as elusive as ever for low-income communities and communities of color. In one place an impoverished central city might struggle with urban disinvestment and an exodus of residents, services, and jobs, while the surrounding suburbs reap the benefit of this urban flight, with new employment opportunities, a robust tax base, increased political clout, and dramatic growth. In another city the existing residents of a resurgent downtown might strain to pay rising rents and risk displacement from gentrification. Despite *Brown v. Board of Education*, over 50 years later many public school districts are in effect resegregating according to regional residence patterns, neighborhood concentration of poverty, and a lack of affordable housing—locking many children in failing, overcrowded schools with woefully limited resources.[5] Fair-housing laws bar the rental, sales, and mortgage lending practices that once discriminated against African Americans, but many suburban and exurban communities now rely on zoning codes to restrict affordable, rental, or multifamily housing development, effectively excluding low-income people of color.

Equity offers a new paradigm for understanding and working to remedy these disparities. Whereas equality is the practice of treating everyone the same, equity is only realized when all people have equal access to opportunity. Equality in an employment context, for example, may consist of civil rights laws that bar employers from hiring or firing based on race. An equity-focused approach probes not only the legal but the practical barriers to opportunity: even if a person of color living in a low-income urban community is protected by antidiscrimination laws, does that worker have the means of transportation to connect to a stable, living-wage job that is likely located far from the central city?[6] Are there affordable housing options in job-rich areas that would allow the worker to move closer to employment opportunity? Did she or he have economic or geographic access to the higher education— or even a sound basic education from disinvested neighborhood public schools—that may be required to qualify for that "equal-employment-opportunity" job in the first place? Equal-rights legislation is rendered hollow without policies that comprehensively address those practical barriers to economic and social parity. Equity, in essence, makes real the promises of equality.

BUILDING COMPETITIVE REGIONS

It is more critical than ever for the United States to address persistent regional inequity. Scores of academics, authors, economists, and pundits emphasize the need for America to keep pace in a rapidly innovating world, and the way to remain competitive in our globalized economy is through strong metropolitan regions. Communities are the building blocks for a vibrant, competitive region, and a region cannot thrive if some of its communities are neglected, disinvested, and isolated from economic opportunity. Ending poverty requires a commitment to eliminating regional disparities by creating opportunity in low-income communities and communities of color and ensuring that those residents can connect to other opportunity-rich areas throughout the region.

To do this will require a new generation of public policies at every level of government—as well as private-sector policymaking—focused on economic and social equity. "Policy" may seem confined to congressional conference committees, governors' offices, or local zoning board meetings, but in fact it shapes every aspect of life. A "free market" did not create urban-suburban inequity, for example, or decimate the postwar streetcar systems of many American cities; policy did that through specific decisions to federally subsidize suburban mortgages or prioritize highway spending at the expense of public transportation. Quite simply, policy matters.

Low-income people of color suffer disproportionately from a jobs-housing mismatch and a "geographic concentration of school failure."[7] When children in low-income, disinvested communities are trapped in failing schools, for instance, their chances of receiving a solid education, gaining living-wage employment, and providing a better future for their own children are severely compromised—and all too often, inequity begets inequity. Fortunately, just as decades of inequitable policymaking exacerbated regional disparities, policy can be the vehicle to address poverty and achieve sustainable social change.

OPPORTUNITY AND EQUITABLE DEVELOPMENT

Where we live has become a proxy for opportunity: entrenched regional disparities mean that the neighborhoods we call home determine the affordability of our housing, the quality of our public schools, our ability to access jobs, and the availability of public transportation. Our address even influences how healthy we are. Bus depots and other facilities that contribute to poor air quality are disproportionately sited in low-income neighborhoods; aging schools with maintenance problems and poorly maintained housing stock in disinvested communities are also frequent sources of mold, lead, and vermin, exacerbating asthma and environmental allergies, especially in children. Neighborhood amenities such as parks and supermarkets also affect health. The "grocery gap" in many low-income communities of color means that residents lack convenient access to fresh produce and other healthy foods and are instead served by a proliferation of convenience stores, liquor outlets stocking snack foods, and fast-food restaurants. Additionally, communities with few parks or recreation centers—and crime rates that keep residents indoors—offer few options for physical activity. Lack of exercise and poor access to nutritious foods, in turn, increase risks for obesity, diabetes, high blood pressure, and other chronic health conditions that studies show significantly contribute to mortality disparities in the United States. Researchers have found that African Americans in high-risk urban areas and western Native Americans primarily living on reservations—two communities that suffer from disinvestment and economic isolation—had life expectancies below those of many other groups.[8] Obesity and related conditions sometimes dismissed as "lifestyle" consequences are in fact a reflection of low-income communities' scarcity of resources for healthy living.

Equitable development connects the quest for full racial inclusion and participation to local, metropolitan, and regional planning and development. This framework embraces complexity and comprehensiveness and consistently asks who benefits from policy and development decisions to ensure that low-income communities and communities of color reap their fair share. Equitable development is grounded in four guiding principles:

1. *Integrate "people" and "place" strategies.* Sustainable revitalization requires a combination of the people-focused programs that support community residents and strengthen families (such as job training, asset building, and health education) and place-focused efforts that stabilize and improve the neighborhood environment (such as affordable housing, supermarket development, local job creation, and public transportation improvements).

2. *Reduce local and regional disparities.* Federal, state, and local policy solutions should focus on simultaneously improving outcomes for low-income communities and building healthy metropolitan regions. Metropolitan areas that pay systemic attention to both regional growth and central-city, suburban, and rural poverty issues are more likely to be competitive for national and international economic opportunities.

3. *Promote "double bottom line" investments.* The business community can and should collaborate with policymakers, planners, and antipoverty advocates to advance equitable development. Public and private investments that produce a "double bottom line"—fair financial returns for investors and community benefits for residents (e.g., jobs, affordable housing, businesses)—are a win-win strategy to achieve regional equity.

4. *Prioritize meaningful community voice, participation, and leadership.* Community residents need access to the tools, knowledge, and resources that can guarantee their meaningful participation and full engagement in development decisions. Policymaking must move beyond a "top-down" process to instead involve local communities and local wisdom in policy development.

Promising examples of equitable development across the United States are demonstrating how the public, private, and nonprofit sectors can work together to alleviate poverty and create stronger communities and regions.

EQUITABLE DEVELOPMENT IN ACTION

Connecting to Employment Opportunities: Equitable Transit Investment

Creating accessible employment opportunities for low-income people is a core goal of equitable development. The connections between work and housing are especially strong. Too often, low-income families face a catch-22 of few decent jobs where they live and little affordable housing in job-rich outer suburbs. This spatial mismatch is exacerbated by racially and economically disparate rates of car ownership: nationally, 19 percent of African Americans and 13.7 percent of Latinos lack access to an automobile, compared with 4.6 percent of whites; 33 percent of poor African Americans, 21.4 percent of near-poor African Americans, 25 percent of poor Latinos, and 14 percent of near-poor Latinos lack automobile access, compared with 12.1 percent and 9 percent of poor and near-poor whites, respectively.[9] Reverse commuting programs such as Bridges to Work in St. Louis focus on helping central-city residents reach jobs in the region's employment-rich suburbs. In partnership with employers, the area's metropolitan planning organization, social service organizations, and transportation agencies, Bridges to Work helps participants design a transportation plan for reaching a MetroLink transit station and provides shuttle service from MetroLink to individual employers located in areas of job growth.

Of course, no program, however successful or broad in scale, is a substitute for fair public transportation investment. In too many metropolitan areas transportation infrastructure resources are disproportionately channeled to suburban and exurban highway or commuter rail projects at the expense of public transportation in more densely populated central-city areas. Residents and transportation equity advocates have begun to recognize the power of metropolitan planning organizations (MPOs) in allocating state and federal transportation dollars. MOSES (Metropolitan Organizing Strategy Enabling Strength),[10] an urban-suburban faith-based coalition serving the Detroit region, is advocating for reform of the Southeast Michigan Council of

Governments (SEMCOG) voting system; the MPO, which is responsible for critical transportation investment decisions, allocates three executive committee votes to the city of Detroit (which has a population of over 900,000), but four votes each to suburban Monroe and Livingston counties (which have less than a quarter of Detroit's population). MOSES is also working to ensure that new transportation initiatives, especially ones backed by tax dollars, promote more balanced growth patterns and allow equal representation by urban core and inner-ring suburban communities in decision-making processes.[11]

This nexus of jobs and transit is a key example of the need to integrate place- and people-focused urban and regional development strategies. Job training and skill building are important people-oriented pieces of the puzzle, but absent a way to bridge the transportation gap between underemployed residents and jobs, training efforts alone will ultimately fail to combat poverty on a large, sustainable scale. Similarly, transportation investment without careful attention to the needs of low-income communities will only serve to perpetuate the employment isolation of low-income communities of color.

Living Near Opportunity: Zoning Reform and Transit Oriented Development

Equitable development advocates are also working to implement policy strategies that allow low-income residents to live in communities that already offer employment opportunities, quality education, and other resources. Because neighborhood geography greatly influences our access to these resources, housing is truly a linchpin of opportunity. Housing policy is, in effect, education policy, health policy, employment policy, and wealth-building policy, all rolled into one. Subtly practiced housing discrimination, including "steering" home seekers to homogeneous communities and discouraging racial or economic integration, still exists despite fair-housing laws, yet the primary means of legal discrimination remains exclusionary land-use and zoning practices that function to maintain regional inequity. These regulations— such as minimum square footage or large lot and setback requirements—serve to deny whole groups and classes of people access to opportunity-rich neighborhoods. A survey in the 25 largest metropolitan areas revealed that low-density zoning consistently reduced rental housing, and the resulting shortage limited the number of African Americans and Latinos in those neighborhoods.[12]

Throughout the United States local jurisdictions of all sizes are turning to zoning ordinances as a way to increase affordability and create economically integrated neighborhoods. Under inclusionary zoning (IZ), a percentage of units in each new (or rehabilitated) housing development is set aside at rents or sale prices affordable to low- to middle-income residents.[13] In return, developers receive tax abatements, credits, density waivers that allow construction of additional units, or other zoning variances. While IZ is not a substitute for a comprehensive affordable housing policy, it is one effective strategy for leveraging public and private investment to create and preserve affordable housing and foster the development of mixed-income communities. Montgomery County, Maryland, which was the first jurisdiction in the country to implement inclusionary zoning, has used its Moderately Priced Dwelling Unit program to develop over 11,000 affordable housing units across the county since 1976, facilitating the creation of mixed-income communities and economic integration in schools.[14] When IZ is crafted with income targets and an implementation plan that ensures affordability for low-income residents, it helps reduce local and regional disparities by expanding access to mixed-income neighborhoods with greater employment, service, and education opportunities.

Transit oriented development (TOD) is another promising strategy for closing the spatial gap between jobs and housing for low-income residents. Transit oriented development is development centered around rail or bus stations to improve both transit accessibility and the surrounding community. TODs are typically high-density, mixed-use, pedestrian-friendly developments located within a quarter mile of shops, housing, and office space around transit hubs. TODs reduce dependence on cars while linking residents to resources throughout the region.

Community development corporations (CDCs) and advocates are increasingly turning to TODs as a strategy for revitalizing disinvested neighborhoods. The CDC philosophy for neighborhood revitalization focuses on the assets that exist in poor neighborhoods—such as transit stops—rather than the deficits and aims to rebuild communities by leveraging these assets. One inspiring example of a CDC-led TOD is the work of Bethel New Life in Chicago's West Garfield Park. For years Bethel New Life had been fighting the Chicago Transit Authority to keep the Lake Pulaski stop on the Green Line open to serve the surrounding low-income neighborhood. Recognizing the transit station's potential as an anchor for commercial and real estate activity, Bethel New Life embarked on a series of development projects culminating in the Bethel Center, a mixed-use facility adjacent to the stop. The center includes six storefronts, a community technology center, and childcare and employment services. Opened in January 2005 after 10 years of organizing, advocacy, lobbying, and planning, the $4.5 million center was built in partnership with the Chicago Transit Authority and financed with a combination of federal, state, city, nonprofit, and private commercial funding sources. Bethel New Life built 50 affordable new homes within walking distance of the center. The homes sell for $165,000, and families may qualify for subsidies of up to $40,000 through New Homes for Chicago, a federal program administered by the city. The organization also plans to add 66 new affordable condominium units and construct a Lake Pulaski Commercial Center on the site of an old building facing the transit stop. Bethel New Life envisions the Lake Pulaski Commercial Center as a catalyst for the complete rejuvenation of the industrial and residential areas surrounding the center—an anchor for the community and a magnet for future investment and development.

Displacement can be an unintended consequence of transit oriented development as people of all races and income levels are increasingly attracted to the idea of walkable communities and less strenuous commutes to work; rents or home prices typically rise as an area becomes more desirable. It is imperative, therefore, that TOD developers and advocates plan ahead for affordable housing provisions that will allow low-income residents to remain in the community and benefit from the amenities the TOD can offer.

Leveraging Public Subsidies for Opportunity: Community Benefits Agreements

Cities and suburban jurisdictions compete endlessly for jobs and tax revenue, particularly in the form of major business, retail, or sports and entertainment complexes prized by many local officials as showpieces of municipal success and prosperity. These large-scale development projects overwhelmingly receive public subsidies, either directly, in the form of tax abatements and similar concessions, or indirectly, through government-financed modifications to roads, sewers, and other infrastructure. Economic benefits to residents often prove elusive, however. Baltimore's Camden Yards, for example, was found to bring in approximately $3 million in annual revenue for Maryland, but cost the state's taxpayers about $14 million a year in operating and capital expenses.[15] Though Harborplace, the city's Inner Harbor waterfront development, became a successful tourist destination, the jobs created by the project were mostly low-wage and part-time; all but three of the city's nonmanagerial tourism job titles pay less than the federal poverty line for a family of four.[16]

Major commercial development projects that fail to produce tangible, lasting public benefits will only serve to widen income gaps and inequality, particularly in regions struggling to attract livable-wage jobs and economic development. Over the past decade local workforce development advocates, community and faith-based organizations, unions, environmental justice groups, and policymakers have used community benefits agreements (CBAs) to ensure that their neighborhoods reap the returns of large-scale commercial projects along with developers and big business. CBAs are based on the premise that public investments must yield defined public benefits, including good jobs, affordable housing, green space, and child care.

CBAs follow the equitable development principle of the double bottom line and show planners, policymakers, and economic development officials the possibilities for achieving not only financial returns for investors, but meaningful, sustaining benefits for local residents. One of the most comprehensive CBAs to date was negotiated by the Figueroa Corridor Coalition for Economic Justice around the development of the downtown Los Angeles Sports and Entertainment District (anchored by the Staples Center); the agreement included living-wage jobs, local hiring requirements, job training, a 20 percent set-aside of affordable housing, and a commitment of $1 million for community parks and recreation in exchange for organized community support of the project.[17]

As the community benefits movement matures, advocates are broadening their focus from CBA negotiation to long-term implementation and enforcement. For CBAs to be effective, they must impose penalties on developers who stray from the agreed-upon benefits. It is also essential that a CBA provide for monitoring and community oversight. The idea that communities should benefit from publicly subsidized development is spreading rapidly, with CBAs at the forefront of project negotiations in metropolitan regions across the country, including Atlanta, Boston, Milwaukee, New York, Seattle, and Washington, D.C.[18]

Those closest to our nation's most persistent challenges of urban, suburban, and rural poverty are central to the solutions. In each of these examples, local communities and organizations are key to the policy process. The cornerstone of equitable development is full and meaningful community voice, participation, and leadership. Policymakers must go beyond simply informing residents of revitalization or economic development plans—beyond holding perfunctory town halls or meetings to gather public comment—to bring low-income residents and community organizations into the policy and decision-making process as real partners.

CHALLENGES FOR THE FUTURE

As equitable development gains momentum, the policymakers, planners, government officials, labor unions, faith- and community-based organizations, business leaders, and neighborhood advocates that comprise this broad and diverse movement are confronting new challenges and opportunities for inclusive, sustainable policy change. Beginning in the 1990s, antipoverty and equitable development advocates were thrown into an environment where communities such as Harlem were gentrifying with astonishing speed. Where black people once struggled to live where they could afford, many in gentrifying neighborhoods were suddenly fighting to afford where they lived as market-rate rents, home sale prices, and property taxes rose.

As urban revitalization projects and an influx of higher-income professional residents into formerly blighted neighborhoods were celebrated, community activists worried about affordability and sometimes resented that neighborhoods long desperate for restaurants, stores, and services only appeared to draw business interest once white newcomers began moving in.[19] Early applications of the equitable development approach often focused on understanding the race and class complexities of gentrification and advancing strategies to ensure that low-income communities and communities of color benefited from dramatic urban turnaround in places such as New York, San Francisco, Boston, Washington, D.C., Seattle, and Portland, Oregon. Nevertheless, longtime low-income residents continue to fear displacement, and even in areas where displacement has been minimal,[20] many residents are able to remain in the neighborhood only through tenuous mechanisms such as doubling or tripling up, paying a burdensome percentage of their income toward rent, or agreements with sympathetic landlords to temporarily hold rents below increased market rates. Preserving affordable housing for low-income residents in revitalized neighborhoods remains an important part of equitable planning and policymaking.

Equitable development advocates and practitioners have also increasingly recognized the importance of developing policy strategies for the substantially different predicament of "older core," "undercapitalized," or "weak-market" cities. Primarily northeastern and midwestern urban centers such as Detroit, Cleveland, Newark, New Jersey, or Hartford, Connecticut, continue to suffer from precipitous job loss and disinvestment and are particularly stark examples of the "donut" effect—a struggling city in a region of prosperous suburbs. As William Julius Wilson notes in this volume, the incidence and consequences of concentrated black poverty in older core cities are especially severe. In these places the key challenge of equitable development will be to implement strategies that draw economic investment to the region while including provisions at the front end that seamlessly allow low-income residents to share in the benefits of revitalization.[21]

Rural communities' role in the regional dynamic is also a pressing issue for equitable development advocates and practitioners. As Anita Brown-Graham discusses elsewhere in this volume, rural communities would benefit from equitable development's integration of place-focused and people-focused strategies. Brown-Graham's discussion of rural America's diversity also underscores the need for equitable development to turn greater attention to the relationship between metropolitan and rural areas—particularly the overlap between rural communities and encroaching far-flung exurbs—to determine how metropolitan development can be leveraged to benefit both cities and rural areas. Whether bucolic farming communities fighting to stave off suburban sprawl, southern hamlets grappling with desperate poverty and isolation, or High Plains towns facing extinction, rural communities are confronting diverse issues that have been off the radar screen of city and suburb dwellers for far too long. Though the context varies, rural areas face similar struggles with equity and access to opportunity, often compounded by spatial isolation and greater infrastructure challenges than the average metropolitan region.

Ultimately, the power of equitable development lies in its ability to cross race, class, and geographic boundaries and provide a comprehensive framework for confronting poverty in urban, suburban, and rural communities of all sizes. By integrating people- and place-based policies and programs and fully engaging local residents in policymaking and planning, equitable development can help create communities of opportunity where all residents can participate and prosper. Whether in Congress, state legislatures, city councils, corporate boardrooms, or community meetings, the policy and resource-allocation cycles that shape our neighborhoods and lives continually ask: who pays, who decides, and who benefits? Equitable development answers: we all can.

NOTES

The author wishes to acknowledge the writing contributions of Katrin Sirje Kärk, PolicyLink.

1. For a detailed analysis of the rise in urban poverty and structural and employment isolation, see William Julius Wilson, *When Work Disappears* (New York: Knopf, 1996).

2. William H. Frey, "Diversity Spreads Out: Metropolitan Shifts in Hispanic, Asian, and Black Populations Since 2000" (Brookings Institution, March 2006), available online at http://www.brook.edu/metro/pubs/20060307_Frey.pdf.

3. Frank D. Roylance, "Swelling Suburbs, Growing Diversity," *Baltimore Sun*, March 20, 2001.

4. Audrey Singer, "The Rise of New Immigrant Gateways" (Brookings Institution, February 2004).

5. John Charles Boger and Gary Orfield, eds., *School Resegregation: Must the South Turn Back?* (Chapel Hill: University of North Carolina Press, 2005).

6. See William Julius Wilson's discussion of suburban employment growth and job-spatial mismatch in this volume.

7. Xavier de Souza Briggs, ed., *The Geography of Opportunity: Race and Housing Choice in Metropolitan America* (Washington, DC: Brookings Institution Press, 2005), 29.

8. Christopher J.L. Murray, et al., "Eight Americas: Investigating Mortality Disparities Across Races, Counties, and Race-Counties in the United States," *Public Library of Science Medicine* 3, no. 9 (September 2006), available online at http://medicine.plosjournals.org/archive /1549-1676/3/9/pdf/10.1371_journal.pmed.0030260-S.pdf.

9. Steven Raphael and Alan Berube, "Socioeonomic Differences in Household Automobile Ownership Rates: Implications for Evacuation Policy" (March 2006), available online at http:// socrates.berkeley.edu/~raphael/Berube%20and%20Raphael%20fed%20paper.pdf. "Poor" is defined as households with incomes below 100 percent of the federal poverty line; "near-poor" households are those with incomes between 100 percent and 200 percent of the federal poverty line.

10. MOSES is an affiliate of the Gamaliel Foundation, an organizing network of 60 affiliates in 21 states across the United States and five provinces of South Africa.

11. Angela Glover Blackwell and Radhika K. Fox, "Regional Equity and Smart Growth: Opportunities for Advancing Social and Economic Justice in America" (Funders' Network for Smart Growth and Livable Communities, 2004), available online at http://www.policylink .org/pdfs/TranslationPaper.pdf.

12. Rolf Pendall, "Local Land-Use Regulation and the Chain of Exclusion," *Journal of the American Planning Association* 66, no. 2 (2000): 125–42, cited in PolicyLink and the Funders' Network for Smart Growth and Livable Communities, "Regional Equity and Smart Growth: Opportunities for Advancing Social and Economic Justice in America" (2004).

13. See PolicyLink (http://www.policylink.org/Projects/IZ/) or refer to the work of David Rusk (http://www.gamaliel.org/DavidRusk/default.htm) for further analysis.

14. David Rusk, *Inside Game, Outside Game* (Washington, DC: Brookings Institution Press, 1999).

15. Noll, Roger G., and Andrew Zimbalist, eds., *Sports, Jobs, and Taxes: The Economic Impact of Sports Teams and Stadiums* (Washington, DC: Brookings Institution Press, 1997).

16. Good Jobs First, *Subsidizing the Low Road: Economic Development in Baltimore* (Washington, DC: Good Jobs First, 2002).

17. See Strategic Action for a Just Economy and Figueroa Corridor Coalition for Economic Justice, http://saje.net/programs/fccej.php.

18. For more information on Community Benefits Agreements, see the PolicyLink Equitable Development Toolkit, http://www.policylink.org/EDTK/default.html; Los Angeles Alliance for a New Economy, http://www.laane.org/; Strategic Actions for a Just Economy, http://saje.net/; and Good Jobs First, http://www.goodjobsfirst.org/.

19. Lance Freeman, *There Goes the 'Hood: Views of Gentrification from the Ground Up* (Philadelphia: Temple University Press, 2006).

20. Lance Freeman, "Displacement or Succession? Residential Mobility in Gentrifying Neighborhoods," *Urban Affairs Review* 40, no. 4 (March 2005): 463–491.

21. For more information on older core cities and a six-point action agenda for equitable revitalization, see PolicyLink, "Shared Prosperity, Stronger Regions: An Agenda for Rebuilding America's Older Core Cities," available online at http://www.policylink.org/Research/OlderCoreCities/.

Conclusion: Ending Poverty in America

Senator John Edwards

America is the richest nation on the face of the earth. It is the richest nation in all of history. Yet in the midst of this abundance 37 million of us live in poverty.

If you are reading this book, you have almost certainly heard that statistic before, probably many times. The problem is that a number lacks a human face. Statistics do not struggle. They do not go to bed hungry, wake up cold, or give up on hope.

The real story is not the number but the people behind the number. The men, women, and children living in poverty—one in eight of us—do not have enough money for the food, shelter, and clothing they need. One in eight. That is not a problem. That is not a challenge. That is a plague. And it is our national shame.

Most of us rarely see the terrible effects of poverty. We sigh in frustration as the person in front of us at the grocery line slowly separates purchases into items covered by food stamps and those that are not. Then, every once in a rare while, something comes along to rip the veneer away and expose the plague that has been among us all along. And then we see.

When Hurricane Katrina struck the Gulf Coast in 2005, suddenly the 37 million had a face, had thousands and thousands of faces. They were in our living rooms, on the evening news, packed into the Superdome, hungry and thirsty and desperate, unable to flee, without the means even to remove themselves from the path of harm. There was nowhere for the poor to go. Americans saw their faces and they—we—responded with support, with resources, and with an awakened will to make a difference.

The task before us is to harness that awakened will to conquer this plague once and for all. The sad truth is that Katrina exposed only the smallest fraction of poverty's victims. They live across this country in circumstances as varied as they are terrible. Many of them are jobless, but many are working. Many are homeless, but many are packed into failed housing projects far from available work. Many live in inner cities, but many live in forgotten rural communities. Many lack a good education, and many are children who desperately need good schools they do not have.

Poverty is America's great moral challenge in our time, and it will take all of us to meet it. This is not a problem that can be left to the government alone. This is a problem that requires the will and commitment of all of us, working as voters, as citizens, and as neighbors. It requires us to make demands of our leaders and ourselves. And it begins with opening our eyes before the next storm strikes.

Over the last two years, I have traveled across America and talked to people living on the margins of our society. I met a single mother in Kansas City with two children. She has a job that pays $9.50 an hour. She told me about winters where "the choice was between lights and gas." She chose the lights. And she said to me, "When my kids go to bed, I tell them to wear as many clothes as they can. And when they go to school, I tell them, 'don't tell anyone you don't have gas because somebody might come and take you away.'" No one who works hard in this country should ever be faced with that kind of choice or that kind of worry.

Ending poverty may seem impossible, but it is not. If we can put a man on the moon, nearly double the length of a human life, and put entire libraries on chips the size of a postage stamp, then we can end poverty for those who want to work for a better life. Once we have the will, we will find the way.

A RENEWED SEARCH FOR SOLUTIONS

Poverty's greatest ally is pessimism. Too many people believe that we can do nothing to fight poverty. Instead of hearing the biblical admonition that "the poor will always be with us" as a call to action, they hear a reason to be quiet.

The truth is that ambitious goals, creative ideas, and practical solutions can make great progress against poverty. They already have. Amid the misery of the Great Depression, President Franklin Roosevelt signed the Social Security Act. Today Social Security lifts 13 million seniors out of poverty.[1]

Thirty years later our nation made more progress through the War on Poverty. Since Medicare's creation in 1965, poverty among the elderly has been reduced by nearly two-thirds.[2] Medicaid provides health care for more than 52 million Americans.[3] Head Start has improved the health and school readiness of more than 20 million children.[4]

The record of the past is not perfect. We made mistakes in the War on Poverty. At times, new government programs failed to reflect our belief in the values of work, family, and responsibility. They gave too much money to bureaucracies and not enough to people. Nonetheless, in a single decade more than 13 million people moved out of poverty; their lives and communities were changed for the better.[5]

Despite the successes, more recent decades have seen a pervasive skepticism toward the government's ability to solve large social problems. Today few speak of eliminating poverty. Few even acknowledge it.

Nonetheless, there have been pockets of progress. In the 1990s President Clinton dramatically expanded the Earned Income Tax Credit, which President Ford created and President Reagan supported. As John Karl Scholz explains, the EITC reduces the taxes of low-income workers, which gives them an incentive to earn money and helps them save for the future.[6] In 2003 it helped 22 million low-income working families, and the EITC alone lifted 4.4 million people out of poverty, including 2.4 million children.[7]

Welfare reform in 1996 based upon the values of work and responsibility helped reduce the number of welfare recipients from 12.2 million to 4.5 million over a decade.[8] Although the law was not perfect, it reassured Americans that the government could fight poverty in a way that was consistent with their values. And the poverty rate for single mothers and their children significantly declined.[9]

However, when we step back, it becomes clear that progress has stalled. The poverty rate is higher today than it was 30 years ago.[10] The public debate on poverty policies is stuck in a rut. One side downplays the importance of strong families and personal responsibility. The other side is driven by a deep skepticism of what government can accomplish. Both sides are right, and both sides are wrong: greater government efforts and greater personal responsibility are both necessary.

Poverty is such a low priority in Washington that politicians are not even interested in developing an accurate statistic. The official measure of Americans living in poverty is incomplete and out-of-date, according to the National Academy of Sciences, and probably undercounts the number of the poor.[11] We do not even count all the poor; this is a perfect metaphor for how poverty is ignored.

If we think back on our past successes, it is clear that they have been possible because we have linked ambitious goals with practical policy solutions. Today we need to apply that formula once again. And we need a nimbleness that allows us to respond to the wide variety of circumstances that drive Americans into poverty and that hold them there. There is not one answer;

there are many. We need the wisdom to identify what works, the imagination to aim high, and the determination to keep working until we succeed. If we have those, anything—including the eradication of poverty—is possible.

This volume is a collection of some of the best ideas from some of the nation's most creative thinkers, activists, and community leaders for addressing the greatest moral challenge facing the country. It represents the cutting edge of what we hope will be a nationwide resurgence of innovative thinking and practical solutions for ending poverty in America. And it represents the work of the Center on Poverty, Work and Opportunity at the University of North Carolina at Chapel Hill, where leaders and thinkers like those in this book are reigniting this essential national debate. Our challenge is to take the best ideas and the most innovative thinking and couple them with the determination and commitment to put them into action so that we as a nation can finally end the plague of poverty.

A NEW DIRECTION IN POVERTY POLICY

Poverty is more than a single issue. David Shipler begins this book by describing how the seemingly unrelated problems faced by poor Americans are actually inextricably connected. The problems of poverty—too few jobs, debt, bad housing, bad schools, illness, and fragile families—cannot be understood or solved in isolation.

However, these problems do share one characteristic: the surest route to addressing them is by applying the time-tested ideals at the heart of the American bargain. Our nation was built on the values of hard work, equal opportunity, thrift, and strong families. Today these principles light the way forward.

First and foremost, Americans believe deeply in the value of work. As laws since the Homestead Act of 1862 have recognized, Americans have wanted only the chance to work hard and collect the rewards of their own labor. Work is the pathway to success and security, but it is even more than the source of a paycheck. It is also a source of dignity and independence and self-respect.

Second, our nation was founded as the land of opportunity, and we should strive to provide equal opportunity. Americans willing to work should have access to entry-level jobs. Equality is one of the abiding principles on which America is based; we need to make it an active principle, not a passive one. Every single child should attend a good school, and every adult should be able to get the job training he or she needs.

Third, antipoverty programs should recognize the importance of savings. Every family needs something to fall back on during hard times, such as an illness or a lost job or even a hurricane. This is true for poor families more than anyone else. Without any cushion, every blow—and all lives have them—consigns the poor more and more to lives of poverty and hopelessness. Saving and investing are also the way for families to get ahead, buy a home, send their children to college, and have a secure retirement.

Finally, Americans believe in the importance of community, responsibility, and, most of all, family. We need to strengthen this institution that—for most of us—is the central work of our lives and the foundation of our own and our children's success. The first cushion we need is a stable family, and the first lessons we learn about responsibility are learned in our homes.

Jobs and Wages

Shortly after Katrina I visited shelters in Baton Rouge where evacuees were living. One man told me, "I've worked hard all my life—it's what I know. And the people here tell me that if I wait outside the shelter at 5 A.M. every morning, sometimes, maybe, someone will come by in a pickup looking for workers. So since the day I got here, for a week and a half, I've been out there every morning at 5 A.M.—just on that chance, because I just want a chance to work."

This man had lost everything he had, but he still believed that in America, if you did your part and were willing to work hard, you would be rewarded in the end. This belief in the value of hard work is not the property of one group; Americans of every race and class share this belief. Our policies must be geared toward building a nation where this belief is translated into reality for all Americans, not allowed to remain just an empty promise for those who happen to live in poverty.

We must build an economy that values work. For starters, that means reversing tax cuts that have shifted the tax burden away from wealth and onto work. Americans aspire to wealth, surely, but we honor and respect work, and our tax code should reflect that. It also means guaranteeing workers a meaningful right to organize. With strong unions, service jobs can be the foundation of the middle class, as manufacturing jobs once were. As Beth Shulman argues, it means raising the minimum wage, which in 2006 reached its lowest point since 1955.[12]

It is important not to overlook rural America, as policymakers too often do. Anita Brown-Graham explains the unique challenges facing impoverished rural communities. We should invest in community colleges, which provide practical job training, and rural small-business centers to help entrepreneurs get off the ground.

Finally, some willing workers cannot find jobs without skills, experience, or references. We know that innovative programs such as those described by David Spickard, Ruston Seaman, and Michael Ferber can help these workers.

And we know—because we have seen it work—that the government can create short-term jobs to serve as stepping-stones, helping people work their way out of poverty now and get the experience they need for better jobs in the future.[13]

Savings and Assets

Savings are a key to financial security and a better future, but they are a missing part of the equation for many American families. The poorest 25 percent of American households have a negative net worth.[14] As Melvin Oliver and Thomas Shapiro have documented, the asset gap divides Americans along racial lines.[15] While the typical white family has nearly $90,000 in assets, the typical Hispanic family has only about $8,000 and the typical African American family only about $6,000.[16]

There are a variety of strategies to give more Americans a stake in our economy. As Michael Sherraden points out, Children's Savings Accounts have real potential. Imagine how a few thousand dollars in the bank can transform a poor child's sense of hope and possibility for the future. Michael Stegman explains the importance of homeownership in promoting economic security and building household wealth.[17] A progressive tax credit could remedy inequalities in our tax code and help millions of first-time homebuyers. I have previously proposed a work bonds tax credit that would give low-income workers $500 toward a new bank account or safe investment fund.

Peter Orszag's "automatic 401(k)" proposal is a proven method to encourage retirement saving. Michael Barr suggests an initiative to establish bank accounts for the 22 million American households without them. These families—who can ill afford any unnecessary expenses—pay check cashers billions of dollars every year for services most banks provide for free.[18] Finally, strong protections against predatory lending would protect the assets that families have worked hard to build. Martin Eakes' experience has demonstrated that low-income families are dependable borrowers when given loans with fair terms. When you spend time with a group of Self-Help borrowers, as I recently did, it becomes abundantly clear that all many families need is a real opportunity.

Housing

Too many struggling families live in neighborhoods of concentrated poverty, often with inferior schools, high crime, and high rates of joblessness.[19] Unable to afford cars, they are cut off from the entry-level jobs that are increasingly located in the suburbs. Yet, despite its importance, housing policy is barely on the national agenda.

As William Julius Wilson suggests, we should fight concentrated poverty with a combination of strategies for both inner-city neighborhoods and the broader regional economies. We should also expand housing vouchers. Vouchers—rather than housing projects built in low-income areas—allow families to escape to safe communities with good schools. We can get better results at lower cost by radically overhauling the federal Department of Housing and Urban Development and giving more authority to states and cities. Angela Glover Blackwell details some of the successful experiments with inclusionary zoning and transit-oriented development.

Education

There is no challenge more central to the fight against poverty than giving every American the opportunities created by a good education, as Dennis Orthner and Hugh Price point out. But our nation is failing to offer an adequate education to every child. Today almost one in three students does not graduate from high school.[20] The numbers are even higher for minority students, who, on average, are four years behind their peers by the end of high school.[21] Meanwhile, those students who do graduate from high school are finding college tuition growing faster than family incomes, student debt rising, and scholarship aid failing to keep pace. Not surprisingly in this environment, qualified students from low-income families are far less likely to enroll in college than their peers.

We need to transform education at every level, from expanding preschool opportunities to paying teachers more to teach where we need them most, from reforming our underperforming high schools to creating "second-chance" schools to help former dropouts get back on track. As Harry Holzer notes, low-wage workers need relevant job training. And as Holzer and Katherine Newman point out, larger Pell grants would expand college opportunity.

For years I have talked about a program I call "College for Everyone," which would make the first year of college free for all qualified students who take a part-time job. Over the last two years this idea has become a reality. A pilot program in Greene County, North Carolina, has provided over $300,000 in aid to more than 80 students, and college enrollment has increased by 25 percent. Many of these students never dreamed of going to college, and they now know that if they are willing to work hard, college is a real option. Every child in America deserves the same opportunity.

Strengthening Families and Communities

In too many poor communities marriage is the exception, and male responsibility is not what it should be. As Sara McLanahan describes, children who grow up without fathers are much more likely to be poor and at greater risk for a host of problems into adulthood.

To strengthen families, we should address the marriage penalty that still hits many poor workers with a massive tax increase if they choose to get married. Welfare reform has helped reduce poverty rates among single mothers, but as Ronald Mincy and Hillard Pouncy argue, too many young men, particularly young black men, remain cut off from the hopes and routines of ordinary American life. We need to finish the job of welfare reform by encouraging young fathers to work and take responsibility for their children. As William Julius Wilson pointed out years ago, low employment levels for single men are linked to low levels of marriage and high levels of out-of-wedlock births.

Encouraging fathers to take responsibility is about much more than money. Recently I visited a faith-based community development corporation in Chicago called Bethel New Life and saw a display of T-shirts that young boys had designed about their fathers. One shirt said, "You won't be there. Should have, could have, would have." And the T-shirt had a hole in the shape of a heart. This is only one of the heartbreaking messages I read. When fathers are absent, children suffer emotionally as much as they do financially.

We can build on recent progress in reducing teen pregnancy by investing in proven programs. At the same time, we must recognize that the government cannot do everything. Carol Mendez Cassell makes an important, but often overlooked point: teens are profoundly influenced by the attitudes and behaviors of adults. All of us—parents, clergy, teachers, public officials—need to send an unambiguous message to the young people in our communities. We need to say clearly that it is wrong when young men father children but do not support them. And it is wrong when girls and young women bear children they are not ready to raise.

AMERICA'S STRUGGLING MIDDLE CLASS

Advocates for the poor can never forget that people living in poverty are not the only families who are struggling. Millions of additional Americans battle daily uncertainty and even material deprivation. As Elizabeth Warren and Jacob Hacker explain, millions of families have only the most tenuous hold on their middle-class status.

While corporate profits have increased over the last several years, most working Americans have not reaped the benefits. Median household income fell by 2.7 percent between 2000 and 2005 after inflation.[22] Corporate profits now make up a larger portion of America's gross domestic product than at any time since the 1960s. In contrast, wages and salaries now make up a lower share of the economy than they have at any time since the government began recording the data in 1929.[23] And as Jared Bernstein details, the rate of upward mobility—the core of the American dream—is stagnant or even declining.

At the same time that wages have stagnated, family expenses have surged. After adjusting for inflation, the indebtedness of American households has alarmingly increased by more than 40 percent over the last five years. Employment-based health-care premiums even surpassed that: they have risen 87 percent over the last six years.[24] And for the first time since the Great Depression, the personal savings rate is negative.[25]

Early last year in South Carolina I met Jim, a 60-year-old man who personified the precarious situation that many middle-class families are in. Jim's wife had worked for the same company for 28 years before suddenly being laid off. Jim was a Navy veteran and former high school teacher. A heart attack and lingering health problems had rendered him unable to hold a steady job for years. When his wife lost her job, they lost everything. Two cars and a four-bedroom house with over half the mortgage paid were gone in what seemed like an instant.

Fortunately, many of the same policies that will help America's poor will also help America's struggling middle class. One of the reasons that poverty declined greatly in the 1960s was a tight labor market that drove strong, broad-based growth. The same combination was critical to the reduction in poverty in the late 1990s. In today's global economy, creating widely shared growth has new dimensions—from making smart investments in technology and human capital, as Richard Freeman suggests, to encouraging entrepreneurs, as Jack Kemp proposes, to overhauling our social insurance programs to create more security and encourage more risk taking, to ensuring smart trade policies, to much else besides. Elizabeth Warren has suggested a Financial Product Safety Commission to protect Americans against predatory and other abusive lending. And we must provide every American with health-care coverage. Too many Americans work hard and contribute to our economy but do not have the peace of mind and protection against financial ruin that health insurance provides. The spiraling costs of health care result in the relocation of too many American businesses and the loss of too many American jobs. We know that when our economy again creates good jobs and strong incomes, it will be our greatest antipoverty program and our best engine of opportunity for all Americans.

LOOKING TO THE FUTURE

Even the most brilliant policy ideas will not make a difference in anyone's life without the determination and commitment to turn them into reality. If we are ever going to end poverty, the American people will have to demand action from their leaders. And I believe that they will when they understand what is at stake.

Too often, politicians sell voters short. When I was serving in the U.S. Senate, lots of so-called political experts told me that nobody cares about poverty except the poor. I did not believe that then, and I do not believe it now. When Americans see people suffering, they care. When Americans see inequality, they care. When Americans see people denied the opportunity to build a good life simply because of the circumstances into which they are born, they care. They care a lot.

Hurricane Katrina exposed us to heartbreaking images of extreme poverty, but it also reminded us of the extraordinary compassion of the American people. Millions opened their hearts, homes, and wallets after the storm.

I have seen this compassion firsthand over the last two years as I have traveled across the country supporting state minimum-wage increases. From Ohio to Montana, the popular support for these initiatives has been overwhelming. The American people understand that no one who works full-time should live in poverty.

I have seen a profound concern about poverty among America's young people in the thoughtful questions asked by University of North Carolina students at our Center on Poverty, Work and Opportunity panels. I saw it when I visited college campuses around the country to encourage young people to get involved with the fight against poverty. At every school the turnout was extraordinary. Seven hundred college students skipped their spring break in 2006 and joined me in St. Bernard Parish, Louisiana, to clean up Katrina damage that had ravaged that community. They could have been on the beach with their friends, but they chose to pick up a hammer and put on a pair of work boots to help their fellow citizens.

Do not underestimate the power of young people to form a movement for change. Our history makes clear that when young Americans rise up against injustice, indifference, and intolerance, they can move mountains. In the 1960s young Americans rose up against racism, freedom-riding across the South to fight discrimination. In the 1970s young Americans protested the war in Vietnam, helping bring an end to that quagmire. In the 1980s young Americans demanded that the government, the private sector, and institutions of higher learning stop supporting the brutal apartheid regime in South Africa. Now, in the first part of the twenty-first century, I believe that young people can lead the way to ending poverty.

Galvanizing the American people will not be easy. Many families are understandably immersed in their own struggles. And many people worry that new government programs will just waste their hard-earned money. These are legitimate concerns, but we can overcome them if our ideas about alleviating poverty are based on our values—equal opportunity for everyone, real responsibility from everyone. People who are capable of working should be expected to work, and people should be accountable for their choices.

People often ask me what they can do to fight poverty. Getting involved in your own community is the first step. That is as simple as getting out the phone book and finding some place to volunteer—as a mentor for a young person, a caregiver for an elderly person, or a volunteer homebuilder for a homeless family.

But if we are going to build a national movement that demands action from our leaders, each of us also needs to vocally participate in the policy debate and raise awareness among our friends and neighbors. We should all pledge to keep talking about poverty until it is at the top of the national agenda. And we should pledge to hold our government accountable for ignoring the suffering of so many for so long.

There is a reason we chose to title this book *Ending Poverty in America*. We should not be satisfied with a modest improvement. Let us set a national goal—the elimination of poverty in America in 30 years. It will not be easy, but I believe in the unlimited power of the American people to accomplish anything we set our hearts and minds to achieve. If we do not rest until poverty is history, it will be.

NOTES

1. Isaac Shapiro and Arloc Sherman, "Social Security Lifts 13 Million Seniors Above the Poverty Line: A State by State Analysis" (Center on Budget and Policy Priorities, February 24, 2005).

2. Carmen DeNavas-Walt, Bernadette D. Proctor, and Cheryl Hill Lee, "Income, Poverty, and Health Insurance Coverage in the United States: 2005" (Current Population Reports, U.S. Bureau of the Census, August 2006), 23.

3. Kaiser Commission on Medicaid and the Uninsured, "Who Needs Medicaid?" (April 2006), available online at http://www.kff.org/medicaid/7496.cfm.

4. Children's Defense Fund, "Head Start Basics" (March 2005), available online at http://campaign.childrensdefense.org/earlychildhood/headstart/headstartbasics2005.pdf.

5. U.S. Census Bureau, "Historical Poverty Tables" Table 2, http://www.census.gov/hhes/www/poverty/histpov/hstpov2.html.

6. Jason A. Levitis and Nicholas Johnson, "Together, State Minimum Wages and State Earned Income Tax Credits Make Work Pay" (Center on Budget and Policy Priorities, July 12, 2006).

7. Robert Greenstein, "The Earned Income Tax Credit: Boosting Employment, Aiding the Working Poor" (Center on Budget and Policy Priorities, July 19, 2005).

8. Robert J. Samuelson, "A Reform That Worked: Lessons from Welfare," *Washington Post*, August 3, 2006.

9. U.S. Census Bureau, "Historical Poverty Tables" Table 4, http://www.census.gov/hhes/www/poverty/histpov/hstpov4.html.

10. U.S. Census Bureau, "Historical Poverty Tables," Table 2.

11. Constance F. Citro and Robert T. Michael, eds., *Measuring Poverty: A New Approach*, (Washington, DC: National Academy Press, 1995).

12. Economic Policy Institute, "Minimum Wage Facts at a Glance" (August 2006), available online at http://www.epinet.org/content.cfm/issueguides_minwage_minwagefacts.

13. Anne Kim, "Transitional Jobs: A Bridge into the Workforce for Hard-to-Employ Welfare Recipients" (Progressive Policy Institute, March 2001).

14. David Shipler, "No Masking the Poverty," *Los Angeles Times*, March 3, 2006.

15. For a thorough discussion, see Melvin L. Oliver and Thomas M. Shapiro, *Black Wealth/White Wealth: A New Perspective on Racial Inequality* (New York: Routledge, 1995).

16. Nell Henderson and Griff Witte, "Wealth Gap Widens for Blacks, Hispanics," *Washington Post*, October 18, 2004.

17. Homeownership is also associated with better educational outcomes for children. For a discussion, see Dalton Conley, "A Room of One's Own or a Room with a View? Housing and Educational Stratification," *Sociological Forum*, 16, no. 2 (2001): 263–80.

18. Katy Jacob, "Meeting Them Where They Work: The Promise of Financial Services Distribution in the Workplace" (Center for Financial Services Innovation, August 2005).

19. Alan Berube and Bruce Katz, "Katrina's Window: Concentrated Poverty Across America" (Brookings Institution, Special Analysis in Metropolitan Policy, October 2005).

20. Jay P. Greene and Marcus A. Winters, "Leaving Boys Behind: Public High School Graduation Rates" (Civic Report no. 48, Manhattan Institute for Policy Research, April 2006). The Economic Policy Institute has calculated a slightly lower rate. But no matter which numbers you believe, the rate is far too high.

21. For information on Latino students, see Education Trust, "Latino Achievement in America" (2003). For information on African American students, see Education Trust, "African American Achievement in America" (2003). Both are available online at www.edtrust.org.

22. Jared Bernstein and Elise Gould, "Working Families Fall Behind" (Economic Policy Institute, August 29, 2006).

23. Aviva Aron-Dine and Isaac Shapiro, "In First Half of 2006, Wages and Salaries Captured Lowest Share of Income on Record" (Center on Budget and Policy Priorities, August 31, 2006).

24. Henry J. Kaiser Family Foundation, "2006 Employer Health Benefits Survey" (September 26, 2006).

25. Ross Eisenbrey and Lawrence Mishel, "What's Wrong with the Economy?" (Economic Policy Institute Policy Brief, June 12, 2006).

About the Editors

MARION CRAIN, Director of the Center on Poverty, Work and Opportunity at the University of North Carolina School of Law, earned her B.S. from Cornell University and her law degree from the UCLA School of Law. She is the Paul Eaton Professor of Law at the University of North Carolina at Chapel Hill, an appointment she received in 1998. Crain is a nationally recognized scholar in the law of work, with a particular emphasis on how work law structures gender, race, and social class. She has authored two textbooks and multiple articles in leading academic journals dealing with the role of work in providing economic security, shaping identity, defining citizenship, and enhancing political participation in a democratic society. She has focused particularly on law's role in creating and maintaining the ever-widening disparity of income and wealth between the upper class and the working class, and the role of labor unions as a voice for working people. Her research has been funded by the National Science Foundation and the AFL-CIO Lawyers' Coordinating Committee.

JOHN EDWARDS, founder and first Director of the Center on Poverty, Work and Opportunity, is a graduate of North Carolina State University and the School of Law at the University of North Carolina at Chapel Hill. He practiced law for 20 years and then served as a senator from North Carolina in 1998–2004. During his time in the Senate he focused on ways to expand opportunity and move more people into the middle class. In his presidential and vice-presidential campaigns in 2004 he brought the nation's attention to the issue of poverty and has carried that work forward to the Center. In addition to his work as Director of the Center, Edwards held an Alumni Distinguished Professorship from 2005–2006 and delivered a series of lectures on domestic and foreign policy issues at the university.

ARNE L. KALLEBERG is Kenan Distinguished Professor of Sociology and Senior Associate Dean for Social Sciences and International Programs in the College of Arts and Sciences at the University of North Carolina at Chapel Hill. He also serves on the Advisory Board of the UNC Center on Poverty, Work and Opportunity. He received his B.A. from Brooklyn College and his M.S. and Ph.D. from the University of Wisconsin at Madison. He was a professor of sociology at Indiana University–Bloomington before joining the faculty at UNC–Chapel Hill in 1986. He has published more than 100 articles and chapters and 10 books on topics related to the sociology of work, organizations, occupations and industries, labor markets, and social stratification. His most recent book is *The Mismatched Worker* (2007). He will serve as President of the American Sociological Association in 2007–8.

About the Contributors

MICHAEL S. BARR is Professor of Law at the University of Michigan, and a nonresident senior fellow at the Brookings Institution. He is currently engaged in a large-scale survey of low- and moderate-income households as the faculty investigator for the Detroit Area Household Financial Services Study. His recent publications include *Global Administrative Law: The View from Base* (with G. Miller), *Credit Where It Counts: The Community Reinvestment Act and Its Critics*, and *Banking the Poor*. He served in senior positions in the U.S. government from 1994 to 2001: Special Advisor and Counselor on the Policy Planning Staff of the State Department, Treasury Secretary Robert E. Rubin's Special Assistant, Deputy Assistant Secretary of the Treasury for Community Development Policy, and Special Adviser to President William J. Clinton.

JARED BERNSTEIN is Director of the Living Standards Program at the Economic Policy Institute. His areas of research include income and wage inequality, technology's impact on wages and employment, low-wage labor markets and poverty, minimum-wage analysis, and international comparisons. Between 1995 and 1996 he held the post of deputy chief economist at the U.S. Department of Labor. He has published extensively in popular and academic journals, including the *American Prospect* and *Research in Economics and Statistics*, and is the co-author of eight editions of the book *The State of Working America*, and author of the book *All Together Now: Common Sense for a Fair Economy*.

ANGELA GLOVER BLACKWELL is founder and Chief Executive Officer of PolicyLink. A renowned community-building activist and advocate, she served as senior vice president of the Rockefeller Foundation, where she oversaw the foundation's Domestic and Cultural divisions. She also developed Rockefeller's Building Democracy program, which focused on race and policy, and created the Next Generation Leadership program. A lawyer by training, she gained national recognition as founder of the Oakland (California) Urban Strategies Council, where she pioneered new approaches to neighborhood revitalization. From 1977 to 1987 she was a partner at Public Advocates, a nationally known public interest law firm. She is the co-author of *Searching for the Uncommon Common Ground: New Dimensions on Race in America* (2002).

ANITA BROWN-GRAHAM is Director of the Institute for Emerging Issues at North Carolina State University. Previously, she was a professor at the School of Government at the University of North Carolina at Chapel Hill, where she specialized in affordable housing, economic and community development, and public liability. She has provided significant training to community leaders in these fields and has written books and articles focused on developing the economic base of distressed communities. She currently serves on the boards of several development organizations and foundations. Before joining the faculty of the School of Government in 1994, she served as law clerk to the Honorable William B. Shubb in the eastern district of California and as a business litigation counsel in a Sacramento, California, law firm.

CAROL MENDEZ CASSELL is a senior health scientist with the University of New Mexico, School of Medicine, Department of Pediatrics, Center for Health Promotion and Disease Prevention. Recently she was Project Director of the Centers for Disease Control and Prevention Community Coalition Partnerships for the Prevention of Teen Pregnancy. She has authored four books, including *Straight from the Heart: How to Talk to Your Teenagers About Love and Sex.*

MARTIN EAKES is the co-founder and CEO of the Center for Community Self-Help. His goal in creating Self-Help was to complete the second half of the civil rights movement: to close the wealth gap between rich and poor by helping low-income North Carolinians buy homes and start businesses. From very modest beginnings, under Eakes' leadership Self-Help has grown into a community development lender that has provided over $1.78 billion in financing to 25,800 homebuyers, small businesses, and nonprofits. Self-Help reaches people who are underserved by conventional lenders—particularly minorities, women, rural residents, and low-wealth families—through the support of socially responsible citizens and institutions across the United States. Eakes is the recipient of the 1996 MacArthur Award.

MICHAEL FERBER serves as Marketing and Development Director for World Vision Appalachia in Philippi, West Virginia, and teaches urban geography and urban planning courses at West Virginia University. He is a Ph.D. candidate in geography at West Virginia University and has completed a master of arts in education from West Virginia University, a master of divinity from Asbury Theological Seminary, and a bachelors degree in geography from West Virginia University. He is the managing editor of the journal *Geographies of Religions and Belief Systems* and has published articles in academic journals such as the *Annals of the Association of American Geographers*, *Geocarto International*, and *American Religious Experience*.

RICHARD B. FREEMAN is Ascherman Professor of Economics at Harvard University, Co-Director of the Labor and Worklife Program at the Harvard Law School and Director of the Labor Studies Program at the National Bureau of Economic Research. He is also Senior Research Fellow in Labour Markets at the Centre for Economic Performance at the London School of Economics. His research interests include the job market for scientists and engineers, the growth and decline of unions, the effects of immigration and trade on inequality, restructuring European welfare states, international labor standards, Chinese labor markets, transitional economies, youth labor-market problems, crime, self-organizing nonunions in the labor market, employee involvement programs, and income distribution and equity in the marketplace.

JACOB S. HACKER is Professor of Political Science at Yale University and a fellow at the New America Foundation. He is author of *The Divided Welfare State* and *The Road to Nowhere* and co-author of *Off Center: The Republican Revolution and the Erosion of American Democracy*. His latest book, published in October 2006, is *The Great Risk Shift: The Assault on American Jobs, Families, Health Care, and Retirement—And How You Can Fight Back*. A frequent commentator on NPR, PBS, and CNN, Hacker has written for *The New Republic*, *The Nation*, *The New York Times*, the *Los Angeles Times*, *The Washington Post*, and other publications.

HARRY J. HOLZER is a Professor of Public Policy at Georgetown University and a Visiting Fellow at the Urban Institute in Washington, D.C. He is also currently a Senior Affiliate of the National Poverty Center at the University of Michigan, a National Fellow of the Program on Inequality and Social

Policy at Harvard University, a Research Fellow at IZA (in Germany), and a Research Affiliate of the Institute for Research on Poverty at the University of Wisconsin at Madison. Before coming to Georgetown, he served as Chief Economist for the U.S. Department of Labor and Professor of Economics at Michigan State University. He has also been a Visiting Scholar at the Russell Sage Foundation and a Faculty Research Fellow of the National Bureau of Economic Research (NBER). Holzer's research has focused primarily on the labor-market problems of low-wage workers and other disadvantaged groups.

JACK F. KEMP is founder and Chairman of Kemp Partners, a strategic consulting firm. Secretary Kemp received the Republican Party's nomination for vice president in August 1996 and since then has campaigned nationally for reform of taxation, Social Security, and education. Before founding Empower America, a non-profit think tank promoting free market principles, he served for four years as Secretary of Housing and Urban Development, where he was the author of the Enterprise Zones legislation to encourage entrepreneurship and job creation in urban America. He continues to advocate the expansion of homeownership among the poor through resident management and ownership of public and subsidized housing. Before his appointment to the cabinet, he represented the Buffalo area and western New York in the U.S. House of Representatives from 1971 to 1989.

SARA McLANAHAN is Professor of Sociology and Public Affairs at Princeton University. She is a faculty associate of the Office of Population Research and is founder and Director of the Bendheim-Thoman Center for Research on Child Wellbeing. She currently serves as Editor in Chief of the *Future of Children*, a journal dedicated to providing research and analysis to promote effective policies and programs for children. She is the past president of the Population Association of America and has served on the National Academy of Sciences–Institute of Medicine Board on Children, Youth, and Families and the boards of the American Sociological Association and the Population Association of America. She currently serves on the Advisory Board for the National Poverty Center, the Board of Trustees for the William T. Grant Foundation, and the selection committee for the William T. Grant Young Scholars Award.

RONALD B. MINCY is the Maurice V. Russell Professor of Social Policy and Social Work Practice at Columbia University's School of Social Work. He formerly served at the Ford Foundation in several programmatic positions related to the treatment of low-income fathers by U.S. welfare, child-support, and family-support systems. He previously taught in the economics departments at Purdue University, Bentley College, the University of Delaware, and Swarthmore College and also worked at the U.S. Department of Labor and the Urban Institute. He is a former co-chair of the Grantmakers Income Security Taskforce and is a board member of the Grantmakers for Children, Youth, and Families.

KATHERINE S. NEWMAN is the Malcolm S. Forbes Class of 1941 Professor of Sociology and Public Affairs at Princeton University. She has previously taught at Columbia, Berkeley, and Harvard, where she served as the Wiener Professor of Urban Studies at Harvard University's John F. Kennedy School of Government and the Dean of Social Science for the Radcliffe Institute for Advanced Study. Her interests lie in the qualitative study of social stratification, with a special emphasis on the cultural meaning of mobility, work, poverty, and violence. Her 2006 book *Chutes and Ladders: Navigating the Low Wage Labor Market* completes her eight-year study of the occupational mobility of African American and Latino workers in Harlem. With Victor Chen, she is currently completing a book on the near poor in America, titled *The Missing Class: The Near Poor Next Door*. Newman holds a Ph.D. in anthropology from the University of California, Berkeley.

MELVIN L. OLIVER is Dean of the Social Sciences Division at the University of California, Santa Barbara, and Professor of Sociology. Previously, he was Vice President for Asset Building and Community Development at the Ford Foundation. He has co-authored a book with Thomas M. Shapiro titled *Black Wealth/White Wealth: A New Perspective on Racial Inequality*, which won the American Sociological Association's Distinguished Scholarly Publication Award and the C. Wright Mills Award from the Society for the Study of Social Problems.

PETER ORSZAG is the Joseph A. Pechman Senior Fellow in Economic Studies at the Brookings Institution, Co-Director of the Tax Policy Center, a joint venture of the Urban Institute and the Brookings Institution, Director of the Retirement Security Project, and Research Professor at Georgetown University. He previously served as special assistant to the President on economic policy and as senior economist and senior adviser on the Council of Economic Advisers during the Clinton administration. His current areas of research include pensions, budget and tax policy, Social Security, higher education, and homeland security.

DENNIS K. ORTHNER is Professor of Social Work at the University of North Carolina, Associate Director for Policy Development and Analysis of the Jordan Institute for Families, and an adjunct professor in the Department of Public Policy, College of Arts and Sciences. He was also a member of the program planning committee for former Vice President Al Gore's Conference on Families and Communities. He was a special assistant for human services reform to the secretary of the Department of Human Resources for the state of North Carolina from 1993 to 1994. He has been a federal consultant for the Department of Health and Human Services, the Department of Defense, the Department of the Air Force, the Department of the Navy, the Department of State, the Department of the Army, the Department of Labor, and the Women's Bureau.

HILLARD POUNCY is a visiting lecturer at the Woodrow Wilson School of Public Policy and International Affairs at Princeton University. He is also the co-author of a book in progress, *Strengthening Fragile Families: Reforming Income Security Policy for Modern American Childhood Poverty*, with Ronald Mincy of Columbia University. This publication is supported by a grant from the Century Foundation.

HUGH B. PRICE is a senior fellow at the Brookings Institution, focusing on issues of equal opportunity, nonprofit governance, K–12 education, criminal justice, and civil rights. He was formerly president and CEO of the National Urban League, as well as vice president of the Rockefeller Foundation. He is the author of two books, *Achievement Matters: Getting Your Child the Best Education Possible* and *Destination: The American Dream*.

JOHN KARL SCHOLZ is Professor of Economics at the University of Wisconsin–Madison. He is a former deputy assistant secretary at the U.S. Department of the Treasury and also served as a senior staff economist at the Council of Economic Advisors.

RUSTON SEAMAN is Executive Director of World Vision Appalachia and has dedicated his adult life to helping others who live and work in rural, under-resourced communities. His work began in 1980 and continues today in Chestnut Ridge, West Virginia. He is a graduate of Eastern Baptist Theological Seminary with a master's degree in Christian faith and public policy. Seeking practical solutions to the root causes of poverty, he has given leadership to numerous organizations, including serving as a board member of the Christian Community Development Association.

THOMAS M. SHAPIRO is Director of the Institute on Assets and Social Policy, and is the Pokross Professor of Law and Social Policy at the Heller School for Social Policy and Management, Brandeis University. His book *Black Wealth/White Wealth*, co-authored with Melvin Oliver, won the American Sociological Association's Distinguished Scholarly Award and the C. Wright Mills Award from the Society for the Study of Social Problems. He has been active in the emerging area of asset policy. His work on assets and the transmission of racial inequality, *The Hidden Cost of Being African American: How Wealth Perpetuates Inequality*, was published in 2004.

MICHAEL SHERRADEN works on creating, implementing, and studying policy and community innovations, focusing on the least advantaged and drawing lessons from historical and international examples. Research on asset building, community and family development, service, productive aging, welfare reform, working poor households, and urban education occurs at the Center for Social Development (CSD) at Washington University, which Sherraden founded and directs. Sherraden has served as an adviser and consultant to the White House, the Department of the Treasury, the Department of Housing and Urban Development, the Department of Health and Human Services, the Progressive Policy Institute, the Carnegie Council, and other organizations. His work has been funded by many foundations and government agencies, including the Ford Foundation, the Rockefeller Foundation, the Charles Stewart Mott Foundation, the German Marshall Fund of the United States, and the National Science Foundation.

DAVID K. SHIPLER is a Pulitzer Prize–winning author and former foreign correspondent of *The New York Times*. He worked for The *New York Times* from 1966 to 1988, reporting from New York, Saigon, Moscow, and Jerusalem before serving as chief diplomatic correspondent in Washington, D.C. He has also written for the *New Yorker*, *The Washington Post*, and the *Los Angeles Times*. He is the author of *The Working Poor*; *Russia: Broken Idols, Solemn Dreams*; *Arab and Jew: Wounded Spirits in a Promised Land* (which won the Pulitzer Prize); and *A Country of Strangers: Blacks and Whites in America*.

BETH SHULMAN is the author of *The Betrayal of Work: How Low-Wage Jobs Fail 30 Million Americans and Their Families*. She is a lawyer and consultant on work-related issues and currently directs a project to increase public awareness about the problems of low-wage work and the need for policy change. She works with the Russell Sage Foundation's Social Inequality and Future Work projects. Previously, she was a vice president of the United Food and Commercial Workers International Union.

DAVID SPICKARD is the President and Chief Executive Officer of Jobs for Life (JfL). Having joined JfL in 1999 as its Chief Operating Officer, Spickard was appointed JfL's CEO in January 2006. Under his leadership JfL has grown from a local effort in Raleigh, North Carolina, to a national organization equipping churches and Christian organizations in over 25 U.S. cities. By mobilizing these leaders across the country, he has played an integral role in helping make

JfL one of the most distinctive and effective job-training strategies in the country—one that has been highlighted by both the Clinton and Bush administrations, the Department of Labor, the Department of Housing and Urban Development, the U.S. Chamber of Commerce, Bank of America, CVS/pharmacy, Promise Keepers, and many other prominent organizations.

MICHAEL A. STEGMAN is Director of Policy for the Program on Human and Community Development at the John D. and Catherine T. MacArthur Foundation. He serves as the foundation's lead observer of domestic policy issues. Stegman is also a fellow of the Urban Land Institute and has served on several national boards, including those of the Initiative for a Competitive Inner City and One Economy Corporation. He has been a consultant to the Fannie Mae Foundation, the Department of Housing and Urban Development (HUD), the Treasury Department, the Community Development Financial Institutions Fund (CDFI), and the U.S. General Accounting Office. He served as Assistant Secretary for Policy Development and Research at HUD and was the MacRae Professor of Public Policy, Planning, and Business at the University of North Carolina at Chapel Hill until June 2006.

ELIZABETH WARREN is the Leo Gottlieb Professor of Law at Harvard Law School, where she teaches contract law, bankruptcy, and commercial law. She is the co-author of *All Your Worth* and *The Two-Income Trap: Why Middle Class Mothers and Fathers Are Going Broke*, which has been cited by senators and presidential candidates. Her earlier award-winning books include *As We Forgive Our Debtors: Bankruptcy and Consumer Law in America*, *The Fragile Middle Class*, *Business Bankruptcy*, and three leading casebooks.

WILLIAM JULIUS WILSON is the Lewis P. and Linda L. Geyser University Professor at Harvard University and the Director of the Joblessness and Urban Poverty Research Program at the Malcolsm Wiener Center for Social Policy at Harvard University. A MacArthur Prize fellow from 1987 to 1992, Wilson has been elected to the National Academy of Sciences, the American Academy of Arts and Sciences, the National Academy of Education, and the American Philosophical Society. In June 1996 he was selected by *Time* magazine as one of America's 25 most influential people. He is a recipient of the 1998 National Medal of Science, the highest scientific honor in the United States, and was awarded the Talcott Parsons Prize in the Social Sciences by the American Academy of Arts and Sciences in 2003.

Index